BY GARDNER DOZOIS

NOVELS

Strangers

Nightmare Blue (with George
Alec Effinger)

Hunter's Run (with George R. R. Martin
and Daniel Abraham)

SHORT-STORY COLLECTIONS

When the Great Days Come

Strange Days: Fabulous Journeys with
Gardner Dozois

Geodesic Dreams

Morning Child and Other Stories

Slow Dancing Through Time

The Visible Man

EDITED BY GARDNER DOZOIS

The Year's Best Science Fiction #1–34

The New Space Opera (with
Jonathan Strahan)

The New Space Opera 2 (with
Jonathan Strahan)

Modern Classics of Science Fiction

Modern Classics of Fantasy

The Good Old Stuff

The Good New Stuff

The "Magic Tales" series 1–37 (with
Jack Dann)

Wizards (with Jack Dann)

The Dragon Book (with Jack Dann)

A Day in the Life

Another World

The Book of Swords

CO-EDITED WITH GEORGE R. R. MARTIN

Warriors I–III

Songs of the Dying Earth

Songs of Love and Death

Down These Strange Streets

Old Mars

Old Venus

Dangerous Women

Rogues

The
Book of
Swords

The
Book of
Swords

EDITED BY

GARDNER DOZOIS

BANTAM BOOKS
NEW YORK

Copyright © 2017 by Gardner Dozois
Introduction copyright © 2017 by Gardner Dozois
Individual story copyrights appear on pages 523–524.

Published in the United States by Bantam Books, an imprint of Random House, a division of Penguin Random House LLC, New York.

BANTAM BOOKS and the HOUSE colophon are registered trademarks of Penguin Random House LLC.

LIBRARY OF CONGRESS CATALOGING-IN-PUBLICATION DATA
Names: Dozois, Gardner R. editor.
Title: The book of swords / edited by Gardner Dozois.
Description: New York : Bantam Books, 2017.
Identifiers: LCCN 2017011852| ISBN 9780399593765 |
ISBN 9780399593772 (ebook)
Subjects: LCSH: Fantasy fiction, American. | Short stories, American. | American
fiction—21st century.
Classification: LCC PS648.F3 B663 2017 | DDC 813/.0876608—dc23
LC record available at https://lccn.loc.gov/2017011852

Printed in the United States of America on acid-free paper

randomhousebooks.com

2 4 6 8 9 7 5 3 1

First Edition

Book design by Caroline Cunningham

For George R. R. Martin, Fritz Leiber, Jack Vance,
Robert E. Howard, C. L. Moore, Leigh Brackett, L. Sprague de Camp,
Roger Zelazny, and all the other authors who ever wielded an
imaginary sword, and for Kay McCauley, Anne Groell, and
Sean Swanwick, for helping me bring this to you.

Contents

Introduction

By Gardner Dozois

One day in 1963, I stopped in a drugstore on the way home from high school (at that point in time, spinner racks full of mass-market paperbacks in drugstores were one of the few places in our town where books were available; there was no actual bookstore), and spotted on the rack an anthology called *The Unknown*, edited by D. R. Bensen. I picked it up, bought it, and was immediately enthralled by it; it was the first anthology I ever bought, and a purchase that would have a long-term effect on my future career although I didn't know that at the time. What it was was a collection of stories that Bensen had culled from the legendary (if short-lived) fantasy magazine *Unknown*, edited by equally legendary editor John W. Campbell, Jr., who at about the same time as he was revolutionizing science fiction as the editor of *Astounding* was revolutionizing fantasy in the pages of *Astounding*'s sister magazine *Unknown* from 1939 to 1943, when the magazine was killed by wartime paper shortages. In the early sixties, in a decade when the publishing industry was still coming out from under the shadow of postwar grim social realism, there was very little fantasy being published in a format affordable to purchase by a short-of-funds high-school student (except for the stories in genre magazines such as *The Magazine of Fantasy & Science Fiction*, which I didn't know about at the time), and the rich harvest of different types of fantasy story available in *Unknown* was a revelation to me.

The story that had the biggest effect on me, though, was a bizarre, richly atmospheric story called "The Bleak Shore," by Fritz Leiber, in which two seemingly mismatched adventurers, a giant swordsman from the icy North named Fafhrd and a sly, clever, nimble little man from the Southern climes called the Gray Mouser, are compelled to go on a doomed mission which seems destined to send them to their death (which fate, however, they cleverly avoid). It was a story unlike anything I'd ever read before, and I immediately wanted to read more stories like that.

Fortunately, it wasn't long before I discovered another anthology on the drugstore spinner racks, *Swords & Sorcery*, edited by L. Sprague de Camp, this one not only containing another Fafhrd and the Gray Mouser story, but dedicated entirely to the same kind of fantasy story, which I learned was called "Sword & Sorcery," a name for the subgenre coined by Leiber himself; in the pages of this anthology, I read for the first time one of the adventures of Robert E. Howard's Conan the Barbarian and C. L. Moore's Jirel of Joiry, as well as stories by Poul Anderson, Lord Dunsany, Clark Ashton Smith, and others. And I was hooked, becoming a lifelong fan of Sword & Sorcery, soon haunting used-book stores in what was then Scollay Square in Boston (now buried under the grim mass of Government Center), hunting through piles of moldering old pulp magazines for back issues of *Unknown* and *Weird Tales* that featured stories of Conan the Barbarian and Fafhrd and the Gray Mouser and other swashbuckling heroes.

What I had blundered into was the first great revival of interest in Sword & Sorcery, a subgenre of fantasy that had at that point lain fallow for decades, with almost all of the material in those anthologies and those old pulp magazines having been published in the thirties or forties or even earlier, about the time that stories that took place in distinct fantasy worlds instead of seventeenth-century France or imaginary Central European countries began to precipitate out from the larger and older body of work about swashbuckling, sword-swinging adventurers written by authors such as Alexandre Dumas, Rafael Sabatini, Talbot Mundy, and Harold Lamb. After Edgar Rice Burroughs in *A*

Princess of Mars and its many sequels sent adventurer John Carter to his own version of Mars, called Barsoom, to rescue princesses and have sword fights with giant four-armed Tharks, a closely parallel form to Sword & Sorcery sometimes called "Planetary Romance" or "Sword & Planet" stories developed, most prominently in the pages of pulp magazine *Planet Stories* between 1939 and 1955, with the two subgenres exchanging influences, and even many of the same authors, including authors such as C. L. Moore and Leigh Brackett, who were highly influential in both forms. The richly colored tales that made up Jack Vance's classic *The Dying Earth*, also published about then, were also technically science fiction, but with their interdimensional intrusions, strange creatures, and mages who wielded what could either be looked at as magic or the highest of high technology, they could also function as fantasy as well.

Probably not coincidentally, interest in Sword & Sorcery, which had faded over the wartime years and throughout the fifties, began to revive in the sixties, after the Mariner and Venera and other space probes were making it increasingly obvious that the rest of the solar system was incapable of supporting life as we knew it—no ferocious warriors to have sword fights with or beautiful princesses in diaphanous gowns to romance. Nothing but airless balls of barren rock.

From now on, if you wanted to tell those kinds of stories, you were going to have to do it in fantasy.

Throughout the early sixties, Sword & Sorcery boomed, with D. R. Bensen, L. Sprague de Camp, and Leo Margulies mining the rich lodes of *Unknown* and *Weird Tales* magazines for other anthologies (Bensen—an important figure in the development of modern fantasy, now, sadly, mostly forgotten—was the editor of Pyramid Books, and also mined the pages of *Unknown* for classic fantasy novels such as de Camp and Fletcher Pratt's *The Incomplete Enchanter* and *The Castle of Iron* to reprint), collections of the original Conan stories being reissued, new Conan stories and novels being produced by other hands, Michael Moorcock producing his hugely popular stories and novels about Elric of Melniboné (which have continued to the present day), and obvious imitations of Conan such as John Jakes's "Brak the Barbarian" stories being turned out. (At about this time, Cele Goldesmith, the editor of

Amazing and *Fantastic* magazines, began to coax Fritz Leiber out of semiretirement and got him to write new Fafhrd and the Gray Mouser stories for *Fantastic,* which, once I noticed that, induced me to begin regularly picking a genre magazine up off the newsstands for the first time, which in turn induced me to begin buying science-fiction magazines such as *Amazing, Galaxy,* and *Worlds of If*—which means that, ironically, although I'd later become associated with science fiction, and would edit a science-fiction magazine myself, I came to them first because I was looking for more Fafhrd and the Gray Mouser stories in the pages of a fantasy magazine . . . although to be fair I was at the same time reading SF such as the Robert A. Heinlein and Andre Norton "juveniles," and stuff such as Hal Clement's *Cycle of Fire* and—also published by Pyramid Books—*Mission of Gravity.*)

Then came J.R.R. Tolkien.

J.R.R. Tolkien's The Lord of the Rings trilogy is often cited these days as having single-handedly created the modern fantasy genre, but, while it is certainly hard to overestimate Tolkien's influence—almost every subsequent fantasist was hugely influenced by Tolkien, even, haplessly, those who didn't like him and reacted against him—what is sometimes forgotten these days is that Don Wollheim published the infamous "pirated" edition of *The Fellowship of the Ring* (the opening book of the trilogy) as an Ace paperback in the first place because he was casting desperately around for something—anything!—with which to feed the hunger of the swelling audience for Sword & Sorcery. The cover art of the Ace edition of *The Fellowship of the Ring* (by Jack Gaughn, of a wizard waving a sword and a staff aloft on top of a mountain) makes it clear that Wollheim thought of it as a "sword & sorcery" book, and his signed interior copy makes that explicit by touting the Tolkien volume as "a book of sword-and-sorcery that anyone can read with delight and pleasure." In other words, in the United States at least, the genre audience for fantasy definitely predated Tolkien, rather than being created by him, as the modern myth would have it. Don Wollheim knew very well that there was a genre fantasy audience already out there, already in place, a hungry audience waiting to be fed—although I doubt if even he had the remotest idea just how tremendous a response there would be to the tidbit of "sword & sorcery" that he was about to feed them. The Tolkien novels had already appeared in expensive hard-cover editions in Britain, but the Ace paperback editions—and the "authorized" paperback editions that followed from Ballantine Books—made them available for the first time in editions that kids like me and millions of others could afford to buy.

After Tolkien, everything changed. The audience for genre fantasy may have already existed, but there can be no doubt that Tolkien widened it tremendously. The immense commercial success of Tolkien's work also opened the eyes of other publishers to the fact that there was an intense hunger for fantasy in the reading audience—and they too began looking around for something to feed that hunger. On the strength of Tolkien's success, Lin Carter was able to create the first mass-market paperback fantasy line, the Ballantine Adult Fantasy line, which brought back into print long-forgotten and long-unavailable works by writers such as Clark Ashton Smith, E. R. Eddison, James Branch Cabell, Mervyn Peake, and Lord Dunsany. A few years later, Lester del Rey took over from Lin Carter and began to search for more commercial, less high-toned stuff that would appeal more directly to an audience still hungry for something as much like Tolkien as possible. In 1974, he brought out Terry Brooks's *The Sword of Shannara*, and although it was dismissed by many critics as a clumsy retread of Tolkien, it proved hugely successful commercially, as did its many sequels. In 1977, Del Rey also scored big with *Lord Foul's Bane*, the beginning of the somewhat quirkier and less derivative trilogy, The Chronicles of Thomas Covenant the Unbeliever, by Stephen R. Donaldson, and *its* many sequels.

Oddly, as fantasy books began to sell better by far than ever before, interest in Sword & Sorcery began to fade. Sword & Sorcery had always been a subgenre mostly driven by short fiction, but, inspired by Tolkien, the new fantasy novels began to get longer and longer and spawn more and more sequels, and now began to be largely thought of as a distinct subgenre, "Epic Fantasy." It's sometimes difficult for me to make a distinction between Epic Fantasy and Sword & Sorcery—both are set in invented fantasy worlds, both have thieves and sword-wielding adventurers, both take place in worlds in which magic exists and there are sorcerers of greater or lesser potency, both feature fantasy creatures such as dragons and giants and monsters—although some critics say they can distinguish one from the other by criteria other than length. Be that as it may, as books thought of as Epic Fantasy became more and more prominent, people talked less about Sword & Sorcery. It never disappeared entirely—Lin Carter edited five volumes of the *Flashing Swords!* anthology series between 1971 and 1981, Andrew J. Offutt, Jr. edited five volumes of the *Swords Against Darkness* anthology series between 1977 and 1979, Robert Lynn Asprin started the long-running series of *Thieves' World* shared-world anthologies in 1978, Robert Jordan produced a long sequence of Conan novels throughout the eighties before turning to his multivolume Wheel of Time Epic Fantasy series, Glen Cook produced recognizable Sword and Sorcery work (notably his tales about the Black Company) throughout the same period, as did C. J. Cherryh, Robin Hobb, Fred Saberhagen, Tanith Lee, Karl Edward Wagner, and others; Marion Zimmer Bradley edited a long sequence of *Sword and Sorceress* anthologies, with the emphasis on female adventurers, throughout the seventies, and Jessica Amanda Salmonson produced a similarly female-oriented set of anthologies, *Amazons* and *Amazons II*, in 1979 and 1982 respectively.

Nevertheless, as the eighties progressed into the nineties, Sword & Sorcery continued to fade as a subgenre, until it was rarely ever mentioned and was in danger of being altogether forgotten.

Then, at the end of the nineties, things began to turn around.

Why they did is difficult to pinpoint. Perhaps it was the enormous commercial success of George R. R. Martin's *A Game of Thrones*, published in 1996, and its sequels, which influenced newer writers by showing them a grittier, more realistic, harder-edged kind of Epic Fantasy, one with characters who were often so morally ambiguous that it was impossible to tell the good guys from the bad guys. Perhaps it was just time for a new generation of writers, who had been influenced by the classic work of writers like Leiber and Howard and Moorcock, to take the stage and produce their own new variations on the form.

Whatever the reason, the ice began to thaw. Soon people began to talk about "The New Sword and Sorcery," and in the last few years of the twentieth century and the early years of the twenty-first century, there were writers such as Joe Abercrombie, K. J. Parker, Scott Lynch, Elizabeth Bear, Steven Erikson, Garth Nix, Patrick Rothfuss, Kate Elliott, Daniel Abraham, Brandon Sanderson, and James Enge making names for themselves, there were new markets in addition to existing ones such as *F&SF* for Sword & Sorcery, such as the online magazine *Beneath Ceaseless Skies* and print magazine *Black Gate*, and new anthologies began to appear, such as my own *Modern Classics of Fantasy* in 1997, which featured classic Sword & Sorcery stories by Fritz Leiber and Jack Vance, *The Sword & Sorcery Anthology*, edited by David G. Hartwell and Jacob Weisman, a retrospective of some of the best old stories of the form, and *Epic: Legends of Fantasy*, edited by John Joseph Adams, an anthology reprinting newer work by newer authors. Most importantly, *new* short work began to appear, collected in anthologies such as *Legends* and *Legends II*, edited by Robert Silverberg, and later in *Fast Ships, Black Sails*, edited by Ann VanderMeer and Jeff VanderMeer, and *Swords & Dark Magic: The New Sword and Sorcery*, edited by Jonathan Strahan and Lou Anders, the first dedicated anthology of the New Sword and Sorcery.

All at once, we were in the middle of another great revival of interest in Sword & Sorcery, one which has so far not faded again as we progress deeper into the second decade of the twenty-first century. Already there's another generation of newer writers such as Ken Liu, Rich Larson, Carrie Vaughn, Aliette de Bodard, Lavie Tidhar, and others, taking up the challenges of the form, and sometimes evolving it in unexpected directions—and behind *them* are yet more new generations.

So, call it Sword & Sorcery, or call it Epic Fantasy, it looks like this kind of story is going to be around for a while for us to enjoy.

I've edited other anthologies with new Sword & Sorcery stories in them, such as the Jack Vance tribute anthology *Songs of the Dying Earth*, *Warriors*, *Dangerous Women*, and *Rogues* (all edited with that other big-time Sword & Sorcery fan, George R. R. Martin), but I've always wanted to edit an anthology of nothing but such stories, which is what I've done here with *The Book of Swords*, bringing you the best work of some of the best writers working in the form today, from across several different literary generations.

I hope that you enjoy it. And it's my hope that to some young kid out there, it will prove as enthralling and inspirational as *Unknown* and *Swords & Sorcery* did to me back in 1963—and so a new Sword & Sorcery fan will be born, to carry the love of this kind of swashbuckling fantasy tale on into the distant future.

The
Book of
Swords

K. J. Parker

• • •

One of the most inventive and imaginative writers working in fantasy today, K. J. Parker is the author of the bestselling Engineer trilogy (*Devices and Desires*, *Evil for Evil*, *The Escapement*) as well as the previous Fencer (*The Colours in the Steel*, *The Belly of the Bow*, *The Proof House*) and Scavenger (*Shadow*, *Pattern*, *Memory*) trilogies. His short fiction has been collected in *Academic Exercises*, and he has twice won the World Fantasy Award for Best Novella, for "Let Maps to Others" and "A Small Price to Pay for Birdsong." His other novels include *Sharps*, *The Company*, *The Folding Knife*, and *The Hammer*. His most recent novels are *Savages* and *The Two of Swords*. K. J. Parker also writes under his real name, Tom Holt. As Holt, he has published *Expecting Someone Taller*, *Who's Afraid of Beowulf*, *Ye Gods!*, and many other novels.

Here he gives us a compelling look at a determined pupil seeking out a master for instruction—with some surprising results.

• • •

The Best Man Wins

K. J. PARKER

He was in my light. I didn't look up. "What do you want?" I said.

"Excuse me, but are you the sword-smith?"

There are certain times when you have to concentrate. This was one of them. "Yes. Go away and come back later."

"I haven't told you what I—"

"Go away and come back later."

He went away. I finished what I was doing. He came back later. In the interim, I did the third fold.

Forge-welding is a horrible procedure and I hate doing it. In fact, I hate doing all the many stages that go to creating the finished object; some of them are agonisingly difficult, some are exhausting, some of them are very, very boring; a lot of them are all three, it's your perfect microcosm of human endeavour. What I love is the feeling you get when you've done them, and they've come out right. Nothing in the whole wide world beats that.

The third fold is—well, it's the stage in making a sword-blade when you fold the material for the third time. The first fold is just a lot of thin rods, some iron, some steel, twisted together then heated white and forged into a single strip of thick ribbon. Then you twist, fold, and do it again. Then you twist, fold, and do it again. The third time is usually the easiest; the material's had most of the rubbish beaten out of it, the flux usually stays put, and the work seems to flow that bit more readily under the hammer. It's still a horrible job. It seems to take forever, and you can wreck everything you've done so far with one split second of carelessness; if you burn it or let it get too cold, or if a bit of scale or slag gets hammered in. You need to listen as well as look—for that unique hissing noise that tells you that the material is just starting to spoil but isn't actually ruined yet; that's the only moment at which one strip of steel will flow into another and form a single piece—so you can't chat while you're doing it. Since I spend most of my working day forge-welding, I have this reputation for unsociability. Not that I mind. I'd be unsociable if I were a ploughman.

He came back when I was shovelling charcoal. I can talk and shovel at the same time, so that was all right.

He was young, I'd say about twenty-three or -four; a tall bastard (all tall people are bastards; I'm five feet two) with curly blond hair like a wet fleece, a flat face, washed-out blue eyes, and a rather girly mouth. I took against him at first sight because I don't like tall, pretty men. I put a lot of stock in first impressions. My first impressions are nearly always wrong. "What do you want?" I said.

"I'd like to buy a sword, please."

I didn't like his voice much, either. In that crucial first five seconds or so, voices are even more important to me than looks. Perfectly reasonable, if you ask me. Some princes look like rat-catchers, some rat-catchers look like princes, though the teeth usually give people away. But you can tell precisely where a man comes from and how well-off his parents were after a couple of words; hard data, genuine facts. The boy was quality—minor nobility—which covers everything from overambitious farmers to the younger brothers of dukes. You can tell immediately by the vowel sounds. They set my teeth on edge like bits of grit in bread. I don't like the nobility much. Most of my customers are nobility, and most of the people I meet are customers.

"Of course you do," I said, straightening my back and laying the shovel down on the edge of the forge. "What do you want it for?"

He looked at me as though I'd just leered at his sister. "Well, for fighting with."

I nodded. "Off to the wars, are you?"

"At some stage, probably, yes."

"I wouldn't if I were you," I said, and I made a point of looking him up and down, thoroughly and deliberately. "It's a horrible life, and it's dangerous. I'd stay home if I were you. Make yourself useful."

I like to see how they take it. Call it my craftsman's instinct. To give you an example; one of the things you do to test a really good sword is make it come compass—you fix the tang in a vise, then you bend it right round in a circle, until the point touches the shoulders; let it go, and it should spring back absolutely straight. Most perfectly good swords won't take that sort of abuse; it's an ordeal you reserve for the very best. It's a horrible, cruel thing to do to a lovely artefact, and it's the only sure way to prove its temper.

Talking of temper; he stared at me, then shrugged. "I'm sorry," he said. "You're busy. I'll try somewhere else."

I laughed. "Let me see to this fire and I'll be right with you."

The fire rules my life, like a mother and her baby. It has to be fed, or it goes out. It has to be watered—splashed round the edge of the bed with a ladle—or it'll burn the bed of the forge. It has to be pumped after every heat, so I do all its breathing for it, and you can't turn your back on it for two minutes. From the moment when I light it in the morning, an hour before sunrise, until the point where I leave it to starve itself to death overnight, it's constantly in my mind, like something at the edge of your vision, or a crime on your conscience; you're not always looking at it, but you're always watching it. Given half a chance, it'll betray you. Sometimes I think I'm married to the damn thing.

Indeed. I never had time for a wife. I've had offers; not from women, but from their fathers and brothers—he must be worth a bob or two, they say to themselves, and our Doria's not getting any younger. But a man with a forge fire can't fit a wife into his daily routine. I bake my

bread in its embers, toast my cheese over it, warm a kettle of water twice
a day to wash in, dry my shirts next to it. Some nights, when I'm too
worn-out to struggle the ten yards to my bed, I sit on the floor with my
back to it and go to sleep, and wake up in the morning with a cricked
neck and a headache. The reason we don't quarrel all the time is that it
can't speak. It doesn't need to.

The fire and I have lived sociably together for twenty years, ever since
I came back from the wars. Twenty years. In some jurisdictions, you get
less for murder.

"The term sword," I said, wiping dust and embers off the table with my
sleeve, "can mean a lot of different things. I need you to be more specific.
Sit down."

He perched gingerly on the bench. I poured cider into two wooden
bowls and put one down in front of him. There was dust floating on the
top; there always is. Everything in my life comes with a frosting of dark
grey gritty dust, courtesy of the fire. Bless him, he did his best to pretend
it wasn't there and took a little sip, like a girl.

"There's your short riding sword," I said, "and your thirty-inch arm-
ing sword, your sword-and-shield sword, which is either a constant flattened diamond section, what the army calls a Type Fifteen, or else with
a half length fuller, your Type Fourteen; there's your tuck, your falchion,
your messer, side-sword or hanger; there's your long sword, great sword,
hand-and-a-half, Type Eighteen, true bastard, your great sword of war
and your proper two-hander, though that's a highly specialised tool, so
you won't be wanting one of them. And those are just the main head-
ings. Which is why I asked you; what do you want it for?"

He looked at me, then deliberately drank a swallow of my horrible
dusty cider. "For fighting with," he said. "Sorry, I don't know very much
about it."

"Have you got any money?"

He nodded, put his hand up inside his shirt and pulled out a little
linen bag. It was dirty with sweat. He opened it, and five gold coins
spilled onto my table.

There are almost as many types of coin as there are types of sword.

These were besants; ninety-two parts fine, guaranteed by the Emperor. I picked one up. The artwork on a besant is horrible, crude and ugly. That's because the design's stayed the same for six hundred years, copied over and over again by ignorant and illiterate die-cutters; it stays the same because it's trusted. They copy the lettering, but they don't know their letters, so you just get shapes. It's a good general rule, in fact; the prettier the coin, the less gold it contains; the uglier, conversely, the better. I knew a forger once. They caught him and hanged him because his work was too fine.

I put my cup on top of one coin, then pushed the other four back at him. "All right?"

He shrugged. "I want the very best."

"It'd be wasted on you."

"Even so."

"Fine. The very best is what you'll get. After all, once you're dead, it'll move on, sooner or later it'll end up with someone who'll be able to use it." I grinned at him. "Most likely your enemy."

He smiled. "You mean I'll reward him for killing me."

"The labourer is worthy of his hire," I replied. "Right, since you haven't got a clue what you want, I'll have to decide for you. For your gold besant you'll get a long sword. Do you know what that—?"

"No. Sorry."

I scratched my ear. "Blade three feet long," I said, "two and a half inches wide at the hilt, tapering straight to a needle point. The handle as long as your forearm, from the inside of your elbow to the tip of your middle finger. Weight absolutely no more than three pounds, and it'll feel a good deal lighter than that because I'll balance it perfectly. It'll be a stabber more than a cutter because it's the point that wins fights, not the edge. I strongly recommend a fuller—you don't know what a fuller is, do you?"

"No."

"Well, you're getting one anyway. Will that do you?"

He sort of gazed at me as if I were the Moon. "I want the best sword ever made," he said. "I can pay more if necessary."

The best sword ever made. The silly thing was, I could do it. If I could be bothered. Or I could make him the usual and tell him it was the best sword ever made, and how could he possibly ever know? There are maybe ten men in the world qualified to judge. Me and nine others.

On the other hand; I love my craft. Here was a young fool saying; indulge yourself, at my expense. And the work, of course, the sword itself, would still be alive in a thousand years' time, venerated and revered, with my name on the hilt. The best ever made; and if I didn't do it, someone else would, and it wouldn't be my name on it.

I thought for a moment, then leant forward, put my fingertips on two more of his coins, and dragged them towards me, like a ploughshare through clay. "All right?"

He shrugged. "You know about these things."

I nodded. "In fact," I said, and took a fourth coin. He didn't move. It was as though he wasn't interested. "That's just for the plain sword," I said. "I don't do polishing, engraving, carving, chiselling, or inlay. I don't set jewels in hilts because they chafe your hands raw and fall out. I don't even make scabbards. You can have it tarted up later if you want, but that's up to you."

"The plain sword will do me just fine," he said.

Which puzzled me.

I have a lot of experience of the nobility. This one—his voice was exactly right, so I could vouch for him, as though I'd known him all my life. The clothes were plain, good quality, old but well looked after; a nice pair of boots, though I'd have said they were a size too big, so maybe inherited. Five besants is a vast, stunning amount of money, but I got the impression it was all he had.

"Let me guess," I said. "Your father died, and your elder brother got the house and the land. Your portion was five gold bits. You accept that that's how it's got to be, but you're bitter. You think; I'll blow the lot on the best sword ever made and go off and carve myself out a fortune, like Robert the Fox or Boamund. Something like that?"

A very slight nod. "Something like that."

"Fine," I said. "A certain category of people and their money are easily parted. If you live long enough to get some sense beaten into you, you'll get rather more than four gold bits for the sword, and then you can buy a nice farm."

He smiled. "That's all right, then."

I like people who take no notice when I'm rude to them.

"Can I watch?" he asked.

That's a question that could get you in real trouble, depending on context. Like the man and woman you've just thought of, my answer is usually No. "If you like," I said. "Yes, why not? You can be a witness."

He frowned. "That's an odd choice of word."

"Like a prophet in scripture," I said. "When He turns water into wine or raises the dead or recites the Law out of a burning tree. There has to be someone on hand to see, or what's the good in it?"

(I remembered saying that, later.)

Now he nodded. "A miracle."

"Along those lines. But a miracle is something you didn't expect to happen."

Off to the wars. We talk about "the wars" as though it's a place; leave Perimadeia on the north road till you reach a crossroads, bear left, take the next right, just past the old ruined mill, you can't miss it. At the very least, a country, with its own language, customs, distinctive national dress and regional delicacies. But in theory, every war is different, as individual and unique as a human being; each war has parents that influence it, but grows up to follow its own nature and beget its own offspring. But we talk about people en masse—the Aelians, the Mezentines, the Rosinholet—as though a million disparate entities can be combined into one, the way I twist and hammer a faggot of iron rods into a single ribbon. And when you look at them, the wars are like that; like a crowd of people. When you're standing among them, they're all different. Step back three hundred yards, and all you see is one shape: an army, say, advancing toward you. We call that shape "the enemy," it's the dragon we have to kill in order to prevail and be heroes. By the time it reaches us, it's delaminated into individuals, into one man at a time, rushing at us waving a spear, out to do us harm, absolutely terrified, just as we are.

We say "the wars," but here's a secret. There is only one war. It's never over. It flows, like the metal at white heat under the hammer, and joins up with the last war and the next war, to form one continuous ribbon. My father went to the wars, I went to the wars, my son will go to the wars, and his son after him, and it'll be the same place. Like going to Boc Bohec. My father went there, before they pulled down the White Temple and when Foregate was still open fields. I went there, and Foregate was a marketplace. When my son goes there, they'll have built houses on Foregate; but the place will still be Boc Bohec, and the war will still be the war. Same place, same language and local customs, slightly altered by the prevailing fashions in valour and misery, which come around and go around. In my time at the wars, hilts were curved and pommels were round or teardrop. These days, I do mostly straight cross hilts and scent-bottle pommels, which were all the rage a hundred years ago. There are fashions in everything. The tides go in and out, but the sea is always the sea.

My wars were in Ultramar; which isn't a place-name, it's just Aelian for "across the sea." Ultramar, which was what we were fighting for, wasn't a piece of land, a geographical entity. It was an idea; the kingdom of God on Earth. You won't find it on a map—not now, that's for sure; we lost, and all the places we used to know are called something else now, in another language, which we could never be bothered to learn. We weren't there for the idea, of course, although it was probably a good one at the time. We were there to rob ourselves a fortune and go home princes.

Some places aren't marked on maps, and everybody knows how to find them. Just follow the others and you're there.

"There's not a lot to see at this stage," I told him. "You might want to go away for a while."

"That's all right." He sat down on the spare anvil and bit into one of my apples, which I hadn't given him. "What are you doing with all that junk? I thought you were going to start on the sword."

I told myself; he's paying a lot of money, probably everything he's got in the world; he's entitled to be stupid, if he wants to. "This," I told him, "isn't junk. It's your sword."

He peered over my shoulder. "No it's not. It's a load of old horse-shoes and some clapped-out files."

"It is now, yes. You just watch."

I don't know what it is about old horseshoes; nobody does. Most people reckon it's the constant bashing down on the stony ground though that's just not true. But horseshoes make the best swords. I heated them to just over cherry red, flipped them onto the anvil, and belted them with the big hammer, flattening and drawing down; bits of rust and scale shot across the shop, it's a messy job and it's got to be done quickly, before the iron cools to grey. By the time I'd finished with them, they were long, squarish rods, about a quarter-inch thick. I put them on one side, then did the same for the files. They're steel, the stuff that you can harden; the horseshoes are iron, which stays soft. It's the mix, the weave of hard and soft that makes a good blade.

"What are they supposed to be, then? Skewers?"

I'd forgotten he was there. Patient, I'll say that for him. "I'll be at this for hours yet," I told him. "Why don't you go away and come back in the morning? Nothing interesting to see till then."

He yawned. "I've got nowhere in particular to go," he said. "I'm not bothering you, am I?"

"No," I lied.

"I still don't see what those bits of stick have got to do with my sword."

What the hell. I could use a rest. It's a bad idea to work when you're tired, you make mistakes. I tipped a scuttle of charcoal onto the fire, damped it down, and sat on the swedge block. "Where do you think steel comes from?"

He scratched his head. "Permia?"

Not such an ignorant answer. In Permia there are deposits of natural steel. You crush the iron ore and smelt it, and genuine hardening steel oozes out, all ready to use. But it's literally worth its weight in gold, and since we're at war with Permia, it's hard to get hold of. Besides, I find it's too brittle, unless you temper it exactly right. "Steel," I told him, "is iron that's been forged out over and over again in a charcoal fire. Nobody has the faintest idea how it works, but it does. It takes two strong men a whole day to make enough steel for one small file."

He shrugged. "It's expensive. So what?"

"And it's too hard," I told him. "Drop it on the floor, it'll shatter like glass. So you temper it, so it'll bend then spring back straight. But it's sulky stuff; good for chisels and files, not so good for swords and scythe-blades, which want a bit of bounce in them. So we weave it together with iron, which is soft and forgiving. Iron and steel cancel out each other's faults, and you get what you want."

He looked at me. "Weave together."

I nodded. "Watch."

You take your five rods and lay them side by side, touching; steel, iron, steel, iron, steel. You wire them tightly together, like building a raft. You lay them in the fire, edge downwards, not flat; when they're white-hot and starting to hiss like a snake, you pull them out and hammer them. If you've got it right, you get showers of white sparks, and you can actually see the metal weld together—it's a sort of black shadow under the glowing white surface, flowing like a liquid. What *it* is, I don't know, and not being inclined to mysticism I prefer not to speculate.

Then you heat the flat plate you've just made to yellow, grip one end in the vise and twist your plate into a rope, which you then forge flat; heat and twist and flatten, five times isn't too many. If you've done it right, you have a straight, flat bar, inch wide, quarter-inch thick, with no trace of a seam or laminations; one solid thing from five. Then you heat it up and draw it out, fold it and weld it again. Now can you see why I talk about weaving? There is no more iron or steel, no power on earth will ever separate them again. But the steel is still hard and the iron is still yielding, and that's what makes the finished blade come compass in the vise, if you're prepared to take the risk.

I lose track of time when I'm forge-welding. I stop when it's done, and not before; and I realise how tired and wet with sweat and thirsty I am, and how many hot zits and cinders have burnt their way through my clothes and blistered my skin. The joy isn't in the doing but the having-done.

You weld in the near dark, so you can see what's going on in the heart of the fire and the hot metal. I looked to where I know the doorway is, but it was all pitch-dark outside the orange ring of firelight. It's just as well I have no neighbours, or they'd get no sleep.

He was asleep, though, in spite of all the noise. I nudged his foot and he sat up straight. "Did I miss something?"

"Yes."

"Oh."

"But that's all right," I said. "We've barely started yet."

Logic dictates that I had a life before I went to Ultramar. I must have had; I was nineteen when I went there, twenty-six when I came back. Before I went there, I seem to recall a big comfortable house in a valley, and dogs and hawks and horses and a father and two elder brothers. They may all still be there, for all I know. I've never been back.

Seven years in Ultramar. Most of us didn't make it past the first six months. A very few, the file-hard, unkillable sort, survived as long as three years; by which point, you could almost see the marks where the wind and rain had worn them down to bedrock, or the riverbeds and salt stalactites on their cheeks; they were old, old men, the three-year boys, and not one of them over twenty-five.

I did three years and immediately signed on for another three; then another three after that, of which I served one. Then I was sent home, in disgrace. Nobody ever gets sent home from Ultramar, which is where the judge sends you if you've murdered someone and hanging is too good for you. They need every man they can get, and they use them up at a stupid rate, like a farmer with his winter fodder in a very bad year. They say that the enemy collects our bones from the battlefields and grinds them down for bonemeal, which is how come they have such excellent wheat harvests. The usual punishment for really unforgivable crimes in Ultramar is a tour of duty at the front; you have to prove genuine extenuating circumstances and show deep remorse to get the noose instead. Me, though, they sent home, in disgrace, because nobody could bear the sight of me a moment longer. And, to be fair, I can't say I blame them.

I don't sleep much. The people in the village say it's because I have nightmares, but really I simply don't find the time. Once you've started welding, you don't stop. Once you've welded the core, you want to get on and do the edges, then you want to weld the edges to the core, then the job's done, and there's some new pest nagging you to start the next one. I tend to sleep when I'm tired, which is roughly every four days.

In case your heart is bleeding for me; when the job's done and I get paid, I throw the money in an old barrel I brought back from the wars. I think originally it contained arrowheads. Anyway, I have no idea how much is in there, but it's about half-full. I do all right.

Like I told you, I lose track of time when I'm working. Also, I forget about things, such as people. I clean forgot about the boy for a whole day, but when I remembered him he was still there, perched on the spare anvil, his face black with dust and soot. He'd tied a bit of rag over his nose and mouth, which was fine by me since it stopped him talking.

"Haven't you got anything better to do?" I asked.

"No, not really." He yawned and stretched. "I think I'm starting to get the hang of this. Basically, it's the idea that a lot of strands woven together are stronger than just one. Like the body politic."

"Have you had anything to eat recently? Since you stole my apple?"

He shook his head. "Not hungry."

"Have you got any money for food?"

He smiled. "I've got a whole gold besant. I could buy a farm."

"Not around here."

"Yes, well, it's prime arable land. Where I come from, you could buy a whole valley."

I sighed. "There's bread and cheese indoors," I said, "and a side of bacon."

At least that got rid of him for a bit, and I closed up the fold and decided I needed a rest. I'd been staring at white-hot metal for rather too long, and I could barely see past all the pretty shining colours.

He came back with half a loaf and all my cheese. "Have some," he said, like he owned the place.

I don't talk with my mouth full, it's rude, so I waited till I'd finished. "So where are you from, then?"

"Fin Mohec. Heard of it?"

"It's a fair-sized town."

"Ten miles north of Fin, to be exact."

"I knew a man from Fin once."

"In Ultramar?"

I frowned. "Who told you that?"

"Someone in the village."

I nodded. "Nice part of the world, the Mohec valley."

"If you're a sheep, maybe. And we weren't in the valley, we were up on the moor. It's all heather and granite outcrops."

I've been there. "So," I said, "you left home to seek your fortune."

"Hardly." He spat something out, probably a hard bit of bacon rind. You can break your teeth on that stuff. "I'd go back like a shot if there were anything left for me there. Where were you in Ultramar, precisely?"

"Oh, all over the place," I said. "So, if you like the Mohec so much, why did you leave?"

"To come here. To see you. To buy a sword." A decidedly forced grin. "Why else?"

"What do you need a sword for in the Mohec hills?"

"I'm not going to use it there."

The words had come out in a rush, like beer spilt when some fool jostles your arm in the taproom. He took a deep breath, then went on, "At least, I don't imagine I will."

"Really."

He nodded. "I'm going to use it to kill the man who murdered my father, and I don't think he lives round here."

I got into this business by accident. That is, I got off the boat from Ultramar, and fifty yards from the dock was a forge. I had one thaler and five copper stuivers in my pocket, the clothes I'd worn under my armour for the last two years, and a sword worth twenty gold angels that I'd never sell, under any circumstances. I walked over to the forge and offered to give the smith the thaler if he taught me his trade.

"Get lost," he said.

People don't talk to me like that. So I spent the thaler on a third-hand anvil, a selection of unsuitable hammers, a rasp, a leg-vise and a bucket, and I lugged that damned anvil around with me—three hundredweight—until I found a half-derelict shed out back of a tannery. I offered the tanner three stuivers for rent, bought a stuiver's worth of rusty files and two barley loaves, and taught myself the trade, with the intention of putting the other smith out of business within a year.

In the event it took me six months. I grant you, I knew a little bit more about the trade than the foregoing implies; I'd sat in the smithy at home on cold mornings and watched our man there, and I pick things up quickly; also, you learned to do all sorts of things in Ultramar, particularly skills pertaining to repairing or improvising equipment, most of which we got from the enemy, with holes in it. When I decided to specialise, it was a toss-up whether I was going to be a sword-smith or an armourer. Literally; I flipped a coin for it. I lost the toss, and here I am.

Did I mention that I have my own water-wheel? I built it myself and I'm ridiculously proud of it. I based it on one I saw (saw, inspected, then set fire to) in Ultramar. It's overshot, with a twelve-foot throw, and it runs off a stream that comes tumbling and bouncing down the hill and over a sheer cliff where the hillside's fallen away. It powers my grindstone and my trip-hammer, the only trip-hammer north of the Vossin, also built by me. I'm a clever bugger.

You can't forge-weld with a trip-hammer; you need to be able to see what you're doing, and feel the metal flowing into itself. At least, I can't; I'm not perfect. But it's ideal for working the finished material down into shape, takes all the effort out of it, though by God you have to concentrate. A light touch is what you need. The hammer-head weighs half a ton. I've had so much practice I can use it to break the shell on a boiled egg.

I also made spring-swedges, for putting in fullers and profiling the edges of the blade. You can call it cheating if you like; I prefer to call it precision and perfection. Thanks to the trip-hammer and the swedges I get straight, even, flat, incrementally distal-tapered sword-blades that don't curl up like corkscrews when you harden and quench them; because every blow of the hammer is exactly the same strength as the previous one, and the swedges allow no scope for human error, such as you inevitably get trying to judge it all by eye.

If I were inclined to believe in gods, I think I'd probably worship the trip-hammer even though I made it myself. Reasons; first, it's so much stronger than I am, or any man living, and tireless, and those are essential qualities for a god. It sounds like a god; it drowns out everything, and you can't hear yourself think. Second, it's a creator. It shapes things, turns strips and bars of raw material into recognisable objects with a use and a life of their own. Third, and most significant, it rains down blows, tirelessly, overwhelmingly, it strikes twice in the time it takes my heart to beat once. It's a smiter, and that's what gods do, isn't it? They hammer and hammer and keep on hammering, till either you're swaged into shape or you're a bloody pulp.

"Is that it?" he said. I could tell he wasn't impressed.

"It's not finished. It has to be ground first."

My grindstone is as tall as I am, a flat round sandstone cheese. The river turns it, which is just as well because I couldn't. You have to be very careful, with the most delicate touch. It eats metal, and heats it too, so if your concentration wanders for a split second, you've drawn the temper and the sword will bend like a strip of lead. But I'm a real artist with a grindstone. I wrap a scarf three times round my nose and mouth, to keep the dust from choking me, and wear thick gloves, because if you touch the stone when it's running full tilt, it'll take your skin off down to the bone before you can flinch away. When you're grinding, you're the eye of a storm of white and gold sparks. They burn your skin and set your shirt on fire, but you can't let little things like that distract you.

Everything I do takes total concentration. Probably that's why I do this job.

I don't do fancy finishes. I say, if you want a mirror, buy a mirror. But my blades take and keep an edge you can shave with, and they come compass.

"Is this strictly necessary?" he asked, as I clamped the tang in the vise.

"No," I said, and reached for the wrench.

"Only, if you break it, you'll have to start again from scratch, and I want to get on."

"The best ever made," I reminded him, and he gave me a grudging nod.

For that job I use a scroll monkey. It's a sort of massive fork you use for bending scrollwork, if that's your idea of a useful and productive life. It takes every last drop of my strength (and I'm no weakling), all to perform a test that might well wreck the thing that's been my life and soul for the last ten days and nights, which the customer barely appreciates and which makes me feel sick to my stomach. But it has to be done. You bend the blade until the tip touches the jaw of the vise, then you gently let it go back. Out it comes from the vise, and you lay it on the perfectly straight, flat bed of the anvil. You get down on your knees, looking for a tiny hair of light between the edge of the blade and the anvil. If you see it, the blade goes in the scrap.

"Here," I said, "come and look for yourself."

He got down beside me. "What am I looking for, exactly?"

"Nothing. It isn't there. That's the point."

"Can I get up now, please?"

Perfectly straight; so straight that not even light can squeeze through the gap. I hate all the steps on the way to perfection, the effort and the noise and the heat and the dust, but when you get there, you're glad to be alive.

I slid the hilt, grip, and pommel down over the tang, fixed the blade in the vise, and peened the end of the tang into a neat little button. Then I took the sword out of the vise and offered it to him, hilt first. "All done," I said.

"Finished?"

"Finished. All yours."

I remember one kid I made a sword for, an earl's son, seven feet tall and strong as a bull. I handed him his finished sword; he took a good grip on the hilt, then swung it round his head and brought it down full power on the horn of the anvil. It bit a chunk out, then bounced back a foot in the air, the edge undamaged. So I punched him halfway across the room. You clown, I said, look what you've done to my anvil. When he got up, he was in tears. But I forgave him, years later. There's a thrill when you hold a good sword for the first time. It sort of tugs at your hands, like a dog wanting to be taken for a walk. You want to swish it about and hit things with it. At the very least, you do a few cuts and wards, on the pretext of checking the balance and the handling.

He just took it from me, as though I'd given him a shopping list. "Thanks," he said.

"My pleasure," I replied. "Well, good-bye. You can go now," I added, when he didn't move. "I'm busy."

"There was something else," he said.

I'd already turned my back on him. "What?"

"I don't know how to fence."

He was born, he told me, in a haybarn on the moor overlooking his father's house, at noon on midsummer's day. His mother, who should have known better, had insisted on riding out in the dog-cart with her maid to take lunch to the hawking party. Her pains came on, and there wasn't time to get back to the house, but the barn was there and full of clean hay, with a stream nearby. His father, riding home with his hawk on his wrist, saw her from the track, lying in the hay with the baby on her lap. He'd had a good day, he told her. They'd got four pigeons and a heron.

His father hadn't wanted to go to Ultramar; but he held of the duke and the duke was going, so he didn't really have any choice. In the event, the duke died of camp-fever a week after they landed. The boy's father lasted nine months; then he got himself killed, by his best friend, in a pointless brawl in a tavern. He was twenty-two when he died. "The same age," said the boy, "as I am now."

"That's a sad story," I told him. "And a very stupid one. Mind you, all stories from Ultramar are stupid if you ask me."

He scowled at me. "Maybe there's too much stupidity in the world," he said. "Maybe I want to do something about it."

I nodded. "You could diminish the quantity considerably by dying, I grant you. But maybe it's too high a price to pay."

His eyes were cold and bright. "The man who killed my father is still alive," he said. "He's settled and prosperous, happy, he's got everything he could possibly want. He came through the nightmare of Ultramar, and now the world makes sense to him again, and he's a useful and productive member of society, admired and respected by his peers and his betters."

"So you're going to cut his throat."

He shook his head. "Not likely," he said. "That would be murder. No, I'm going to fight him sword to sword. I'm going to beat him and prove myself the better man. Then I'll kill him."

I was tactfully silent for a moment. Then I said; "And you know absolutely nothing about sword-fighting."

"No. My father should've taught me, it's what fathers do. But he died when I was two years old. I don't know the first thing about it."

"And you're going to challenge an old soldier, and you're going to prove yourself the better man. I see."

He was looking me straight in the eye. I always feel uncomfortable when people do that even though I spend my life gazing at white-hot metal. "I asked about you," he said. "They reckon you were a great fencer."

I sighed. "Who told you that?"

"Were you?"

"*Were* implies a state of affairs that no longer prevails," I said. "Who told you about me?"

He shrugged. "Friends of my father. You were a legend in Ultramar, apparently. Everybody'd heard of you."

"The defining characteristic of a legend is that it isn't true," I said. "I can fight, a bit. What's that got to do with anything?"

"You're going to teach me."

I remember one time in Ultramar, we were smashing up this village. We did a lot of that. They called it *chevauchee*, but that's just chivalry talk for burning barns and stamping on chickens. It's supposed to break the enemy's will to fight. Curiously enough, it has exactly the opposite effect. Anyway, I was in this farmyard. I had a torch in my hand, and I was going to set fire to a hayrick, like you do. And there was this dog. It was a stupid little thing, the sort you keep to catch rats, little more than a rat itself; and it jumped out at me, barking its head off, and it sank its teeth into my leg, and it simply would not let go, and I couldn't get at it to stab it with my knife, not without stabbing myself in the process. I dropped the torch and danced round the farmyard, trying to squash it against walls, but it didn't seem to make any odds. It was the most ridiculous little thing, and in the end it beat me. I staggered out into the lane, and it let go, dropped off, and sprinted back into the yard. My sergeant had to light the rick with a fire-arrow, and I never lived it down.

I looked at him. I recognised the look in his silly pink face. "Is that right," I said.

"Yes. I need the best sword and the best teacher. I'll pay you. You can have the fifth coin."

A gold besant. Actually, the proper name is *hyperpyron*, meaning "extra fine." The enemy took so many of them off us in Ultramar that they adopted them in place of their own currency. That's war for you; the enemy turn into you, and you turn into them, like the iron and steel rods under the hammer. The only besants you see over here are ones that got brought back, but they're current everywhere. "I'm not interested in money," I said.

"I know. Neither am I. But if you pay a man to do a job and he takes your money, he's obliged."

"I'm a lousy teacher," I told him.

"That's all right, I'm a hopeless student. We'll get on like a barn on fire."

If ever I get a dog, it'll be one of those rat-like terriers. Maybe I just warm to aggressive creatures, I don't know. "You can take your coin and stick it where the sun doesn't shine," I told him. "You overpaid me for the sword. We'll call it change."

The sword isn't a very good weapon. Most forms of armour are proof against it, including a properly padded jerkin, it's too long to be handy in a scrum and too light and flimsy for serious bashing. In a pitched battle, give me a spear or an axe any time; in fact, nine times out of ten you'd be better off with everyday farm tools—staff-hooks, beanhooks, muck-forks, provided they're made of good material and properly tempered. Better still, give me a bow and someone in armour to hide behind. The fighting man's best view of a battlefield is down an arrow, from under a pikeman's armpit. For self-defence on the road, I favour the quarterstaff; in the street or indoors, where space to move is at a premium, the knife you cut your bread and peel your apples with is as good as anything. You're used to it, for one thing, and you know where it is on your belt without having to look.

About the only thing a sword is really good for is sword-fighting—which in practice means duelling, which is idiotic and against the law, or fencing, which is playing at fighting, good fun and nobody gets hurt, but not really my idea of entertainment—and showing off. Which is why, needless to say, we all went to Ultramar with swords on our hips. Some of us had beautiful new swords, the more fortunate ones had really old swords, family heirlooms, worth a thousand acres of good farmland, with buildings, stock, and tenants. The thing is—don't say I told you so—the old ones aren't necessarily the best. There was even less good steel about two hundred years ago than there is now, and men were stronger then, so old swords are heavier, harder to use, broader, and with rounded points for cutting, not thrusting. Not that it mattered. Most of those young swashbucklers died of the poisoned shits, before the desert sun had had a chance to fade the clothes they arrived in, and their swords were sold to pay their mess bills. You could pick up some real bargains back then, in Ultramar.

"I don't know how to teach," I said, "I've never ever done it. So I'm going to teach you the way my father taught me, because it's the only way I know. Is that all right?"

He didn't notice me picking up the rake. "Fine," he said. So I pulled the head off the rake—it was always loose—and hit him with the handle.

I remember my first lesson so well. The main difference was, my father used a broom. First, he poked me in the stomach, hard, with one end. As I doubled up, gasping for breath, he hit my knee-cap, so I fell over. Then he put the end of the broom-handle on my throat and applied controlled pressure.

I could only just breathe. "You didn't get out of the way," he explained.

I was five when I had my first lesson, and easier to teach to the ground than a full-grown man. I had to tread on the inside of his knee to get him to drop. When eventually he got his breath back, I saw he was crying; actually in tears. "You didn't get out of the way," I explained.

He looked up at me and wiped his nose with the back of his hand. "I see," he said.

"You won't make that mistake again," I told him. "From now on, whenever a fellow human being is close enough to hit you, you're going to assume that he's going to hit you. You'll keep your distance, or you'll be ready to avoid at a split-second's notice. Got that?"

"I think so."

"No exceptions," I said. "Not any, ever. Your brother, your best friend, your wife, your six-year-old daughter, it makes no odds. Otherwise you'll never be a fighter."

He stared at me for a moment, and I guessed he'd understood. It was like that moment in the old play, where the Devil offers the scholar the contract, and the scholar signs it.

"Get up."

I hit him again when he was halfway to his feet. It was just a light tap on the collarbone; just enough to hurt like hell without breaking anything.

"This is all for my own good, I take it."

"Oh yes. This is the most important lesson you'll ever learn."

We spent the next four hours on footwork; the traces, which is backwards and forwards, and the traverses, which is side to side. Each time I hit him, I laid it on a bit harder. He got there eventually.

My father wasn't a bad man. He loved his family dearly, with all his heart; nothing meant more to him. But he had a slight, let's say, kink in his nature—like the cold spot or the inclusion you sometimes get in a weld, where the metal wasn't quite hot enough, or a bit of grit or crap gets beaten into the joint. He liked hurting people; it gave him a thrill. Only people, not animals. He was a fine stockman and a humane and conscientious hunter, but he dearly loved to hit people and make them squeal.

I can understand that, partly because I'm the same though to a lesser degree, and I control it better. Maybe it's always been there in the blood, or maybe it was a souvenir from Ultramar; both, probably. I rationalise it in forge-welding terms. You can heat the metal white-hot, but you can't just lay one bit on top of the other and expect them to weld. You've got to hit them to make the join. Carefully, judiciously, not too hard and not too soft. Just enough to make the metal cry, and weep sparks. I hate it when they burst into tears, though. It makes me despise them, and I have to take pains to control my temper. Anyway, you can see why I like to stay out of people's way. I know what's wrong with me; and knowing your own flaws is the beginning of wisdom. I'm sort of a reverse fencer. I stay well out of distance, partly so that people can't hit me, mostly so I can't hit them.

Once you've learned footwork, the rest is relatively easy. I taught him the eight cuts and the seven wards (I stick to seven; the other four are just elaborations). He picked them up quickly, now that he understood the essence—*don't let him hurt you*, followed by *make him safe*.

"The best way to make a man safe," I told him, "is to hurt him. Pain will stop him in his tracks. Killing doesn't always do it. You can stab a man and he'll be past all hope, but he can still hurt you very badly before he drops to the ground. But if you paralyse him with pain, he's no longer a threat. You can then despatch him, or let him go, at your pleasure."

I demonstrated; I flicked past his guard and prodded him in the stomach with my rake-handle; a lethal thrust, but he was still on his feet. Then I cracked him on the knee, and he dropped. "Killing's irrelevant," I told him. "Pain wins fights. That's unless you've absolutely set your heart on cleaving him to the navel, and that's just melodrama, which will get you killed. In a battle, hurt him and move on to the next threat. In a duel, win and be merciful. Fewer legal problems that way."

I was rather enjoying being a teacher, as you've probably gathered. I was passing on valuable knowledge and skill, which is in itself rewarding, I was showing off and I was hitting an annoying sprig of the nobility for his own good. What's not to like?

You learn best when you're exhausted, desperate, and in pain. Ultramar taught me that. I kept him at it from dawn till dusk, and then we lit the lamp and did theory. I taught him the line and the circle. Instinctively you want to fight up and down a line, forwards to attack, backwards to defend; parry, then lunge, then parry. All wrong. Idiotic. Instead, you should fight in a circle, stepping sideways, so you avoid him and can hit him at the same time. Never just defend; always counterattack. Every handstroke you make should be a killing stroke, or a stopping stroke. And for every movement of the hand, a movement of the foot—there, I've just taught you the whole secret and mystery of swordsmanship, and I never had to hit you once.

"Most fights," I told him, giving him a chance to wipe the blood out of his eyes before we moved on, "in which at least one party is competent, last one to four seconds. Anything more than that is a fitting subject for epic poetry." Judging that he wasn't ready yet, I shot a quick *mandiritto* at the side of his head. He stepped back and left out of the way without thinking, and my heart rejoiced inside me, as I side-stepped his riposte in straight time and closed the door with the Third ward. So far he hadn't hit me once, which was a little disappointing; but he'd come close four times, in six hours. Very promising indeed. He just lacked the killer instinct.

"The Fifth ward," I went on, and he lunged. I almost didn't read it, because he'd disguised the Boar's Tooth as the Iron Gate; all I could do was trace back very fast and smack the stick out of his hands. Then I whacked him, for interrupting me when I was talking. He very nearly got out of the way, but I wanted to hit him, so he couldn't.

He had to pick himself up off the ground after that. I took a long step back, to signal a truce. "I think it's time for a progress report," I said. "At the moment, you're very good indeed. Not the best in the world, but more than capable of beating ninety-nine men in a hundred. Would you like to stop there and save yourself further pain and humiliation?"

He got up slowly and dabbed at his cut eye. "I want to be the best," he said. "If that's all right."

I shrugged. "I don't think you ever can be," I told him. "In order to be the best, you have to lose so much. It's just not worth it. Being the best will make you into a monster. Stick with just plain good, you'll be so much happier."

He was a pitiful sight, all cuts and bruises. But still, under all the blood and discoloured tissue, a hopeful, pretty boy. "I think I'd like to carry on just a bit longer if you don't mind."

"Please yourself," I said, and let him pick up his stick.

Actually, he reminded me a lot of myself at his age.

I was a brash, irritating boy when I went to Ultramar. I'd known all along that I wasn't going to get the land, having elder brothers in good health. Probably I'd always resented that. I think I'd have made a good farmer. I was always the one who wasn't afraid of hard work, who saw the need to get things done—not tomorrow, or when we've got five minutes, or when it stops raining, but now, right now; before the roof-tree breaks and the barn falls down, before the fence-posts snap off and the sheep get out into the marsh, before the oats spoil on the stalk, before the meat goes off in the heat; now while there's still time, before it's too late. Instead, I saw the place gradually falling to pieces—and decline and decay are so peacefully gradual; grass takes so long to grow up through the cobbles, it's imperceptible, therefore not threatening. But my father and my brothers didn't share my view. I was keen to get away from them. I wanted to take a sword and slice myself a fat chunk of the world off the bone. There's good land in Ultramar, they told me, all it needs is a bit of hard work and it could be the best in the world.

The very best; that's a concept that's danced ahead of me, just out of reach, all my life. Now, of course, I am the very best, at one small corner of one specific craft. I'm stuck, wedged in by my own pre-eminence, like a rafter lying across your leg in a burning house.

But never mind; I went to Ultramar aiming to be a farmer. When I got there, I found what was left after seventy years of continual recipro-cal *chevauchees*. I recognised it at once. It was what was going to happen to my father's land back home, but in macrocosm. All the barns fallen, all the fences broken down, all the crops spoilt, briars and nettles neck-high in all the good pastures; the effects of peace and idleness acceler-ated and forced (like you force early crops, under straw) by the merely instrumental action of the wars. Cut myself off a slice of *that*, I said to myself; why the hell would I want to bother? So I started hurting people instead.

And the thing is, if you do it in war, they praise you for it. Strange, but true.

In war, there's so much scope, you can afford to be selective. You can afford to limit yourself to hurting the enemy, of whom there are plenty to go round, and twice as many again once you've finished what's on your plate. I survived in Ultramar because I was having the time of my life, for a while.

Odd thing about farmers; they love their land and their stock and their buildings, fences, trees, but give them the chance to wreck someone else's land, kill their stock, burn their buildings, smash their fences, maim their trees, and after a brief show of reluctance they go to it with a will. I think it's just basic revenge; take that, agriculture, that'll learn you. Volunteers for a *chevauchee*? My hand was up before I had time to think.

And then I did something bad, and I had to come home. I cried when they pronounced sentence. I despise men who cry. They told me I was to be spared the noose in recognition of my years of valiant and honourable service. I don't think so. I think they were just being very, very spiteful.

There came a moment, very sudden and unexpected, when it was over, and I'd succeeded. I went to smack him—a feint high followed by a cut low—and he simply wasn't there to be hit; and then my ear stung horribly, and while I was confused and distracted by the pain, he dug me in the pit of the stomach with his broom-handle.

He wasn't like me. He took a long step back and let me recover. "I'm sorry," he said.

It took me quite awhile to get back enough breath to say, "No, don't apologise, whatever you do." Then I squared up into First. "Again."

"Really?"

"Don't be so bloody stupid. Again."

I let him come at me, because attacking is so much harder. I read him like a book, swung easily into a traverse and the devastating *volte*, my speciality; and he cracked me on the elbow as I floundered past him, then prodded me in the small of the back, just before I overbalanced and fell over.

He helped me up. "I think I'm starting to get the hang of this," he said.

I went for him. I wanted to beat him, more than I've ever wanted anything. I couldn't get anywhere near him, and he kept hitting me, gently, just to make a point. After a dozen or so passes, I dropped to my knees. All my strength had drained out of me, as though one of his gentle prods had punctured right to my heart. "I give up," I said. "You win."

He was looking down at me with a sort of confused frown. "I don't follow."

"You've beaten me," I said. "You're now the better man."

"Really?"

"What do you want, a bloody certificate? Yes."

He nodded slowly. "Which makes you the best ever teacher," he said. "Thank you."

I threw away the rake-handle. "You're welcome," I said. "Now go away. We're finished with each other."

He was still looking at me. "So am I really the best swordsman in the world?"

I laughed. "I don't know about that," I said, "but you're better than me. That makes you very good indeed. I hope you're satisfied because as far as I'm concerned, this has been a pretty pointless exercise."

"No," he said, and his tone of voice made me look at him. "This was all for a purpose, remember."

Actually, I'd forgotten, briefly. "Oh yes," I said, "it's so you can kill the man who murdered your father." I shook my head. "You still want to do that."

"Oh yes."

I sighed. "I'd hoped I might have smacked some sense into you," I said. "Come on, you must've learned something. Think about it. What's that possibly going to achieve?"

"It'll make me feel better," he said.

"Right. I don't think so. I've killed God knows how many people, all of them the enemy, and believe me, it never makes you feel better. It just hardens you, like forging the edges."

He grinned. "And hard is brittle, yes, I know. The extended metaphor hasn't been lost on me, I assure you."

It didn't hurt quite so much by then, and I was breathing almost normally. "Well," I said, "I guess it's something you've got to get out of your system, then you can get on with your life. You carry on, and good luck to you."

He smiled at me, awkwardly. "So I have your blessing, then?"

"That's a bloody stupid way of putting it, but if you want to, then yes. My blessing goes with you, my son. There, is that what you wanted?"

He laughed. "As a father you have been to me, for a little while." It was a quotation from somewhere, though I can't place it. "You think I can beat him?"

"I don't see why not."

"Neither do I," he said. "It's always easier the second time."

Now I'm not particularly slow on the uptake, not usually. But I admit, it took me a moment. And in that moment, he said, "You never asked my name."

"Well?"

"My name is Aimeric de Peguilhan," he said. "My father was Bernhart de Peguilhan. You murdered him in a brawl, in Ultramar. You smashed his skull with a stone bottle, when his back was turned." He dropped the broom-handle. "Wait there," he said, "I'll fetch the swords and be right back."

I'm telling this story, so you know what happened.

He had the best sword ever made, and I'd taught him everything I ever knew, and he ended up better than me; he was always better than me, just like his father. Nearly everybody's better than me, in most respects. One way in which he excelled me was, he lacked the killer instinct.

But he made a pretty fight of it, I'll give him that. I wish I could have watched that fight instead of being in it; there never was better entertainment, and all wasted, because there was nobody to see. Naturally you lose all track of time, but my best educated guess is, we fought for at least five minutes, which is an eternity, and never a hair's breadth of difference between us. It was like fighting your own shadow, or your reflection in the mirror. I read his mind, he read mine. To continue the tedious extended metaphor, it was forge-welding at its finest. Well; I look back on it in these terms, the same way I look back on all my best completed work, with pleasure once it's over but hating every minute of it while I'm actually doing it.

When I wake up in the middle of the night in a muck-sweat, I tell myself I won because he trod on a stone and turned his ankle, and the tiny atom of advantage was enough. But it's not true. I'm ashamed to say I beat him fair and square, through stamina and the simple desire to win: killer instinct. I made a little window of opportunity by feigning an error. He believed me, and was deceived. It was only a tiny opportunity, no scope for choice; I had a fraction of a second when his throat was exposed and I could reach it with a scratch-cut with the point, what we call a *stramazone*. I cut his throat, then jumped back to keep from getting splashed all over. Then I buried him in the midden, along with the pig-bones and the household shit.

He should have won. Of course he should. He was basically a good kid, and had he lived he'd probably have been all right, more or less; no worse than my father, at any rate, and definitely a damn sight better than me. I like to tell myself, he died so quickly he never knew he'd lost.

But; on the day, I proved myself the better man, which is what sword-fighting is all about. It's a simple, infallible test, and he failed and I passed. The best man always wins; because the definition of *best* is *still alive at the end*. Feel at liberty to disagree, but you'll be wrong. I hate it, but it's the only definition that makes any sense at all.

Every morning I cough up black soot and grey mud, the gift of the fire and the grindstone. Smiths don't live long. The harder you work, the better you get, the more poisonous muck you breathe in. My pre-eminence will be the death of me, someday.

I sold his sword to the Duke of Scona for, I forget how much; it was a stupid amount of money, at any rate, but the Duke said he wanted the very best, and he got what he paid for. My barrel of gold is now nearly full, incidentally. I don't know what I'll do when the level reaches the top. Something idiotic, probably.

I may have all the other faults in the world, but at least I'm honest. You have to grant me that.

Robin Hobb

· · ·

New *York Times* bestseller Robin Hobb is one of the most popular writers in fantasy today, having sold more than one million copies of her work in paperback. She's perhaps best known for her epic fantasy Farseer series, including *Assassin's Apprentice*, *Royal Assassin*, *Assassin's Quest*, as well as the two fantasy series related to it, the Liveship Traders series, consisting of *Ship of Magic*, *The Mad Ship*, and *Ship of Destiny*, and the Tawny Man series, made up of *Fool's Errand*, *The Golden Fool*, and *Fool's Fate*. She's also the author of the Soldier Son series, composed of *Shaman's Crossing*, *Forest Mage*, and *Renegade's Magic*, and the Rain Wild Chronicles, consisting of *Dragon Keeper*, *Dragon Haven*, *City of Dragons*, and *Blood of Dragons*. Most recently she's started a new series, the Fitz and the Fool trilogy, consisting of *Fool's Assassin*, *Fool's Quest*, and, coming up in 2017, *Assassin's Fate*. Hobb also writes under her real name, Megan Lindholm. Books by Megan Lindholm include the fantasy novels *Wizard of the Pigeons*, *Harpy's Flight*, *The Windsingers*, *The Limbreth Gate*, *Luck of the Wolves*, *The Reindeer People*, *Wolf's Brother*, and *Cloven Hooves*, the science-fiction novel *Alien Earth*, and, with Steven Brust, the collaborative novel *The Gypsy*. Lindholm's most recent book is a "collaborative" collection with Robin Hobb, *The Inheritance: And Other Stories*.

In the chilling tale that follows, FitzChivalry Farseer visits a village caught up in the Red Ship Wars, where the unhappy villagers face some very hard choices, none of them good—and some of them worse than others.

◆　◆　◆

Her Father's Sword

ROBIN HOBB

Taura shifted on her lookout's platform. Cold was stiffening her, and calling two skinny logs tied across a couple of outreaching branches a "watchtower platform" was generous. A flat surface would have been kinder to her buttocks and back. She shifted to a squat and checked the position of the moon again. When it was over the Hummock on Last Chance Point, her watch would be over and Kerry would come to relieve her. In theory.

They'd given her the least likely point of entry to the village. Her tree overlooked the market trail that led inland, to Higround Market where they sold their fish. Unlikely that Forged would come from this direction. The kidnapped people had been forced from their homes and down to the beach. Past their burned fishing boats and the ransacked smoking racks for preserving the catch the captured townsfolk had gone. A boy who had dared to follow his kidnapped mother said the raiders had forced their folk into boats and rowed them out to a red-hulled ship anchored offshore. As they had been taken to the sea, so they would return from the waves.

Taura had seen them go from her hiding place in the big willow that overlooked the harbor. The raiders hadn't seemed to care who they took. She'd seen old Pa Grimby, and Salal Greenoak carrying her nursing baby. She'd seen the little Bodby twins and Kelia and Rudan and Cope. And her father, roaring and staggering with blood sheeting down the side of his face. She had known the names of almost every captive. Smokerscot was not a big village. There were perhaps six hundred folk here.

Well. There had been perhaps six hundred. Before the raid.

After the raid, Taura had helped stack the bodies after they'd put out the fires. She'd stopped counting after forty, and those were just the people in the stack on the east end of the village. There'd been another pyre near the rickety dock. No. The dock wasn't rickety anymore. It was charred pilings sticking out of the water next to the sunken hulks of the small fishing fleet. Her father's boat was among them. The changes had all happened so fast that it was hard to remember them. Earlier tonight, she'd decided to run back home and get a warmer cloak. Then she'd recalled that her home was wet ash and charred planks. It wasn't the only one. The five adjoining houses had burned, and dozens of others in the village. Even the Kelp's grand house, two stories, not even finished, was now a smoking pile of timbers.

She shifted on her platform and something poked her. She'd sat on her whistle on its lanyard. The village council had given her a cudgel and a whistle to blow if she saw anyone approaching. Two blasts from her whistle would bring the strong folk from the village with their "weapons." They would come with their poles and axes and gaff hooks. And Jelin would come, wearing her father's sword. What if no one came to her whistle? She had a cudgel. As if she were going to climb down from the tree and try to bash someone. As if she could bear to club people she had known since she was a babe.

A rhythmic clopping reached her ears. A horse approaching? It was past sundown, and few travelers came to Smokerscot at any time, save the fish buyers who came at the end of summer to dicker for the fall run of redfish. But in winter, and after dark? Who would be coming this way? She watched the narrow stripe of hard-packed earth that led through the forested hills to Higround, peering through the darkness.

A horse and rider came into sight. A single rider and horse, bearing a lumpy bundle on the saddle before him and two bulging panniers behind him. As she stared, the bundle wriggled and gave a long whine, then burst into the full-throated fury of an angry child.

She blew a single blast on her whistle, the "maybe it's danger" signal. The rider halted and stared toward her perch. He did not reach for a bow. Indeed, it looked to be all he could do to restrain the child that he held before him. She stood, rolled her back a bit to remove some of the chill-stiffened kinks, and began the climb down. By the time she reached the ground, Marva and Carber had appeared. And Kerry, long past his time to come and relieve her. They stood with tall poles, blocking the horse's path. Over the sound of the child's wailing, they were trying to question him. By their torches, she saw a young man with dark hair and eyes. His thick wool cloak was Buck blue. She wondered what was in his horse's panniers.

He finally shouted, "Will someone take this boy from me? He says his name is Peevy and his mother's name is Kelia! He said he lived in Smokerscot, and pointed this way. Does he belong here?"

"Kelia's boy!" Marva exclaimed, and came closer to examine the kicking, wriggling child. "Peevy! Peevy, it's me, Cousin Marva. Come to me, now! Come to me."

As the man started to lower the child from his tall black mount, the small boy twisted to hit at him shouting, "I hate you! I hate you! Let me go!"

Marva stepped back suddenly. "He's Forged, isn't he? Oh, sweet Eda, what shall we do? He's just four, and Kelia's only child. The raiders must have taken him when they took her. I thought he'd died in the fires!"

"He's not Forged," the rider said with some impatience. "He's angry because I had no food for him. Please. Take him." The youngster was kicking his heels against the horse's shoulder and varying his now-incoherent wails with shouting for his mother. Marva stepped forward. Peevy kicked her a few times before she engulfed him in her arms. "Peevy, Peevy, it's me, you're safe! Oh, lovey, you're safe now. You're so cold! Can you calm down?"

"I'm hungry!" the boy shouted. "I'm cold. Mosquitoes bit me and I cut my hands on the barnacles and Mama threw me off the boat! She threw me off the boat into the dark water and she didn't care! I screamed and the boat left me in the water. And the waves pushed me and I had to climb up the rocks, then I was losted in the wood!" He aired all his grievances in a child's shrill voice.

Taura edged up beside Kerry. "Your watch, now," she reminded him.

"I know that," he told her in disdain as he stared down at her. She shrugged. She'd reminded him. It wasn't her task to see he did his share. She'd done hers.

The stranger dismounted. He led his horse into the village as if certain of that right. Taura marked how everyone fell in around him, forgetting to challenge him at all. Well, he wasn't Forged. A Forged one would never have helped a child. He gave the boy in Marva's arms a sympathetic look. "That explains a great deal." He looked over at Carber. "The boy darted out of the forest right in front of my horse, crying and shouting for help. I'm glad he has kin still alive to take him in. And sorry that you were raided. You aren't the only ones. Up the coast, Shrike was raided last week. That's where I was bound."

"And who are you?" Carber demanded suspiciously.

"King Shrewd received a bird from Shrike and dispatched me right away. My name is FitzChivalry Farseer. I was sent to help at Shrike; I didn't know you'd been raided as well. I cannot stay long, but I can tell you what you need to know to deal with this." He lifted his voice to address those who had trooped out to see what Taura's whistle meant. "I can teach you how to deal with the Forged ones. As much as we know how to deal with them." He looked around at the circle of staring faces, and said more strongly, "The king has sent me to help folk like you. Man your watch stations, but call a meeting of everyone else in the village. I need to speak to all of you. Your Forged ones may return at any time."

"One man?" Carber asked angrily. "We send word to our king that we are raided, that folk are carried off by the Red-Ship Raiders, and he sends us one man?"

"Chivalry's bastard," someone said. It sounded like Hedley, but Taura couldn't be certain in the dusk. Folk were coming out of the houses that remained standing and joining the trailing group of people following the messenger and his horse. The man ignored the slur.

"The king did not send me here but to Shrike. I've come out of my way to bring the boy back to you. Did the raiders leave your inn standing? I'd appreciate a meal and a place to stable my horse. Last night we were out in the rain. And the inn might be a good place for folk to gather to hear what I have to say."

"Smokerscot never had an inn. Not much call for one. The road ends here, at the cove. Everyone who lives here sleeps in his own bed at night." Carber sounded insulted that the king's man could have imagined Smokerscot had an inn.

"They used to," Taura said quietly. "Now a lot of us don't have beds to sleep in." Where was she going to sleep tonight? Probably at her neighbor's house. Jelin had offered her a blanket on the floor by his fire. That was a kind thing to do, her mother had said. The neighborly thing to do. Her younger brother Gef had echoed her words exactly. And when Jelin had asked for it, they'd given him Papa's sword. As if they owed it to him for doing a decent thing. The sword was one of the few things they had saved from their house when the raiders set it on fire. "Your brother is too young, and you will never be strong enough to swing it. Let Jelin have it." So her mother had said and sternly shushed her when she'd discovered what they had done. "Remember what your father always said. Do what you must to survive and don't look back."

Taura recalled well when he'd said that. He and his crew of two had dumped most of their catch overboard so they could ride out a sudden storm. Taura thought it was quite one thing to surrender something valuable to stay alive and quite another to give away the last valuable thing they had to a swaggering braggart. Her mother might say she'd never be strong enough to swing it, but she didn't know that Taura could already lift it. Several times when her father had taken it out of an evening to wipe it clean and oil it fresh, he'd let her hold it. It always took both her hands, but the last time, she'd been able to lift it and swing it, however awkwardly. Papa had given a gruff laugh. "The heart but not the muscle. Too bad. I could have used a tall son with your spirit." He'd given Gef a sideways glance. "Or any sort of a son with a mind," he'd mutter.

But she had not been a son, and instead of her father's size and strength, she was small, like her mother. She was of an age to work the boat alongside her father, but he'd never taken her. "Not enough room on the deck for a hand who can't pull the full weight of a deckhand's duties. It's too bad." And that was the end of it. But still, later that month, he'd again let her lift the bared sword. She'd swung it twice before the weight of it had drawn the point of it down to the earth again.

And her father had smiled at her.

But now Papa was gone, taken by the Red-Ship Raiders. And she had nothing of his.

Taura was the elder; the sword should have been hers, whether she could swing it or not. But the way it had happened, she'd had no real say. She'd come back from dragging bodies to the pyre, come back to Jelin's house to see the sword standing in its sheath in the corner, like a broom! She and her mother and Gef could sleep on the floor of Jelin's house, and he could have the last valuable item her family owned. And her mother thought that good. How was that a fair trade? It cost him nothing for them to sleep on his floor. Clearly her mother had no idea of how to survive.

Don't think about that.

". . . the fish-smoking shed," Carber was saying. "It's mostly empty now. But we can start up the fires for heat instead of smoke and gather a lot of folk there."

"That would be good," the stranger said.

Marva smiled up at him. Peevy had stopped struggling. He had his arms around his cousin's neck and his face buried in her cloak. "There is room in our home for you to sleep, sir. And too much room now in our goat shed for your horse." Her smile twisted bitterly. "The raiders left us few animals to shelter. What they did not take they killed."

"I'm sorry to hear that," he said wearily, and it seemed to Taura it was a tale he had heard before and perhaps that was what he always replied to it.

Carber sent runners through the village, calling the folk to gather in the fish-smoking shed. Taura felt childish satisfaction when he ordered Kerry to take up his watch. She followed the crowd to the shed. Several families were already sheltering there. They had a fire going and had set up makeshift households in different parts of the shed.

Had her mother thought of coming here? At least they would still be a separate family, a household. They would still have had Papa's sword.

Carber tipped over a crate for the messenger to stand upon, as the villagers gathered in the barn-like shed that always smelt of alder smoke and fish. The folk trickled in slowly and Taura could see the stranger's impatience growing. Finally he climbed onto his small stage and called for silence. "We dare not wait any longer. The Forged will be returned to your village at any time now. That we know. It is a pattern the Red-Ship Raiders have followed since they first attacked Forge and returned half its inhabitants as heartless ghosts of themselves." He looked down and saw the confusion on the faces that surrounded him. He spoke more simply. "The Red Ships come. The raiders kill and they plunder, but their real destruction comes after they have left. They carry off those you love. They do something to them, something we don't understand. They hold them for a time, then give them back to you, their families. They will return tired, hungry, wet, and cold. They will look like your kin and they will call you by name. But they will not be the folk who left here."

He looked out over the gathered folk and shook his head at the hope and disbelief that his words had stirred. Taura watched him try to explain. "They will recall your faces and names. A father will know his children's names and a baker will recall her pans and oven. They will seek out their own homes. But you must not let them into your village or homes. Because they will care nothing for you, only for themselves. Theft and beatings, murders and rape will come with them."

Taura stared up at him. His words made no sense. Other faces reflected the same confusion, for the man shook his head sorrowfully. "It's difficult to explain. A father will snatch food from his little boy's mouth. If you have something they want, they will take it, regardless of how much violence they must use. If they are hungry, they will take all the food for themselves, drive you from your homes if they wish shelter." His voice dropped as he added, "If they feel lust, they will rape." His gaze roved over them, then he added, "They will rape anyone."

He shook his head at the disbelief on their faces. "Listen to me, please! Everything you have heard about the Forged, every rumor you have heard is true. Go home and fortify your homes now. Tighten the shutters on your windows, be sure the bars on your doors are strong. Organize the people who will protect this village. Assemble them. Arm yourselves. You've set a watch. That's good."

He drew breath and Taura called into the pause, "But what are we to do when they come?"

He looked directly at her. Possibly he was a handsome man, when he was not cold and weary. The tops of his cheeks were red and his dark hair lank with rain or sweat. His brown eyes were agonized. "The people who went away are not coming back to you. The Forged will not change back into those people. Ever." His next words came out harshly. "You must be prepared to kill them. Before they kill you."

Abruptly, Taura hated him. Handsome or not, he was talking about her father. Her father, big, strong Burk, coming back from a day's fishing, unarmed and unprepared to be clubbed down and dragged away. When her mother had screamed at her to run and hide, she had. She'd been so sure that her father, her big strong Papa, would fight his way clear of his captors. So she had done nothing to help him. She'd hidden in the thicket of the willow's branches while he was dragged away.

The next morning, she and her mother found each other when they returned to the remains of their house. Gef had stood outside their burned home, wailing as if he were five instead of thirteen. They'd let him stand and weep. Both Taura and her mother knew there was no getting through to her simple brother. In a light drizzle of freezing rain, they'd poked through the scorched timbers and the thick ash of the fallen thatch that had been their home. There had been little to salvage. Gef had stood and bawled as Taura and her mother had poked through the smoldering wreckage. A few cooking pots and three woolen blankets had been in a heavy cupboard that had somehow not burned through. A bowl and three plates. Then she'd found, sheltered beneath a fallen timber and unscorched, her father's sword in its fine sheath. The sword that would have saved him if he'd had it with him.

Worthless Jelin now claimed it as his. The sword that should have been hers. She knew how her father would have reacted to her mother's bartering the sword for shelter. She pinched her lips tight as she thought of Papa. Burk was not the kindest, gentlest father one could imagine. He was, in fact, very much as the king's man had described a Forged man.

He ate first and best at their meals and had always expected to be deferred to in all things. He was quick with a slap and slow to praise. In his early life, he'd been a warrior. If he needed something, he found a way to get it. She knew a tiny flame of hope. Perhaps, even Forged, he would still be her father. He might come home, well, back to the village where their home had stood. He might still rise before dawn to take their small boat out to . . .

Oh. The boat that now rested on the bottom, with only a handspan of its mast sticking up.

But she knew her father. He'd know how to raise it. He'd know how to build their house again. Perhaps there might be some return to her old life. Just her family, sitting beside their own fire in the evening. Their food on the table, their beds . . .

And he'd take back his sword, too.

The king's man wasn't having a great deal of luck persuading the village that their returning kin should be barred from the village, let alone murdered. She doubted he knew what he was about; surely if a mother remembered her child's name and face, she would remember that she cared about that child! How could it be otherwise?

He soon saw he was not swaying them to his thinking. His voice dropped. "I will see to my horse and spend one night here. If you want help to fortify some of your homes or this shed, I'll help with that. But if you will not ready yourselves, there is little I can do here. And yours is not the only village to be Forged. The king sent me to Shrike. Chance brought me here."

Old Hallin spoke up. "We know how to take care of our own. If Keelin comes back, he'll still be my son. Why wouldn't I feed him and give him shelter?"

"Do you think I will kill my father because he behaves selfishly? You're mad, man! If you are the sort of help King Shrewd sends us, we're better off without it."

"Blood is thicker than water!" someone shouted, and suddenly everyone seemed angry at the king's messenger.

His face sank into deeper lines of weariness. "As you will," he said in a lifeless voice.

"As we will indeed!" Carber shouted. "Did you think no one would look in the panniers on your mount! They're full of loaves of bread! Yet seeing how devastated we are, you said nothing and made no offer to share! Who is heartless and selfish now, FitzChivalry Farseer?" Carber lifted his hands high and cried out to the crowd, "We ask King Shrewd to send us help, and he sends one man, and a bastard at that! He hoards bread that would ease our children's bellies and tells us to slay our kin. This is not the help we sought!"

"I hope you touched none of it," the man replied. His eyes, so earnest before, had gone distant and dark. "The bread is poisoned. It's to use against the Forged in Shrike. To kill them and put an end to the murders and rapes there."

Carber looked stunned. Then he shouted, "Get out! Leave our village now, tonight! We've had enough of you and your 'help!' Begone."

The Farseer didn't quail. He looked out over the gathered folk. Then he stepped down off the crate. "As you will." He did not shout the word but his words carried. "If you will not help yourselves, there is nothing I can do here. I'll be on my way. When I have finished my tasks at Shrike, I will come back this way. Perhaps by then, you will be ready to listen."

"Not very likely," Carber sneered at him.

The king's envoy walked slowly to the door. His hand was not on his sword hilt, but the crowd flowed back to make way for him. Taura was one of those who followed him. His horse was still tethered outside. The lid of one pannier was loosened. The man paused to secure it. He patted the horse's neck, untethered her, mounted, and rode off into the darkness without a backward glance. He left the way he had come and the sound of his mount's hooves faded slowly.

In the morning, the rain continued and the day dragged by. None of the kidnapped folk returned. The red-hulled ship was no longer anchored at the edge of the bay. Jelin began to assert his authority over her family. Her mother helped with the cooking, and Gef salvaged wood that could be used to rebuild or as firewood. When Taura came in from standing her watches, Jelin commanded her to tend his brat so his wife Darda could rest. Cordel was a spoiled, snotty two-year-old who toddled about knocking things over and shrieking when he was reprimanded. His clothing was constantly soiled and they expected Taura to rinse out his dirtied napkins and hang them on the line above the fireplace to dry. As if anything could dry on the chill, damp days that followed the raid. When Taura complained, her mother would hastily remind her that some folk were sheltering under salvaged sails or sleeping on the dirt floors of the fish-smoking shed. She spoke low at such times, as if fearful that Jelin would overhear her complaints and turn them out. She told Taura that she should be grateful to help the household that had taken her in.

Taura did not feel grateful at all. It grated on her to see her mother cooking and cleaning like a servant in a house that was not theirs. Even worse was to see how Gef followed Jelin about, as anxious to please as a hound puppy. It was not as if Jelin treated him well. He ordered the boy about, teased and mocked him, and Gef laughed nervously at the taunts. Jelin worked the boy as if he were a donkey, and they both came home from trying to raise Jelin's fishing boat soaked and weary. Gef didn't complain; rather he fawned on Jelin for his attention. He had never behaved so with their father; her father had always been distant and gruff with both his son and daughter. Perhaps their own father had not been affectionate, but, simple or not, it was wrong for Gef to forget him so soon. Likely their father wasn't even dead yet. Taura seethed in silence.

But worse came the next night. Her mother had made a fish stew, more like a soup for she had stretched it to feed all of them. It was thin and grey, made from small fish caught from shore, and the starchy roots of the brown lily that grew on the cliffs and kelp and small shellfish from the beach. It tasted like low tide smelled. They had to eat in shifts, for there were not enough bowls. Taura and her mother ate last, with Taura given a small serving and her mother scraping out the kettle for her dinner. As Taura slowly spooned up the thin broth and small pieces of fish and root, Jelin sat down heavily across from her. "Things have to change," he said abruptly, and her mother gaped silently.

Taura gave him a flat look. He was staring at her, not her mother.

"It's plain to see that there's not enough in this house to go around. Not food, not beds, not room. So. Either we have to find a way to create more of those things or we have to ask some people to move out."

Her mother was silent, gripping the edge of the table with both hands. Taura gave her a sideways glance. Her eyes were anxious, her mouth pinched tight as a drawstring poke. She'd get no help there. Her father taken less than five days ago and her mother already abandoning her. She met Jelin's gaze and she was proud her voice didn't shake as she said, "You're talking about me."

He nodded once. "It's plain to see that caring for little Cordel doesn't suit you. Or him. You stand your watches for the village, but that doesn't put more food in the house or more firewood on the stack. You step over a chore that plainly needs doing, and what we ask you to do, you do grudgingly. You spend most of each day sulking by the fire."

A coldness was running through her as he recounted her faults. It made her ears ring. Her mother's silence was condemnation. Her brother stood away from the table, looking down, shamed for her. Frightened perhaps. They both felt Jelin was justified. They'd both surrendered their family loyalty to Jelin at the moment that they gave him her father's sword. He was talking on and on, suggesting that she could go with some of the people who were scavenging the beaches at low tide for tiny shellfish. Or that she might walk for four hours to Shearton, to see if she would find work there, something she could do for a few coins a day to bring some food into the house. She made no reply to any of his words nor did she let her face change expression.

When he finally stopped talking, she spoke. "I thought our room and board here were well paid for in advance. Did not you take my father's sword in its fine leather sheath, tooled with the words of my family's motto? 'Follow a Strong Man,' it says! That's a fine sword Buckkeep made. My father bore it in his days in King Shrewd's guard when he was young and hearty. Now you have the sword that was to be my inheritance!"

"Taura!" her mother gasped, but it was a remonstrance for her, not a heart-stricken realization of what she had given away.

"Ungrateful bitch!" Jelin's wife gasped as he demanded, "Can you eat a sword, you stupid child? Can it keep the rain from your back or warm your feet when the snow falls?"

Taura had just opened her mouth to reply when they heard the scream. It was not distant. Someone pelted past the cottage, shrieking breathlessly. Taura was first to her feet, opening the door to peer out into the rainy night as Jelin and Darda shouted, "Close the door and bar it!" As if they had learned nothing from the folk who had been burned to death when the raiders had torched their cottages.

"They're coming!" someone shouted. "They're coming from the beach, out of the sea! They're coming!"

Her brother came crowding behind her to slip under her arm and peer out. "They're coming!" he said in foolish approval. A moment later, the whistles sounded. Two blasts, over and over again.

"El's balls, close that damn door!" Jelin roared. The sword he had so decried a moment before was bared in his hands now. The sight of it and the fine sheath discarded on the floor raised Taura's fury to white-hot. She pushed past her brother, seized the edge of the door, and slammed it shut in his face. An instant later, she wished she had thought to take her cloak with her, but it was too fine of a defiant exit to spoil by going back for it.

It was raining, not heavily but in penetrating small insistent drops. Other folk were emerging from their homes, to peer out into the night. Some few had seized their pathetic weapons, cudgels and fish-knives and gaff hooks. Tools of trades that were never intended for battle or defense were all they had. A long scream rose and fell in the night.

Most folk stayed within their doorways, but some few, the bold or the hopeless, ventured out. In a loose group they walked through the dark streets toward the whistle. One of the men carried a lantern. It showed Taura damaged homes, some burned to cinders and others skeletons of blackened beams. She saw a dead dog that had not been cleared from the street. Perhaps his owner was no longer alive. Some homes stood relatively intact, light leaking from shuttered windows. She hated the smell the rain woke from the burned homes. Items that the raiders had claimed then dropped were scorched and sodden in the street. The scream was not repeated and to Taura that seemed more frightening than if it had gone on.

The lantern bearer held it high and by its uncertain light Taura saw several figures coming toward them. One of the men in the group suddenly called out "Hatilde! You live!" He ran toward a woman. She made no reply to his greeting. Instead, she abruptly stopped and stared at the rubble of a home. Slowly Taura and the others approached them. The man stood beside Hatilde, a questioning look on his face. Her hair was lank, her wet clothes hung limp on her. He spoke gently to her. "They burned your cottage. I'm so sorry, Hatilde."

Without a word, she turned from him. The house next to her rubble had survived the attack. She walked to it and tried the door, and then pounded on it. An elderly woman opened it slowly. "Hatilde! You survived!" she exclaimed. A tentative smile began to form on her face.

But the Forged woman said nothing. She pushed the old woman out of her way and entered the cottage. The old woman stumbled after her. From within Taura heard her querulous cry of, "Please don't eat that! It's all I have for my grandson!"

Before Taura could wonder about that, a woman came running down the street toward them. She shrieked in terror as she passed two plodding silhouettes then, as she saw the huddled group, she sobbed out, "Help me! Help me! He raped me! My own brother raped me."

"Oh, Dele!" a man in Taura's group cried out, and doffed his cloak to offer it to cover her torn garments. She accepted it but shrank back from his touch.

"Roff? Is that you?" the lantern-bearer asked as a tall man strode out of the darkness toward them. The man was bare-chested and barefoot, his skin bright red with cold. He made no response but abruptly knocked a young man in the group to his knees. He tore the cloak from the youngster's shoulders, half choking him in the process. He wrapped himself in it, glared at the gawkers, then turned and stalked toward a house.

"That's not your house, Roff!" the lantern bearer cried as others helped the shaken lad to his feet. They huddled ever closer together, like sheep circled by wolves.

Roff did not pause. He tried the door and found it latched. He backed up two steps and then, with a roar, he charged the door and kicked it hard. It flew open. From within came angry shouts and a shriek. Taura stood openmouthed as Roff walked in. "Roff?" asked a man's voice, and moments later, the sounds of a fight filled the night. Several of the men moved purposefully toward the door. A woman carrying a small child ran out toward them, crying, "Help, help! He's killing my husband! Help."

As two men ran in, Taura stood still in the darkened street. "This is what he meant," she informed herself quietly. He'd been right. She'd thought the king's man had been mad, but he'd been right.

Into the street stumbled Hatilde and the old woman. They were locked in fierce battle while a small child stood in the doorway and wailed his terror. Some folk sprang to separate them while others went to drag out Roff. In the midst of the shouting and the struggling fighters, Taura looked down the street and saw by the light of the open doorways more Forged ones coming. Folk opened their doors, peered out, and slammed them again. Dread and hope warred in her; would she see her father's silhouette among them? But he was not there.

The youngster whose cloak Roff had stolen leaped onto his back when the other men dragged him out of the cottage. He wrapped an arm around Roff's neck shouting, "I want my cloak back!" Another man tried to pull him off Roff while three others fought to detain Roff as someone shouted, "Roff! Give up, Roff! Let us help you! Roff! Stop fighting us."

But he didn't stop and while his opponents attempted only to restrain him, he struck out with full force, as pleased to kill them as to drive them off. Taura saw the moment when the other men lost all their restraint. Roff was borne to the ground under the weight of the other fighters. The one man pleaded for Roff to give up but the others were cursing and hitting and kicking Roff. But Roff kept fighting. A savage kick to his head ended it, and Taura cried out as she saw Roff's neck snap and his ear touch his shoulder. Abruptly, he was still. Two more kicks from different men. Then, like rebuked dogs, they were suddenly, silently stepping back from his body.

In the street, the man who had first greeted Hatilde still gripped her from behind, pinning her arms to her side. The old woman was sitting up in the street, weeping and wailing. Hatilde was flinging her head back, her teeth snapping wildly and kicking her bare heels into the man's legs. Taura had a flash of insight. The raiders had deliberately released them cold and hungry and soulless, so they would immediately have reasons to attack their families and neighbors. Was this why they had burned only half the village? Was it so that those who remained would know the fury of their own people?

But there was no quiet moment to mull over that thought.

"Sweet Eda!" A man shouted some distance away, and Roff's friend cried out, "You've killed him! Roff! Roff! He's dead! He's dead!"

"Hatilde! Stop it! Stop it!"

But Roff was sprawled on the ground, his tongue thrust out of his bloody mouth, and Hatilde went on silently snapping, struggling and kicking. And in that moment of shocked unsilence, Taura heard the cries, the crashes, the shrieks and the furious roars from elsewhere in the village. Someone was blowing a whistle, desperately, over and over. Their folk had come back, Forged as King Shrewd's messenger had warned them they would be. But now Taura knew what it meant. They would, indeed, take anything they wanted or needed. And some, like Roff, would not be stopped by anything short of death.

The villagers would kill her father. Taura abruptly knew that. Her father was a strong and stubborn man, the strongest man she'd ever known. He would not stop until he had what he needed. The only way to stop him from taking what he needed would be to kill him.

Papa.

Where would he be? Which way would he come? The whistles and shouts and screams were coming from every direction. The Forged were returning and it was worse than the night the raiders had come, setting fires and stealing and raping and killing. That attack had been a shock. But they had known their folk would return. Their dreads and hopes had risen, and fallen. And now, just when the villagers had begun to resume their lives, to rebuild houses and pull the boats ashore to repair them, the raiders struck again. With their own folk as weapons. With her father as their attacker.

Where would he be?

And she knew. He would go home.

Taura ran through the dark streets. Twice she dodged Forged ones. She knew them even in the dim light leaking from shuttered windows. They walked stiff and cold, as if puzzled at being thrust back into a life they had once shared. She ran past Jend Greenoak kneeling in the streets and sobbing, "But the baby? Where is our baby?"

Taura slowed her steps and stared unwillingly. Jend's wife Salal stood in the street, her garments still dripping seawater, her arms empty of the babe she had carried off to the Red Ship. She stared at the burned rubble of their home. She spoke harshly. "I'm cold and hungry. The baby did nothing but cry. It was useless." Her words carried no emotion, not regret nor anger. She stated her truth. Jend swayed where he knelt and she walked away from him, her arms embracing herself against the cold as she strode down the street toward a lit cottage. Taura knew what would come next.

But the woman who stepped out of the cottage held a cudgel and called over her shoulder, "Bar the door. Open for no one but me!"

Nor did the woman wait for Salal to try to enter. She strode forward to meet her, cudgel swinging. Salal did not retreat. Instead, she voiced her fury at being thwarted with an inhuman shriek and ran at the woman, her hands lifted to claw.

"NO!" shouted Jend, and found his feet to rush to his wife's defense. So it would go, Taura suddenly knew. Some would stand with their loved ones, Forged or not, and others would defend their homes at any cost. Jend took a smashing blow to his gut and went down in the street but Salal fought on regardless of a dangling and crooked jaw. The defending woman was screaming wordlessly, turned just as savage as the Forged one she fought. The men who had fought Roff were standing and shouting at one another. Taura dashed past them, powered by both horror and fear. She did not want to see another person die tonight.

"Stand with your family," her father had always told her. She remembered the day well. Someone had cursed Gef for dashing into the street, entranced by a flock of geese flying overhead.

"Keep your half-wit boy tethered to your porch!" the teamster had shouted at them. He'd had to rein in sharply and his slippery load of fresh fish had nearly slewed out of his cart. Papa had dragged him down from the seat of his cart and thrashed him in the street. No matter how her father might shun his simple son within the walls of his own home, in public he defended him. Her mother had echoed those words when her father came in with his bloodied knuckles and blackened eyes. "We always stand with our blood," she'd told Taura. Then, Taura had not doubted that she meant it. Perhaps tonight, her mother would recall where her loyalties should be.

Taura was out of breath. She trotted rather than ran now, but her thoughts raced far ahead of her destination. She could well be on the path back to her old life. She would find her father and he would know her. She would warn him, protect him from villagers who might not understand. Even if he never showed affection for any of them again, he would still be Papa, and her family would be together again. She would rather sleep on cold earth with her family than sleep on the floor by the fire in Jelin's house.

She ran past Jelin's house and on, past the partially burned homes, away from the dim light that leaked from windows. This part of the village was dead; it stank of burned wood and burned flesh. She had lived in the same house all her life, but in all the destruction, she was suddenly not sure which burned wreckage had been their home. Thin moonlight reached down and glinted faintly only on wet wood and stone. She trotted through a foreign landscape, a place she had never been before. Everything she had ever known was gone.

She almost crashed into her father before she saw him. He was standing motionless, staring at where their house had been. She recoiled then stood still. He turned slowly toward her and for an instant the moonlight glinted in his eyes. Then darkness claimed his face again. He said nothing.

"Papa?" she said.

He didn't respond.

The words vomited from her. "They burned the house. We saw them take you away. Your head was bloody. Mother told me to run and hide. She went to find Gef. I hid high in the old willow that overlooks the harbor. They took you out to their ship. What did they do to you? Did they hurt you?"

He was very still. Then he shook his head, a small quick shake as if a mosquito had buzzed in his ear. He walked past her toward the dimly lit part of the village that still stood. She hesitated then hurried after him.

"Papa. The others in the village know you were taken. A man came from the king. He told the village to defend themselves against Forged ones. To kill them if we had to."

Her father kept walking.

"Are you Forged, Papa? Did they do something to you?"

He kept walking.

"Papa, do you know me?"

His steps slowed. "You're Taura. And you talk too much." After he'd spoken he resumed his pace.

It was all she could do to keep from dancing after him. He knew her. He had always mocked and teased her that she was such a talker! His voice was flat, but he was cold and wet, hungry and tired. But he knew her. She hugged herself against the cold and hurried after him. "Papa, you have to listen to me. I've seen them killing some of the others who were kidnapped. We have to be careful. And you need a weapon. You need your sword."

For five steps he kept his pace. Then he said, "I need my sword."

"It's at Jelin's house. Mother and Gef and I have been staying there, sleeping on their floor. Mother gave him your sword, to let us stay with him. He said he might need it, to protect his wife and baby." She had a stitch in her side from all the running, and despite hugging herself, the cold was seeping into her bones. Her mouth was dry. But she pushed all that to one side. Once Papa was inside the house, with his sword, he'd be safe. They'd all be safe again.

Her father turned toward the first lit house.

"No! Not there! They'll try to kill you. First, we have to get your sword. Then you can get warm and have some food. Or a hot drink." Now that she thought of it, there was probably no food left. But there would be tea and perhaps a bit of bread. Better than nothing, she told herself. He was walking on. She dashed ahead of him. "Follow me!" she told him.

A piercing scream rang out in the night, but it was distant, not nearby. She ignored it as she had ignored the angry shouts that came and went. She did not slacken her pace but walked backwards hastily, motioning for him to follow her. He came on doggedly.

They reached Jelin's cottage. She ran up to the door and tried to open it. It was barred. She banged on it with her fists. "Let me in! Open the door!" she cried.

Inside, her mother lifted her voice. "Oh, thank Eda! It's Taura: she's come back. Please, Jelin, please let her in!"

A silence. Then she heard the bar lifted from its supports. She seized the handle and pulled the door open just as her father came up behind her. "Mother, I've found Papa! I've brought him home!" she cried.

Her mother stood in the door. She looked at Taura, then at her husband. A terrible hope lit in her eyes. "Burk?" her mother said, her voice cracking on his name.

"Papa!" Gef's voice was both questioning and fearful.

Jelin pushed them both to one side. Papa's sword was naked in his hand. He lifted it and pointed it at Papa. "Get back," he said in a low and deadly voice. His gaze flickered to Taura. "You stupid little bitch. Get in here and get behind me."

"No!" It wasn't just that he'd called her a bitch. It was the way he held the blade unwavering toward her father. Jelin wasn't even going to give him a chance. "Let us in! Let Papa in, let him get warm and have some food. That's what he needs. It's all that any of the Forged ones need, and I think if we give it to them, they'll have no reason to hurt us." At Jelin's flat stare, she grew desperate. "Mother, tell him to let us both in. This is our chance to be a family again."

The words tumbled from her mouth. She stepped, not quite in front of Papa, but closer to him, to show Jelin that he'd have to stab her before he could fight Papa. She wasn't Forged. He had no excuse to stab her.

Papa spoke behind her. "That is *my* sword." Anger rose in his voice on that last word.

"Get inside, Taura. Now." Jelin shifted his stare to her father. He spoke sternly. "Burk, I've no wish to hurt you. Go away."

Back inside the cottage, the baby started crying. Jelin's wife began to sob. "Make him go away, Jelin. Drive him off. And her with him. She's nothing but trouble. Oh, Sweet Eda, mercy on me and my child! Drive him away! Kill him!"

Darda's voice was rising to hysteria and Taura could see in Jelin's eyes that he was listening to her. Maybe he would stab her. Her voice rose to shrill despite herself. "Mother? Will you let him kill both of us? With Papa's own sword?"

"Taura, get inside. Your father is not himself." Her mother's voice shook. She had hugged Gef to her side. He was sob panting, his prelude to one of his total panics. Soon he would race in circles, sobbing and shrieking.

"Mother, please!" Taura begged.

Then her father seized her by the back of her neck and her shirt collar. He flung her into the cottage. She collided with Jelin then fell at his feet. He was off balance and flailing when Papa reached in, past the tip of his own sword, to seize Jelin's wrist. Taura knew that clamping grip. She'd seen him haul big halibut up off the bottom, his hands seized tight on the line. In a moment it happened as she knew it would. Jelin gave a cry and the sword fell from his nerveless hand. It was right next to her. She seized the hilt and scrabbled back into the room.

"Papa, I've got it! I've got your sword for you."

Papa said nothing. He had not released his grip on Jelin's wrist. Jelin was shouting and cursing and fighting Papa's one hand, as if by breaking that grip he could win. Her father's lips were pulled back from his set teeth. His eyes were empty. Jelin put all his efforts into pulling away. But Papa jerked the smaller man toward him. His free hand went to Jelin's throat. He caught him there, his big hand right under Jelin's jaw. He squeezed, and then abruptly released Jelin's wrist and put both hands on his neck. He lifted Jelin up on his toes and Papa's eyes were very intent, his mouth flat as he throttled the man. He tilted his head to one side and regarded Jelin's darkening face with intent interest.

"No!" shrieked Darda, but she did nothing but retreat into the corner clutching her child. Gef seized two handfuls of his own hair and wailed loudly as he shook his own head. Taura's mother was the one who charged in. She seized one of Papa's thick arms and tugged at it. She hung her weight from it as if she swung from a tree branch.

"Burk! No, no, let him go! Burk, don't kill him! He was kind to us, he gave us shelter! Burk! Stop!"

But Papa did not stop. Jelin's eyes were wide, his mouth open. He had been clutching at Papa's hands but now his hands fell away to hang limply at his sides as Papa shook him. Taura looked down at the sword in her hands. She lifted it in a two-handed grip, unsure of what she was going to do. She was shaking and the sword was heavy. She braced her feet and squared her shoulders and steadied the blade just as Papa dropped a floppy Jelin to the floor. He looked at his wife still clinging to his arm. He snapped his arm straight, flinging her aside, and she flew backwards.

And onto the sword.

Taura dropped the blade as her mother crashed into it. It stuck, sank, then fell away as her mother tumbled down. Papa took two steps forward and backhanded Gef. The blow drove him to the floor. "Quiet!" he roared at his idiot son. And for a wonder, Gef obeyed. Gef drew his knees tight to his chest and clapped both hands over his bleeding mouth as he looked up in terror at his father. The command almost silenced Darda as well. Jelin's wife had one hand clapped over her own mouth and with the other she held Cordel tight to her body, muffling his cries.

"Food!" Papa commanded. He moved toward the fire and held out his hands to the warmth. Jelin did not move. Taura's mother sat up, moaning and clutching her ribs. Taura looked down at the sword on the floor.

"Food!" her father said again. He glared round at them all, and his eyes made no distinction between his own bleeding wife and Jelin's cowering one. Neither spoke nor stirred and Gef, as always, was useless.

Taura found her tongue. "Papa, please, sit down. I'll see what I can find for you," she told him, and went to Darda's larder. The raiders had not burned Jelin's home but had looted any foodstuffs they could find. She doubted she would find much on the shelves. In a wooden box, Taura found half a loaf of bread. That was all. But as she pulled the box down to get the bread, she saw something hidden behind the box. A clean cloth wrapped several sides of dry fish and a big wedge of cheese. Her outrage rose as she pushed it aside to see a trove of potatoes in a bag, a pot of honey, and a pot of rendered lard. Dried apples at the very back of the shelf. A braid of garlic! Darda had hidden all that rich food and forced them to exist on thin soup!

"You were holding the good food back from us!" she accused Darda, speaking toward the cupboard in a low voice. She broke a piece from the cheese and crammed it into her mouth. Behind her, her father roared, "NOW! I want food now!"

As Taura glanced over her shoulder, her father bared his teeth at her. His eyes were narrowed and he made a threatening noise in his throat. Taura carried the bread, honey, and cheese to the table. He didn't wait for her to set it out nicely, but snatched the loaf in both his dirty hands. She dropped the cheese and set down the honey.

She backed away from the table. She spared a sideways glance for Darda and spoke in a low voice. "Mother, they were cheating us. Jelin said there wasn't enough to go around but Darda hid food from us!"

Darda's voice shook with fear and defiance. "It was our food before all this happened! We didn't owe it to you! It was food for my boy; he needs it to grow! Jelin and I weren't eating it! It was food for Cordel!"

Her father appeared to hear none of this. He had lifted the loaf to his mouth and was worrying a tremendous bite from it. Around that mouthful he yelled, "Drink! Something to drink. I am thirsty!"

Water was what there was, and Taura filled a mug with it and took it to him. Her mother had risen, staggered, then folded up to huddle by Gef. Her idiot brother was rocking back and forth. Instead of seeing to her own wound, her mother was trying to calm him. Taura took the cloth that had wrapped the loaf and went to her. "Let me see your wound," she said as she crouched down beside her.

Her mother's eyes flashed dark fire. "Get away from me!" she cried, and pushed Taura so she sprawled on the floor. But she did snatch up the cloth and hold it to her ribs. It reddened with blood, but only slightly. Taura guessed that the blade had sliced her but not deeply. She was still appalled.

"I'm sorry!" she said stiffly. "I didn't mean to hurt you! I didn't know what to do!"

"You did know. You just didn't want to do it. As is ever your way!"

"Family first!" she cried out. "You and Papa always say that. Family first!"

"Does he look like he is thinking of his family?" her mother demanded. Taura looked over at her father. The cheese was almost gone. He had pushed a piece of bread into the pot of honey and was wiping it clean of sweetness. As she watched, he shoved it into his mouth. The discarded honeypot rolled to the edge of the table and fell to the floor with a crash.

Her mother levered herself to her feet, leaning on Gef's shoulder. "Get up, boy," she said quietly, tugging on him, and he rose. She took his hand and led him back to where Darda and Jelin's son huddled. "Stay there," she warned him, and he sank down on his haunches beside them. Clutching her side, she stood between them and her husband. Taura got slowly to her feet. She backed to the wall and looked from her father to her mother.

The fire crackled and Papa ate noisily, tearing at the bread with bared teeth. Rain and wind came in the open door. In the distance, people still shouted. Darda clutched her baby and sobbed into him and Gef made his babyish crooning in sympathy. Jelin was silent. Dead. Taura crept closer to the table. "Papa?" she said.

His eyes turned toward her then back to the bread. He tore off another mouthful.

"Family first, Papa? Isn't that right? Shouldn't we stay together, to fix our house and raise our boat?"

His gaze roved around the room and her hopes rose that he would speak. "More food." That was his response. His eyes had a glitter in them she had never seen. As if they were shallow now, like puddles in the sun. Nothing behind them.

"There isn't any," she lied.

He narrowed his eyes at her and showed his teeth. Her breath caught in her throat. Papa crammed the last of the bread into his mouth. He stuffed the cheese in after it. He rocked from side to side in the chair as he chewed it then stood. She backed away from him. He picked up the mug, drank the last of the water and dropped it. "Papa?" Taura begged him.

He looked past her. He walked to the couple's bed. He took Jelin's extra shirt from its peg on the wall. He put it on. It was too small for him. Jelin's wool cap fit him well. He peered around the cottage. Jelin's winter cloak was on a hook beside the door. He took that, too. He swung it around his shoulders. Then he rounded to look at her accusingly.

"Please, Papa?" Could not he be who he had been, just for a time?

Even if he cared nothing for them as the bastard had said, could not he be the man who always knew what they must do next to survive?

"More food?" He scratched his face, his blunt nails making a sound in his short beard. His gaze was flat.

That was all he said. He was thinking only of what he needed now. Nothing for what tomorrow might bring. Nothing for where he had been, what had happened to him, what had befallen the village. "You ate it all," Taura lied quietly. She scarcely knew why she did so. Papa gave a grunt. He nudged at Jelin's body and when he didn't move, he stepped over it to stand in the open door. His head turned slowly from side to side. He took one step out the door and stopped.

His sword was still on the floor. Not far from it, the sheath lay as well. She heard her mother's breathed prayer. "Sweet Eda, make him go away."

He walked out into the night.

The other villagers would kill him. They would kill him and they would hate Taura forever because she hadn't killed him. Because she'd let him kill Jelin. Darda would not be silent about that. She would tell everyone.

Taura looked over at her mother. She'd taken a heavy iron pan from the cooking shelf. She held it by the handle as if it were a weapon. Her eyes were flat as she stared at Taura. Yes. Even her mother would hate her.

Taura stooped to pick up the sword. It was still too heavy for her. The point of it dragged on the floor as she reached for the sheath. "Follow a Strong Man" the carved lettering told her.

She shook her head. She knew what she should do. She should close the door behind Papa and bar it. She should say she was sorry a hundred, a thousand times. She should bind Mother's wound and help Darda compose her husband's body. She should take Papa's sword and stand in the door and guard them all. She was the last person they had who might stand between them and the Forged ones roaming the streets.

She knew what she should do.

But her mother was right about her.

Taura looked back at them all, then took Darda's cloak from the hook. She put it on and pulled the thick wool hood up over her damp hair. She heaved the sword up so it rested on her shoulder like a shovel. She stooped and took up the fine sheath in her free hand.

"What are you doing?" her mother demanded in outrage.

Taura held out the sheath toward her. "Following a strong man," she said.

She stepped out into the wind and rain. She kicked the door shut behind her. A moment longer she stood in the scant shelter of the eaves. She heard the bar slammed down into the supports on the door. Almost immediately, Darda began shrieking, anger and grief in furious words.

Taura stepped out into the night. Her father had not gone far. His hunched shoulders and stalking stride reminded her of a prowling bear as he moved through the rain toward his prey. A decision came to her. She pushed the empty sheath through her belt and gripped the sword's hilt in both hands. She considered it. If she killed him, would her mother forgive her? Would Darda?

Not likely.

She ran after him, the bared sword heavy and jouncing with every step she took. "Papa! Wait! You'll need your sword!" she called after him. He glanced back at her but said nothing as he halted. But he waited for her. When she caught up with him, he walked on.

She followed him into the darkness.

Ken Liu

• • •

K en Liu is an author and translator of speculative fiction, as well as a lawyer and programmer. His fiction has appeared in *The Magazine of Fantasy & Science Fiction*, *Asimov's Science Fiction*, *Analog*, *Clarkesworld*, *Lightspeed*, and *Strange Horizons*, among many other places. He has won a Nebula, two Hugos, a World Fantasy Award, and a Science Fiction & Fantasy Translation Award, and been nominated for the Sturgeon and the Locus awards. In 2015, he published his first novel, *The Grace of Kings*. His most recent books are *The Wall of Storms*, a sequel to *The Grace of Kings*, a collection, *The Paper Menagerie and Other Stories*, and, as editor and translator, an anthology of Chinese science-fiction stories, *Invisible Planets*. He lives with his family near Boston, Massachusetts.

Here a young girl pressed into service as an assassin faces one final test of her skills—if she lives through it.

• • •

The Hidden Girl

KEN LIU

Beginning in the eighth century, the Imperial court of Tang Dynasty China increasingly relied on military governors—the jiedushi—whose responsibilities began with border defense but gradually encompassed taxation, civil administration, and other aspects of political power. They were, in fact, independent feudal warlords whose accountability to Imperial authority was nominal.

Rivalry among the governors was often violent and bloody.

On the morning after my tenth birthday, spring sunlight dapples the stone slabs of the road in front of our house through the blooming branches of the pagoda tree. I climb out onto the thick bough pointing west like an immortal's arm and reach for a strand of yellow flowers, anticipating the sweet taste tinged with a touch of bitterness.

"Alms, young mistress?"

I look down and see a bhikkhuni. I can't tell how old she is—her face is unlined but there is a fortitude in her dark eyes that reminds me of my grandmother. The light fuzz over her shaved head glows in the warm sun like a halo, and her grey kasaya is clean but tattered at the hem. She holds up a wooden bowl in her left hand, gazing up at me expectantly.

"Would you like some pagoda-tree flowers?" I ask.

She smiles. "I haven't had any since I was a young girl. It would be a delight."

"If you stand below me, I'll drop some into your bowl," I say, reaching for the silk pouch on my back.

She shakes her head. "I can't eat flowers that have been touched by another hand—too infected with the mundane concerns of this dusty world."

"Then climb up yourself," I say. Immediately I feel ashamed at my annoyance.

"If I get them myself, they wouldn't be alms, now would they?" There's a hint of laughter in her voice.

"All right," I say. Father has always taught me to be polite to the monks and nuns. We may not follow the Buddhist teachings, but it doesn't make sense to antagonize the spirits, whether they are Daoist, Buddhist, or wild spirits who rely on no learned masters at all. "Tell me which flowers you want; I'll try to get them for you without touching them."

She points to some flowers at the end of a slim branch below my bough. They are paler in color than the flowers from the rest of the tree, which means they are sweeter. But the branch they dangle from is much too thin for me to climb.

I hook my knees around the thick bough I'm on and lean back until I'm dangling upside down like a bat. It's fun to see the world this way, and I don't care that the hem of my dress is flapping around my face. Father always yells at me when he sees me like this, but he never stays angry at me for too long, on account of my losing my mother when I was just a baby.

Wrapping my hands in the loose folds of my sleeves, I try to grab for the flowers. But I'm still too far from the branch she wants, those white flowers tantalizingly just out of reach.

"If it's too much trouble," the nun calls out, "don't worry about it. I don't want you to tear your dress."

I bite my bottom lip, determined to ignore her. By tightening and flexing the muscles in my belly and thighs, I begin to swing back and forth. When I've reached the apex of an upswing I judge to be high enough, I let go with my knees.

As I plunge through the leafy canopy, the flowers she wants brush by my face and I snap my teeth around a strand. My fingers grab the lower branch, which sinks under my weight and slows my momentum as my body swings back upright. For a moment, it seems as if the branch would hold, but then I hear a crisp snap and feel suddenly weightless.

I tuck my knees under me and manage to land in the shade of the pagoda tree, unharmed. Immediately, I roll out of the way, and the flower-laden branch crashes to the spot on the ground I just vacated a moment later.

I walk nonchalantly up to the nun and open my jaw to drop the strand of flowers into her alms bowl. "No dust. And you only said no hands."

In the shade of the pagoda tree, we sit with our legs crossed in the lotus position like the Buddhas in the temple. She picks the flowers off the stem: one for her, one for me. The sweetness is lighter and less cloying than the sugar-dough figurines Father sometimes buys me.

"You have a talent," she says. "You'd make a good thief."

I look at her, indignant. "I'm a general's daughter."

"Are you?" she says. "Then you're already a thief."

"What are you talking about?"

"I have walked many miles," she says. I look at her bare feet: the bottoms are calloused and leathery. "I see peasants starving in fields while the great lords plot and scheme for bigger armies. I see ministers and generals drink wine from ivory cups and conduct calligraphy with their piss on silk scrolls while orphans and widows must make one cup of rice last five days."

"Just because we are not poor doesn't make us thieves. My father serves his lord, the Jiedushi of Weibo, with honor and carries out his duties faithfully."

"We're all thieves in this world of suffering," the nun says. "Honor and faith are not virtues, only excuses for stealing more."

"Then you're a thief as well," I say, anger making my face glow with heat. "You accept alms and do no work to earn them."

She nods. "I am indeed. The Buddha teaches us that the world is an illusion, and suffering is inevitable as long as we do not see through it. If we're all fated to be thieves, it's better to be a thief who adheres to a code that transcends the mundane."

"What is your code then?"

"To disdain the moral pronouncements of hypocrites; to be true to my word; to always do what I promise, no more and no less. To hone my talent and wield it like a beacon in a darkening world."

I laugh. "What is your talent, Mistress Thief?"

"I steal lives."

The inside of the cabinet is dark and warm, the air redolent of camphor. By the faint light coming through the slit between the doors, I arrange the blankets around me to make a cozy nest.

The footsteps of patrolling soldiers echo through the hallway outside my bedroom. Each time one of them turns a corner, the clanging of armor and sword marks the passage of another fraction of an hour, bringing me closer to morning.

The conversation between the bhikkhuni and my father replays through my mind.

"*Give her to me. I will have her as my student.*"

"*Much as I'm flattered by the Buddha's kind attention, I must decline. My daughter's place is at home, by my side.*"

"*You can give her to me willingly, or I can take her away without your blessing.*"

"*Are you threatening me with a kidnapping? Know that I've made my living on the tip of a sword, and my house is guarded by fifty armed men who will give their lives for their young mistress.*"

"*I never threaten; I simply inform. Even if you keep her in an iron chest ringed about with bronze chains at the bottom of the ocean, I will take her away as easily as I cut your beard with this dagger.*"

There was a cold, bright, metallic flash. Father drew his sword, the grinding noise of blade against sheath wringing my heart so that it leaped wildly.

But the bhikkuni was already gone, leaving behind a few loose strands of
grey hair floating gently to the floor in the slanted rays of the sunlight. My
father, stunned, held his hand against the side of his face where the dagger had
brushed against his skin.

The hairs landed; my father removed his hand. There was a patch of de-
nuded skin on his cheek, as pale as the stone slabs of the road in the morning
sun. No blood.

"Do not be afraid, Daughter. I will triple the guards tonight. The spirit of
your dear departed mother will guard you."

But I'm afraid. I *am* afraid. I think about the glow of sunlight around
the nun's head. I like my long, thick hair, which the maids tell me resembles my mother's, and she had combed her hair a hundred times
each night before she went to sleep. I don't want to have my head shaved.

I think about the glint of metal in the nun's hand, quicker than the
eye can follow.

I think about the strands of hair from my father's beard drifting to
the floor.

The light from the oil lamp outside the closet door flickers. I scramble to the corner of the closet and squeeze my eyes tightly shut.

There is no noise. Just a draft that caresses my face. Softly, like the
flapping wings of a moth.

I open my eyes. For a moment, I don't understand what I'm seeing.

Suspended about three feet from my face is an oblong object, about
the size of my forearm and shaped like the cocoon of a silkworm. Glowing like a sliver of the moon, it gives off a light that is without warmth,
shadowless. Fascinated, I crawl closer.

No, an "object" isn't quite right. The cold light spills out of it like
melting ice, along with the draft that whips my hair about my face. It is
more like the absence of substance, a rip in the murky interior of the
cabinet, a negative object that consumes darkness and turns it into light.

My throat feels parched and I swallow, hard. Fingers trembling, I
reach out to touch the glow. A half second of hesitation, then I make
contact.

Or no contact. There is no skin-searing heat nor bone-freezing chill.
My impression of the object as a negative is confirmed as my fingers
touch nothing. And neither do they emerge from the other side—

they've simply vanished into the glow, as though I'm plunging my hand into a hole in space.

I jerk my hand back out and examine my fingers, wiggling them. No damage as far as I can see.

A hand reaches out from the rip, grabs my arm, and pulls me toward the light. Before I can scream, blazing light blinds me, and I'm overwhelmed by the sensation of falling, falling from the tip of a heaven-reaching pagoda tree toward an earth that never comes.

The mountain floats among the clouds like an island.

I've tried to find my way down, but always, I get lost among the foggy woods. *Just go down, down*, I tell myself. But the fog thickens until it takes on substance, and no matter how hard I push, the wall of clouds refuses to yield. Then I have no choice but to sit down, shivering, wringing the condensation out of my hair. Some of the wetness is from tears, but I won't admit that.

She materializes out of the fog. Wordlessly, she beckons me to follow her back up the peak; I obey.

"You're not very good at hiding," she says.

There is no response to that. If she could steal me from a cabinet inside a general's house guarded by walls and soldiers, I suppose there's nowhere I can hide from her.

We emerge from the woods back onto the sun-drenched peak. A gust of wind brushes past us, whipping up the fallen leaves into a storm of gold and crimson.

"Are you hungry?" she asks, her voice not unkind.

I nod. Something about her tone catches me off guard. Father never asks me if I'm hungry, and I sometimes dream of my mother making me a breakfast of freshly baked bread and fermented beans. It's been three days since the bhikkhuni had taken me here, and I've not eaten anything but some sour berries I found in the woods and a few bitter roots I dug from the ground.

"Come along," she says.

She takes me up a zigzagging path carved into the face of a cliff. The path is so narrow that I dare not look down but shuffle along, my face and body pressed against the rock face and my outstretched hands clinging to dangling vines like a gecko. The bhikkhuni, on the other hand, strides along the path as though she's walking in the middle of a wide avenue in Chang'an. She waits patiently at each turn for me to catch up.

I hear the faint sounds of clanking metal above me. Having dug my feet into depressions along the path and tested the vine in my hands to be sure it's rooted securely to the mountain, I look up.

Two young women, about fourteen years of age, are fighting with swords in the air. No, *fighting* isn't quite the right word. It's more accurate to call their movements a dance.

One of the women, dressed in a white robe, pushes off the cliff with both feet while holding on to a vine with her left hand. She swings away from the cliff in a wide arc, her legs stretched out before her in a graceful pose that reminds me of the apsaras—flying nymphs who make their home in the clouds—painted on scrolls in the temples. The sword in her right hand glints in the sunlight like a shard of heaven.

As her sword tip approaches her opponent on the cliff, the other woman lets go of the vine she's hanging on to and leaps straight up. The black robe billows around her like the wings of a giant moth, and as her ascent slows, she flips herself at the apex of her arc and tumbles toward the woman in white like a diving hawk, her sword arm leading as a beak.

Clang!

The tips of their swords collide, and a spark lights up the air like an exploding firework. The sword in the hand of the woman in black bends into a crescent, slowing her descent until she is standing inverted in the air, supported only by the tip of her adversary's blade.

Both women punch out with their free hands, palms open.

Thump!

A crisp blow reverberates in the air. The woman in black lands against the mountain face, where she attaches herself by deftly wrapping a vine around her ankle. The woman in white completes her arced swing back to the rock, and, like a dragonfly dipping its tail into the still pond, pushes off again for another assault.

I watch, mesmerized, as the two swordswomen pursue, dodge, strike, feint, punch, kick, slash, glide, tumble, and stab across the webbing of vines over the face of the sheer cliff, thousands of feet above the roiling clouds below, defying both gravity and mortality. They are graceful as birds flitting across a swaying bamboo forest, quick as mantises leaping across a dew-dappled web, impossible as the immortals of legends whispered by hoarse-voiced bards in teahouses.

Also, I notice with relief that they both have thick, flowing, beautiful hair. Perhaps shaving is not required to be the bhikkhuni's student.

"Come," the bhikkhuni beckons, and I obediently make my way over to the small stone platform jutting into the air from the bend in the path. "I guess you really are hungry," she observes, a hint of laughter in her voice. Embarrassed, I close my jaw, still hanging open from shock at seeing the sparring girls.

With the clouds far below our feet and the wind whipping around us, it feels like the world I've known all my life has fallen away.

"Here." She points to a pile of bright pink peaches at the end of the platform, each about the size of my fist. "The hundred-year-old monkeys who live in the mountains gather these from deep in the clouds, where the peach trees absorb the essence of the heavens. After eating one of these, you won't be hungry for a full ten days. If you become thirsty, you can drink the dew from the vines and the springwater in the cave that is our dormitory."

The two sparring girls have climbed down from the cliff onto the platform behind us. They each take a peach.

"I will show you where you'll sleep, Little Sister," says the girl in white. "I'm Jinger. If you get scared from the howling wolves at night, you can crawl into my bed."

"I'm sure you've never had anything as sweet as this peach," says the girl in black. "I'm Konger. I've studied with Teacher the longest and know all the fruits of this mountain."

"Have you had pagoda-tree flowers?" I ask.

"No," she says. "Maybe someday you can show me."

I bite into the peach. It is indescribably sweet and melts against my tongue as though it's made of pure snow. Yet, as soon as I've swallowed a mouthful, my belly warms with the heat of its sustenance. I believe that the peach really will last me ten days. I'll believe anything my teacher tells me.

"Why have you taken me?" I ask.

"Because you have a talent, Yinniang," she says.

I suppose that is my name now. The Hidden Girl.

"But talents must be cultivated," she continues. "Will you be a pearl buried in the mud of the endless East Sea, or will you shine so brightly as to awaken those who only doze through life and light up a mundane world?"

"Teach me to fly and fight like them," I say, licking the sweet peach juice from my hands. *I will become a great thief,* I tell myself. *I will steal my life back from you.*

She nods thoughtfully and looks into the distance, where the setting sun has turned the clouds into a sea of golden splendor and crimson gore.

Six years later.

The wheels of the donkey cart grind to a stop.

Without warning, Teacher rips the blindfold away from my eyes and digs out the silk plugs in my ears. I struggle against the sudden bright sun and the sea of noise—the braying of donkeys; the whinnying of horses; the clanging of cymbals and the wailing of erhus from some folk-opera troupe; the thumping and thudding of goods being loaded and unloaded; the singing, shouting, haggling, laughing, arguing, pontificating that make up the symphony of a metropolis.

While I'm still recovering from my journey in the swaying darkness, Teacher has jumped down to the ground to leash the donkey to a roadside post. We're in some provincial capital, that much I know—indeed, the smell of a hundred different varieties of fried dough and candied apples and horse manure and exotic perfume already told me as much even before the blindfold was off—but I can't tell exactly where. I strain to catch snippets of conversation from the bustling city around me, but the topolect is unfamiliar.

The pedestrians passing by our cart bow to Teacher. "*Amitabha,*" they say.

Teacher holds up a hand in front of her chest and bows back. "*Amitabha,*" she says back.

I may be anywhere in the empire.

"We'll have lunch, then you can rest up at the inn over there," says Teacher.

"What about my task?" I ask. I'm nervous. This is the first time I've been away from the mountain since she's taken me.

She looks at me with a complicated expression, halfway between pity and amusement. "So eager?"

I bite my bottom lip, not answering.

"You will choose your own method and time," she says, her tone as placid as the cloudless sky. "I'll be back on the third night. Good hunting."

"Keep your eyes open and your limbs loose," she said. "Remember everything I've taught you."

Teacher had summoned two mist hawks from nearby peaks, each the size of a full-grown man. Iron blades extended from their talons, and steel glinted from their vicious curved beaks. They circled above me, alternately emerging from and disappearing into the cloud-mist, their screeches mournful and proud.

Jinger handed me a small dagger about five inches in length. It seemed utterly inadequate for the task. My hand shook as I wrapped my fingers around the handle.

"What can be seen is not all," she said.

"Be aware of what is hidden," Konger added.

"You will be fine," Jinger said, squeezing my shoulder.

"The world is full of illusions cast by the unseen Truth," Konger said. Then she leaned in to whisper in my ear, her breath warm against my cheek, "I still have a scar on the back of my neck from my time with the hawks."

They backed off and faded into the mist, leaving me alone with the raptors and Teacher's voice coming from the vines above me.

"Why do we kill?" I asked.

The hawks took turns swooping down, feinting and testing my defenses. I leapt out of the way reflexively, brandishing my dagger to ward them off.

"This is a time of chaos," Teacher said. "The great lords of the land are filled with ambition. They take everything they can from the people they're sworn to protect, shepherds who have turned into wolves preying on their flocks.

They increase the taxes until all the walls in their palaces are gleaming with gold and silver; they take sons away from mothers until their armies swell like the current of the Yellow River; they plot and scheme and redraw lines on maps as though the country is nothing but a platter of sand, upon which the peasants creep and crawl like terrified ants."

One of the hawks turned to dive at me. A real attack, not a test. I crouched into a defensive stance, the dagger in my right hand held up to guard my face, my left hand on the ground for stability. I kept my eyes on the hawk, letting everything fade into the background except the bright reflections from the sharp beak and talons, like a constellation in the night sky.

The hawk loomed in my vision. A light breeze brushed the back of my neck. The raptor extended its talons and flapped its wings, trying to slow its dive at the last minute.

"Who is to say that one governor is right? Or that another general is wrong?" she asked. "The man who seduces his lord's wife may be doing so to get close to a tyrant and exact vengeance. The woman who demands rice for the peasantry from her patron may be doing so to further her own ambition. We live in a time of chaos, and the only moral choice is to be amoral. The great lords hire us to strike at their enemies. And we carry out our missions with dedication and loyalty, true and deadly as a crossbow bolt."

I got ready to spring out of my crouch to slash at the hawk, then I remembered the words of my sisters.

". . . What can be seen is not all . . . I still have a scar on the back of my neck."

I dropped to the ground and rolled to the left, the talons of the hawk who had been trying to sneak up behind me missing only by inches. It collided with its companion in the spot where my head had been but a moment ago like a diver meeting her reflection at the surface of the pool. There was a tangle of beating wings and angry screeching.

I lunged at the storm of feathers. One, two, three slashes, quicker than lightning. The hawks tumbled down, their wings crumpling as they struck the ground. Blood from the clean cuts in their throats pooled on the stone platform.

There was also blood seeping from my shoulder where the rough rocks had scraped the skin during my roll. But I had survived, and my foes had not.

"Why do we kill?" I asked again, still panting from the exertion. I had

killed wild apes before, and forest panthers and bamboo-grove tigers. But a pair of mist hawks were the hardest kill yet, the height of the assassin's art. "Why do we serve as the talons of the powerful?"

"We are the winter snowstorm descending upon a house rotten with termites," she said. "Only by hurrying the decay of the old can we bring about the rebirth of the new. We are the vengeance of a weary world."

Jinger and Konger emerged from the mist to sprinkle corpse-dissolving powder on the hawks and to bandage my wound.

"Thank you," I whispered.

"You need to practice more," said Jinger, but her tone was kind.

"I have to keep you alive." Konger's eyes flashed mischievously. "You promised to get me some pagoda-tree flowers, remember?"

The thin crescent of the moon hangs from the tip of a branch of the ancient pagoda tree outside the governor's mansion as the night watchman rings the midnight hour. The shadows in the streets are thick as ink, the same color as my silk leggings, tight tunic, and the cloth mask over my nose and mouth.

I'm upside down, my feet hooked to the top of the wall and my body pressed against the flat surface like a clinging vine. Two soldiers pass below me on their patrol route. If they looked up, they'd think I was just a part of the shadows or a sleeping bat.

As soon as they're gone, I arch my back and flip onto the wall. I scramble along the top, quieter than a cat, until I'm opposite the roof of the central hall of the compound. Snapping my coiled legs, I sail across the gap in a single leap and melt into the shingles on the gentle curve of the roof.

There are, of course, far stealthier ways to break into a well-protected compound, but I like to stay in this world, to remain surrounded by the night breeze and the distant hoots of the owl.

Carefully, I pry off a glazed roofing tile and peek into the gap. Through the latticed under-roof I see a brightly lit hall paved with stones. A middle-aged man sits on a dais at the eastern end, his eyes intent upon a bundle of papers, flipping through the pages slowly. I see a birthmark the shape of a butterfly on his left cheek and a jade collar around his neck.

He is the jiedushi I'm supposed to kill.

"Steal his life, and your apprenticeship will be completed," Teacher said. *"This is your last test."*

"What has he done that he deserves to die?" I asked.

"Does it matter? It is enough that a man who once saved my life wants this man to die, and that he has paid handsomely for it. We amplify the forces of ambition and strife; we hold on to only our code."

I crawl over the roof, my palms and feet gliding over the tiles smoothly, making no sound—Teacher trained us by having us glide across the valley lake in March, when the ice is so thin that even squirrels sometimes fall through and drown. I feel one with the night, my senses sharpened like the tip of my dagger. Excitement is tinged with a hint of sorrow, like the first stroke of the paintbrush on a fresh sheet of paper.

Now that I'm directly above where the governor is sitting, once again I pry off one tile, then another. I make a hole big enough for me to slink through. Then I take out the grappling hook from my pouch—painted black to prevent reflections—and toss it to the apex ridge so that the claws dig in securely. Then I tie the silk cord around my waist.

I look down through the hole in the roof. The jiedushi is still where he was, oblivious to the mortal danger over his head.

For a moment I suffer the illusion that I'm back in the great pagoda tree in front of my house, looking through a hole in the swaying leaves at my father.

But the moment passes. I'm going to dive through like a cormorant, slit his throat, strip off his clothes, and sprinkle corpse-dissolving powder all over his skin. Then, as he lies there on the stone floor, still twitching, I will take flight back to the ceiling and make my escape. By the time servants discover the remains of his body, barely more than a skeleton, I will be long gone. Teacher will declare my apprenticeship to be at an end, myself an equal of my sisters.

I take a deep breath. My body is coiled. I've trained and practiced for this moment for six years. I'm ready.

"*Baba!*"

I hold still.

The boy who emerges from behind the curtains is about six years old, his hair tied into a neat little braid that points straight up like the tail of a rooster.

"What are you doing still up?" the man asks. "Be a good boy and go back to sleep."

"I can't sleep," the boy says. "I heard a noise, and I saw a shadow moving on the courtyard wall."

"Just a cat," the man says. The boy looks unconvinced. The man looks thoughtful for a moment, then says, "All right, come over."

He sets the papers aside on the low desk next to him. The boy scrambles into his lap.

"Shadows are nothing to be afraid of," he says. Then he proceeds to make a series of shadow puppets with his hands held against the reading light. He teaches the boy how to make a butterfly, a puppy, a bat, a sinuous dragon. The boy laughs in delight. Then the boy makes a kitten to chase his father's butterfly across the papered windows of the large hall.

"Shadows are given life by light, and they also die by light." The man stops fluttering his fingers and lets his hands fall by his side. "Go to sleep, child. In the morning you can chase real butterflies in the garden."

The boy, heavy-eyed, nods and leaves quietly.

On the roof, I hesitate. The boy's laughter will not leave my mind. Can the girl stolen from her family steal family away from another child? Is this the moral pronouncement of a hypocrite?

"Thank you for waiting until my son has left," the man says.

I freeze. There's no one in the hall but him, and he's too loud to be talking to himself.

"I prefer not to shout," he says, his eyes still on the bundle of papers. "It would be easier if you came down."

The pounding of my heart is a roar in my ears. I should flee immediately. This is probably a trap. If I go down, he might have soldiers in ambush or some mechanism under the floor of the hall to capture me. Yet, something in his voice compels me to obey.

I drop through the hole in the roof, the silk cord attached to the grappling hook looped about my waist a few times to slow my descent. I land gently before the dais, silent as a snowflake.

"How did you know?" I ask. The bricks at my feet have not flipped open to reveal a yawning pit and no soldiers have rushed from behind the screens. But my hands grip the cord tightly and my knees are ready to snap. I can still complete my mission if he truly is defenseless.

"Children have sharper ears than their parents," he says. "And I have long made shadow puppets for my own amusement while reading late at night. I know how much the lights in this hall usually flicker without the draft from a new opening in the ceiling."

I nod. It's a good lesson for the next time. My right hand moves to grasp the handle of the dagger in the sheath at the small of my back.

"Jiedushi Lu of Chenxu is ambitious," he says. "He has coveted my territory for a long time, thinking of pressing the young men in its rich fields into his army. If you strike me down, there will be no one to stand between him and the throne in Chang'an. Millions will die as his rebellion sweeps across the empire. Hundreds of thousands of children will become orphans. Ghostly multitudes will wander the land, their souls unable to rest as beasts pick through their corpses."

The numbers he speaks of are vast, like the countless grains of sand suspended in the turbid waters of the Yellow River. I can't make any sense of them. "He saved my teacher's life once," I say.

"And so you will do as she asks, blind to all other concerns?"

"The world is rotten through," I say. "I have my duty."

"I cannot say that my hands are free of blood. Perhaps this is what comes of making compromises." He sighs. "Will you at least allow me two days to put my affairs in order? My wife departed this world when my son was born, and I have to arrange for his care."

I stare at him. I can't treat the boy's laughter as an illusion.

I picture the governor surrounding his house with thousands of soldiers; I picture him hiding in the cellar, trembling like a leaf in autumn; I picture him on the road away from this city, whipping his horse again and again, grimacing like a desperate marionette.

As if reading my mind, he says, "I will be here, alone, in two nights. I give you my word."

"What is the word of a man about to die worth?" I counter.

"As much as the word of an assassin," he says.

I nod and leap up. Scrambling up the dangling rope as swiftly as I ascend one of the vines on the cliff at home, I disappear through the hole in the roof.

I'm not worried about the jiedushi's escaping. I've been trained well, and I will catch him no matter where he runs. I'd rather give him the chance to spend some time saying good-bye to his little boy; it seems right.

I wander the markets of the city, soaking up the smell of fried dough and caramelized sugar. My stomach growls at the memory of foods I have not had in six years. Eating peaches and drinking dew may have purified my spirit, but the flesh still yearns for earthly sweetness.

I speak to the vendors in the language of the court, and at least some of them have a passing mastery of it.

"That is very skillfully made," I say, looking at a sugar-dough general on a stick. The figurine is wearing a bright red war cape glazed with jujube juice. My mouth waters.

"Would you like to have it?" the vendor asks. "It's very fresh, young mistress. I made it only this morning. The filling is lotus paste."

"I don't have any money," I say regretfully. Teacher gave me only enough money for lodging, and a dried peach for food.

The vendor considers me and seems to make up his mind. "By your accent I take it you're not a local?"

I nod.

"Away from home to find a pool of tranquility in this chaotic world?"

"Something like that," I say.

He nods, as if this explains everything. He hands the stick of the sugar-dough general to me. "From one wanderer to another, then. This is a good place to settle."

I accept the gift and thank him. "Where are you from?"

"Chenxu. I abandoned my fields and ran away when the Jiedushi Lu's men came to my village to draft boys and men for the army. I had already lost my father, and I wasn't interested in dying to add color to his war cape. That figurine is modeled after Jiedushi Lu. It gives me pleasure to watch patrons bite his head off."

I laugh and oblige him. The sugar dough melts on the tongue, and the succulent lotus paste that oozes out is delightful.

I walk about the alleyways and streets of the city, savoring every bite of the sugar-dough figurine as I listen to snatches of conversation wafting from the doors of teahouses and passing carriages.

"... why should we send her across the city to learn dance? ..."

"The magistrate isn't going to look kindly on such deception ..."

"... the best fish I've ever had! It was still flapping ..."

"... how can you tell? What did he say? Tell me, sister, tell ..."

The rhythm of life flows around me, buoying me up like the sea of clouds on the mountain when I swing from vine to vine. I think about the words of the man I'm supposed to kill:

Millions will die as his rebellion sweeps across the empire. Hundreds of thousands of children will become orphans. Ghostly multitudes will wander the land.

I think about his son, and the shadows flitting across the walls of the vast, empty hall. Something in my heart throbs to the music of this world, at once mundane and holy. The grains of sand swirling in the water resolve into individual faces, laughing, crying, yearning, dreaming.

On the third night the crescent moon is a bit wider, the wind a bit chillier, and the hooting of the owls in the distance a shade more ominous.

I scale the wall of the governor's compound as before. The patrolling patterns of the soldiers have not changed. This time, I crouch even lower and move even more silently across the branch-thin top of the wall and the uneven surface of roofing tiles. I'm back at the familiar spot; I pry up a roof tile that I had put back two nights earlier and press my eye against the slit to block the draft, anticipating at any moment masked guards leaping out of the darkness, to spring their trap.

Not to worry—I'm ready.

But there are no shouts of alarm and no clanging of the gong. I gaze down into the well-lit hall. He is sitting in the same spot, a stack of papers on the desk by him.

I listen hard for the footsteps of a child. Nothing. The boy has been sent away.

I examine the floor of the hall beneath where the man sits. It's strewn with straw. The sight confuses me for a moment before I realize that it's an act of kindness. He wants to keep his blood from staining the bricks so that whoever has to clean up the mess will have an easier time.

The man sits in the lotus position, eyes closed, a beatific smile on his face like a statue of the Buddha.

Gently, I place the tile back in place and disappear into the night like a breeze.

"Why have you not completed your task?" Teacher asks. My sisters stand behind her, two arhats guarding their mistress.

"He was playing with his child," I say. I hold on to the explanation like a vine swaying over an abyss.

She sighs. "Next time this happens, you should kill the boy first, so that you're no longer distracted."

I shake my head.

"It is a trick. He is playing upon your sympathies. The powerful are all actors upon a stage, their hearts as unfathomable as shadows."

"That may be," I say. "Still, he kept his word and was willing to die at my hand. I believe other things he's told me may be true as well."

"How do you know he is not as ambitious as the man he maligns? How do you know he is not only being kind in service of a greater cruelty in the future?"

"No one knows the future," I say. "The house may be rotten through, but I'm unwilling to be the hand that brings it tumbling down upon the ants seeking a pool of tranquility."

She stares at me. "What of loyalty? What of obedience to your teacher? What of carrying out that which you promised to do?"

"I'm not meant to be a thief of lives," I say.

"So much talent," she says; then, after a pause, "Wasted."

Something about her tone makes me shiver. Then I look behind her and see that Jinger and Konger are gone.

"If you leave," she says, "you're no longer my student."

I look at her unlined face and not unkind eyes. I think about the times she bandaged my legs after I fell from the vines in the early days. I think about the time she fought off the bamboo-grove bear when it proved too much for me. I think about the nights she held me and taught me to see through the world's illusions to the truth beneath.

She had taken me away from my family, but she has also been the closest thing to a mother I know.

"Good-bye, Teacher."

I crouch and leap like a bounding tiger, like a soaring wild ape, like a hawk taking flight. I smash through the window of the room in the inn and dive into the ocean that is night.

"I'm not here to kill you," I say.

The man nods, as if this is entirely expected.

"My sisters—Jinger, also known as the Heart of Lightning, and Konger, the Empty-Handed—have been dispatched to complete what I cannot."

"I will summon my guards," he says, standing up.

"That won't do any good," I tell him. "Jinger can steal your soul even if you were hiding inside a bell at the bottom of the ocean, and Konger is even more skillful."

He smiled. "Then I will face them alone. Thank you for the warning so that my men do not die needlessly."

A faint shrieking noise, like a distant troop of howling monkeys, can be heard in the night. "There's no time to explain," I tell him. "Give me your red scarf."

He does, and I tie the scarf about my waist. "You will see things that seem beyond comprehension. Whatever happens, keep your eye on this scarf and stay away from it."

The howling grows louder. It seems to come from everywhere and nowhere. Jinger is here.

Before he has time to question me further, I rip open a seam in space and crawl in to vanish from his sight, leaving only the tip of the bright red scarf dangling behind.

"Imagine that space is a sheet of paper," Teacher said. "An ant crawling on this sheet of paper is aware of breadth and depth, but has no awareness of height."

I looked at the ant she had sketched on the paper, expectant.

"The ant is terrified of danger, and builds a wall around him, thinking that such an impregnable barrier will keep him safe."

Teacher sketches a ring around the ant.

"But unbeknownst to the ant, a knife is poised above him. It is not part of the ant's world, invisible to him. The wall he has built will do nothing to protect him against a strike from a hidden direction—"

She throws her dagger at the paper, pinning the painted ant to the ground.

"You may think width, depth, and height are the only dimensions of the world, Hidden Girl, but you'd be wrong. You have lived your life as an ant on a sheet of paper, and the truth is far more wondrous."

I emerge into the space above space, the space within space, the hidden space.

Everything gains a new dimension—the walls, the floor tiles, the flickering torches, the astonished face of the governor. It is as if the governor's skin has been pulled away to reveal everything underneath: I see his beating heart, his pulsating intestines, the blood streaming through his transparent vessels, his gleaming white bones as well as the velvety marrow stuffed inside like jujube-stained lotus paste. I see each grain of shiny mica inside each brick; I see ten thousand immortals dancing inside each flame.

No, that's not quite accurate. I have not the words to describe what I see. I see a million billion layers to everything at once, like an ant who has always seen a line before him suddenly lifted off the page to realize the perfection of a circle. This is the perspective of the Buddha, who comprehends the incomprehensibility of Indra's net, which connects the smallest mote at the tip of a flea's foot to the grandest river of innumerable stars that spans the sky at night.

This was how, years ago, Teacher had penetrated the walls of my father's compound, evaded my father's soldiers, and seized me from within the tightly sealed cabinet.

I see the approaching white robe of Jinger, bobbing like a glowing jellyfish in the vast deep. She ululates as she approaches, a single voice making a cacophony of howling that sends terror into the hearts of her victims.

"Little Sister, what are you doing here?"

I lift my dagger. "Please, Jinger, go back."

"You've always been a bit too stubborn," she says.

"We have eaten from the same peach and bathed in the same cold mountain spring," I say. "You taught me how to climb the vines and how to pick the ice lilies for my hair. I love you like a sister of the blood. Please, don't do this."

She looks sad. "I can't. Teacher has promised."

"There's a greater promise we all must live by: to do what our heart tells us is right."

She lifts her sword. "Because I love you like a sister, I will let you strike at me without hitting back. If you can hit me before I kill the governor, I will leave."

I nod. "Thank you. And I'm sorry it's come to this."

The hidden space has its own structure, made from dangling thin strands that glow faintly with an inner light. To move in this space, Jinger and I leap from vine to vine and swing from filament to filament, climbing, tumbling, pivoting, lurching, dancing on a lattice woven from starlight and lambent ice.

I lunge after her, she easily dodges out of the way. She has always been the best at vine fighting and cloud dancing. She glides and swings as gracefully as an immortal of the heavenly court. Compared to her, my moves are lumbering, heavy, lacking all finesse.

As she dances away from my strikes, she counts them off: "One, two, three-four-five . . . very nice, Hidden Girl, you've been practicing. Six-seven-eight, nine, ten . . ." Once in a while, when I get too close, she parries my dagger with her sword as effortlessly as a dozing man swats away a fly.

Almost pityingly, she swivels out of my way and swings toward the governor. Like a knife poised above the page, she's completely invisible to him, falling upon him from another dimension.

I lurch after her, hoping that I'm close enough to her for my plan to work.

The governor, seeing the red scarf I dangle into his world approach, drops to the ground and rolls out of the way. Jinger's sword pierces through the veil between dimensions and, in that world, a sword emerges from the air and smashes the desk the governor was sitting behind into smithereens before disappearing.

"Eh? How can he see me coming?"

Without giving her a chance to figure out my trick, I launch a fusillade of dagger strikes. "Thirty-one, thirty-two-three-four-five-six . . . you're really getting better at this . . ."

We dance around in the space "above" the hall—there's no word for this direction—and each time, as Jinger goes after the governor, I try to stay right next to her to warn the governor of the hidden danger. Try as I might, I can't touch her at all. I can feel myself getting tired, slowing down.

I flex my legs and swing after her again, but this time, I'm careless and come too close to the wall of the hall. My dangling scarf catches on the sconce for a torch and I fall to my feet.

Jinger looks at me and laughs. "So that's how you've been doing it! Clever, Hidden Girl. But now the game is over, and I'm about to claim my prize."

If she strikes at the governor now, he won't have any warning at all. I'm stuck here.

The scarf catches fire, and the flame erupts into the hidden space. I scream with terror as the flame engulfs my robe.

With three quick leaps, Jinger is back on the same strand I'm on; she whips off her white robe and wraps it around me, helping me smother the flames.

"Are you all right?" she asks.

The fire has singed my hair and charred my skin in a few places, but

I'll be fine. "Thank you," I say. Then before she can react, I whip my dagger across the hem of her robe and cut off a strip of cloth. The tip of my dagger continues to slice open the veil between dimensions, and the strip drifts into the ordinary world, like flotsam bobbing to the surface. We both see the governor's shocked face as he scrambles away from the white-silk patch on the floor.

"A hit," I say.

"Ah," she says. "That's not really fair, is it?"

"Nonetheless, it's a strike," I say.

"So that fall . . . it was all planned?"

"This was the only way I could think of," I admit. "You're a far superior sword fighter."

She shakes her head. "How can you care for a stranger more than your sister? But I gave you my word."

She climbs up and glides away like a departing water spirit. Just before she fades into the night, she turns to look at me one last time. "Farewell, Little Sister. Our bond has been severed as surely as you've cut through my dress. May you find your purpose."

"Farewell."

She leaves, ululating all the while.

I crawl back into ordinary space, and the governor rushes up to me. "I was so frightened! What kind of magic is this? I heard the clanging of swords but could see nothing. Your scarf danced in the air like a ghost, and then, finally, that white cloth materialized out of nowhere! Wait, are you hurt?"

I grimace and sit up. "It's nothing. Jinger is gone. But the next assassin will be my other sister, Konger, who is far more deadly. I do not know if I can protect you."

"I'm not afraid to die," he says.

"If you die, the Jiedushi of Chenxu will slaughter many more," I say. "You must listen to me."

I open my pouch and take out my teacher's gift to me on my fifteenth birthday. I hand it to him.

"This is a . . . paper donkey?" He looks at me, puzzled.

"This is the projection of a mechanical donkey into our world," I say. "It's like how a sphere passing through a plane would appear as a circle— never mind, there's no time. Here, you must go!"

I rip open space and shove him through it. The donkey looms now before him as a giant mechanical beast. Despite his protests, I push him onto the donkey.

Tightly wound sinew will power the spinning gears inside and move the legs on cranks, and the donkey will gallop off in a wide circle in the hidden space for an hour, springing from glowing vine to vine like a wire walker. Teacher had given it to me to help me escape if I'm hurt on a mission.

"How will you defend against her?" he asks.

I pull out the key and the donkey gallops away, leaving his query unanswered.

There is no howling; no singing; no terrifying din. When Konger approaches she is completely silent. If you don't know her, you will think she has no weapon. That is why she is nicknamed the Empty-Handed.

The robe is hot and the dough makeup on my face heavy. The hall is filled with smoke from the scattered straw on the floor I've set on fire. I crouch down on the floor where the air is clearer and cooler so I can breathe. I put on a beatific smile but keep my eyes slitted open.

The smoke swirls, a gentle disturbance that you'd miss if you weren't paying attention.

I know how much the lights in this hall usually flicker without the draft from a new opening in the ceiling.

Moments earlier, I had carefully cut a few fissures in the veil between dimensions with my dagger and kept them open with strands of silk torn from Jinger's robe. The openings were enough to let a draft through from the hidden space, enough to let me detect an approaching presence beyond.

I picture Konger with her implacable mien, gliding toward me in hidden space like a soul-taking demon. A needle glints in her right hand, the only weapon she needs.

She prefers to approach her victims in the unseen dimension, to prick the inside from the undefended direction. She likes to press the needle into the middle of their hearts, leaving the rib cage and the skin intact. She likes to probe the needle into their skulls and stir their brains into mush, driving them insane before their deaths but leaving no wound in the skull.

The smoke stirs some more, she's close now.

I imagine the scene from her point of view: a man dressed in the robe of a jiedushi is sitting in the smoke-filled hall, a birthmark the shape of a butterfly on his cheek. He's terrified into indecision, the rictus of a foolish smile frozen on his face even as his home burns around him. Somehow the air in the hidden space over him is murky, as though the smoke from the hall has transcended the veil between dimensions.

She lunges.

I shift to the right, moving by instinct rather than sense. I have sparred with her for years, and I hope she moves as she has always done.

She meant to press her needle into my skull, but since I've moved out of the way, her needle pierces into the world at the spot where my head was, and with a crisp clang, strikes against the jade collar I'm wearing around my neck.

I stagger up, coughing in the smoke. I wipe off the dough makeup from my face. Konger's needle is so fragile that after one impact it is bent out of shape. She never attacks a second time if the first attempt fails.

A surprised giggle.

"A good trick, Hidden Girl. I should have gotten a better look through all that smoke. You've always been Teacher's favorite student."

The crevices I carved between the worlds were for more than just warning. By filling the hidden space with smoke, her view of the ordinary world had become indistinct. Ordinarily, from her vantage point, my mask would have been but a transparent shell, and the bulky robe would not have concealed the slender body underneath.

But maybe, just maybe, she chose to not see through my poor disguise, the same way she once chose to warn me of the hawk swooping down behind me.

I bow to the unseen speaker. "Tell Teacher I'm sorry, but I won't be returning to the mountain."

"Who knew you would turn out to be an anti-assassin? We will see each other again, I hope."

"I will invite you to share some pagoda-tree flowers then, Elder Sister. A tinge of bitterness at the heart of something sweet makes it less cloying."

Peals of laughter fade, and I collapse to the ground, exhausted.

I think about heading home, about seeing my father again. What will I tell him about my time away? How can I explain to him that I've changed?

I will not be able to grow up the way he wants. There is too much wildness in me. I cannot put on a confining dress and glide through the rooms of the compound, blushing as the matchmaker explains which boy I will marry. I cannot pretend to be more interested in my sewing than I am in climbing the pagoda tree next to the gate.

I have a talent.

I want to scale walls like Jinger, Konger, and I used to swing from vine to vine over the cliff face; I want to cross swords against worthy opponents; I want to pick a boy to marry—I'm thinking someone who is kind and has soft hands, maybe someone who grinds mirrors for a living so that he will know that there is another dimension beyond the smooth surface.

I want to hone my talent so that it shines brightly, terrorizing the unjust and lighting the way for those who would make the world better. I will protect the innocent and guard the timid. I do not know if I will always do what is right, but I am the Hidden Girl, and my loyalty is to the tranquility yearned by all.

I am a thief after all. I've stolen my life for myself, and I will steal back the lives of others.

The sound of beating, mechanical hooves approaches.

Matthew Hughes

. . .

Matthew Hughes was born in Liverpool, England, but has spent most of his adult life in Canada. He's worked as a journalist, as a staff speechwriter for the Canadian Ministers of Justice and Environment, and as a freelance corporate and political speechwriter in British Columbia before settling down to write fiction full-time. Clearly strongly influenced by Jack Vance, as an author Hughes has made his reputation detailing the adventures of characters like Henghis Hapthorn, Guth Bandar, and Luff Imbry who live in the era just *before* that of *The Dying Earth*, in a series of popular stories and novels that include *Fools Errant, Fool Me Twice, Black Brillion, Majestrum, Hespira, The Spiral Labyrinth, Template, Quartet and Triptych, The Yellow Cabochon, The Other,* and *The Commons*, with his stories being collected in *The Gist Hunter and Other Stories* and *The Meaning of Luff and Other Stories*. He's also written the Urban Fantasy To Hell and Back Trilogy, *The Damned Busters, Costume Not Included,* and *Hell to Pay*. He also writes crime fiction as Matt Hughes and media tie-in novels as Hugh Matthews. His most recent books are the Luff

Imbry novellas, *Of Whimsies & Noubles* and *Epiphanies*, the science-fantasy novel, *A Wizard's Henchman*, and the collection *Devil or Angel and Other Stories*.

In the flamboyant story that follows, a wizard's henchman bungles an important mission and finds that he has to deal with a cascading sequence of wildly extravagant consequences.

◆　◆　◆

The Sword of Destiny

MATTHEW HUGHES

Baldemar ran across the flat roof at his best speed, though he was hampered by the scabbarded sword thrust through his broad belt. When he had lifted it out of its cradle, he had slipped it through at his hip, but during the race up the stairs it had somehow worked its way around to the rear and now it struck the back of his left calf with every other step. But there was no time to stop and adjust matters; the erbs that guarded the house were already emerging from the trapdoor and at once their preternatural sensory organs locked onto the fleeing thief. A strange, wavering cry, like that of a weak and hungry child, rose from each of the three long, scaly throats, and Baldemar heard the click of razor-edged claws on the roof's flagstoned surface.

The neighboring building overtopped this one by several stories and from its ornamental cornices hung a rope. Baldemar had arranged it to be his emergency escape should the operation go amiss. But between the two buildings was a space as wide as Baldemar was tall and that gap was still a good ten paces away—or a very bad ten paces, if the erbs caught him before he reached it.

There was nothing for it but to drag out the sword and let it drop, in the hope that the watchbeasts would stop to guard it, that being their function. He yanked the eldritch weapon free and let it fall. But the staccato clicking of claws did not break its rhythm and now the eerie howl of the creatures was loud in his ears, its pitch rising. *That's the sound,* the thought went through his head, *they make just before they seize their prey.*

Two more strides and the lip of the roof was below the ball of his right foot. He kicked off, flung himself into space, just as a reaching claw sliced through the cloth of his shirt and left a long vertical scratch down the middle of his back. But the lead erb—it would have been the big female—was not poised to leap and could not stop. She tumbled over the edge of the roof and the cry she gave as she plummeted to the pavement below was almost human in its disappointment.

But the other two—her grown pups—were lighter and younger. They pulled up at the brink, their jaws clacking in fury, as Baldemar's fingers connected with the rope and, unfortunately, with the brick wall against which it hung. He felt a bone snap in the middle finger of his left hand, but he ignored the pain and clung to the thick hemp, immediately reaching up with his right to haul himself higher while the toes of his boots scrabbled for purchase against the wall.

He began to climb but had scarcely risen a body length before he heard again the sound the erbs' dam had belled just before her claw had raked his skin—followed immediately by a thump as the body of one of her brood struck the wall below him.

Down you go, too, was his happy thought, until he discovered he was celebrating too soon. The creature's forearms had reached out as it leapt the gap and one of its grasping hands made contact. A talon tore through his right legging and gouged his calf muscle, the pain lancing up through his body to resonate with the ache in his broken finger.

Baldemar gave his own cry now, of pain and fear, as the erb's weight caused the claw to slice downward through the leg muscle until it met the curled-over leather at the top of his boot. Now he had the beast's weight as well as his own hanging from his diminished grip on the rope. The injured hand told him it was not up to the task and he knew that he must change the situation or join the erb and its mother down below in a welter of broken bones and burst bodies.

With his unencumbered foot, he kicked at the paw hooked into his boot just as the watchbeast reached up with its other limb and sank another claw into the curled top, its strong hind legs scrabbling against the brick. Baldemar's efforts availed him nothing and he looked down into the erb's yellow eyes and saw its jaws gape in anticipation of the first bite, a long, pointed tongue licking across the rows of teeth like serrated daggers.

The sight caused him to give a reflexive jerk of the seized leg. A moment later, he felt the boot slide off his foot and the watchbeast fell into the darkness below. Relieved of the erb's weight, he disregarded the complaints from his finger and calf, as well as the plaintive chirps from the surviving watchbeast, and scrambled up the three stories to the roof of the building.

Coiling the rope and carrying it with him, he limped to where he had left Thelerion's flying platform, stepped aboard, and said the words that compelled the two indentured imps to lift it into the air and carry him away. The platform's floor pushed against his feet as they climbed into the sky, and Baldemar lowered himself into the plush, high-backed chair and rested his tired limbs on its gilded arms.

One of the creatures that powered the platform raised itself enough to peer through the surrounding railing. It was the one with skin like fired clay. The nostrils of its pug nose distended to sniff the scent of blood and its red-and-black eyes inspected the wizard's henchman closely.

In a voice that had the creak of stiff leather, it said, "I do not see the Sword of Destiny."

Baldemar was gingerly pressing his swollen finger, feeling for the break. "Tend to your own affairs," he said.

"Thelerion will not be pleased."

That was an unfortunate truth, and now that the man had the leisure to consider his situation, he faced the fact that the perils avoided at the beginning of this flight were nothing to what awaited him at the end. They were already far above the rooftops of High Marsan, the platform arcing west to where its owner waited in his eyrie overlooking the sparsely settled caravan stop called Khoram-in-the-Waste.

Thelerion had spent years assembling a unique ensemble: The Sword of Destiny would have completed the set. What the wizard intended to do with the items was unknown. Baldemar thought he would probably construct an invincible champion to wreak revenge on some adversary. Sorcerers were a tetchy lot, always eager to wreak revenge.

The Sword's acquisition would have allowed Baldemar to retire from his thirty years of service to the wizard. Or so Thelerion had said though his word was not to be relied upon. But now the Sword of Destiny was *not* to join Thelerion's collection of magic armor. And Baldemar's employer was not forgiving of failure. Indeed, lately he had begun to suspect that the thaumaturge had contracted a condition to which members of the Wizards Guild were susceptible: creeping figmentia. It was often accompanied by delusions of grandeur and outbursts of misdirected violence.

"Change direction," he instructed the red imp. "Go due south."

The compressed features of its diminutive face drew even closer together. "The master awaits," it said.

"What was his last instruction to you?"

"To obey you until you returned to his manse."

"And have we returned there?"

The reply was grudging. "No."

"Then obey me."

"But—"

"Tell me," Baldemar said. "Is Thelerion such a wizard as to encourage his underlings to second-guess his wishes? To embroider upon them their own whims and fancies?"

A shiver shook the small shoulders. "He is not such."

"Then take us south, at more speed."

"Still—"

"And do not speak to me again until I require it."

The stars above rearranged their positions as the platform turned south. Its velocity increased until the wind of their passage drew tears from Baldemar's eyes. But it was not just the chill of the upper air that made him shiver.

Soon they had left the city of Vanderoy—home to Baldemar since he had arrived as a young man to be taken on as a junior henchman to Thelerion the Exemplary—far behind. Now the platform flew south over the forest of Ilixtrey until the grand old trees gave way to heathered downs where the villages were few and the sheep many. Soon the rolling land climbed to where it abruptly fell away. Baldemar looked back and saw the alabaster cliffs of Drorn gleaming in the starlight and knew that he was over the Sundering Sea, its faint salty reek tainting the wind that blustered against his face.

He calculated as best he could their speed, the distance to the sea's farther shore, and the time remaining before Thelerion would begin to wonder why the platform was not landing on the terrace of his mountainside-hugging manse, with his henchman stepping down to hand him the prize he had been sent to bring.

Baldemar had no doubt that the thaumaturge would be able to reach out to his imps, and the moment he did so the platform would reverse course and leave him with the choice between returning to Thelerion's wrath—legendary for its depth and inventive display—or leaping to a quick, cold death in the gray waters far below.

But no, he thought, *the imps would bring the platform down beneath me faster than I could fall. They would catch me then they would make sure I did not try again.*

He voiced a short word that was out of context yet appropriate to the gravity of his situation, folded his arms across his chest, and shivered. His agile mind began rapidly considering plans, but just as quickly discarding them. Evading vengeful wizards was a complex task, even for a man with ten working fingers and both his boots.

The dark sky was paler off to his left. Baldemar limped to the portside rail and cupped a hand against the side of his face to shelter his eyes from the wind. The faint light became less pallid, and now he could see a line of gray that gradually resolved into an overcast that stretched from every horizon to every other. Ahead, the cloud layer became darker and soon he was flying through a cold rain.

He leaned against the balustrade and looked down. Darkness still ruled the world below but after a few more shivers he saw that the sea was no longer beneath him. He was flying above another forest, this one of dark conifers stretching unbroken as far as he could see, except far off to his right, dim in the distance, where he saw cleared land, and beyond, on the slopes of an eminence, a conglomeration of buildings of various sizes surrounded by a wall, with towers set in it at intervals. Atop the heights sat a more imposing structure of gray stone, with its own crenellated walls and a tall keep from which flew a gold-and-black banner.

He began to look around for a clearing to land in. He would send the platform on its way farther south and hope that some southern thaumaturge might seize it for his own. But even as he spotted a distant opening in the forest, the floor beneath him tilted as the platform heeled over and began to head for the castle.

He shouted for the imps' attention. "Not that way!" he said. "Over there!" he added, pointing.

But the red imp poked its head up through the balustrade, and said, "We are summoned thence."

"Can you not resist the summons?" Baldemar said.

The creature gave an equivocal toss of its head. "Perhaps. But we really don't care to."

The platform pursued a slanted course over the town then spiraled down toward a flat-roofed round tower on the castle. A lean old man in a figured robe stood there, his mouth pursed in concentration and a short length of black wood loose in one veined hand. The imps set the vehicle down softly, as if eager to demonstrate their capabilities, then both scuttled out from under to bob and bow in front of the wizard. Baldemar remained seated in the platform's chair, his posture and face indicative of one who expects an explanation for rude and boisterous behavior.

But the man in the robe addressed himself first to the imps. "Explain yourselves."

This the red one did, with much more prostrating and head-nodding, declaring that they were indentured to Thelerion the Exemplary, Grand Thaumaturge of the Thirty-Third Degree, while the spotted one mimicked every movement to support what was being said.

"And *that* one," the wizard asked, gesturing with the wand toward Baldemar. "What of him?"

"Don't answer that!" Baldemar said, leaping to his feet. "I will speak for myself."

But the interrogator made a motion with the wand and the red imp burst out with, "Oh, he's a terrible man, and a willful liar! Trust not a word he utters!"

"Hmm," said the wizard. He pointed the black wood at Baldemar and said a few syllables audible only to himself. The man felt a cold shiver enter through the sole of his right foot, swiftly climb his leg, torso, and neck, then exit his left ear after performing what felt like a scouring of his skull with icy water. One hand trembled uncontrollably and he had difficulty suppressing an intense urge to urinate.

"Now," said the man with the wand, "what's this all about?"

Baldemar had been preparing a tale of misadventure and surprise, in which he featured as a creature of purest innocence. But when he opened his mouth to speak, his tongue rebelled, and he heard himself giving an unadorned version of how his employer, Thelerion the Exemplary, had sent him to recover the Sword of Destiny, in which endeavor he had failed. "Dreading my master's wrath, I fled across the sea on this, his flying platform," he finished.

The wizard tugged at his nose, causing Baldemar to fear that another spell would be launched his way. Instead, he was told to accompany the wand-wielder down to his workroom. The imps were told to remain where they were. "I'll send you up some hymetic syrup," said the wizard.

"Ooh!" said the red imp, as the two looked at each other with widened eyes.

"Yum!" said the spotted one.

The wizard's workroom was depressingly familiar. Thelerion's had much the same contents: shelves crammed with ancient tomes, mostly leatherbound, some of the hides scaly; glass and metal vessels on a workbench, one of them steaming though no fire was set beneath it; an oval looking glass hanging on one wall, its surface reflecting nothing that was in this chamber; a small cage suspended on a chain in one corner, containing something that rustled when it moved.

The wizard gestured for Baldemar to sit on a stool while he went to pick through a shelf of close-packed books. "Don't try to run away," he said, over his shoulder. "I've been having trouble with my paralysis spell.

The fluxions have altered polarity and the last time I used it . . ."—he looked up at a large stain on the ceiling—"well, let's just say it was an awful mess to clean up."

Baldemar sat on the stool.

The wizard sorted through the next shelf down, made a small noise of discovery, and pulled out a heavy volume bound in tattered black hide. He placed it on a chest-high lectern and began to leaf through the parchment pages. "The Sword of Destiny, you said?"

"Yes," said Baldemar.

The thaumaturge continued to hunt through the book. "Why did he want it, this Fellow-me-whatsit of yours?"

"Thelerion," said Baldemar, "the Exemplary. It was to complete a set of weapons and armor." He named the other items in the ensemble: the Shield Impenetrable; the Helm of Sagacity; the Breastplate of Fortitude; the Greaves of Indefatigability. As he spoke, the wizard found a page, ran a finger down it, and his face expressed surprise.

"He was going to put these all together?"

"Yes."

"To what purpose?"

"I don't know."

The long face turned toward him. "Speculate."

"Revenge?" said Baldemar.

"He has enemies, this Folderol?"

"Thelerion. He is a thaumaturge. Do they not attract enemies as a lodestone attracts nails?"

"Hmm," said the other. He consulted the book again, and said, "But these items do not . . . care for each other. They would not gladly cooperate."

He tugged a thoughtful nose and continued in a musing tone, "The helmet and the shield *might* tolerate each other, I suppose, but the greaves would pay no attention to any strategy those two agreed upon. And the sword . . ."

The wizard made a sound of suppressed mirth. "Tell me," he said, "your master, he is a practitioner of which school?"

"The green school," Baldemar said.

The wizard closed the book with a clap and a puff of dust. "Well, there you go," he said, after a discreet sneeze. "Green school. And a northerner, at that. Say no more." He shook his head and made a noise that put Baldemar in mind of an elderly spinster contemplating the lusts of the young.

The wizard put the book back where he'd found it and favored his visitor with a speculative assessment. "But you're an interesting specimen. So, what to do with you?"

He was stroking his long chin while the series of expressions on his other features suggested that he was evaluating options without coming to a conclusion, when another man appeared in the doorway, clad in black-and-gold garments of excellent quality. He was even leaner than the wizard, his face an intricate tracery of fine wrinkles spread over a noble brow, an aristocratically arched blade of a nose, a well-trimmed beard as white as the wings of hair that swept back from his temples. A pair of gray eyes as cold as an ancient winter surveyed Baldemar as the man said, "Is he anything to do with that contraption on the roof?"

"Yes, your grace," said the wizard. "He arrived in it."

The aristocrat's brows coalesced in disbelief. "He's a thaumaturge?"

"No, your grace. A wizard's henchman who stole his master's conveyance."

The man in the doorway frowned in disapproval and Baldemar shuddered. The fellow had the aspect of one who enjoyed showing thieves the error of their ways. Indeed, he looked the type to invent new and complex forms of education, the kind from which the only escape is a welcome graduation into death.

But then the frown disappeared, to be replaced by the look of a man who has just come upon an unsought but useful item. "Stole from a thaumaturge, you say? That's an accomplishment, isn't it?"

The wizard did not share the aristocrat's opinion. "His master is some northern hedge-sorcerer. Green school, for Marl's sake."

But the man in the doorway was yielding no ground. "Say as you will, it's an accomplishment!"

Understanding dawned in the thaumaturge's face. "Ah," he said, "I see where your grace is going."

"Exactly. We could cancel the race."

"Indeed." The thaumaturge now again wore the face of a man who mentally balances abstract issues. After a while he said, "There is great disaffection this time around. The townspeople and the farmers have lost confidence in your . . . story." He gestured toward the looking glass. "I have heard grumblings in many quarters."

The aristocrat's stark face became even starker. "Revolt?" he said.

A wave of a wizardly hand. "Some vague mutterings in that vein. But more are talking about packing up and moving to another county. The Duke of Fosse-Bellesay is founding new towns and clearing forest."

The aristocrat grimaced. "Little snot-nose," he said.

"Actually, your grace, he is now in his fifties."

The other man waved away the implication. "I remember his great-great-grandfather. He was just the same. Tried to steal my lead soldiers."

"Yes, your grace."

The conversation, Baldemar saw, had meandered off and left both participants temporarily stranded. Then the aristocrat seemed to recollect himself. He rubbed his hands against each other, their skin so dry it was like hearing two sheets of parchment frictioned together, and said, "So that's settled. He's *accomplished*. He'll do."

The wizard considered for but a moment, then said, "I'll need him for a little while first. I think I can get an interesting paper out of him for *The Journal of Hermetic Studies*. But yes, he'll do."

"Do for what?" Baldemar said.

But the aristocrat had already gone, and the thaumaturge was looking for another book, humming to himself as he ran a finger over their spines. Baldemar thought about easing out the door, then glanced again at the stain on the ceiling, and decided to stay.

Over the ensuing few days, Baldemar learned several things: he had landed in the County of Caprasecca, which was ruled by Duke Albero, he of the papery skin. The wizard was Aumbraj, a practitioner of the blue school. The race the Duke had mentioned was a contest held every seven years to discover a "man of accomplishment" who would be sent as an emissary of the Duke to some hazily referenced realm. He would be accompanied by a woman who had bested all others in a test of domestic skills.

"My companion is a beautiful woman?" he asked, when this news was given him by the Duke's majordomo, a man who wore a large panache in his high-crowned black hat and was given to sniffing in disapproval at virtually everything that existence contrived to offer him.

"Comeliness is not a factor," the functionary said, with a mocking smile. "Certainly not in this case."

Baldemar's hopes faded. He had briefly liked the idea of becoming an ambassador accompanied by some long-necked, pale aristocratic beauty, until the majordomo described the women's champion as a lumbering rural wench who had been a bondsmaid on a dairy farm. "The things that were stuck to her boots defy description," the servant said, adding a sniff of double strength.

Aumbraj had repaired Baldemar's injuries and given him new clothing and boots. He was a prisoner but could wander the castle's confines at will though if he saw Duke Albero at a distance, he should immediately endeavor to make that distance even greater. "But don't try to leave," said the thaumaturge. "You have opened up an interesting avenue of research, and I will want to question you further. That may not be possible if I have to restrain you with the paralysis spell."

They both glanced at the workroom ceiling and agreed that Baldemar would not venture beyond the castle's walls. However, he did stand on the battlements facing the town and saw the Duke's men-at-arms disassembling a succession of barriers and obstacles strewn along a taped course that followed the curve of the curtain wall. There were narrow beams over mud pits, netting that must be crawled under, some barrels that had to be foot-rolled up a gentle incline, and a series of rotating drums from which protruded stout wooden bars at ankle, chest, and head height, plus some clear patches of turf for sprinting.

"It is some sort of obstacle course?" he asked a sentry.

"Yes, you could call it that," said the guard. "The townies and bumpkins don't like it, though. We have to wield whips to keep them running."

"And the winner becomes the Duke's ambassador?"

The man-at-arms regarded Baldemar as if his question had revealed him to be a simpleton. "Sure," he said, after a moment, "his grace's ambassador."

Baldemar would have pressed him for a proper explanation, but at that moment he was summoned by Aumbraj. Since the summons consisted of a loud clanging in his head that only lessened when he went in the direction of the summoner and did not cease until he found him, Baldemar did not linger.

"Describe the Sword of Destiny," the thaumaturge said when he arrived breathless in his workroom.

Baldemar did so, mentioning the ornate basket hilt and its inset jewels.

"And you just seized it?"

"Yes."

"Show me your hand." When the man did so, the wizard examined his palm and the inside flesh of his fingers. "No burns," he said, apparently to himself.

Aumbraj tugged his nose again, then said, "You said you tricked the guardian erbs into entering another room then locked them in."

"I did."

"But once you had the Sword, they appeared and gave chase."

"Yes." The how of that had puzzled Baldemar. The lock had been securely set.

"And yet, they did not catch you."

"I ran very quickly."

"But they were *erbs*," said Aumbraj. "Were they decrepit?"

"No, it was a mature dam and her two grown pups."

"Hmm." The wizard made a note on a piece of parchment before him on the workbench. "You ran onto the roof and there you left the Sword behind."

"It was hampering me, poking me in the leg."

"Just poking? Not slashing, gouging, stabbing?"

"It was still in its scabbard, just stuck through my belt," Baldemar said. "No one was wielding it."

Aumbraj's pale hand batted away his last remark as irrelevant. "Now, this Flapdoodle who sent you after it, did he equip you with any thaumaturgical aids?"

"Only the flying platform. I used my own rope and grapnel, my own lock picks."

"Hmm, and you're quite sure that the Sword did not seek to kill you?"

Baldemar showed surprise. "Quite sure."

"Hmm."

Another note on the parchment. The wizard rubbed a reflective chin then raised a finger to launch another question. But at that moment, Duke Albero appeared in the doorway, his face congested with concern. "He needs to go," he said, flicking a finger in Baldemar's direction.

"I may be on the verge of a significant discovery," Aumbraj said. "This man may be more . . . accomplished than the usual candidate. I need another day, at least."

The Duke's expression brooked no argument. He consulted a time-piece he drew from his garments. "The seven years end this very afternoon. There can be no extensions."

"But—" the wizard began.

"No buts." The Duke was adamant. "No just-untils, or a-moment-mores. If he does not go, You-know-who will arrive. So he goes, and he goes now."

He stepped aside and the majordomo, accompanied by two men-at-arms, entered the workroom. Baldemar found himself once more under restraint.

The Duke gestured for them to take him away but blocked the doorway long enough to tell Aumbraj, "And you will do nothing to interfere with his fulfillment of the requirements."

The thaumaturge looked as if he might have argued but dipped his head, and said, "I will do nothing to hinder him."

"Good." Albero once more consulted his timepiece then said to his majordomo, "You have the medal?"

"Yes, your grace."

"Then let's go."

Baldemar was taken to the castle's forecourt, just past the gatehouse. There he stood, his attendants keeping hold of him while the majordomo took from a pouch at his belt a bronze medallion on a chain. Stamped into the metal were the words: *For Merit*. He showed it to the Duke, who stood in the doorway of the tower from which they had come and moved a hand in a gesture that urged speed.

The functionary hung the chain around Baldemar's neck. Meanwhile another pair of guards emerged from a timber outbuilding leading a plump young woman in a nondescript gown whose life experiences to this point had developed in her the habits of smiling nervously and wringing her hands. She wore an identical medal.

No introductions were made. Instead the majordomo cocked his head toward a waist-high circle of masonry some distance across the courtyard, and said, "Here we go."

"What happens next?" Baldemar said, but no one thought the question worth answering. The stone circle had the look of a well, and when he arrived at it, he peered over and saw a deep shaft descending into darkness. The young woman also took a look into the depths and her smiling and hand-wringing intensified.

"In you go," said the man in the hat.

"What?" Baldemar adopted an explanatory tone. "I am to be an ambassador. Where is the coach to carry me, my sash of office?"

He looked about him, but saw only the woman, the guards and majordomo, the Duke, who was agitatedly gesturing, and high in the tower, at the workroom's window, Aumbraj pointing his black wand in their direction and speaking a few syllables. The young woman gave a little start, as if someone had pinched her behind, but then the functionary was pointing toward the dark depths.

"You and she go down," he said. "As you see, we have provided the convenience of a ladder. Or we can offer you a more rapid descent."

The woman tried to withdraw but the guards were practiced at their task. In a moment, her arm was pinned back and she was forced to the brink of the well. "All right," she said, "I'll climb down."

The functionary considerately helped her over the rim and saw her firmly onto the iron ladder. When she had descended a few rungs, Baldemar accepted the inevitable and took his place above her. Steadily they made their way down into darkness while the circle of sky overhead relentlessly shrank. Then it disappeared altogether as the guards slid a wooden cover over the well. Baldemar heard a clank of iron against stone as it was locked into place.

He had expected water, but when they came to the foot of the ladder, they were standing on dry rock. It was too dark to see anything, but a cold wind was blowing from somewhere.

He said to the woman, "What happens now?"

He could not see but could imagine her nervous smile and busy hands. "I don't know," she said. "They said it would be a journey to the land of Tyr-na-Nog and we would be received by princes and princesses. But . . ." She let her voice trail off.

"Tyr-na-Nog?" Nothing more was forthcoming so Baldemar pressed her. "Has anyone ever come back from this paradise?"

"No. But then, who would want to?"

Baldemar realized he wasn't dealing with the realm's most intelligent specimen of womanhood. "Did you have to run an obstacle race?" he said.

"No, that's just for the boys. We have our own competition of women's skills: sewing, milking a cow, baking bread, plucking a chicken."

"And you won?"

"I was surprised," she said. "There were better seamstresses and bakers in the contest, yet somehow they all faltered and it was I who received the accolade!"

"Which is at the bottom of a dry well."

She said nothing, but he could hear the faint sound of her hands comforting each other.

"Stay here," Baldemar said, "I'll explore a little." He felt his way around the wall until he found a gap, then he got down on hands and knees to cross it until the wall resumed again. While he crawled, he was chilled by a river of cold air. He stood up, and said, "Say something."

"What?" Her voice came from the darkness; he oriented himself and found his way back to her side.

"There's a tunnel," he said.

Her voice came quavering. "Where does it go?"

He told her he did not know and had no desire to find out. They stood in the darkness and felt the wind. The flow of air must mean that the tunnel connected with the outside world, but he had no desire to grope his way through blackness in which anything might lurk.

Time passed. The woman introduced herself as Enolia. Baldemar gave her his name. They sat on the rock, backs against the wall on either side of the ladder. After a time, Baldemar let his mind wander and found himself thinking about the wizard's questions about the Sword of Destiny. Enolia's voice brought him back to the here and now.

"I smell something."

His head came up and now he caught it, too: a sour odor, almost sulfurous, with a nose-tickling peppery overtone that made him want to sneeze. "It's coming from the tunnel," he said. A moment later, he added, "And there's a light."

They stood up, backs against the wall. Baldemar missed his knife, which was still in his boot, far away to the north. Then he found himself missing the Sword.

The tunnel was long and the light was far down it. It did not flicker like a flame nor throw a beam like a mirror-backed lantern. He saw a shapeless yellow glow that gradually resolved into a sphere with a flattened bottom, the shape of the tunnel. The closer it came, the stronger grew the taint of brimstone with a strong underlay of putrefaction.

He felt motion beside him and realized that the woman was trying to fit herself between him and the wall. "Stop that," he said, but she did not.

"I'm frightened," she said.

So was Baldemar, but there was no point dwelling on it. He couldn't quite bring himself to try to hide behind her, so he let her peep over his shoulder as the light came nearer. When it was a hundred paces away, he saw that there was something within the sphere. At fifty paces, he could almost make out what it was; at thirty, he could see it clearly and wished he did not have to. The stench became the olfactory equivalent of deafening.

A moment later, the yellow glow filled the mouth of the tunnel and the bottom of the well. There was neither torch nor lantern; the light somehow came sourcelessly from the creature before him. It regarded them from several eyes, then an orifice that resembled no mouth that

Baldemar had ever seen spoke in a voice that was somewhere between a hiss and a gobble.

"Well, here we are again."

"It is the first time for us," said Baldemar. He felt Enolia's head nodding against his shoulder in strident agreement.

"I don't suppose," said the demon—the man couldn't think of another word that did the thing justice—"that you bring me a message from Duke Albero? Something along the lines of, 'I'm ready. Take me'?"

Baldemar said that no message had been vouchsafed to him and felt the woman's nose rub his shoulder as she signaled the same was true for her. "But," he added, "I'm willing to climb the ladder and ask for one if you can give me some help with the lid up there."

The demon made a sound that might have been a sigh, if a sigh could sound that horrible. "We might as well get on with it, then," it said.

"With what?" Despite the almost unbreathable air, Baldemar felt a strong urge to extend this part of the encounter rather than discover just what "get on with it" might entail.

"The usual."

"And what is the usual?"

The demon focused all of its eyes on the man. Baldemar felt an uncomfortable pressure in his skull and a terrible itching of his palms and soles, but he bore the sensations as best he could while maintaining an expression of polite interest.

Part of the glowing creature moved and settled. Baldemar thought he might have just witnessed how a demon shrugged. "Very well," it said, "Duke Albero made one of those agreements I'm sure you've heard about. Wealth, power, health, longevity, and so on, until he should grow weary of the eternal sameness of existence. Meanwhile, I have to hang about and do his bidding."

"He seems to have fended off the weariness," Baldemar said. "Indeed, he looks capable of doing so indefinitely."

"Hence the escape clause," said the demon. "Every seventh year, he must send me a man and a woman of accomplishment. I ask them three riddles. If they can answer them, I go up and collect the Duke and take him back with me."

"And if they can't?"

Again the complex set of strange motions. "I take the messengers."

"By any chance, would you take them to a paradise?"

"No, not a paradise," was the answer. "Certainly not for *them*. Indeed, I find it rather confining, myself. I would much prefer to collect the Duke and go home."

"Oh," said Baldemar. The gibbering from behind him increased, but he forced himself to focus his mind, and said, "What is the first riddle?"

The demon said, "What walks on four legs in the morning, on two at noon, and three in the evening?"

"Seriously?" said Baldemar.

"You can't answer?" Another demonic sigh; a limb festooned with hooks and grapples reached for him.

"Of course I can answer," said Baldemar. "Everybody knows that one."

The arm or leg or whatever it was withdrew into the glow. "None of the Duke's messengers has ever answered it correctly," the creature said.

Baldemar realized that the seven-yearly contests were not intended to determine who among the Duke's subjects were the most learned. They were instead tests of gullibility.

"The answer," he said, "is 'man.' As an infant he crawls on all fours; that is the morning of his life. In maturity, his noon, he walks on his own two feet. And in the evening, which is his dotage, he relies on a cane."

All the demon's eyes again concentrated their gazes upon the man and again he had to resist the urge to rub itchy palms and soles together. "It's hard for me to think when you do that," he said.

The creature sent most of its eyes looking in other directions. "I was just surprised," it said. "No one has got it right before."

"The 'accomplishments' of the Duke's previous messengers," said Baldemar, "were not in the arena of intellect."

"I should have specified scholars," the demon said, "but now I'm encouraged. Here is the second conundrum. Do take your time." The man thought that the contortion of its facial parts might approximate a smile. Shivering, he looked away and listened to the riddle.

"There are two sisters; each gives birth and death to the other. What are they?"

The conundrum rang a faint chime in the back of his mind, but he could not quite close a mental grip upon it. He said to Enolia, "Do you know it?"

"No, it makes no sense," she said. She began to snuffle against his shoulder. "Poor me! I shall never see another dawn. Oh, woe—"

"Dawn! That's it!" Baldemar said. "The sisters are night and day. Each gives birth to the other, each ends the life of the other."

"Very good!" said the demon. "Very, very good!" The man could not be sure, but beneath the pure horror of its hideous voice and writhing facial parts, it sounded actually pleased. "And now the last, and simplest." It paused portentously then said, "What do I have in my hand?"

Instinctively, Baldemar looked at the limb that had reached for him, then at another that arched up and over what he thought might be the demon's head if it had a neck, finally at a third appendage that more or less curled at its more or less feet.

"Is there a clue?" he said.

"I wish there could be," said the demon. "I have long wanted to leave here and install the Duke in my collection."

"Let me think."

"Yes, do."

The first riddle had been easy. The second had come courtesy of a prompt from the woman. He now spoke to her over his shoulder. "Anything?"

Her voice was a whisper, "Nothing," and he could feel she had gone back to wringing her hands.

"Can you repeat the question?" he said.

"What is in my hand?"

"Which hand?"

"No clues," said the demon. "Oh, dear. Does this mean you're falling at the last jump?"

"Give me a minute."

Baldemar was mentally cudgeling his brain. *What would a demon have in its hand? What would this particular demon have in its particular hand?* For some reason, or no reason at all, he wanted to blurt out, *A piece of cake!*

The young woman began to blub, her tears and nasal flows wetting his shirt. "It's not fair," she said. "It doesn't even *have* a hand!"

A sensation came upon Baldemar, like a cooling flow of water on a searing summer day. "Nothing," he told the demon. "You have nothing in your hand because you don't *have* a hand. Just a kind of paw, and a crabby claw thing, and . . ."—he couldn't find the words—"and whatever that other thing is, but I know it's not a hand!"

There was a silence at the bottom of the well, broken only by the woman's stifled sobs. Then the yellow glow around the demon deepened to gold and became tinged with red around the edges. "Good-bye," it said then swept up the shaft of the well at great speed, taking most of its stench with it.

Baldemar looked up and saw the timber lid fly apart into splinters. He pulled Enolia into the tunnel as a rain of sharp wood briefly fell, then said, "Come on!"

He threw himself at the ladder and climbed with as much alacrity as his still-trembling legs could deliver. The young woman matched him step for step. When they climbed over the rim of the well, it was early evening. He saw the flying platform, far off in the distance, framed against the dying light.

From the castle came shouts and screams, the clatter of boots on stone flags. In the nearby stables, hooves were pounding against stalls. Then, from on high, came one great cry of despair.

"Get back!" he warned the woman as a pulsing sphere of red light appeared at the top of the keep, leapt into the air, and arrowed down toward the well. It paused above the opening and Baldemar had a glimpse of the Duke wrapped in what might have been a tentacle bedecked with curved thorns, the circles of his eyes and mouth forming a perfect isosceles triangle. He was making sounds that were not quite words.

The demon had all of its eyes trained on the new addition to its collection but it let one stray toward the man. "He who made me ordained that gratitude may never be part of my nature," it said, "but I am required to seek equipoise."

Baldemar said, "I am not prepared to make a bargain with you. No offense meant."

"None taken," said the demon. "But I cannot be obligated and I find that I am, to both of you. You may each ask a service of me at no further charge."

Baldemar took this statement and turned it over to examine it from several angles, demons being what they were. But the woman said, "I would like a nice farm, with good crop fields and healthy livestock, a warm well-furnished house with a pump right in the kitchen."

"Done," said the fiend. "It used to belong to the Kazakian family."

"I was their servant," she said. "They were always cruel to me, said I was not good enough to clean their muddy boots. The girls pulled my hair and the boys clutched me in private places."

"I know," said the fiend, then as an aside to Baldemar it added, "Equipoise, as I said."

To Enolia, it said, "The Kazakians are now *your* indentured servants." A claw handed her several scrolls and a cane fashioned from black, spiraled wood. "Here are all the necessary documents, and a stout stick to beat them with."

The woman took them and clasped them to her bosom. A smile briefly softened her features before they assumed an aspect of determination. "I have to go now," she said, and left without further ceremony.

Baldemar had finished his examination of the demon's offer. "Free of charge?" he said. "No comebacks?"

"No comebacks, but hurry up and decide. I am eager to introduce Duke Albero to his new circumstances."

"Can we leave it open? Can I call you when I have need?"

"If it is not too long," said the demon. "I experience obligation as a nagging itch. When you know what you want, say the name *Azzerath*, and I shall arrive forthwith." Then it disappeared down the well with the gibbering addition to its collection.

The castle was empty of people though filled with the odor the demon had left behind. Baldemar breathed through his mouth and found it bearable. He had not gone far before he came upon the majordomo's hat, the man's head still in it. From a room dedicated to trunks and lidded baskets he took a capacious satchel. In the Duke's quarters, he changed into richer garments then examined the coffers and cupboards, choosing items that were valuable yet sturdy—precious metals and gems, mostly—along with as much weight in gold coins as he could carry. He also filled a purse with silver bits and bronze asses for incidentals.

The coins all bore the likeness of the Duke. Baldemar studied the aquiline profile on one then turned it to see the obverse. It showed a date from a previous century and Albero's motto in an extinct tongue: *Miro, odal miro.*

Baldemar thought back to his school days and found he could translate it. "Mine, all mine," he said. He dropped the coin into the purse, put the purse in the satchel, and patted its comforting bulk. Then he smiled the exact smile as the woman had before she set off.

The black horse the Duke had ridden was in its stall, half-maddened by the smell of demon. But Baldemar was an experienced horse handler and soon calmed the beast. He saddled and bridled it with the Duke's own gold-chased tack and affixed the satchel securely behind. He walked it out into the courtyard, still clucking and cooing to comfort it, and saw that some of the men-at-arms had abandoned their weapons when the fiend arrived. He picked up a serviceable sword, and, since he was riding, a long-shafted lance. It had a black-and-gold pennant that he tore off.

The animal's iron shoes beat solid notes on the drawbridge as it carried Baldemar out of the castle. The fortification's surrounds were empty and he suspected that he would find the town similarly deserted. Demons had that effect.

"Now," he said to himself, "I'll ride to the land's edge and take passage on a ship sailing north. I'll buy myself a house in one of the Seven Cities of the Sea and invest in the fiduciary pool. Maybe I'll get a boat and take up fishing."

He touched his heels to the black's sides and the horse began to canter toward the town. Just then, a voice from above him said, "There you are!"

Baldemar looked up. The flying platform was just overhead, Aumbraj leaning on the balustrade. It settled to the turf, and the wizard said, "Come aboard. We have to go."

The man was tempted to urge the horse to a gallop. But the thaumaturge was tapping the palm of one hand with the wand. He climbed aboard and the flying platform turned north. Past the town, he looked down and saw Enolia marching along a lane that led to a capacious stone farmhouse. She paused to roll up her sleeves then used her stick to take a few practice swipes at the weeds that grew beside the track before resuming her methodical progress toward the house. When the platform's shadow passed over her, she did not look up.

"The thing is," the thaumaturge said, "you really ought to be dead."

They were flying north over the Sundering Sea at an even faster speed than Baldemar had come south. Aumbraj had fed the imps well on hymetic syrup and conjured an invisible shield to protect him and Baldemar from the shrieking wind of their passage.

The wizard's henchman had been watching the waves ripple the surface of the sea. Now he turned to the thaumaturge. "The demon would have given me a fate worse than death," he said. "He would have taken Enolia and me for playthings."

"I'm not talking about the demon. I'm talking about the Sword of Destiny. It is known to be very—touchy about being touched."

He grinned at his play on words but Baldemar bored in on the substance of his remark. "You're saying the Sword . . . has a will of its own?"

"A will—and a history of seeing that will turned into ways. And means, if you get what I'm saying."

Baldemar said, "So Thelerion was sending me to be killed?" His disaffection for his employer plumbed new depths.

"I doubt that," said Aumbraj. "He simply didn't know what he was getting into—or, more properly, getting *you* into. But it's clear from my researches that the moment your hand touched the Sword, you should have found yourself looking at a charred stump somewhere between your wrist and elbow."

Baldemar shuddered. But the thaumaturge went on, oblivious to his distress. "Instead, the Sword merely freed the erbs you had sequestered so that they could chase you away. Even then, it did not allow them to catch you, as they certainly should have. The man has not yet been born who can outrun an erb, especially up stairs."

Baldemar forced from his mind the image of what would have happened if the beasts had caught him.

"Then, instead of hacking off a leg, it hampered you just enough to make you leave it behind."

"So it didn't want to kill me, yet it didn't want me to take it away."

Aumbraj thoughtfully tugged his nose, then pointed a conclusive finger at Baldemar. "It did not want you to take it to this Fallowbrain who sent you," he said, "but I think we have to deduce that it didn't mind your touch."

Baldemar turned back to the sea. "I am confused," he said.

"As you ought to be. You're probably not used to thinking of yourself as a man of destiny."

"Indeed, I am not."

"Well, you'd better *get* used to it. Once it makes up its mind, the Sword can be quite adamant."

Aumbraj went on to describe the Sword's history and attributes. Forged on some other Plane of existence, its exact circumstances of origin were now completely forgotten. On the Plane where it was created, it probably had some other shape and function altogether. But here on the Third Plane, it presented as an invincible weapon. Yet it was more than that. It had the inclination sometimes to single out "persons of interest"—that was the Sword's own term—and assist them to become grand figures of the age.

"Its own term?" Baldemar said. "It speaks?"

"When it cares to," said the wizard. "But to continue, persons possessed of overweening ambition will seek out the Sword and grasp its hilt. Most of them meet with a swift and decisive end of all their dreams. It is not a forgiving entity and hates to be harassed. But, occasionally, it picks out some seeming nonentity and raises him to heights of glory. Some have taken that as a sign the Sword possesses a sense of humor."

"Amazing," said Baldemar.

"You have never heard of any of this?"

"My education was largely informal and centered on acquiring practical skills."

"Hmm," said the thaumaturge and spent some time studying Baldemar, after which he said, "You don't show any signs of being a candidate for glory, but then again, you might be one of those seeming nonentities."

Baldemar did not know whether to be insulted or pleased. Situations involving thaumaturges and magical weapons were often hard to read.

"Well, we'll just have to see," Aumbraj said.

The sun had set long before they crossed the southern downs and the forest of Ilixtrey. Soon the lights of Vanderoy showed themselves, strung atop a long ridge and its lower slopes. Baldemar offered to direct Aumbraj to the building where the Sword resided, but the wizard waved the proposal away.

"I can find it," he said. "To one of my abilities, it emits the equivalent of a blinding light and an earsplitting noise." He made a small sound of contempt, and added, "Your employer, the Great Fullbean, probably managed to catch a faint glow and a fading whisper."

They crossed the city wall and began to spiral down toward the rooftop Baldemar remembered so well. "I suppose," he said, "that's not really a building at all."

"Of course, it is," said Aumbraj. "But it is an edifice unremarked by even its neighbors, who pass by daily with never a thought as to what lies within. Even the city's tax collectors will overlook it."

"The Sword's doing?" the man said.

"As I said, it prefers not to be harassed."

The roof was in darkness but as they descended closer, Baldemar saw motion on its flat surface. "Look," he said.

The wizard peered, then made a gesture and muttered something. Immediately, the top of the building was bathed in bright light, revealing that someone was bent over the trapdoor, tugging at it with both hands.

"Oh, my," said Aumbraj. "Truly a skimpwit of the first water."

The figure looked up, shading its eyes against the light, and Baldemar saw that the skimpwit was Thelerion, clad in the Greaves of Indefatigability, the Breastplate of Fortitude, and the Helmet of Sagacity.
The Shield Impenetrable lay on the rooftop beside him, but now he
snatched it up and slipped an arm through it while his other hand produced a wand tipped with a large, faceted emerald.

Baldemar knew that wand well. He flinched in anticipation. But
Aumbraj said, "Oh, really!" and made a shooing gesture with the backs
of his fingers. The Shield glowed briefly as it was thrust back against
Thelerion, who stumbled backward and ended up on his rump.

Aumbraj had the imps bring the platform to a gentle landing. He
opened the gate in the balustrade and stepped down onto the rooftop.
Baldemar followed, being careful to keep the southern thaumaturge between him and his employer.

But not careful enough, because now Thelerion laboriously rose to
his feet, leaning on the Shield, and his gaze locked on his missing
henchman. His unappetizing features twisted in rage.

"Ahah! Miscreant! Faithless turd! Slackarse!" He had dropped his
emerald-tipped wand. Now he stooped and took it up, and said, "Receive your just punishment!"

"I would not do that here," said Aumbraj. "The Sword might not like
it."

Thelerion focused on Aumbraj just long enough for outrage to expand his eyes and mouth, then all his features contracted and his gaze
again bored into his lackey. "You told!" he cried. "The Sword was my
great secret, and you told this . . . this—"

"Aumbraj the Erudite," said the object of his inarticulacy, "blue school,
ninety-eighth degree. And I advise you to lower that thing you probably
think of as a wand before something truly awful happens to you."

Thelerion looked from henchman to wizard, then back and forth
several times. His mouth made sounds that were neither words nor in-
cantations, and spittle appeared on his lips. Finally, he emitted a noise
that came straight out of his lower throat and pointed the wand at
Baldemar. He spoke a portentous syllable and the instrument's tip
glowed a baleful green. A vindictive smile spread across his lips and he
opened his mouth to speak again.

At the moment, the trapdoor behind him flew open and struck the rooftop with a heavy slam. Light shot up from a great brightness within the stairwell, and, as Thelerion turned to see, the head, neck, and then the shoulders of a young erb serenely emerged from the glowing rectangle.

Baldemar's employer made another wordless sound, this one expressive of surprise and horror. He pointed his wand at the beast that, continuing its rise from the stairwell, now showed its clawed hands—which clutched the Sword of Destiny.

At this juncture, Thelerion made two decisions: one wise, one not. The wise move was to drop his wand; the unwise choice was to assume that the erb was bringing him the Sword, and that he ought to reach for it. His grasping fingers made contact with the scabbard.

Another blast of light illuminated the rooftop, though this one entirely conformed to the shape of Thelerion the Exemplary. His person was limned by a glare so bright that his body seemed to be a black silhouette at its center.

Then the light faded and the seeming became the reality. Where the wizard had been there now stood a figure of deepest black, dull and unreflective. It remained standing just long enough for the shape to be recognized and for its armor and shield to fall away with a clatter. Then the silhouette fell apart into granules of coarse grit that cascaded down to become a cone of stygian cinder. Scarcely had it formed a conical shape before its mass spread out under its own weight to lie as a circular mat of black sand—sand that crunched under the clawed feet of the erb as, still clutching the Sword, it stepped out of the trapdoor and approached Baldemar.

He whirled to leap onto the flying platform only to find that it was now high above him and moving off, with Aumbraj leaning over the balustrade to observe the scene he had left. A glance to one side told Baldemar that the rope and grapnel he had left on the adjacent building were no longer there.

He turned back and saw the beast coming on at a steady pace, the Sword now held in its paws so that the jewel-bedecked hilt offered itself to him.

Baldemar experienced a moment of sharp mental clarity. There were two outcomes to accepting the erb's offer: in one, he would be instantly, and probably painfully, converted into black grit, as Thelerion had been; in the other, he would rise as a man of destiny, to carve out a kingdom or an empire, and rule by whim and fiat. The momentary appeal of the latter prospect swiftly faded as he recalled the ruler of the County of Caprasecca, Duke Albero.

I don't want that life, he heard his inner voice saying. He remembered his plan to find a nice house in one of the Seven Cities of the Sea and a boat to fish from.

That option, however, did not seem to be available at this moment. But the thought of the parchment-skinned Duke brought up another possibility—a desperate gamble fit for a desperate situation.

As the Sword's hilt almost touched his fingers, Baldemar said, "Azzerath!"

He was immediately enveloped in a hideous odor and yet another bright light. Between him and the erb, which had leapt back, stood the repellent form of the demon. "What can I do for you?" it said.

Baldemar pointed and the fiend turned to regard the beast and what it held in its claws. All of its eyes focused on the Sword and a kind of ripple went through its being that the man could only interpret as an expression of delight.

"There you are!" said the demon, reaching out and taking the Sword from the erb, which promptly fainted from terror. The fiend folded the weapon in two of its limbs, clutching it to what might have been its torso. It seemed to Baldemar that the Sword also shivered in pleasure.

"I thought I'd lost you forever!" Azzerath said. "What have you been up to all this time?"

The fiend stood still, attentively listening to whatever the Sword was telling it. Finally, it stroked the scabbard, and said, "Well, never mind. That's all over now. We'll go home and it will be as if none of this ever happened. I've got a nice, fresh Duke for us to play with."

It became aware of Baldemar again and the man thought he was seeing a demonic frown. "It seems," the creature said, "that I am even more in your debt." Its body shook like thorned jelly. "The itch is quite uncomfortable."

Baldemar did not hesitate. "Can you arrange for me to have," he said, "a nice house in Golathreon, overlooking the Sundering Sea, with a sturdy boat to go fishing in? And perhaps a satchel of gold and jewels?"

"Done," said Azzerath. Two scrolls appeared at the man's feet. "Those are the deed and the boat registration. "You'll find the satchel in the library. Shall I transport you there now?"

"No, thank you. I think the wizard will carry me."

But Azzerath's attention had returned to the Sword of Destiny. "You arranged all this?" it said. "Just to find me again? What a smart little woozums you are." It stroked the scabbard again, making cooing noises, then disappeared.

The flying platform touched down. Aumbraj offered no apology for deserting Baldemar, who expected none. If their positions had been reversed, he would have made the same hasty exit. The wizard did enthuse about the events he had witnessed, chortling and saying, "I feel a wonderful scholarly paper coming on!"

"It seems," Baldemar told the wizard, stepping over the recumbent erb to where Thelerion's ashes were scattering in the wind, "that I have acquired a few pieces of magical armor. Would you care to purchase them? For scholarly purposes, of course."

A brief haggle followed, concluded to both participants' mutual satisfaction. A purse was conjured into existence and passed over. Then Baldemar helped the wizard gather the items and load them aboard the platform. Aumbraj also swept up some of the grit that had been Thelerion the Exemplary and stowed it in a brass cylinder with a tightly fitting lid.

"You never know," he said.

Meanwhile, Baldemar picked up his scrolls and read the address on one of them.

"Will you be passing near the City of Golathreon?" he asked Aumbraj.

"I can do."

"I would appreciate a ride."

The wizard shrugged. "If you'll fill in a few more details about your association with the demon. I mean to make the editor of *Hermetic Studies* clap for joy."

"Done," said Baldemar.

As they flew over the city, Aumbraj observed, in a carefully idle tone, "Even a scholarly thaumaturge can always use a good henchman."

"I was never a good henchman," Baldemar said. "Could never manage the required depth of self-abnegation. I was not even a very good thief. But I think I just might make a passable fisherman."

Kate Elliott

• • •

Kate Elliott is the author of twenty-six fantasy and science-fiction novels, including her *New York Times* bestselling YA fantasy, *Court of Fives* (and its sequels, *Poisoned Blade* and *Buried Heart*). Her most recent epic fantasy is *Black Wolves* (winner of the RT Award for Best Epic Fantasy of 2015). She's also written the alt-history Spiritwalker Trilogy (*Cold Magic*, *Cold Fire*, *Cold Steel*), an Afro-Celtic post-Roman gas-lamp fantasy adventure with well-dressed men, badass women, and lawyer dinosaurs. Other series include the Crossroads Trilogy, the seven-volume Crown of Stars epic fantasy, the science-fiction Novels of the Jaran, and a short-fiction collection, *The Very Best of Kate Elliott*. Her novels have been finalists for the Nebula, World Fantasy, and Norton awards. Under her real name of Alis A. Rasmussen, she's written the novels *The Labyrinth Gate*, *A Passage of Stars*, *Revolution's Shore*, and *The Price of Ransom*. Born in Iowa and raised in farm country in Oregon, she currently lives in Hawaii, where she paddles outrigger canoes for fun and exercise. You can find her on Twitter at @KateElliottSFF.

Here she introduces us to the self-proclaimed handsome man Apollo Crow—who turns out to be a lot more, and a lot stranger, than merely someone with a pretty face.

◆　　◆　　◆

"I Am a Handsome Man," Said Apollo Crow

KATE ELLIOTT

"**I** am a handsome man," said Apollo Crow, fixing the emperor of Rome with a look that dared that august ruler to disagree. "If your desire is to have a woman kidnapped without alerting her confederates until it is too late to rescue her, look no further. My skills are subterfuge, tracking down people who don't wish to be found, and an ability to lie with a straight face. I am also an exceptionally skilled swordsman."

The emperor set chin upon hand with thoughtful consideration, a pose suited to the stage, as he was well aware. "I was warned you always lie about something."

"Alas, so I do. It is a curse." His charming smile made a witticism of the remark.

"I am sure to a ruffian like you such a claim seems an amusing challenge. However, your situation is easy enough for a man such as me to expose. We'll start by process of elimination. Are you truly an exceptionally skilled swordsman?"

"I will duel any among your soldiers, or two or three at once. Bring them forth."

The emperor flicked up his fingers, straightening. "Will you duel me?"

One eyebrow only Apollo Crow raised, a neat trick many an opponent had admired to their cost. "It seems dishonorable, considering your age."

The emperor extended his right hand. An attendant guardsman settled a steel blade into the imperial fingers. He rose, took three steps down from the dais onto the marble floor of the audience chamber, and indicated that he was ready to begin.

Naturally Apollo Crow wore a hip-length black cape of the sort that swirls dashingly with any swift movement. He spun a full circle, the fabric floating like a whirl of shadow. When he again faced the emperor he held his blade in his right hand, as if it had appeared there by magic rather than sleight of hand.

The emperor shifted stance, taking his sword into his left hand. Apollo Crow smiled and did the same.

Light pouring from high-arched windows framed their shapes to dazzling effect as uniformed soldiers and gaudily robed officials admired the show.

"What is your fee?" A probing flurry by the emperor, easily parried by Apollo Crow.

"That depends upon the distance to be traveled and the circumstances under which I must put myself at risk."

They circled.

"The woman is a beauty, so that part of the job is no risk."

"What one man calls beauty another may find trifling. But that you call her a beauty tells me a good deal. Is she a woman who spurned you, the very emperor of shrunken Rome?"

The emperor laughed. "Quite the opposite, if you must know."

"Or at least so you feel obliged to claim." Crow assayed a thrust, and the emperor of all Rome and its few remaining provinces turned it aside.

"I need affect no lies, Crow. I am hiring you to do a job and ascertaining whether you can succeed. The woman is secondary to my interest. I need her sketchbook, which she carries with her everywhere. She is herself exceptionally well guarded and her movements well concealed by her many allies."

The emperor feinted left, then rapidly attacked right. Apollo Crow replied with a vicious riposte.

"Of what possible use can a sketchbook be to you? Are there compromising images that you seek to recover and burn?"

A flurry of parries and thrust rang through the hall. Both stymied, they broke apart.

"These are tedious attempts at provocation," said the emperor, scarcely out of breath. "Can you manage it?"

"It seems a simple enough job. Where do I start?"

"My agents report there will be a secret meeting in the town of Nikaia, a gathering of criminals and malcontents who harbor revolutionary sentiments. We don't know in which disreputable tavern it will take place. They change their meeting places every week. In any case, even if we did know, were my soldiers to appear in force, it would scare her off. Any violence done at the gathering will merely strengthen their querulous voices. So this is where you come in, Crow."

"Why, a seditious gathering with one foot into the empire itself! No wonder you are eager to crush this assembly before it can seed its roots into Roman soil. Yet what has a beautiful woman to do with such masculine pursuits as revolution?"

The emperor flashed an annoyed look toward a tapestry on the wall whose bright colors and bold design depicted his famous Amazon regiment striding into battle. As with the strike of an agitated viper, he pressed a bold attack straight at the other man. The ring of their blades striking and sliding, the scuff and stamp of their feet, and the movements of their bodies as they sought each to gain the upper hand were for a time the only dance in the chamber. The emperor pressed with his greater height and weight, while Apollo Crow answered with a speed and precision that made him seem to almost float above the ground.

At length they disengaged and the emperor stepped back to indicate the bout had ended.

"You disappoint me with your conventional thinking."

"That you are a rejected lover anxious to avenge yourself on an arrogant woman by stealing from her a personal item that is precious to her?"

A smile fluttered and faded. "That women cannot foment revolution. Indeed, they are the more dangerous, once roused. I had thought one such as you, who makes a living outside of the law, would not indulge in too much of convention."

"One such as me? What sort of one is that?"

"Among other things, a person who makes a living outside of the law." The emperor shook his head. "But I am finished dueling with you. Perhaps I can find a better person for the work."

"You cannot. If you have come to me, it means you have failed in your previous attempts to obtain the sketchbook."

"True enough," agreed the emperor with a gracious nod.

At a gesture from the ruler, an official walked forward and handed a substantial pouch of coins to Apollo Crow.

The man weighed them without opening the pouch.

"I know what you are lying about," added the emperor.

"Do you, indeed?"

"So we shall discover." With a decisive nod, the emperor indicated the doors, which were promptly opened by waiting attendants.

Apollo Crow smiled. He had a winning smile, a seductive smile, a handsome smile, and he knew it. With a flourish made into a mocking bob of a bow, he took his leave of the imperial palace.

Nikaia was a port town, seething with travelers, sailors, and merchants: a volatile and lucrative brew spiced with rumor, poverty, and discontented plebeians whose ears itched the more fiercely as more promises of suffrage were whispered into them. The haunts where radical sentiments pooled like wraiths awaiting release on Hallow's Eve were many, and Apollo Crow only one man, with one pair of legs. Yet he had other means of gathering intelligence.

A week after he arrived a crow fluttered to land on the open windowsill of the room at the inn where he was staying. Since he hated being alone he always found a way to have company.

The woman in his bed raised herself up on an elbow, her beautiful eyes opening wide as the crow bobbed a greeting. "What dreadful omen is this?" she gasped.

"You think like a Celt," he said as he slipped from under the covers.

He grabbed a bit of bread off a platter on the sideboard and went to the window to offer it to the bird. "The crow is sacred to my namesake, the Hellene god."

The bird snapped up the bread, then cawed for so long a stretch that the woman laughed.

"Is it thanking you for the meal? Or boring you with a complaint?"

"Not at all. Just giving me a welcome scrap of information in exchange."

"What an amusing tale-teller you are! Crows would make magnificent conspirators and agents if only they could talk and spy." Her voice turned coaxing. "You standing there naked has quite obliterated all thoughts of omens, battlefields, and carrion crows from my mind. I would take another welcome scrap, if you have a mind to come back to bed, for I certainly have no complaints."

"I am compliant in all things that harmonize with my wishes," he assured her truthfully, turning away from the window. "Are you acquainted with a tavern called The Four Abreast?"

"By rumor only, not from setting foot in it myself. You wouldn't want to go there."

"Why not?"

"It's in a very poor part of town, frequented by sailors, washerwomen, and cutthroats." She beckoned him closer with a pretty frown. "But I see from your expression you are determined to get yourself killed in that dreadful district. So be it. Come over here so I don't waste this chance while you are still among the living."

Later he made his way amid the dregs of twilight down a dismal avenue lined with shuttered shops, on the trail of The Four Abreast. Dark, empty streets made him melancholy, pining for the open land he had once called home. Ahead, a man pushed a cart of refuse while whistling a cheerful melody that lightened the lonely night. He quickened his pace to catch up, and just as he was about to make a friendly remark the carter halted next to a dank alley. A pair of ragged children crept out of the darkness.

"Go ahead but be quick," murmured the carter.

The children pawed through the stench-ridden garbage for anything they might use, eat, or sell.

"There's a coin in it for each of you if you can lead me to The Four Abreast," Apollo Crow said to the children.

The carter slapped away their reaching hands. "Don't go walking with strange men."

"I meant no harm. Can you tell me, Maester? I know I'm bound for the streets below Castle Hill but by what means may I recognize the tavern?"

"Why do you want to know?"

"I've served a cruel master and escaped. It seems right to see what I can do to help others who may wish for a different way of life."

The carter grunted, not entirely convinced.

"For your trouble, then." Apollo Crow tossed a coin to each child, pressed a third into the man's hand, and walked away.

"Juniper wards the entrance," the carter called after him. "That's all I'll say."

The neighborhood crowded up against the flanks of Castle Hill, straight streets collapsing into a confusing web of cramped lanes. The night lamps that illuminated the harbor walk and main avenues were absent. Gloom spilled like an incoming tide, turning every doorway and alley into a pool of shadows. A figure detached itself from a wall, swinging a club. Apollo Crow made a great drama of drawing his sword, and the shape thought better of attacking him and slid away into the night.

The harsh laughter of women drew him to a dilapidated gate framed by wreaths of strong-smelling juniper beneath candle lanterns, two on each side. Because it was set ajar he pushed on it, then realized it was stuck. Anyone going in would have to squeeze through, making them easy prey to an ambush.

He cocked his head to one side, listening, and identified two heart-beats waiting beyond. Sheathing the sword, he stepped sideways, back to the wall, and found himself in a hazy courtyard redolent of fish being smoked. A pair of burly guards shined a light on him. They hadn't even gotten out their swords.

"You're a looker and that's for sure," said one. He looked at his companion as if they were both about to burst out laughing. "But there isn't no one hereabouts who can afford the likes of you, if it's yourself that you're selling. No fancy personages up to your scratch of the type you must be accustomed to."

He tossed them each a coin. "I've a fancy to try the brew, that's all. I hear that late at night the tap flows with speeches and songs of a sort that interest me."

"At your own risk." They waved him on.

Beyond the reek of the smokehouses lay the more pleasant aroma of a stable and, beyond it, another courtyard overlooked by a portico in the Roman style, supported by old stone pillars. The building that rose up against the ancient columns was modern, built of wood. Lamps shone within to illuminate people seated in a spacious common room, their figures distorted by thick window glass. A pair of fiddles unfurled a dancing tune into the air, two voices weaving around each other as people stamped along to the rhythm.

He made a cautious entrance to find himself in the cheerful clamor of a tavern common room, divided in the Kena'ani fashion with a rope fence down the middle so men and women sat separately. He took a step toward the right, corrected himself, and went to sit on the men's side.

A blond lad of Celtic fairness and stern Roman disposition brought him a mug of the house beer so golden it might have been brewed from sunlight. He struck up a conversation with a group of local men whose callused hands and sun-weathered faces proclaimed them dockhands.

"Where do you hail from?" they asked him. "What ship did you come in on? Perhaps you came overland from the east, for you have a bit of that eastern look about you."

He entertained them with fanciful tales, all of which were true but sounded false to their ears: that he was born in a place where every fresh tide altered the contours of the land; that a dragon ate his father; that his mother was a crow. All the while he surreptitiously studied the women crowded at their ease on the other side of the fence as at a cheerful roost. They were all females of the laboring class: washerwomen with lye-scarred hands; street sellers whose baskets of walnuts and onions sat at their feet; street sweepers dozing against their brooms. It had long been his observation that women labored from before sunrise to long after sunset. Sitting in a tavern late at night to hear the pronouncements of a radical who wielded words like the deadliest of swords might well be the most restful patch of their year.

His gaze caught on a young woman with a lively face who seemed unable to sit still. She had brought a bit of mending to do as women were wont, there always being some tear or fray that needs repair as a bird must endlessly tend to its feathers. Sewing kept her hands busy. But it was her long, thick braid of hair, as glossy a black as his own, that made him twitch, as if he'd been pricked by a needle wielded by an invisible hand.

"What do you think of our fine harbor, and the countryside hereabout?" they asked, for he had fallen inexplicably silent.

"The provinces of Rome I call a fair and lovely land, for all that its skies and earth are so very different from my homeland," he answered. "Yet this is the first time here in Roman territory I've seen women seated in a tavern as if they are accustomed to take their ease where men usually perch. Usually Roman women stay home."

"We're a port town, not a staid Roman oppidum. Anyway, women as much as men flock to any meeting where there's a chance the Honeyed Voice will speak. Men for her beauty, and women for her exhortations and her knife."

"The Honeyed Voice?" He sat up straighter. "What knife does she wield?"

"The knife of persuasion."

The fiddles ran down a cadence and ceased. One man elbowed another as a table was cleared at the far end of the room.

"Here she comes," cried one of his interlocutors with an eager smile.

The crowd made way for three figures: a short, curvaceous woman flanked on either side by a tall individual of the people known as the feathered ones. These two had narrow jaws, vicious claws, and the slightly bobbing walk of a people who seemed a blend of human, bird, and lizard. Although soberly dressed as respectable lawyers, the feathered ones betrayed their true nature in having the toothy grins of dangerous beasts. In a chamber so filled with the strong scent of humanity their dry, summer-burnt smell faded away almost to nothing, but he took in a deep breath to make his chest bigger and himself thus more threatening, lest they look his way and think they must attack. Then, recalling prudence, he hunched instead so neither would mark him with its roving gaze. Not that the feathered ones had any reason to recognize him for what he was. Like humans, they were creatures of this world. He was truly alone, the only murder of his kind he had ever found in all the long and lonely years living in exile.

A shout arose from the company all around as the feathered ones helped the petite woman up to stand on the tabletop.

Taken utterly by surprise by her exquisite features and magnificent poise, Apollo Crow jumped to his feet to get a better look. With delighted remonstrations his companions tugged him back down to the bench.

"Did we not say she would astound you?" They laughed as the vision raised her arms with a gesture that invited the chattering audience to be quiet. "Listen, and you will hear."

"My comrades. My friends. *My sisters.*"

The women in the room ululated, then hushed expectantly.

"I am come into a hostile land bearing a message for those of you who seek freedom. The yoke of tyranny harnesses you, yet it can be thrown off here as it has been elsewhere in Europa."

She spoke in a compelling tone that without apparent effort filled the large room so no listener need strain to hear. With effortless eloquence she lectured on the means by which the rich and powerful arrogate wealth and favor for themselves and exploit those who toil under their lash. She described in convincing detail the creation of a governing Assembly in the city of Havery, presided over by the prince of that territory but subject to no master except itself. Half the room leaned forward as she detailed how the elections for representatives to this Assembly included women, while the other half exchanged troubled looks. Yet all listened, for she had the gift of speech that made every word bloom from her mouth into a flower and so that every sentence became a fragrant bouquet.

"It is true that by ancient Roman law women are forbidden from holding magistracies, priesthoods, triumphs, badges of office, or spoils of war. But what is law if not words written by hands?" she went on, as if the men's surly glances and hot murmurs impelled her to harden her phrases. "What the hand works can be made or unmade, as times change and philosophies take new paths. This is our new path, if we wish to walk it."

"Is she an actress?" Apollo Crow demanded of his new friends.

The men hushed him with slaps on the arm, for however appalled they might be by her rhetoric they were also entranced by her person and her voice.

"No actress! She has roused the hearts of people all across Europa. They say the emperor would imprison her if only he could catch her."

A dangerous woman, indeed, if you were emperor over all the Romans and feared the discontent that simmered beneath the surface of the normally silent plebeians. She was the fire coaxing the water to boil, and a fine fierce blaze she was, but whatever else he might think he had a job to do and a curse that bound him.

When at length she finished her speech to thunderous applause, he winkled a gold chain from one of the many pockets secreted about his clothing where he kept the bits and bobs he collected on his travels. He caught the collar of a passing child young enough to be allowed to wander both sides of the fence.

"There is a denarius in it for you if you take this gold chain to the Honeyed Voice and let her know what man sent it."

"What if I just steal the chain and run away and never come back?" the child asked, perplexed by such a naïve offer and also staring greedily at the glittering links.

"Let me assure you I never forget a face." Apollo Crow's smile made the child shudder. "If you disoblige me, then I promise that one day you will find yourself set upon by crows and pecked to death, with no one the wiser."

The child pretended to laugh to save face but at the same time cast a frightened look to either side, seeking escape. Yet the possibility of earning a denarius was no trivial inducement. After less of a hesitation than Apollo Crow had expected, the child fished both chain and coin out of his hand and ducked under the rope.

As he had known they would, the women pressing forward to speak to the Honeyed Voice allowed the child to slip through their ranks, for women always made room for hatchlings. She dipped to listen as the child spoke. Her shoulders tensed in surprise and she looked up to scan the chamber.

Her gaze met his. The light was a little too dim and she a little too far away for him to read the subtleties of her reaction, but he could guess by her shifts in posture that she was displeased, and yet also tickled by an incurable swell of curiosity. Hard not to notice that she took in several bosom-heaving breaths. He lifted his mug to salute her. The men around him, captured by the gesture, applauded and laughed, praising him for his steely nerve. Everyone knew, they said, that the Honeyed Voice had no patience for men who tried to bribe her with gifts; she chose as she wished for interest, not for gain.

She handed the gold chain to a woman who stood beside her and indicated that the other woman should return the rejected bauble to him. Then, with an empty hand pretending to hold a nonexistent cup, she saluted him back.

He was abruptly head over tail in love with the challenge.

Oddly enough, the woman entrusted with the necklace was the very same seamstress he had noticed before. He hadn't noticed her leaving her bench and therefore studied her more closely as she approached. Her clothes were sturdy, not fancy, her boots worn by much walking.

"Maester, I've been asked by the maestra to return this to you."

"No, no, I insist you keep it for your trouble."

"A generous offer." She swung the chain between her fingers. "I'd best not, for that would put me in your debt in a way you might misinterpret."

"Not at all. It is a mere bauble, a token of appreciation for the fine speech by the Honeyed Voice that so entertained me. Since she rejects me so cruelly, my sole request is that you be so kind as to exchange a few words with me, a gentle balm to my aching heart. What is your name?"

"Catherine, Maester. And yours?"

"I am Apollo Crow, a traveler. Please sit."

The seamstress seated herself on an empty bench beside the rope and smiled. She was attractive, with the grace of a fighter about her long limbs and easy physical confidence. He might find a way to the other woman through this one: jealousy and competition sometimes fired women's interest when a handsome man became involved.

He called for a round of drinks and seated himself close enough to talk to the seamstress across the fence. He essayed teasing banter, but she wanted only to discuss the coming revolution.

"Many speak against the radical proposal to allow women to vote. You must have a thought on this topic, Maester."

"What is your opinion, Maestra?" he parried.

"Why, do you really wish to hear my opinion? I'm often told I talk too much. Many men say women are formed for bread and butter and not for philosophical debate. What do you think, Mr. Crow?"

"I come from a people where everyone talks a great deal, women and men equal in their vociferousness. As for what I think, I am new to this town and thus prefer to discover what the locals may think. How else may I come to an understanding of how people get on here? Your compatriot speaks compellingly. I would wish nothing more than an evening of innocent conversation with such a persuasive voice. Perhaps in your company?"

He had a smile that melted women and when he used it now she leaned closer, and even closer still, gaze alight with interest. Over her shoulder he noticed the Honeyed Voice moving toward the exit, then pulled his gaze back to the seamstress.

Her lips parted as if in delight at his advances. In a low, husky, sensuous voice, she said, "She's well guarded, Mr. Crow. Don't believe otherwise. It's best if you leave us alone."

She rose and cut her way smoothly through the crowded common room and out the door to the courtyard, through which the Honeyed Voice had departed.

His new friends laughed. "Well, well, you've been put in your place and lost your coin besides!"

"I shall need a drink to drown my sorrow!" He gestured to the server. "Fill my friends' cups again."

As the youth moved forward, Apollo Crow surreptitiously tipped the bench so as to knock the server in the legs and send him sprawling. A great splash from the pitcher, and a mighty shout from everyone around as they got wet, distracted his male companions. In the ensuing commotion he slipped the chain into the server's pocket, then left as quickly as possible, elbowing through the crowd to get out the door in his haste. Outside he had to pause and set an elderly man to rights who had lost hold of his cane and stumbled in the crush. Then he strode on the path of his target, who was even now slipping out the gate.

As he hurried past the reeking smokehouses a slender young man fell into step beside him. He had hair as long and black as the seamstress's and indeed there were other signs of a family resemblance in coloring and the shape of their eyes.

"A word of advice," said the young fellow with a smile that was more a baring of teeth. "If the Honeyed Voice has rejected your offer, as she has, then do not press your suit."

"My thanks," replied Apollo Crow with the sardonic eyebrow lift he had perfected as a means to intimidate people who thought to spar with him. "What business is it of yours?"

"I am her kinsman. Therefore her well-being is my responsibility." His new companion eyed him as a cat would a bird. "Just a warning, Maester. Personally I find the Honeyed Voice bossy and impatient but I understand that for men of your type she presents an irresistible attraction. The need to prove that her beauty and her fierce confidence will yield to you, and you alone, where lesser men have failed."

"My type? What type do you believe that to be?"

The young man braced himself in the narrow opening of the gate so no one—and particularly not Apollo Crow—could pass. He sniffed the air, then frowned just as if he could sift through the fug of the courtyard's air and tease out threads of information.

"Now I'm not so sure. Where did you say you come from?"

"I didn't say. What was your name?"

"I didn't say," said the young man with another of those smiles filled with charm and menace. "If you have family, you'll understand we look out for each other."

"I understand the sentiment very well. I am in every possible way a family man."

The fellow kept standing there, meaning to block the gate until it was too late to follow. While Apollo Crow was never averse to a headlong attack he judged the other man too much of a puzzle to assay with so little to go on. There was a coiled energy about him that reminded him of . . . himself, that sense of a body lodged in this world and a spirit anchored in the world beyond. But he had learned the hard way not to speak to strangers and ordinary people about mortal worlds and spirit worlds because no one believed him. He had learned to turn truth into tales that people accepted as entertainment.

He bowed as if in gracious retreat, acknowledging the right of family to protect its own. But upon stepping away from the gate he at once sought out the darkest and most isolated corner of the courtyard. Behind a smokehouse amid the crunch of ashy scales and discarded refuse he paused, looking around one last time to make sure he was entirely alone. The night was not kind to his eyesight, and he could never rely on his sense of smell. Cocking his head to one side, he listened. Fiddles and stamping feet adrift in the air made it hard to pick out any softer noise but then the young man spoke over by the gate, addressing the guards.

"Where did he go? I didn't see him go back into the tavern."

With a sigh he sloughed the self he wore. In a flurry of one hundred and thirty-four pairs of wings—because it takes many crows to make a man—they flew out over the night-drenched streets in search of a woman.

The flock followed the woman and the two feathered ones to a respectable inn on the waterfront in a well-lit and prosperous district of the town. In a dense cloud they descended onto the rooftop of the inn as if coming to roost for the night. Individuals flapped down to spy. One even got into the common room and perched watchfully in a smoky corner as the Honeyed Voice sat down to supper, as drinks were sent to her table by hopeful suitors and shy admirers. A crow flew to every windowsill looking into every room, awaiting her arrival in one of them. But it was the crow stationed at the kitchen yard who saw her leave by a back door and slip away into the night, joined by the seamstress and the young man while the two much more conspicuous feathered ones remained behind to make it seem she hadn't left yet. A cunning scheme, indeed, to throw off the scent of people who would be following her. Cawing in excitement at this simple ruse, some of the younger crows had to be hushed lest they draw attention.

Her route took her into the humbler streets along the riverbank where lived folk of modest circumstance and law-abiding habit. She came to rest at last in a small two-story inn with a ramshackle window-less exterior. Despite their unprepossessing appearance the gate and walls presented a formidable challenge for a person on the street who wanted to get a look inside without being noticed. The crows merely settled all around the roof overlooking an interior courtyard. No fire burned in the courtyard's hearth, ashes as cold as if they hadn't been lit in days.

Even this late at night a solitary soul sat at a table intent on reading by the illumination of a floating sphere of cool white light. Several crows hopped forward to get a better look. He was a well-dressed and well-preened man who might be said to be as handsome as a crow, not that that was possible. When the others hurried in through the gate he rose to greet them. By the intimate kiss he gave the seamstress, it was evident that a plan to seduce her in order to instigate the envious attention of the Honeyed Voice would probably not work. Indeed, by the way the four conversed with casual remarks and overlapping interruptions, they themselves had the manners of a flock.

After a short wait the two feathered ones appeared. Once they were inside and the gate closed the target crossed the courtyard and entered a gated stairwell, alone.

The inn was really two old buildings stitched together: a set of rooms facing inward around the courtyard and a separate wing stuck on at right angles. This extra wing protruded over the water, a relic from a now-derelict ancient bridge that no longer reached the opposite shore. The repurposed bridge had no lower story, only the arched foundation, so the rooms atop were unreachable except by the guarded stairwell and an interior passage.

The windows of these rooms overlooked the river. Soon enough a pair of shutters were opened from inside. The woman leaned out and took in a deep breath of night air, then winced at the smell of refuse and smoke. The moment she retreated into the room two crows landed on the windowsill to watch. She lit a candle and, by its light, locked the door from the inside and tucked the key into her sleeve. Then she set the candle into a brass holder on a dressing table. Flame glimmered in the mirror as she opened a sketchbook and sat down to draw.

One crow flew to a perch atop the wardrobe.

Although flight and landing made no discernible noise, her hand paused.

"Was there something more you needed to tell me?" she said to the air.

The air offered no reply.

Both the crow on the windowsill and the one on the wardrobe hopped out of sight as she closed the book and rose. After a puzzled glance around the chamber, she opened the door into the passage and went out. As soon as she shut the door, crows mobbed into the chamber.

He quickly stitched himself into a single shape, all but for three parts. First he tested the door to the passage but she had locked it from outside. No chance escaping with the sketchbook out that way, not without the key. Taking a seat at the dressing table, he weighed the sketchbook in a hand. Too heavy to fly with even if he created a net for crows to carry.

Therefore he reluctantly had to accept the third option although he liked it least and would have to play for time. He tore a scrap of blank page out of the back of the book and filled it with exceedingly precise and tiny writing. This scrap he slipped into a message tube, which he fixed to the leg of one crow. Thus dismissed, it flew, and the other two parts took up watch outside.

At last he opened the sketchbook. With the greatest interest and delight he examined the first drawing, which depicted a crowned young woman riding a bull—clearly meant to be the Phoenician queen Europa—and a lion sneaking up behind them dragging a length of chain. As a metaphor for the shrunken empire of Rome wishing to re-capture the lands it had lost hundreds of years ago it was, if anything, a little obvious.

A key tumbled the lock. He shut the book, set his elbows on the dressing table, and in the mirror examined his lean face, his glossy black hair, his nimble fingers. Was there anything wrong with him? Something he could shape better? Why, was there a man in this world handsomer than he was?

The hinges creaked. A figure loomed up behind him like a stain expanding in the mirror. Candlelight glinted on the edge of a slim sword, but it wasn't as sharp as the pique of her smile. He met the reflection of her gaze and smiled in lazy reply.

She had an interrogative eyebrow not unlike his own, and she used it now. "You are sitting in my chair."

"It is hard to resist admiring myself when I have the chance, for I am certainly a sleek and shiny fellow."

Her gaze had a measuring look. "Indeed, it is hard to resist wondering how such a sleek and shiny fellow as you could have gotten into this locked chamber."

"You are irresistible. Therefore, no barrier can keep me from you."

"Really?" Her posture had the angles and muscle of someone who knew how to fight. "The passage to these rooms is guarded day and night which, as you may imagine, is why people who have enemies like to sleep here. The door from this chamber into the passage can be locked both from the inside and from the outside, and I have the key. So common sense suggests you came in through the window. Yet the roof is too steep to negotiate and the wall too steep to climb. Even if you could climb it, you aren't wet as you would have to be if you'd come up from the river."

"I might have arrived in a boat."

She went to the window and looked down, then turned back to him. "There's nowhere to tie it up. Do you care to explain this mystery?"

He rose carefully, held his hands palms out to show himself unarmed, and offered a courteous bow, hand to heart. "I am not the only mystery in this chamber. The greatest mystery is your allure."

"You should have tried that line earlier, before your back was to the wall. Why are you here?"

"Perhaps you and I may trade secrets. Why has the emperor of Rome hired me? That your revolutionary agitation troubles the Roman regime is one answer but I sense it is not the only one. I fear I am afflicted with an implacable curiosity."

"I could placate your curiosity by running you through with my sword."

"Ah, but what about your own curiosity? Do you not wish to know by what cunning and skill I appeared in your chamber? Imagine those same attributes turned solely to the task of . . . pleasing you."

"Pleasing me?" She considered the whole of him, a twist of amusement playing about her lips. He took the opportunity to turn his head so she would see his best profile. With a rueful laugh, she shook her head. "Before or after you turn me over to the emperor of Rome?"

He considered this question with the seriousness it deserved. "Before would be a sure thing. After would be determined by his whim."

"I can see you are a strategist," she said, a scrape like swallowed laughter in her tone that annoyed him. Was she mocking him? "But what if I don't want to be kidnapped and taken to the emperor of Rome?"

"Perhaps you could match his price and thus dissuade me."

"I do not have access to the same sort of funds. Or were you offering a different sort of trade?" Her gaze measured him from top to toe.

"Naturally you like what you see, and I certainly am formed in all ways to please you, if you like how I am formed. But I fear money is the only coin I trade in."

"Naturally! Anyway, you don't want to make an enemy of the emperor of Rome, not if you are, as I am coming to suspect, some form of hired ruffian who makes his living doing dirty work so the rich and powerful can keep their hands clean."

"Your peaceable acquiescence will make this all go so much more easily. I'll wait while you gather a cloak and such traveling niceties as you desire." He carefully did not pat the sketchbook although it rested alongside his left hand. "I have a ship waiting to leave within the hour."

"You do not. We are an hour away from low tide. No ships will be departing for some time. So that, my mysterious miscreant, was your first lie."

"My first lie?"

"You've cleverly avoided a second lie, I note. I gave you several opportunities to agree that the emperor wants to kidnap me, and you never quite did. So I think he wants something else, and I know what it is."

Faster than he expected, she snatched the sketchbook from the table, leaped backward, and tapped the point of her sword to his chest.

"You may fight, or you may retire gracefully from the field. I'm not in a mood to hand over my sketchbook."

He leaned away from the point but thereby found himself backed up against the dressing table. This was proving much more exciting than he had hoped. So he crossed his arms and relaxed. Fearlessness in the face of blades always impressed people.

"Why does the emperor of Rome want your sketchbook? What have you drawn that he feels such a desperate need to possess?"

"Ah. That would be telling." She fished a key from her sleeve. "Because I am merciful and you have entertained me, however briefly, you may unlock the door and leave."

When she tossed the key, he allowed it to strike his thigh and fall with a quiet clunk to the floor. She cocked her head with corvid-like grace, a question without words.

"Just one," he said, because he still had to stall for time.

"Just one what?"

"Show me just one page from the sketchbook. If you would be so kind. He told me what treasures it holds and why he wants it."

"No, he didn't tell you. Why do you keep lying?"

"It's a curse." His insouciant smile was one of his great gifts, a little higher on one side than the other so that it promised both pleasure and mischief. "I always lie about something."

"And if your lie is found out? What then?"

"Curses fall in threes. Three lies caught out, or three lies uncaught."

"And then?"

He shrugged.

"How interesting. Two lies caught so far. You'd best be careful."

He was a little disturbed that she probed no further but rather retreated to the bed, just far enough that if he lunged, she could sidestep and attempt to skewer him. She set down the sketchbook and flipped through it. He could see that the first half of the book was filled in while the latter remained blank, pages as yet unfilled. From this angle he could not discern what exactly she liked to draw except dense shadows and crisp lines. At one point she studied a two-page spread, lifted her keen gaze to him, then back down to the page.

"Oh!" She smiled in an assessing way that puzzled him as greatly as it excited his inquisitive nature. "That explains it."

A crow landed on the windowsill and cawed thrice.

"Among the Hellenes, crows are considered divine messengers," she remarked as she slapped shut the sketchbook, slid it into a pouch, and slung it over her back with every appearance of making ready to depart.

Politeness had taken him as far as he could go. He expected her to grab for the key but instead she flung open the door of the wardrobe, jumped inside, and slammed it shut. With a leap he grabbed the wardrobe door and tugged. It was like dragging on weighted chains. With a croak of frustration he yanked with all his strength. The door gave way as if she had let go. He fell back, thumping into the bed, then spun a full circle to unsheathe his sword out of the adamant shadows that weave together the world he was in and the spirit world he came from.

Besides a set of shelves on which traveling gear was neatly folded and stacked, the wardrobe had a false back that formed a passage into the adjoining bedchamber. This chamber's door stood wide open. Her footsteps slapped as she raced down the passage. He pursued on foot although the dim light and the low ceiling hampered his speed, and he tripped once on a loose plank.

She halted at the top of the stairwell just as the sound of clashing weapons broke out in the courtyard below. A voice shouted, "You are all under arrest by order of the emperor of Rome."

Her frown fell like a sledge blow upon him. "You led them to us. I do not call that a kindness."

She lunged, driving him back with a series of fierce, tight thrusts that he scarcely had time to turn aside. Just as he got his bearings and turned the force of his greater height and skill against her, he bumped the back of his head on the ceiling. As he flinched, she attacked, and he skipped back to gather himself and again hit his head on a low beam. She suffered no such vicissitudes, being short and, more importantly, knowing her ground. Her blade flashed but it was the force behind it that dismayed him, the relentless press he parried once twice and thrice as his head pounded in time to the slap of her feet on the floor.

Then of course he tripped on that cursed loose plank.

He went down hard on his backside. Sucking in a sharp breath, he took hold of the threads that stitched him together, making ready to release them. He was bound by the curse to never reveal to any inhabitant of this world what he truly was, and doing so would trap him in this world forever, but to survive a killing blow he would have to scatter.

Yet no steel pierced him. She pelted back to the stairwell. By the time he picked himself up and ran after, she and the mysterious sketchbook were halfway down the steps.

He plunged after, sure there must be a side gate through which she would escape. Instead a stunning sight met his startled gaze: Despite the disparity in numbers, the imperial soldiers had defensively backed together into an outward-facing circle. They were hampered by a lack of light, for none of the lanterns they carried flickered with even the weakest flame. Only a cold white sphere of light drifted above the head of the particularly handsome man, who stood over to one side away from the altercation, leaning against a wall with his arms crossed like he was annoyed that his reading had been so rudely interrupted.

Round and around the soldiers prowled the two feathered ones with their claws and teeth and height and speed proving a formidable barrier. One of the soldiers made a probing stab, only to have a claw slash the sword right out of his grip. It clattered away onto the pavement. As the soldier leaped boldly forward to retrieve it the young man Apollo Crow had met at the tavern gate bolted out of the shadows. He melted in a smear and twist of shadow and became a large black saber-toothed cat.

Apollo Crow stared, almost losing control of his selves as a shock of recognition pulsed through him. Here was another creature like himself, a denizen of the spirit world who like all the inhabitants of the spirit world had the capacity and necessity to change.

The huge cat roared into the soldier's startled face. The man staggered back to the safety of his soldierly flock, drawing a knife. By now all were quaking.

The Honeyed Voice marched forward to confront the hapless men. She looked very powerful with her flock around her.

"Throw down your swords and you may go in peace, my friends. You labor for a power that will happily sacrifice you for its own selfish purposes."

"What strengthens Rome strengthens us all," said one of the soldiers stoutly.

Her back was to Apollo Crow, and the bag slung there invitingly, gapping open, as he crept on soft feet forward. She kept talking, perhaps a little too accustomed to hearing herself speak.

"They who rule give you just enough rope that you feel you can walk freely, while they keep all the advantage to themselves. They pay you a pittance while they sit on a vast treasury . . ."

He slid the sketchbook out of the bag and took a step back.

". . . They allow you to till the land as long as you pay a tithe to them for the honor."

A flutter of air disturbed his senses for he was adept at adapting to any slight change in the loft and direction of the winds. The currents of movement suggested something moving alongside him and yet he saw no one. Not until the seamstress appeared as out of the air itself. Her edged blade pressed across his chest.

"Stop there," she said.

Apollo Crow laughed out of sheer surprise. Her sudden materialization where she had not been before caused the poor soldiers to lose their tenuous hold on courage. As one, they bolted for the street. The feathered ones stood politely aside to let them pass. The big cat chased them to the gate and lashed its tail with vigor.

"What manner of creature are you?" he asked the seamstress.

"I might ask the same of you," she said. "For you are wrapped in many threads, a skein of shadows, but I don't know what it means."

"Those are the threads of a curse laid on me when I was exiled from my home."

"How interesting!" said the seamstress, looking as delighted as a child settling in for a thrilling tale. "Why were you exiled?"

"I took back something that belonged to me, but it was deemed theft by those with more power than me. So I was cursed into exile on the charge of being a thief."

The Honeyed Voice turned to meet his gaze, her attention as bold and solid as truth. Just for an instant it seemed that within her eyes he glimpsed a vast and silent vision of shapes and colors tumbling like flashes of light and line.

"That is the most honest thing I've heard you say," she began, but broke off as a crow fluttered down to land on his shoulder.

The big cat hissed.

The seamstress vanished, like a thread pulled out of the fabric of the world.

The emperor of Rome and a company of imperial soldiers marched through the gate, their ranks bristling with spears, swords, and crossbows. The cat retreated, teeth bared. The feathered ones lifted their crests threateningly, while the well-dressed and unfortunately handsome man remained standing quietly in the shadows, easy to overlook.

The Honeyed Voice faced down the emperor with the look of a person sure that her confederates will back her up, that as a flock they are stronger together than alone.

"As much as this may come as a surprise to you, I confess I did not expect to meet you in Nikaia," she remarked, as if she and the emperor were well acquainted and accustomed to sparring.

"Foment revolution among the principalities if you must, my dear Beatrice." His avuncular tone made her lips pinch. "The turmoil you and your associates create among the border lords serves me well enough."

"You mean to expand the empire to its old borders. You will start by moving your troops into areas where you think the ruling princes are too weak to resist or will be grateful for imperial protection against radical agitators."

"Do you say that with certainty, or is it a guess?"

"What do you think?"

"I think I do not intend to share my plans with you. When you bring your radical ideas into my empire, then you become my business."

"Is it your intention to arrest me?"

The emperor of Rome looked past her. "Do you have it?"

Apollo Crow tucked the sketchbook under his arm. "Yes."

One luxuriant eyebrow the Honeyed Voice raised, and her lips quirked in a silent laugh.

There came a pause, a sort of expectant silence, a drawing in as of breath.

The emperor of Rome suddenly caught sight of the man standing almost hidden at the wall. "Archers! Kill him!"

"Your mistake," uttered the Honeyed Voice.

Crossbows raised, the archers targeted the man just as the temperature in the courtyard plunged from a summery balm to an eye-stinging freeze. The cold hit like a hammer, slamming the emperor and his troops to the ground.

The magic hit so hard, like an invisible downward slap, that Apollo Crow almost came undone. He held himself together by sheer will, kneeling on the ground as his thoughts swirled. In his time in this world he had encountered magic rarely; he stayed away from mages as a wise bird avoids sunning itself on a rock beside snakes: They might not wish to harm him but it was better not to find out.

By the time the emperor and his soldiers picked themselves up from the ground, the Honeyed Voice and her associates had fled into the darkened streets. The soldiers turned toward the gate, then paused, awaiting orders.

"Let me see," said the emperor, extending a hand.

Apollo Crow handed him the sketchbook.

A soldier lit a lamp, and by its light the emperor flipped through the pages, at first with a self-congratulatory smile then with an increasingly furrowed frown.

"This isn't her sketchbook!" he roared, and flung the book so abruptly at Apollo Crow that he didn't have time to dodge. It thumped against his chest and thudded to the ground in a crush of paper.

"Curse it!" shouted the emperor. Then, "Go after them! Search the premises. And arrest this useless thief."

Apollo Crow hastily picked up the sketchbook but since he was immediately surrounded by bristling spears and angry soldiers who acted as if this was all *his* fault, he had no chance to look at it. The puzzling question of what he had stolen and why it wasn't the right thing nipped at his heels all the long march to Castle Hill and down ill-lit steps to a corridor of prison cells dug into the rock. Rough hands shoved him into a narrow chamber, then slammed shut the door, leaving him alone with the smell of old urine. High up, right against the ceiling, some manner of opening allowed in a breath of salty sea air. It was too dark to see anything so he groped around until he found a cot. There he sat.

Not long after, light gleamed beneath the cell door amid the drum of footsteps and the jangle of keys. The door clanged open, and he hastily got to his feet as two soldiers entered, carrying lamps. The emperor appeared.

"You shouldn't promise what you can't deliver," said the great man without preamble.

Apollo Crow let the book fall open into the glow of lamplight. A blank page greeted him, and another, and another: all blank.

"She substituted this unused one for the other one."

"They played you." The emperor shook his head, jaw set with anger. "And to think I actually believed you could manage what you promised."

"From your description I thought there was only the woman involved, a persuasive speaker hiding secrets from you in her journal. I thought she'd be accompanied by a few fellow radicals and malcontents. I didn't realize her comrades would be two feathered ones, a shape changing saber-toothed cat, a woman who can vanish at will, and a powerful mage. Had you warned me, I would have changed my strategy."

"So you say now that you've failed." The emperor walked to the door and, pausing at the threshold, spoke to the guards. "Keep her locked in here until I return."

"Her?" said Apollo Crow.

After a generous pause, like an actor deciding whether to give the final flourish to a bow the audience is anticipating, the emperor turned back.

"I have my own spies. You are in fact Apollonia Crow, a notorious lady thief and smuggler, whose last known residence was the Illyrian city of Salona." The emperor eyed the fine, glossy black garments Crow wore, then gave a grimace of disgust. "There is a simple way to reveal the truth about you but I disdain violent and humiliating methods."

"But you are an emperor. Empires are always violent."

"Empires bring peace and order and justice when an enlightened person rules."

"If that enlightened person is you?"

"This sparring is pointless. What I know is that when it suits your purpose, you use a male disguise, as now."

"In this world I find my path is better smoothed when people believe I am a man."

"So you admit I have seen through your lie?"

Crow offered a polite bow and tried very hard not to make it mocking although he wanted to laugh out loud. "I disguised myself as a man when I am really a woman. Allow me to introduce myself properly, Your Excellency. I am Apollonia Crow, espionage agent and recoverer of stolen objects, at your service."

"You are a thief and a swindler. You'll serve a year in Nikaia's prison for your crime."

He stepped out into the passage, followed by the guards.

To his back, Apollo Crow remarked, "Three lies uncaught."

"What?" said the emperor impatiently over his shoulder.

, "The curse forces me to accept any offer of employment made to me, and compels me to finish the work to my employer's satisfaction whatever I may think of the job. But three lies uncaught allow me to walk away from the contract as long as I tell the truth about the curse to the employer I'm leaving. As I am leaving you now."

"I've heard enough of this farrago. Close the door!"

The cell door slammed shut. Bars dropped into place. Locks clicked. The sound of footsteps receded.

Apollo Crow tossed the blank sketchbook on the cot and waited a little longer to make sure everyone had gone back to their expected routine. Then he unstitched the threads that held him together and became a murder of crows, one hundred and thirty-four pair of wings. Each crow easily fit through the barred slit built to be too narrow to admit a human body.

Most of the flock flew down to the harbor and roosted in the masts until the crack of dawn as ships began to sail with the tide. Although they circled in their numbers, they saw no sign of the Honeyed Voice or her confederates on any deck, escaping by sea. At length two of the farthest-flung scouts returned with news of a coach fleeing west on the coastal road. By the time the flock caught up with the coach, the vehicle had crossed out of Roman territory and into the bordering nation of Oyo, beyond reach of any but the most foolhardy of imperial soldiers.

Crows are perfect scouts. They accompanied the travelers all day without being spotted. At dusk the coachman and groom put into a well-guarded inn. Soon after the woman opened the shutters to an upstairs room. She sat down at a small table, opened her sketchbook, and began to draw.

Apollonia Crow took shape in the carriage house and thus avoided the guards at the gate. Climbing the back steps, she knocked on the appropriate door and, when it was opened, stepped inside with a charming smile.

"You!" said the Honeyed Voice.

"You recognize me?"

"You're very striking. What are you doing here? And why, Mr. Crow, have you affected this disguise as a woman? Did you think to confuse me with a fashionable gown and your hair styled in the antique Hellene fashion?"

Apollonia Crow paused to look at her reflection in the dressing-table mirror. Her black hair fell in pleasing ringlets past her shoulders, but perhaps her chin was a little too square for this face. What a wonder it always was to know that a mere change of clothing and outward presentation altered so radically how people responded to you, whether they thought you too manly for beauty or too feminine for handsomeness.

"The emperor discovered my ruse." Apollonia Crow's gaze slid toward the sketchbook.

The woman closed it and sat on it. "Your ruse? What ruse is that?"

"That I disguised myself as a man when really I am a woman."

She tilted her head to one side, examining him as if to untangle the threads of his being. "No, you aren't."

"I'm not?"

The Honeyed Voice seated herself prettily at the table, opened the sketchbook, and resumed her drawing with a speed and precision that made the images emerge as if by magic although it was merely skill. Crows and yet more crows flowed out of her pencil and across the page, flocking, roosting, arguing, spying. They were handsome crows, too, not a single ugly caricature among them.

"Do you know, I was once infatuated with the emperor of Rome, before he became emperor. I offered to marry him, even though he is old enough to be my father, and yet he turned me down even though he wanted my dreaming for his own uses. How strange that he rejected such a facile way to gain my undying loyalty."

"I should think it puzzling he did not choose you as his life-mate when he had the chance."

She pressed a hand against her bosom and fluttered her beguiling eyes. "Do you think so?"

"Yes, of course. You are loquacious and intelligent."

"Why, you flatter me."

"Why would I need to flatter you when you are already so fine a figure, almost as fine as me?"

"Why, indeed!" she said with a laugh. "Alas that he had scruples and was loath to take advantage of my infatuation in that particular way. Yet it was a fortunate escape on my part, for otherwise I might be a very different person with a very different outlook on the world than I am now. Rather than calling for revolution I would be standing among those trying to stamp it out. An irony, do you not think?"

"What are your dreams to him?"

She set down her pencil. "I can see the future in a manner of speaking. My dreams give me glimpses of what is to come. Often I cannot interpret the visions because they appear as details without context. A hat. A flowering branch. A broken tea set. So I draw the visions I see in my dreams in my sketchbook. If their details and context can be properly untangled—which is no simple task—my drawings may be said to predict the future."

"A lion—that would be the emperor—chaining Queen Europa."

"Ha! That was no dream. That was just a metaphorical sketch." She tapped the pencil against the page. "For example last week I dreamed of crows. One hundred and thirty-four crows. Isn't that an unusual number?"

For once, Crow had no answer.

"Crows are messengers. Of all creatures, they can pass most easily from the spirit world to this world. If a saber-toothed cat can become a man, then why not a flock of crows become a man, or a woman for that matter? Since a flock contains both male and female crows, why be limited to one or the other?"

Almost the crows fell apart, so shocked by how casually the Honeyed Voice dropped the truth upon them.

"What brought you across from the spirit world to bide in this world?"

"None of your business." The words came out more of a harsh caw.

"But you already told us, didn't you? You just thought we wouldn't believe you, that we'd think you were telling a tale. What did you steal?"

"I stole back part of myself," Crow snapped. "Two of my number, stolen by a power greater than mine to serve his needs, as kings and emperors do. That is why I was punished, and exiled to this world, cursed to serve anyone who offered to pay me as if I am nothing more than a petty mercenary."

"And here you have landed. Are you back to make another attempt on my sketchbook?"

"No. I am no longer obligated to serve the emperor of Rome. Now I have come to make an offer to you."

"To me?"

"You caught me in three lies. Therefore, I must henceforth always tell you the truth."

She frowned consideringly and made no retort.

"You told me earlier that you are low on funds."

"We are not as well funded as we'd like to be, it's true. Revolution is an expensive business. Often we spend what funds we have on charitable work. Also we have an exceedingly large household to feed. None of this is a secret. Why do you care?"

"I don't like powerful people who punish me, which means, to start with, that I don't like the emperor of Rome. Crows hold grudges. You can help me."

"How is that?"

"A woman who can catch glimpses of the future, a vanishing seamstress, a saber-toothed cat, two fearsome feathered ones, and an annoyingly handsome mage. I've had the chance to take a good look around the imperial compound in Rome. I know where an extensive treasury is kept. With the right flock, we can steal it."

Dark eyes flashed up to meet Crow's gaze in the mirror. The Honeyed Voice smiled in a gratified and appreciative way that jolted all one hundred and thirty-four crow hearts.

"When do we start?"

Walter Jon Williams

◆ ◆ ◆

In the fast-paced story that follows, a dashing and adventurous young man sets out in hot pursuit of a miscreant, only to find that sometimes it's perhaps better to leave well enough alone . . .

Walter Jon Williams was born in Minnesota and now lives near Albuquerque, New Mexico. His short fiction has appeared frequently in *Asimov's Science Fiction*, as well as in *The Magazine of Fantasy & Science Fiction*, *Wheel of Fortune*, *Global Dispatches*, *Alternate Outlaws*, and in other markets, and has been gathered in the collections *Facets* and *Frankensteins and Foreign Devils*. His novels include *Ambassador of Progress*, *Knight Moves*, *Hardwired*, *The Crown Jewels*, *Voice of the Whirlwind*, *House of Shards*, *Days of Atonement*, *Aristoi*, *Metropolitan*, *City on Fire*, a huge disaster thriller, *The Rift*, and a Star Wars novel, *Destiny's Way*, and the half-dozen installments of his acclaimed Modern Space Opera epic, Dread Empire's Fall, which begins with *The Praxis*. Among his recent books are the novels *Implied Spaces*, *This Is Not a Game*, *Deep State*, and *The Fourth Wall*, the chapbook novella *The Boolean Gate*, and a new collection, *The Green Leopard Plague and Other Stories*. His most recent book is a new novel in the Praxis series, *Impersonations*. He won a long-overdue Nebula Award in 2001 for his story "Daddy's World," and took another Nebula in 2005 with his story "The Green Leopard Plague."

The adventurer Quillifer, who narrates the following story, is the hero of his own series, the first installment of which, *Quillifer*, appears from Saga Books in November 2017.

◆　◆　◆

The Triumph of Virtue

WALTER JON WILLIAMS

I s it a very great fault, do you think, for a prominent person to display a married lover to the world? Before friends, relatives, the in-laws, the lover's unhappy spouse?

Is it a lesser fault if the prominent person is the monarch? For it was none other than our new Queen Berlauda who had fallen in love with the married Viscount Broughton of Hart Ness, and who I could now view together with him in the swan-boat the latter had built for her, a boat covered with thousands of actual swan feathers that trembled in the breeze like sea-foam. In the boat was room for no more than two passengers. The couple were together beneath the canopy in the back, their heads together, as twelve oarsmen in Broughton livery rowed them about the lake of Kingsmere.

The viscount was a pretty young man, it is true, blond like the Queen, and with a face as lively as hers was impassive. Dressed in the satin and silk of court finery, gems winking from their fingers and from the great collars of lace that draped over their shoulders, they made a resplendent couple.

During the early days of Berlauda's reign, with her royal father dead on a distant shore and her scheming half-brother Clayborne plotting for the throne, Broughton had ridden into the capital of Selford with a troop of companions to declare their allegiance and pledge their swords to her service. She appointed him Master of the Hunt, and now he played host to the Queen at her own hunting lodge.

The viscount's poor neglected wife was nowhere in sight. She had declared that she did not like boats, and so had retired to the Kingsmere Lodge to nurse a headache, and very possibly a broken heart.

But how great a fault lay in our royal Berlauda? Her much-married father, the late King Stilwell, had often sought the wives and daughters of his noble companions, and few had dared to object. A great king, it was supposed, possessed appetites as vast as his majesty, and was not bound by the laws that constrained the meiny . . . Why should a queen be so bound, merely on account of her sex?

These complexities were not abstract to me, for I too had a married lover. Though, as I was an eighteen-year-old lawyer's apprentice and not a monarch, I did not dare parade Amalie in front of the court. She paraded proudly but alone, walking languorously along the verge of the lake with her fan dangling from her wrist; and since our arrival at Berlauda's hunting lodge two days before I'd had no opportunity to speak with her, let alone speak privately. Yet I was constantly alert to her presence, a kind of tremor in the atmosphere of which I was subtly aware, as if she were radiating some sort of invisible beam that prickled over my skin. She was always present, yet always unavailable. I was impatient and filled to the eyebrows with frustration, and it was with great relief that I saw her leave the lawn and stroll into one of the lodge's formal gardens. With a feigned casualness I followed.

The garden was symmetrically laid out, square in area, and at its center stood a worn statue of an old man or a venerable god, so eroded that he seemed all gaping black eyes and hollowed-out beard. The flowers were brown and dead, and the avenues lined with autumn leaves that crackled beneath my boots. I affected to be surprised by the presence of a fair lady in this place, and I took off my cap and louted low, as the saying is. A cool breeze floated past, and autumn leaves rained down from the trees and skittered along the gravel walks.

"Goodman Quillifer," she said, "do you come to view dead flowers?"

"I come to view something far more beautiful," said I. "More lovely than all the brilliant autumn leaves, more perfect than Bernaudi's statue of the Graces, finer than—"

"Ah," she said, "you come to see Viscount Broughton of Hart Ness. He is not here, but you will find him on the lake."

I straightened and put on my cap. "I have viewed him. That fair face charmed me not."

A wry smile touched her lips. "It charms the only person that matters."

I contemplated my lover, Amalie Brilliana Trevil, the seventh child and fifth daughter of the Count of Culme. Such was the abundance of daughters in his gloomy northern stronghold that Culme rather haphazardly gave Amalie in marriage to his friend the widowed Marquess of Steyne, for the express purpose of breeding an heir. Married at sixteen, Amalie was now seventeen and had been carrying the heir for five months. The *nausea gravidarum* having passed, and her husband having ridden off on a military adventure that got him captured and held for ransom, I had been fortunate to find Amalie ready for her own adventure. I was only a few months older than she and had been recently orphaned, a misfortune which, as a result of a fluke of patronage, had resulted in my being presented at court. Yet I held no office and had but little money, and possessed nothing in abundance but time—time which I was willing to devote to Amalie.

As Amalie was with child, she had dispensed with the corsets and farthingales and bumrolls of feminine fashion, and wore a garment of black velvet very like a dressing gown, but held closed with swags and braid and silver-gilt buttons arrayed in artful disorder on its front. Its sleeves were puffed and purfled, its hem embroidered with gold thread and cat's-eye chrysoberyls. Pearls wound their way through Amalie's tawny hair, and a carcanet of jet beads and diamonds held her long throat in a close embrace. A fan of black swan feathers hung carelessly from one hand. She gazed at me with long, lazy dark eyes that made her seem as if she had just risen from a lengthy, luxurious sleep.

She walked past me with slow, languorous steps. I restrained my desire to put my arms around her, and instead followed just behind her left shoulder.

Amalie looked at me over that velvet-clad shoulder. She still wore that amused smile. "The Queen's mother is beside herself with fury. She planned a greater husband for Berlauda than a little penniless viscount."

"I can't imagine any viscount being penniless," said I. At one point in my life I had actually *been* penniless, and did not recall sharing my status with nobles.

"He is a pauper indeed compared to foreign princes," said Amalie. "The King of Varcellos has sons to spare, and offers them to Berlauda severally, or all together, according to her taste. And the King of Loretto has but only one prince, though he is the heir, and the suitor the Queen Mother most favors."

"Loretto?" I said. "Leonora favors Loretto? Have we not fought a score of wars with that kingdom? Are they not our great enemies?"

"In the event of marriage," said she, "they would not be our enemies but our loving kin."

"Then," said I, "the Queen Mother greatly underestimates the sorts of quarrels that can arise in families."

Amalie turned to me and touched her chin with the tip of her closed fan.

"Did you hunt this morning?"

I had, in fact, pursued stag through her majesty's deer park. I am not a natural horseman, and I was happy to ride toward the back of the pack. When I could not avoid a jump, my courser took me over it rather than the other way around, and in the end I was pleased not to have pursued deer, but to have avoided a broken neck.

"I did well enough." I looked at her. "Yet I hope some other manner of hunting will prove more lucky for me."

She looked at me from her long eyes. "What manner is that?"

"I hope to track you to your den, my lady."

She flashed her little chisel-shaped white teeth, a feature that in a lesser person might have been a defect, but which in Amalie I found enchanting.

"I would bite you if you did," said she. She let fall her fan. "But your hunt would fail. The guest rooms are crowded, and I share a room with my two maids. We would not be alone."

I fell into step with her. "It is a fine day," I said, "and perhaps we might find a mossy nook in the forest."

"Too many eyes," she said.

"Tonight, then, after the play?" I paused by the corroded old statue and turned to face her. "We could meet here. I could bring blankets and a flask with a warming libation."

She smiled and touched my arm with her fan. "I will not say no, but I can make no promises."

Other people came into the garden then, and Amalie and I parted. I procured blankets and a flask of brandy, which I rolled up and hid beneath a bench in a shadowed part of the garden, then I returned to the lake. More boats had joined Broughton's swan-boat on the surface of the water, and there was a barge with music, where the tenor Castinatto sang surrounded by a group of girl-children dressed as water nymphs. Berlauda's mother, the Dowager Queen Leonora, sped about the lake in her own little galley and kept a stony eye on her daughter.

That night we supped out-of-doors, this time by torchlight, a great venison feast that had been cooking all afternoon. There were dishes of roast venison, venison stewed with vegetables and herbs, venison breaded and fried, venison backstrap wrapped in bacon and broiled. Alongside were sweet sauces composed of cherry and apricot, plum and raspberry. Venison pie was presented at the high table, with pastry sculptures of harts and does. Several varieties were offered each of venison soup, venison patties, and venison sausage. There were kidneys seared, or deviled along with the liver, or fried and doused with sherry and mustard. The deer hearts were cut up, marinated in sweet vinegar, fried, and served on greens. The liver was fried with butter, bacon, parsley, onions, and rosemary, or mixed with venison to make the large meatballs called "faggots." The tongue was roasted and served sliced thin on salad or braised and served on simnel bread with gravy.

With the venison was served the traditional frumenty, done in a dozen different ways, both sweet and savory.

I supped vastly, then we went to the outdoor theater and watched my lord Roundsilver's company perform *The Triumph of Virtue,* a masque written by the poet Blackwell.

Few of the company's actors were involved, for most of the parts in the masque that did not involve singing were taken by members of the court, all dressed in extravagant costumes that no acting company could possibly afford. The story was an allegory—which made it tedious—and involved the singer Castinatto as the demon Iniquity, who was rejoicing in the fact that he'd succeeded in capturing and imprisoning Virtue and her friends Honor, Purity, and Piety.

Whatever dungeon he'd put them in, it was a place with a lot of music and dancing. My eyes turned to the great throne-like chairs where sat the Queen and her party. Her favorite Broughton was on her right, and the two leaned toward each other and shared smiles and glances. On the left was her mother Leonora, who looked from the play to her daughter and back, thwarted fury glittering in her eyes. Near them were the ambassadors of Varcellos and Loretto, faces set in attitudes of thoughtful calculation. Of Lady Broughton there was naught to be seen.

I wondered if Virtue, Honor, Purity, and Piety were in truth held in captivity somewhere while this royal tableau played itself out, and the court sang and danced and knew better than to break the virtues out of prison. I turned to view my lover Amalie, the Marchioness of Steyne, and saw her half-reclined in a large chair, her fine long eyes half-closed in languor, the pearls in her hair gleaming softly in the torchlight. At that moment I felt perhaps a little sympathy for the demon Iniquity, his fine voice, and his lovely, seductive songs.

Virtue and her comrades eventually broke free, and the company celebrated with a galliard. I applauded with the rest and hastened through the cold wind to my lodgings for my old tweed overcoat, which I brought with me to the garden, where I retrieved my bundle and waited for Amalie. I stood in the lee of the wind by the old statue and watched high cloud scud across the stars, and when the wind blew cold up my neck I reached for the bottle of brandy and took a swallow of its fire.

A spatter of rain came down, and another spatter, then the heavens opened and black rain pelted down. I realized that Amalie would not come, and ran for the lodge.

◆   ◆   ◆

By morning the wind had strengthened and freezing rain was slashing down. The lake was so turned to froth that it looked like milk, and the Queen's swan-boat pitched at its mooring while the wind tore at its feathers. The lodge was filled with hunters unable to hunt, and their mood was sour and irritable. Some played at cards for more money than I could afford, and others played chess.

The Queen was not in view, for she was closeted with her spiritual advisors for a round of chants and prayers. Her favorite Broughton must have been praying alongside her, for he was not present, either.

I watched a few games of chess, but I found myself frustrated in the same way that I had been when I'd first learned the game. The board presented a rigid field of sixty-four squares, and the pieces maneuvered about in ways that were inflexible. A knight had to move a certain way, and the abbot another, and the king a third. Yet I had never understood why any of this was necessary: why should not a queen move like a knight, or a cunning abbot dissolve the boundaries between its white square and the black square adjacent, and so occupy it? Wherefore should not a mighty king move with the same range and power as the queen—and for that matter, why should only one piece move at a time? A proper king should be able to martial his forces and move his whole army at once, to the thunder of drums and the clangor of trumpets.

It seemed to me that chess did not represent the world as I understood it, or at any rate as I wished it to be. Were I a pawn on that board, I would have slipped away from that confining arrangement of sixty-four squares, taken advantage of cover available on the tabletop—a cup here, a candlestick there—to march unobserved behind the enemy, and from there launch a surprise attack to capture a castle or stab the enemy king. But alas, the pieces are confined to their roles, and pawns may not leave the board unless captured, and once captured they may not escape. I could not help but feel that all the pieces lacked proper imagination.

Chess is a game I could much improve if only given the opportunity.

While the chess games went on, the wind died down, and the rain decreased to a misty drizzle. Some of the guests began to talk hopefully of going out to shoot some rabbits. I grew tired of watching lords play chess badly and walked through a series of drawing-rooms toward another room where I had seen a table of skittles. So involved were my musings on chess that it took me a few seconds to react to the shrieks of women.

I spun toward the sound, and a door banged open right in front of me. A tall cavalier, hat and long coat starry with rain, burst out of the door and ran into me as he dashed through the room. I felt a savage impact on my shoulder and the breath went out of me in a great rush. I had just turned and was unbalanced even before the stranger struck me, and the blow knocked me sprawling. The shrieks continued, accompanied now by the clank of the cavalier's rowelled spurs, and the uproar scraped my nerves as I strove to still my whirling mind. I got my feet under me and stood, and as I staggered toward the screams I groped at myself to find if the stranger had stabbed me.

I reeled through the open door and found myself in a withdrawing-room full of ladies. The Viscountess Broughton sat on the carpet clutching at her abdomen with both hands, and everyone else was frozen in postures of surprise and horror.

Only a few seconds had passed since I first heard the screams.

I knelt by the stricken noblewoman and touched her cold pale hands. "Are you all right, my lady?"

She looked at me with wide eyes. "He stabbed me!" she said.

I gently parted her hands. I saw no blood, no deadly gash in the daffodil-yellow silk of her gown. I looked then at her lap, and saw the blackened steel of a dagger blade lying in the folds of her skirt. I plucked it forth, and saw that it had broken near the hilt.

"I think you may be unwounded, madame," I said.

She gasped and searched her gown, finding only a small tear over her abdomen. Tears spilled from her eyes. "My busk!" she said. "I'm wearing a steel busk!"

At this point other men arrived, demanding to know what had happened, and more kept arriving over the next few minutes, and everything kept having to be explained all over again. They were all members of the nobility, and all wanted to be in charge. One of them snatched the knife-blade away, and I never got it back.

Then someone called out "Hue and cry!" and half the gentlemen ran from the room. The words "hue and cry" were then shouted out all over the lodge, pointlessly because a hue and cry was supposed to be raised when the criminal was in sight, to keep him from escaping, and the cavalier had not been in sight since he vanished from the parlor with spurs clanking, and not one of the pursuers knew what he looked like.

Then more cries rose—"Guard the Queen!"—and more men ran off to form a wall around the monarch. Lady Broughton ignored all the questions hurled at her and continued to weep, slow tears dropping steadily from her eyes. The floral aroma of a cordial floated through the air, and I looked to see Amalie offering a delicate crystal cup. I had not noticed her in the room till that moment. "I think perhaps Lady Broughton needs a restorative," she said.

I passed the glass to Lady Broughton, and she drank. This action seemed to bring her a little more into an awareness of her situation, and she looked around at the circle of ladies. "Who was he? Does anyone know him?"

No one seemed to have recognized him, and they all began to discourse at length concerning how little they knew. "Perhaps we could shift Lady Broughton to a couch?" suggested one lady, and they all agreed. The ladies clustered around the stricken woman—neither I nor any other man was permitted to assist—and they helped her to rise and placed her on a couch, where they arranged satin cushions beneath her back.

Being useless, I let my attention wander over the scene, and I saw the hilt of the dagger lying on the floor near the door. I bent to retrieve it. It was what is called a sword-hilt dagger, as the hilt resembles the cross-hilt of a sword, with a disk-shaped pommel. The blade had snapped off about an inch below the hilt, leaving the smith's hallmark visible where it was stamped on the blade, a triangular shield holding an imperial crown. The pommel was made of red jasper, and was carved in a strange design: an arm with a wing where the shoulder should be, and carrying a mace with a tip that resembled a crown. I tried to read it as a rebus: wing-arm-mace-crown. Mace-crown-arm-feathers. Flying-arm-club. Clearly I was misreading the message, whatever it was.

I was still puzzling over this when a compact yellow-haired man arrived wearing that very design embroidered into his doublet: Viscount Broughton of Hart Ness, the husband of the victim, and the Queen's lover. As soon as he came into the room, all conversation ceased. He approached his wife, hesitated a moment, then took her hand. If there were affection or concern in his heart, it did not show on his face. Instead he was very pale, and was no doubt considering what this would mean regarding his relationship with the Queen.

His wife's life had been spared because she was wearing her corset, as did all well-bred ladies of fashion. The busk, usually a piece of wood or bone, was a wedge-shaped stiffener worn at the front of the corset, and intended to flatten the bosom to conform to the dictates of current fashion. I do not know why fashion insisted that women alter their natural shapes in order to display chests as flat as those of young boys, but fashion saved Lady Broughton's life that morning, as did the fact that she could afford a high-quality steel busk, which being more flexible than wood was more comfortable.

We were all pretending not to watch Lord and Lady Broughton when a sergeant of the Yeoman Archers arrived, carrying a half-pike so as to skewer any available traitors. He demanded information, which was given by all the ladies at once. No sooner had he sorted all this out than his lieutenant appeared, his hand on the hilt of his sword, and he had to sort through the clamor all over again. The lieutenant was just beginning to make sense of this when his captain arrived, and it all had to be gone through once more.

"Her majesty is safe." The captain wanted to reassure everyone on that point. "The house is being searched, and the ruffian will be found."

"He came in from out-of-doors," I said. "His hat and coat were wet from the rain." I pointed. "He ran that way, probably to flee the lodge."

The captain looked at the lieutenant, who looked at the sergeant. "That next room leads outside, ay," he said. "We make sure the door is locked on our nightly patrols."

I handed the captain the hilt of the broken dagger. "This is the knife that broke," I said. "I know not where the blade has gone—someone took it."

The captain examined the dagger, saw the device on the red-jasper pommel, and looked up at Broughton in cold surmise. He seemed about to say something, then decided against it. He turned and left the room, followed by the other Yeoman Archers, and he followed the assassin through into the next room with its skittle tables. I followed the gang of Archers along with some of the remaining gentlemen. It seemed the excitement in Lady Broughton's room was over.

A sturdy oaken door led from the room to the grounds outside. The rain had died down to a soft mist that caressed my face with cool fingers. The air smelled of broken, beaten vegetation.

A wide gravel drive circled around the house, and on the far side was a garden. A stooped gardener, in big boots, cloak, and hat, was attempting to repair storm damage to the garden.

"You, there!" called the captain. "Did you see anyone leave by this door?"

Raindrops slid from the sagging brim of his hat as the gardener straightened. He was an old man with a long beard that stretched out over his chest in wet serpentine fingers.

"Ay, sir!" he said. "He asked me to hold his horse."

The captain quickly ascertained that the man had ridden up, paid the gardener a crown to hold his horse, then gone into the lodge. A few minutes later he'd come out, mounted his horse, and trotted away, in the direction of the gate.

"We must pursue him, sir!" said the lieutenant, stoutly.

"Hue and cry!" said one of the gentlemen.

"Not just yet." The captain turned to the gardener. "What kind of horse did the fellow ride?"

"A chestnut, sir."

The captain turned to his lieutenant. "Choose a party to ride in pursuit. Good riders, good horses. We should only need a half-dozen or so. I will report to her majesty."

"Hue and cry!" shouted the gentleman again, and they all rushed off. I looked down the gravel drive in the direction the cavalier had fled. The pursuers would ride two leagues through the forest to the main gate, then have to decide whether the cavalier had turned right, to the capital of Selford, or to the left, for Blacksykes and the north.

That was assuming the cavalier took the road at all, instead of riding off through the Queen's forest to some hidden destination of his own.

I approached the gardener. "Father," said I. "You say the horse was a chestnut?"

"Yes, sir." He leaned on his rake. "What they call a liver chestnut, very dark, more brown than red."

"Did you get a good look at him?"

"Nay, sir. His collar was up, and he wore his hat pulled low over his face. I think he may have had a beard, sir."

A beard he shared with most of the men in the kingdom. "Did you mark his voice, father? Where he might have come from?"

"He talked somewhat like they of Bonille," said the gardener. "Like most of them at the big house."

Indeed, most of those at court tended to soften their consonants in the style of Bonille, whether they were born there or not.

"And the tack?"

"Finely made, sir. A saddle such as they use here for the chase, brown leather. There were steel roundels on the breast collar. Medallions like, for decoration."

"Of any particular pattern?"

"They had like rays on them, sir."

"Any other ornaments on the saddle?"

"Nay, I can think of none."

"The leather was not tooled or ornamented?"

"Nay. It was plain, but well made and nearly new. Brown leather, as I said."

"The bridle likewise?"

"Ay."

I supposed I could continue to ask about the girth and the stirrups and the bit, but I was already feeling this line of inquiry was hopeless. And then I remembered the crown-and-shield hallmark on the broken dagger, and I felt a flush of icy water flood my veins and shock me into sudden alertness.

"Was there a mark on the saddle? A hallmark, stamped on the saddle by a maker?"

The old man's eyes brightened. "Ay, sir! There was the figure of a bird stamped on the flap, near the rider's left knee. I noticed it when I helped his foot into the stirrup."

"A hawk? Eagle?"

"Nay, sir. A small bird. A sparrow, maybe, or warbler or some such."

I gave the gardener a silver crown. "Thank you, father. That is very useful."

He touched the brim of his hat. "I'm very grateful, sir. It's a proper gentleman you are."

I grinned at him. "I'm no gentleman at all!" I returned to the lodge.

A pair of Yeoman Archers stood guard outside the withdrawing-room where Lady Broughton was undergoing an examination by the royal physician. Broughton leaned on the wall of the next room, pensive eyes fixed on the floor-boards, his heel kicking idly at the wainscoting.

I returned to the parlor, where cards were scattered on the tables, and chessmen stood abandoned in their ranks and files. Events had over-leaped the boundaries of the game, and only a piece that had already left the board could possibly be of use. Small groups of people clustered together and spoke in low voices. I saw Amalie with some of her friends by the fire-place, and I walked to join them, standing politely and wait-ing my turn to speak.

Two gentlemen dashed into the room, booted, cloaked, and spurred, on the way to the stables. They paused long enough for a cup of wine apiece, then continued on their way. One of Amalie's friends looked at me.

"You are not joining the pursuit?"

"My horse is a stout animal," said I, "but not a racer." Which referred not so much to the horse but to myself. I turned to Amalie. "Lady Broughton is no worse?"

She pulled her green-satin gown close about her. "It was a dreadful shock," said she. "I cannot speak to the state of her mind, but I think her body is unharmed."

"I do not understand how Broughton can survive this," someone said. "He will be accused of trying to make away with his wife in order to marry the Queen."

"The attempt failed," said one of the gentlemen.

"That does not matter," said the first. "What matters is that he will be accused."

"He will be accused," said I. "But he may not be guilty."

Amalie's long eyes shifted along the company, and apparently de-cided those within hearing were safe for this line of conversation. "There are easier ways of making away with one's wife," she said, "than having it done in front of half a dozen witnesses."

"And a better way of arranging it," said I, "than to leave behind a dagger that will point straight to you."

The others had not heard of this development. While I was explaining about the carved jasper pommel, the sounds of the chase came from the front of the building, yips and shouts, as a pack of gentlemen raced off in pursuit of the assassin. They had come for the chase, had been confined indoors to their frustration, and now launched themselves on this new hunt with all the joy and vigor they would have applied to the pursuit of a stag.

While those around the fire-place discussed Broughton's future, I considered my own. I was not involved in this assassination save as a witness. Therefore, I decided, I was free to act on my own.

An equerry arrived from the Queen asking members of the Great Council to attend her majesty, and many of the company left while the party around the fire-place dispersed. I found myself with Amalie, the two of us disposed around a chess table. I reached down and picked a carved walnut knight from the table.

"I think I may ride out," I said.

She looked up at me. "Are you going to pursue the assassin after all? Can you catch him after all this time?"

"I think I may be able to identify him if I ride to Selford."

She looked off through the diamond-pane windows at the Yeoman Archers on the lawn, preparing to depart. She frowned.

"I wonder if that knowledge would be to anyone's benefit?" she wondered.

I was surprised. "If your ladyship thinks I should not go," I said, "I will remain here."

"I cannot say whether your errand is for good or ill," she said. "And I hardly think the Queen's party will remain at the lodge in any case. I'm sure the Council will recommend a return to Selford, but it will take the rest of the day to organize it, and her majesty will not leave till tomorrow."

"Then if I may have your leave?"

She looked at me with some slight surprise, as if she were surprised

I asked her permission. "Of course. Try not to be captured by brigands or assassins on the way."

I smiled. "I will happily comply."

"And, should you find the villain, think carefully what you do."

This seemed curious advice, so I merely said that I would, bowed, and went to my room. I changed into boots, leather riding jerkin, and trousers, and stuffed everything else in my saddlebags. I donned my overcoat and also brought a hooded cloak against rain.

I stopped by the kitchens and begged a pair of venison pies, which I put in my coat pockets. I filled my leather bottle with small beer, then I made my way to the stables, where the captain of the Yeoman Archers was just departing with his party of pursuers, all armed with swords and pistols.

Though I had no hopes of riding down the assassin, I intended to set a brisk pace, for I had twelve leagues to cover before nightfall, when the city gates would be closed against me. I knew not whether I could bribe my way past the guards, and I preferred not to have to test their honesty one way or another.

The Yeoman Archers spurred away. Perhaps I should remark that I never saw a man of the Yeoman Archers carrying a bow, as the corps was armed entirely with pikes, swords, and firelocks. Modern warfare may have made the bow obsolete, but so devoted to tradition was the Palace that its guards remained Archers in name, and probably would remain Archers so long as the Palace continued to stand.

As I was saddling my mount Amalie appeared, with her maids, coachman, footmen, and baggage. I looked at her in surprise.

"I've decided to follow your example, Goodman Quillifer," said she, "and abandon this 'sad cockpit of ruined ambition.'"

"I am. And that is a quote from Bello, is it not?"

"I know not and I care not," said she. "You may join me in the carriage, if you like."

I debated with myself whether or not to accept her offer—I truly wanted to get to the city as soon as I could, and though a ride with Amalie would be diverting, there would almost certainly be delays.

Yet, I thought, if the assassin was in Selford tonight, he would probably still be there tomorrow.

I joined Amalie in her carriage. She ordered the carriage's top low-ered, so we might enjoy the air, but we and her servants had to wrap warmly in furs against the cold day. Her four horses were matched and of the breed called cremello, white with rose-pink noses and brilliant blue eyes. Not only were they a striking and beautiful quartet, they set a rattling pace, and my fears of being delayed soon faded. Indeed, my bor-rowed beast, following on a lead, was hard put to keep up.

We wound our way through the Queen's forest, splashed through puddles and detoured around fallen limbs. It was not long before we encountered the first of the pursuers returning. They had galloped after their quarry as though he were a stag, and soon enough their horses were blown, and they were forced to return. You would think that this possibility might have occurred, even to the nobility, well before they spurred off. Those who actually cared about their animals led them home on foot, and the rest rode lathered, staggering, pitiful beasts.

Once we were on the main road Amalie had a bottle of wine opened, and I shared my meat pies. Our conversation was lively, for the maids remained excited by the morning's developments, and during their ten-ure in the servants' quarters had managed to absorb quite a number of rumors, for instance was the would-be assassin hired by Berlauda's scheming half-brother Clayborne, by the ambassador from Loretto, by Broughton, or by the Queen herself.

"Why would Clayborne want to kill the Viscountess?" Amalie scorned. Though she did put some effort into an examination of the theory that one or another ambassador was behind it, in order to secure the Queen for his prince.

While this speculation was taking place, I was able to take Amalie's hand beneath the fur that we shared, and now and again stroke her thigh, causing her to take a little intake of breath. But I dared not risk that intake of breath too often, not under the sharp eyes of the two maidservants, nor take any other liberties.

Howsoever, judging by the gleam in her eye, I believe that at least one of the maids was very taken with me during that ride though I did not put this surmise to the test.

As we rode we encountered more and more of the pursuers, all re-turning to the lodge. Though none of these had blown their horses in an over-hasty pursuit, they had all concluded they stood no chance of catching the assassin, and turned around in time to enjoy supper at the lodge.

Last of all was the dispirited troop of Yeoman Archers, who had pursued longer than the others. The lieutenant had been sent on to warn the capital's gate guards, just in case the fugitive had spent part of the day hiding and rode in after nightfall, but the rest were riding their weary way back to the lodge, to report their failure to Queen Berlauda.

Even though the carriage maintained a good pace when the road was clear, still we followed the storm, and the road was full of mud and muck and fallen limbs, some of which were so heavy that the footmen and I could barely shift them. This meant delays, and shadows were growing long by the time we passed Shornside's royal castle.

"We will probably not make Selford before nightfall," I said. "Your ladyship might want to look for an inn."

"Oh! That will not be necessary." She gave me a look from out of those long eyes. "We have a country house not far from here, and I've sent word ahead, and will sleep and sup there. The steward will find a bed for you somewhere, if you are not bent on galloping for the capital tonight." And, as her hand grazed along my thigh as she spoke her invitation, I overcame feigned reluctance and accepted.

The fugitive will still be there tomorrow, I decided. Assuming he is there at all.

The promised bed was on the same floor as Amalie's chambers, and was very comfortable, not that I spent a lot of time in it. For as soon as the house grew quiet, I stole down the hall to quietly knock on Amalie's door, and the two of us spent a delightful night beneath the grand canopy of her bed, thoughts of murder and conspiracy forgotten beneath pleasure and laughter. When I finally fell asleep, I slept so well that, in the morning, I was hard put to scramble back to my room before the servant came up to bring me my shaving water.

After breakfast I put on my grateful suppliant face, kissed Amalie's hand, and rode off to the capital, where I arrived before mid morn. Low clouds hung over the day, and the wind was brisk. I returned my horse

to the livery stable in Mossthorpe and walked across the bridge to Selford with my saddlebags on my shoulder, then to my lodgings on Chancellery Street. I emptied my saddlebags, then without changing out of
my riding leathers walked to Clattering Lane, where all the knife- and
swordmakers clustered, and viewed the signs overhanging the street.
With the ringing sound of hammers on anvils echoing on either hand,
I found the sign shaped like a shield, with a crown in its center, and
entered the shop of Roweson Crowninshield—whose surname, as I discovered when I asked for the master, was pronounced something like
"Grunsel."

I asked Master Crowninshield about the sword-hilted dagger with
the Broughton badge, and he remembered it quite well. He had made
the dagger himself, and it had been on display in his shop. A customer
had walked in from the street and bought it on condition that the plain
steel pommel be replaced by one with the Broughton blazon. Crowninshield customarily worked with a cameo-carver on such commissions,
and both were paid extra for carving and mounting the jasper carving
swiftly.

Crowninshield was told that the dagger was a gift for Broughton's
son. He was hardly to be blamed for not knowing that no such son existed.

"Who commissioned the dagger?" I asked, and was surprised to hear
that it was a lady. I asked for a description.

Crowninshield's lengthy description, given with many digressions
over four or five minutes, amounted to the lady being generally lady-
shaped, and having a face similar in large degree to that of a lady. Her
accent was either that of Bonille, or of south Fornland, neither of which
resembled one another. I made a note to myself that, should I ever be
qualified as a lawyer, never to call Crowninshield as a witness.

"Not a grand lady, mind," he added. "But respectable. Maybe a servant, but a superior sort of servant. A housekeeper, or a governess."

In order to protect myself from any housekeepers and governesses
and their murder plots, I bought a sword-hilted dagger of my very own
and thrust it into my belt behind, under my cloak, where I could draw it
easily with the right hand. I then thanked Master Grunsel and made my
way to Saddlers Row, where I failed to find any shop signs displaying a

sparrow, warbler, or any small bird. This sent me farther up the row to the Honourable Companie of Loriners and Saddlers, where a helpful apprentice showed me the book of marks used by members of the guild, and found the bird mark straightaway.

"That would be the shop of Dagobert Finch, sir," he said.

"Where would I find it?"

"Across the river, in Mossthorpe."

So I retraced my steps across the great bridge to the House of Finch in Mossthorpe. The shop was rich with the scent of leather and prime neat's-foot oil, and saddles hung beneath the roof beams like carcases at my father's butchery. Master Saddler Finch was a short, peppery man with a bristly mustache. "I sell a great many saddles, younker," said he.

"This would have been sold to a gentleman about my height," I said. "Wore a beard when I met him yesterday. He rides a liver chestnut."

I saw from a sudden gleam in Finch's eye that he recognized my description, but then his look grew cautious. "Why do you want to know?"

"I owe him money," said I. "We were both at the hunt at Kingsmere two days ago, and we wagered on one of the gentlemen fighting a stag with a sword, and I lost. Yet in the excitement of the betting, I failed to note the gentleman's name."

"Yet it is unusual for a man to pursue another, and all to willingly give money away."

"I can afford it," I said. "I won my other bets." And, to demonstrate my prosperity, I passed a couple of crowns across the table.

"Sir Hector Burgoyne," said Finch. "A military gentleman, yes? He will be glad of your money. He commissioned the saddle over a year ago, but I only gave it to him last month when he finally paid the balance on his account."

"Know you where he lives?"

"Nay, younker. But he keeps his courser at Mundy's on the main road, and they will probably know."

So off I went to Mundy's livery stable, and one of the grooms, once I had given him his vail, was able to direct me to Burgoyne's garrett in Selford, in the stew called Ramscallion Lane. Wearing my hood over my head, I found the building without trouble, a half-timbered structure sagging over the street, with ancient thatch hanging over the eaves like untidy bangs over a scarred forehead. It hardly seemed the sort of place for a knight to lodge unless he was desperate for money—desperate enough to commit murder, I supposed.

A fetid, rank odor hung about the lane, both from the rubbish thrown in the streets and the ditch that ran behind the neighborhood, a ditch full of the sewage of the district as well as that which had run down the hill. I kept my hand on my purse the entire visit, to avoid being robbed by the thieves, custrels, apple-squires, and trulls that infested the district. I could see my silver reflected in their pouched, greedy eyes.

I now had a number of choices. I could apprehend Burgoyne myself but cared little for the idea of nabbing a desperate villain in a rathole like Ramscallion Lane. I could hire some professional thief-takers, but that would cost money.

I could disdain the thief-takers and go to a magistrate, who would give me a warrant, but then I would still have to find someone to serve the warrant, and be scarcely any better than I had before.

I might go to the sheriff if he was in the city and not elsewhere in the county. But then he would bring his own thief-takers and probably claim credit for the arrest.

I could not go to the Attorney-General, for the simple reason that Queen Berlauda had not yet appointed one.

The one place I absolutely could not go was the barracks of the Yeoman Archers. The City of Selford rejoiced in its traditional liberties, which included freedom from interference by the Queen's Army. The army was forbidden to apprehend lawbreakers, or otherwise disturb the orderly business of criminality, unless there was hue and cry (in which case soldiers could apprehend a felon while acting in the character of private individuals, rather than members of a military company), or if there was a riot or insurrection and a magistrate certified that the Act to Prevent Tumult applied, in which case the army was allowed to massacre at will.

Should the pursuing Archers have caught the assassin, I thought, it would have raised an interesting point. Could Sir Hector Burgoyne claim at his trial that his arrest was illegal, as the army had no right to apprehend him?

Of course, the prosecution could claim that a hue and cry had been raised, but the defense could counter that a hue and cry only applied when the quarry was actually in sight.

I would have enjoyed arguing it either way.

To apprehend Burgoyne, I might go to a member of the Watch. But the Watch were mostly elderly pensioners who wandered the city at night calling that all was well while ringing a bell. (The point of the bell was to let everyone know they weren't sleeping on duty.) If a watchman discovered a fire or a crime in progress, he did not intervene, but rang the bell continuously and called for help.

The decrepit, underpaid members of the Watch were unlikely to provide enough brawn to apprehend a vigorous, unscrupulous man in Ramscallion. Selford and the law provided any number of ways to take up a criminal, and none of them were of any use to me.

So it must be the thief-takers after all. I went up Chancellery Road to the courts, where such people made themselves available for hire, and acquired for three crowns each, and a share in any reward, the services of two very large men named Merton and Toland. From their broken noses, missing teeth, and the scars on their pates I marked them as former prizefighters, which meant they had practical experience in the ring against opponents carrying broadswords, halberds, and flails. Toland, indeed, looked as if his entire face had been flattened in a collision with a buckler.

I explained that Burgoyne was wanted for attempted murder and warned that he was a former military man and probably dangerous.

"Should I not hire some more men?" asked I.

"Nay, sir." Merton spoke in a plausible, peaceful voice that belied his formidable appearance. "We two are used to taking felons quietly, and if we bring a large group into the Ramscallion, we're asking for trouble. Let's keep the reward between the three of us." Merton nodded sagely. "And I will need another couple of crowns."

"For what purpose?"

"For the landlady, so she won't make a fuss."

This was sensible, and I passed over the silver. I was a little surprised when, even after my warnings, the thief-takers armed themselves only with wooden cudgels, which they hid beneath their cloaks.

"Are you sure those clubs will do the job?" I asked.

Merton seemed offended. "Sir, they haven't failed yet—our veteran crown-knockers must have tamed a hundred villains, and turned them docile as little fuff-cats."

We made our way down the hill to Ramscallion Lane, and while the stench of the ditch clawed at the back of my throat, I pointed out Burgoyne's building. Merton and Toland gave it a professional survey, then Merton disappeared inside. I followed, and in the deep interior darkness of the hall saw one of my crowns make an appearance and vanish into the grimy hands of a beak-nosed slattern on the ground floor.

"Sir Hector?" Merton inquired.

"Top of the stair. Uphill side."

Merton wasted no time with thanks but stuck his head out the door and gestured to his partner.

"Master Toland will stay outside the house," he explained, "to make certain that Sir Hector does not escape by his window. You should stand with him, if you please, and I'll howster out this villain."

"I'll go with you," said I.

Merton made no reply and went to the stair—I doubt he cared whether I lived or died, but he had done his duty in trying to keep me away from any violence. There was no light on the stair, and its upper reaches were black as midnight. The steps creaked and shuddered under Merton's weight. My hand reached for the hilt of my new dagger. Then there was a flash and a shot louder than thunder, and Merton pitched backward, dead into my arms.

I struggled with the weight of the body as I gaped in astonishment up the stair, and there in the gloom I saw Burgoyne looking more or less as I'd last seen him, in a hat and a long coat, but this time with a big horse pistol in his fist. He looked down at me in a searching, contemplative way, as if he were trying to work out where he'd seen me before, then he turned and vanished into the murk. My ears, still ringing from the shot, could still mark the clank of his rowelled spurs as he retreated.

I laid Merton down on the steep stair, and one look told me that he was dead, having been shot with a heavy pistol ball right in the middle of his forehead. I was staring down at the man's face, my heart beating high in my throat, when Toland came running in and staggered to a halt at the sight of his partner.

Anger and excitement blazed up in me like sparks in a forge. "Burgoyne shot him!" I said. *"Let's take him!"*

I drew my dagger and hurled myself up the stair, stumbling over the body as I went. The top of the stair reeked of powder, but that scent was fresh and wholesome compared to the other smells of the place. I got to the top and saw gray light at the end of the passage, and I lurched toward it, stumbling over rubbish that people had left in the corridor.

I burst through the low doorway at the end of the hall and found myself outside, at the top of another steep stair, made of weathered planks, that dropped onto the narrow path that ran alongside the sewer-ditch behind the Ramscallion. A dark, sinister muck thicker than treacle oozed down the ditch. Dead dogs floated belly-up in the mire, and the place stank worse than a charnel house.

Burgoyne was fifty feet down the path, loping comfortably along as he looked over his shoulder at me. Even at this distance I could see that he retained that thoughtful expression with which he had viewed me from the top of the stair. If my blood hadn't been burning hot in my veins, if I hadn't been half-mad with the frenzy of pursuit, I would have understood that look for what it was, the calculating glance of a professional as he evaluated his foe.

Burgoyne had taken out the lever used to rewind his pistol, and he was cranking the wheel-lock as he hastened down the path. Even in my state of excitement I calculated that he couldn't possibly have had time to pour powder and ball down the barrel, or primed the pistol to fire, and I knew that I had to catch him before he could reload.

I dived down the steep, rickety stair three steps at a time and charged after him. Apparently he realized the futility of reloading, and he turned away and began to run faster. "Stop!" I shouted. "Stop!" The words *hue and cry* flashed through my mind, and I realized that "Stop!" and "Stop, thief!" were probably heard twenty times a day in the Ramscallion, only to raise laughter and derision on the part of the inhabitants.

"Stop, murderer!" I shouted. *"Reward for the murderer!"*

I guessed that the promise of reward might *well* bring more aid than a plea for help, and indeed as we ran along I saw windows opening, and faces peering past shutters.

"Reward!" I cried *"Reward for the murderer!"* At the words Burgoyne cast a choleric look over his shoulder but kept running.

The path was slippery and choked with rubbish and a truly astounding array of dead animals, and we both had trouble keeping our feet under us. Still, I closed the distance. Looking ahead, I could see a broad gray expanse of water, the Saelle swollen at high tide and backing the water up into the ditch, and I realized that Burgoyne was going to have to turn left, to run along the river's bank, or else wade across the horrid ditch, which I could not imagine him doing if he had a choice.

And indeed he went neither left nor right. At the end of the path he turned, drew his rapier, and directed its point at my breast.

My blood went from scalding hot to frigid cold in an instant. I stopped in mid-career, my feet sliding in the mud five yards away from the point of the sword. I stared at the weapon, which seemed long as a lance. My dagger now seemed preposterously inadequate as a weapon.

"Thus, boy," said Burgoyne, "your chase is brought to an end." His accent was that of northern Bonille.

I gasped, my heart thrashing in its cage, then drew in a breath and called out. *"Reward for the murderer!"*

He snarled at me, his teeth flashing white in his beard. "Pursue me further and I'll murder you in truth."

I saw an old bottle lying by the path, and I bent and flung it at him. He dodged it with an easy, contemptuous shift of his hips. Next to me was a tumbled-down stone wall, once a part of a shed, and I bent to pick up a stone. Burgoyne turned and vanished down the Saelle embankment.

For an instant I readied myself to chase again, then I thought that he might lurk just around the corner of the last building before the embankment, waiting for me to run into range of his rapier. I looked at the old shed on my left, with its broken wall and half-fallen roof-beams. I put my dagger in my teeth—an expedient I would have found ridiculous had I seen it in a play—and I jumped atop the half-fallen wall, and hoisted myself from thence to the roof-beams. I jumped along the beams, the shed shaking under my weight, then leaped from there to the moldy old thatch of an ancient, decrepit house. My footfalls nearly silent on the straw, I rustled across the roof's ridge, then down the other side.

I saw that my shouts and the promise of reward had brought out some of the more enterprising inhabitants of the district, men rough and dubious, and some of these stood at the end of Ramscallion Lane, looking along the side of the building on which I stood. It was no great deduction on my part to conclude that their neighbor Burgoyne stood there.

I ventured to peer over the edge of the roof, and I saw from above Burgoyne's broad hat at the corner of the building. He was, as I suspected, waiting for me to come dashing around to be skewered like a capon. I disappointed him, apparently, because the hat tilted as he peered around the corner and failed to see me. Then he turned and appeared in plain sight, walking toward Ramscallion Lane with his rapier still in his hand.

He called to his neighbors. "D'ye see that troublesome urchin anywhere?" Some of them looked up at me on the thatch, and I knew he'd follow their glance and realize I was above him; and so I snatched the dagger out of my teeth and leaped.

I landed behind and to his left side, near enough that I fell into him and knocked him toward the Saelle, but more importantly I'd brought the pommel of the dagger down on top of his head as I came down. His hat protected his crown somewhat, but he was dazed, and when I rose from the crouch into which the fall had sent me, I was on him, my left hand clutched around his coat-collar while my right struck again with the hilt of the dagger. As long as I stayed close, he couldn't use the rapier.

I did not want to stab him. It was clear Burgoyne was a hireling merely, and I wanted to haul him before a magistrate for interrogation and have him reveal the source of the conspiracy.

As I pummeled my quarry I could hear shouts of joy from the Ramscallions in the lane. I'm sure they loved nothing so much as a fight.

Burgoyne managed to fend off most of my blows as I wrenched him around by his collar, shaking him as a terrier shakes a rat. He tried to strike with the hilt of the rapier, but I parried with my own weapon and cut a gash in his overcoat sleeve. I smashed at his head again and was warded off. I know not what happened next, but somehow he twisted under me, I felt a hand grasp my left wrist, and suddenly I was tumbling through the air.

I landed on my back with some force, but panic picked me from the ground and rolled me forward to my feet. Plain murder gleamed pale in his eyes. My heart sank as I realized that he could now use his rapier, and I leaped back and parried with the knife as the narrow blade sprang for my vitals. He charged on and I skipped away, out into Ramscallion Lane, with our audience scattering as the blades gleamed in the day's dull light.

Burgoyne paused in his pursuit as he gasped for breath. I pointed at him.

"Reward!" I cried. *"Reward for the murderer!"*

Burgoyne snarled and lunged at me again, and I danced away. We were in a growing half-circle of observers, men and women and laughing children. Anticipation, cruelty, and greed shone in their eyes, as if we were dogs fighting in a pit for their entertainment. I pointed again.

"Knock him down!" said I. "Throw rocks! Throw bottles! Trip him up! There's a reward!"

"How much?" asked some pragmatist, but a young man hurled a bottle, and it whistled past Burgoyne's head. He glared at his neighbor and mouthed a curse.

More bottles followed, and pans, and stones. A slop pot, hurled from an upper storey, landed at his feet, and spattered him with its contents. I had turned the neighborhood into my accomplices. Burgoyne fended off most of the missiles but they slowed him down, and then one caught him on the forehead, and after that blood poured into his eyes, and he had to keep wiping them.

I could see the resolve building in him, and so I was ready when he made another attempt to kill me, running at me with the sword thrusting for my heart—and I would have got away if the growing crowd hadn't hampered me. Suddenly I was within range of the blade, and I frantically twisted away from it as it plucked at the buttons of my leather riding jerkin. I stabbed at him with my knife, and felt the blade enter the right shoulder. And then one of the crowd failed to get out of the way in time, and I tripped over him and fell . . . and there I was, helpless as the killer stood over me with growing triumph in his eyes. His arm came back for the final thrust.

At which point the thief-taker Toland, who had come up through the crowd, swung his cudgel and caught Burgoyne behind the ear, and so laid the murderer out atop me.

Amalie and I lay like spoons in my lodgings off Chancellery Road, my hand warm on her pregnant belly. She wore only her jewelry, gems on her fingers and a carcanet of gold and rubies about her throat. The strands of pearls she'd woven into her hair had come loose and lay on the pillow. Her languorous tones were regretful, and I vibrated with resentment. Nothing had ended as I planned.

"I regret extremely to give you this advice," she said. "But I think it best if you stayed away from court for the present."

I felt defiance straighten my spine. "I have done nothing wrong," said I. "I have in fact done the Queen a service. Why should I hide?"

"The whole world knows of the Queen's distaste for your presence," said she. "Should you appear at court, any who hope for royal favor will be obliged to shun you. It will be humiliating and will do your cause no good."

I thought for a long moment. Anger boomed dully in my veins. "I understand," said I.

"Other matters will soon occupy the court's attention. After that, you may return."

She turned and looked at me, compassion showing in her long eyes. "I warned you, did I not, that you should think before you acted?"

"You did," said I.

"A court conspiracy," said she, "is sometimes better left unmasked. If you meant to help Broughton, you failed. If you meant to uncover the guilty, you succeeded all too well. The Queen was forced to take action, and well does she resent you for making her take notice of the intrigue at her court."

After the capture of Burgoyne, Toland and I had taken the renegade knight to a magistrate, accompanied by a pack of the inhabitants of

Ramscallion Lane. The sheriff's men turned out, not because of the prisoner, but because they thought a riot was about to begin.

While Burgoyne was marched to jail, I led the mob to one of the counting-houses where I kept my funds. At the sight of this pack of unruly stew-dwellers, the good bankers began locking doors and slamming shutters, certain they were about to be stormed by an angry rabble. It took a bit of negotiation, but eventually I was allowed inside to collect some of my silver, after which I paid the mob to go away.

That same morning, before leaving Kingsmere for the capital, the Queen announced a reward of three hundred royal for the assassin, then appointed Lord Slaithstowe to be the new Attorney-General and put the investigation into his hands. Slaithstowe rode ahead of the Queen's party and arrived late in the afternoon, to find Burgoyne already in custody.

The next day Slaithstowe spent in putting the assassin to the question before the Court of the Siege Royal and coercing him to name his accomplices. What Slaithstowe heard probably had him tearing his beard out by the roots, but he did his duty, copied the transcript of the interrogation in his own hand—not trusting anyone else—and reported to the Queen first thing the next morning.

For Burgoyne admitted that he was in the pay of the Queen's own mother, the divorced Queen Leonora. Leonora rejoiced in her place near the Queen and feared losing the Queen's love to the interloper Broughton—and in addition Leonora, for reasons of policy, favored Berlauda's marriage to Loretto's prince and heir, not to a minor viscount with a pretty face.

Leonora's father had been Burgoyne's liege lord, before Burgoyne had gone abroad to serve in foreign wars. He had come home to Bonille with a competence, but being a rake and gambler had lost it all. Leonora gave him a few crowns now and again and kept him in reserve, in case she needed someone to intercept a messenger or cut a throat. And then came the inspiration to kill Broughton's wife and blame the husband for the deed. It was one of the Dowager Queen's ladies who commissioned the dagger with the Broughton badge.

Queen Berlauda must have been appalled and devastated by the news, but she lacked neither courage nor resolution. Burgoyne was sent to the gallows that very day. Queen Leonora was ordered to the royal residence and fort at West Moss, beyond the Minnith Peaks, as far from the capital as it is possible to travel without actually wading out into the ocean. She would remain there indefinitely, at the Queen's pleasure.

As for Broughton, the scandal was too great for a man without powerful friends to survive. Though he was innocent of anything but ambition, he was obliged to resign his post as Master of the Hunt, given the new office of Inspector-General of Fortifications, and sent off to view and report on the state of every fort, castle, and city wall in the kingdom. And, as he had borrowed heavily to outfit himself as a great man at court, and to provide the entertainments at Kingsmere, he would be pursued on this pilgrimage by his creditors, or their representatives.

Whether Lady Broughton rejoiced in the return of her husband, I do not know.

An official announcement was made that Burgoyne had been hanged after an attempt to assassinate the Queen. No mention was made of Dowager Queen Leonora though everyone at court knew the story within hours.

Those responsible for the violence were punished, but the punishment did not stop there, for Berlauda deeply resented losing everyone she loved and trusted, and viewed without charity those who had brought her to this pass. She could not abide the sight of Lord Slaithstowe, and found the pain of his presence too much to bear. He kept his office less than a week, which must have been a great blow, as he had performed his duty as well as it could be done—and he lost also the sweeteners he would have been paid by anyone whose business brought them before the Attorney-General, a sum that over time would have been a great fortune. Instead he was appointed commissioner of the royal dockyard in Amberstone, where the opportunities for enrichment were small by comparison.

And as for me—I, who had been the subject of praise and the object of envy on my return to court, the day after my capture of Burgoyne—I was told merely that the sight of me was disagreeable to her majesty and that I should keep clear of the royal presence. Unlike Slaithstowe I was not offered a job, lest the offer be construed as a reward rather than a punishment.

I still waited for the three hundred royals promised for Burgoyne. If I ever received it, I would divide it evenly between Toland, Merton's family, and my own declining fortune.

Amalie was still willing to see me, but then a Marchioness of Steyne was almost as grand as the Queen, and she could set her own fashions. Still, she could not be seen with me in public, and only visited my lodgings for a few hours now and again. Our dalliance, like the season, would soon enough reach its wintertide, for in a few months she would give birth to Steyne's heir, and Steyne himself would return from captivity. Sometimes I missed her even when she was in my arms.

I wondered if Virtue had triumphed over Iniquity, as in Blackwell's masque. Berlauda's court had been cleansed of one conspirator and one adulterous nobleman, but no doubt there were many of that sort who remained. The court was also rid of one half lawyer who trusted too much to his own luck and had suffered the consequence of that trust. I could almost hear the laughter ringing down from the roof-beams.

Was it Virtue who laughed in her chaste home, or was the laughter that of her demicolleague, Iniquity?

Whoever it was who laughed, it was clear that I was not in Virtue's camp as long as Amalie visited my bed. And so I kissed the fine tawny hair that grew at the base of her neck, thanked her for her advice, and set myself to amuse her, that she might soon choose again to visit me in my exile.

Daniel Abraham

• • •

Daniel Abraham lives with his family in Albuquerque, New Mexico, where he is Director of Technical Support at a local Internet service provider. Starting off his career in short fiction, he made sales to *Asimov's Science Fiction*, *SCI FICTION*, *The Magazine of Fantasy & Science Fiction*, *Realms of Fantasy*, *The Infinite Matrix*, *Vanishing Acts*, *The Silver Web*, *Bones of the World*, *The Dark*, *Wild Cards*, and elsewhere, some of which appeared in his first collection, *Leviathan Wept and Other Stories*. Turning to novels, he made several sales in rapid succession, including the books of The Long Price Quartet, which consist of *A Shadow in Summer*, *A Betrayal in Winter*, *An Autumn War*, and *The Price of Spring*. He's also written the The Dagger and the Coin series, which consists of *The Dragon's Path*, *The King's Blood*, *The Tyrant's Law*, *The Widow's House*, and, most recently, *The Spider's War*. He also wrote *Hunter's Run*, a collaborative novel with George R. R. Martin and Gardner Dozois; as M.L.N. Hanover, wrote the four-volume paranormal romance series Black Sun's Daughter; and with Ty Franck, writing as James S. A. Corey, the Space Opera Expanse novels (which have been made into a popular TV series), consisting of *Leviathan Wakes*, *Caliban's War*, *Abaddon's Gate*, *Gods of Risk*, *Cibola Burn*, *Nemesis Games*, and *Babylon's Ashes*.

Here he takes us along with companions trying to penetrate to the heart of a daunting and deadly mystery, and discovering that what they find is not at all what they expected to find.

♦　♦　♦

The Mocking Tower

DANIEL ABRAHAM

Old Au saw the thief first.

Squatting in the garden, she commanded a long view of the east road; gray flagstone straighter than nature amid the green scrub and bramble. Rich soil breathed its scent around her as she took an offending root in one hand and her garden knife in the other. Between the moment she began sawing and when she pulled the first tangle of dirt and pale vegetable flesh out of the ground, the thief appeared, a dot on the horizon. She worked as he approached. His cloak hung limp in the humid summer air. His hat, wide as his shoulders, shadowed his eyes. He wore an empty scabbard across his back. Old Au paused when he grew close. When he reached the wall of ancient stone that marked the border between the greater world and the protected lands within, he paused and looked toward the Mocking Tower.

The tower shimmered as the tales all said it would, appearing to change shape between one breath and the next. A great thrusting pillar of alabaster studded with living torches became an ancient palace of gray stone and moss became a rose-colored complication of terraces stacked one atop another toward the sky. The thief took in the illusionist's art with an air of haughtiness and satisfaction. Old Au watched the man watch the tower, cleared her throat, and nodded to the stranger.

"What news?" she asked.

His gaze shifted to the old woman. His eyes looked as if they'd been dyed the same blue as a storm cloud. The lines around his mouth and eyes spoke of age and weather, but Old Au thought she saw a boyishness in them as well, like the image of an acorn worked in oak. Something in him reminded Old Au of a lover she'd taken years before. A man of high station who dreamed of living as a gardener. Dead now and his dreams with him except for what she carried with her. When the thief spoke, his voice carried the richness and depth of a reed instrument, softly played.

"The throne stands empty," the thief said. "King Raan rots in his grave, and the princes vie to claim his place."

"All seven of them?"

"Tauen, Maush, and Kinnin all fell to their brothers' blades. Another—Aus by name—rose from the south with a foreign army at his back to lay a new claim. Five armies still cross the land and blight wherever they pass."

"Shame, that," Old Au said.

"Wars end. Even wars of succession. They also create certain unexpected opportunities for the bold," he said, then shifted as by moving his shoulders, he moved the conversation. "These lands belong to the Imagi Vert?"

Old Au shrugged, pointing to the stone wall with her chin. "Everything within the border, and all the way round. Not subject to the throne, nor the one before it. Nor to whatever comes next either. The Mocking Tower stands apart from the world and the Imagi Vert sees to that, once and eternal. You've come on behalf of one of the princes? Plead the Imagi to take a side, maybe?"

"The tale I hear told says the Imagi Vert took King Raan's soul when he died and fashioned it into a blade. And the blade lies somewhere in that tower. I have come to steal it."

Old Au wiped a soil-darkened hand across her cheek, squinting first at the thief then at the Mocking Tower and back to the thief. His chin lifted as if in challenge. The empty scabbard tapped against his back as if asking for attention. Green lacquer and brass fittings, and long enough to hold even a fairly large sword. As though a king's soul surely required a palatial blade to hold it.

"You make it a habit to announce that sort of thing, do you?" Old Au said as she brushed the soil off the length of pale, stubborn root still in the earth. "Seems an odd way to get what you want."

The thief's attention returned to her. A smile both bright and brief flickered on his lips. "I'm sure you know a great deal about gardening. I know a great deal about theft. This road leads to the township at the tower's base?"

Old Au nodded. "Another hour down the road. Keep left at the crossing or you'll find yourself heading south without much besides grain silos and the mill for company. But take the warning. Everyone you find there is loyal to the Imagi Vert. Anyone not tends to leave fair quick."

"I don't plan to stay."

"You have a name, friend?" Old Au asked.

"Many of them."

The thief slid a hand into his sleeve and drew it back out. Something small and bright between his fingers caught the sunlight. He tossed the coin to Old Au, and she caught it without thinking. A square of silver with a young man's likeness pressed into the metal. Some prince or another. One of the dead king's warring brood.

"This for my silence?" Old Au asked.

"For your help in directing me," the thief said. "Anything more lies between you and your conscience."

Old Au chuckled, nodded, and tucked the coin in her belt. The thief and his empty scabbard stepped off down the road. His stride shifted his cloak from side to side like the flourish of a street magician's right hand distracting from the actions of the left. His hat carried shadow under its brim like a veil. The Mocking Tower changed to a soaring complex of chains hanging from a stonework tree taller than clouds to a spiral of basalt with stairways cut into the sides. Old Au shook her head and bent back down to her work. The stubborn root defied her, but she was stern and hard and well practiced with a garden knife. When it came out, long as her arm and pale as bone, she squatted in the churned black soil, wiped the sweat from her face, and looked west after the thief. The curve of the road and the trees hid him already.

The township that served the Imagi Vert pretended normalcy even in the shadow of magic. Only the central square boasted flagstone. Dust, dirt, and weeds made up all the streets. The small stables reeked like stables anywhere, and pisspots stood in the alleys waiting to be taken and their contents sold to the launderer to whiten cloth or the tanner to soften hide. The flowers of early summer drew bees and flies. The sun warmed thatched roofs until they stank a little. Birds chattered and warned each other from their nests. Dogs ran here as they did anywhere, chasing squirrels and each other. A few hundred feet to the north, the Mocking Tower loomed, a spire of bone and glass, then a pillar of plate-thin stones stacked one atop the other toward the sky, then a spiral of what looked like skinned flesh, then an ivy-clad maiden of granite with a crown of living flame.

The people of the township viewed the thief as the greater curiosity. He walked through the streets, eyes hidden but with a cheerful smile. The empty scabbard bumped against his back with every step.

The Traveler's Hearth stood just down from the square and at an angle, like a servant with eyes politely averted. The thief went to it as if he stayed there often. The keeper—a fat man wearing the traditional iron chain of hospitality wrapping his left arm—greeted him in the courtyard.

"I need only a small room," the thief said.

"No small rooms, nor any big ones either," the fat man said. "Just rooms is all."

"All people claim the same dignity before the Imagi?" the thief said as if joking.

"Just so. Just so. Simin can take your horse if you have one."

Simin—a lanky, dark-haired boy with a simple, open face—nodded hopefully. The thief shook his head and handed three of the square, silver coins to the fat man. "I only take what I can carry."

The keeper considered the coins as if they spelled out the future, then pressed his lips tight and shrugged. The iron chain clinked as if offering its own metallic thoughts. Simin broke the silence. "I can show you the way anyhow."

"Very kind of you," the thief said.

Simin trotted ahead, leading the thief down short halls and into a hidden courtyard of cherry trees. A stone cistern loomed in a corner where a thin-limbed girl scrubbed away moss with a black-bristled brush and tried not to stare. The thief nodded to her. She blushed and nodded back.

Simin stopped at a high door the color of fresh cream, opening the brass latch with a click. The thief stepped into his private room and the boy trotted along behind him. The air smelled of soap and lilac. Shadows clung to the pale walls, like stepping into a sudden twilight. A modest bed with a dark brown, rough-woven blanket of the sort common to the southern tribes a hundred years before. An ironwork sculpture of an iris in a frame hung on the wall opposite the only window. An earthenware jug and cup sat on a low table beside three unlit candles. Simin, smiling, closed the shutters as if the thief had asked him to. The shadows grew deeper.

The thief sank slowly to the bed. The empty scabbard clattered on the floor where he dropped it. He swept off his hat and let it sit beside him, covered in pollen and dust. Sweat-dark locks of hair stuck to his balding scalp. His cheerful smile vanished and fear took its place. He shook his head, pressed a palm to his brow, and shook his head again.

"I can't. I can't do this."

"You can," Simin—whose name was not Simin—snapped, his own affectation of boyish goodwill falling away. "And you will."

"Did you see that tower? I've heard tales of the Mocking Tower, everyone has. I thought it would . . . I don't know. Catch the sunlight oddly. Cast weird shadows. 'Seems to shift moment by moment' they say, ah? Too damned true. How do I put myself against a wizard who can do that?"

Simin leaned against the wall, arms folded across his chest. "You don't. I do."

"We're making a mistake. We should go back."

"Back to what? Fire and death? We keep to the plan," the boy said. "Get the sword. End the war."

The thief sagged forward, elbows against his knees, head in his hands. "If you say. If you say." Then, gathering himself. "Did you find it?"

Simin poured water from the jug into the cup and handed it to the thief as he spoke. "No. But with you here, they'll show me. Whatever changes, wherever the guard increases, whatever they keep you from.

That's how I'll know. You strike the drum, and I listen to the echoes for answers. It works that way. And the more they watch you, the less they watch me."

"I know, I know," the thief said, then paused to drink the cup dry. He handed it back, wiping his lips with a sleeve. "I liked this plan better before I came here. Successions and thrones and blood and armies in the field. Now magic swords and wizards and a tower like something that's crawled out of a bad dream. I don't belong in something like this."

"Go in the morning. Talk to everyone you can find. Ask about green glass."

"Green glass? Why?"

"I found a private temple not far from the tower fashioned from it. I think the blade may be there."

"Green glass, then. And boasting about crossing the Imagi Vert in front of the people most loyal to him. And acting mysterious and charming. When the wizard kills me over this, you can carry the guilt."

"What news from the war?" Simin asked, and his tone said he already knew. The swamping of Loon Channel. The murder of Prince Tauen. The starvation in Cai Sao Station. A question that carries its own answer argues something more than its words. The thief understood.

"The payout justifies the risk," the bald man said to the boy. "I never said otherwise."

"We start tomorrow, then," the boy said, and left, closing the door behind him.

"I already started today," the thief muttered to an empty room.

King Raan took the throne, and with it control of the Empire, a week before his twentieth name day. A boy still with the glow of youth in his skin, he sat in a chair of gold and gemstones and bones. He ruled for six decades through peace and strife, famine and plenty. Many people born on the day of his ascension lived out their whole lives not knowing any other ruler. The idea of governance and King Raan grew together in the minds of his subjects like two saplings planted side by side twining around each other until neither could exist without the other. King

Raan and the Empire and the right function of the world all named the same thing.

Easy enough, then, to forget the man who bore that weight. He alone of everyone from the Sea of Pearls to the knife-peaked Dai Dou mountains, the ice sheets of High Saral to the deserts of the Heliopon, understood that the man called King Raan who controlled the Empire as a normal person commanded their own hands, and the one named Raan Sauvo Serriadan born of Osh Sauvo, princess of Hei Sa and third wife to King Gaudon, did not share everything. The man and the office that demanded all his days only appeared at peace with each other. If anything, Death's shadow oppressed him more than it did others because he could not pretend that more power and influence would bring a deeper meaning to his life. Wealth and status could not dispel the questions that haunted him. He sought his consolation in sex and philosophy and—near the end—the occult.

The sex led to a legion of children both within and outside the political labyrinths of marriage; the philosophy, to a series of melancholy letters which detailed his conception of the human soul and the nature of a well-lived life; and the occult, inevitably, to his friendship with the Imagi Vert.

The Imagi Vert: a name that conjured up a whole mythology of threats and wonders. Even more than the bodiless voice of the Stone Oracle at Kalafi or the Night Children that played in the waves off the coast of Amphos, the Imagi Vert embodied the deeper mysteries of the world. Some claimed that the Imagi began life as a human and suffered transformation by falling down a cliff and into a flaw in the universe. Others, that God could not breathe life into the clay of the world without opening a crack between heaven and earth, and the scar from that wound took a name and a tower and a circle of land for itself. Or that a great wizard cheated death itself by learning to live backward to the beginning of all things. All the different versions agreed on three things: the Imagi held the Mocking Tower and the land around it inviolate, those who sought to bend the Imagi to mere human will ended poorly, and wonders beyond the understanding of the most outlandish imagination lay hidden in the shadow of that changing and eternal tower.

King Raan's studies of the occult drew him to the low stone wall and the town and the tower as inevitably as water running down.

No one can know the nature of that first meeting, but many have guessed. Perhaps the emperor could only experience humility before the ageless, timeless thing that called the Mocking Tower home. Or perhaps two people set so far above humanity that power became isolation more resembled refugees in a vast wilderness clinging to each other. No one witnessed the time those two kept in each other's company, and King Raan shared little with his court. His trips to the Mocking Tower became first a yearly pilgrimage, then once in the high summer and another in winter's depth. And then, as his years thinned him and travel from the palaces became impossible, a beloved memory that outlasted all others.

Death came to King Raan as with anyone. The throne of Empire did not exempt him. Physicians came from every corner of the world bearing vials of salt and herb, charms and chants and leeches. King Raan allowed them all to minister to him like an uncle indulging his nieces and nephews in their games. If he held any real hope of prolonging his life, he didn't express it. The princes and princesses gathered around the palaces. The eldest—Prince Kinnan—bore his diadem on hair already grown thin and pale by fifty-eight years of life. Princess Magren, the youngest present, still wore braids like a child, celebrating a youth she had not quite outgrown. The palaces grew dense with the volume of servants and wealth and ambition, like a tick ready to pop with blood.

At the moment of his death, a darkness passed over the palaces. The torches and lamps and the fires in their grates all shuddered and went out. Some claim to have heard the sound of wings, as if the blackness hid a vastness of huge birds. Others, a low, musical whistling that came from the walls themselves. Only King Raan's nurse and Prince Tauen, who fortune placed at his bedside, heard King Raan's last words—*You remembered your promise*—and at the time, they placed no great importance upon them. When the servants finished rekindling the torches and candles, fire logs and lanterns, King Raan lay dead and the Empire changed.

For a time, it seemed as if this new order might fall close to the old. The legal scholars and priests who studied the arcana of dignified bloodlines identified those of King Raan's children with just claims to the throne. As eldest, Kinnan held the strongest claim, but Naas—younger but of a higher-born mother—ran a near second. Then Tauen and Clar, Maush, and Tynnyn. Princess Saruenne of Holt cut her hair and her name together, declaring herself Prince Saru in a gesture which the priests said had many precedents. For the weeks of mourning, the Empire held its breath. Then Prince Kinnan announced the date of his ascension and invited his siblings to come in peace to honor the memory of the father they shared.

Even now, the identity of the men who slaughtered Kinnan's wife and children remained unclear. But they failed to kill the prince, and the War of Seven Princes began.

In the years since the first blood spilled, only chaos reigned. News traveled across mountains and plains, lakes and oceans, and it spoke of death and loss and palace intrigue. And, sometimes to those who cared to listen for it, of the Imagi Vert. A fisherman whose cousin worked in the palace kitchens said that on the night of King Raan's death, when the fires died, a shape—human or nearly so—had been seen flying across the face of the moon. It came from the direction of the Mocking Tower and returned the same way. A woman traveling through the lands of the Imagi Vert at that same time reported that the townsfolk had kept inside that night, leaving the mild summer evening as empty as if a wild storm had raged.

Some tales could even be verified. Yes, agents of the Imagi had sought out half a dozen of the best swordsmiths in the Empire in the months of King Raan's decline. Yes, a forge had been built in the lee of the Mocking Tower, then—a month after the death of the king— collapsed. Yes, a stranger had arrived at the library of Ahmon Suer in the weeks after the king's first decline and demanded an obscure treatise on the nature of the soul.

Little more than whispers in a high wind, yet the links between the Imagi Vert and the death of the king began to tell a larger tale. This new mythology began in the king's dying words and ended in one man's plan to end the war.

The patchwork of truth and surmise came together this way: In his age, King Raan came to fear death, or if not fear it, at least regret its necessity. He appealed to his deathless friend and companion, the Imagi Vert. Together, they plotted a way that King Raan might shed the clay of his flesh and yet remain undying. The Imagi Vert, through means unknown to the pious, collected the king's soul when it fled his body, returned with it to the Mocking Tower, and there forged it into a sword. Steel and fire formed a blade in which Raan could escape all endings.

And then ... what would the wizard who lived outside of time do with such a blade? What power could a true soulsword give? Mere human guesses seemed unlikely to plumb the depths of the Imagi's schemes and plots. Perhaps the sword gave some advantage a thousand years hence. Perhaps it only offered the pleasure of accomplishing a task no other alchemist dared to hazard. But for the heirs of the Empire? For the men and women and children who faced the prospect of war, it was an object of even greater power.

And so, in the capital of a small nation where King Raan had made one of his last visits, in the home of a woman who, almost two decades before, had been charged with the raising of young Prince Aus, the heir farthest from his father's throne built schemes of his own.

He had lived alone his whole life, knowing nothing of his father and mother beyond a direction over the sea and an assurance that his blood gave him honor and dignity, if not love. He covered the fine stone walls in charcoal and wax as he mapped out his journey, the paths of his little armies. The eighth in the War of Seven Princes, and the one with the least hope of victory in the field.

The field did not concern him. For Aus, the path of victory wound through no battlefields. Only the gardens and grounds of the Mocking Tower. The ruins where ivy already overgrew the charred bones of a forge. A temple of green glass. The streets and stables, mills and kitchens and farmyards of the lands that no king claimed. There or nowhere lay the key to the ambitions of Aus, the Forgotten Prince.

Aus, whose name was not Simin.

"I have always had a fondness for ... *green glass*," the thief said and smiled knowingly. The woman standing before him—dark-haired and broad-shouldered—rested her axe on her shoulder and said nothing.

The thief smiled as if the two of them were sharing a joke, tipped his wide-brimmed hat, and moved on down the street. The town betrayed no trace of its eerie status apart from the Mocking Tower itself. Men and women went about the business of their days here as they would anywhere. Dogs and children chased each other over rough stone paving and through wide puddles of standing mud. Birds watched from the tree branches thick with leaves. So long as the constantly changing tower remained hidden, forgetting it seemed possible. And the thief found ways to keep the tower out of sight.

A thick-faced man hauling a cartload of fresh-cut hay made his way along the street, a creature of soft grunts and sweat. The thief stepped in front of him. "A fine morning. I wonder, friend, if you might know something interesting about green glass? I have good silver to trade for good words."

The hauler paused, scowled, and shrugged his shoulders before he shoved on. The thief smiled after him as if his reticence told a clearer tale than all the eloquence in the world. He drew an old tin sextant from his robe, hung a plumb line with a lump of gem-bright crimson glass for a bob, and pretended to take readings of the tops of the trees. He felt like an idiot, and a frightened one at that. He expected to end the day facedown in a ditch with fish eating his eyes. But he also took his work seriously, so he made a mysterious ass of himself and hoped for the best without being too specific about what that best might be.

In the stables, Prince Aus played at Simin, nodding and helping wherever he found a chance, and above all else listening.

The keeper to his wife as they tended to the grapevines behind the main house: *Of course I sent word to the tower. Went there myself as soon as I saw him off to his room. Expect the Imagi knew well before I said anything, though.*

The cleaning girl to her mother as they walked toward the market with the day's eggs: *The Imagi sent instructions in the night. Little finches with hollowed eyes that carried bits of parchment in their beaks. Bir—*(who Simin knew as the blacksmith's apprentice)*—got one, and so did Soylu.*

One of the little girls wearing as much mud as dress as she clapped her hands in the filthy water by her house: *Thieves and rats, thieves and rats, and all of us are blades and cats.*

Everyone knew, as Simin hoped they would. But if any panicked, he didn't see it. Like a man walking toward a dog on a road at twilight, the town watched, calm and steady, as it judged the threat. But at least it felt threatened or amused or at least *interested*. Of his greatest fears—boredom, complaisance, indifference—he saw nothing. The thief loomed in the news of the town, and that sufficed.

After lunch, when Simin traditionally slipped away to the hayloft for a long nap, Prince Aus slipped away down the track that pretended to be a deer trail. He walked carefully, his ears straining over the buzzing of summer flies and the hushing of the high grass. The midday heat drenched him with sweat and the thick air went into his lungs like steam. The Mocking Tower shifted: a spiral of smooth white stones reaching to the sky; a pair of massive yellow curves nesting one within the other like the beak of an impossible huge bird; a single uncarved block of smoky obsidian. As he neared the site of the green-glass temple, he slowed even more.

The little marks set to warn of others passing along the track remained. The long blade of grass bent at knee height still leaned across the path. The thread thin as spider's web at waist height still caught the thick, sluggish breeze between a dead tree and a thick, sharp-leaved bush. Prince Aus felt the disappointment growing in his heart even before he made the last turn and the green-glass temple came into view.

Perhaps it had grown smaller since first he'd discovered it—anything seemed possible so close to the Mocking Tower. Or perhaps the first dissonant chords of disappointment only made it seem so. The afternoon sun shone against the undulating emerald surfaces, but he only saw the dust now. When he stepped inside and stepped to the low altar, he felt none of the sense of wonder and certainty that bore him up the night he'd found it. The dust he'd spread so carefully in hopes of showing where the footsteps of the unwary had passed remained unstirred.

The thief had come, made his threat, and no one had reacted. Not the townsfolk. Not the Imagi Vert. Prince Aus told himself to be pleased. He preferred finding the blade's true hiding place, but knowing for certain that the temple did not hold it added to his knowledge, subtracted from the possibilities that remained. He cultivated patience. Mostly. His single frustrated shout set the birds in the treetops to flights, but only once. He didn't repeat it.

He walked back along the trail, hurrying to get back to the hayloft before anyone expected Simin to wake. Even as he broke into a trot, he felt his false persona slipping into place. Simin the vagabond. The boy too dull to have a story of his own worth knowing. Simin the unremarkable. And perhaps it was because of this—the role he'd inhabited before fitting so well into place—that the cleaning girl walking along the road away from town and tower failed to notice him.

The market lay nowhere near. The girl's mother no longer limped at her side. And something bounced and bobbled against her back. A little cloth bag, grease-stained. The sort that might hold a bit of food carried for not too long a journey.

Aus or Simin paused, pulled between two impulses: return to safety before anyone could penetrate his disguise or else . . . or else see what this girl meant by traveling alone so far from where her usual paths led her. And with food. And—yes—just the faintest air of furtive excitement. Aus felt his belly tighten, a knot form in the back of his throat.

He turned, following her at a distance, and with all the stealth he could.

The girl led him to the north, away from the green-glass temple, and around to the uncanny, shifting tower. The sun caught the crimson of her scarf and the sway of her hair as brightly as a banner on the field. The sun's heat stood on the edge between pleasant and oppressive. The thickness of the air felt like a coming storm. He kept to the shadows under boughs and edges of the tall grass where the path's curve took her nearly out of sight. His fear of being seen grew in him, changing as it did into a vibrating excitement. At any moment, the keeper of the Traveler's Hearth would come looking for him. The urge to break off tugged at him, but the sense of teetering on the edge of something critical pulled him forward. The girl, unaware that his world now centered on her, walked and skipped, paused and looked back, walked on. A patch of sweat darkened the back of her dress.

And in a stretch of dappled shade where two trees overhung the path, she vanished.

A cold rush of panic filled the prince's chest. The girl had been an illusion, the bait in a trap. Or she had escaped him and even as he stood there, she hurried to raise the alarm. He waited, his body stiff as wood, and only when nothing happened for ten long, shuddering breaths together did he move forward. The path between the trees stood empty. The leaves shuddered in a barely felt breeze. The rough-worn earth went before and behind. Nothing seemed odd or out of place apart from his memory of the girl and her present absence. The prince turned slowly, blinking in confusion and wonder.

The complication of air nearly escaped him. Made from nothing, it looked like nothing. Only a flaw in the light like the smallest ripple in a glass. Even when he saw it, he doubted. But he stepped forward, one foot before the other, and the landscape unfolded around him as if by walking straight ahead, he rounded a bend in the path and exposed new and unseen vistas. A hillside rose green-grassed and dandelion-spattered to the very foot of the Mocking Tower. A lintel of stone stood at the mouth of a cave, and in the place of twilight between the darkness underground and the shining daylight, the cleaning girl sat with Bir, the blacksmith's apprentice, beside her. A lunch of chicken and bread spread out by their side and the little cloth bag collapsed behind them. The two saw nothing but each other, but Prince Aus saw everything. The girl's awkward smile. The apprentice blacksmith's ill-fitting armor and leather-handled axe. The shuddering shape after shape after shape of the tower. He walked backward, the world refolding itself around him until he stood alone on the path again, in the same place but no longer entirely the same man.

A pathway hidden by magic. A man set to guard it even at the cost of his usual duties. The abandoned temple no longer pained him. What he'd sought, he'd found. The Imagi Vert, alarmed by the thief, drew up his defenses, and in doing so, showed what wanted defending. Simin or Aus retreated to the town, walking often forward and often backward, hurrying to avoid suspicion in his absence but also committing the path to memory for the time when he returned.

The rest of the day Prince Aus committed himself to being Simin. He mucked out the stalls and repaired the place in the chicken run where something from the woods failed to force its way in. He hauled water from the well to the hearth's kitchen and carried pies from the kitchen to the miller as exchange for the uncooked flour. When the keeper made a joke, he laughed. When the cleaning girl trotted by near sundown with her cheeks bright and her sleeve stained green with grass, he pretended not to notice. The Mocking Tower changed: a moon-pocked shaft of white and gray; a block of iron like a great anvil with glowing windows around the top; a ramshackle construction like all the buildings of a rough village stacked one atop the other and swaying in the slight breeze.

The thief came to the common room for dinner, ate and drank and laughed without appearing to have a care in the world or any interest in Simin. His merry blue eyes danced and glittered in the candlelight, and he drank wine and sang songs as if everything that happened fit in with some unimaginably complex plan. Near midnight, when Prince Aus snuck across the grounds to the thief's room, the door stood ajar, and the man hunched on the bed seemed like someone else entirely. The thief's eyes watered and deep grooves of concern bordering on fear carved themselves into his forehead and the corners of his mouth.

"I can't keep doing this," he said, as the prince stepped into the room. "They smile and talk when I face them, but as soon as I turn my back, they plot murder. A day more, two at most, and a knife's going to sprout right between my shoulder blades. I can feel it already."

"Can you, now?" the prince said, shutting the door.

"I can. It itches." The thief ran a hand over his scalp, disarranging his hair.

The prince sat beside him. "Good that we leave tonight, then."

The thief started then went still. His wide eyes flickered over the Prince's face. "Seriously?"

"I found a place. A hidden cave at the base of the tower. Guarded by a man who isn't a guard by trade and shrouded by magic."

"Well," the thief said, then laughed like a brook in flood. "The plan worked? The plan actually worked? I'm damned. I figured us both for dead."

"Working," the prince said. "Not worked. Not yet. You stay here. Rouse no more suspicions. But when I come back, we ride."

"Understood," the thief said. And as the prince rose to go, he leaped to his feet, scrabbled under the bed, and stood again. He held out the green-and-brass scabbard. "Take this. To carry the blade when you find it."

Gently but firmly, the prince pushed the scabbard back. The thief blinked his confusion.

"I don't want to *claim* my father's soul," the prince said. "I came here to destroy it."

The prince moved through the darkness, a shadow among shadows. The night held no terror for him. His tightly cut black cloak and the sheathed knife at his hip, soft boots and dirtied face, left him feeling like a dock-side cutthroat. He told himself that the tightness in his throat and the tripping of his heart only meant excitement, not fear, and the telling made it true.

The scrub and grass along the path had lost its green. Moonlight remade the world in black and gray. Animals shuffled in the darkness of the scrub. The trees rubbed their leaves together with a sound like soft rain. The Mocking Tower shifted and changed like a sleeper made uneasy by spoiled dreams, but in the darkness he could not make out the details. Without so much as a candle, the prince retraced the way the cleaning girl had brought him.

Where the two trees spanned the path, he paused. Gloom made the fissure of light and air invisible, but he remembered it. Crouching low, he crept forward. His eyes strained. The glamours and spells of the Imagi Vert might not hold to the laws of human experience. What worked in daylight could fail in the night. But no, the world shifted as it had before. The mere wild unfurled a path, a hill, a cave. And the shifting tower where his father's soul lay, fashioned now in steel. A flicker of light from the mouth of the cave. A lantern imperfectly shuttered. He slipped forward, cultivating silence.

He recognized the night guard but didn't know his name. Simin had perhaps nodded to him at the market or waved to him at the mill; the simple exchange of fellow citizens. But circumstances transformed them now to a prince of the Empire and the servant of his enemy. Aus attacked from the dark, killing the man before he could cry out. The prince watched the life fade from the man's eyes. The war claimed other people all across the Empire. Children and women died in the streets of Low Shaoen. Soldiers irrigated the fields of Mattawan Commons with their blood. The guard choking on surprise and his own blood deserved no more or less than the other thousands of dead. Prince Aus stood over him as man became corpse. The murder didn't belong to him. King Raan put all of it in motion, and so the responsibility lay with him and his still-unjudged soul. If the prince's hands trembled after the violence, it only proved that death still moved him. That his humanity still stood higher than that of the man who sired him.

He took the keys from the dead man's hip and the lantern from beside the guard stool that now stood empty, and moved deeper into the cave. The walls of rough stone, simple and uncarved, curved and dipped and rose without offering any corners or doorways. Cool air carried the smell of soil. The profound silence made even his stealthy footsteps seem like shouts. And in one stretch of hallway, unremarkable from all that came before, the prince's ears ached suddenly and the air pressed in on him like a storm front, and he knew the Mocking Tower stood above him.

A glimmer came from the deeper darkness before him, something catching the lantern's fragile beam. Part of the prince's soul warned him to turn back, but the stronger command of his purpose drove him on. The glimmer grew and brightened until it resolved into a wide brass doorway with three panels and carvings of glyphs and designs that teased him from the edge of legibility. Had he seen it anywhere else, Prince Aus would still have recognized it as the entrance to the Imagi Vert's sanctuary and seat of power. It took long, anxious minutes to find the keyhole hidden among the carvings—a tiny plate of brass that shifted to reveal a darkness just the right shape—but the dead guard's key fit and it turned and the door opened.

Prince Aus stepped into the chamber beyond.

Candles burned along the walls but without any scent of tallow or wax, and their light settled softer than snow. In all, the chamber reached no deeper or wider than the common room of the Traveler's Hearth, but rather than stools and tables and the long, low fire grate, plinths stood scattered about the space as if the stone had grown up from the bones of the earth. On each, an object stood. A cut gem the red of blood and the size of two clenched fists together. A rough doll fashioned from a twist of rope and a handful of dried grass. The skull of a child so young a staggered row of teeth still haunted the jawbone, waiting for a chance to displace tiny, sharp milk teeth. Aus walked slowly. No sounds troubled him. The stillness of the room felt profound. Even his breath seemed close to sacrilege in the space. A cup formed to resemble a cupped, thick-knuckled hand. A simple clay pot painted over with black lines as fine as a feather. Treasures, the prince thought, of a life prolonged centuries beyond its due. A sheet of vellum with a handprint in green. A bird's nest made of long, thin bones.

A sword.

The prince's throat went tight, his mouth suddenly dry. The blade lay on its side. Gems and worked silver formed a hilt like the writhing body of a man. Knotwork etching ran the length of the blade, twisted as a labyrinth. He reached out to it, hesitated, then, almost against his will, took it in his hand. It felt cooler than the room, as if eating the warmth of his flesh. It balanced perfectly. The finest sword ever forged. A sword of empires. A sword forged from steel and dark magic and his father's willing soul. He swung it gently, half expecting its edge to cut the air itself.

"You admire it?"

The voice, harsh and low as stone dragged over earth, came from behind him. The man stood in the candlelight where the prince would swear no one had been only a moment before. The man's dark robe moved stiffly, like the bark of a tree remade as cloth. Dark veins welled up under flesh as pale as bone. His mild eyes considered the prince.

"I admire it too," the pale man said. "Good workmanship deserves respect, I think. However much you may disapprove of the project." He tried a smile, then sighed.

"You are the Imagi?" the prince said, his voice high and tight. Fear vibrated in his blood and his grip on the sword tightened.

"Am I?" the pale man said, and tilted his head. "Before, I was part of something greater than myself, and darkness was my home. But now? I play the role of the Imagi now, I suppose. Yes. For this I might as well be the Imagi Vert."

"I am Aus, son of Raan. You have stolen something from me and from my people. I have come to restore the balance of the world."

The pale man seemed to settle into himself. Not a movement of peace or acceptance, but a grounding like a bull setting himself in place and refusing to be moved. A vast stillness radiated from him like cold from ice. The prince felt the sword pulsing in his hand, but it might only have been the beating of his own half-panicked heart.

"What balance is that?" the Imagi Vert asked, as if the matter held some trivial interest but no more than that.

"My father sinned against the gods," the prince said, his voice wavering. "He used your powers to cheat death. To live forever. All the evil that the world has seen flows from that sin. The war raging through the Empire now? It's because no one can take the power of the Empire while the former emperor still lives."

"Is that the case?" the Imagi Vert said, lifting pale, hairless brows. "Ah."

"My brothers die at each other's hands. The wonders of the Empire burn. The right order of the world lies scattered like bones on the plain. Because of this." The prince raised the sword between them. "Because one cowardly old man feared too much to die as he should have. And because his pet wizard chose to break the world. Do you deny it?"

"Would you like me to?" The Imagi's smile could have meant anything. "If you wish. Let me think on it. Yes. Yes, all right. The war first, yes? You say it comes because the rightful heir cannot claim while the emperor still lives. But there have been usurpers before now. If the rightful king cannot rise, an unrighteous one could but hasn't. The history of the world is studded with kings who have abdicated out of weariness or love or religious zealotry. Consider that the war came not because King Raan was a greedy man or an evil one but because he was unhappy."

"Unhappy," the prince said. Neither a question nor an agreement. A distance had come into his eyes and the feeling of hearing everything said before him as if he were eavesdropping from another room.

"His life was never his own. Duty and necessity kept him in the most glorious prison humanity could devise, and the envy of others made that confinement solitary as a monk's. Even when among the throngs who worshipped him, your father lived his life alone. Others dream of power and kingship. Of more money and more sex and more respect. Just as you do. You say you've come here to . . . what? Save the world from your father? By taking your revenge upon the man who left you behind? And the confluence of those motives gave no pause, eh?"

The prince took a step back. The floor felt as if it had shifted beneath him, but the candle flames stood straight. None of the treasures in their places shook.

The Imagi shrugged, a slow, powerful gesture. "All right. All right. Let's imagine you get what you claim you want. You kill the undying king and take his throne. What will you want then? When the loneliness and melancholy come upon you and you already have everything you aspired to and there is no higher reach, what will you wish for as a balm?"

"I would not need one."

"You're mistaken," the Imagi said, and the words struck his chest like a blow. "Your father wished for a life he had not lived. A simple one with the freedoms invisible to you and the others. A baker, perhaps, spending his early hours kneading dough and smelling yeast and salt. Sweating before the oven. Or a fisherman mending nets with his brothers and sisters, daughters and sons. A brewer or a gardener or the manager of a dye yard. These were as sweet and exotic to him as he was to the lowborn. And he longed for the things denied to him. Badly.

"He lost sight of the challenge his children faced. Bearing his misery in silence cost him the strength to be a good father. Kept him from preparing his sons for the prison cell. Perhaps he thought of it as a kindness, yes? In some subterranean way, he hoped that by cutting you and your brothers away, he could protect you from all that he bore. Love's cruel that way, and men are fools. But wouldn't that be enough to explain why so many of you—yes, and yourself not the least—are so desperate to slaughter each other for what your father didn't want?"

"The sword," the prince said. "My father's soul."

The pale man shook his head, but whether his expression meant sorrow or disgust, the prince didn't know. "You have misunderstood everything. There is no soul in that blade. It's well made, but it means nothing. Take it if you think it will help you. Melt it if you'd rather. I'm beyond caring."

Aus looked down at the sword in his hand. The complications along the blade felt like writing in a language he almost knew. His breath came hard, like he'd run a race. Or fled for his life. He tried to put names to the emotions that spat and wrestled in him: humiliation, anger, despair, grief. The coldness of the hilt grew intense, as if he held a shard of ice. He gripped it harder, inviting the chill into his flesh. Into his mind. Something to stand against the raging armies in his heart.

He shouted before he knew he meant to shout. Swung the blade hard, the movement starting in his legs, his hip, reaching out with a single flowing gesture, extending the sword as if it were part of him. The Imagi's eyes went wider, and the tip of the blade split his jaw. It made a sound like an axe splitting wood. No blood fell from the wound, only a thin runnel of clear fluid.

The prince wrenched the blade free and struck again, screaming as he did. The Imagi lifted a hand to block the attack, and the bloodless fingers scattered on the floor. Great gashes opened in the pale flesh, the body splintering and falling apart under the assault. If he called out, the prince's war cries drowned out his words. Prince Aus found himself standing with feet on either side of the pale corpse, swinging down and down and down, his wrist and shoulder aching from his effort. The Imagi lay still and dead, his head a pale pulp with neither muscle nor bone nor brain. Prince Aus lifted the sword again, in both hands this time, and drove it deep into the pale man's torso, then put his weight upon it. He drove it deeper and twisted, his strength and his weight and his mad will pressing at the metal, bending it past its tolerance. All the power he possessed, he threw into this one terrible moment.

And the sword broke.

Prince Aus fell to his knees. The stump of the blade stood a few inches from the twisted hilt. The labyrinthine pattern was open now, its puzzles solved by violence. A shard of metal fallen at his knee glittered in the soft candlelight. The motionless body of the Imagi Vert looked like a hillside, the greater half of the sword standing proudly from it like a tower. Aus gasped for air and dropped the freezing hilt. His whole body ached, but the physical pain claimed the least of his attention.

The blade broken, his hopes fulfilled, he waited for something. A sense of release. Of victory. The soundless scream of his father's soul at last set free from the world. A rush of the mystic energy that had forged the deathless vessel. Anything.

The candles shed their light. The plinths held their treasures. The silence folded around him until his own chuffing sobs broke it.

He rose unsteady as a drunk, stumbled against a plinth. The hilt of the broken sword slipped from his numb fingers and clattered on the floor. A sweet, earthy smell rose from the dead man, and the nausea it called forth drove the prince back toward the brass door. He'd dropped the lantern somewhere. He couldn't recall. The passage back to the world stood dark as a tomb, but he made his lightless way. One foot before the other, hands out before him to warn him before he walked into the stone. His mouth tasted foul. His arms trembled. He wept empty tears with no sense of grief or catharsis. For a time, he felt certain that the cave would go on forever, that the death of the Imagi Vert had sealed him also in the immortal's tomb. When he stumbled out into the starlit mouth of the cave, he more than half thought it a dream. The visions of a man with a broken mind. The dead guard, lying in his pool of blood brought the prince back to himself. It was a war. It was the war. Terrible things happened here.

The night sky glittered with stars. The trees shifted in the open air. All the world seemed terrible and beautiful and empty. Prince Aus turned toward the path, the town. Behind him, the Mocking Tower whose roots he had dug changed and changed and changed again: a threefold tower with bridges lacing between the spires like a web, a vast tooth pointing toward the sky with a signal fire blaring at its tip, a glasswork column that rose toward the stars and funneled their dim light into its heart. The prince didn't watch it. The night before him carried terrors and wonders enough.

He made his way to the path between the trees, toward the town where he'd lived—it seemed now—in some previous lifetime. To the Traveler's Hearth, where the keep once sheltered and offered fair work to a boy named Simin, who in fact had been a being of skin and lies.

The thief's door was barred from within, but candlelight flickered at the edges. The prince pounded until he heard the hiss of the bar lifting and the door swung open. The thief blinked at him, uncertain as a mouse.

"You look terrible."

"We have to go," the prince said, and his voice seemed to belong to some other man.

"You did it? It's done?"

"We have to go now. Before the changing of guards, first light I'd guess. But it could be earlier. Could be now."

"But—"

"*We have to go!*"

Together, the two men ran to the stable, chose which horses to steal, and galloped out to the road. They turned east, toward the first threads of rose and indigo where the light would rise to meet them. A dawn that would rise elsewhere on army camps and burned cities, fields left uncultivated for want of hands to farm them and river locks broken open for fear that an enemy would make use of them. The ruins of empire, and a war still raging.

And in the depths of the Mocking Tower, something stirred.

At first, the body moved only slightly, reknitting the worst of its wounds with a vegetable slowness. Then, when it could, the body levered itself up to unsteady feet. Pale eyes looked all around the chamber of treasures without suffering or joy. The rough cloak creaked and crackled as the body—neither alive nor dead but something of both—stepped out of the light and into the darkness. It felt a vague comfort in the darkness underground, to the degree that it felt anything.

The mouth of the cave came all too soon. A human body lay there, a cast-off forgotten thing. The pale man, jaw still hanging from his skull by woody threads, turned away from town and tower, walking into the trees where no path existed. He moved with the same deliberation and speed as he would have on the road and left no trail behind him. The Mocking Tower at his back shifted, fluttering from shape to shape, miracle to miracle, as compelling as a street performer's scarf fluttering to draw attention away from what the other hand was doing.

Birds woke, singing their cacophony at the coming dawn. The light grew, and the wild gave way to a simple garden. Wide beds of dark, rich soil, well weeded so that no unwelcome plant competed with the onion, the beets, the carrots. A short, ragged-looking apple tree bent under the combined weight of its own fruit and a thin netting that kept the sparrows from feasting on it. In the rear near a well, a rough shack leaned, small but solid with a little yard paved in unfinished stone outside it. A little fire muttered and smoked as it warmed a pot of water for tea.

The pale man folded his legs under him, rested his palms on his knees, and waited with a patience that suggested he could wait forever. A yellow finch flew by, its wings fluttering. A doe tramped through the trees at the garden's edge but didn't approach.

Old Au came from the shack and nodded to him. She wore long trousers with mud-crusted leather at the knees, a loose canvas shirt, and boots cracked and mended and cracked again. A thin spade and gardener's knife hung from her belt, and she carried an empty cloth sack over her shoulder. Heaving a sigh, she sat across from the pale man.

"Went poorly, then, did it?"

The pale man tried to say something with his ruined mouth, then made do with simply nodding. Old Au looked into the gently boiling water in the pan as if there might be some answers in it, then lifted it off and set it on the stone at her side. The pale man waited. She pulled a little sack from her pocket, plucked a few dried leaves from it, and dropped them in the still-but-steaming water. A few moments later, the scent of fresh tea joined the smells of turned earth and dew-soaked leaves.

"Did you explain that the war was only a war? That humanity falls into violence every few generations, and that his father, if anything, was too good at keeping the peace?"

The pale man nodded again.

"And could the boy hear it?"

The pale man hesitated, then shook his head. *No, he could not.*

Old Au chuckled. "Well, we try. Every generation is the same. They think their parents were never young, never subject to the confusions and lust they suffer. Born before the invention of sex and loss and passion, us. They all have to learn in their own way, however much we might wish we could counsel them out of it." She swirled the tea. "Did you warn him what it will be like once he takes the throne?"

The pale man nodded.

"He didn't hear that either, did he? Ah well. I imagine he'll look back on it when he's old and understand too late." Old Au reached out her well-worn hand and took the pale man's fingerless palm in hers. She shook him once, and he became a length of pale root again. Scarred now and ripped, paler where the bark peeled back. She hefted the root back close to the shed. She might break it down for mulch later, or else use it to carve something from. A whistle, maybe. Return it to the cycle or transform it to something Nature never dreamed for it. They were simple magics, and profound because of it.

She poured the tea into an old cup and sipped it as she squinted into the sky. It looked like a good day. Warm in the morning, but a bit of rain in the afternoon she guessed. Enough for a few hours of good work. She took the spade from her hip and broke a little crust of mud from just below the handle with the nail of her thumb, humming to herself as she did. And then the gardener's knife with its serrated edge for sawing through roots and the name Raan Sauvo Serriadan scratched into the blade in a language no one had spoken in centuries.

"There are some bulbs in the west field that want thinning," she said. "What do you think, love?"

For a moment there, the breeze and the chirping of the birds seemed to harmonize, making some deeper music between them. Something like the murmur of a voice. Whatever it said made Old Au laugh.

She finished her tea, poured what remained out of the pot, and started walking toward the gardens and the day's work still ahead.

C. J. Cherryh

. . .

C. J. Cherryh is the author of more than forty novels, the winner of the John W. Campbell Award and four Hugo Awards, and a figure of immense significance in both the science-fiction and fantasy fields. In science fiction, she's published the eighteen-volume Foreigner series, the seven-volume Company Wars series, the five-volume Compact Space series, the four-volume Cyteen series, and many other series and standalone novels; in fantasy, she's the author of the four-volume Morgaine series, the three-volume Rusalka series, the five-volume Tristan series, the two-volume Arafel series, and, as editor, the seven-volume Merovingen Nights anthologies. Some of her best-known novels include *Downbelow Station*, *The Pride of Chanur*, *The Betrayal*, *Gate of Ivrel*, *Kesrith*, *Serpent's Reach*, *Rimrunners*, *Festival Moon*, *The Dreamstone*, *Port Eternity*, and *Brothers of Earth*. Her short fiction has been collected in *Sunfall*, *Visible Light*, and *The Collected Short Fiction of C. J. Cherryh*. Her most recent books are two new novels in the Foreigner series, *Visitor* and *Convergence*. She lives in Spokane, Washington.

Almost everyone knows the story of Beowulf, one of the most famous pieces of mythological poetry ever written—but what happens a generation *after* the deadly events at Heorot, when the ruins lie quiet and wreathed in weeds? Here Cherryh takes us for a look at the aftermath, and plunges us into an adventure no less perilous for a young man in search of his family heritage than those that took place on that fateful, monster-haunted night long before.

❖   ❖   ❖

Hrunting

C. J. CHERRYH

"May your journey be swift. May the gods greet you with strong mead and beautiful women."

Halli smoothed his muddy hands across the sad little mound and blinked away the drizzle that clouded his vision, trying not to think of that withered body curled beneath his hand, tried not to imagine mud seeping through the stones they had laid and curdling around the wise old face. Great lords lay in stone ships out across the meadow, or slept in massive barrows, rich in grave goods.

A thrall might be buried in a muddy pit. They had at least done better than that. Grandfather's cup, his drinking horn, and one of the pigs went with him. They had combed his beard, braided his hair. They had cut his nails, so at Ragnarok the Jotunn could not summon him to build the Nauglfar ship. Best of all hopes, Grandfather might be safe behind Valhalla's walls. He had died no hero's death, to be swept up to the skies, but Odin called great men, too. And Grandfather had been a brehon, a judge, a wise counselor. That his lord had not listened to him—could the Allfather fault that?

The drizzle fell and stood in puddles on the trampled ground. The sun had shone fair this morning. This evening, overtaking them at their sad work, the rain had started. Halli and his father had kept working, building up the earthen mound, few words exchanged, breath saved for digging up muddy ground and piling earth into a mound atop the stones. At the last, it was mud they piled on, and the place where they had dug the dirt had turned to a puddle.

Father slung a wet load onto the mound, which stood only knee high. The shovelful ran with water. "Enough. Enough. The light's leaving. We've done what we can."

"I can keep going."

"He was a crotchety, demanding old man. At least he won't walk. We gave him the best damned pig."

Father hadn't been happy about that. Halli had picked the pig, brought it out, and slaughtered it at the grave before Father had come back with the stones.

"You go get warm, pabbi. I'll finish."

Father just stared at him, water trickling off his hat, dripping off his beard. They'd broken a shovel on the job. They'd owned two. Now it was one, the other to be mended, another job to be done, an endless chain of jobs to be done before the leaves fell. And that was all it was to his father, Eclaf, son of Unferth son of Eclaf, hero of the Skyldings, wielder of the great sword Hrunting. Father gathered up the broken pieces and the surviving shovel, flung them into the muddy little cart, and hauled it off, empty now, an easier job than the stones had been.

Grandfather's death was a relief for his father. Grandfather had needed everything at the last. Old age had robbed him of every faculty. And Father had said it, over Grandfather's grave—Grandfather Unferth was a constant reminder of their family's fall from grace; and they had chosen this place, near one of the great barrows, but screened off by brush, so that the village could forget it was there.

So that the village would forget.

"It's wrong," Halli had said. "It's wrong that it's just us to witness, it's wrong that he's out here alone."

"He's got a lord beside him," Father had said. "Best we can do for him. Gods know he's done nothing for us. We'll drink the sjaund for him seven days from now, and we'll have all the inheritance he's left us. A house and three pigs. At least he didn't lose that."

He didn't lose the sword, Halli wanted to say. He'd lent it. He'd only lent it.

But they didn't talk about the sword.

Everybody else did, when they talked about Grandfather. Nobody ever forgot it.

Halli had other memories. Alone in the fading light, he smoothed down the mud, patted it even. He tried to imagine Grandfather youthful and strong, entering Valhalla with the heroes. A raven had flown over this afternoon, and he hoped it was Odin's eye, scouting out Grandfather, to call him up to the halls of the gods, young again, but wise as he had ever been. The Allfather knew the truth about things. And the Allfather, who himself had given an eye for wisdom, surely knew the value of it in an honest judge, who had dared challenge his lord's judgment and question a guest's reputation.

Grandfather had risked his lord Hrothgar's anger, and had no way to prove his case, when Hrothgar's boon companion, Aeschere, an older man, white-bearded, had taken him to task for discourtesy to a guest. Handsomely had Grandfather atoned for it—handsomely, if Beowulf had been the hero he claimed.

Grandfather had lent the family treasure, the sword Hrunting, ancient, and infallible if a hero wielded it. It never failed, for a hero true in battle.

Until then.

He squeezed his eyes shut. He concentrated on the mud, on patting it down smooth, making it as fine as he could.

He had never seen Heorot in its glory. He had never seen Hrunting. His father said he had no memory of either. He had been too young. His father remembered only fire, when Heorot had gone down. Grandmother had died in that fire. Grandfather had gotten Father out. That was all. Then Grandfather had built the little house in Lejre village, near the ruin, near the burials of the great lords and heroes.

His own first memory of Grandfather was of a wrinkled face peering nearsightedly at him, wondering why a fool of a five-year-old had tried to slop the pigs himself. He had had as much mud on him that day as now. It had been a day like this, drizzling summer rain, and the hungry old sow had knocked him down. Father had rescued him and cuffed him so his ears had rung—from fear, having almost lost him.

Grandfather had asked him why he had done it. That was always Grandfather's way with things. Why? and Why not? were Grandfather's favorite questions. He imagined Grandfather in his days as a judge, wearing gold, and always, before judgment, challenging people with that one question.

The sun was sneaking below the earth, and the rain was down to a mist. It was a treacherous hour, a time to fear ghosts. But not Grandfather's. If any draugr got up from his stone bed and went walking, Grandfather would rise up and protect his grandson, he had every confidence.

"Ha!"

His heart froze. He turned about, seeing shapes in the mist—but not ghosts, those. Young men. Four of them. The very ones he'd hoped would never visit this place.

"Well, well, well. What have we here? A beggar, a worm, burrowing in the mud?"

Halli stiffened, slowly, deliberately smeared a muddy hand across his face and even more slowly rose to face the owner of that voice.

Not alone, no. Eileifr was never alone. Egill. Hjallr. Eileifr's cousin Birgir. They were always together. Halli thought of the shovel, but Father had taken that. He had not a rock, not a stick for a weapon. He was standing ankle deep in mud and water with no defense.

"Oh, leave him alone," Birgir said, who was no friend of his either. "He's burying the old nithing. In seven days his father can drink the sjaund and claim the title for his own."

Not even a belt with a buckle on it. He could take them all on. But Birgir alone outweighed him and topped him by a head. Never doubt they were armed.

"What did you put with the old man?" Eileifr asked. "Gold rings? A great sword?"

That raised laughter from Eileifr's hangers-on. Eileifr was Ragnbjorg's heir—the richest man in Lejre. Eileifr was a gray ghost in the fog at the moment, but never doubt he had a sword, and fine gear. Eileifr would afford a ship, next summer, and maybe, Halli hoped, he would take his friends aboard it and all sink in the deep sea.

"Where is the sword, Nithing's-heir? Where is your inheritance? Will you kill all your pigs and invite the village in for the funeral-feast?"

"Those scrawny pigs might feed Birgir," Egill said, to more laughter.

Saying anything invited a fight, and in a fight, he would lose. He might die out here, and his father would be alone in his own old age. They had no kin. They lived at the edge of the village. They would spend the winter keeping the pigs alive, and hunting such as they could.

"Where is the sword?" Egill asked, taking up the theme. "Is it buried with him?"

"Heorot's luck is," Eileifr said. "Buried in that muddy heap. Lejre's luck. The old lord's luck with it, under heaps of mud. Look at him, the nithing, the moon all waned to a sliver of itself, no glory, no gut, the hollow, hungry moon. Burying this old fool won't end the curse. Gold will. Beg me, nithing, beg me to go a-viking with us next summer."

"Ha!" was the most Halli could muster of the anger boiling up in him, anger tempered with Grandfather's cold good sense. Time to walk out of a fight, or at least gain ground less boggy. Run? He'd walk. If they attacked him, he'd take down one of them. Egill, maybe. He'd concentrate on Egill. Eileifr went in ring mail, with rings on his fingers.

He walked. He walked past them, and heard their hooting and their jeering, but he kept walking, and they chose not to attack him . . . or to give him a fair challenge, either. They fell behind him in the fog and the gathering night, and as he walked he thought it was time for a rock to come at his back—that was one of their amusements in the village— except all the rocks to be had were in the mound with Grandfather.

And if they had not set on him, it was only because a beating there, over Grandfather's grave, at that hour, might come back on them in village gossip. There were blind eyes turned to what Eileifr did, and if the weak suffered, that was their fault for being weak, but attacking him at night, while he was burying his grandfather—that attached them to his grandfather's legend, just one more sorry, ugly deed that hovered over Grandfather's extended and cursed existence. Halli Eclafssen to die weaponless, battered to death at Grandfather's feet? It was no noble deed, and Eileifr was hungry for glory . . . like someone else he could name, but the world never would.

Beowulf the Geat. The man Hrothgar had trusted most in the world, since Hrothgar had spent gold on Beowulf's uncle, and bought off a death-feud, paying the man-price for the Geat and saving him from his fate. Hel would not be cheated. Gold would not end all hatred. Hrothgar had disregarded Grandfather's counsel, rebuked him through his friend Aeschere, and silenced his good advice. Yet the skjalds made Beowulf a true man.

Why? Because Beowulf had become king in Geatland. And gave gold he had gained from Hrothgar. With all of that to give, Beowulf fared very well in legend.

So had Hrothgar . . . for a season.

But Beowulf had taken more than gold. He had taken Hrunting, the sword that could not fail in battle . . . more, he had reported it a failure, a lie and a deception.

And now the Danes had a dog for a king. A small, one-eyed dog, a cur that the king of the Swedes had set over them, saying that if any man came to him to say that dog was dead, that man would die the death.

That was to say, preserve this king, you bickering Danes, since your lords have all killed one another. Preserve this king. Keep this little dog alive. And learn restraint.

Could a people fall any lower?

All for the loss of a sword. The loss of their luck.

Mist hazed the village, veiled the little house, veiled everything. Halli pulled the latchstring, pushed the door open, and smelled ale, a great deal of it, ale, no little of it spilled on the boards. His father, still in his muddy clothes and boots, sat by the fire, drinking. Halli dipped up a cup for himself and sat down.

The bench was scant one person now. But it had been, through Grandfather's illness. So they drank, and his father asked:

"Are you satisfied?"

Halli asked himself that question. He thought, and drank two long sips that did nothing to quiet the anger roiling in him.

He said, finally: "Eileifr and his gang have already found the place."

"Did you fight them?"

"Am I dead? No. I didn't." A third sip, that went down like bitter shame. "Did you ever see the sword, Father?"

"Not to my memory," his father answered.

"I know why Grandfather lent it."

"Hrothgar ordered him to lend it. Because he insulted a guest in Heorot."

"Grandfather questioned a guest's reputation. He gave ample room for the man to come back with a good tale in good humor if he could deny it. Beowulf only half denied it. No. I know the lord was upset at Grandfather that morning. But Grandfather said Hrunting's enchantment was just one simple thing. It would never fail a hero in battle. It failed Beowulf. So it proved Grandfather was right to challenge the man."

"Small good being right could do us. Beowulf lost the sword. And still came back alive."

"And Hrothgar gave him the gold. Hrothgar loaded him with all the gold he could carry. And Beowulf sailed away with it, never looking back. Hrothgar thought the gold he gave would bring warriors to bring more gold. But the luck all went with Hrunting. And the warriors all went with the gold. Beowulf's Geats have all fled to Sweden and left us to face the Franks and the White God, with no king but a flea-bitten dog. Our luck is lying at the bottom of that lake, with Grendel's bones, and the truth is lying with it."

"Nothing we can do about it." His father got up, dipped up another cup of ale. "The old man's gone. The sword's gone. We're facing a sjaund in seven days apt to lose the house and land if we don't slaughter at least half the pigs and put on a feast for the village. We go hunting tomorrow. We see if we can come up with hide to trade and a way to save our pigs."

It was the law. It was the sjaund, the drink for the dead, that confirmed an inheritance, and what his father inherited came down to a small house with only room for pigs in the underside, and maybe no pigs, because they had to feed the village and share the ale, so that all the village would admit the inheritance was rightfully theirs.

Eileifr and his crew would be there, boasting about their boat, boasting about great plans, and their good fortune.

Eileifr's father and mother would be there, looking down their noses at their little house and its poor goods.

Great-grandfather Eclef had wielded Hrunting himself, had gained battle-gold, had helped raise Hrothgar to the height he had reached. A great man. A real hero, who had never lost a battle, who had helped keep the Franks from Danish soil.

And Eileifr would sneer at them, while Father tried to plan a way to save their pigs.

"No," he said. "You hunt, Father, and Odin guide your arrows—but I am going to Grendel's lake."

"No! No. No such thing."

Halli stood up. He had been cold through. He had never shed his coat nor his boots, either, and the ale had warmed him to the point of sweating. He went to the pegs where they hung their hunting gear and took his own, and a knife they used for butchering.

"Son." Father was on his feet. "Son, it's the ale talking. Come to your senses."

"I have, Father. I have come to my senses. I am going to Grendelsjar to see what I can see. Grendel is dead, is he not? His mother, too. What danger can there be?"

"It's a foul marsh. A cursed place."

"The curse is our giving up. The sword isn't lost until we give up. And I'm not giving it up. Grandfather will rest easier when he has it. And maybe we will not have a dog for a king." He strung a piece of leather through the hole in the butchering knife, tied it, and slung it from his shoulder. "You hunt for a deer, Father. I'll hunt for the sword. And I'll be back before the sjaund."

"You're mad." Father went to the table in the corner, took the ashy loaf of bread that was yesterday's baking, took it in muddy fingers, and gave it to him. "Take this with you, at least. Have a look at the place. And come back early. I'll have a deer. I'll need that knife."

"I'll hope to bring you better," he said, and hugged his father, clapped him on the back. "Find us a deer, at least, pabbi."

He did not walk through the night. He did not stay under the roof with Father, either, to be persuaded of his folly. He found a place in old Olaf's haystack, not the first night he had spent in that snug shelter, and was gone in the morning, in the first glimmering of sun in the fog. The fields about Lejre he well knew, but when he had reached the end of the last barrow, he took the old traders' track, the way the children of Lejre dared each other even to set foot on. It was no more than a game trail now, but so long as he could make it out, he walked it, well beyond any venture he had made before—walked on determination and with a ragged remnant of last night's encounter still lively in him—dark thoughts, on an ill-omened track, memories of Grandfather's poor burial, and their neighbors—

Their neighbors had not turned out when they bore Grandfather to his burying. The few out and about had changed direction, gone back in, shut their doors, as if Grandfather, dead, were shedding bad luck on them all. Not a one had come to help or offer regret.

Eileifr had seen them. Eileifr and his lot had taken on a load of ale and watched, waiting for him to come back with Father, and when he had not, why, they had come looking. But the whole village had known Grandfather was gone. Gossip spread like wildfire. It would be spreading now.

Have you seen Eclef this morning? Have you seen his son? Well, it's a relief to the whole village, the old man finally in his grave, good riddance to him.

If neither he nor his father ever made the sjaund and lost the house and all, it going up to be claimed as ownerless, why, who else would claim house and land and all, but Ragnbjorg, Eileifr's father? Not to live there, no. Ragnbjorg had a fine house. He'd probably house goats on the property, use the house for a shed. Or let Father live there as a tenant, working for him.

There was a worse turn for their luck to take. He could not abide the thought.

But even anger ran out, when hunger began to turn him light-headed, and by then the fog lay still thicker, so he began to fear he might have gotten off the track.

Well, so, it was the better course to sit down for a while, stay warm, and take a bit of the bread Father had sent with him. The fog might lie thickest in low spots, but even so, it had stopped raining, and when the sea wind came, past noon, the fog would thin out. He had every confidence it would, even if he had walked into a low place and come into one of those places fog loved.

He was careful, in sitting down, to face the same direction he had been going, not to make that mistake, and end up turned about—trolls might prowl about in such lonely places, and try to trick people into bogs and pits. Trolls might look like trees, of which there had been a few along the way, or stones, of which there was no scarcity here, and a butchering knife was not much defense against them, but he was curiously beyond fear of that sort of harm.

Grendel was dead, he had reminded Father. If that was not true, then there was the worst of all trolls to fear, him, and his mother, sun-fearing, going about by night, and fog, and in dark places. But—dead, he said to himself. Grandfather had been convinced of that. Never had the pair troubled Heorot after Beowulf had come back, bearing the mere hilt of a sword that had availed against the troll-mother, where Hrunting had failed. Halli had heard the story sung, how the great hero had prevailed, though Hrunting had not—how Beowulf had cast Hrunting aside, and found another sword amid the hoard of gold, a Jotunn-forged sword that had melted clean away when it touched a troll's hard heart.

From the bottom of Grendelsjar, the deep lake, the great hero had brought up Grendel's head, and the Jotunn sword hilt.

Yet, the same song had said—on departing Heorot with a massive load of Hrothgar's gold, Beowulf had sent a man to deliver a sword to Grandfather. Sent a man. And sent a sword. As if that paid all, for casting away the treasure of Eclaf's line.

One could all but pity the trolls, the old folk of stone and earth and water, old as the hills, and living under them. Jotunn themselves, such creatures, born of the land, and preferring places where men did not dwell. The Allfather let them live, while they kept to their places. The great Jotunn, the Frost-giants, were another matter, but trolls—generally kept to themselves, doing no harm.

Grendel had crossed that line and become a menace. He had kept coming at Heorot, as trolls had to travel, at night, entering in the great mead hall, and killing—killing the warriors Hrothgar's gold had drawn to him.

Grandfather had seen him. "Tall as a tree," Grandfather had said, himself standing tall before the fire in the hearth. Grandfather had flung his arms wide. "Wide as a bear, and roaring like one. That was his voice.

Like timbers breaking. Like great stones rolling. No one could understand his speech, but they were words he spoke. His brow was sloped. His hair and beard were wild. He wore bits and pieces of armor, and wielded a sapling tree for a staff, all knotty, still bearing some twigs. He was a shadow and he was quick. Warriors scrambled for their armor, and Grendel climbed, he threw over benches, he swung on the great beam, and he was gone out into the dark, leaving dead in his wake. Three of the warriors were never seen again, whether they fled or whether he killed them."

Halli had asked for that story over and over, and sometimes it was tall as a tree and sometimes shaped like a bear, but overall, Grandfather had been sure about the three warriors.

Troll, maybe, but he had been this land's troll. Part of their stones, their earth, raving mad at Hrothgar's men. Or at Hrothgar, for what cause the songs told no tale.

Hrothgar had not treated Grandfather well, either. Hrothgar had not cast Grandfather out, but Grandfather had had no honor in that hall afterward. Grandfather had told Hrothgar not to marry his daughter to Ingeld; Hrothgar had coldly spurned his advice, offered peace to his old enemy, and sowed distrust in his own house—bringing down a spate of kinslaying and bloodletting unmatched in legend. Four lords in one year, two in a single hour—that had brought Heorot down.

Halli ate a portion of the bread, spat out bits of sand—their millstone was not the best and getting worse, and one was always careful. He protected the loaf inside his shirt, under his coat, seeing it might have to last him a little. A meal a day. Three days was the most he allotted.

A meal, and a little rest. His feet were warm for the moment. There was nothing stirring, no sound in all the world. And fear of trolls was low by daylight, such as it was. He pulled the badger-skin hood over his head, tucked down and slept a little, catching just a little rest before another tramp toward—what? What would he see? A lake he'd heard about all his life? A pit of a lake, rock-rimmed, where trolls had lived?

He was too tired, too sore to think much on it. He had a direction, that was all, and for a moment he was warm, saving all his body warmth inside wet wool clothes and a leather cloak.

Nothing stirred, until a breeze slipped inside the hood and touched his face.

He was elsewhere warm, sun-warm; but a brisk wind was whispering in the grass, and there was bright sunlight on the stones. He gathered himself up, and above him and a little distant, formerly unseen in the fog—rose a hill. On that hill, charred timbers, black and broken, rose against a blue sky.

Heorot. The cursed place.

It had been a great hall, indeed, larger than Ragnbjord's house and any three of the village houses combined. He felt constrained to go up to it, at least, to say that he had been there, and he had touched the beams, which were too thick to have burned. Those timbers, set deep in the earth of the hill, and the stones of the hearth, were all that had survived the fire.

Grandmother had died here. So had all Hrothgar's line, all the Skyldings, sons of the Half-Dane.

He wandered what would have been the center of the hall, where warriors had stood and fought against Grendel. He saw a stone edge where Hrothgar's seat would have been, lord of the hall and all the land roundabout. He saw a gap where the door would have stood.

How had Grendel gotten in? Through the doors? Grandfather said they had been barred inside—how not, with an enemy abroad? The smoke vents? Those were small.

Enchantment? Perhaps. Surely runes and charms of every sort were about the place. Halli stood at the very place Hrothgar would have sat, at the head of the hall. All about the walls, under the high roof, would have been benches, and there the warriors would have sat, exchanging tales, drinking, joking in the way men would. The feasting platters would go round, every night, in such a great hall. There would be every sort of good thing, a feast such as Lejre had never held, he was sure. Strong men and battle-skilled had gathered here, every night a feast, every day a wager and a contest, drawn by the gold and the glory of a great lord ...

Strong men and battle-skilled, armed and in numbers. A ring fort would doubt its safety, if such a war band came up against it.

And Grendel had made them all his helpless prey?

Yet lost an arm to one man's grip?

A bear's strength could do it. A great bear could do it.

Had Beowulf shape-shifted? Had he changed his skin, even for a moment?

That would answer for everything. He felt a chill, even by summer noon, thinking of such a battle, troll against skin-changer. Beowulf. Bee-wolf. Honey-eater. The old folk, the small dark folk who moved their dwellings about and made no villages, they would never say the name bear. To speak a name was to call it, and they feared the great forest-walkers, that went on two feet like a man.

Honey-eater, they called it. Such a man—monster, himself, grappling hand-to-hand with the night-walking troll who made Hrothgar's hall his larder: what ordinary man could do it? And in the night and the smoke and the fear, who might see the true shapes? In the screaming and the shouting, who could tell the roaring of one from the other?

Halli gave a twitch of his shoulders, a sort of shiver, looking toward the stumps of doorposts—west, it had faced. So also Lejre looked west, toward Nerthus' Grove, toward the sacred places, to the dark old ones that ruled the earth and the night, that pulled down Lady Sun and claimed the world until the dawn.

Heorot honored that tradition of facing doors toward the west. But it had been unlucky. Unlucky as its lord. Mist persisted beyond those ruined posts, far downhill. And that way, surely, Grendel had come.

That way, too, lay Grendelsjar, the lake where Hrunting rested.

The troll was dead, dead, too, the troll-wife who had spawned him—so he had no fear of them. Heorot and the old powers had had their duel, and Heorot had lost its luck.

But this was not the place to linger. Ill omened the lake where he was going, but worse, this, where so many had died. He walked from there, walked through the fire-ravaged doorway and down the hill westward, steadily west, where no sign of man persisted.

The land grew rougher, overgrown with brush where Heorot's axes had hewn down woods for hall timbers and firewood. Saplings had grown

up, and wild scrub—deer did not browse here. That was what it said to
Halli's eye. There was no natural restraint on wild growth, and trees,
seeds chance-sown, had not yet shaded the ground. Two generations of
summers and winters had passed, and yet the deer did not browse here.
Closer to Lejre, one could see straight through the forests easterly, and
they were bold enough now and again to come right up to the village.

Not here. No sign of deer. Not even marten or rabbit. Nor even birds,
now that he marked it. There was a hush over the place, and a rock dis-
lodged roused nothing as it rolled, the only sound roundabout.

He came at last to a forest long uncut, a woods surrounding a stream
that gave easier passage for his journey, but no game tracks showed along
its margins, and the forest grew darker and more tangled on either hand.

Had this been Grendel's path, this shallow place, this thread of water
running down among the stones?

There began to be larger rocks, and the way grew darker with the
setting of the sun somewhere beyond the woods. He struggled among
rocks, anxious to find an end of the tangle, loath to spend a night in this
dead place.

And quite suddenly he saw fading daylight through the branches
and the scrub, light, and the pure wan gold of the sun itself. He redou-
bled efforts, shoved branches aside, and drove toward it with all his
strength, relieved that there was an edge to this woods, and that the sun
was not yet gone.

The forest stopped there, abruptly, roots driven stubbornly into rock,
seeking purchase. And abruptly—there was the sun, and an edge, a cliff,
and the golden sky, and a lake far below his feet, water gathered in the
riven rock.

Halli caught his balance with a grasp at a dry branch—it cracked,
but held, and he stood solidly on the rocky edge, looking out from the
rim of a little waterfall that ran under his feet and vanished over the
edge, to what surely was Grendelsjar. Forest rimmed it, sparse, some
trees white and dead, fallen or canted sharply over the edge. It was that
abrupt, and still, he thought, apt to crumble. He got down to hands and
knees on solid rock and looked over, where that thread of water fell
down, white, where it plunged into the lake below, not the only such
stream to end here.

Grendelsjar. His heart beat higher in the realization he had indeed found the place, that Grandfather's treasure lay under that black water, which might not be so deep as it looked down, or so dark as it seemed at twilight.

It was six or seven times a man-height down to the lake, if he had fallen, a sorry cold surprise after a long walk, and one which might well have landed him on jagged rock, a little shy of the thread of waterfall. This side of the lake was a cliff on which he stood. The other was a low marshy shoreline, which might require a far walk to reach.

But there was a second ledge, and a rockfall. Very large boulders had come down from this edge and made a ladder to that lower level. Sapling trees had taken hold in it—it was no recent slide, but a stair all the way to the water.

This might have been the troll's own stairway, and the stream above his highway through the woods. In that dark water below was Grandfather's sword, as good as calling to him, wanting him to come down to it and bring it back. He started down in the chancy light, and the massive rocks were steady enough, but the shapes turned treacherous and difficult, delivering him not all the way to the water's edge but to a ledge above it.

There sat a white stone, so his eyes made it out in the fast-fading light, a curious thing, different from the gray rock. But a shift in view made it no stone at all but a bleached skull.

It was not a companion he wanted in the dark, on this narrow ledge above the water. But to climb up again was foolish. Fear was foolish. He had only reached the ledge, down a chancy climb, and was it not what the skalds sang? Did he not know what ornament the troll-wife had set above her door?

Aeschere, Hrothgar's friend and advisor—his head, the blood price the troll-wife had taken for her son's life. She had taken Aeschere's head and set it above her door.

"Well, sir," Halli said, sinking down to sit on a tumbled boulder, "well, the great hero might have brought you home to bury. And did not. So many things the skalds say he did that he did not."

"Unferth? Is it Unferth here?"

His heart half stopped. He drew in a breath, telling himself at first he was mistaken, that it was the blood pounding in his ears, the exertion that had brought him down here. But the voice repeated: "Is it Unferth?"

"Unferth's grandson." One hardly dared give a hostile ghost a name, but Aeschere had been no enemy of his grandfather's. "Are you Aeschere?"

"Aeschere. Yes." The voice grew stronger. "I have slept the night through, I think." Was there a glimmering of light in the gathering murk, an upright figure composed of fog, when there was no fog about at all. "I was in the hall." What might be an arm flung outward. "I slept. I waked. She was among us!"

"She's dead now," Halli said. Fear went out from the ghost, like a drowning wave, speeding the heart, making the skin cold. "She is dead, sir, in the lake below us. Be calm. She can't harm us now."

"How fares Heorot? How fares my lord?"

"It was years ago, sir, years ago that you fell asleep. Heorot is gone. Lord Hrothgar is gone. My grandfather Unferth is gone." It was the first time he had said the words to anyone, and it made an ache in his throat. "Just now gone, sir. Day before yesterday. He was an old, old man."

"Your grandfather." The ghost was still for a moment but seemed brighter now as sunlight faded. A bearded face appeared, with braided hair, a collar of gold links. "Unferth. My friend. Dead."

Aeschere had been a good man, a true man, and brave, Grandfather had said. Brave, but not wise—far too ready to undertake anything Hrothgar wanted, taking Hrothgar's side, Grandfather had said, in any great folly.

And in Heorot, that night, Aeschere had thrown himself, unarmed, between his lord and Grendel's mother, a warrior's death, though weaponless; but she had taken his head with her. "Here my vengeance is taken," that act had signified, the head set above the entry to her domain. "The blood debt is ended unless you pursue it."

Beowulf had pursued it. But still Aeschere remained here, unsatisfied and restless.

The ghost had faded in that news, face eclipsed by shadowy hands, big hands, a warrior's hands, without power now to grasp a weapon. Rings of honor and scars of warfare were evident on those hands. And they shut out the sight of him, shut out his presence, perhaps, while Aeschere tried to remember events he had not lived to see.

"Beowulf came," the ghost said, and the hands fell. "He went under the water. And came out again. She is dead."

"Your watch is well kept, sir. You did all you could. I have made my grandfather's grave. I'll make yours if you wish. He remembered you as a friend though you disagreed. Your lord has gone on. The heroes all have gone on to the gods' feast, my grandfather, too. He would welcome you."

"Unferth's grandson. Son of his son."

"Halli is my name. Halli Eclefssen." He gave the ghost assurance, a measure of reckless trust. A ghost's blessing might be lucky in this undertaking. But ghosts were chancy creatures who saw only their own purpose, their reason for lingering. "My grandfather is waiting for his sword, that Beowulf abandoned there. Bless me with luck, warrior, while I go down and find it, and when I come up again, I will free you from this place so you can go join the others. More, I'll tell your tale and give you a warrior's glory so long as they sing songs."

The ghost brightened until the man stood there, just his feet absent. "Unferth's grandson has all the luck I can lend. Tell me the songs you know. Tell me how Heorot fared."

Dared he lie? It might bring a curse when the ghost found out the truth.

He could gloss the truth and stop while the telling was still fair. Gods knew the skalds did it.

"Beowulf killed your killer, sir. Hrothgar grieved for you so much he sent Beowulf away loaded down with gold. Beowulf became a king himself, and Hrothgar and his great gold-giving became a legend of its own. The heroes you knew in Heorot became great lords themselves in the lands all about, and made the land so strong, the king of the Franks and his White God turned aside from us. The Frankish king found it much easier to make war in the south, rather than here, where such great men live, and has not yet come back. The Skyldings you knew all have great mounds above them, and their songs still are sung. Now the world will know your part in all that happened here."

The world became less clear. Halli found a mist all about him, but there was no chill in it. Rather he felt separated from the world, and he thought he should be afraid, but he could not think what to do about it, if he was being dragged down to his own death. He found himself sinking into sleep, and warm, and simply too weary even to lift his head and protest.

Had he told too much truth? Could the ghost know what he had not said of Hrothgar's ending?

The dark was all about him, silent, so still he heard only the little waterfall burbling away in its plunge off the cliff, a thin thread, a thread so thin a breath could sever it. It was all that held him to the world.

Until a bird sang.

Halli opened his eyes. The sun beat down on his face, blazing white in a pure blue sky.

He sat where he had sat last night. A skull sat gazing out over the ledge, white and weathered, but never touched by beast or bird.

The far shore bristled with pines all twisted and strange. It was as if the earth had split here, with this rocky face on one side, a low forest on the other, and the midst of it filled up with murky water.

Yet when he stood up, the dark water seemed clear below, shadowed like dark glass, and very still, no wind disturbing the waters. He stood, if the skalds sang true, on the very lintel of the troll cave, where the trollwife had set her grim trophy. He was as near to his goal as he ever could be, without going under the water. And the moment was before him, as near as ever it could be, without his going in. He cast off his cloak. He laid by the last of the bread he had. He stood on the brink. He looked down into that glassy darkness, and hesitated, thinking how cold it might be, how changed appearances might be, of something left long beneath the water, and how, if he left this place and only said he had gone down into that depth—there was no witness to make him a liar. It was a coward thought. He hated it. And still his feet stayed on solid ground.

No. He could not go back with a lie. He drew in deep, deep breaths, then took a running step and jumped clear of the edge, feetfirst, chin tucked.

His feet hit the water, and water rushed up, cold, and apt to drive the breath from his body. Down and down he went with that force, then, when the water grew still around him, he opened his eyes on a darkened view of lumps of rock, fallen from the cliff, they might be.

Among them, as he turned about in the water, was a deeper darkness, nothing distinct, just a place where no light reached—a cave, perhaps. A place to be trapped, airless, and drowned even in still water. But he swam toward it, chill and desperate, scanning all the rocks for any hint of gold, Hrunting's pommel, as Grandfather had described it, a puzzle-knot of gold, noble metal, that never would rust or blacken.

Current took him. He grew desperate for air, chest burning, heart beating in his ears, and if he once gave way to the urge to breathe, he was done. He felt the rocks with bare hands, tried to fight the current, but his fingers found no purchase. He was caught, turned, moved against his will.

The weight of water lessened. He was rising, somehow, rapidly, and fought to hold his breath until he reached the surface, gasping, flailing out to stay afloat in utter darkness.

His feet found a surface, a shallow where he could go on hands and knees, cold and dripping wet and blind.

"See," a voice said.

He flung his head up, and immediately with the voice came warmth, and with the warmth came the faintest of lights, like the light that took the rigging of ships on god-touched nights. The blue fire grew, ran across a pile of bones, skulls and ribs of sheep and cattle, a midden heap of long feasting. About it, scattered among the bones, were five, six swords, and helms, and armor, broken shields. Amid it all, standing aslant through the eyehole of a cow's skull—a sword, unsheathed, shining bright, from its blade to the gold puzzle-knot that gave it balance.

Halli staggered forward, laid his hand on it, drew it out, and colors came to the place, as if the sword were a torch bright as the sun. Grandfather had never told such a thing. But it knew him, Hrunting did. It blazed bright. It showed him all the cave, and with it, on its rocky shore, a troll-wife's home, table and benches, neat shelves, with homely, humble pots all in order, like any good householder would arrange, well aside from the midden heap.

He was still breathing hard. He turned all about, and saw a bed, and in the bed—someone sleeping, he thought at first glance. A dark-haired someone, with long, braided hair. A white shift. And a dagger jutting from its back. A corpse, a woman, and one long dead, by the condition of the cloth and, as he moved closer, the withered flesh.

Who? he wondered. What woman had there been, but the troll-wife herself, and could a troll be so slight as this?

And what great battle had there been, with a sword thrust through the back of a woman lying abed.

That was not the tale the skalds told.

He held Hrunting aloft, like a torch, but the colors it showed all blurred and went blue again. And the woman moved, turned her head.

He stepped back, appalled. But the face that showed was a face comely enough, neither young nor old, a middling age—she began to sit up, transparent, with her lifeless form beneath her. She looked up at him and everything seemed to hush. The water ceased to lap at the rocks. And the cave was touched with ghost-fire.

"Woman," he said, his own voice hardly a whisper, "woman, what happened here?"

"They killed my son," the ghost said. "And I killed them."

This slight woman, a woman in features and size like the old ones that dwelled in the deep woods, had killed men in Heorot? Had come away with a head and set it above her gate?

There was more to her than seemed. He half expected the ghost to grow, and tower above him, gnashing fangs, grasping with cold hands . . .

But she simply stared at him with eyes black as night itself, and he felt cold, bitter cold.

"Our sacred place you took for your feasting. Our forests you cut for your cookfires. Our meadows you gave to your great slow beasts. You hunted our deer and our hares. You hunted us for sport. How shall we not take your cattle? How shall we not take food from your tables?"

"Lady," he said—respect seemed the only safety. "I did none of these things. I shall go and leave you to your rest."

Her eyes rolled back until the whites showed plain, and she threw back her head and gave a trilling shriek. Then those black eyes fixed on him, dark fire. "Rest? Rest, is it? I warned my son. But he was young, he was foolish, he was angry. He came bare-handed against your swords. He fought. He took food. And you wounded him, and he died. I buried him. With my own hands, I buried him. And when I had buried him I went to that den of thieves and I took the blood price I was due. I set it for a warning. I was done with you unless you offended me again."

"You slept. You slept, and one came here, and killed you. He carried my grandfather's sword, lent him against a monster, so the story was—but this sword he said failed him." He stood facing a righteous ghost, with power crackling all about, and knew he was dead if he misspoke. "This sword is bespelled—and its geas is that it will never fail a hero in battle. Hrunting never failed him. He failed its conditions. He struck from behind, as you slept. It was no battle. And greater shame, he told it otherwise."

"Truth," a voice said out of the depths of the cave. Halli flinched but did not look that way, fearing the ghost facing him would take advantage. Was it the son? Was it Grendel himself?

"Lady," Halli said, "you were wronged. I believe it. Let me leave this place and I'll tell others what happened here, I swear it."

"One knows," the troll-wife said. "One who is living knows. The rest are dead. The killer himself will die. The thieves are gone from the hill. The meadows and the woods will mend themselves. And my house is mine again. You may dismiss the watcher to his gods."

She seemed taller of a sudden, taller and more formidable, hair unbraiding and flying in a wind that didn't touch Halli at all. He looked up at her and stood his ground.

"What shall I call you?" he asked. "What shall I call you, lady, when I tell the skalds?"

"I have no name," she said, in a voice like the sea itself. "I am everything now. Return!"

He was in the deep water, in the dark, and rising, rising to break through into sunlight, chest aching for that next breath—hand encumbered—

Hrunting broke the surface and shone in the light as Halli kicked and swam toward the rocks. He crawled out, sodden, dripping, and lay on sun-warmed stone until he could breathe without gasping, until the blood flowed back to his sword hand, and he dared look at it.

No whit diminished, the gleam of its gold puzzle-knot, or its gray-steel blade.

Halli stared at it, the whole jumble of ghosts and darkness trying to escape memory, for all the world like a dream—except the substantial evidence in his grip, the sword with its puzzle-knot, and its geas . . . never to fail a hero in battle.

Did he have the wielding of such a thing? He didn't think so. Yet it was in his hand, and it was real, and unblemished, It would have looked exactly like this when Grandfather lent it to Beowulf that morning in Heorot. The pommel would have gleamed like that, a puzzle-knot posing a question.

Why such an ornament? And Grandfather—a judge, a brehon, not a warrior—how the heroes must have looked at him, a man not great of stature, not known for battles. A pity such a potent sword rests in those hands, they would have said. A treasure, indeed, a way to glory for any hero who bore it. More, protection for any kingdom defended by such a hero—sure salvation for the Skyldings and defeat for any enemy who dared confront them. It was an embarrassment that the bearer of it was such a lily-handed fellow—nobody feared Unferth. They taunted him to his face, the folk of Lejre had, with being soft, a man who won with words, and who dealt sharply, a stingy man, who served a gold-giving lord, Hrothgar the Generous, Hrothgar the Ring-giver.

Halli blinked, squeezed his eyes shut, opened them to be sure Hrunting was still safely in his hand.

How could such a fellow wield a sword like this? Grandfather was no hero. Grandfather had never claimed to be. Judge was his claim. Advisor, except that Hrothgar preferred Aeschere's advice, which always agreed with him.

Why had Grandfather given the sword to a stranger? Grandfather had been, of all things, deep-thinking and deliberate, nor wont to back down from his positions.

Such an ornament as the puzzle-knot bespoke the blade's character.

He could not unbind it. It was as it was. He dragged himself, dripping, up to his knees, and thought of practical things, like his dry, warm cloak up on the ledge, and a small portion of stale bread.

He looked up, where the rockslide, by full daylight, showed him a way to get up to that ledge, and honor a promise.

It was a small tomb he made, of the smallish rocks he could safely free from the slide. He made it, and he gave Aeschere half the bread he had left. He thought hard about it, but he added the butchering knife to the grave goods, not that they had another, but that he had his life, and Aeschere had, he felt, wished him well. He had Grandfather's sword with him for protection, and maybe Grandfather's ghost with it—he had no idea.

"Go take care of Father if you can," he wished his grandfather. "I'm all right. It's Father who needs you. Go bring him luck with the deer. I'll be there as soon as I can."

So he set the last stones in place, giving Aeschere the best he could, and all he could spare, and he ate the last of the bread and set out to climb the slide, no small risk in that—he set his feet carefully, and he tested every step, some of which were boulders as large as he was. He had not cheated Aeschere's ghost, he had not dealt badly with the troll-wife. If either could send him luck now, he would take it gratefully, and he wished he had told Grandfather to linger just until he reached the top of the slide.

He was ever so glad to crawl up onto the crumbling edge of the forest, and anxious to be far back from the cliff, where a step sent pebbles and small rocks rattling and bouncing down the ledges. Likely it was that some spring thaw, when ice had forced its fingers into rocks and crevices in hills, that it would all let go, and half a forest plunge down into the lake.

He was not disposed to linger, not another moment. He wrapped his cloak about his wet clothes and the sword and all, bowed his head, and walked, eastward now, homeward with his treasure.

He had said he would be back before the sjaund. He brought nothing that would feed the village. He arrived in sight of the great mounds footsore, limping—he had taken strips of his shirt to bind his feet within his boots, which he had not gotten dry—and hungry, since a lump of stale bread had been his last meal, and nothing since but a few berries from a bush and a few seeds he had come on. He had not delayed to hunt, nor tried to build a fire. He had simply walked with the strength he had, and found no challenge on the way, but no trace of game, either.

He limped his way, at last, to Grandfather's grave, and found the endmost stones disarranged—the grave not violated, but stones kicked about. Such was Eileifr and his lot.

He put back the stones one by one, angry, but too weary to rage at fools. He smoothed the earth. When he had done, he simply sank down by the grave mound and folded back his cloak. He laid Hrunting on Grandfather's grave, a shining treasure atop the mud.

"Grandfather," he said. "I have it. I brought it back. I don't think I should wield it. I think I'd have to be as wise as you were, and know as much, and be a hero besides, which I'm not. The heroes are gone away and the gold is all given and gone. Except this. I found it where the man threw it, and I know why he threw it. It wouldn't strike. He tried to murder a woman in her bed, and the sword wouldn't obey him. That was why he didn't bring it back. It might have done it again. It never failed him. He failed it. That's what I learned."

Aeschere had talked to him. The troll-wife had. He rather hoped that Grandfather would, now, just once.

"Hrunting will never fail a hero in battle," he murmured. "And its pommel is a puzzle-knot. It's a puzzle I can't solve. You lent it to a stranger. Why, Grandfather? Was it what I thought, that it was to prove you were right about the man? But you never doubted you were right, did you?"

The silence went on a moment.

Then a thought came to him. "He couldn't commit murder with it, could he? You were a judge, and a good one. Grendel's mother said she was justified, and she was. They'd killed her son. She had every right to take a price. And she did. You were an honest judge. Always an honest judge, weren't you, Grandfather? The law, you'd say. Save the law. Wise men made it. We have to save it. You gave him Hrunting so he couldn't kill her. So he couldn't do what he did."

A mother's curse was a potent one. And Grendel's mother was no ordinary woman.

Heorot had burned. Its lords had killed one another in a frenzy of succession—one within an hour of the last. The gold had gone with Beowulf and the land had a dog for a king.

"Is that the puzzle, Grandfather? You didn't lend Hrunting for battle. You lent it for judgment, because your lord would not listen and Beowulf certainly wouldn't. It wouldn't kill her. It wouldn't bring down a curse. Only Beowulf found the place littered with weapons he could use. That was the troll-wife's misfortune, and Heorot's. Her curse came down, sure as death, despite your trying to prevent him. Is that Hrunting's riddle?"

Silence still. He got up, picked up the sword. "I'll bring this back in a little while, Grandfather. I'll show it only to Father, not to the village, so that fool Eileifr won't go looking for it. Though it would be a judgment if he did steal it and go a-viking. He's no hero, that's certain. It's a sword that would make its own way in the world, and lucky only so long as you can keep from using it."

He walked on past the great mound, sword wrapped again in his cloak and hidden. He walked within view of the house.

There was a deer carcass hanging. That cheered him immensely. One deer would not feed the village except as massive pots of stew, but that was good enough. They might barter hide for ale. He was sorry to have to report he'd lost the butchering knife, and he could not, gods, he could not suggest they take the sword to it.

But he thought his father would forgive him. Father forgave him most everything.

He hailed the door, pulled the latchstring without ceremony, and walked into a house warm and bright from a strong fire, his father leaping up to welcome him with a huge hug, all relief and gladness. He pounded his father's shoulder one-handed, and pushed his way back to show him the sword.

"Gods," was all Father could say.

"I didn't want to leave it with him before I showed it to you. I don't want the village to see it."

"They should!"

"Father, you know Eileifr and his dogs. They'll dig. And I promised Grandfather. Listen. I know the sword's secret, and its luck. That's the important thing."

"What secret?"

"That it's better to have than to use. I know why Grandfather gave it, and I know why Beowulf threw it away. There's a lot about Grendelsjar that's chancy, and I don't think it will even be there in years to come. I think the sword needed to come home. But it's not for us to use."

"I remember the heroes," Father said. "They were given to a lot of drink and shoving little kids out of the way. It's not what I wanted to be, either."

"Good," Halli said. "Good. I'm glad. I'm glad you had a good hunt."

"Three deer."

"Three!"

"Best day ever. One after the other. Meat and hide and bone, traded every bit of it. Ale in plenty. Meat for the sjaund. We'll send the old man off in style."

"I lost the knife. Well, I gave it." A glance at the wall showed a fine new knife, a blade gray and bright and sharp as ever a smith these days could make it. "That's new."

"Luck," his father said. "Sheer luck. I was never a great hunter. But now I have a name."

"Luck. Warm fire. Enough to eat and feast the neighbors." Halli longed to cast himself down on the bench before the fire and have some of that stew he smelled. His feet hurt miserably and his legs were all but shaking from exhaustion. But it came to him that Hrunting's luck was perilous, and Grandfather had managed it well enough, no shame to him. He knew that now.

And if the sword in the ground was as good as the sword in a man's hands, then let it rest there with its riddle for good and all.

"I want to go back to Grandfather's grave and leave this before I sleep," he said. "Come with me. Let us give it to him, both of us. He'll be satisfied."

"The luck's back," Father said. "Never such a day as that in my life, three deer. And if the luck's back, then our family will have it, and if we have it, they'll forget all the bad things about Grandfather and remember he was a good judge."

"He was that," Halli said, and wrapped his cloak about himself and the sword. "He was all of that."

Garth Nix

· · ·

New York Times bestselling Australian writer Garth Nix worked as a book publicist, editor, marketing consultant, public-relations man, and literary agent whilst also writing, becoming a full-time author with the success of the bestselling Old Kingdom series, which consists of *Sabriel, Lirael, Abhorsen,* and two more recent additions: *Clariel* and *Goldenhand.* His other books include the Seventh Tower series, consisting of *The Fall, Castle, Aenir, Above the Veil, Into Battle,* and *The Violet Keystone,* the Keys to the Kingdom series, consisting of *Mister Monday, Grim Tuesday, Drowned Wednesday, Sir Thursday, Lady Friday, Superior Saturday,* and *Lord Sunday,* as well as standalone novels such as *The Ragwitch, Shade's Children,* and *Newt's Emerald.* His short fiction has been collected in *Across the Wall* and *To Hold the Bridge.* Among his recent books are the Troubletwisters series with Sean Williams, a standalone SF novel, *A Confusion of Princes,* and a new collection, *Sir Hereward and Master Fitz: Three Adventures.*

His most recent novel is *Frogkisser!* Born in Melbourne, raised in Canberra, he lives in Sydney, Australia.

Here we join Sir Hereward and Master Fitz hard on the trail of their most dangerous adversary yet, one they dare not actually catch up to if they want to stay alive . . .

◆　◆　◆

A Long, Cold Trail

GARTH NIX

Sir Hereward drew his heavy fur cloak tighter around himself and lifted his feet higher, his sealskin boots coming out of the snow with a discouraging sucking noise.

"You're *sure* the road is under here?" he asked, apparently to the empty air, for no one strode next to him, and the bleak landscape of bare snow dotted here and there with dying, stunted trees appeared to be entirely bereft of life.

"Yes," came the short reply from inside the tall wicker basket he carried upon his back. A moment later, Mister Fitz emerged, the hairless top of his round, papier-mâché head flipping back the lid of the basket, which up until two days ago had served to hold the laundry of a country squire. That squire was now dead, along with every occupant of his manor, both human and animal. Since Sir Hereward's battlemount had also been slain by the effect of proximity to the godlet that killed the squire, and the huge riding lizard's saddlebags were unsuitably large for pedestrian movement, the laundry basket had been pressed into service to carry blankets, tarpaulin, carbine, powder, ball, water bottles, and food.

Mister Fitz had climbed inside the basket when the snow got too deep, as he stood only three feet six and a half inches tall on his carved wooden feet. A sorcerous puppet, imbued with magical life, he did not feel the cold but did find deep snow an inconvenience. Not so much to travel, as he was preternaturally strong and could bull his way through the deepest drift, but because he didn't like being surrounded by snow with the consequent diminution of vision.

The snow was not a natural phenomenon. As with the desiccated corpses sprawled about the manor half a league behind them, it was an indication and by-product of the passage of a godlet inimical to both life and the regular weather patterns of the area. The depth of the snow and the heaviness of the fall, as evidenced by the steady flakes now settling on Sir Hereward's woolen watch cap (his three-bar visored helmet was currently tied to his belt) indicated that the godlet and its unwilling and contrary host were only three or four hundred yards ahead of them.

This was the closest the duo of man and puppet had got to it after six days of dogged pursuit in increasingly bad weather, and the closest they wanted to get, at least until one of Sir Hereward's cousins got around to delivering the relic they would need to destroy, or rather banish, the godlet.

The whole matter had the air of a mordant family affair, thought Sir Hereward, as he galumphed through the snow, exerting his weary senses to be alert for any sign the godlet might have stopped to lie in wait or had begun to turn back. For in addition to waiting on his cousin to deliver the necessary relic, the reluctant host the godlet rode was Sir Hereward's great-great-aunt Eudonia. A notable witch and thus also an agent of the Council for the Treaty of the Safety of the World, she had been tasked with banishing the newly rediscovered proscribed godlet Xavva-Tish-Laqishtax.

But Laqishtax had proven far stronger than expected and had managed to attach itself to Eudonia's person. As neither witch nor godlet was initially able to subdue the other in a clash of wills, the godlet had sought to grow stronger by sucking the life force from any living thing around that was unable to resist—which was usually everything alive for several hundred yards from its foul presence. Eudonia had countered this tactic by walking them both off into the sparsely populated wastelands of the former Kingdom of Hrorst.

However, at some point in the last week, Xavva-Tish-Laqishtax had clearly found an additional source of power—some poor shepherd and a flock of goats or the like—and had managed to overcome Eudonia sufficiently to redirect their path back out of the wastelands toward the prosperous, well-populated lands of the Autarchy of Kallinksimiril. More grist for the godlet's mill.

The border manor where the godlet had just consumed everything with even the faintest spark of life was but the first of many that lay ahead, not to mention the walled town of Simiril itself. If Xavva-Tish-Laqishtax got that far, and subsumed the life force of not only the inhabitants but also their patron godlet—the benign lesser deity the locals called the Whelper—then it would be almost impossible to overcome.

Hence, Sir Hereward and Mister Fitz stalked Xavva-Tish-Laqishtax at a safe distance, and hoped very much the relic would soon be delivered, so they could attack.

"Kishtyr had best speed her travels," complained Sir Hereward as he stumbled and fell forwards into a drift. Standing up to brush snow from his front, he added, "Simiril lies less than five leagues ahead, and I doubt the lake they call the Smallest Sea will slow the godlet one whit. I fail to see why Kishtyr did not arrive last night, or at least this morning. Also, I believe my nose is becoming frostbitten."

"It is no simple matter to retrieve a relic from the crypt," said Mister Fitz in his instructional voice. He had been Sir Hereward's nanny then teacher, and in truth had taught a great many godslayers over the centuries, so he still veered to the didactic at the least temptation. "Being of necessity items that contain the specially distilled and controlled essence of particularly inimical godlets, the relics held by the Council are secured in a number of different ways. Nothing can be removed in a hurry, it takes several witches several days and is not without hazard. There may easily have been a complication."

"It's been a *week*," grumbled Sir Hereward, quickly wrinkling his nose several times in an attempt to warm it.

"It has been six days and we are some considerable distance from the High Pale," commented Mister Fitz. "Hmmm . . ."

"What was that?" asked Sir Hereward. The puppet's senses were far more acute than his own, particularly for things beyond the ordinary. And even more so when Hereward had a cold coming on. His ears were beginning to be blocked as a consequence of that cold, but he did think he might have heard a distant, fading scream, suddenly cut off.

"Xavva-Tish-Laqishtax has found some more people to consume," said Mister Fitz. "No . . . not entirely, it seems. It has left some fragment of spiritual essence within the husks."

Sir Hereward grimaced at the word "husks" and almost remonstrated with Mister Fitz for describing people in such a fashion. But he did not, for he knew the term was entirely accurate and Mister Fitz did not welcome sentimentality over verisimilitude. Whatever was left of the people after the godlet's devouring passage would indeed be no more than husks, things of flesh without thought or purpose. Unless they were given purpose by a greater power.

"It fills them with its will," reported Mister Fitz. "And sends them against us."

Sir Hereward swore and dumped the basket, unclasping his cloak in the same motion, letting it drop behind. Mister Fitz leapt from basket to shoulder and thence into the snow.

The knight's two long-barrelled wheel-lock pistols were already charged with powder and loaded with silver-washed shot, but they were not wound. Sir Hereward wore the spanner on a thong about his wrist and from years of practice flipped it into his hand and began to wind the first pistol even as Mister Fitz pushed out of the drift and climbed swiftly up the dead, grey trunk of a tree that up until the god's passage a half hour before had been a luxuriant beech. Its former foliage and much of its bark was now no more than dust below its branches, dirtying the snow.

"How many?" asked Sir Hereward. In a scant minute and a half he had spanned both pistols, loosened the basket-hilted mortuary sword in the sheath at his side, undone his helmet from his belt and slapped it on, and was now extracting his carbine—a more common flintlock—from the basket.

"Eight," said Mister Fitz.

"Unarmed?" asked Sir Hereward hopefully. Those recently dispossessed of the majority of their spiritual essence often retained some bodily memory of how to use arms and implements, which meant they could still fight with considerable competence even when directed by a puppeteering godlet rather than their own will.

"Farmers," said Mister Fitz. "They have hayforks, a scythe, and such-like."

Sir Hereward grunted and primed the carbine from the small powder flask that slotted into the butt of the weapon. He had seen sufficient mortal wounds delivered by hayforks and reaping hooks to have a healthy respect for even such agricultural weaponry.

"I cannot spare the use of my sole remaining sorcerous needle," said Mister Fitz. "We may need it to protect ourselves from the godlet's ravening. However, I shall assist as best I may in a more mechanical fashion."

As he spoke, the puppet reached behind his back, and withdrew from a hidden sheath a short triangular blade made to follow the proportion of the Golden Ratio, so it looked rather broader than it should. Some opponents—soon disabused of their fallacious notions—thought such a blade too small to be dangerous, particularly in the hands of a puppet. Most sorcerous puppets were mere entertainers and would not or could not fight under any circumstances. Mister Fitz did not follow that stricture, though it was true he fought hand to hand only when no more elegant alternative presented itself.

"How close?" asked Sir Hereward. He reached up and quickly fastened his helmet strap and turned up the thick, high collar of his buff coat to protect his neck.

"As you see," answered Mister Fitz, pointing.

Hereward could see them now, dark figures stark against the snowy backdrop, moving in the disturbing, stop-start, jagged fashion of the spirit-shorn.

"There are nine," said Sir Hereward, with some surprise, pointing to one far off to the right of the main group.

"That is not one of the godlet's playthings," said Mister Fitz, after a moment's pause. "It is a whole man . . . and he has an aura which suggests something of the sorcerer, to boot. Which perchance explains why he approaches on the diagonal, rather than fleeing as one might expect."

"Should I shoot him first?" asked Sir Hereward. Stray sorcerers of unknown allegiance on the field of battle were generally best removed from consideration in the overall military equation.

Mister Fitz did not answer for a few seconds, his pale blue eyes staring through the falling snow at that distant figure sloshing and leaping through the lesser drifts in an alley between rows of dead trees.

"No," he said finally. "It is Fyltak, the man who calls himself the God-Taker."

"That charlatan!" exploded Sir Hereward. "If he gets any closer, I'll finish him with steel, rather than waste my silvered shot on his—"

"He is not entirely a charlatan, and he may be useful," interrupted Mister Fitz. "In any event, the soul-reaped will be upon us well before he gets here."

"I make no warranty for his life," snapped Sir Hereward. His previous experience with Fyltak the God-Taker was recent, and had consisted of the latter successfully taking the credit for the banishment of the Blood-Sipping Ghoul, a minor but still sufficiently deadly godlet whose nocturnal predations on the burghers of Lazzarenno had actually been put to an end by Mister Fitz, with Sir Hereward taking care of the godlet's hematophagic minions. While Sir Hereward did not want his true business known, Fyltak had messed up their careful plans. The knight cared nothing for the false claims and subsequent rewards. He could not forgive Fyltak's bumbling interference.

"He bears an interesting sword," mused Mister Fitz, sharp gaze still fixed on Fyltak, who was leaping in great bounds through the snow, a blade bare in his hand. "I had not occasion to mark it previously, but I believe it is the source of the sorcerous emanations I have felt before. Not Fyltak himself, after all."

"Hmmph!" growled Sir Hereward. Sorcerous swords were generally even more trouble than sorcerers. Particularly the sentient variety, who were almost always crazed from centuries of bloodletting, or had adopted strange and annoying philosophies about when or even if they would deign to be wielded, and by whom.

The knight looked about for some better shooting position and sloshed through the snow to climb upon an exposed rock, which on closer examination proved to be a rectangular-shaped obelisk of marble, a fallen milestone of the old Empire of the Risen Moon. Perhaps a good omen as that state was one of the founding members of the Council that Sir Hereward and Mister Fitz served. Or perhaps the reverse, as the empire, like the milestone, had fallen many centuries ago. So had the moon the empire was named after, Hereward suddenly recalled, feeling a frisson of melancholia. It had only been a very small moon, but it had made a very large crater when it fell.

The soul-reaped were drawing closer. They employed no tactics, no stratagems, the godlet in all likelihood simply filling them with thoughts of moving in a straight line and killing everything that got in their way. There were five men and three women, none of them young, for which Sir Hereward was grateful. Even knowing they were already dead in all ways that mattered, it was still easier to give grace to those who had experienced some extent of life.

He raised his carbine when they were some sixty paces away, sighted carefully, and fired. The heavy, silvered ball struck the closest scythe-wielding relict in his chest, hurling him backwards as it blew out lungs and heart. The godlet's essence within tried to lift the corpse back up out of the snow, but the silver on the ball had disrupted Xavva-Tish-Laqishtax's hold, and after a few moments of thrashing and reaching, the former farmer lay still.

Sir Hereward placed the carbine down carefully at his feet. There might be a chance to reload. Taking out his first pistol, he took aim again, supporting his shooting arm under the elbow with his left hand, locking in his left elbow as he had been taught long ago. Squeezing the trigger, the wheel spun, showering sparks. The pistol barked its characteristic sharp roar and another silvered ball struck the next closest spirit-shorn, exploding his head like an overripe melon kicked at the market by a disgruntled customer.

"Two," remarked Sir Hereward, returning the pistol to his belt and drawing its twin. Xavva-Tish-Laqishtax's servitors were moving faster now, doubtless infused with more of the godlet's essence as it became aware of opposition. They were jumping high out of the snowdrifts, leaping ahead in great bounds.

There would not be time to reload and shoot again, Sir Hereward judged. He let out a long, foggy exhalation, slowing his breath, which had become quicker than he liked, and took aim once more.

The third shot was not so good, for any one of many reasons. He did not think it was from the fear he kept well clamped within. Sir Hereward was used to fear, and used to managing it, calling on it for energy and direction, rather than letting it use him. He did not trust those who claimed to feel no fear.

In any case, the ball struck the side of a woman who carried a pruning hook, setting her aback several paces but no more. If she'd still been alive, or more alive, the shock would have put her down, blood loss finishing the job in a matter of minutes. But her wounded body was no longer guided by a fearful human mind. She pushed on, leaving a red trail behind her on the snow, her vicious, long-shafted hook raised high.

"Take the wounded one!" shouted Sir Hereward, thrusting the second pistol through his belt and drawing his sword in an oft-practiced movement.

Mister Fitz sprang from his perch in the dead beech, landing on the shoulders of the pruning-fork woman, cutting her throat clear to the backbone and jumping again almost in one motion. This time he landed in the snow, disappearing under the legs of one of the remaining five attackers, who strode on, only to fall a few paces later, his tendons cut. The puppet reappeared on his back, only his head and sticklike arm visible above the snow, the arm vanishing as he struck down into the base of the fallen man's brain with his short dagger.

Four others came at Sir Hereward, where he stood high on the old milestone. They all bore hayforks, and again showed no trace of tactical thought, colliding together at the front of the stone and thrusting with their weapons, the shafts clashing together. Sir Hereward trod down one fork, dodged another, and thrust first one and then another of the relicts through their eyes. Even as he pulled the slightly stuck blade from the skull of the second farmer, Mister Fitz dispatched the remaining two, stabbing them in the brain stem, leaping from the shoulders of one to the other then to the stone.

Dying bodies flopped in the snow around the duo as the godlet tried to reanimate the corpses. But both Sir Hereward's sword and Mister Fitz's dagger were well washed with silver, and with brain or spinal cord destroyed, the godlet could not take hold of anything to continue the fight.

"Hold hard! I come to your aid!"

Fyltak the God-Taker was still leaping through the snow toward them, waving his sword above his head. He moved very fast, considering the difficulty of the ground.

Sir Hereward grunted, wiped his sword clean on the sackcloth tunic of the closest no-longer-writhing farmer, sheathed it, and bent down to retrieve his carbine. He reloaded it swiftly, taking cartridge and ball from his belt pouch.

"No," said Mister Fitz. "I think he will be useful."

"I wasn't going to shoot him," lied Sir Hereward. "I am just preparing for the next half-eaten meal Xavva-Tish-Laqishtax will disgorge and send against us."

Though Fyltak arrived far sooner than Sir Hereward had expected, the knight had still managed to reload his pistols as well as the carbine. He had also resumed his cloak and picked up the basket. Mister Fitz rode in it again, his knife once more invisible. He had licked it clean with his blue, stippled leather tongue before sheathing the blade, something Sir Hereward still found somewhat disquieting though the puppet assured him he had no appetite for blood. His tongue was merely an effective cleansing agent and upon occasion, the taste would reveal something of import that otherwise might be missed.

"Thank the kind gods you yet live!" gasped Fyltak. "But know had it been otherwise, I would have avenged you!"

He sheathed his sword and took several deep, racking breaths, indicating what Sir Hereward considered a lack of acquaintance with physical exertion, or perhaps too great a dedication to cakes and ale, though against this supposition he was quite a lean individual.

"I care not for your bravado, Fyltak," said Sir Hereward. "You could no more avenge us against Xavva-Tish-Laqishtax than I could unassisted fly to the closest moon."

"That voice is known to me," muttered Fyltak. He rummaged inside the neck of his somewhat oversized cuirass, to produce a lorgnette on a cord of silk. Placing the glasses on his nose, he gazed up at Sir Hereward, whose face was shadowed by the bars of his visor. The knight noted that looking down at Fyltak the lenses greatly magnified the man's eyes, and were thus presumably extremely necessary and Fyltak should wear them all the time. Furthermore, he probably hadn't seen the detail of the combat that had just occurred, which was useful to know.

"Sir Hereward!" exclaimed Fyltak, letting the lorgnette fall back inside the neck of his breastplate. "Well met, fellow justiciar and executioner of wicked gods!"

"I am not your fellow!" barked Sir Hereward. "You are to me and mine as a . . . a flea is to a dog. Damnably irritating and hard to shift!"

"Ah, the growl of one who has not breakfasted well!" exclaimed Fyltak. "I understand. Nay, I feel the lack myself, but fortunately I bear within this most cunning canister coffee still hot from the kitchens of the Duke of Simiril and within this round tin, pastries fresh-baked from that same kitchen. Allow me to spread a cloth upon this stone and set forth a repast!"

"A man must eat," said Mister Fitz, standing up on the back of the basket. "The godlet has paused in its travel, in any case. We cannot go closer for the nonce."

"Ah, the most wondrous puppet!" exclaimed Fyltak. "Perhaps you might play a cheerful gigue or sing us a roundelay, to lift our spirits while we eat and drink?"

Clearly Fyltak had no conception of what kind of puppet Mister Fitz actually was and had made the common mistake that he was one of the standard performing variety. This further confirmed Hereward's deduction that the man needed his eyeglasses and only pretended to use them as an affectation. A kind of double blind. The knight's mouth quirked at this wordplay, and he wished he could share it with Mister Fitz. Though the puppet would doubtless not find it amusing. He considered nearly all of Sir Hereward's jokes and witticisms foolish, or at best, not worth the breath required to make them.

"I fear it is too cold for my lute, and my throat is a little rusty and wants sweet oil," replied Mister Fitz. "Would a poem suffice? I must cogitate a little to create, but I do not wish to hold you gentlemen from your coffee."

"I do not want any coff—" Sir Hereward started to say angrily, but he stopped as he felt the pressure of Mister Fitz's fingers on his shoulder. The puppet saw some use in Fyltak, or in his sword, so with some effort Hereward forced down his ire. Besides, the God-Taker had opened the "cunning canister" and the delightful aroma of hot coffee had reached Sir Hereward's nose.

"I do not normally drink coffee among corpses," continued Hereward, climbing down to sit on his fur cloak at the far end of the stone, as far away as possible from the bloodied snow and the fallen bodies at the other end. "But there is nowhere else to sit in this new wasteland the godlet has made."

Fyltak handed him a steaming demitasse of coffee. Hereward raised one eyebrow at the delicate pale blue and silver porcelain cup, surely not long to survive any serious travel or fighting, and sipped.

Mister Fitz recited his poem as the two men drank.

> *Soft, the snow falling*
> *Steam spiralling from coffee*
> *The slain cold and still*

Fyltak nodded several times in appreciation. Sir Hereward, who considered himself a far more skillful and talented poet than Mister Fitz, privately made a face at his companion that indicated he could do better but would refrain so as not to raise doubts about the puppet's nature.

"Which ... err ... godlet is causing the trouble?" asked Fyltak, after a suitable pause to absorb the full beauty of the poem. "There is considerable panic in Simiril, many already flee the town."

"Very wise," said Mister Fitz. He moved closer to Fyltak and reached out with one hand toward his sword, wooden fingers making an understated grasping motion, quickly quelled. Sir Hereward noted this. Fitz really was interested in the charlatan's weapon. It seemed unremarkable to the knight, an old-fashioned sword with a dull blackened steel hilt and from the look of the plain scabbard, a heavy blade made for hacking and slashing, rather than for any finesse with the point, which was very likely dull.

"Your sword interests me," continued the puppet. "I am something of a student of antiquities. I perceive it is of an ancient make."

"What? This old blade?" asked Fyltak. "Been in the family forever, but it's nothing special. I bear it for reasons of sentiment, no more."

"I see," murmured Mister Fitz, bending closer to examine the hilt. Fyltak swapped his demitasse to his left hand and draped his right over the hilt, obscuring the puppet's view.

"As I said, it is quite an ordinary weapon," he blustered. "But tell me of our business! Which godlet is it? What are its powers and weaknesses?"

"Our business!" exclaimed Sir Hereward. He would have gone on, but Mister Fitz glanced at him meaningfully again, so the knight subsided. Fyltak handed him a pastry, which was as excellent as the coffee.

"It is properly known as Xavva-Tish-Laqishtax," said Sir Hereward reluctantly, in between bites, after he saw that Mister Fitz was not going to enlighten Fyltak. Presumably so the God-Taker continued to think him one of the harmless entertaining puppets. "However, it was better known in its heyday as Xavva the Soul-Gorger."

"Ah!" exclaimed Fyltak.

"You know of it?" asked Sir Hereward curiously. The godlet had only been identified by the witches after some considerable research in their incomparable archives, and that only after Eudonia managed to get a fresh sample of the "spoil" left behind by the godlet's predations, revealing the unique prismatic band of the godlet's sorcerous signature. Unfortunately, after procuring the sample, Eudonia had not waited for the confirmation of identity before taking on the godlet by herself.

"Not as such," replied Fyltak. "That was merely an expression of punctuation, as it were. And its weaknesses?"

"Not very apparent," replied Sir Hereward. He hesitated, wondering how much he could tell Fyltak before he would have to kill him. The man seemed innocuous, an innocent, or near enough. Only his sword made him of some account, though he was either deluded on that score or did not wish others to know of it.

"It must have some weakness," replied Fyltak. "As Hereshmur describes in *Banishing and Imprisonment: Methods for Dealing with Unruly Gods*, all extradimensional entities are flawed."

"Ah, a scholar," said Sir Hereward.

"What do you mean?" asked Fyltak, his eyebrows drawing together as he frowned, quick to detect offence or sarcasm.

"Merely punctuation," replied Sir Hereward blandly. "Hereshmur may well be correct, but he is perhaps countered by that famous quotation of Lorquar, Executioner of Gods."

"Oh yes," said Fyltak, nodding.

Sir Hereward, who had made up "Lorquar, Executioner of Gods" on the spur of the moment, kindly did not tell Fyltak so, but ascribed a frequent saying of his own mother to this mythical personage.

"If an inimical godlet's weakness cannot be discerned, does one exist? Act against its strengths for a greater chance of success."

"And this Xavva . . . err . . . godlet . . . what are its strengths?"

"It devours souls," said Sir Hereward bleakly. "It sucks the life out of anything that gets too close, and it grows stronger. Should it garner enough spiritual essence, it will become well-nigh impossible to banish."

"But doubtless you have a plan, Sir Hereward?"

"I have an ally," replied Hereward. "Who is extremely late arriving!"

"And who would that be, sir?" asked Fyltak, drawing himself up and inflating his chest. "For dare I say, an ally already stands before you!"

"Yes," replied Hereward dubiously. "However, the specific ally I await is . . ."

Once again the knight hesitated, reluctant to give this imposter more knowledge than it would be safe to allow him to retain. Fyltak struck an expectant attitude, indicating that possibly not telling him might lead to death by curiosity in any case.

"You have heard of the Witches of Har?" asked Sir Hereward. "Agents for the ancient Council for the Treaty of the Safety of the World?"

"Have I not!" exclaimed Fyltak. "Am I not one of those agents myself?"

Momentarily puzzled by the double negative, Sir Hereward didn't respond for a moment. Then he exploded.

"No, you're not, so stop talking nonsense! And before you go fulminating about the place like a turkey-cock with singed tail feathers think about what I just told you. A Witch of Har—a real agent of the Council—should be here shortly, and they do not take lightly to impersonators. Furthermore, she will be bringing with her a weapon which we, and by that I mean the Witch and I and Mis—that is, the Witch and I—will use to banish Xavva-Tish-Laqishtax. And you, sir, should immediately face about in the opposite direction and go as fast as you can as far as you can and hope that we succeed!"

"You are offensive, sir!" exclaimed Fyltak. "And when this godlet has been dealt with you shall answer to me for a lesson in manners!"

"Did you not hear a word I said?" expostulated Sir Hereward. He stood up and thrust the demitasse back at Fyltak, who reflexively took it. "This is a serious business, not for moongazers and dilettantes!"

"Perhaps we should let the Witch of Har decide who is the dilettante!" Fyltak snapped back. As he spoke, he put both porcelain cups back in a well-padded box and slipped it into a pouch inside his cloak. "A notable such as myself, or a brutish wanderer who travels about with a capering puppet, aggrandizing himself as a godslayer!"

Sir Hereward's hand went to his pistol as Fyltak's went to his sword.

"Enough!" said Mister Fitz, very loudly. "The godlet has turned back toward us!"

Fyltak looked to the puppet, but Sir Hereward gazed up to the sky. The snow was beginning to fall thicker and faster, and he felt the air suddenly grow colder, ice forming on his nose and cheeks.

"How far away is it?" he asked, urgently.

"Four hundred yards and closing swiftly," replied Mister Fitz. He jumped to the basket even as Sir Hereward leapt from the milestone and began to force his way back the way they had come. Already the path they had made was beginning to disappear under the fresh snow.

"Why do you flee?" called out Fyltak, adding, "Coward!"

"If it gets closer than a hundred yards, Xavva-Tish-Laqishtax will draw the spirit from your body as easily as a man quaffing a pint of ale!" shouted Sir Hereward over his shoulder, not pausing to do so. "Stay and have your soul consumed! Your small life will not be a great weight in the scales! That's if you don't freeze first!"

A few minutes later, he heard Fyltak puffing up behind him.

"So do we simply flee?"

"Going back on its own trail, the godlet will diminish, finding no new life to consume," explained Sir Hereward shortly. "If it follows us for a sufficient time, it may become weak enough to dispatch even without the weapon I await from the Witches."

"It grows cold," said the self-professed God-Taker. His breath came out as dense fog, icicles forming around his mouth as he spoke. "Very cold."

"The cursed godlet is applying its strength to bring an even greater freeze, staking all on this pursuit," huffed Sir Hereward. It hurt to breathe in, the air was so intensely cold. "Fitz! We cannot long go on like this."

"A little farther!" urged Mister Fitz from within the basket. "I am calculating. We must make the godlet use as much of its stored energy as possible, because with only one needle, I cannot hold it off for more than twenty or perhaps thirty minutes."

"Ww-what is this . . ." asked Fyltak, his teeth chattering. He was staggering now, wading through icy, brittle snow that was building higher than his thighs, the air so thick with flakes neither man could see much farther than their own outstretched arms. "W-w-hat talk of n-n-needles?"

"The mathematics are simple," continued Mister Fitz, ignoring Fyltak's question. "If the godlet depletes its reserves sufficiently in pursuing us or trying to break down the defences I will raise, it will not be able to retain control over Eudonia's body. She will reassert dominance and walk away, back along the path they took, where the godlet will only grow weaker. We can follow, await Kishtyr and proceed as required."

"W-h-at if . . . if it doesn't weaken enough?" asked Sir Hereward. He couldn't stop shivering, and he could barely see now, his eyes thin slits surrounded by ice. "Or we freeze first? We have to stop and shield ourselves!"

"Ten more steps!" commanded Mister Fitz.

Sir Hereward pushed on, but every step took him a smaller distance forward. The snow was waist high and more tightly packed, indicating he had wandered off their previous path. Or so much snow had fallen so quickly it didn't matter where he went. He couldn't hear Fyltak, but then he couldn't hear much of anything, save the echo of his own straining heartbeat. His ears were frozen under his woolen cap, he felt as if the only sound he picked up now was coming from within him.

Dimly he heard Fitz shouting something, and he felt a vibration on his back. The puppet leaping clear of the basket, he supposed. He tried to walk on, but instead he fell face-first in the snow, which was weirdly warmer than the air above it. For a moment he welcomed this, before realizing it was a trap. If he didn't get up again straightaway, he would lie here and freeze to death. Groaning, the knight rose up on one knee and with frantic but feeble swimming motions, managed to clear the snow away from his chest and stand.

Fitz spoke again, a phrase Hereward couldn't properly make out, save it included the word "eyes." He knew what that meant—Mister Fitz was about to use a sorcerous needle—so he forced his ice-ridden eyes completely closed and buried his face in his buff coat sleeve.

Even with this protection, a violet radiance burst through, seeming to illuminate the insides of his eye sockets and skull. Sir Hereward cried out at that, and at the blast of welcome but painful heat. His ears suddenly cleared. He heard Fyltak groaning and Mister Fitz reciting instructions as if they were back in the schoolroom at the High Pale.

"Hereward, Fyltak. Do not move. I have inscribed a sorcerous barrier about us, which will resist the godlet's ravening and also make the air much more clement. But it is of a small radius and should you cross the boundary, flesh and bone would be bisected and death instant."

Slowly, very slowly, Sir Hereward opened his eyes, blinking away the melted ice. He was now standing in a pool of melted snow that was trickling about his ankles, finding its way to the lowest point of the ground nearby. Mister Fitz, sodden to his neck, was crouched next to him, his wooden fingers cupped around a needle that even so shrouded, shone with a light too bright to address save out of the corner of one's eye. A radiant trail, not so brilliant, marked where the puppet sorcerer had drawn a circle around the three would-be godslayers.

Xavva-Tish-Laqishtax stalked around the circle, ice instantly forming in thick sheets under its feet. Hereward looked at the godlet's current physical form with rather mixed feelings. Eudonia had always hated him, always called him an aberration, even to his face: a boy-child born to a Witch, when the Witches only gave birth to girls. She had wanted him exposed at birth on the cliff tops of the High Pale, a fate only averted because Hereward's mother was one of the Three, the ruling council. Eudonia had also opposed his being taught by Mistress Fitz (as she was then), and later had tried to prevent Hereward and the puppet being sent out as companions on the eternal mission to rid the world of inimical godlets.

Hereward feared her and returned her hatred.

But now he also felt pity.

Xavva-Tish-Laqishtax had retained Eudonia's shape, at least in torso and head. But somewhere along its ravening trail it had obviously felt the need for faster locomotion, because there were two extra sets of human legs fused to Eudonia's middle, with repellent growths of flesh and skinless bundles of muscles and nerves bulging out where the godlet had stuck everything together willy-nilly.

Eudonia's harsh, unforgiving face with its ritual scars was unchanged, save that the stubs of sorcerous needles were embedded in her forehead and through both cheeks, all three still sparking faintly with susurrations of violet energy. Clearly she had resorted to draconian measures in an effort to resist the godlet. Looking at her white, rolled-back eyes, Sir Hereward wondered if deep inside she still fought against the extradimensional being who had invaded her mind and flesh.

Xavva-Tish-Laqishtax approached the circle, reaching out with Eudonia's hands, only to draw them back as sorcerous energy flared, its fingers smoking and blackened. It paid these hurts no heed, not even dipping its hands in the snow, so the fingers continued to slowly burn, skin crackling back to bone. The awful stench wafted across to Hereward, Fitz's sorcerous defence on this occasion not designed to forestall odors.

"Will the circle hold?" croaked Sir Hereward.

"For a time," confirmed Mister Fitz. The puppet was watching the godlet intently. After a few moments, he made a clicking sound with his tongue, which was pierced with a silver stud, perhaps just for this purpose. "I fear I have miscalculated."

"What?" asked Fyltak, his voice quavering.

"It is more cunning than I expected," remarked Mister Fitz, facing the horrific, malformed thing that hosted the godlet's presence in the world.

Xavva-Tish-Laqishtax smiled at the puppet too widely, the skin around Eudonia's mouth splitting like rotten cloth at each end, revealing bone. No blood came from this new wound. Then the godlet turned

and moved away, using all three sets of legs clumsily in a lopsided wad-
dle through the drifts. Snow swirled and followed it, a localized flurry.
Though the godlet moved slowly, within half a minute it was lost to
sight in the gloom of the perpetual winter that followed it everywhere.

"The godlet's turn and pursuit was a bluff," continued Mister Fitz.
He closed his fist completely, concentrating for a moment. When he
opened his hand, the needle he held was nothing more than a sliver of
cold iron, all radiance gone, and the circle around them faded into nothing more than a line of melted snow. "To make me use my remaining
needle in defence. It clearly never intended to press its attack home.
Worse, it has more stored energy to sustain it than I estimated, enough
to reach the manors on the far shore of the Smallest Sea. There it will
gorge itself beyond chance of retribution."

"Yet it is weakened now?" asked Sir Hereward. He was vigorously
rubbing his extremely cold nose, so his words were only just intelligible.
"There was less snow and ice about it then, as it departed, and it was
definitely slower."

"It is diminished," confirmed Mister Fitz. "Our brassards would give
us sufficient protection to close with it now and not be frozen. But we
still do not have any armament that might force it from Eudonia's body,
let alone send it out of this world."

Hereward looked to the sky, shook his fist, and exclaimed, "Kishtyr!"

"Unless, of course there is more to *your* sword than has been supposed," mused Mister Fitz, his round head slowly turning on his thin
neck to fix his gaze upon Fyltak, who stood shivering and wild-eyed at
Hereward's side.

"What kind of puppet are you really?" he asked, his voice as unsteady
as his shivering body.

"A singular one, made for a most particular purpose: dealing with
proscribed extradimensional entities," said Mister Fitz. Though he spoke
in his usual matter-of-fact tone, there was an air of menace in his next
words. "Doing whatever must be done for the safety of the world."

"Mister Fitz is a sorcerer, as much as any of the Witches of Har,"
added Sir Hereward. "More so, in many ways. Come, tell us about your
sword. It might be the only chance for the people whose souls will otherwise be fodder for Xavva by tomorrow's dawn."

"I told you before . . ." Fyltak started to say, but his voice withered under the combined stare of Mister Fitz and Sir Hereward. There was something about the puppet's piercing gaze, in particular, the man was not eager to meet.

"The sword has been in my family a long time," he finally said. "I don't know exactly how long. We have always known it was made to kill . . . banish, I suppose in actuality . . . godlets."

"Show me the blade," commanded Mister Fitz. He drew closer, while Sir Hereward stepped behind Fyltak. The knight's fingers closed slowly into a fist, ready to smash the other man on the side of the head if he chose that moment to try to use his sword rather than merely show it.

But the God-Taker drew the weapon slowly and held it low across his body, angling the sword so the light fell upon the blade. The sky was already clearing, only a few scant snowflakes falling now, and there was even a hint of the sun's presence in the west, a kind of golden backlight to the dissipating clouds. To the east, where Xavva-Tish-Laqishtax was inexorably staggering toward the Smallest Sea, the sky might as well have been painted with coal dust, being entirely black.

Mister Fitz inspected the sword, peering closely at the rippled surface of the blade. There were no obvious marks or inscriptions, at least none visible to Sir Hereward's mortal eyes. But the puppet saw something there.

"Interesting," he said. "This might actually be one of the fabled God-Taker swords of sunken Herenclos."

"Herenclos?" asked Sir Hereward. "But that is an abyss, a molten cleft . . ."

"It was a city once," said Mister Fitz. "Before the earth swallowed it. The city sat above a deep vent that tapped the fires of the underworld, which they used in their smithing. That vent was kept from yawning open by their patron godlet Heren-Par-Quaklin. When that godlet disappeared, the city quite literally fell."

The puppet leaned closer still to the sword and touched the blade with the very tip of his blue tongue.

"Yes," he said. "It is of Herenclos. The last captive of the sword still lingers within. Greatly reduced, but still with some remnant power. Perhaps enough."

"Captive?" asked Fyltak and Sir Hereward, speaking together.

"Yes," said Mister Fitz. "The God-Taker swords were not made to banish the extradimensional, but rather to entrap and use their powers. The smiths of Herenclos were not particular about which godlets served this purpose, often enslaving benign entities as well as those proscribed. I do not know which particular godlet lingers in this blade, nor is there time to capture a slide of its essence . . . what powers does the weapon exhibit, Fyltak?"

"When I wield it, I can see in the dark," said Fyltak slowly. "The world around me moves more slowly, I become impossibly swift and consequently deadly. But this slowing continues . . . if I hold too long to the sword, then everything about me drags to a standstill, people and animals. Everyone and everything, they become as statues and it seems so too does the movement of the air, for however I gasp and struggle, I can draw no new inhalation into my lungs."

"So you can only use the sword as long as you can hold your breath?" asked Sir Hereward.

"Yes," replied Fyltak. "But my family has long raised its children to practice the arts of the sponge divers of Zhelu. I can go without new breath for four or even five minutes at a time. That is why I was given the sword, I was the best of us. So equipped, I took the name of the sword and became known as the God-Taker!"

He was evidently recovering his former boisterous self, the shock of the cold and the close encounter with Xavva-Tish-Laqishtax wearing off.

"Have you actually tried to use the sword against any godlets?" asked Mister Fitz. "Or did you just merely adopt the sword's title and not its activity? I ask because the entity within is very old and somewhat faded, and the sorcerous structures within the steel likewise degraded. I would presume that the sword's use against another godlet would result in the banishment of *both* entities and destruction of the physical hosts."

"With this very hand and blade I slew the Blood-Sipping Ghoul of Lazzarenno!" exclaimed Fyltak.

"No you didn't," said Hereward crossly. "Remember who you're talking to."

"That would be wise," said Mister Fitz. "For any number of reasons."

"Oh, yes, that's right," said Fyltak. He looked nervously at the puppet. "In truth, while I have slain a number of . . . I suppose you might call them hedge wizards and shop sorcerers, I have not yet had the chance to test my mettle against an actual godlet."

"Hedge wizards I am familiar with," said Sir Hereward. "What by Hroggar's beard is . . . what is a shop sorcerer?"

"You know, someone whose powers come from sorcerous trinkets they have purchased," said Fyltak. "Invariably they are scoundrels seeking an easy path to power."

Hereward blinked at this assessment from a man whose own sorcery derived entirely from a sword he had inherited.

"Though you have not proven its worth against a godlet as yet, I think the sword may still be strong enough to do what is needed," said Mister Fitz. "We had best take it and test this assumption before Xavva gets too far ahead."

"Take it? None but I can wield this sword!"

Sir Hereward glanced aside at Mister Fitz, who gave the slightest shake of his head, forestalling the action he knew full well Hereward wanted to undertake: smack Fyltak down and take the weapon.

"Well then, you had best accompany us and wield it against the godlet," said the puppet. He jumped to the basket on Hereward's back. "Let us go, forthwith!"

They had barely gone three steps when Fyltak moved past and began to walk half-backwards so he could face knight and puppet, talking all the while.

"Ah, while of course I wish to take action against this vile godlet," said Fyltak. "What with the cold, and the . . . er . . . spirit-gorging . . . do you have a plan on how to proceed, taking these things into account?"

"It is weakened," said Mister Fitz. "We have sorcerous brassards that provide some protection against such things as Xavva-Tish-Laqishtax. We will don them at a suitable proximity."

"Oh, the agent's brassard!" exclaimed Fyltak. He reached inside his cloak and drew forth a broad silk armband some five fingers wide, embroidered with a symbol of great familiarity to Sir Hereward and Mister Fitz, that of the Council of the Treaty for the Safety of the World. Though the symbol did not glow as it should from the sorcerous thread used to sew it, it was unquestionably genuine and merely quiescent.

Sir Hereward stopped, boots crushing ice emphatically.

"Where did you get that?"

His face was set and hard, his eyes narrowed, his body tensed to take action. The brassards were supposed to fall into dust if they left their owner's possession for more than a night and day, and were carefully handed down from one agent to the next, often as a deathbed ritual.

Once again, Mister Fitz touched Hereward's shoulder, restraining the knight from sudden, lethal action.

"It is also a family heirloom," said Fyltak, oblivious to his danger. "With the sword. Though the old tales say it should light up, brighter than a lantern."

"It will," said Mister Fitz. "May I hold it a moment?"

Fyltak passed the brassard to Mister Fitz, who tasted the silk with his tongue. A ripple of light passed through the silken threads, fading as the puppet handed it back.

"Curious," said Mister Fitz. "It is very old, not some recent find, Hereward. Fyltak must indeed be a descendant of some long-lost agent. The brassard will answer to the invocation, in due course. Come, we must hurry!"

They marched on, the weather around them returning to its more natural state, the air warming and the snow melting. There was still a clot of darkness ahead, but clearly Xavva was saving its strength, for the black cloud no longer stretched across the horizon but was concentrated in an area of a few hundred yards about the godlet.

A few times they caught sight of Xavva itself, for they were descending a broad slope toward the Smallest Sea and there were several sections where it was quite steep and the height extended their view, cloud notwithstanding. But always the snow swirled and closed about the godlet, so they saw little beyond that it was still using three sets of legs in an ungainly motion that provided slightly slower locomotion than the pursuers could manage on their own better-twinned pairs of legs.

"The Simirila have thrown down the bridges," remarked Mister Fitz, who could see more clearly through the snowy cloud. The Smallest Sea was little more than a lake, dotted with many islands, which were connected by a multitude of bridges of many different makes and load capacities, forming a veritable maze of water crossings that usually required a local and not inexpensive guide to navigate, particularly if requiring bridges that might support wagons or draft animals.

"We will catch it on the shore, then," said Sir Hereward. "What do you intend? Don the brassards and close? We two distract Xavva as best we may while Fyltak takes off Eudonia's head with the God-Taker?"

He spoke lightly, but with the clear knowledge that the godlet was almost certainly still potent enough to draw out the life essence of any or all would-be distractors, regardless of the protection offered by the brassards. The only question would be if the godlet could do it quickly enough to avoid the banishing stroke from Fyltak's sword.

"I fear the lack of a bridge does not halt the godlet," replied Mister Fitz, blue eyes bright. "It is making its own, of ice. Come, we must be on the ice it makes before it melts again!"

Sir Hereward broke into a run, the basket bobbing up and down on his back. Fyltak ran at his side, exhibiting none of the puffing and blowing he had done before when they had met him earlier that day, adding credence to his story about how brandishing the sword slowed all around him, including the air.

There was a layer of ice on the muddy shore, which cracked under their bootheels, but the broad swathe that led out across the water looked considerably thicker, much to Sir Hereward's relief. He paused by the shore to drop the basket before testing the ice with his sword. It held against several blows, and he stepped out upon it, causing no cracks or disturbing movement. Despite the thick ice underfoot, it was not particularly cold.

"Xavva expends much of its strength upon the ice bridge," said Mister Fitz, bending down to inspect the newly frozen surface of the lake. "That is good. It is only fifty or sixty yards ahead of us now. Come, don the brassards. We shall do as you suggest, Hereward, the two of us distracting it for Fyltak to make the banishing blow. Fyltak, you must strike for the neck and take the head off with a single blow. Can you do that?"

Fyltak licked his lips nervously, then nodded. He hesitated further for a moment, then drew the lorgnette out of his cuirass and wrapped the cord around his head to keep the lenses balanced on his nose.

"Not the best eyes," he said. "But I can do what must be done. I am Fyltak the God-Taker!"

"After this, you will be indeed," muttered Sir Hereward, who was pulling his brassard over the sleeve of his buff coat, not an easy operation with fingers still numb from cold. He thought, but did not say aloud, "if you live."

"Remember to drop the sword as soon as the stroke is through," instructed Mister Fitz. "Now, slide the brassard up your arm, and we will do the declaration as we hurry along. Repeat what Sir Hereward and I say. Are you ready?"

"Yes. I . . . I am ready."

Knight and puppet spoke together, with Fyltak a few moments behind. The symbol on their brassards shone more brightly with every word, the God-Taker's no less brilliant, for all its antiquity.

"In the name of the Council of the Treaty for the Safety of the World, acting under the authority granted by the Three Empires, the Seven Kingdoms, the Palatine Regency, the Jessar Republic, and the Forty Lesser Realms, we declare ourselves agents of the Council. We identify the godlet manifested on the ice ahead as Xavva-Tish-Laqishtax, a listed entity under the Treaty. Consequently, the said godlet and all those who assist it are deemed to be enemies of the World and the Council authorizes us to pursue any and all actions necessary to banish, repel, or exterminate the said godlet."

When they finished the declaration, Fyltak had a broad smile upon his face.

They had been walking while they spoke, but now Mister Fitz urged them to move more quickly.

"Faster! The godlet sprints for an island, and the fools have only thrown down the closer bridges!"

The puppet ran ahead, bending almost double and using his hands as well as his feet, his spindly limbs making him all too reminiscent of some injured spider that had lost half its legs. Sir Hereward galloped after him, both pistols drawn, with Fyltak close behind, who had not yet drawn his sword.

As they ran, the snow cloud ahead dissipated, pulling apart to become mere streaks across the sky. They saw Xavva clearly, a hundred yards short of the closest island. But it was not moving straight for the shore. Two of its legs were trying to take it back the way it had come, and the others were straining to go forwards, resulting in a crabwise, sprawling motion.

"Eudonia has risen within it!" cried Mister Fitz. "Quickly now!"

He matched action to his words, drawing his triangular blade to send it whirring through the air as fast as a crossbow bolt. It struck one of the added-on legs above the knee, inflicting a terrible wound, but not severing it as he had hoped. The knife, deeply embedded in bone, stuck there. Fitz reached inside his sleeves and drew two more blades, longer and sharper versions of the sorcerous needles he more commonly used.

Sir Hereward paused, went down on one knee, aimed for a second and fired both pistols at the midsection of the godlet. One ball whizzed past. The other struck, but as far as he could tell had no effect. The knight threw the pistols aside and drew his sword, charging onward with a wild shout he hoped would serve to distract the attention of the godlet from the real attack, delivered by Fyltak.

Who slipped over on the ice and fell, the God-Taker sword sliding from his grasp.

At that moment, Xavva stopped, reached down to break a splintered piece of fallen bridge out of the ice, and turned to its pursuers, raising its makeshift weapon over its head. An oak beam longer than Hereward was tall, this terrible club was liberally dotted with iron bolts, and a single blow would doubtless be fatal.

The godlet advanced on Hereward, who slipped and skidded backwards in an effort to arrest his forward momentum. Mister Fitz circled around the godlet, needles ready, but even if he could successfully close, it was doubtful sharp steel could do more than irritate it.

Fyltak got to his feet. His lorgnette had fallen off, but he still spotted his sword upon the ice. He staggered over to it and lifted it with both hands.

But the godlet paid him no attention, apparently completely fixated on Sir Hereward. It was only as it got closer he saw that Eudonia's eyes were open now, albeit crazed and washed with the violent violet light of remnant energy from the sorcerous needles.

"Aberration!" spat the witch's mouth. Clearly, the godlet was no longer fully in charge of the body, but this was not the hoped-for improvement Sir Hereward and Mister Fitz had counted on, as his great-

great-aunt's animosity to the boy-witch had remained when so much else of her personality had been eroded in the long contest with the godlet.

"Aunt Eudonia!" cried Hereward. He retreated again, but he could feel the ice cracking and shifting under his bootheels. Now the witch was back in charge, the godlet was not freezing the water. "I charge you to assist us as an Agent of the Treaty!"

"Vile spawn," muttered the witch, following these words with a sudden smashing blow with the bridge timber that sent a fountain of exploded ice up into the air. Hereward leapt aside as the club came down, and scuttled sideways for more solid ice, but his foot broke through and he fell forwards. Twisting around, he raised his sword in a futile attempt to block a further blow, just as Mister Fitz jumped to the witch's shoulders and plunged his needles into the witch's insane eyes.

Eudonia—or the godlet, or both—screamed. But it was a scream of rage rather than pain. It threw the timber away, narrowly missing Sir Hereward, and one hand grabbed Mister Fitz and hurled him away too, far away, over the ice and into the water.

Sir Hereward freed his foot and crawled on his elbows and knees over the ice, faster than he had ever crawled before. Half of him hoped the godlet or Eudonia or Xavva or whatever the thing behind him currently was would follow and be distracted, and half of him desperately hoped it wouldn't.

At the edge of the island, he hit mud instead of ice, rolled over, and looked back. Xavva *was* following him, blind face pressed close to the lake surface, nose sniffing, hands reaching, head twitching from side to side as it sought to catch sounds as well as scent.

Fyltak was behind it, moving with a peculiarly swift and liquid grace, the God-Taker sword raised high, the brassard bright upon his arm.

"Eudonia! Xavva! Over here!" screamed Sir Hereward, as he drew himself to his feet and readied himself to run as best he could.

The godlet sprang up too, its legs bunched to spring forwards, just as Fyltak swung his sword. The blade met the thing's neck and cut through with a sound like the mainmast of a great ship snapping in a hurricane or an overpowered siege cannon blowing itself apart. The blade burned away like a powder trail as Fyltak finished the cut, but the head toppled from the neck and rolled across the ice, which in that same moment was crazed with a thousand cracks.

Fyltak dropped the sword hilt, emitted a euphoric shout, took one step and fell through the ice into the Smallest Sea. A moment later the unnaturally chilled waters also claimed the God-Taker sword hilt and burned-out stub of a blade, and the body and head of Eudonia, with or without the godlet still within.

Sir Hereward took three swift steps into the now-open water, which was littered with tiny chunks of ice similar to those chipped into the cool drinks of that same city of Simiril which lay ahead and supplied Fyltak's coffee, but he stopped when the water came to his waist. He was too heavily clothed and booted to swim, and the water was very cold. Besides, there was a small chance that Xavva-Tish-Laqishtax was not in fact banished after all.

He looked around for Mister Fitz, fully expecting the puppet to have swum ashore. The puppet had done so, but Sir Hereward was shocked to see Mister Fitz's upper body in its dripping blue jacket was canted to one side at an odd angle. Though made of papier-mâché and wood, the puppet was constructed of sorcerous versions of said materials, which were extraordinarily difficult to damage. But here he was, most evidently damaged.

"You are injured!" exclaimed Hereward, rushing to his side. But the puppet waved him off.

"It is nothing," he said. "Merely the alignment of a joint in my spine, which I will adjust as soon as my sewing case is replenished. Have you seen any sign the godlet persists? Movement under the water?"

"No," replied Hereward, turning to gaze upon the ice-cube-spattered waters. "Yes! There!"

A shadow was moving under the water. Sir Hereward and Mister Fitz drew back as it broke through the surface in a sudden explosion of ice cubes.

Fyltak stood there, huffing and blowing and shivering, before quickly wading in to be greeted with a comradely backslap from Sir Hereward, who was rapidly readjusting his views on his unlooked-for ally.

"I thought you drowned for certain!" exclaimed the knight. "In cuirass and boots and cloak, no man could swim ashore!"

"Nor could they," coughed Fyltak. "I walked upon the bottom of the lake. I told you I was trained in the arts of the sponge divers of Zhelu."

"And I am glad of it!" exclaimed Sir Hereward. "Ah, did you perchance see anything of Xavva-Tish-Laqishtax while you were down there?"

Fyltak jumped and twisted about to look behind him.

"No!" he cried, suddenly shaking even more. "I had thought . . . it is banished is it not!"

"I am not certain it is," replied Mister Fitz. "The water clouds my sight . . ."

The lopsided puppet shifted clumsily, turning his whole body rather than just his head, to gaze upon a stretch of water some fifty yards distant.

"It is still here," he said. "Greatly diminished, but still here."

Even as he spoke, a ghastly, headless thing crawled out of the lake on all fours. It had lost not only its head, but the extra legs as well, torn off in the explosion caused by the conjoining of godlet-possessed sword and the entity within Eudonia's body. Despite raw gaping wounds at neck and hip, no blood flowed.

It did not attempt to stand, but moved fully onto the land, pausing to shake itself, an unnerving sight given that it had no head.

"What . . . what do we do?" asked Fyltak.

"Move away quietly," said Mister Fitz in a whisper. The puppet followed his own advice, stepping out swiftly and surely though his torso remained twisted. "Tread lightly, breathe shallowly, stay calm."

"But it has no head, it cannot hear . . . or see us," said Fyltak as he too hurried away, glancing anxiously back over his shoulder.

"There are other senses," replied Mister Fitz. "I fear it will be swift, once it locates us. But if we make that bridge, perhaps we can lure it into the water once more . . . Hereward! Why do you stop?"

Fyltak ran on for several steps, only stopping when he realized Fitz had turned back. Puppet and knight were looking to the sky, but Fyltak could not tear his gaze away from the headless, broken thing that was now scuttling like a spider in a zigzag, backwards and forwards where Fyltak had first left the water, somehow finding a trail of energetic scent or something of that kind.

Suddenly, a vast shadow passed over men and puppet, accompanied by a long, falling shriek of titanic proportion. Fyltak thrust his hands against his ears and cowered down, all courage leeched away by this new addition to their woes.

But Sir Hereward kept looking up, a smile lifting the corner of his mouth. A moonshade swept past overhead, its enormous leathery wings spread wide, a hundred and twenty feet or more. It turned its big-as-a-house, furred, bat-like head down and fixed Sir Hereward with one sharp black eye, an eye greater in diameter than the knight was tall. Opening its pink-lined, sharp-toothed, elongated jaw, it gave vent once more to its greeting call.

The witch who sat securely on the tall chair on its back, seemingly grown of the same shiny black bone as the creature's spine, added to the creature's screech with a jaunty wave. Sir Hereward smiled, for though she was very late, Kishtyr was one of his favorite cousins, and a former lover besides, who might well be one again. The Council back at the High Pale would not be expecting her to return for at least another week.

But far more significantly Kishtyr was suitably equipped with both a god-slaying relic and a full sewing desk of sorcerous needles. The husk of Eudonia and the diminished extradimensional entity Xavva-Tish-Laqishtax within would offer her no challenges. She would swiftly banish the godlet and give whatever might remain of the woman peace.

Hereward lost his smile at the thought of Great-great-aunt Eudonia's head still somewhere out there under the lake's clouded surface. Pierced by three sorcerous needles and infused with an indomitable will that would not even surrender to a godlet, it was possible that Eudonia still lived—after a fashion—inside that sunken head. Kishtyr's task might not be as straightforward as he had supposed, and worse, she might enlist him to go fishing. He most certainly did not want to hook and land Eudonia's separated head . . .

"What is that?" asked Fyltak, creeping up to man and puppet. He could see that whatever it was, its arrival had disturbed the remnant relict of Xavva-Tish-Laqishtax, which had retreated back to the lakeshore and was now trying to bury itself in the mud, presumably in an effort to conceal itself from this new, airborne nemesis.

"It is a moonshade, bearing a Witch of Har," answered Mister Fitz, responding literally, as was his wont. "The long-awaited Kishtyr, in fact."

The huge flying creature turned about to land on the longer and broader shore on the northern side of their current island. Despite their enormous size, moonshades were nimble and agile flyers, and could set down in a space only a little longer than their own length. Once landed, they could fold their wings up remarkably small, as this one was in the process of doing. They were in fact deceptive in their size, being mostly leathery skin and thin bones, with a little black fur dabbed here and there. Though, even when all was said and done, it was still a monster roughly the size of a watchtower laid on its side.

"More to the point," said Sir Hereward, dragging the smaller man upright and draping his arm over his shoulder in a comradely fashion. "The moonshade and the witch who rides it represent an opportunity which I believe we should take at once."

"An opportunity?"

"To shuck off our cares and responsibility, and hie ourselves to yonder Simiril, where I will purchase both of us some more of that excellent coffee."

He paused and added with a wink to the puppet: "And some sweet oil, for I, for one, would like to hear Mister Fitz sing!"

Ellen Kushner

• • •

Ellen Kushner's first novel, *Swordspoint*, introduced readers to Riverside, home of the city to which she has since returned in *The Privilege of the Sword* (a Locus Award winner and Nebula nominee), *The Fall of the Kings* (written with Delia Sherman), a handful of related short stories, and, most recently, the collaborative Riverside prequel *Tremontaine* for SerialBox.com and Saga Press. The author herself recorded all three novels in audiobook form for Neil Gaiman Presents/Audible.com, winning a 2012 Audie Award for *Swordspoint*. With Holly Black, she coedited *Welcome to Bordertown*, a revival of the original urban-fantasy shared-world series created by Terri Windling. A popular performer and public speaker, Ellen Kushner created and hosted the long-running public radio show *Sound & Spirit*, which Bill Moyers called "the best thing on public radio." She has taught creative writing at the Clarion and Odyssey workshops, and is an instructor in Hollins University's Children's Literature M.F.A. program. She lives in New York City with Delia Sherman and no cats whatsoever, in an apartment full of theater and airplane ticket stubs.

Here she introduces us to a young man newly arrived in Riverside to seek his fortune, one who, like many young men come to the big city before him, finds that he's got a lot to learn to succeed—and that many of the lessons aren't pleasant.

◆ ◆ ◆

When I Was a Highwayman

ELLEN KUSHNER

"Do it," Jess said. "It'll be fun."

I had no wish to be a highwayman, even for a day, but we needed the money. So I considered it.

Since I had come to Riverside, I had learned that not everyone there gives a stranger from the country good advice. If Riversiders advise a new blade to challenge that guy over there by the fire to a duel—you can take him, no problem!—well, it's lucky that you do turn out to be better than he is. Of course, now he hates you and won't recommend you for any jobs uptown, which is where the glory and the money are. Bad advice.

But since Jessamyn and I had begun keeping company toward the end of winter, I'd learned she usually had my best interests at heart, especially when it came to advice about making money. She was expert at that herself: the cleverest con artist the city had to offer, according to her admirers, and the slyest shyster ever to pick a pocket, according to the others.

Jessamyn was pretty, too. A mane of moon-pale hair such as I'd never seen before, fun to get tangled in at night, fun to braid up tight in the morning so she looked like a middle-city girl, decent yet delectable. That was how she played her game.

We made a good pair. *Silver and smoke; ice and steel,* people said. I could go anywhere with her: suddenly, all the taverns of Riverside were open to me, even the Maiden's Fancy, where women like Flash Annie and Kathy Blount told one another their secrets. Everyone knew Jess, and if they didn't like her, at least they admired her skill—and the way she took marks in uptown. She knew the handkerchief trick, the Lost Baby trick, the Pigeon Drop, and the Lover's Dare.

I never went on jobs with her, though, because it was important for people to know my face if I was going to get work—and it was very, *very* important that no one remember hers.

Jessamyn had a wardrobe a duchess would envy, for quantity if not for quality: velvet with the nap rubbed away in back, raveled silk stockings, lace frontlets and silk shawls stained underneath, ribbons in every color imaginable to trim and retrim her many hats, feathers picked up on the street—

"It just has to *look* right, Richard," she'd explain. "No one's going to lift up my fine linen skirt to see the patched petticoats underneath. If I paint a thing gold, and wear it like it's gold, only a jeweler will know it's not." She arched her neck, laughing. "And I never get anywhere near a real jeweler, so that's no problem."

I stroked the nape of her smooth neck, where the soft hair grew in an arrow shape. "I'll get you near a real one. We're going to make money, Jessamyn—*I'm* going to make it. A swordsman can get rich in this town. Look at Rivers. And de Maris, before his last fight. I'm going to be better than them. And then we'll go up to Lassiter's Row and buy you gold earrings with jewels in them, the biggest they've got!"

I didn't know much about jewels, then; not their names, nor what they were worth, really. I just liked the way they sparkled, catching the sun with a rainbow's fire. I'd only seen my first diamond, at a merchant's wedding I was playing guard at. I'd thought it was a composite of all other jewels, compressed into one, till someone set me right.

Jess and I shared a couple of rooms upstairs in a crumbling old house on a narrow street full of them. Like its neighbors, it had been grand and glorious once, before the rich abandoned Riverside to move over the Bridge into the rest of the city. Our two rooms still had carvings and fancy molding clinging to the peeling walls. There was plenty of space for Jess's massive collection of costumes. The house's owner was a laundress who plied her trade in the courtyard's ancient stone well and rented out her upstairs rooms by the week, which suited us fine.

Whenever either of us got—or did—a job, we'd pay Marie her rent first, then go out and spend the rest on whatever pleased our fancy: dresses and hats and fine cloaks for Jessamyn (really just business, she explained), and whatever pretty flotsam had turned up in the Old Market at the heart of Riverside: stuff salvaged from crumbling houses, things no one could pawn, like cracked porcelain vases, a fragment of gilded picture frame, a carved boxwood figure with its arms missing.

The money for that, I got from working a wedding uptown: the most boring job in the world. I always felt ridiculous with my sword out and that stupid wreath on my head, marching behind the bridal party to the temple, then standing there on display while the priests read the same words over each couple. It's not as though anyone was ever coming to actually steal away the bride.

Jess said it was a way to get noticed, and I was lucky I looked good in a wreath. "You're, what, barely eighteen?" she'd ask, knowing perfectly well I wasn't even that yet. "There's time."

But I hadn't come to the city to stand around watching people get married. Everyone here in Riverside knew I was a serious duelist; sometimes I was able to prove it there, when another swordsman got fresh with Jess, or a new blade came down looking for trouble and decided to see if I was any good.

Still, it was from working a wedding that I finally got a chance to prove myself to the ones who counted. I'd gotten the job because Hugo Seville was already scheduled for a demonstration duel at some Hill noble's birthday party, lucky stiff, so he'd passed the wedding job on to me.

"I'm recommending you because I know you'll do your best," he said pompously, as though there was real effort involved in standing very still and not scratching your nose. "These people are important, Richard. Lord Hastings never comes to town, but he's here to marry off his seventh daughter to Condell's eldest."

I could never remember their names; I just put on my clean shirt and my blue doublet, polished my boots, and went over the Bridge.

It was a very fancy wedding. A whole band of musicians walked us to the temple, not just one or two flute players. Little girls tossed lavender and rosemary in the bride's path; when we stepped on the herbs, the scent made me suddenly homesick for my mother's garden.

I wasn't the only swordsman, either. Lord Hastings had a House Sword who walked beside me, a tall, quiet, older man who didn't want trouble; I could tell by the way he gave me enough space, and I appreciated that.

Lord Hastings' blade and I left the temple together, well after the musicians had played the wedding party and their guests away. Our part was done; I guess the bride belonged to her husband's family, now. Hastings' swordsman was no Riversider: maybe one of those men who learn from an academy, or even from their fathers, and make their way up in a nobleman's service, fighting exhibition duels, doing weddings, showing off grace and form, and standing ready in case anyone tries to challenge their noble masters. I'd never really gotten the chance to talk to one of them; the last wedding with two swords, the other wouldn't answer any questions, and when I challenged him after, he spat and called me Riverside guttertrash, the poser.

I was beginning to think about asking Lord Hastings' quiet swordsman how to get work as a duelist uptown, when suddenly he staggered and fell against the wall.

"Are you hurt?" I said. He was very pale.

A woman in a simple dress with bright starched cap and collar came running up. "Oh, George, George, I told you you were too ill for this today!"

"Marjorie." He grinned feebly at her. "How could I disappoint his lordship, after all this time? And little Amilette . . . Lucky Seventh, right? Didn't she look lovely?"

"You're going to disappoint him even more, now, for you're in no fit shape to duel for the guests at the party."

He'd started shivering; some kind of fever, I guessed. There were a lot of those in the city. "They've seen me fight before. Many times. They'll like seeing someone new. What's your name, boy?"

I let the "boy" go because he was so ill.

"Richard St. Vier."

"Of the banking St. Viers?" the woman asked.

"Do I look like a banker?" But I said it with a smile; I'd gotten used to that question here. (My mother had once been a daughter of that family—but that was no one's business but hers.) "I am a swordsman, madam, and I would be happy to take up this duel if you will tell me where to go."

"Come, George." She had her arms around him. "I'll take you home. And you, Master St. Vier, if you could just give me a hand with him—No, of course you don't need one, George, but I do!—I'll give you directions to Lord Condell's. You've got plenty of time; there's all the eating and drinking before the entertainment."

I'd never been up on the Hill before, where the nobles' fine houses were. They didn't want you there if you weren't working for them. But this time I was, so I walked boldly along the wide, open streets lined with the walls and massive iron gates of great houses on either side. An occasional carriage passed me—one of theirs, flash with high-headed horses and glitzy harness—or a liveried servant, on foot, out on some errand I couldn't imagine.

At Lord Condell's house I gave my name, explained my business, and assured them that I was not there to challenge their master at his son's wedding feast. They reminded me that I was to use the *back* entrance, but that Cook might have something hot for me.

Lord Condell's servants were all madly busy with the feast and didn't have time for me. So I went out to the side yard to warm up and practice my moves until someone came out to tell me it was time.

The duel was to be held in the entry hall of the house. Very dressed-up people encircled the space, many of them on the landing to the main stairs, and more of them crowding the stairs themselves or leaning from the upstairs balcony. I walked slowly, trying to look like I knew what I was doing. The people didn't matter, but my opponent did.

He was a fair man of about my size and reach. I stood across the hall from him while a liveried man announced:

"For the honor and pleasure of the bride and groom, the duel will be to first blood, or until one man yields."

I knew about first blood. It could mean a scratch, a slash, or a deep puncture wound. I imagined duels at a wedding feast called for just a scratch, and took a long breath to remind myself to go no further in this bout.

After a few more formalities, it began.

My opponent and I moved slowly, testing, observing, as is right. We circled each other. The crowd was silent. In Riverside, they would have started shouting bets already. I made a feint to see what he'd do, and he did nothing but raise his eyebrows and cock up one corner of his mouth at me. Not easily drawn. This was going to be a longer fight than I'd expected.

We let the swords converse a little, back and forth, feeling each other's strength in the pressure of the blades, trying to hide our real abilities from each other. Suddenly his high wrist dropped and he struck low, like a swooping falcon; but I'd felt it coming and countered easily. He stepped back, surprised, to give himself time to assess, and to avoid me.

Once they start stepping back, you have them. I pressed forward, forward, forward, quickly, not giving him time to think, showing off a new move every time for those who could see fast enough, wanting to impress them all. He defended himself ably, but I never let him pick up an attack, just kept pushing him back.

He was a pleasure to fight because I knew it would be hard to make my touch on him but that he didn't stand a chance at hitting me. When we closed together with our *quillons* crossed, he hissed at me, "What are you doing? Fall back!"

I understood his words only well enough to gasp, "What? No!"

He turned his blade so that we half circled each other, still close together. "This is for their entertainment! They want to see some back-and-forth!"

I disengaged, sliding my blade back along his, until their tips alone touched. We messed around like that for a bit, like some kind of kiddie training exercise, circling each other, circling the blades ... The noble guests were enchanted. They seemed to think something was happening, and started shouting encouragement. I saw a woman's face, very white, her hands twisting a handkerchief as though there were real danger here. Were these the arbiters of skill, the people I was so eager to impress?

My opponent thought he held the match in his hand, that having acceded to his suggestion, I would let him control the finish. With a triumphant grin, he advanced ferociously.

I fell back just long enough to gauge my distance and leap in over his blade, touching him in the upper breast as gently as I could manage. It drew blood. The bout was over.

My opponent bowed, and was helped away by a footman. I stood there in the hallway with shouts of "Blood!" and "Bravo!" ringing in my ears, wondering what I should do next. A servant brought me a silver cup filled with a cool drink. When I'd emptied it, the nobles started crowding around me, congratulating me, asking my name, how long had I been in Lord Hastings' employ, did I take commissions, what was my next fight, where could they find me . . . ?

To be honest, it was a little too much. Success was wonderful, new jobs were wonderful, but the people all moving in and out of my vision, arms and hands and heads, right after I'd been fighting—

"Richard St. Vier," I said. "My name is St. Vier, and you can find me in Riverside. At the, ah, the Maiden's Fancy. Thank you. Yes, thank you. I must—I have to go and clean my blade. Really. It's important. If you'd just let me through—"

"Absolutely."

A young man with soft, curling brown hair and one red jewel in his ear raised a hand where I could see it, and slowly put his arm around my shoulder. They fell back a little when he did that, and I was grateful. "You must go and refresh yourself, Master St. Vier. Allow me to assist you."

The crowds parted for us. He was in lace and velvet: one of them. "Have you been paid?" he murmured. I shook my head. "Well, never mind. Condell is busy now; you can come back tomorrow. "

Instead of away toward the kitchens, he led me out the big front door. The air on the steps was cooler. "Just a moment," he said. "Stay here while I send for my carriage."

The seats in the nobleman's carriage were soft as down. It smelt a little of leather, a little of horses, and a little of the man himself, a scent like roses and amber.

"My name is Thomas Berowne," he told me. He rested his gloved hand on my leg for a moment, and I let him. "Please allow me to take you wherever you wish to go." He ducked his head slightly. "This includes my own rooms if you would be so kind as to have it so."

I thought, Why not? Jess wouldn't mind; she was out some nights herself, keeping up contacts, solidifying friendships, forging alliances or just plain having fun. She might even be pleased to learn that I had been taken home by a lordling.

Lord Thomas Berowne was courtesy itself. When we came to his family town house, we took a side entrance, "so as not to alarm my parents," and went up one set of stairs then another, into a room all rosy with velvet and firelight, shadows playing on a glint of painting here, a fall of tapestry there.

He was beautiful without his clothes on, and he knew how to please me. My boyhood friend Crispin and I had had our little rituals, but Thomas Berowne was a grown man who clearly had a lot of practice. All that night, when I woke to the fall of the light on his skin, or the candles guttering, or a glass of wine being sleepily handed to me, I felt oddly safe, and oddly happy. He asked very few questions, but I found myself telling him about my hopes for work, my wish to challenge worthy opponents, to duel to my utmost strength and skill. Until I had come to the city, I hadn't realized I was that good. I thought everyone could do what I do, more or less, with the right training. My drunk old master, a wanderer my mother had taken in off the road out of pity, who had trained me mercilessly, always told me not to be too sure of myself. I took that to heart. But he had also taught me how to assess an opponent and how to take advantage of their every weakness. The men I'd fought so far in the confines of Riverside were no match for me; those who were steered clear of my sword. There were no demonstration bouts in Riverside.

Thomas Berowne was only a little older than me—not yet twenty, as he admitted, and so, though his father was rich, he wasn't, and he was also a second son. What funds he had went to collecting objects of art, and he hoped I didn't take offense if he said I was one of the finest, ". . . not that I could afford your true price."

I asked what he thought that was, wondering uneasily if he was planning to pay me. That would make me a nobleman's whore, which was far from my ambition. He kissed me, said this was an open exchange of willing hearts. He said that my skill with the sword might be for the marketplace, but when it came to . . . Well, I can't honestly remember what he said, but it was along those lines.

You couldn't exactly call it morning when we finally got out of bed to drink the chocolate his valet had brought in. It was amazing stuff; you couldn't get anything like that in Riverside. There were crisp white rolls, too, and butter so sweet it must have come from the country.

In the light of day, I admired the nobleman's treasures: the tapestry of lovers in a rose garden that covered half a wall; the ancient chest carved with deer and oak leaves, gleaming with beeswax . . . even the bed curtains were works of art, embroidered with moons and stars.

I picked up something small, an ivory statue of a boy king, with his many braids and naked chest, barely bigger than my palm. "I know you can't afford a swordsman," I told him lightly, trying not to want it too much. "But I'd fight a challenge for this."

Thomas Berowne's lips curved. His curly hair was tousled, and his mouth was the kissable color of certain roses. "You have good taste," he said. "You could fight a dozen challenges for that, and still not come near its worth."

I put it down carefully.

"Now then." Lord Thomas kissed my shoulder. "I am expected somewhere, and I imagine you are, too. It will, however, take me much longer to be made presentable to the outside world, so if you'd like me to call my carriage to carry you up to Lord Condell's—"

I shook my head. Their houses were so close I was amazed that he felt the need to ride between them.

"Well, then," Lord Thomas said; "let me assist you in dressing, to make up for being so eager to undress you last night."

As he slipped the linen shirt over my head, I realized that it was much finer than my own. I didn't say anything; he probably had chests full of them, and if this was the gift he wanted to give me, well, having a third shirt to my name was only to the good.

I found Jessamyn at the Maiden's Fancy, drinking with our friend Kathy Blount.

"Well, if it isn't the great St. Vier!" Jess tipped her chair back. "And here I thought you'd run off with the bride."

"She wouldn't have me," I said casually. "So I fought a duel instead."

"Yeah, at Lord Condell's; I heard." I'd been looking forward to telling her myself. "Nimble Willie was just up there, checking it out for Kathy's ma and her gang. He went as a delivery boy, and they were all bragging about your fight in the kitchens."

I spilled Lord Condell's coins on the table in front of her. Kathy, at least, had the grace to look impressed. Jess just grabbed one and held it up like a prize. "Rosalie! This is for the tab—and for another round. For the house! For luck! For Annie."

She was far from sober. "Where's Annie?" I said. "What happened?"

Kathy wiped her eyes with the back of her hand. "Annie got nabbed. Yesterday morning. They whipped her today, in Justice Place. Jessamyn went, and I went with her. So she knew we both was there in the crowd."

"*Were* there," Jess corrected savagely. "You'll never make it uptown if you talk like that, Kath. You'll end up just like Annie, rotten straw from the jail in your hair, your dress torn open for them to see your tits while they whip you for stealing what they wish they had—"

"Shut up!" Kathy pushed back from the table so fast her bench tipped over. "You just shut up, Jessamyn Fancypants! You think you're any better? You may be able to pass uptown for an hour's grift, but you drink and you fuck down here in Riverside with the rest of us."

I knew Kath had a knife up her sleeve, but she made no move to use it, so I just watched as she knuckled her eyes with her fist, rose, and dashed out of the tavern.

Jess made a face.

"Cheapskate didn't even pay her tab," she said. She took another coin from my pile. "But that's all right. We've got plenty to spend, now, love, haven't we? Let's go see if Salamander still has that snake-headed dagger you liked."

I put my hand over hers. "Rent first," I said. "That's the rule. And while we're back there, maybe we should go upstairs." I put my hands behind her head, weaving my fingers in her moonlight hair, and I kissed her there in the tavern, I wanted her so much.

She slid her free hand down my thigh. "Rules are rules," she said. "Let's go pay the rent and have some fun."

The snake-headed dagger was gone, but Salamander had a plain one with a balance so perfect it could have been made for me. We got that, and a dagger made of glass because it was just so unbelievable, and bangles for Jess that Sal said came from Cham, and five silver forks that ended in nymph's heads. Then we went over to Maddie's to see what clothing she had in. Jessamyn carefully scrutinized all the servants' cast-offs for the best, dresses made over from hand-me-downs of generous mistresses that could be tarted up to look new. She found a skirt and petticoat almost perfect, and a bundle of collars and neckerchiefs Mad let her have for cheap because they'd been scorched by a careless ironing maid. Jessamyn spent some time cooing over an old bodice of gold thread brocade, most of its tiny silk rosettes still intact, but then said she had no use for it. I bought it for her anyway, just for fun. We found plenty of use for it back home.

We went on spending freely because we knew there would be more. And, that spring, there was. Nobles started sending emissaries down to the Maiden, offering me jobs. Demonstration bouts, mostly, for parties and things—still no actual duels, but Jess and our friend Ginnie Vandall said to be patient, that was how you got noticed. Ginnie knew everything about swordsmen.

She didn't like it when I turned down Lord Condell's offer to spend a month on his summer estates. I told her I'd just come from the country, and I didn't want to turn around and go back there. I didn't say I didn't want to leave Jess for so long, but that was clear.

◆　◆　◆

Then Jess got pregnant, despite all our care, and it was expensive to get rid of it. She was sick for a while after and couldn't go out on jobs. That was when the money started drying up for me, too. I went over all my recent paying duels, trying to figure out what I'd done wrong. Was I too predictable? Should I have let someone beat me, just the once?

"I could have told you," Ginnie said. "Take all the work while you can get it! Yeah, even the weddings, Richard. Because guess what? Summer's coming, and they all go to the country. Not just Lord Condell. No one needs a swordsman here in summer."

"Richard only takes the jobs he wants, now." Jess coiled around me on the settle like a big white cat. We both knew Ginnie fancied me like mad, but whatever I got up to on the Hill, I had only one love in Riverside. "He's sick of weddings. Everyone knows he's the best. We'll be just fine till their lordships come home in the fall and start having fun again."

First we had to pawn the nymph forks. And sell the brocade bodice, then pawn Jessamyn's winter clothes. "I'll get them back," she said with a shrug. "Soon as I'm better."

When that day came we braided her hair up tight again, and she went across the Bridge to find a mark and make some money with the Turned-Out Servant Girl trick.

"I'm thin enough now." She grinned at me. "It'll be a snap."

Jess came home with a kerchief full of apples, bread and new cheese, and we gorged ourselves on food and kisses. But when I lifted her skirts, I found her petticoats were gone.

"I'll get them back," she said fiercely. "It's my stuff, I can do what I want with it. I just wasn't ready, yet."

I sold the green glass, and the armless statue, because the Salamander wouldn't take them in pawn. Maddie bought back most of Jess's linen—"Your luck will turn," she said, and pressed one of the scorched collars back into Jessamyn's hands. "A girl's got to earn a living. Don't worry, love, I've seen it before. You'll come around."

If there were any wedding jobs, I would have taken them. But it seemed summer wasn't a good time for weddings, either.

That was when Marco and Ivan came up with their grand scheme.

We were drinking at Rosalie's, because her tavern is underground, in the cellar of an old town house. The cellar was god-awful damp in winter, but in summer it was a blessing. Even her beer was relatively cool—and Rosalie was one of the few who still let us eat on credit.

"Richard St. Vier!" They strolled on up to our table, feathers in their hats and a swagger in their stride. "Have you ever been on the highway?"

"Of course I've been on the highway. How do you think I got here?"

Ivan poked Marco in the ribs. "I like this kid. He's got a sense of humor."

Jess just sat there with a little smile at the corner of her lips, watching the show.

"Richard." Marco leaned into the table. He was unarmed, so I let him. "Where do you think this hat came from? Or these buckles? Or these shoes?" I waited. They were really ugly buckles. "From noblemen's coaches, that's where. Out on the highway. Where they pass to and fro without a care, just waiting for gentlemen like us to stop and relieve them of some of their gold."

"And personal effects," said Ivan, stroking the world's gaudiest hat-pin.

Marco turned to Jessamyn. "There are ladies, too, you know. Miserable old hags wearing silks and jewels they shoulda left off long ago, to adorn some younger, sprightlier dame."

Jessamyn nodded. "Go on, Richard," she said brightly. "You should try it! You can get me some new petticoats."

I asked, "What would I have to do?"

"There's a carriage coming by," Marco said. "Tomorrow morning. Carrying all kinds of fancy stuff. I had it from Fat Tom, whose brother's wife's cousin works up on the Hill and knows the guy who's driving. All we have to do is lie in wait at a particular bend in the road we happen to be familiar with, well hid from any passersby. You step out and challenge the driver. The coach stops, and—"

Who did they think I was? "I'm not challenging any driver!" A sword fights only other swords.

Jess stroked my arm. "You don't challenge him, not really. Just get him to stop."

"Or we can do that," Ivan said hastily. "We can stop him, if you want. It just looks better when you do it. You know, with a sword."

"But there's a guard," Marco explained. "A footman, usually, not a blade, but trained with knives and stuff. Sometimes two of them. Plus the coachman. That's where you come in."

"Scare 'em off. They'll know what swords can do. They respect that. You just round 'em up and keep 'em still. Look menacing. Don't let 'em pull any tricks, while we rifle the coach, then we're off!"

"Off in the bushes, or off on a horse?" Jess asked.

Marco looked pious. "We always rent Brown Bess. She is most reliable, and has a very smooth trot."

"She's not going to carry three."

"They're not going to chase after a swordsman."

It sounded like hell to me. "I'd rather do weddings." But that wasn't entirely true. And Jess knew it.

"At least you'll get to fight, Richard," she said; "or pretend to, anyway. You can fix them with that awful stare you get when you're practicing. And I promise you won't be bored."

"Easy money," Marco said.

"Do it," Jess said. "It'll be fun!"

I was plenty bored.

Marco and Ivan appeared on Brown Bess at the white part of dawn, when many Riversiders were just coming home off jobs. They let me ride up behind them, and we plodded along the highway for a long time, until we came to their particular spot. Ivan tied up Bess in the woods, and we lay on a verge in the still-damp grass, watching the road.

And watching the road. And watching the road. I fell asleep for a little bit; then Ivan nudged me with a "Here they come!" but it was only a delivery cart, its two mules laboring slowly up the slope.

"Remember," Marco murmured when it had passed. "Don't kill anyone. It is very important that you don't kill anyone."

"Why?"

"For robbery, you get jailed and lashed. For murder, you swing. All of us."

I said nothing. "Yeah," said Ivan; "it's a funny old world. You kill a guy in a duel for them, it's right as rain, no questions asked. We kill someone by accident while trying to make a living, and it's up the gibbet to do the Solo Jig."

"Of course," Marco added, "if you do kill anyone—if we do, I mean— you'd better kill them all."

"Why?"

"So they don't tell. That way, we've got a chance."

I was very, very sorry I'd come. This was all I needed, to be marked out a common murderer, and with a true blade, yet. That would be the end of me as a swordsman, the end of everything my old master had taught me. All for nothing.

"Hey, now." Marco must have seen my frown. "Nobody's getting killed, here. The highway life is all gold and glory, don't let anyone tell you otherwise. They may even write a song about you! You know, like that one about Dapper Dan, or whatever his name is." He started singing: "Dapper Dan, Dapper Dan, steals your wife and bones your—"

"Shhh!" Ivan flapped his hand at us. "They're coming!"

This time, they truly were.

Matched white horses pulled a gorgeous carriage. It looked strangely familiar to me—and when Ivan and Marco had stopped it, pulled the coachman off his perch while I held the horses, then had me threaten the footman with my blade until he and the coachman were safely tied up together, I found out why.

Marco banged on the door of the carriage with the butt of his knife, scarring the painted coat of arms with a certain pleasure. The young nobleman who emerged was very familiar, indeed.

"Hello, Thomas," I said.

"Richard!" He looked almost pleased. "What are you doing here?"

"I'm afraid my associates and I are going to take all your money and jewels, now."

Lord Thomas Berowne was scared, I could tell—but he handled it well: Though his hand was shaking, he kept his voice even and his head high.

"If you must, you must," he said. "My father will be very upset, but when I explain how you outnumbered us, I'm sure he'll understand."

"This is messed up," Ivan said, craning around the horses to see what was going on. "Stop talking and knock him out."

I hesitated. It was messed up. Marco sighed gustily. "All right, we get it, Richard: the one noble in town you actually know, you've worked for him, you don't want to lose a patron. Just our luck. As usual. You should've come masked."

"Just so," said Lord Thomas, in that soft and friendly way of his. "It is unfortunate that we had to meet again like this, Master St. Vier. The Watch—and my father—will demand a full description of the criminals." He pointed his chin at Marco. "You gentlemen, of course, I do not know."

Both his hands were shaking badly now. I was surprised he was still standing, because usually the knees go first. "My father is hard to lie to, but I will try."

"How kind," Marco sneered. "What for?"

Berowne turned to me. "If I might ask, in return, that you would consent to visit me again? Soon?"

"Yes," I said, surprised. "I would like that."

"See, Richard," Marco crowed. "And you even got a job out of it! Now let's bash him on the head and get this over with."

Berowne paled, and Marco said with savage cheer, "Fathers like it when we bash you on the head."

"I'd rather you didn't," Thomas said desperately. "I have a very soft head—my father says so—"

"Shut up," snapped Marco, but I said:

"Wait."

"Richard, what the hell are you doing?"

"Knocking him out," I said.

I knew Thomas closed his eyes when he kissed, and kept them closed. So I sheathed my sword and put my arms around him, and my damp cloak, as well, hiding Ivan and Marco from his sight and he from theirs. It was sort of lovely, the way his whole body was shaking against me. I kissed him, and after a while he started kissing back, a thing he does very well.

Behind us, Marco and Ivan were looting the carriage. I murmured with pleasure, so Thomas wouldn't hear them, wouldn't think about it. He pressed in closer to me. His hands had stopped shaking, were moving against my back. I wasn't sure how long either of us was going to be able to remain standing. I wanted to shove him up against the side of the carriage, which would be foolish, or against one of those god-awful trees, which would be difficult. The more I thought about it, the more I wanted to—so it was a relief when I heard Marco say, "Let's go."

"What about his rings?" Ivan whined.

I unpeeled myself from Thomas Berowne. "Leave the goddamned rings," I said harshly, not quite master of my breath. "Get in the coach, Thomas, and keep your head down." Luggage was scattered across the road; shirts and stockings and waistcoats and broken-open boxes and books. "Leave it! Leave it and get in. No, don't, Marco—"

But this time, they didn't heed me. Marco elbowed him in the kidneys, then bound his hands with a neckcloth, stuffed a stocking in his mouth, and left Lord Thomas Berowne in his coach for the next traveler to find.

As arranged, we met up at the Four Horse Quarters, a tavern on a side road to Azay, about a mile outside of town. Marco and Ivan were in the back room, organizing their takings, which ranged from plentiful coins to jeweled neck pins. They were delighted to see me.

"So," Ivan said, practically bouncing on his toes; "we're gonna do that again, right?"

"Not really."

"Not really? But it was perfect! You're even more than a Gentleman Robber—you're the Robber Lover! There'll be songs out there in a week. Less!"

"Not just songs"—Marco leered—"they'll be lining up on the high road to get 'knocked out' by you!"

"Just watch you don't knock 'em *up*!" said Ivan, which was his idea of humor.

"No," I said again, taking the flagon from in front of him and drinking it straight down. "I spent hours in the grass getting bored and wet. I'm going to have to oil my sword again, and I didn't really use it. I had to walk all the way back here. And I missed a whole day's practice."

Marco sat back a little, his hands on the table. "And the money?"

"I'll take it."

◆ ◆ ◆

Jess and I lived well for a few weeks. We got her linen back, and I bought her a dress, nearly new, white with bright flowers scattered all over it. She put it on to go uptown to do the Missing Pocket trick, her braids tidy, her skirts neat, looking for all the world like the pampered daughter of a country gentleman.

She came home late, red-faced and drunk, her hair in a half-knot, the rest straggling down her front. I hadn't realized how dark it had gotten: I'd been practicing, which is important whether you have work or not, and I don't really need to see if there's no one else there.

"Look!" she said. "Look what he gave me!"

She parted her hair to display a gold necklace, curlicued and jeweled. "Dipped," she said. "And fake. But it'll be real next time." Her kiss tasted of brandy. That was her favorite, when she could get it. "I'm coming up in the world!"

I didn't ask her what happened. Sometimes, things just did. I had to hear it from Nimble Willy, that Jess had nearly been nabbed up on Tilton Street. But the man with the necklace had stepped forward and vouched for her to the Watch, then he offered her a drink.

She sold the necklace, and bought more dresses. When she came back from her expeditions in town, she didn't boast of her sharp cons, the way she used to. Sometimes, she didn't want to talk at all.

That gave me more time to practice. It was a hot summer, and our rooms were stifling. Jess thought I should go drill out in the courtyard, but that was too public: the moves I practiced were mine. A winning fight is where they don't have any idea what you're likely to do next.

Jess said my endless practice was no fun, and she started spending more time out at Riverside taverns. That might not have been such a great idea. I could see for myself that her hands were shaky sometimes. Picking gentlemen's pockets would be out of the question. And yet she came home with all kinds of gauds and bangles. "Coming up in the world," she'd tell anyone who asked her. "Marks can be so stupid if you know how to manage them." And no one contradicted her. Maybe because she shared some of her trinkets out with her friends at the Maiden's Fancy, the ones she didn't keep, the ones she didn't sell.

You'd think she had enough stuff to play with, but she started messing with my things, as well: prancing around the room in nothing but my sword belt, playing childish games with my dragon candlesticks, going through all my shirts looking for holes, over and over . . . When she tried to mess with my good knives, I'd had it. Those edges are perfect, and needed to remain that way. "They're not toys," I told her; "and they're not yours. Leave them be."

So she picked up the glass dagger, and wound her bright, heavy hair up off her neck with one hand, pinning it in place with the blade. It looked good, and I told her so. She just tossed her head—"Glad you like it"—and went out.

From then on, I kept both knives on me, the weight balancing my hips.

It was a warm evening, and I was practicing. Jessamyn and I had woken early that morning and taken our pleasure together slowly and lazily for once, until the sun blazed through the cracks in the shutters, and we unstuck ourselves from the sweaty unit we had become. I lay in bed, drying myself with a corner of the sheet, watching Jessamyn sponge herself off with the water in the basin. She was like an ivory statue herself, pale body with its smooth and perfect curves, hair pale in the shadows, falling like a river carved by a careful hand.

She didn't ask me for help braiding her hair. Quickly and efficiently, she did it in one long, thick plait, and then she gave it a twist and secured it with the glass dagger. She dressed in a white linen smock, and a blue linen kirtle and bodice, then started draping herself with some of the trinkets she'd been collecting. I thought they looked garish, but I didn't say anything; she didn't like it when I had opinions. She said she knew her business best.

"I'm off," she said.

I said, "D'you have to go?"

"Oh, yes," she answered brightly. "He's taking me to luncheon at the King's Head."

I'd never heard of the place. I fell back asleep for a bit. Then I got up, and washed in the courtyard, dressed and went out to find something to eat. There were no messages of employment for me at the Maiden's Fancy. Rosalie hadn't heard of any stray jobs, either. So I went home to practice.

I was working on a new move that a blade in my last duel had nearly taken me down with. First I had to see my opponent clearly, and then I had to become him, executing the sequence so slowly that a child could have pierced through it, before speeding up, faster and faster.

The light was fading when Jess came waltzing in with a bright, fringed shawl. She tried to tickle me with the fringe. I shook her off, the way you do a fly: She knew better than to disturb me when I was working, I'd told her a dozen times.

"Rich-a-ard," she sang, "how do you like my new duds?"

"Later." Sweat was pouring down my chest. But I had to get the new move solid in my body so I knew it was there to count on next time, so fast my next opponent would never even see it coming.

"Oh, come on," she teased. She darted in to flick me with that shawl, like a kid taking a dare, and darted back out.

"Stop it, Jess." It's not wise to come at a swordsman unannounced.

"No, *you* stop it!" She started marching around the edges of my vision, in a distracting little semicircle. "You can practice later. Don't you want to have some fun?"

"I don't like 'fun.'"

"You don't, do you? Not anymore." She worked her bodice loose, bared a shoulder to me like some girl on the street. I saw it out of the corner of my eye, but I ignored her. "Like what you see?"

"Will you please—"

"I'm not just here to decorate the room, you know."

"I know." I tried to keep my sharpness and attack for my drill, but it came out in my voice: "I know, I know, now will you please shut up?"

"*I will not shut up!*" she shrieked, a sudden explosion, and she grabbed my free arm, a move I was not expecting. "You *look* at me! And you listen to me!"

Sweat was dripping into my eyes so I could hardly see. "*You don't care about me, you country son of a bitch! All you care about is your sword. You'd be dead if it weren't for me!*" I don't know how I even understood the words, they were so loud and high. "*You think you're too good to go out and earn your living like the rest of us, well, let me tell you, I do what I can to survive, do you even notice? You think you're some nobleman? You think you're too fine to do anything but practice until your next big duel?"* The noise was intolerable. *"When did you get so fancy, huh? When did you get too good for the rest of us?"* I didn't know how to make her stop. *"Look at you, waiting here at home for me to come back with whatever I can get for whatever I have to do and it's hard but you think I've lost my style I've got plenty of style, more than you'll ever have, you can't even get a job I haven't lost my nerve I have plenty of nerve left when it comes to whoresons like you Riverside doesn't want you I don't want you."*

She pulled the glass dagger from her hair. Silver tumbled all around her, so there must have been moonlight. She was coming at me with the knife still saying those things. I had to make her stop.

The moon was so bright it cast shadows all around.

Kathy Blount came by in the morning, with the sun barely up. She knocked on the door again and again, and when she opened it she stared at what she saw and stuck both fists in her mouth.

"She was screaming," I tried to tell her, and Kathy turned and ran.

After that, people steered clear of me for a while. It was a respectful distance, and I didn't mind. I never like it when people crowd me. Then a new swordsman came to town, flashy and boastful, annoying as hell. I challenged him on the street, killed him clean and fair with one blow, straight to the heart, and after that I was Riverside's own true blade again. Ginnie Vandall was annoyed because she'd just taken up with Hugo Seville, and it would be dangerous to dump him now, not to mention foolish. Hugo did weddings; Hugo did demonstration bouts; Hugo would fight a golden retriever if it made him popular with the nobles, or the merchants paid him enough.

I didn't go back to the Maiden's Fancy, even at summer's end. The stew at Rosalie's was better, and my credit seemingly inexhaustible.

So it was there that Marco and Ivan found me, back from their summer jaunt up north, and greeted me like a long-lost friend. Did I want to go back on the highway? they asked. Did I want to make some real money, this time? The summer had been tough on me, they'd heard, and hardly any of the nobles back in town yet, so jobs must be scarce, and the nights were getting cold. They'd missed me, up in Hartsholt, truly they had, though my style would be wasted up there, and now they were back in the city, how about it?

I told them *No*. It didn't matter what they offered, or how hard up I was.

I wasn't doing that again.

It leads to things I'd rather not think about.

And it wasn't any fun.

Scott Lynch

. . .

Fantasy novelist Scott Lynch is best known for his Gentleman Bastard series, about a thief and con man in a dangerous fantasy world, which consists of *The Lies of Locke Lamora*, which was a finalist for both the World Fantasy Award and the British Fantasy Society Award, *Red Seas Under Red Skies*, and *The Republic of Thieves*. His most recent book is another Gentleman Bastard story, *The Thorn of Emberlain*. He maintains a website at scottlynch.us. He lives with his wife, writer Elizabeth Bear, in Massachusetts.

Here he takes us along on an insanely dangerous quest with a down-on-his-luck thief who has nothing left to lose, and who finds that by finding everything, he gains nothing—except for a rousing story to tell on a cold winter's night.

. . .

The Smoke of Gold Is Glory

SCOTT LYNCH

S ail north from the Crescent Cities, three days and nights over the
rolling black sea, and you will surely find the tip of the Ormscap, the
fire-bleeding mountains that circle the roof of the world like a scar.
There in the shallows, where the steam rises in a thousand curtains,
you'll see a crumbling dock, and from that dock you can still walk into
the scraps and tatters of a blown-apart town that was never laid straight
from the start. It went up on those rocks layer after layer, like ten eyeless
drunks scraping butter onto the same piece of bread.

The southernmost Ormscap is still called the Dragon's Anvil. The
town below the mountain was once called Helfalkyn.

Not so long ago it was an enchantment and a refuge and a prison,
home to the most desperate thieves in all the breathing world. Not so
long ago, they all cried out in their sleep for the mountain's treasure.
One part in three of every gleaming thing that has ever been drawn or
dredged or delved from the earth, that's what the scholars claimed.

That's what the dragon carried there and brooded over, the last
dragon that will ever speak to any of us.

Now the town's empty. The wind howls through broken windows in
roofless walls. If you licked the stones of the mountain for a thousand

days, you wouldn't taste enough precious metal to gild one letter in a monk's manuscript.

Helfalkyn is dead, and the dragon is dead, and the treasure might as well have never existed.

I ought to know. I'm the man who lost a bet, climbed the Anvil, and helped break the whole damn thing.

I tell this story once a year, on Galen's Eve, and no other. Some of you have heard it before. I take it kindly that you've come to hear it again. Like any storyteller, I'd lie about the color of my eyes to my own mother for half a cup of ale-dregs, but you'll affirm to all the new faces that to this one tale I add no flourishes. I deepen no shadows and gentle no sorrows. I tell it as it was, one night each year, and on that night I take no coin for it.

Heed me now. Gather in as you will. Jostle your neighbors. Spill your drinks. Laugh early at the bad jokes and stare at me like clubbed sheep for all the good ones, and I shall care not, for I am armored by long experience. But this bowl of mine, if we are to part as friends, must catch no copper or silver, I swear it. Tonight pay me in food, or drink, or simple attention.

With that, let me commence to tell:

FIRST, HOW I FELL IN WITH THE CHARMING LUNATICS WHO ENDED MY ADVENTURING CAREER

It was the Year of the Bent-Wing Raven, and everything went sour for me right around the back side of autumn.

One week I was in funds, the next I was conspicuously otherwise. I'm still not sure what happened. Bad luck, worse judgment, enemy action, sorcery? Hardly matters. When you're on the ground getting kicked in the face, one pair of boots looks very much like another.

I have long been candid about the nature of my previous employment. Those of you who find this frank exchange of purely historical details in any way disturbing are of course welcome to say a word or two to Galen on my behalf, and I shall thank you, as I doubt an old thief can really collect such a thing as too many prayers. In those days I would have laughed. Young thieves think luck and knee joints are meant to last forever.

I started the summer by lifting four ivory soul lanterns from the Temple of the Cloud Gardens in Port Raugen. Spent a few weeks carving decent wooden replicas and painting them with a white cream wash, first. I made the switch at night, walked out unnoticed, presented the genuine articles to my client, and set sail on the morning tide as a very rich man. I washed up in Hadrinsbirk a few weeks later with a pounding headache and a haunting memory of money. No matter. I made the acquaintance of an uncreatively guarded warehouse and appropriated a crate of the finest Sulagar steel padlocks. I sold the locks and their keys to a corner-cutting merchants' guild, then sold wax impressions of the keys to their bitter rivals for twice that sum. So much for Hadrinsbirk. I cast off for the Crescent Cities.

There I guised myself as a gentleman of leisure, and wearing that mask, I investigated prospects and rumors, looking for easy marks. Alas, the easy marks must have migrated in a flock. I took the edge off my disappointment by indulging all the routine questionable habits, and that's when the bad time crept up behind me. The gaming tables turned. Easy credit went extinct. All the people who owed me favors locked their doors, and all the people I needed to avoid were thick in the streets. Before I knew it I was sleeping in a stable.

I stretched a point of courtesy then and slipped an appeal to the local practitioners of my trade. My entreaty was coolly received. There was a sudden plague of honesty in the land, and schemes simply weren't hatching, or so they claimed. Nobody needed to arrange a kidnapping, or a vault infiltration, or have a barrow desecrated.

This was a bind, and I confess that I partly deserved it. For all my hard-earned professional fame, I was still an outsider, and doubtless should have paid my respects to the thieves of the Crescent Cities a few weeks earlier. Now they were wise to me and watchful for the sorts of jobs I might pull on my own. The wind was sharpening, my belly was flat, and my belt was running out of notches. I needed money! Yet honest employment was out of the question too, as word of my presence spread. Who would make a caravan guard of Tarkaster Crale, bane of a dozen caravan runs? Who'd set Crale the Cracksman to stand guard over a money changer's strongboxes? Awkward! I couldn't beg for so much as an afternoon hauling wash buckets behind a tavern. A larcenist of my caliber and experience? Any sensible local thief would assume it had to be a cover for some grand scheme, which they would have to interrupt.

It's hard to be poor at the best of times, but in my old line of work, to be poor and famous—gods have mercy.

I had no prospects. No friends. I could have won an empty-pockets contest against anyone within a hundred miles. All I had left was youth and a sense of pride that damn near glowed like banked coals.

These were the circumstances that led me to seriously consider, for the first time in my life, the words of the Helfalkyn Wormsong.

I can see some of you nodding, those of you without much hair left. You heard it, too. Nobody repeats it these days, the fortunes of Helfalkyn having diminished so profoundly. But in my youth there wasn't a child in any land who didn't know the Wormsong by heart. It was a message from the dragon itself, the last and greatest of them, the Shipbreaker, the Sky Tyrant. Glimraug.

It went like this:

> *High-reachers, bright-dreamers, bright-enders,*
> *Match riddlesong, venom, and stone.*
> *Carry ending and eyes up the Anvil,*
> *Carry glorious gleanings back home.*

Isn't that a fine little thing?

Friends, that's how a dragon says, "Why not climb up my impenetrable treasure mountain and let me kill you?"

From the first day Glimraug claimed the Anvil, it took pains to welcome and entice us. Don't mistake that for a benevolent and universal hospitality, for of course Glimraug raided half the earth and spread dismay for centuries. No dragon ever deigned to smelt its own gold. But even as Glimraug fell on caravans and broke castles like eggs, it tolerated a small community of outcasts and lunatics in the shadow of its home. Once in a rare while it would even seize someone and haul them to the crest of the Anvil, to make a show of its growing treasure, then set them free to sing the Wormsong louder than ever.

Thousands of people accepted the dragon's invitation over the years. None of them lived. Some very canny customers in that crowd, too, great heroes, names that still ring out, but none of them were ever quite a match for riddlesong, venom, and stone. Still, for every one who dreamed the impossible dream and cacked it hard, two more showed up. The Dragon's Anvil was the last roll of the dice for those who'd played their lives out and bet poorly. It was equally attractive to the brilliant, the mad, and the desperate. I was at least two of those three, and by that simple majority the vote carried. I was on a ship that night, the *Red Swan*, and I scrubbed decks and greased ropes to pay for my passage to the end of the world.

That's what Helfalkyn looked like when I finally saw it—like the last human habitation thrown down by the last human hands at the far end of some mad priest's apocalypse. The sun was the color of bled-out entrails, edging the hulking mountain, and the bruised light showed me a gallimaufry of dark warrens, leaning houses, and crooked alleys down below. We sailed in through veils of warm breath from the mountain's underwater vents, and the air was perfumed with sulfur.

Many of you must be thinking the same thing I was as I trod the creaking timbers of the Helfalkyn docks—how did such a place ever come to thrive? The answer lies at the intersection of greed and perversity. Here came the adventurers, the suicides, the mad ones intent on climbing the mountain and somehow stealing the treasure of ten thousand lifetimes. But were they eager to go all at once? Of course not. Some needed to lay their plans, or drink their brains out, or otherwise work themselves into fits of enthusiasm. Some waited days, or weeks, or months. Some never went at all, and clung to Helfalkyn forever, aging sourly in the shadows of failed ambition. After the adventurers came the provisioners, of inebriation and games and rooms and warm companionship, and the town became a sputtering, improvised machine for sifting the last scraps of currency from those who would surely never need them again. The captains of the few ships that made the Helfalkyn run had a cordial arrangement with the town. They would haul anyone there

for the price of a few days' labor, and charge a small fortune in real valuables for passage back to the world. Any newcomer trapped in Helfalkyn would thus be forced to try the mountain, or toil for years to the
great advantage of the town's masters if they ever wanted to escape.

Mountebanks swarmed as I and a few other neophytes examined the
town warily. The junk-mongers outnumbered us three to one. "Don't
breathe the dragon air without taking a draught of Cleansing Miracle
Water," shouted a bearded man, waving a stone pitcher of what was
clearly urine and mud. "Look around! The dragon air gives you clisters,
morphew, wretched megrims, and the flux like a black molasses! Have
the advantage when you challenge the Anvil! Protect yourself at a fair
price!"

I did look around, and it seemed that none of the other natives were
downing miracle mudpiss to keep their lungs supple, so I judged none
of us likely to perish of the megrims. I moved on, and was offered enchanted blades, enchanted boots, enchanted cheese, and enchanted
handfuls of mountain rock, all for a fair price. How fortunate I felt, to
discover such simple generosity and potent magic in the meanest of all
places! Even if I'd had money, I would have reciprocated this cordial
selflessness by refusing to take advantage of it. Two gracious humanitar-
ians of Helfalkyn then attempted to pick my pockets; the first I merely
spurned with a scolding. The second mysteriously incurred a broken
wrist and lost his own purse at the same time, for in those days my fingers were considerably faster than the contents of my skull. I worried
then about constables, or at least mob-fellowship against outsiders, but
I quickly realized that the only law in Helfalkyn was to win or stay out
of the way. No more creeping fingers tried my pockets after that.

Cheered by the acquisition of a few coins, I hunted for a place to
spend them and tame my tyrant stomach. Ale dens of varying foulness
offered themselves as I strolled, and street hawkers made pitches even
less appetizing than the prospect of Cleansing Miracle Water. Sooner
rather than later, for while Helfalkyn was encysted with diversions it
was not terribly vast, its twisted streets naturally funneled me to the
steps of the grandest structure in town, Underwing Hall. Here would be
food, though the smell wafting out past the cold-eyed guards beside the
doors promised nothing delicate.

Outside it was morning, but inside lay a perpetual smoky twilight. The entrance hall was decorated with bloody teeth and the slumped bodies of those who'd recently had them knocked out of their mouths. Porters, working with the bored air of long practice, were levering these unfortunates one by one out a side entrance. I saw more fisticuffs under way at several tables and balconies in the cavernous space. Given the relaxation of the door guards, I wondered what it took to rouse their interference. The servers, stout men and women all, wore ill-fashioned armor as they heaved platters about, and the kitchen windows were barred with iron. Rough hands thrust forth tankards and wine bottles like castle defenders dispensing projectiles through murder-holes. Though I'd enjoyed some elevated company in my career, this crowd was still an intimately familiar sort, comprised of equal parts stupid, cruel, cunning, blasphemous, and greedy faces. Every corner of the known world had skimmed the scum of its scum to populate Helfalkyn. I resolved to step warily and attract no attention until I learned the order of things.

"CRALE!" bellowed someone from a balcony overhead.

Ah, the feeling of receiving unsought the attention of a great room full of brawlers and carousers. Heads turned, conversations quieted, and even some of the servers halted to stare at me.

"Tarkaster Crale?" came a disbelieving shout.

"Bullshit. Tarkaster Crale's a tall handsome bastard," muttered a woman.

I was about to say something that would have, in all candor, improved nobody's situation, when I was seized from above and hauled into the air. The sheer power of my appropriator was startling, and I kicked helplessly as I was spun a disagreeable number of feet above the stones of the tavern floor. My assailant hung from a balcony rail by one arm and dandled me with the other. I prepared fresh unhelpful commentary and reached for the knives in my belt; and then I saw the man's face.

"Your highness!" I whispered.

"Don't give me the courtesies of cushion-sitters unless you want to get dropped, Crale." Still, there was warmth in his voice as he heaved me over the railing and set me on a stool as easily as anyone here might hang a tunic on a drying line. Here was a man with shoulders as broad as a boat's rowing-bench and arms harder than the oars. He was dark of skin and darker of hair, with gray setting some claim to his temples and beard, and all the lines in his face had been carved by either the sea-winds or the wild grin he wore when facing them. The other patrons of Underwing Hall rapidly lost interest in me, for I had been claimed for the table of none other than my old adventuring companion, Brandgar Never-Throned, King-on-the-Waves, Lord of the Ajja.

Like Helfalkyn, the King-on-the-Waves is little more than a story these days, though it's a good one and an Ajja skald who'll sing it for you is worth the asking price. All the Ajja clans had kings and queens, and keeps and lands and suchwise, but once a generation their mystics would read the signs and proclaim a King-on-the-Waves. This lucky bitch or bastard would be gifted a stout ship to crew with sworn companions, and set sail across the Ajja realms, calling upon cousin monarchs, receiving full courtesy and hospitality. Then they'd usually be asked to undertake some messy piece of questing that would end in unguessable amounts of death and glory. Thus charged was a King-on-the-Waves, to hold no lands, but to slay monsters, retrieve lost treasures, lift curses, and so forth, until they and all their companions had met some horrible, beautiful fate on behalf of the Ajja people. Brandgar was the last so-named, nor is there like to be another soon, for he and his companions were uncommonly good at the job and left few messes for others to clean up. I had fallen in with them on two occasions and done some reaving, all for the best of causes, I assure you, though I am sworn to utter no details. Even my sleeping sense of honor sometimes rolls over in bed and kicks. Onward!

"There's fortune in this. We had not thought to see an old friend here." Brandgar settled himself back on his own stool, over the half-eaten remains of some well-fatted animal I couldn't identify, sauced with sharp-smelling mustard and brown moonberry preserves. "What say you, Mikah?"

I gave a start, for sitting there in the darkness at the rear of the balcony was a shape I hadn't previously noticed. Yes, indeed, here was Mikah King-Shadow, rarely seen unless they chose the time and place. Mikah, my better in all the crafts of larceny, who could pass for man or

lined with the color of iron like her king's, and her round, flushed face was all mischief and mirth.

"That was unworthy," I scowled.

"That was fair as anything," said Brandgar. "For if your eyes had been working as a fine and cunning lookout's should, you'd have seen that there was only one beast upon the wall until a moment before my proposal. Come, Crale. We need you, and you won't find better company if you wait here a hundred years! This is fate."

I partly hated him for being right and was partly thrilled that he was. A warrior-king, a master thief, and a sorceress. Great gods, hope was a terrible and anxious thing! They were indeed allies who had as much chance on the Dragon's Anvil as any mortal born. I pondered my recent poverty and pondered the treasure.

"I have never in my life behaved with any particular wisdom," I said at last. "It would make little sense to start now."

"Ha!" Brandgar pounded the table, stood, and leaned out over the balcony. His voice boomed out, echoing from the rafters and startling the raucous commotion below into instant attention. "HEAR ME! Hight Brandgar, son of Orthild and Erika, King-on-the-Waves! Tonight we go! Tonight we climb the Dragon's Anvil! We, the Never-Throned, the King-Shadow, the Sky-Daughter, and the famous Tarkaster Crale! We go to claim a treasure, so take this pittance! Drink to us, and wait for the word! Tonight we break a legend!"

Brandgar opened a purse, and shook out a stream of silver into the crowds below, where drinkers cheered and convulsed and clutched at his largesse. Gods! If I'd had even that much money just a week before, I'd never have left the Crescent Cities. As the near riot for the coins subsided, a voice rose in ragged chant, and was joined by more and steadier voices, until nearly everyone in Underwing Hall was gleefully serenading us, a single verse over and over again:

> *Die rich, dragon's dinner!*
> *Play well the game that has no winner!*
> *Climb the mountain, greedy sinner!*
> *Die rich, dragon's dinner!*

The chant had the sound of a familiar ritual that had been much practiced. I liked it not a whit.

NEXT, HOW WE PROVED OUR RESOLVE AND BROKE A FEW HEARTS ALONG THE WAY

I dozed fitfully most of the day, in a hired chamber guarded by some of Gudrun's arcane mutterings. Terrified or not, I was still an experienced man of fortune and knew to try to catch a bit of rest when it was on offer.

At dusk the moons rose red, like burnished shields hanging on the wall of the brandywine sky. The mountain loomed, crowned with strange lights that never came from any celestial sphere, and it seemed I could hear the hiss and rumble of the stone as if it were a hungry thing. I shuddered and checked my gear for the tenth time. I had come light from the Crescent Cities, in simple field leathers, dark jacket, and utility belts. I carried a sling and a sparse supply of grooved stones. My longest daggers were whetted, and I wore them openly as I headed for the northeastern side of town with my companions, pretending to swagger. Denizens of Helfalkyn watched from every street, every rooftop, every window, some jeering, some singing, but most standing quietly or hoisting cups to the air, as one might toast a prisoner on the way to the gallows.

Brandgar wore a fitted coat of plate under a majestically ragged gray cloak with parti-colored patchings from numerous cuts and burns over the years; he claimed it was as good as enchanted and that he had sweated most of his considerable luck into it. Gudrun had never offered a professional opinion on this, so far as I knew. She was as scruffy as ever, a study in comfortable disrepute. Strange charms and wooden containers rattled on leather cords at her breast, and she bore a pair of rune-inscribed drums on her back. Mikah were lightly dressed in silks and leather bracers, moving with their familiar fluid grace, concealing their real thoughts behind their even more familiar mask of calculating bemusement with the world. They carried a few coils of sea-spider silk and some climbing gear wrapped in muffling cloth. However detached they seemed, I knew they were fanatics about the selection and care of their tools, more painstaking than any other burglar I had ever worked with, and any professional jealousy I might have felt was rather drowned in comfort at their preparedness.

The only real oddity was the extra weapon Brandgar carried. His familiar spear, Cold-Thorn, had a bare and gleaming tip, and its shaft was worn with use. The other spear looked heavy and new, and its point was wrapped in layers of tightly bound leather like a practice weapon. When asked about this, Brandgar smiled, and said, "Extra spear, extra thief. Aren't I growing cautious in my old age?"

At the northeast edge of Helfalkyn lay our first ascent, an unassuming path of dusty dark stone that was marked by a parallel series of lines, half a foot deep, slashed across the walkway. Though time and weather had softened the edges of these lines, it was not hard to see them for what they were, the claw-furrows of a dragon. An unequivocal message to anyone who wanted to step over them. I suddenly wished I could forget our mutual agreement to go up the Anvil with clear heads and find something irresponsible to pour down my throat.

One by one we crossed the dragon's mark, your nervous narrator lastly and slowly. After that we walked up in silence save for the occasional rattle of gear or boot-scuff on stone. As the odors of the town and the harbor steam faded below us, the indigo edges of evening settled overhead and stars lit one by one like distant lanterns. It would be a clear night atop the mountain, and I wondered if we would be there to appreciate it. This first part of the climb was not hard, perhaps three-quarters of an hour with the switchback path offering nothing more than agreeable exercise. As the light sank the way roughened and narrowed, and when full dark came on it ceased to be a path and became a proper climb, up a sloping black rock face of crags and broken columns. Rugged as it was, this was the only face of the Anvil that could be approached at all. Brandgar shook Cold-Thorn and muttered something to Gudrun, who muttered something in return. A moment later the tip of Cold-Thorn flared with gentle but far-reaching light, and by that pale gleam we made our way steadily up.

"What happened to everyone else?" I asked on a whim during one of our brief pauses. When last I'd sojourned in the Never-Throned's company, he'd had eight of his original boon companions yet unslain, enough to crew his ship and drink up truly heroic quantities of something irresponsible whenever they paid call to a landed king or queen. "Asmira? Lorus? Valdis?"

"Asmira was pitched from the mast during a storm," said Brandgar. "Lorus challenged a vineyard wight to a game of draughts and kept it occupied 'til dawn. It killed him in its fury just before the first light of the sun slew it in turn. Valdis died in the battle against the Skull Priests at Whitefall."

"What about Rondu Silverbeard?"

"The Silverbeard died in bed," chuckled Gudrun.

"Under a bed, to be precise," added Mikah. "The defenders dropped it on us at the siege of Vendilsfarna."

"I hope our friends know joy in the Fields of Swords and Roses," I said, for that is where worthy Ajja are meant to go when they die, and if it's true I suppose it keeps all of our own heavens and hells a bit quieter. "Though I hope I give no offense if I wish we had a few more of them with us tonight."

"They died to bring us here," said Brandgar. "They died to teach us what we needed to know. They died to show us the way, and when our numbers dwindled and our duties grew lean, we three knew where we were called." Gudrun and Mikah nodded with that sage fatalism I had long lamented in my Ajja friends, and though my presence on that mountain reinforced my assertion that I had never in my life behaved with any particular wisdom, neither was I boorish enough to voice my concerns with their philosophy. Perhaps they had always mistaken this tact for fellow feeling. No, I admit I could fight with abandon when cornered, but when I could see a meeting with Death obviously scrawled in the ledger, I always preferred to break the appointment. How any of the Ajja ever survived long enough to span the seas and populate their holdings remains a mystery of creation.

We resumed our climb and soon heaved ourselves over the edge of a cleft promontory where a hemispherical stone ceiling, open to the night like a theater, overhung a darkness that led into the depths of the mountain. The wind had risen and the air was sharp against my skin. We gazed out for a moment at the lights of the town far below us, and the white-foamed blackness of the sea capped with mists, and the hair-thin line of sunset that still clung to the horizon. Then rose a scraping, shuffling noise behind us, and Brandgar turned with Cold-Thorn held high.

Red lights glowed in answer, throbbing like a pulse beat within the cavern. Whether they were lanterns or conjurations I could not discern, but in their rising illumination I saw an arched door wide enough to admit three wagons abreast. I wondered whether the dragon had left itself ample room in setting this passage, or if it could tolerate a tight squeeze. Unhelpful conjecture! In the space between us and the door stood two straight lines of pillars, and beside each pillar stood the shape of a man or woman.

Brandgar advanced, and the man shape nearest us held up a hand. "Bide," it whispered in a hoarse sickbed voice. "None need enter."

"Unless you propose to show us a more convenient door," said Brandgar, "this path is for us."

"Time remains to turn." There was enough light now to see that the hoarse speaker and all of its companions were unclothed, emaciated, and caked with filth. A paleness shone upon their breasts, where each on their left side bore a plate of something like dull nacre, sealed to the edges of the bloodless surrounding flesh by the pulsing segments of what seemed to be a milk-white centipede. The white segments passed into the body like stitches and emerged in a narrow, twitching tail at the back of the neck. From these extremities hung threads, gleaming silver, connecting each man or woman to a pillar. Atop those, in delicate brass recesses, pulsed fist-sized lumps of flesh. I'd been near enough death to know a human heart by sight, and felt a tight horror in my own chest. "The master grudges you nothing. You may still turn and go home."

"Our thanks to your master." Brandgar set his leather-wrapped spear down and spun Cold-Thorn, casting about a light like the sun's rays scattering from rippling water. "We are here on an errand of sacred avarice and will not be halted."

Some enchanted guardians never know when to shut up, but this one had a reasonable sense of occasion, so it nodded and proceeded directly to hostilities. Each of the heart-wraiths took up handfuls of dust, and in their clenched fists this dust turned to swords. Eight of them closed on four of us, and with a merry twirl of my daggers I joined most of my companions in making royal asses of ourselves.

It was plain to Mikah, Brandgar, and me, as veterans of too many sorcerer's traps and devices to enumerate here, that the weakness of these creatures had to be the glittering threads that bound them to their heart-pillars. Dodging their attacks, we wove a dance of easy competence and with our weapons of choice swung down nearly simultaneously for the threads of our targets. What it felt like, to me, was swinging for dandelion fuzz and hitting granite. I found myself on the ground with my right hand spasming in cold agony, and was barely able to seize my wits and roll aside before a blade struck sparks where my head had just been.

"I had thought," muttered Brandgar (shaking Cold-Thorn angrily, for either his rude health or some quality of the spear had let him keep it when Mikah and I had been rendered one-handed), "the obvious striking point—"

"So did we all," groaned Mikah.

"Speak for your cloddish selves," shouted Gudrun, who had cast lines of emerald fire upon the stones, where they flashed and coiled like snakes in response to the movements of her hands, and were holding several of the heart-wraiths at bay.

I sidestepped a new assault, rebalanced my left-hand dagger, and judged the distance to the nearest pillar-top heart. If the threads had been a distraction, the weakness of the magic animating our foes surely had to lie there. I was not left-handed, but I threw well, and my blade was a gratifying blur that arrived dead on target, only to be smacked aside by one thrown with even greater deftness by Mikah, aimed at the same spot.

"Damnation, Crale, we're supposed to be better than this," said the King-Shadow as they whirled and weaved between onrushing heart-wraiths.

"If I live to tell this story in taverns, I shall amend this part to our advantage," I said, though you apprehend, my friends, that I have done otherwise and will sleep soundly in my conscience tonight. Mikah found a fresh dagger and made another cast, this time without my interference. The blade struck true at the visibly unprotected heart, and rebounded as though from an inch of steel. We all swore vicious oaths. Magic does from time to time so boil one's piss.

Mikah rolled one of the silk ropes off their shoulders, and with a series of cartwheels and flourishes deployed it as a weapon, lashing and entangling the nearest heart-wraiths, quickstepping between them like the passage of a mad tailor's needle. I had no such recourse, and my right hand was still useless. I scrambled across the stones, swept up a dropped blade in my left hand once more, and whirled toward the two wraiths assailing me. "Hold," I cried, "Hold! I find I'm not so eager for treasure as I was. Would your master yet give me leave to climb back down?"

"We are here to slay or dissuade, not to punish." The heart-wraith before me lowered its weapon. "Living with yourself is your own affair. You may depart."

"I applaud the precision and dedication of your service," I said, and as the heart-wraith began to turn from me, no doubt to join the fray against my companions, I buried my dagger in its skull with an overhand blow. The segments of the insectoid thing threaded into its abdomen shook, and something like creamy clotted bile poured from the mouth and ears of what had once been a man. It collapsed.

"That was a low trick," rasped the other heart-wraith, and came for me. I wrenched my dagger free, which wafted a sickly vinegar odor into my face, and waved my hands again.

"Hold," said I. "It's true that I'm a gamesome and unscrupulous rogue, but I feared you were playing me false. Are you really prepared to let me go in good faith?"

"Despite your unworthy—"

I never learned the specifics of my unworthiness, as I took the opportunity to lunge and sink my dagger into its left eye. It toppled beside its fellow and vomited more disgusting yellow soup. I am the soul of pragmatism.

"Enough!"

I saw that only one heart-wraith remained, and before my eyes the sword in its hand returned to dust. I had slain two, Gudrun had scorched two with her fire-serpents, and Mikah had at last bound their pair tightly enough to finish them with pierced skulls. Brandgar had beaten one of his foes to a simple pulp, breaking its limbs and impaling it through the bony plate where its heart had once been. As for those hearts, I saw at a glance that those atop seven of the eight pillars had shriveled. Dark stains were running down the columns beneath them.

"You have proven your resolve," rasped the final heart-wraith. "The master bids you onward."

The eerie red lights of the cavern dimmed, and with the crack and rattle of great mechanisms the arched doors fell open. Brandgar advanced on the surviving heart-wraith, spear held out before him, until it rested gently on the white plate set into the thing's chest.

"Onward we move," said Brandgar, "but how came you to the service of the dragon?"

"I sought the treasure and failed, threescore years past. You may yet join me, when you fail. If enough of your flesh remains, the master may choose to knit watch-worms into the cavern of your heart, so be advised . . . to consider leaving as little flesh as possible."

"After tonight your master Glimraug will have no need of us." Smoothly and without preamble, Brandgar drove his spear into the wraith's chest. "Nor any need of you."

"Thank . . . you . . ." the wraith whispered as it fell.

"Did we amuse you in our stumblings, sister Sky-Daughter?" said Mikah, massaging their right hand. My own seemed to be recovering as well.

"Spear-carriers and knife-brains love to overthink a problem," laughed the sorceress. "Feeds your illusionary sense of finesse. The truly stupid and the truly wise would have started with simply bashing at the damn things, but since you're somewhere in between, you tried to kill everything else in the room first. Good joke. This dragon knows how adventurers think." She looked up at the mountain and sighed. "Tonight could be everyone's night to stumble, ere we're through."

THIRD, HOW I PUT MY ASS ON THE LINE AND HOW
WE SOUGHT THE SONG BENEATH THE SONG

Past the arched doors we found ourselves in a vaulted hall, lit once more by pale scarlet fires that drifted in the air like puffs of smoke. For a moment I thought we stood in an armory, then I saw the jagged holes and torn plates in every piece displayed, tier on tier and rank on rank, nearly to the ceiling. Broken blades and shattered spears, shields torn like parchment sheets, mail shirts pierced and burnt and fouled with unknown substances—here were the fates of all our predecessors memorialized, obviously. The dragon's boast.

"Perhaps a part-truth," responded Mikah, when I said as much. "Surely all dragons are braggarts after a fashion. But consider how this one seems determined to play fair with its challengers. The ascent up the mountain, with its gradual reduction of ease. The guardians at the door, willing to forgive and forget. Now this museum show for the faint-hearted. At every step our host invites the insufficiently motivated to quit before they waste more of anyone's time."

Proud to be numbered among the sufficiently motivated, no doubt, I followed my companions through the dragon's collection, uneasily noting its quality. Here were polished Sulagar steel breastplates and black Harazi swords of the ten thousand folds. Here were gem-studded pauldrons of ageless elven silver, and gauntlets of sky iron that glowed faintly with sorcery, and all of these things had clearly been as useful as an underwater fart against the fates that had overtaken their wielders. At the far end of the hall lay another pair of great arched doors, and nested into one like a passage for pets was a door more suited to those of us not born as dragons. On this door lay a sigil that I knew too well, and I seized Brandgar by his cloak before he could touch it.

"That is the seal of Melodia Marus, the High Trapwright of Sendaria," said I, "and I've had several professional disagreements with her. Or, more precisely, the mechanisms she devises for the vaults and offices of her clients."

"I know her work by reputation," said Mikah. "It seems Glimraug is one of those clients."

"She's the reason I once spent three months unconscious in Korrister." I twitch at the memory, friends, but not all of one's ventures can end in good fortune, as we have seen. "And six weeks in a donjon in Port Raugen. And why I only have eight toes."

"Another fair warning," said Gudrun. "A frightful spectacle for all comers, then a more specific omen for those professionally inclined to thievery."

"We have two master burglars to test our way," said Brandgar, who seemed more cheerful with every danger and warning of greater danger. "And if this woman's creations were perfect, surely she'd have more than two of Crale's toes by now."

The craft of trap-finding is much sweat and tedium, with only the occasional thrill of accident or narrow escape, and we spent the next hour absorbed in its practice. All the stairs and corridors in that part of the dragon's domain were richly threaded with death. Some halls were sized to us and some to the transit of larger things, and these networks of passages were neither wholly parallel nor entirely separate. This was no citadel made for any sensible court, but only a playing field for Glimraug's game, a stone simulacrum of what we would call a true fortress. Up we went floor by floor, past apertures in the walls that spat razor-keen darts, over false floors that gave way to mangling engines, through cleverly weighted doors that sprang open with crushing force or sealed themselves behind us, barring retreat from some new devilment.

In one particularly narrow hall both Mikah and I had a rare bout of all-consuming nincompoopery, and one of us tripped a plate that caused iron shutters to slam down before and behind us, sealing our quartet in a span of corridor little bigger than a rich merchant's water closet. An aperture on the right-hand wall began to spew a haze at us, the stinging sulfur reek of which was familiar to me from a job I'd once pulled in the mines of Belphoria.

"Dragon's breath," said Brandgar.

"More like the mountain's breath," I cried, and with a creditable leap I braced myself like a bridge across the narrow space and jammed my own posterior firmly into the aperture. The thin cloud of foulness that had seeped into the hall made my eyes water, but was not yet enough to cause us real harm. Though once a few minutes passed and I could no longer maintain such an acrobatic posture, my well-placed buttocks would no longer avail us. "It's what miners call the stink-damp, and it will dispatch us with unsporting speed if I can't hold the seal, so please conjure an exit."

"Fairly done, Crale!" Brandgar waved a hand before his face and coughed. "To save us, you've matched breach to breeches!"

"All men have cracks in their asses," said Gudrun, "but only the boldest puts his ass in a crack."

"Henceforth Crale the Cracksman will be celebrated as Crale the Corksman," said Mikah.

I said many unkind things then, and they continued making grotesque puns which I shall not torture any living soul with, for apparently to ward off a stream of poisonous vapor with one's own ass is to summon a powerful muse of low comedy. Eventually, moving with what I considered an unseemly attitude of leisure, Mikah tried and failed to find any mechanism they might manipulate. Then even the strength of Brandgar's shoulder failed against the iron shutters, and our salvation fell to Gudrun, who broke a rune-etched bone across her knee and summoned what she called a spirit of rust.

"I had hoped to reserve it for some grander necessity," said she. "Though I suppose this is a death eminently worth declining."

In a few moments the spirit accomplished its task, and the sturdy iron shutters on either side were reduced to scatterings of flaked brown dust on the floor. I unbraced with shudders of relief in every part of my frame, and we hurried on our way, kicking up whorls of rust in our wake to mingle with the lethal haze of the broken trap. We moved warily at first, then with more confidence, for it seemed that we had at last cleared that span of the mountain in which Melodia Marus had expressed her creativity. I do hope that woman died in a terrible accident, or at least lost some toes.

The red lights the dragon had graciously provided before were not to be found here, however, so we climbed through the darkness by the silver gleam of Gudrun's sorcery on our naked weapons. Eventually we could find no more doors or stairs, and so with painful contortions and much use of Mikah's ropes we ventured up a rock chimney. I prayed for the duration of the ascent that we had discovered nothing so mundane as the dragon's privy shaft.

Eventually we emerged into a cold-aired cavern with a floor of smooth black tiles. Scarlet light kindled upon a far wall, and formed letters in Kandric script (which I had learned to read as a boy, and which the Ajja had long adopted as their preference for matters of trade and accounting), spelling out the Helfalkyn Wormsong.

"As if we might have forgotten it," muttered Mikah. At that instant, a burst of orange fire erupted from the rock chimney we had ascended and burned like a terrible flickering flower twice my height, sealing off our retreat. White-hot lines spilled forth from the ragged crest of this flame, like melted iron from a crucible, and this burning substance swiftly took the aspect of four vaguely human shapes, lean and graceful as dancers. Dance they did, whirling slowly at first but with ever-increasing speed, and toward us they came, gradually. Inexorably.

"*Seek the song beneath the song,*" rang a voice that touched my heart, a voice that echoed softly around the chamber, a voice blended of every fine thing, neither man's nor woman's but something preternaturally beautiful. To hear it once was to regret all the years of life one had spent not hearing it. Even now, merely telling of it, I can feel warmth at the corners of my eyes, and I am not ashamed. The four fire-dancers glided and spun, singing with voices that started as mere entrancement and became more painfully beautiful with every verse.

> "*The fall of dice in gambling den*
> *The sporting bets of honest men*
> *Will bring them round again, again*
> *To their fairest friend, distraction . . .*"

It was not the words that were beautiful, for as I recite them here I see none of you crying or falling over. But the voices, the voices! Every hair on my neck stood as though a winter wind had caught me, and I felt the sorcery, sure as I could feel the stones beneath my feet. There was a compulsion weighing on us. The voices drew us on, all of us, cow-eyed, yearning to embrace the gorgeous burning shapes that called with such piercing loveliness. And that was the horror of it, friends, for I knew with some small part of my mind that if I touched one of those things, my skin would go like candle wax in a bonfire. Still, I couldn't help myself. None of us could. With every moment they sang, the pull of the fire-dancers grew, and our resolve withered.

"When beauties into mirrors gaze
Nor look aside for all their days
Until they lose all chance for praise
They wake too late from distraction . . ."

I groaned and forced myself backwards, step by step, though it felt like hooks had been set in my heart and it was ten hells to pull against them. I saw Mikah, reeling dizzily, seize Brandgar by the collar.

"Forgive me, lord!" Mikah cuffed their king hard, first across one cheek then the other. Terrible fury flared for an instant beneath Brandgar's countenance, then he seemed to remember himself. He clutched at his King-Shadow like a man being pulled away from a pier by a riptide.

"Gudrun," yelled Brandgar, "give us strength against this sorcery, or we are all about to consummate very painful love affairs!"

Our sorceress, too, had steeled her will. She swung the strange drums from her back, gasping as though she'd just run a great distance, and began to beat a weak, hesitant counter rhythm in the casual Ajja style:

"Heart be stone and eyes be clear
Gudrun sees the puppeteer—
Fire sings eights, Gudrun sevens
This spell your power leavens . . ."

I felt the rhythm of Gudrun's drumming like the hoofbeats of cavalry horses, rushing closer to bring aid, and for a moment it seemed the terrible lure of the fire-dancers was fading. Then they spun faster, and glowed fiercely white, and ribbons of smoke curled from their feet as they pirouetted across the tiles. Their voices rose, more lovely than ever, and I choked back a sob, balanced on the edge of madness. Why wasn't I embracing them? What sort of damned fool wouldn't want to hurl himself into that fire?

"The fly with hateful flit and bite
The swordsman's feint that wins the fight
The thief enshrouded in the night
The world's true king is distraction . . ."

Mikah knelt and punched the tiles, hard, screaming as their knuckles turned red. "I can't think," they cried, "I can't think—what's the song beneath the song?"

> *"The lasting truths poets compose*
> *The lowly tavern juggling shows*
> *Friends over card games come to blows*
> *You're chained like dogs to distraction . . ."*

"Fire!" bellowed Brandgar, who was stumbling with the eerie movements of a sleepwalker toward his destined fire-dancer, which was a scant few yards away. "Fire is beneath the song! No, stone! Stone is below the dancers! No, the mountain! The mountain is below us all! Gudrun!"

None of Brandgar's guesses loosened the coils of desire that crushed my chest and my loins and my mind. Gudrun shifted tempo again, and beat desperately at her drums in the stave rhythm of formal Ajja skaldry:

> *"Now to sixes singing,*
> *Ajja Gudrun knows well:*
> *Hellfire dancer's contest*
> *Can be met with no spell.*
> *Grimly laughs the king-worm,*
> *Mortal toys must burn soon;*
> *Fly now spear of Wave-King,*
> *Breaking stones before ruin!"*

With that, Gudrun fixed herself like a slinger on a battlefield and pitched her rune-stitched drums straight at Brandgar's head. Their impact, or the repeated shock of such treatment at the hands of his companions, brought him round to himself one final, crucial time.

"The wall," shouted Gudrun, falling to her knees. "The song of distraction is the distraction! The song beneath the song . . . is beneath the song on the wall!"

Heat stabbed the unprotected skin of my face like a thousand darting needles. Smoke curled now from the sleeves and lapels of my jacket; I breathed the scent of my own burning as my fire-dancer leaned in, looming above me at arm's reach, and I had never known anything more beautiful, and I had never ached for anything more powerfully, and I knew that I was dead.

In the corner of my vision, I glimpsed Brandgar steady on his feet, and with the most desperate rage I ever saw, he charged howling past his grasping fire-dancer and drove the point of Cold-Thorn into the center of the Helfalkyn Wormsong that glowed upon the chamber wall. Rock and dust exploded past him, and revealed there beneath the fall of shattered stone were lines of words glowing coldly blue. Quickly, clumsily, but with true feeling Brandgar sang:

> *"From the death here, all be turning*
> *Still the song, forsake the burning*
> *Chance at mountaintop our earning*
> *Though golden gain is distraction!"*

Instantly the blazing heat roiling the air before my face vanished; the deadly whites and oranges of the fire-dancers became the cool blue of the new song on the wall. An easement washed over me, as though I had plunged my whole body into a cold, clear river. I fell over, exhausted, groaning with pleasure and disbelief at being alive, and I was not alone. We all lay there gasping like idiots for some time, chests heaving like the near drowned, laughing and sobbing to ourselves as we came to terms with our memories of the fire-song's seduction. The memory did not fade, and has not faded, and to be free of it will be both a wonder and a sorrow until the day I die.

"Well sung, son of Erika and Orthild," said one of the gentled fire-dancers in a voice nothing like that which had nearly conquered us with delight. "Well played, daughter of the sky. The gift you leave us is an honor. Your diminishment is an honor."

The blue shapes faded into thin air, leaving only the orange pillar of fire which still poured from the rock chimney; it seemed our host was done with offering chances to escape. Then I saw that Brandgar was on his feet, staring motionless at a pair of objects, one held in each hand.

The two halves of the broken spear Cold-Thorn.

"Oh, my king," sighed Gudrun, wincing as she stood and retrieved her drums. "Forgive me."

Brandgar stared down at his sundered weapon without answering for some time, then sighed. "There is nothing to forgive, sorceress. My guesses were all bad, and your answer was true."

Slowly, reverently, he set the two parts of Cold-Thorn on the floor.

"Nine-and-twenty years, and it has never failed me. I lay it here as a brother on a battlefield. I give it to the stories to come."

Then he hefted his second spear over his shoulder, though he still refused to unbind the leather from its point, and his old grin appeared like an actor taking a curtain call.

"Bide no more; the night is not forever, and we must climb. With every step, I more desire conversation with the dragon. Come!"

FOURTH, HOW WE PASSED FROM THE BRITTLE BONES
OF THE MOUNTAIN TO THE SNOW OF DEATH

Shaken but giddy, we wandered on into many-pillared galleries, backlit by troughs and fountains of incandescent lava that flowed like sluggish water. The heat of it was such that to approach made us mindful of the burning we had only narrowly escaped, and by unspoken agreement we stayed well clear of the stuff. It made soft sounds as it ran, belching and bubbling in the main, but also an unnerving glassy crackling where it touched the edges of its containers, and there darkened to silvery black.

"A strangeness, even for this place," said Gudrun, brushing her fingers across one of the stone pillars. "There's a resting power here. Not merely in the drawing up of the mountain's boiling blood, which is not wholly natural. There are forces bound and balanced in these pillars, as if they might be set loose by design."

"A new trap?" said Brandgar.

"If so, it's meant to catch half the Dragon's Anvil when it goes," said Gudrun. "Crale won't be shielding us from that with his bottom."

"Is it a present danger to us?" I asked.

"Most likely," said Gudrun.

"I welcome every new course at this feast," said Brandgar. "Come! We were meant to be climbing!"

Up, then, via spiral staircases wide enough for an Ajja longship to slide down, assuming its sails were properly furled. Into more silent galleries we passed, with molten rock to light our way, until we emerged at last beneath a high ceiling set with shiny black panes of glass. Elsewhere they might have been windows lighting a glorious temple or a rich villa, but here they were just a deadness in the stones. A cool breeze blew through this place, and Mikah sniffed the air.

"We're close now," they said. "Perhaps not yet at the summit, but that's the scent of the outside."

This chamber was fifty yards long and half as wide, with a small door on the far side. Curiously enough, there was no obvious passage I could see suited for a dragon. Before the door stood a polished obsidian statue just taller than Brandgar. The manlike figure bore the head of an owl, with its eyes closed, and in place of folded wings it had a fan of arms, five per side, jutting from its upper back. This is a common shape for a *barrow-vardr*, a tomb guardian the Ajja like to carve on those intermittent occasions when they manage to retrieve enough of a dead hero for a burial ceremony. I was not surprised when the lids of its eyes slowly rose, and it regarded us with orbs like fractured rubies.

"Here have I stood since the coming of the master," spoke the statue, "waiting to put you in your grave then stand as its ornament, King-on-the-Waves."

"The latter would be a courtesy but the former will never happen," said Brandgar, cheerfully setting his wrapped spear down. "Let us fight if we must though I will lose my temper if you have another song to sing us."

"Black, my skin will turn all harm," said the statue. "Silver skin forfeits the charm."

"Verse is nearly as bad," growled Brandgar. He sprinted at the statue and hurled himself at its midsection, in the manner of a wrestler. I sighed inwardly at this, but you have seen that Brandgar was one part forethought steeped in a thousand parts hasty action, and he was never happier than when he was testing the strength of a foe by offering it his skull for crushing. The ten arms of the barrow-vardr spread in an instant, and the two opponents grappled only briefly before Brandgar was hurled twenty feet backwards, narrowly missing Gudrun. He landed very loudly.

Mikah moved to the attack then with short curved blades, and I swallowed my misgivings and backed them with my own daggers. Sparks flew from every touch of Mikah's knives against the thing's skin, and the air was filled with a mad whirl of obsidian arms and dodging thieves. Mikah were faster than I, so I let them stay closer and keep the thing's attention. I lunged at it from behind, again and again, until one of the arms slapped me so hard I saw constellations of stars dancing across my vision. I stumbled away with more speed than grace, and a moment later Mikah broke off the fight as well, vaulting clear. Past them charged Brandgar, shouting something brave and unintelligible. A few seconds later he was flying across the chamber again.

Gudrun took over then, chanting and waving her hands. She threw vials and wooden tubes at the barrow-vardr, and green fire erupted on its arms and head. Then came a series of silver flashes, and a great ear-stinging boom, and the thing vanished in an eruption of smoke and force that cracked the stones beneath its feet and sent chips of rock singing through the air, cutting my face. Coughing, wincing, I peered into the smoke and was gravely disappointed, though perhaps not surprised, to see the thing still standing there quite unaltered. Gudrun swore. Then Brandgar found his feet again and ran headlong into the smoke. There was a ringing metallic thump. He exited the haze on his customary trajectory.

"I believe we might take this thing at its word that we can do nothing against it while its substance is black," said Mikah. "How do we turn its skin silver?"

"Perhaps we could splash it with quicksilver," said Gudrun. "If we only had some. Or coat it with hot running iron and polish it to a gleam, given a suitable furnace, five blacksmiths, and most of a day to work."

"I packed none of those things," muttered Mikah. Little intelligent discourse took place for the next few minutes, as the invulnerable statue chased us in turns around the chamber, occasionally enduring some fresh fire or explosion conjured by Gudrun without missing a step. She also tried to infuse it with the silvery light by which we had made our way up the darker parts of the mountain, but the substance of the barrow-vardr drank even this spell without effect. Soon we were all scorched and cut and thinking of simpler times, when all we'd had to worry about was burning to death in dancing fires.

"Crale! Lend me your sling!" shouted Mikah, who were badly beset and attempting not to plunge into a trough of lava as they skipped and scurried from ten clutching hands. I made a competent handoff of the weapon and a nestled stone, and was neither swatted nor burned for my trouble. Mikah found just enough space to wind up and let fly—not at the barrow-vardr, but at the ceiling. The stone hit one of the panes of black glass with a flat crack, but either it was too strong to break or Mikah's angle of attack was not to their advantage.

I admit that I didn't grasp Mikah's intent, but Gudrun redressed my deficiency. "I see what you're on about," she shouted. "Guard yourselves!"

She gave us no time to speculate on her meaning. She readied another one of her alarming magical gimmicks and hurled it at the ceiling, where it burst in fire and smoke. The blast shattered not only the glass pane Mikah had aimed for, but all those near it, so that it rained sharp fragments everywhere. I tucked in my head and legs and did a creditable impersonation of a turtle. When the tinkling and shattering came to an end, I glanced up and saw that the sundering of the blackened windows had let in diffuse shafts of cold light, swirling with smoke. Mikah had been right; we were indeed close to open sky, and in the hours we had spent making our way through the heart of the Anvil the moons had also risen, shedding the red reflection of sunset in favor of silvery-white luster. This light fell on the statue, and Brandgar wasted no time in testing its effect.

Now when he tackled the barrow-vardr it yielded like an opponent of ordinary flesh. The king's strength bore it to the stones, and though it flailed for leverage with its vast collection of hands, Brandgar struck its head thrice with his joined fists, blows that made me wince in overgenerous sympathy with our foe. Imagine a noise like an anvil repeatedly dropped on a side of beef. When these had sufficiently dampened the thing's resistance, Brandgar heaved it onto his shoulders, then flung it into the nearest fountain of molten rock, where it flamed and thrashed and quickly sank from our sight.

"I shall have to look elsewhere for a suitable watch upon my crypt."
Brandgar retrieved the wrapped spear he had once more refused to employ and wiped away smears of blood from several cuts on his neck and
forehead. "Presuming I am fated to fill one."

The small door swung open for us as we approached, and we were all
so battle-drunk and blasted that we made a great show of returning the
courtesy with bows and salutes. The room beyond was equal in length to
the chamber of the barrow-vardr, but it was all one great staircase, rising
gently to a portal that was notable for its simplicity. This was no door,
but merely a passage in stone, and through it we could see more moonlight and stars. The chamber was bitterly cold, and drifting in flurries
across the stairs were clouds of scattered snow that came from and
passed into thin air.

"Hold a moment," said Gudrun, kneeling to examine a plaque set
into the floor. I peered over her shoulder and saw more Kandric script:

> *Here and last cross the serpent-touched snow*
> *In each flake the sting of many asps*
> *To touch skin once brings life's unmaking*

"To be stymied by snow in the heart of a fire-mountain," I said,
shuddering at the thought of death from something as small as a grain
of salt brushing naked skin. "That would be a poor end."

"We won't be trying it on for fit," said Gudrun. She gestured, and
with a flash of silver light attempted the same trick I had seen in Underwing Hall, to move herself in the blink of an eye from one place to another. This time the spell went awry; with an answering flash of light she
rebounded from some unseen barrier just before the stairs, and wound
up on her back, coughing up pale wisps of steam.

"It seems we're meant to do this on foot or not at all," she groaned.
"Here's a second ploy, then. If the snow is mortal to this flesh, I'll sing
myself another."

She made a low rumbling sound in her throat and gulped air with
ominous croaks, and with each gulp her skin darkened and her face
elongated, stretching until it assumed the wedge shape of a viper's head.
Her eyes grew, turning greenish gold while the pupils narrowed to dark

vertical crescents. In a moment the transformation was complete; she flicked a narrow tongue past scaled lips and smiled.

"Serpent skin and serpent flesh to ward serpent bite," she hissed. "And if it fails, I shall look very silly, and we can laugh long in the Fields of Swords and Roses."

"In the Fields of Swords and Roses," intoned Mikah and Brandgar.

But there would be no laughing there, at least not on this account, for wearing the flesh of a lizard Gudrun hopped up the stairs, clawed green hands held out for balance, through twenty paces of instant death, until she stood beside the doorway to the night, unharmed. She gave an exaggerated curtsy.

"And can you do the same for us?" shouted Mikah.

"The changing-gift is in the heart of the wizard," she replied, "else I would have turned you all into toads sometime ago and carried you in my pack, loosing you only for good behavior."

Mikah sighed and pulled on their gloves. They studied the waft and weft of the snow for some time, nodding and flexing their hips.

"Mikah," I said, kenning their intentions, "this seems a bit much even for one of your slipperiness."

"We've each come here with all the skills of lives long lived," they said. "This is the test of those lives and skills, my friend."

Mikah went up the steps, fully clothed, but still their face and neck and wrists were unprotected. I understand it must be hard to credit, but that is only because you never saw Mikah move, and any attempt to describe it with words must be a poor telling, even mine. Swaying and weaving, whirling at a speed that made them seem half ghost, they simply dodged between the falling snowflakes as you or I might step between other people walking slowly along a road. In less time than it takes for me to speak of it they had ascended the deadly twenty paces and stood safe beside Gudrun. They stretched idly, in the manner of a cat pretending it has always been at rest, and that no mad leap or scramble has just taken place.

"Well done!" said Brandgar. "This is embarrassing, Crale. Those two have raised the stakes, and I am not sure how to make a show to match theirs, let alone surpass it."

"My concerns are more prosaic," I said. "I have no powers or skills I can think of to get myself out of this room."

"We would be poor friends to leave you here at the threshold," said Brandgar. "And I fear it would disappoint our host. I have a notion to bear us both across; can you trust me, as I have trusted you, absolutely and without objection?"

"You needn't use my affections as a lever, Brandgar," said I, though truthfully, in the face of the serpent-touched snow, he rather did. "Anyway, I am famous among my friends for having never in my life behaved with any particular wisdom."

"Be sure to make yourself small in my arms. Ho, Mikah!" Brandgar threw his wrapped spear up and over the snow, and Mikah caught it. Without taking any further measures to brace my resolve, Brandgar unclasped his cloak. Then he seized me, crushing me to his chest as if I were an errant child about to be borne away for punishment. Apprehending his intentions, I clung to him with my legs, tucked my head against his armored coat, and once again commended my spirit to whichever celestial power was on guard over the souls of fools that night. Brandgar spun his cloak over the pair of us like a tent, covering our arms and heads, blotting out my vision as well as his. Then, shouting some Ajja battle blather that was lost on me, he charged blindly up the steps. My world became a shuddering darkness, and I vow that I could hear the hiss and sizzle of the venomous snow as it met the cloak, as though it were angry at not being able to reach us. Then we bowled over Gudrun and Mikah, and wound up tangled in a heap, cloak and spear and laughing adventurers, safe and entirely bereft of dignity at the top of the steps. Save for a lingering smell in our clothes and gear, the power of the snow seemed to promptly evaporate outside the grasp of the sorcerous flurries.

We were all gloriously alive. The light of moon and stars drew us on.

FINALLY, WHAT AWAITED US AT THE
TOP OF THE DRAGON'S ANVIL

Atop the mountain lay a caldera, a flat-bottomed cauldron of rock wider than a longbow shot, and the stars were such brilliant figures of fire overhead that we could have seen well by them had it been necessary.

But it was not, for here was the treasure of the dragon Glimraug, and the dragon was clearly much taken with the sight.

Arched pavilions of wood and stone ringed the caldera, each multiply tiered and grand as any temple ever set by human hands. A thousand glass lanterns of the subtlest beauty had been hung from the beams and gables of these structures, shedding warm gold and silver light that scintillated on piles of riches too vast to comprehend, even as we stood there gaping at them. Here were copper coins in drifts twenty feet high and silver spilling like the waters of an undammed river; gold nuggets, gold bars, gold discs, gold dust in ivory-inset barrels. Here were the stolen coins of ten centuries, plunder from Sendaria, the Crescent Cities, Far Olan, and the Sunken Lands. Here were the cold dead faces of monarchs unknown to us, the mottos stamped in languages we couldn't guess, a thousand currencies molded as circles, squares, octagons, and far less practical shapes. There were caskets beyond counting, rich varnished woodcrafts that were treasures in themselves, and each held overflowing piles of pearls, amethysts, citrines, emeralds, diamonds, and sapphires. To account it all in meanest summary would double the length of my telling. Here were gilded thrones and icon-tables, gleaming statues of all the gods from all the times and places the human race has set foot, crowns and chalices and toques and periapts and rings. Here were weapons crusted with gems or gleaming enchantments, here were bolts of silk and ceramic jars as tall as myself, full of gauds and baubles, drinking horns and precious mechanisms. All the mountaintop was awash in treasure, tides of it, hillocks of it the size of houses.

There was nothing pithy to say. Even getting it down would become the work of years, I calculated. Years, and hundreds or thousands of people, and engineers and machinery, and ships—if we could indeed force the dragon to part with this grand achievement, Helfalkyn would have to double in size just to service the logistics of plunder. I would need galleons to carry a tenth part of my rightful share, and then vaults, and an army to guard the vaults. These riches loosed upon the world would shake it for generations. My great-great-great-great-grandchildren would relieve themselves in solid gold chamber pots!

"Gudrun," said Brandgar, "is all here as we see it? Is this a glamour?"

The mere thought broke me from the hypnotic joy of my contemplation. Gudrun cast a set of carved bones on the ground. We all watched anxiously, but after consulting her signs only briefly she giggled like a giddy child. "No, lord. What's gold is gold, as far as we can see. And what's silver is silver, and what's onyx is onyx, and thuswise."

"This is the greatest trap of all," I said. "We shall all die of old age before we can carry it anywhere useful."

"We are missing only one thing," said Brandgar. "And that is our host, who will doubtless prefer to see us die of other causes before we take any of it. But I am content to let it come when it will; to walk amidst such splendor is a gift. Let us stay on our guard but avail ourselves of the courtesy."

And so we wandered Glimraug's garden of imponderable wealth, running our hands over statues and gemstones and shields, caught up in our private entrancements. So often had I won through to a rumored treasure in some dusty tower or rank sewer or mountain cave, only to discover empty, rusting boxes and profitless junk. It was hard to credit that the most ridiculous legend of wealth in all the world had turned out to be the most accurate.

Plumes of smoke and mist drifted from vents in the rock beyond the treasure pavilions, and my eyes were drawn to another such plume rising gently from a pile of silver. From there my attention was snared by a scattering of dark stones upon the surface of the metal coins. I approached, and saw that these were rubies, hundreds of them, ranging in color from that of fresh pumping blood to that of faded carnations. I have always been a particular admirer of red stones, and I shook a few into my hands, relishing the clink and glimmer of the facets.

The silver coins shifted, and from within them came a blue shape, a yard wide and as long as I was tall. So gently did it rise, so familiar did it seem that I stared at it for a heartbeat before I realized that it was a hand, a scaled hand, and the dark things glistening at the near ends of its digits were talons longer than my daggers. Delight transmuted to horror, and I was rooted with fear as the still-gentle hand closed on mine from beneath, trapping me with painless but inescapable pressure. The difference in scale? Imagine I had elected to shake hands with a cat, then refused to let go.

"Tarkaster Crale," rumbled a voice that was like a bolt of the finest velvet smoldering in a furnace. "The rubies are most appropriate for contemplation. Red for all the blood that lies beneath this treasure. The million mortals who died in vaults and towers and ships and armies so that we could take these proud things into our care."

The pile of silver shuddered, then parted and slid to the ground in every direction, displaced by the rising of the creature that had lain inside it, marked only by steaming breath curling up from nostrils as wide as my head. The arms rose, each a Brandgar-weight of scaled strength. I gaped at the lithe body the color of dark sapphire, its back ridges like the thorns of some malevolent flower, its impossibly delicate wings with membranes that glistened like a steel framework hung with nothing more than moonlight. Atop the sinuous neck was a head somehow vulpine and serpentine at once, with sharp flat ears that rang from their piercings, dozens of silver rings that would have encircled my neck. The dragon had a mane, a shock of blue-white strands that vibrated with the stiffness of crystal rather than the suppleness of hair or fur. The creature's eyes were black as the sky, split only by slashes of pulsing silver, and I could not meet them; even catching a glance made my vision flash as though I had stared at the sun. I could not move as the dragon's other hand reached out and closed around my waist, again with perfect care and unassailable strength. I was lifted like a doll.

"I ... I can put the stones back," I burbled. "I'm sorry!"

"Oh, that is not true," said the dragon. Its breath smelled like burning copper. "And if it were, you would not be the sort of mortal to which we would speak. No, you are not sorry. You are terrified."

"Hail, Glimraug the Fair!" shouted Brandgar. "Hail, Sky Tyrant, Shipbreaker, and Night-Scathe!"

"Hail, King-on-the-Waves, Son of Erika and Orthild, Landless Champion, Remover of Others' Nuisances," said Glimraug, setting me down and nudging me to run along as if I were a pet. I gladly retreated to stand with my companions, judging it prudent to toss the rubies back onto the dragon-tossed pile of silver first. "Hail, companions to the king! You have endured every courtesy provided for our visitors, and glimpsed what no mortal has for many years. Have you been dispatched here to avenge some Ajja prince? Did we break a tower or two in passing? Did we devour someone's sheep?"

"We have come for our own sakes," said Brandgar. "And for yours, and for your treasure as a last resort. We have heard the Helfalkyn Wormsong."

I had no idea what Brandgar meant by any of that, but the dragon snorted and bared its teeth.

"That is not the usual order in which our visitors lay their priorities," it said. "But all who come here have heard the song. What is your meaning?"

"There are songs, and there are songs beneath songs, are there not?" Brandgar removed the leather wrappings of his unused spear. Ash-hafted, the weapon had the lethal simplicity of a boar spear, with a pyramidal striking tip forged of some dark steel with a faint mottle, like flowing water. "Others heard the song of gold, but we have heard the song of the gold-taker, the song of your plan, the song of your hope. We have brought ending and eyes."

"Have you?" whispered the dragon, and it was wondrous to see for an instant, just an instant, a break in its inhuman self-regard. It caught its breath, and the noise was like a bellows priming to set a furnace alight, which might have been closer to the truth than I preferred. "Are you in earnest, o king, o companions? Are we in sympathy? For if this is mere presumption, we will give you a death that will take five lifetimes to unravel in your flesh, and while you rot screaming in the darkness we will pile the corpses of Ajja children in a red mound higher than any tower. Your kinfolk will gray and dwindle knowing that their posterity has been ground into meat for the flies! This we swear by every day of every year of our age, and we have known ten thousand."

"Hear this. For long months we sought and strove," said Brandgar, "in Merikos, where the dragon Elusiel fell, where the wizards were said to keep one last jar of the burning blood that had seeped from her wounds."

"We lost many companions," added Gudrun. "The wizards lost everything, including the blood."

"For another year we dispensed with a fortune in Sulagar," said Mikah, "engaging the greatest of the old masters there in the crafting of black-folded steel."

"Twenty spears they made for me," resumed Brandgar. "Twenty I tested and found wanting. The twenty-first I quenched in the blood of Elusiel, and carried north to Helfalkyn, and have carried here to be used but once. Its makers called it *Adresh*, the All-Piercing, but I am the one who gave it purpose, and I have named it Glory-Kindler."

Glimraug threw back its head and roared. We all staggered, clutching our ears, even Brandgar. The sound rattled the very air in our lungs, and I did not merely imagine that the mountain shook beneath us, for I could see the lanterns bobbing and the treasure piles shaking. Lightning flashed at the rim of the caldera, bolt after bolt, splitting the darkness and painting everything in flashes of golden white, and the thunder that followed boomed like mangonel stones shattering walls.

"Perhaps it is you," said the dragon, when the terrific noises of this display had faded. "Perhaps it *is* you! But know that we are not so base as to tip the scales. Achieve us! Hold nothing back, for nothing shall be held in turn."

"This is an excellent doom," said Brandgar, "and we shall not take it lightly."

The dragon flared its wings, and for an instant their translucence hung like an aura in the night. Then, with a fresh roar of exultation, Glimraug hurled itself into the air, raising a wind that lashed us with dust and shook lanterns from their perches. I felt something close to seasickness, for in the manner of my profession I had blithely presumed we would make some effort to trick, circumvent, weaken, or even negotiate with our foe rather than honorably baring our asses and inviting a kick.

"Brandgar," I yelled, "what in all the hells are we supposed to be doing here?"

"Something beautiful. Your only task is to survive." He gave me a powerful squeeze on the shoulder, then pushed me away. "Run, Crale! Keep your wits loose in the scabbard. Think only of living!"

Then Glimraug crashed back down, and treasure fountained in a fifty-yard radius. Brandgar, Gudrun, and Mikah evaded the snapping jaws and the buffet of the wings, and now they commenced to fight with everything they had.

Gudrun chanted and scattered glass vials from her collection of strange accoutrements, breaking them against the stone, loosing the powers and spirits bound therein. She held nothing back for any more rainy days—seething white mists rose at Glimraug's feet, and in their miasmic tatters I saw the faces of hungry things eager to wreak harm. The dragon reared, raised high its arms, and uttered darkly hissing words in a language that made me want to loose my bowels. I ran for one of the treasure pavilions, hid behind a stout wooden pillar, and peered around the side to watch the battle unfold.

Brandgar struck for Glimraug's flank but the sapphire-scaled worm flicked its tail like a whip, knocking Brandgar and his vaunted new spear well away. Mikah fared better, dashing under the dragon's forelimbs and heaving themselves into a wing joint, and from there to the ridges of its back. The whorls of Gudrun's spirit-mist became a column, bone-white, wailing as it surged against Glimraug's face and body. It seemed as if the dragon were attempting to climb a leafless winter tree, and failing—but only for a moment.

With a sound like a river rushing swollen in spring's first melt, Glimraug opened wide its maw and sucked Gudrun's ghost-substance into its throat as a man might draw deeply from a pipe. Then it reared again, and blasted the stuff high into the air, trailing flickers of blue-and-white fire. The spirit-mist rose like smoke and quickly faded from sight against the stars, whatever power it had contained either stolen or destroyed. Then the dragon lunged with foreclaws for Gudrun, but with a flash of silver she was safe by twenty yards, and hurling her fire gimmicks without dismay. Orange fire erupted at Glimraug's feet, to little effect.

Now Gudrun sung further spell-songs, and hurled from a leather bag a thousand grasping strands of spun flax, which sought the dragon's limbs and wove themselves into bindings. Glimraug snapped them in a trice, as you or I might break a single rotten thread, and the golden fibers floated to the ground. Then the dragon's dignity broke, for Mikah had made their way up into its gleaming mane, and from there stabbed at one of its eyes. The blade met that terrible lens, I swear, but either luck wasn't with the thief or the weapon was too commonplace to give more than a scratch. Still, neither you nor I would appreciate a scratch against an eye, and the dragon writhed, trying to fling Mikah off. They kept their perch, but only just, and could do little else but hold fast.

Glimraug whirled and leapt away from Gudrun with the easy facility of a cat, once more scattering delicate objects far and wide with the shock of its landing. It struck at a pile of silver coins, jaws gaping, and took what must have been tons of the metal into its mouth as a greedy man might slurp his stew. Then it breathed deep, hissing breaths through its nostrils, and its neck bulged with every passage of air. A glow lit the gaps of the scales in the dragon's chest, faint red at first but swiftly brightening and shifting to blue, then white. Mikah cried out and leapt from the dragon's mane, trailing smoke. Their boots and gloves were on fire.

The dragon charged back toward Gudrun, mighty claws hammering the stones. The sorceress chanted, and a barrier of blue ice took shape before her, thick and overhanging like the crest of a wave. Glimraug drew in another long breath, then expelled it, and for an instant the blazing light of its internal fire was visible. Then the dragon breathed forth a stream of molten silver, all that it had consumed and melted, like the great burst of a geyser, wreathed in crackling white flame. The wave of burning death blasted Gudrun's ice shield to steam and enveloped her in an instant. Then came eruption after eruption of green-and-orange fire as the things she had carried met their fate. I recoiled from the terrible heat and the terrible sight, but to the last she had not even flinched.

I was forced to run to another pavilion as rivulets of crackling metal flowed toward me. Glimraug chuckled deep in its throat, orange-hot streams still dripping from between its fangs and cooling silver-black beneath its chin, forming a crust of added scales. Mikah howled furiously. They had quenched the flames, and however much pain they must have been bracing against, they did not reveal it by slowing down. Glimraug's claws came down twice, and Mikah was there to receive the blow neither time. Once more the thief leapt for the dragon's smoking back, but now they rebounded cannily and clung to the leading edge of the dragon's left wing. Before the dragon was able to flick them away, Mikah pulled out one of their blades and bore down on it with both arms, driving it into the gossamer substance of the dragon's wing membrane. This yielded where the eye had not. Mikah slid down as the stuff parted like silk, then fell to the ground when they ran out of membrane, leaving a flapping rent above them.

Glimraug instantly folded the hurt wing sharply to its side, as an unwary cat might pull back a paw that has touched hot fireplace stones. Then, heaving itself forward, it whirled tail and claw alike at the Ajja thief, whip-smack, whip-smack. Nearly too late I realized that the next stroke would demolish my place of safety. I fled and rolled as Glimraug's tail splintered the pavilion; a hard-flung wave of baubles and jewelry knocked me farther than I'd intended. I slid to a halt one handspan from the edge of a cooling silver stream, and hundreds of coins rolled and rattled past me.

I looked up just in time to see Mikah's fabled luck run its course. Stumbling over scattered treasure, at last showing signs of injury, they tried to be elsewhere for the next swipe of a claw but finally kept the unfortunate rendezvous. Glimraug seized them eagerly and hauled them up before its eyes, kicking and stabbing to the last.

"Like for like," rumbled the dragon, and with two digits of its free hand it encircled Mikah's left arm, then tore it straight out of the socket. Blood gushed and ran down the dragon's scales; Mikah screamed, but somehow raised their remaining blade for one last futile blow. The dragon cast Mikah into a distant treasure pavilion like a discarded toy. The impact was bone-shattering; the greatest thief I have ever known was slain and buried in an explosion of blood-streaked gold coins.

"One died in silver, one died in gold," said Glimraug, turning and stalking toward me.

"Tarkaster Crale won't live to be old," I whispered.

Up went the bloodstained claw. I heaved myself to my knees, wondering where I intended to dodge to, and the claw came down.

Well short of me, clutched in pain.

Brandgar had recovered himself, and buried the spear Glory-Kindler to the full length of its steel tip in the joint of Glimraug's right wing. The blood that spilled from the wound steamed, and the stones burst into flames where it fell on them. Brandgar withdrew the smoking spear and darted back as the dragon turned, but it did not attack. It shuddered, and stared at the gash in its hide.

"The venom of Elusiel, kin of our kin," said the dragon with something like wonder. "A thousand wounds have bent our scales, but never have we felt the like."

Brandgar spun Glory-Kindler over his head, pointed it at the dragon in salute, and then braced himself in a pikeman's stance. "Never have you *faced* the like," he shouted. "Let it be here and now!"

Ponderously the dragon turned to face him; some of its customary ease was gone, but it was still a towering foe, still possessed of fearsome power. With its wings folded tight and burning blood streaming from one flank, it spread its taloned arms and pounced. Brandgar met it screaming in triumph. Spear pierced dragon breast, and an instant later the down sweep of Glimraug's talons shattered the haft of Glory-Kindler and tore through Brandgar's kingly coat-of-plate. The man fell moaning, and the dragon toppled beside him, raising a last cloud of ashen dust. Disbelieving, I stumbled up and ran to them.

"O king," the dragon murmured, wheezing, and with every breath spilling more fiery ichor on the ground, "in all our ten thousand years, we have had but four friends, and we have only met them this night."

"Crale, you look awful." Brandgar smiled up at me, blood streaming down his face. I saw at once that his wound was mortal; under smashed ribs and torn flesh I could see the soft pulse of a beating heart, and a man once opened like that won't long keep hold of his spirit. "Don't mourn. Rejoice, and remember."

"You really didn't want the damned treasure," I said, kneeling beside him. "You crazy Ajja! 'Bring ending and eyes,' meaning, find a way to kill a dragon . . . and bring a witness when you do it."

"You've been a great help, my friend." Brandgar coughed, and winced as it shook his chest. "I was never made to retire quietly from valor and wait for the years to catch me. None of us were."

"It comes," said Glimraug. Shaking, bleeding fire, the dragon hauled itself up, then lifted Brandgar gently, almost reverently in its cupped hands. "We can feel the venom tightening around our heart. The long-awaited wonder comes! True death-friend, let our pyre be shared, let us build it now! To take is not to keep."

"To take is not to keep," answered Brandgar. His voice was weakening. "Yes, I see. It's perfect. Will you do it while I can see?"

"With gladness, we loose our holds and wards on the fires bound within the mountain." Glimraug closed its eyes and muttered some-thing, and the stone shifted below my feet in a manner more ominous than before. I gaped as one of the more distant treasure pavilions seemed to sink into the caldera floor, and a cloud of smoke and sparks rose from where it had gone down.

Then another pavilion sank, then another. With rumbling, cracking, sundering noises, the dragon's treasure was being spilled into reservoirs of lava. Flames roared from the cracks in the ground as wood, cloth, and other precious things tumbled to their destruction.

"What by all the gods are you doing?" I cried.

"This is the greatest of all the dragon-hoards that was ever built," said Brandgar. "A third of all the treasures our race has dug from the ground, Crale. The plunder of a million lives. But there's no true glory in the holding. All that must come in the taking . . . and the letting go."

"You're crazier than the Ajja!" I yelled at Glimraug, entirely forgetting myself. "You engineered this place to be destroyed?"

"Not so much as a shaving of scented wood shall leave with you, Tarkaster Crale." Glimraug carefully shifted Brandgar into one palm, then reached out and set a scimitar-sized talon on my shoulder. Spatters of dragon blood smoked on my leather jacket. "Though you leave with our blessing. Our arts can bear you to a place of safety."

"Wonderful, but what the hell is the *point*?"

Cold pain lashed across my face, and I gasped. Glimraug had flicked its talon upward, a casual gesture—and all of you can still see the result here on my cheek. The wound bled for days and the scar has never faded.

"The point is that it has never been done before," said Glimraug. Another treasure pavilion was swallowed by fire nearby. "And it shall never be done again. All things in this world are made to go into the fire, Tarkaster Crale. All things raise smoke. The smoke of incense is sweet. The smoke of wood is dull haze. But don't you see? The smoke of gold . . . is glory."

I wiped blood from my face, and might have said more, but Glimraug made a gesture, and I found that I could not move. The world began to grow dim around me, and the last I saw of the caldera was Brandgar weakly raising a hand in farewell, and the dragon holding him with a tenderness and regard that was not imagined.

"Take the story, Crale!" called Brandgar. "Take it to the world!"

After a moment of dizzy blackness, I found myself back at the foot of the Dragon's Anvil, on the gentle path that led up to it from Hel-falkyn. The sky was alight with the orange fire of a false dawn; no sooner did I glance back up at the mountaintop than it erupted in an all-out conflagration, orange flames blasting taller than the masts of ships, smoke roiling in a column that blotted out the moons as it rose.

Glimraug the Sky Tyrant was dead, and with it my friends Brandgar, Gudrun, and Mikah. And I, having lost my purse somewhere in the confusion, was now even poorer than I had been before I successfully reached the largest pile of assorted valuables in the history of the whole damn world.

I don't know how I made my way down the path without breaking my neck. My feet seemed to move of their own accord. I could perhaps believe that I was alive, or that I had witnessed the events of the night, but I could not quite manage to believe them both at the same time. A crowd came up from Helfalkyn then, armed and yammering, bearing lanterns and an unwise number of wine bottles, and from their exclama-tions I gathered that I looked as though I had been rolled in dung and baked in an oven.

They demanded to know what had happened atop the Anvil; most of Helfalkyn had roused itself when the thunder and lightning rolled, and by the time the flames were visible there wasn't anyone left in bed. My occasionally dodgy instinct for survival sputtered to life then; I realized that the denizens of a town entirely dedicated to coveting a dragon's treasure might not handle me kindly if I told them I had gone up with my friends and somehow gotten the treasure blasted out of existence. The solution was obvious—I told them I had seen everything, that I was the sole survivor, and that I would give the full and complete story only after I had received passage back to the Crescent Cities and safely dis-embarked from my ship.

Thus I made my first arrangement for compensation as a profes-sional storyteller.

That, then, is how it all transpired. I heard that various scroungers from Helfalkyn sifted the shattered Anvil for years, but the dragon had its way—every last scrap of anything valuable had been dropped into the molten heart of the mountain, either burned or sunk from mortal reach forever. I retired from adventuring directly and took up the craft of sitting on my backside at the best place by the fire, telling glib confabulations to strangers for generally reasonable prices.

But one night a year, I don't tell a single lie. I tell a true story about kindred spirits who chose a doom I didn't understand at all when I walked away from it. And one night a year, I turn my bowl over, because the last thing I want to see for my troubles is a little pile of coins reminding me that I am an old, old man, and I sure as hell understand it now.

Rich Larson

* * *

Rich Larson was born in West Africa, has studied in Rhode Island and Edmonton, Alberta, and worked in a small Spanish town outside Seville. He now lives in Grande Prairie, Alberta, in Canada. He won the 2014 Dell Award and the 2012 Rannu Prize for Writers of Speculative Fiction. In 2011 his cyberpunk novel *Devolution* was a finalist for the Amazon Breakthrough Novel Award. His short work appears or is forthcoming in *Asimov's Science Fiction*, *The Magazine of Fantasy & Science Fiction*, *Clarkesworld*, *Interzone*, *Lightspeed*, *DSF*, *Strange Horizons*, *Apex Magazine*, *Beneath Ceaseless Skies*, *AE*, and many others, including the anthologies *Upgraded*, *Futuredaze*, and *War Stories*. Find him online at richwlarson.tumblr.com

In the tense and atmospheric story that follows, he takes us along to the gritty industrial city of Colgrid in company with two rogues seeking to unlock the secret of a fabulous treasure, and who find that the situation gets stranger and the knots they have to unravel more and more complicated with every step they take.

* * *

The Colgrid Conundrum

RICH LARSON

The channel was skinned with dark ice that squealed and crackled away under the ship's prow; apart from that they entered Colgrid in silence.

For Crane, it was uncharacteristic. He sat spider-like on an overturned crate, elbows resting on bony knees, wide mouth hidden under a thick-knit scarf. His watery blue eyes narrowed to slits as he watched Colgrid's sprawling factories slide closer. Gilchrist stood, sinewy arms folded, breath escaping as a tendril of steam. He was comfortable in silence, but his dark eyes, normally always scanning, always measuring, looked off to nowhere.

On the deck between them sat the strongbox. It was a dull gray cube resting on four small clawed feet, one of which had been cracked in the escape. The sides were filigreed with a carefully crafted pattern of whorls and ripples. The top was ringed with concentric grooves, and in the deepest of them, where Crane's scrubbing hadn't reached, there was still a crust of dried-black blood.

As the ship moved deeper into the city, the smells of oil and machinery spiked through the cold air. Half the factories still churned, belching smog that hung over the city like an inky cloak, blotting out the stars overhead.

"Acrid as ever," Crane finally said. He adjusted his scarf with one long, pale hand. "But from what I've heard of this lock breaker, I surmise our stay will be brief. We should leave with only partially devastated lungs."

"Lucky," Gilchrist said, toneless.

The dock approached, lit by phosphor lanterns that glowed bright green in the darkness. The ship's crew stirred to action, cutting speed, making shouted calculations with the dockhands before the pitons launched with a muzzle flash and sharp crack. Thick cables winched them out of the current, reeling them into the mooring, making the ship's frame shiver and groan.

"It was unavoidable, Gilchrist," Crane said, as gangplanks thumped down and the hubbub of debarking grew around them. "You know that as well as I do."

Gilchrist made no reply, but his hands clenched more tightly. Under one thumbnail, where his scrubbing hadn't reached, there was still a sliver of dried-black blood.

They slipped away from the dock like shades, with the strongbox slung in a makeshift harness between them. The ship's captain had been paid for his averted eyes, and persuaded even further by the feathery white Guild scar Crane had exposed while adjusting his sleeve—no need for him to know that the criminal organization had been more or less dissolved for months now.

Tall lampposts lined Colgrid's streets, topped with the same glowing phosphor as on the dock, lighting a way through thickening smog. A mask vendor was hawking shrilly at the next corner.

"We should," Gilchrist said. "Not many gypsies up here."

Colgrid's denizens were pale-skinned and dark-eyed—Crane blended well enough, but Gilchrist's dusky skin could stick in a passerby's memory. If all went well, they would have the strongbox opened and be sailing for far warmer climes before anyone could identify them.

Crane flicked the vendor two silver coins and received two masks from the stall in return, flimsier versions of the bug-eyed creation that concealed her entire face.

"I'm told they now wear these in the courts," Crane said, slipping the mask over his mouth and nose. "Fashion is an unpredictable beast, is it not, madam?"

"Them ones just for show, they don't have a good filter." The vendor's voice came high and tinny through her mask. "Mine have the best filters."

Gilchrist kept a hand on the strongbox while Crane adjusted his mask, then swapped places to don his own. They continued on, moving deeper into the city, following the directions Gilchrist had memorized in a small filthy bar on Brask's wharf. The hour was late and the streets mostly empty. Both tensed when a tall figure emerged from the gloom on impossibly long, skeletal legs, but it was only a lamplighter, using the clicking mechanical stilts that were still a rarity everywhere but Colgrid. Each metal shin was painted with a scarlet circle.

The same insignia appeared a dozen more times as Crane and Gilchrist wound their way through the twisting streets: sometimes stenciled onto signboards above shops, sometimes painted raggedly straight onto the brick. In the neater versions, they could see it was meant to be a fine-toothed gear.

"I admit I'm unfamiliar with this particular cipher," Crane puffed, nodding his chin toward the closest. "What do you make of it, Gilchrist? A mark of allegiance?"

Gilchrist touched his arm momentarily, where a Guild scar twin to Crane's own was hidden under his sleeve. The Guild had never had a strong hold on Colgrid, and now, not at all. "Vacuums fill quickly," he said.

Crane massaged his shoulder and tightened his grip on the sling. A transient snow was starting to fall, small dirty flakes that didn't touch the ground. They turned into a narrow alley, not marked by any red gear, and startled a small bundle of rags. The child was bony thin, soot-smeared. He, or maybe she, gave a choked sound of surprise and scuttled backward.

Gilchrist blinked. He stuck a hand into his pocket and retrieved a handful of crusts from their last meal on board the ship. "It's too cold tonight," he said, squatting. "You'll lose your toes. There's a heating pipe around back of that smithy two streets over."

The child snatched the bread away and forced all of it at once into a scabby mouth, then scrambled out of the alley, darting past Crane's knees. Gilchrist's dark eyes trailed after. He took a silver coin from his other pocket and wrapped it in the nest of rags the child had left behind.

Crane only watched, expressionless, until Gilchrist stood up and hefted his side of the strongbox. They walked on.

The lock breaker's shop was small, ensconced in shadows, the nearest lamppost smashed. Smoke coiled from a small stack on the roof and grease-yellow light leaked from slits in the barred windows. No light escaped the door, which was a thick slab of reinforced iron that looked better suited to a gaol or a fortress.

"A deceiver imagines everyone is out to deceive him," Crane said, yanking his mask down around his neck. "Perhaps a similar logic applies to lock breakers."

They set the strongbox down on the cobblestone with a dull thunk. Crane rubbed his aching shoulder again; Gilchrist studied the door. There was an ornate sort of knocker, shaped like a jaw, that seemed out of place on the otherwise unadorned surface. Crane blew into his reddening hands, then reached for it and took hold.

A disguised second jaw sprang from underneath and clamped his wrist in place. Crane flinched, but barely. His lips twisted into a smile as he looked down at his trapped extremity.

"How fortunate it has no teeth," he said. Gilchrist snorted. The quick-knife had slid from his sleeve into his fist and he was tensed, scanning for ambush. Crane gave an experimental wiggle and shook his head. The metal jaws were tight as a vise.

The scratch of moving feet came from behind the door, and a slit shuttered open. An eye ringed with kohl appeared in the gap. "Who the fuck are you?" came a woman's hoarse voice.

"A man with a great many uses for his left hand, most of which would be severely diminished by frostbite or broken bones," Crane said. "I am called Crane. My companion is Gilchrist. A mutual acquaintance in Brask informed us you might be able to solve a particularly vexing toy puzzle, for a price."

There was a muffled *click-chunk* from some internal mechanism, and the jaws opened. Crane retrieved his hand, rubbing ruefully at his blue-veined wrist. The cold metal had left a purplish welt.

"He said someone was going to try hitting the Thule Estate. You pulled it off?" The lock breaker's eye widened and her scratchy voice carried a hint of admiration.

"We are gentlemen and I resent the suggestion," Crane said blithely. "Will you aid us with the puzzle or not? It's rather conspicuous and we would prefer to have it off the streets, and out of sight, as soon as possible."

The lock breaker hesitated. "Show me."

Gilchrist slipped the strongbox from its harness and hefted it up to eye level. Its filigreed design gleamed in the yellow light. The lock breaker's eye narrowed. Then another *click-chunk*, a series of rattling scrapes as bolts retracted, and the door swung open at last with a slink of steam.

The lock breaker was wide-shouldered, narrow-hipped, dressed all in black. Her pale hair was slicked backward off an angular face. She had deep-set eyes, made more so by the kohl, that seemed older than the rest of her. There was a gray smudge on her forehead from an unwashed finger.

"Didn't think anyone would actually have the stones to rob that place," she said. "Heard they flay thieves."

"Do you greet all your customers so vigorously?" Crane asked, rubbing his wrist again as they stepped inside with the strongbox, smelling gunpowder and old metal.

"I'm closed," the lock breaker said. "Been closed three weeks now. And I'm careful." She turned back to the door and set to locking it again, spinning a brass wheel that drove the bolts into place. From the back, the simple iron door was a patchwork of moving mechanisms. Crane observed it keenly while Gilchrist scanned the shop's interior.

Oil lamps provided the yellow light, pulling strange shadows over the objects littering the workbench and hanging from the walls. There were glinting skeleton keys, hooks and thick needles, what looked like a hand-cranked drill. Dissected locks sat beside their intact neighbors in a scattering of pins and springs. A floor-to-ceiling rack contained hun-

dreds on hundreds of keys, large and small, sleek and spiky, cheap copper and ornate silver and everything in between.

Traces of the lock breaker's personal effects were scant, but a small
table carrying a cracked mug and half-eaten bowl of food was tucked
into one corner, and a few shirts dangled from improvised hooks in the
ceiling. A shabby rug was tacked unevenly to one wall and a cylindrical
urn sat above the hissing heating pipe.

The lock breaker picked out a square of space on the bench; Crane
and Gilchrist set the strongbox down. She examined it with an almost
hungry expression on her face, leaning in close, peering from every
angle.

"Haven't crossed paths with one of these little bastards for a long
time," she said. "It's a dead-box. You know that, I hope. You try to force
this open with a pry bar, it's spring-loaded to crush whatever's inside."

"We know that," Gilchrist said flatly, pulling off his mask.

"If it was within my abilities, we would not have come seeking yours,"
Crane said. "You've encountered its like before. I assume you can solve
this one as well."

The lock breaker's eyes narrowed again. Her mouth thinned. "I can,
yeah," she said. "For a price, I can."

"Of course," Crane said. "An expert of your caliber demands suitable
compensation. With that in mind, we might be willing to negotiate up
to—"

"A third," Gilchrist cut in.

Crane's face soured. "Yes. That."

The lock breaker was silent for a moment, considering. A muscle
twitched in her cheek. "No," she said.

"No?" Crane echoed, a needle tenting the silk of his voice.

"Without me, that box isn't worth a pig's shit," she said. "Without
me, you did that job for nothing, so I figure I get to name my own price,
thanks."

Behind her, the quick-knife rippled down Gilchrist's sleeve again.

"But I don't want money," she continued. "I want something else. I
want the pair of you to do something for me." She looked across the
room, to the gray urn, and came slightly unfocused. Her thumb drifted

up to her forehead, where the ash stained her skin. "How we mourn a lover, in the north," she said. "A little every day until the ash is gone. I want you to help me avenge him."

The lock breaker dragged a pair of splintering stools over to the heating pipe where Crane and Gilchrist were warming their hands, and told them, like an afterthought, that her name was Merin.

"A pleasure," Crane said.

Merin squatted down, nodding her chin toward the urn. "And his name was Petro. He was my husband. More or less. He's been dead eighteen days now."

"We extend our sincerest condolences," Crane said warily. His gaze flickered back toward the unattended strongbox. Gilchrist, by contrast, was rapt.

"I bet you do." Merin snorted. "I don't need you to care. Just need you to understand the situation, is all." She folded her arms on her knees. "Do you know who runs Colgrid?"

"The Dogue, officially," Crane said. "But I imagine the balance of power now shifts in favor of the merchants and industrialists. The same change has begun in Brask."

"Men of business." Merin's voice was thick with contempt. "Brutes, all of them. They worship money and see the world all in numbers." She clenched her teeth for a moment. "Here in Colgrid, we have the very worst of them. He calls himself Papa Riker. He's nearly as rich as the Dogue himself now. Ten times as ruthless."

"How did he attain his wealth?" Crane asked.

"The New World," Merin said. "Same as the rest of them. He was with the trading companies. Mostly narcotics."

Crane and Gilchrist exchanged a glance that did not go unnoticed.

"You know the trade?" Merin asked.

"A brief foray that proved ill-fated," Crane said. "For a variety of reasons."

"There was a fire," Gilchrist said.

Merin nodded, tonguing her teeth. "You know shiver?"

"Not my preferred vice," Crane said, but his eyes brightened. "But yes. We're quite familiar. Distilled powder from the xoda plant. Hones the nerves to a razor's edge." He tapped the side of his nose.

"Riker is the one who introduced it to the factories," Merin said. "They use it to keep the workers from falling asleep. He owns almost half the city, now. Competition is bought off or killed off. He's ruthless, how I said. Always looking for a new advantage." She looked at the urn again. "Twenty-six days ago, he wanted me to do some work for him. Petro set up the meeting."

"Sabotage?" Gilchrist guessed.

"Security," Merin said. "Not to keep anyone out. To keep the little imps in. Wanted me to rig up a design for adjustable manacles. Their wrists are too skinny, see. And some of them lose a hand altogether in the machinery." Her nostrils flared. "I told him to go fuck himself."

Crane looked over to Gilchrist. "This Riker employs children in his factories?"

"Sweeps them off the streets and puts them to work, yeah, mostly on the south side," Merin said. "Always looking for an advantage, how I said. As close to the devil as you can get. So I refused."

"And there was retribution," Crane surmised.

"Not the kind I was ready for." Merin glared at the urn. "My husband was a strong man in many ways. Weak, in some ways. When it came to drink, or to drug, Petro was weak." She blinked hard. "The last few years, it was shiver. Never too bad. Never bad enough to make me put a stop to it. I even did it with him, every so often." Her voice turned fierce. "A week after I refused the job, I found Petro in our bed, pale as snow. Dead. With shiver smeared around his nose. I tested some of the powder on a rat the next day, and it was how I thought. Someone gave him a tainted pinch. Laced it with cyanide."

Silence seeped into the cramped space. Crane glanced to Gilchrist again, but Gilchrist was staring at the urn almost as intently as Merin. "And in what manner did the rat die?" Crane asked.

The lock breaker's face darkened. "Badly," she said. "So that's my price. That's how Riker has to die. Badly."

"Vengeance is a natural proclivity," Crane said. "I indulge in it myself from time to time. But we are only three, and of the three, only you are familiar with this Riker and with the general environ. Gilchrist and I are strangers here."

"Better that way," Merin said. "Walls have ears these days. Don't know who to trust. That's why not another soul in Colgrid knows what I've got planned."

"To speak frankly, Madam Merin." Crane picked a piece of lint from his knee, peered at it, and cast it aside. "You would do better to open the strongbox and use your more than generous allotment of the contents to hire an assassin. We may even be able to put you into contact with one."

Merin's gaze was defiant. "If you got into that estate, and out in one piece, you can do this job easy. The price stands."

Crane opened his mouth to riposte.

"We'll do it," Gilchrist said. His black eyes were gleaming. "You have a plan?"

Merin exhaled a long breath. She looked more closely at Gilchrist, then nodded. "Yeah. Haven't thought about much else since Petro." She turned to Crane. "You're the talker, he's the doer. Is that it?"

"Such things are never so simple as they first appear," Crane said flatly. "But if no other payment can satisfy you, then Mr. Gilchrist speaks for us both. We will aid you in your revenge."

"Good." Merin rose and went to the urn, hesitating only a moment before she dipped her fingers inside. She turned back to them. The ash was smooth and cool against Gilchrist's hand, then Crane's, as they shook.

The queue of workers stretched from the factory gate all the way around the corner, ragged men and women stamping their feet and rubbing their arms against the cold. Some of them pulled their filter masks down long enough to puff at the clay pipe being passed from hand to grimy hand. Crane and Gilchrist kept theirs on as they tacked themselves to the end of the line.

"A rather ghastly piece of architecture, isn't it?" Crane remarked, tipping his head back to observe the factory. Its high brick walls were stained jet-black from soot and displayed no windows, the wrought-iron gates were topped with wicked-looking spikes, and the scaly roof was dominated by several enormous smokestacks already leaking their ink into the sky.

"Not many points of egress," Gilchrist said.

They stepped out of the queue and reinserted themselves farther along, aided by Crane opening the tin of snuff from his coat pocket and Gilchrist delivering a winding elbow to the gut of the one worker who protested. Up close, they could see the gate itself, guarded by a pair of scowling watchmen with truncheons. The red gear was painted on their chest plates.

Both guards snapped to attention as the clockwork clatter of a strutter echoed up the cobblestones. One of them made his way along the line, brandishing his truncheon, snarling for single file. The workers shuffled themselves; so did Crane and Gilchrist. All of them turned to watch the strutter clack up the street like a massive black insect, limbs churning in perfect synchronization, pulling a black carriage behind.

Whispers traveled up and down the queue as the carriage passed with curtains drawn. The top of it was racked and loaded with three squat barrels, all of them secured tightly by cables. The strutter shuddered to a halt at the gate and its driver dismounted, yanking off her grease-stained gloves before opening the carriage door.

The man who descended was massive, thick-shouldered with a broad chest and sizeable paunch only somewhat disguised by the precise tailoring of his black-and-scarlet waistcoat. His fine clothes were at odds with his bulk, and with the boxer's hands, gnarled and scarred, that escaped his sleeve cuffs. The wide ruff splayed around his neck might have looked affected on another man; on Riker, it gave him the look of a cannibal lizard from the New World. The impression was strengthened by his ornate filter mask, angled like the snout of a beast and inlaid with silver teeth locked in a razor-sharp grin.

Riker adjusted his cuffs while a pock-faced porter started unloading the barrels from the top of the carriage. When he wobbled under the last of them, Riker gave a snort of impatience and took it from his grasp, setting it on one bow-broad shoulder as if it weighed nothing at all.

"Merin failed to mention the man was a virtual colossus," Crane said, watching closely as Riker, accompanied by a swirl of attendants, strode toward the factory doors.

"Moves light," Gilchrist said, watching his gait.

A tremor of anticipation moved through the queue as the other two barrels passed by. One of the men whose thumb was stained from snuff broke into a gapped grin. "Big shipment," he said. "Heard it's purer than last one. Pure, pure."

Crane sucked air between his teeth. "That is a rather extravagant quantity of narcotic, Gilchrist," he murmured. "Three barrels, already processed. Worth a small fortune, I imagine."

Gilchrist calculated. "Double and a half the weight in silver."

"How the conflagration still haunts me," Crane said mournfully.

"Only pennies to what's in the strongbox," Gilchrist reminded him.

One attendant handed Riker a manifest on thick parchment; another stretched to mutter something into his ear. Riker turned toward the line of workers, all of whom fell dead silent. "Fifty only today," he said, in a voice thinned by the filter mask. "Preference to those already marked. Rest of you, fuck off."

Half the queue surged forward excitedly, nearly bowling Crane and Gilchrist over in their hurry to bare their wrists, scratching away grime to expose the blotted red ink stamped there. Others howled in disappointment; a few furtively tried to spit and rub the ink from a neighbor onto their own skin. Small scuffles broke out where the guards moved to establish the cutoff point.

An emaciated woman with wild gray hair broke through and darted at Riker. "My Skadi, my little Skadi, where is she?" she wailed, grabbing for him. "She has a cough, let me in, I'll work harder than anyone, I swear, I swear I will . . ."

Riker half turned and swatted her away with the back of his fist, sending her sprawling. Her skull bounced off the cobblestone with a wet smack. He looked down at her for a moment, watching impassively as she moaned and babbled. Then a guard hurried to drag her away, and Riker continued through the factory gate, returning his attention to the parchment.

Crane and Gilchrist stood still a second longer, then melted back through the clamoring workers, back the way they'd come. Gilchrist's hands were clenched to fists.

◆　◆　◆

They were around the corner and out of sight, moving down a dirty alley, when Crane spoke.

"There is no ledger, Gilchrist."

Gilchrist looked up. "Meaning what, Crane?" His voice was brusque.

"You have a marvelous way with accounts and balances," Crane said. "But in matters of morality, there is no ledger. You cannot wash one man's blood off your hands using another's."

Gilchrist's broad back stiffened. He stopped walking. "You think that's what I'm doing."

Crane yanked the filter mask down from his mouth. "Assuaging your guilt, yes, by assuring yourself there are men far more evil than we are and by removing one from existence," he said. "It's delusional. Self-indulgent. It doesn't become you."

"It's how we get the strongbox open," Gilchrist said.

Crane scoffed. "You were ready to force her to do it," he said. "At knifepoint. It was her tragic tale that swayed you. That and the fact that our target employs children. Or do I misremember?"

Gilchrist gave a tight shrug. "I saw threats wouldn't work. Not on her. She has nothing to lose."

"So she would have us believe," Crane grated. "Yet she was unable to correctly describe the effects of cyanide poisoning. Why is that?"

Gilchrist started to walk again. "Not everyone knows poisons, Crane."

"We would do better to take the strongbox elsewhere." The blue veins of Crane's neck were taut and his voice was ice. "We are working in unfamiliar territory with an ally who, I believe, is not entirely forth-coming." He strode after his companion. "Dealing with the individual we just observed, I suspect any error at all might be disastrous. Riker does not strike me as a man one attempts to kill twice."

Gilchrist kept his eyes forward. "Lucky we only need to do it once."

Crane's long legs overtook him. "Your reticence is growing tiresome," he snapped. "I want to discuss what occurred during our escape from the Thule Estate."

"I remember what happened."

"You slit a man's throat before he could cry warning," Crane said. "Had you not, we would both be dangling from the gallows even now.

You exchanged his life for ours, as I would have done in the same situation." He reached to seize onto Gilchrist's shoulder.

Gilchrist whirled and locked his arm, slamming him into the soot-stained brick of the alleyway. His lips pulled back off his teeth. "The watchman had children," he said. "I saw their shoes after. Outside the guardhouse. You did the reconnaissance. You never mentioned it."

Crane blinked down at the unfamiliar sight of Gilchrist's forearm under his windpipe. Rage twisted across his face for a moment, then receded. "It wasn't pertinent," he said, enunciating each word.

"To you," Gilchrist finished. "And he had ash on his forehead. Saw it while I was stashing the body. That means no mother for them. That means they end up in the street or sold off to some factory."

"There are worse fates," Crane said defiantly. "You survived similar beginnings." His expression was calm but his ears were scarlet red.

Gilchrist stepped back. Dropped his arm. "That's what I mean, Crane." He croaked a half laugh. "The last thing I want is to make more of me."

Crane rubbed his throat. He said nothing.

When they arrived back at the lock shop, Gilchrist forewent the knocker and rapped out the agreed-upon pattern against the door with his fist instead. This time Merin was quicker to let them inside. There was new ash on her forehead.

"You saw him? Saw his mask?" she asked, pulling a rubbery cup away from her ear and flopping its attached tube over her shoulder. The strongbox was sitting in the center of the workbench, surrounded by an array of skeleton keys and picks, one of which was sticking out from the locking groove. "Been listening," she explained, shutting the door behind them. "It's sticky in there. Something spilled on it."

"Wine," Gilchrist said. He took a seat on one of the stools; Crane stood, pale hands sunk in his pockets. "We saw the mask."

"He hardly takes it off," Merin said. "Had it specially made by an artisan from Lensa." She reached under the workbench and produced a thin tracing in carbon. "This wasn't easy to nab. Don't spill no wine on it."

Crane and Gilchrist looked down at the tracing, which showed the mask's design from the front, then in profile, then cross-sectioned.

"It's bigger than it needs to be," Merin said. "Room to make improvements." She overlaid the sheet with another, this one bearing her own pen strokes. Coiled springs and wedges folded against themselves, some sort of trigger mechanism. It was only when she brought the realized product from under the workbench, unwrapping wax paper from its metal shell, that they saw the sharpened spikes studding the inside.

Crane touched his wrist where the spring-loaded knocker had clamped down on it the night before. "How ingenious."

"These won't be visible after I line it," she said, running a finger down one of the spikes. "Hand me that bowl, would you?"

Gilchrist passed her the thick-bottomed clay bowl without speaking. She flipped it over, then set the metal shell down on top of it. The spiked jaws snapped with a deep crack. When she lifted the shell, the bowl fell to the bench in fragments and powder. Her expression was both eager and slightly ill.

"How do we get ahold of the mask?" Gilchrist asked.

Merin chewed the inside of her cheek. "Not from his quarters," she said. "Where he lives, it's a fucking labyrinth and it's locked down tighter than anyplace I've ever seen." She swept the remnants of the bowl off the bench's surface with one hand. "But there's a bathhouse he goes to. That's where you plant it. Then you leave without him ever even seeing you."

Crane looked down at the device. "Remote assassinations do not always go as planned," he said. "What if the mechanism were to fail?"

"It won't," Merin said firmly. "It's been tested plenty."

"Very well." Crane looked down at the schematic, avoiding Gilchrist's eye. "But leaving the sabotaged mask in its proper place, without arousing suspicion, fulfills our contract. If your device fails, it is no responsibility of ours. You will open the strongbox regardless."

"It'll work," Merin said, running her tongue along her gums. "But yes. I open the box regardless."

She inserted a crank into a slot in the metal shell and began to wind it tight again, click after rasping click.

◆   ◆   ◆

The bathhouse was an incongruous slab of gleaming black stone amid the scab-colored brick and slant roofs that surrounded it. Geometric hieroglyphs carved over the doorway and the roof's beveled edges evoked the abandoned ziggurats of the New World, as if the building had been cleaved whole from the rain forests and dropped in the center of Colgrid.

It was a clumsy imitation at best—Crane and Gilchrist had seen the sleeping cities, with their towering temples and intricate catacombs deep under the earth, and knew no living architect could ever approximate them. But perhaps Riker had seen them too, and the bathhouse served him as a small reminder.

"Strutter's coming," Gilchrist said.

Crane drew himself up to his full height, adjusting the brim of a scooped hat with a sewn-in filter mask. The stolen clothes were slightly baggy on his frame, but of good quality, and Merin had assured him many gentlemen's clothes were ill fitting ever since shiver caught on in the courts.

The two of them had spent the better part of the day observing the bathhouse comings and goings, checking its exterior against the stained parchment where Merin had sketched a layout, all with a garrote-wire silence stretched between them.

It was a simple enough plan. According to a former attendant they'd bribed, Riker always went to the steam rooms first, near the back, then made a quick cold plunge before leaving—the whole visit took no more than fifteen minutes. That was time enough for Crane to crack the locked cupboard with Riker's effects in it, especially with Merin's superior tools. Gilchrist would be monitoring the steam room from the outside, ready to call warning should Riker leave early.

Now the distinctive black strutter was rounding the corner, and it was time to part ways: Gilchrist into the alley, Crane toward the bathhouse entrance.

As he swaggered toward the entry, Crane put a thumb to his reddened nostril and snorted sharp. The rush of powder through membrane made him shudder. It wasn't his drug of choice, but shiver was cheap and temptingly plentiful here. He'd bought a pinch in the factory queue and another behind the bathhouse while Gilchrist was otherwise occupied.

Colgrid's dirty streets turned clear and bright and slightly vibrating, the effect that gave the narcotic its name. He felt the high like a razor blade, like his every step and motion was slicing through a slower, thicker world. Riker seemed to move through syrup as he stepped from the strutter, trailed by a sole attendant carrying a fabric bag.

At the entrance, Crane paused his stride, bowed at the precise angle that hid his face entirely, and let the giant man pass first. He managed to seem even larger on shiver, as if the bunched muscles of his arms and shoulders were swelling and straining to escape his skeleton. He gave Crane a brief glance through the lenses of his filter mask.

Crane had an unbidden image of Riker's head imploding and spattering the insides of the lenses with greasy blood and gray matter. He had to lash down his chemical smile as he followed him into the antechamber, flicking a coin to the boy waiting by the door and receiving a cupboard key in return. He took one side of the coal-heated benches and Riker took the other. Riker was half-shielded by his attendant as he stripped down, but from the glimpse Crane caught, the whole of his bulk was netted with scars.

Gilchrist wedged himself into the corner of the furnace room and steam room, cramming low and yanking off his filter mask to put an eye against the knothole he'd drilled earlier. He breathed through his mouth; the back alley had a strong stink of tanning chemicals that he hoped would keep passersby to a minimum. If anyone did see him, the ragged coat he'd fished from the gutter would make him look like a beggar seeking warmth as the sunlight waned.

He blinked. He could see a few silhouettes lounging on the benches, steam swirling around their midsections, but none with Riker's size.

"What are you doing?"

Gilchrist whirled. There was less soot on the child's face this time; he could tell she was a girl. She rocked back and forth on the balls of her feet. Rubbed at her left shoulder.

"You gave me the coin, didn't you," she said vaguely. "Think it was you. Not the tall one." She peered between him and the hole in the wall, then made a wanking gesture in the air. "You a pervert, then?"

Gilchrist took another coin from his pocket. When she snatched for it, he closed his fist and put a finger to his lips. Tapped his wrist where a timepiece would sit, once, twice, three times. She nodded solemnly and clapped a dirty hand over her mouth.

He hunkered down again, squinting through the knothole.

Crane peeled off his stolen clothes and walked to the warm baths, smooth stone whispering against the soles of his feet. He nodded to the other occupants, then lowered himself in at a stretch of gleaming black wall polished reflective. The hot water tingled and stung at his cold skin. His reflection was ghostly, distorted. Deep dark circles beneath the eyes and a bruise blooming at his collarbone where Gilchrist had pinned him.

He traced it gently with one finger, then dug into it and made it sear. Behind his reflection, Riker passed by like a thunderhead, the attendant trailing behind with towel and scrubber. No bather looked up. Crane waited a beat in the water, was tempted to wait longer. But he got out and doubled back to the antechamber. Empty, aside from the boy wiping down the benches.

"What slobbering ignoramus runs the furnace today?" Crane demanded, punching out his syllables in the harsh Colgrid accent.

The boy flinched, nearly dropping the rag.

"I could better warm the baths with my piss," Crane said. "Tell them: more coal. Tell them: a fucking plenitude of coal."

The boy scrambled away. Crane went to his own cupboard first, pulling on his oversized trousers and knotting them with one hand. He took Merin's picks from the inside of the hat, where the skull-crusher was concealed, and moved to the cupboard he'd watched Riker's attendant wrestle shut. The shiver had receded to a clear singing focus that would keep his hands smooth.

Crane eyeballed the lock and selected the second-narrowest pick.

◆　◆　◆

"Were you born in the desert?" the girl asked, for the third time. "You're dark all over."

Gilchrist wiped a trickle of sweat before it could slide into his eye. He focused through the steam. Riker had the room mostly to himself— the other bathers had drifted away when he entered, their body language twitching nervous. Through the other wall, he could hear voices arguing in the furnace room about the definition of a plenitude.

"You and the tall one, you staying in the widow's shop," the girl said, scratching her shoulder. "Followed you from there. Best be careful."

The words prickled the back of his neck, but Gilchrist kept watching the knothole. "Why's that?" he asked, keeping his voice low and even.

The girl's reply came in a solemn whisper. "Because she got a musket, and she shot her husband dead."

Gilchrist looked up. The girl made the shape of a muzzle with her fingers.

"Bam. His skull went all apart like an old fruit." She screwed up her face. "So, best be careful."

"Who told you that story?" Gilchrist asked.

"It's not a story," the girl said scornfully, scratching at her shoulder again, more vigorously. "I seen it. Papa Riker sent me to keep my eyes on her. I seen it happen." She gave a devilish smile. "Made an awful mess on the wall."

Gilchrist stared straight ahead for a moment, recalling the interior of the lock shop. "Crane's a bastard when he's right," he muttered, then put his fingers to his mouth and whistled three long, mournful notes.

Crane was a tumbler away, two at most, when the faint but unmistakable call of a New World carrion bird reached his ears. He froze. Cursed. The clear-out call meant something had gone wrong, meant Riker could be barreling in at any moment, but he was so close. He steadied his hands and leaned in, feeling for the next catch.

The wet slap of approaching feet sounded from the corridor. Close. Crane gritted his teeth. He tore the pick free, seized his shirt and shoes and hat last as he slipped out the door.

◆ ◆ ◆

The inside of the lock shop was thick with shadows. Merin had only lit one lamp. When Gilchrist set the skull-crusher down on the workbench, just inside the pool of light, she stared at it blankly for a moment before she spoke.

"What happened?"

"We have a similar query," Crane said. "Regarding your husband's death. Your version of events is under dispute, and if we cannot trust your information, we cannot trust you to maintain your end of our bargain."

"Why did you kill him?" Gilchrist asked.

Merin gave a choked laugh. "The fuck are you talking about?"

"A musket ball at close range," Crane said. "Here in this very shop." He circled the cramped room in a few long strides, stopping at the threadbare rug hanging on the wall. "Such a death would leave traces." He reached for the corner of the rug.

"Don't." Merin's voice came in a snarl. She was standing, breathing hard, her hands balled into fists. Then all at once, her face crumpled. She dropped back down onto the stool, laying both hands flat on the bench. One of her fingers jumped. "I never meant to fire it," she said, looking at her hands first, then up at Crane and Gilchrist. Her black-rimmed eyes were hollow. "Only to keep him back." She blinked. "He was given laced shiver. That was the truth. But it wasn't laced with poison. It was ichor."

Gilchrist didn't flicker at the word, but Crane's eyes narrowed. "The rage drug," he clarified. "Secreted by a particularly venomous New World toad. Extremely rare."

"That's how I know it was Riker who did it," Merin said. "Only he'd have access to that stuff."

"Describe it." Crane's voice was intent, almost eager. "Describe the effects."

Merin's nostrils flared. "Fuck you."

"You've attempted to deceive us once already," Crane said. "Why would we accept your word now without—"

"His veins were like ropes." Merin paused. Took a shuddering breath.

"When he came down the stairs, he was sweating and all his veins were thick like ropes. His cock was hard. And he was talking. Not in any language, just talking. Gibberish."

"How did he behave?" Crane asked, folding his arms.

"Tranced, at first," Merin said thickly. "I tried to get him to sit down. Then, angry. Like an animal. Like an animal in my husband's body." She waved a hand over her eyes. "There was nothing back there. He was gone in the head. I tried to calm him down." She swallowed. "Tried to calm him down, couldn't. He got his hands around my throat. I barely slipped him. Musket was on the table. He chased me." Her gaze raked around the room, seeing ghosts in motion, then came to rest on the hanging rug. "Told him to back up. He didn't. He grabbed my wrist and I pulled the trigger."

Crane nodded with something like reverence. "Ichor is incredibly potent," he said. "Even in the smallest doses it causes violent hallucinations. Inflames the carnal urges. Occasionally induces a form of glossolalia, as well." He drummed his long fingers against his elbow. "Little wonder it was considered a myth in the early years of exploration."

"Riker helped cover up Petro's killing," Gilchrist said. "Told everyone he'd gone south to dodge a debt. That right?"

"Yes," Merin said bitterly. "He'll ask me for another job someday, and he knows I'll do it if I don't want to end up imprisoned for Petro's murder. You see why I hate him. See why I have to kill him. Don't you?"

Gilchrist looked at her for a moment, then nodded. "You have to kill him because you aren't sure," he said. "You aren't sure if he gave Petro the ichor. Or if Petro took it himself and misjudged the potency."

Merin snarled. "He wouldn't."

"The barflies of the inner city say otherwise," Crane interjected. "By all accounts, your husband was not sound in mind or in spirit during the months leading up to his disappearance. He experimented with the more exotic narcotics. He spoke often of death."

"I know that," Merin snapped. "I know he wasn't well. But he would never."

"Riker might have spread the rumor of your husband's debt in order to deflect attention from his own role," Crane said. "The Dogue would not react kindly to Riker selling ichor to Colgrid's citizenry."

"If you kill Riker without knowing the truth, you'll wonder," Gilchrist said. "Forever."

Merin's eyelids dropped shut. "What are you suggesting, then?" she asked, voice cracked.

"An amendment to our bargain," Crane said. "You need a confession, not a mere execution. Confessions can be extracted with the proper leverage."

"If you think Riker would ever confess to giving Petro the ichor, you're a simpleton."

"Leverage," Crane repeated. "As of this morning, Riker is storing three barrels of shiver in the south-side factory. That represents a sizeable investment."

Merin opened her eyes. "What, steal it?"

"More take it hostage," Gilchrist said. "We know someone who can get us inside. Tonight." He cocked his head toward the sound of a small fist rapping low on the door. "That'd be her."

When the night was sufficiently dark, they trooped out of the shop into the cold streets. The girl scampered ahead of them. Her name was Skadi, and the shoulder she always scratched had a messy red gear tattooed into the skin. She'd shown it to them with a mixture of pride and resentment.

Then, without ever looking at Merin directly, she'd explained how Riker had ordered her to watch the lock shop on the day of Petro's death, and how after relaying the news to him she'd never returned to the factory how she was supposed to.

But she still knew how to get back in without anyone seeing her. She knew where the guards patrolled and half of their names. She knew the third smokestack was no longer in use. She'd hovered over Gilchrist's shoulder, chewing dates from Merin's larder, as he sketched out the factory's dimensions.

Their shadows stretched long and slender as they passed under the first phosphor lamppost. Gilchrist carried coiled rope and the improvised grapple Merin had put together. Crane's long fingers toyed with the phial he'd mixed over the heating pipe. Merin was strapped with her lock-breaking tools.

All of them wore filter masks, and Merin had dug out one for Skadi, too, after the girl emptied her pockets of all the keys she'd filched while they were sketching out the factory's dimensions and arguing about entry and egress.

They stopped a street behind the south-side factory. Crane took out the glass phial and tapped one frayed fingernail against it. Tendrils of luminous yellow swirled inside. Skadi watched with undisguised fascination as he capped it with a tiny pipette.

"I want to use it, too," she said, yanking her mask down.

"Lamprey extract requires successive doses to be effective," Crane said, tipping his head back, peeling back an eyelid. "I'm afraid you would see only a blur." He squeezed a drop into one eye, then the other. When he finished blinking his pupils were swollen wide with a silvery gleam to them. Gilchrist took the phial from him and did the same.

"What do you see?" Skadi asked.

"The light human eyes miss," Gilchrist said. "You ready, Merin?"

Merin pulled down her mask. Her face was drawn, but her voice came steady. "Haven't done a break-in for about a decade," she said. "Always feel a bit sick until the entry. Let's get on with it."

One of the night watchmen was sauntering along the back of the factory, singing hoarsely and occasionally tapping his truncheon against the brick for percussion. They watched from the shadows until he rounded the corner, then Skadi led the way to the wall, almost skipping.

"See the cracks?" she whispered. "You should be able to see 'em. I can barely, but I know where they all are anyways."

Crane and Gilchrist looked up the brick wall to see where the mortar had eroded, leaving the cracks Skadi used for her climb. Large enough for a child's hand- and toeholds, nothing more, but they'd anticipated as much. Gilchrist unspooled the rope and handed the grapple off to Crane. He judged the distance to the carved gutter that rimmed the roof, made two practice swings, and cast it.

The grapple sailed up through the dark, rope ribboning out behind it like a startled snake. Its hooks clattered against the angled surface, sliding, scraping, finally catching. Soot caked on the roof softened the noise, but they still waited, breath bated, for watchmen voices. A moment passed. Another.

Crane tugged the rope taut and offered it to Merin. She dusted her hands with chalk from her pouch and stretched her arms, then started to climb. She was barely over the top when Skadi followed, quick as a cat. Gilchrist reached for the rope next, but paused.

"Why'd you agree to hit the factory?" he asked.

Crane snorted. "Your sketch of the exterior was remarkably detailed, considering it was done from memory," he said. "You would have ended up here whether I agreed or not. In order to liberate a cadre of orphans."

Gilchrist fixed him with a long look. "You came to skim some of the shiver," he said.

"I suppose we are each in our own way predictable." Crane paused. "Will this balance your ledger, then? Will you be satisfied?"

"More than the drug ever satisfies you."

"Two entirely different matters," Crane said, but quietly, as Gilchrist churned up the rope with his feet barely grazing the wall for support. Crane followed, coiling the rope up behind him as he went.

From the top, they could see Colgrid's crooked roofs and belching chimneys spilling into the distance, dotted with the green phosphor blaze of streetlamps. They only lingered long enough for Crane to un-hook the grapple before making their way along the factory's spine, to the disused smokestack Skadi had pinpointed on Gilchrist's crude map.

"Rungs on the inside for when we used to go up to clean it," the girl said. "Nice and easy for you."

Crane cast again, but this time the grapple bounced, clanging off the rim of the smokestack and back to the roof. Merin had to hop backward to avoid its impaling her foot. She hissed a curse; Crane only gave an irritable shrug. He retrieved the grapple, measured, and this time found the edge of the smokestack.

The descent was cramped and slow, the rungs all slippery with soot, the cloying smell of chemical leaking through their masks' filters. Crane and Gilchrist led the way, their augmented vision painting the pipe with silvery brushstrokes, letting them see the accumulated sediment scab-bing the walls and pass up whispered warnings of the rungs that were rusted weak or missing entirely.

Before the bottom, where the shaft connected to the boiler, they found a small metal door in the dark as Skadi had promised. It came open with a sharp creak and Gilchrist squeezed through, twisting his wide shoulders. Crane next, easily as an eel, then Merin contorted herself to follow. Skadi levered herself through last.

It was a short drop to the base of the boiler, and after the tight confines of the smokestack the vaulted factory interior felt the size of a cathedral. Rows of spiky black machinery stretched from back to front, looming out of the dark like mechanical monsters, their bared cogs grinning teeth. Skadi's shoulders hunched at the sight; she rubbed furiously at the left one.

"Storeroom's back there," she murmured, pointing with her whole hand. "Locked up good." She looked around the factory again and shook herself. "I hate this place lots."

She led the way down the row, and as they walked, soles scuffing on soot, pale faces poked out from the machinery. Some of them whispered; one called Skadi's name in a wavering question. Crane put a bony finger to the place where his mask covered his lips. There was straw spread out underneath the machinery, moth-eaten blankets, too. A few of the children huddled alone; most tangled together for body heat or for comfort.

"Hush, hush, hush," Skadi said. "How asleep is the nanny?"

"Two and some," one of the children whispered. "Amalia took the some."

They found the nanny slumped up ahead in a carved wooden chair, three empty bottles lined beside him, grizzled chin resting on his chest. Crane paused long enough to pour laudanum into his half-open mouth, to make sure he stayed that way. More of the children were waking, now, and there was a sound of scraping metal as they shifted.

Merin pointed down at a foot that wasn't tucked under blankets. The child's ankle was cuffed in a heavy iron attached to a long cable that ran the length of the factory floor. "Bastards," she said softly. "Looks like an easy pick, though."

They moved on to the storeroom, which was bricked into the back corner of the factory and secured by a heavy wooden door.

"Go faster with a bit of light," Merin said, running her fingers over its thick lock. "I don't have lamprey shit in my eyes."

Gilchrist turned. "Skadi. Get a candle."

The girl vanished and returned a moment later with a burned-down nub of wax. She crouched, watching intently as Merin laid out her tools on the floor in a neat line. The lock breaker held out a few simple picks. Gilchrist and Crane took one each, then went back down the row. Gilchrist worked one side and Crane the other, rousing the children who were still asleep, muffling the occasional startled yelp, pointing to the ankle iron, jiggering it open.

They'd made it nearly all the way down when voices came from the factory entrance.

"See if the old drunk's got something for us, too," a watchman coughed. "Go on, just check. Fucking dull out here."

Crane and Gilchrist exchanged a look. Crane motioned the children to cover their ankles and be still, then swept toward one side of the entry, pulling on his gloves. Gilchrist took up position at the other, moving like a shadow. The quick-knife was in his hand, the blade telescoping and clicking into place. His jaw clenched.

The iron door swung open, and the watchman's lantern pierced the gloom. In the same instant, Crane sucked in his breath, pulled a burnt-orange pellet from his pouch, and crushed it between his palms.

The watchman took a few steps inside, then hesitated. He fumbled with the strap of his filter mask. Motes of powder from Crane's stained gloves were clouding into the air, a foul peppery smell accompanying. One of the children started to sneeze. Crane's eyes were leaking tears and mucus was spotting his mask. He still hadn't breathed in.

The watchman took another faltering step, then spun. "Ask him yourself, you sheepfucker," he said, hauling the factory door shut behind him, his voice turning faint. "You didn't tell me there was a spill today. Smells like the devil in there."

They waited another heartbeat, another. They waited for the sound of boots to disappear. As soon as the watchmen were gone back to the gate, Crane darted over to the barrel of drinking water and plunged his face inside. He emerged with a curse that made the children's ears prick up as Gilchrist picked the last few cuffs.

"Rather more potent than my previous recipe," Crane muttered, stripping off the stained gloves.

"Good." Gilchrist used the ladle to splash water into his bloodshot eyes. Then they moved back down the row, the freed children trailing after them, murmuring to each other, some of them knuckling their eyes still from the pellet. When they got to the storeroom, Merin was lifting her mask to wipe sweat off her forehead.

"Close thing, that watchman coming in," she said. "Good work. Whatever you did."

She shoved the wooden door and it swung open smoothly on its hinges. Inside, among the crates and stacked metal, the three barrels of shiver stood clustered together.

"They look heavy," Merin muttered.

"Then let's not waste time," Crane said, eyes gleaming. He tipped the first barrel and Gilchrist caught it from the other side, lowering it to the floor to be rolled. The three of them worked quickly, moving the barrels into position by the smokestack. Skadi and a few older girls managed to herd the children into a group, quieting the talkers with hissed admonishments or smacks up the head.

When all three barrels of shiver were in place, Crane gingerly fished more of the orange pellets from his pouch and passed them out among the older children. "These are intended to be thrown, not crushed in hand, and certainly not ingested," he said. "Not for eating. Understood?"

A few nods.

"I have a query, children," he continued. "What happens when one pokes a ball of cave spiders?"

The children looked at each other for a moment. "Go everywhere," one of the boys finally mumbled. Others made scurrying motions with their fingers.

"Yes," Crane said. "So, when we open the factory door, all of you must be little cave spiders. Scattering in all directions." He lifted one of the pellets between two fingers. "And should a watchman move to grab you, these are your stingers."

The children nodded, every single one of them, and Skadi's grin gleamed in the dark.

◆　◆　◆

Morning over Colgrid. The rising sun drenched the sky red outside Merin's window. The lock breaker was boiling a pot of tar-black coffee; Crane and Gilchrist were sitting by the heating pipe, the blankets they'd slept on briefly now piled at their feet. During the chaos created by the fleeing children, they'd gone back up the smokestack and down from the roof. The last they'd seen of Skadi was her leading her little band into the streets, whooping and shrieking.

"Bet he's flogging the watchmen," Merin said. "Bet he thinks they helped us."

"All the better," Crane said, tapping a pen against his cheekbone as he considered the letter lying in midcomposition across his lap. "Ambiguity is our ally. How does this strike you both?" He stroked out the final sentence and raised the parchment to the light. "My dearest Mr. Riker, you are cordially invited to join me at the Corner of the Four Angels at midnight, unaccompanied and unarmed, so that we might negotiate an exchange of goods and services. If I sight anyone in your employ within a block of our meeting point, or sense any threat to my person, your barrels will burn. Signed, your loving thief."

Merin snorted. "Won't think it's me, that's for certain."

"Seal it," Gilchrist said. "With a pinch of the shiver."

Crane grudgingly opened one of the tiny bags he'd filled from the last barrel. He tapped a bit of powder onto the flat of Merin's kitchen knife, then held it over the heating pipe until it bubbled and melted to a distinctive tarry brown Riker would recognize. It smeared like hot wax over the fold of the letter.

"He won't come alone," Merin said, taking the letter as it cooled and stiffened. "Or unarmed."

"You won't, either," Gilchrist said.

Merin hesitated for a moment. Then she set the letter aside and reached under the workbench, hauling the strongbox out into the light and lifting the rough-spun shroud overtop of it. The locking grooves were pinned with calipers and a tiny section of metal had been peeled back, exposing part of the mechanism where two skeleton keys speared inside.

"Had it cracked yesterday already," she admitted. "Once you know the trick to them, they're not so bad." She pointed at the keys. "That one clockways, the other opposite. You can do the honors, if you like."

The men exchanged a glance. Then Crane took the left, Gilchrist the right, and they twisted without hesitation. Rather than simply falling open, the strongbox seemed to bloom. The intricate filigree of the cube's four sides came unlocked and peeled outward onto the floor like the petals of a mechanical flower, revealing a simple mesh cage, and inside that cage . . .

"My lexicon fails me," Crane said. "Gilchrist?"

Gilchrist only shook his head.

"Fucking beauty, isn't it," Merin said. "I peeked earlier." Her mouth twisted. "I can see why you went to the trouble."

The crown was a heavy ring of unblemished gold that turned fiery in the lamplight, veined with new silver and set with gemstones the color of a sparkling clear sea.

"The Thule clan's last link to the ancient kings," Crane murmured. "Far older than the elected Dogues. Older than Colgrid or even Brask." He yanked a work glove over his hand and removed the crown gently, so gently, as if it might shatter under his fingers. Gilchrist's eyes were fixed to it as it revolved gleaming in the light.

"Miraculous," Crane said. "To be in such condition. After so many years." His gaze hardened as he looked up. "You realize we have no compulsion to stay now that you've solved our toy for us. We could leave you and Riker to the fates."

"I realize, yeah." Merin managed half a smile. "But I figured you would want to see it through. Just to see how it all ends." She looked from the crown to the splayed-open strongbox. "And if things go to shit tonight, I wanted to make sure I'd held up my end of the bargain."

News of the factory break-in diffused through Colgrid over the course of the day; Gilchrist and Crane heard snatches of it both times they left the concealment of the shop to buy twine, resin, gunpowder. They never removed their filter masks, and they took circuitous routes back to Merin's to ensure they weren't followed. By the time night fell, a stiff wind was building in the streets, enough to shift part of the smog. It flapped at their clothes as they made their way to the Corner of the Four Angels.

Gilchrist circled the block to ensure none of Riker's men were lying in wait, then the three of them stepped into the sculptures' shadow. They were angels in the style of Brask, harsh and inhuman with geometric faces, archaic script carved into their spindly limbs and spread wings. In the gusting wind, they seemed ready to take flight. Merin climbed up to spread the resin in the crook of a stone elbow. Crane paced out the distance.

It wasn't long before the tap-tap-tap of a strutter echoed up the cobblestone. They took their positions: Crane stood loose and insolent, Gilchrist and Merin spread their feet and clasped their hands behind their backs, a military stance to keep Riker guessing. Gilchrist was massaging his hands in slow patterns, keeping his fingers warm and ready, but Merin's were clenched white.

A silhouette hulked through the gloom, then Riker strode into view, a phosphor lantern clutched in his massive hand like a ball of witch's fire, illuminating the sharklike teeth of his filter mask. The strutter's driver followed him like a shadow, dressed in a long black jacket with the shape of a musket bulging underneath.

"Mr. Riker," Crane greeted. "You've failed to follow instructions. Do you not recall the consequences?"

Riker halted five steps away from them, a gap that his long arms could close in an instant, and planted his feet. The tips of his boots were sharp and pointed toward them like knives. He surveyed them in silence through the lenses of his mask, then passed the lantern backward to his driver.

"Nobody burns three barrels of the pure shit," he said. "Not even a lunatic."

"You seem quite convinced of their value," Crane said. "And yet they were so poorly secured. Removing them was child's play, frankly."

"You think it was clever." Even through the mask, Riker's thin voice was taut with anger. "Using the children."

"Clearly you think the same."

"Everyone in Colgrid knows better than to steal from me," Riker said. "That means you're not from here. Means you don't know winter. If those children stay on the street, they'll all be frozen fucking corpses in a couple months."

"You keep them chained," Gilchrist said, speaking for the first time.

"At night. Better that than have another one climb into a boiler." Riker tapped a gnarled finger against his ornate mask. "Half the little shits are addled in the head right out the womb, from their mothers breathing the smog. They won't last outside."

"They left," Gilchrist said. "First chance they had."

"You didn't do them a fucking favor," Riker snapped. "I feed them. I keep them off the shiver. Out of the whorehouses. The ones with any sense will come back to the factory. The others will freeze."

Crane cleared his throat. "We digress," he said. "Fortunately for you, Mr. Riker, the shiver we stole was not our primary target. Our reconnaissance was flawed, you see." He paused. "We were told there might be ichor."

Riker didn't react.

"We are opportunists, of course, so we took what we found," Crane continued. "But as you ascertained, we are not from Colgrid. Our buyers lie farther south, and receive shiver through more established channels. They want ichor for the fighting pits in Vira and Lensa. That was what we intended to steal. Now we are open to an exchange."

"You'd trade my own shit back to me." Through the mask, Riker's laugh was a dead thing. "You do have some fucking balls on you."

Crane managed a careless shrug. "Assuming you *do* have ichor. And that you've tested it."

Riker regarded them for a long minute through his lenses. "How'd you get the barrels out?"

"With considerable difficulty," Crane said. "The method is irrelevant."

Another long pause, then Riker spoke. "I have ichor. As a curiosity. There's not a market for it up here."

Merin twitched; reined it in. Riker didn't seem to notice.

"Then I propose a deal: your shiver for your ichor. And if our buyers approve of your product, we might be able to establish a standing arrangement lucrative for all parties." Crane's voice hardened. "But we've encountered many would-be vendors returning from the New World, and their product is invariably a crude stimulant mixture that lacks the . . . *specific* ferocity of true ichor."

Riker cocked his head to the side for a moment. "It's real," he said. "Gave it to a few mad beggars. One killed the other and fucked his corpse raw for an hour or so. I put him down as it wore off. More merciful than his having to remember it."

Merin was so still she might have been a statue herself. Crane drew a breath through his mask. "How marvelous," he said. "Though you would have been better served testing it on a more stable individual."

"Those are hard to come by in Colgrid." Riker waved a dismissive hand. "Half this fucking city is mad. But there was one other trial, yeah. When I first got my hands on the stuff. I cut some wastrel's shiver with it and sent him home to his woman."

The words drifted on the cold air. The angels seemed to bend forward, blank faces awaiting revelation.

"Did he know it was tainted?" Crane asked softly. "One must always be wary of the placebo response."

"He didn't," Riker said. "And when it came on, she shot him in the head. Clever cunt must have been waiting for an excuse to do that."

Merin ripped her filter mask down; the sudden motion triggered a flurry as the strutter driver drew her weapon, dropping the phosphor lantern. It smashed, painting a tableau in a burst of pale green: Crane had stepped back, Gilchrist's blade was out, the driver was aiming at Merin's chest . . .

Riker peered at her. His flat laugh was contemptuous. "The clever cunt. The locksmith."

Merin had one hand still behind her back. The other trembled at her side as she spoke. "You know my fucking name."

"I forgot it," Riker said. "But I remember you needed a lesson."

Merin's face was twisted, half anger, half anguish. "You wanted me dead."

Riker looked at Crane and Gilchrist again, then back to Merin. "No," he said coldly. "The beggars got a full dose. Your Petro got barely a trace. He would have fucked you good and hard. Roughed you a bit. Came to his senses and wondered where he'd gotten a spine all of a sudden."

Behind her back, Merin pulled the twine that wrapped around her fist and stretched like spiderweb to the sculptures looming over them.

"All you had to do was take your lesson," Riker said. "Maybe you would've even liked it."

The crack of the concealed musket was deafening. Riker sank; Gilchrist lunged over him. A second crack, splitting the night air and sending shards of stone flying from an angel's ruined face. Gilchrist drove his quick-knife through the driver's arm and the smoking musket spun away in the dark. Then Riker was on his feet again, despite a ragged hole punched through his thigh, and his silence was more terrifying than anything else as he hurtled at Merin.

Crane leapt from the side but Riker swatted him away; Merin was backpedaling as Riker's fist glanced her jaw, snapping her head back. She crumpled to the cobblestone. Gilchrist was tangled with the driver, who was keening and bleeding as she scrabbled for the dropped gun. Riker swung at Merin again, enough force behind it to shatter her face, and Merin slid a metal shell from under her coat and thrust it up like a shield.

Riker's hand caught in the mechanism. He made to pull back, and—

"Don't fucking move," Merin said, thick through a syrup of blood. "Or you'll lose it. Feel the spikes?"

Riker didn't move. Merin got slowly to her feet, still holding her end of the skull-crusher. Crane picked himself up. Gilchrist joined them, delivering a last kick to the strutter driver. He had the musket in hand, first wiping blood off the grip with the edge of his shirt, then loading the second ball.

"You can have the fucking shiver," Riker said, not taking his eyes off his trapped hand. "And I'll get you the ichor, too. For your southern buyers."

"Oh, we have our sights set on far more exotic locales than Vira and Lensa," Crane said, mildly apologetic. "We are bound for the New World once more, you see. Funded by a certain object worth more than all the ichor you could supply." He massaged his chest where Riker's blow had landed. "As for the shiver, it's currently piled in the bottom of your factory's third smokestack."

Gilchrist placed the loaded musket in Merin's free hand. He hesitated. "Do what you want," he said. "But remember there's always a worse man."

"Our ship awaits us," Crane said. "We bid you farewell, Madam Merin. Mr. Riker. The hospitality of your fair city was very ..." He trailed off, wrapping his coat more tightly around himself.

"You ever need another dead box opened," Merin said vaguely. She held the musket trained on Riker's forehead. Her hand was perfectly steady.

Gilchrist pried the other musket from its hiding place and disassembled it with three smooth motions. Then he and Crane departed, plunging back into the winding streets, retrieving their things from a particular alley before heading toward the docks. Both of them listening for the sound of a final gunshot.

The strongbox sat between them on the rail, shifting precariously as the ship began to move. The crown's gemstones had been hidden in various boots, pockets, and pouches, while the crown itself resided inside Crane's wide-brimmed hat. Now the box was empty and stuck halfway open, a bat unsure of whether to unfurl its wings.

"Think she did him?" Gilchrist asked.

Crane cocked his head to the side, contemplating. "I heard no third report," he said. "Though it's possible she marched him to a more secluded location first."

Gilchrist was silent for a moment. "Skadi's tattoo, that was from the factory. But she had older marks on her, too. Scars. From her mother, she said." He grimaced. "Maybe Riker was right about the children. And I only freed them to freeze to death. Maybe in the end I'm worse than he was."

"We are all composed of light and darkness, Gilchrist," Crane said. "Which in turn renders us all the same muddled gray as we stumble toward our respective graves. Better to not meditate long on such matters." He retrieved the bag of shiver he'd scooped from the top of Riker's barrel and tapped a fat white trail onto the back of his hand. "The design of this box is remarkable. I imagine we could resell it."

Gilchrist shook his head. "Not worth finding a fence. We're rich enough as is."

"Indeed." Crane snorted, rubbed his nose. "It's time we started making arrangements for our passage across the ocean. The New World awaits our return. The infamous Crane and Gilchrist, seeking further fortunes, battling the fates . . ."

Gilchrist said nothing. Then he reached forward and pushed the strongbox off the edge of the rail. The winds caught its delicate mechanisms, wrenching it fully open, and it settled on the dark slushy water like a metal flower. Crane fell into uneasy silence, stroking his bruised collarbone, as they watched it sink.

Elizabeth Bear

• • •

Here's a daring raid on a cursed, monster-haunted island by as odd and mismatched a trio of treasure hunters as ever rowed themselves hopefully ashore—only to find that they have no idea at all what they're getting themselves into. If they had, they might have rowed *back* again just as quickly . . .

Elizabeth Bear was born in Connecticut, and now lives in South Hadley, Massachusetts. She won the John W. Campbell Award for Best New Writer in 2005, and in 2008 took home a Hugo Award for her short story "Tideline," which also won her the Theodore Sturgeon Memorial Award (shared with David Moles). In 2009, she won another Hugo Award for her novelette "Shoggoths in Bloom." Her short work has appeared in *Asimov's Science Fiction, Subterranean, SCI FICTION, Interzone, The Third Alternative, Strange Horizons, On Spec*, and elsewhere, and has been collected in *The Chains That You Refuse* and *Shoggoths in Bloom*. She is the author of the five-volume New Amsterdam fantasy series, the three-volume Jenny Casey SF series, the five-volume Promethean Age series, the three-volume Jacob's Ladder series, the three-volume Edda of Burdens series, and the three-volume Eternal Sky series, as well as three novels in collaboration with Sarah Monette. Her other books include the novels *Carnival* and *Undertow*. Her most recent book is an acclaimed novel, *Karen Memory*.

◆　◆　◆

The King's Evil

ELIZABETH BEAR

"I am a servant of King Pale Empire," Doctor Lady Lzi muttered to herself, salt water stinging her lips. "My life at his command."

Brave words. They did not quiet the churning inside her, but her discomfort did not matter. Only the brave words mattered, and her will to see them through.

Lzi told herself it was enough, that this will would see her through to the treasure she sought, and further yet. She held a long, oiled-silk package high and dry as she turned back in the warm surf to watch the metal man heave himself, streaming, from the aquamarine waters of the lagoon. He slogged up the slope beneath breakers rendered gentle by the curving arms of land beyond. The metal man—his kind were a sort of Wizard's servant common in the far West, called a Gage—had a mirrored carapace that glittered between his tattered homespun rags like the surface of the water: blindingly.

Behind him, a veiled man in a long red woolen jacket held a scimitar, a pistol, and a powder horn aloft as he sloshed awkwardly through the sea, waves tugging at the skirts of his coat. He was a Dead Man, a member of an elite—and disbanded—military sect from the distant and exotic West. Right now, ill clad for the heat and the ocean, he looked ridiculous.

Afloat on the deeper water, the *Auspicious Voyage* unfurled her bright patchwork wings and heeled her green hull into a slow turn. The plucky little vessel slid toward the gap where the lagoon's arms did not quite complete their embrace of the harbor. She took with her three hands, a ship's cat, and the landing party's immediate chance of escape from this reputedly cursed island. Even royal orders would not entice the captain to keep her in this harbor while awaiting the return of Lzi and her party.

They could signal with a fire in the morning if they were successful. And if not, well. At least it was a pretty place to die and a useful cause for dying in.

Birds wheeled and flickered overhead. A heavy throb briefly filled the air, an almost-mechanical baritone drone. A black fin sliced the water like a razor, then was gone. Lzi sighed to herself, and wondered if she had made a terrible mistake. True, her feet were on the sand and she hadn't been afflicted with Isolation Island's purported royal death curse yet, but there was water yet foaming around her thighs. Maybe the eaten-alive-by-maggots part wouldn't kick in until she was properly beached.

Or maybe the blessing of her royal mission was enough to protect her. And maybe even the mercenaries, too. She had only hope—and the store of sorcery promised by her honorific.

Determination chilled in her belly. She turned her back on the sea and the splashing mercenaries and marched through the water to the dark gray beach, so different from the pink coral sand of most of the Banner Isles. Each roll of the sea sucked sand from under her, as if the waves themselves warned her away. She forced herself not to hesitate as she stepped from the surf: waiting wouldn't alter anything.

When the solid, wet sand compacted under her bare toes, though, she still held her breath. And . . . didn't die. Didn't sense the gathering magic of a triggered hex, either, which was a good sign. She paused just above the tide line and turned back. While she waited for the mercenaries, she unwrapped her long knife and wrapped the silk around her waist as a sash, then stuck the knife in its scabbard through the sash, where she could reach it easily.

By the time she was done, the Dead Man had also gained the beach. The Gage was still heaving himself forward step by sucking step, his great weight a tremendous handicap.

Lzi threw back her head and laughed. "Well, here I am! Foot upon the sand, and no sign of warbles yet, you cowards!"

Whether the retreating sailors heard her or not, she could not tell. The only one she could spot on deck was Second Mate, and he seemed busy with the sail.

"This was a terrible idea," the Dead Man said, as he found his stability in the sandy bottom. Water pumped from the top of his boots with every stride. He didn't dignify their marooners with a backwards glance. Lzi supposed from the stiffness of his shoulders that the stiffness of his neck was quite intentional.

"At least you'll dry out fast in the heat," the Gage said, conversationally.

"Crusted in such salt as will rub one raw in every crevice."

"You should strip down," said Lzi. "I don't know how you stand it." She wrung out her own bright gauze skirt between her hands.

The Dead Man ignored her and thrust his sword through the sash binding his coat closed.

"I'll be crusted in salt, too, very shortly," the Gage said. Lzi wondered if it would flake and freckle off his metal hide. He didn't seem to have corroded yet. He pointed with a glittering hand to the dark blue water the *Auspicious Voyage* was already slicing through. "How does a coral atoll form in such deep water?"

The Dead Man swept a hand around. "Ah, my friend. You see, this island is unlike the others. It is volcanic. The black sand reveals its nature. That's not a coral ring. It's the caldera."

"You aren't as ill educated as you look," Lzi said. She kept her face neutral, hoping the mercenaries would know she meant to include herself in their bantering. "That's the reason the King from this island chose the name King Fire Mountain Dynasty."

"Is it extinct?" the Gage asked.

Lzi shook out her orange-patterned wrapped skirt so it would dry in the breeze. "It hasn't erupted since about 1600, I think."

The Gage paused—she supposed he was doing a date conversion to his weird Western system of dating by Years After the Frost—and came up with what Lzi hoped was a comforting thousand-year cushion. "That could just mean that it's biding its time."

"I've heard volcanos are so wont." The Dead Man tugged his veil more evenly across his face. According to the books, such soldiers revealed their faces only when they were about to kill. "Do you not care to discover if your magical, impervious hide is magically impervious to molten stone, my brother?"

"Oh," said the Gage. "I think I'll pass on being smelted."

"Anyway," Lzi interrupted, pretending to be impervious to the smirk showing at the corners of the Dead Man's eyes, "there's plenty of fresh water on the island for you to rinse yourself in. There's a stream right there."

A braid of clear water trickled over steel-colored sand. When she stepped toward it, her bare feet left prints like pearls had been pressed into the wet, packed beach beside their parent oyster shells.

The Gage called her attention to the answering marks on the far side of the freshwater rill at the same moment that she noticed them herself—and just an instant after the Dead Man invoked his Prophet and her Goddess. A furrow, as if a boat had been dragged up the beach to be hidden in the greenery, with the divots of striving feet beside it.

Fresh.

"Isn't it a strange thing," the Dead Man said conversationally, "that we should not be the only visitors to such an out-of-the-way, shunned, supposed cursed and abandoned island on the very same day?"

Lzi stopped, staring at the furrow. "Strange indeed."

"I don't suppose there's any significance to this particular date on the calendar?"

After a day's acquaintance, Lzi had already learned that the more casually curious the Dead Man sounded, the more likely he was to have his hand on his wheel lock. She checked. Yes, there it was, resting on the ornately elaborate pistol butt.

She slapped at a mosquito that was insufficiently discouraged by the sea breeze and the brightness of the sun burning white in the rich blue sky.

"Well," she said resignedly. "Now that you mention it. But before we talk about that, I'm going to wash the salt off."

◆　◆　◆

The outrigger was inside the jungle's canopy, screened and shaded by ferns and vines. Lzi and the Gage stood over it, touching nothing, counting the seats, estimating the provisions cached under canvas for when the paddlers returned. Four seats, and they seemed to have all been filled. Leaving not much room for spoils ...

Lzi slapped another mosquito and bent down to peer. She found that what was under the canvas was not food, but blown-glass fishing floats. Perhaps they too were here to steal the dead King Fire Mountain Dynasty's treasure, and they intended to float the treasure back? Or sink it and mark its location? But then anyone could come along and claim it.

"So it's possible," Lzi said, "and perhaps even likely, that His Majesty King Pale Empire was overheard making preparations to rescind the old King's curse on his island, and perhaps they decided to try to beat us to the treasure. If this interloper should succeed, of course, it would be disastrous for the poor, as King Pale Empire means to use these resources to provide for the needy."

"That is a thing that still confounds my understanding. How is it that such treasure has come to be left in a tomb?"

"It's not a tomb," Lzi said, for what felt like the five hundredth time. "It's a palace."

"A tomb," said the Dead Man patiently, "is perforce where a corpse is maintained ..."

"Look at the bright side," the Gage interrupted, coming back. "We just got significantly less marooned."

"You design to steal their canoe and abandon them to the haunted island?" The Dead Man slapped at a mosquito as well, less patiently.

"Well," the Gage said, "I'd still have to walk back. That won't carry me. But I was thinking that they could take a message to the *Auspicious Voyage* for us, if they turn out to be polite. And maybe they'd let you straddle the outrigger."

"Much to the amusement of the sharks," the Dead Man said, slapping. "Doctor Lady Lzi. You're a natural philosopher. Can't you do anything about these mosquitoes?"

"Welcome to the tropics," the Gage said lightly. "Tell him about the parasites, Doctor Lady Lzi."

◆ ◆ ◆

Lzi paused within the canopy and found long-leaved zodia plants. They had a pungent, fecund scent, and a handful of leaves stuffed into a pocket or waistband did a fairly good job of keeping the mosquitoes at bay.

"The fact is," she said a few moments later while holding a tangle of vines aside for the Dead Man, "having all this gold tied up in mausoleums is murder on the economy." Her knife was still sheathed in her sash. Whoever had come before them had done a good job cutting a path. While it was regrowing already, it would be useful for a few days more.

"So the current King wants to rob his ancestor's tomb to put a little cash back into the system?" It was hard to tell when the Gage was being sarcastic. Unless he was always being sarcastic. He was a wicked and tireless hand with the machete, however.

"Not so much rob the tomb as . . . put the treasure back into circulation. To use as relief for the poor. And, King Fire Mountain Dynasty was not King Pale Empire's Ancestor," said Lzi. "Our Kings are not hereditary. Only their Voices are, and that's because of magic. A retired King can only speak through his female relatives."

"It would be less hassle if your Kings all came from the same lineage," the Gage suggested. "Then at least the money would still be in the family, and the new King could use it, instead of its all going to sustain a relic. And the current Kings would keep siring Voices for their Ancestors."

"Sure," said Lzi. "There are absolutely no problems with hereditary dynasties. And everybody wants to spend all eternity being bossed around personally by their Ancestors. Smooth sailing all the way."

"Well," said the Gage. "When you put it like that . . ."

The Dead Man looked at Lzi shrewdly over his veil. "Will you be an interlocutor for the current King, when he is gone?"

"Not gone, exactly, either," Lzi said. "The Kings drink certain sacred potions, which are derived by natural philosophers such as myself. Abstain from most foods, and many physical pleasures. If they have the discipline to stay the course, the flesh hardens and becomes incorruptible. The *processes* of life stop, but . . . the life remains. They may continue for a long time in such a state, far beyond a mortal life span. But eventually the flesh hardens to the point where they cannot move or speak on their own. And then they need interlocutors. Voices."

"Interlocutors like you."

"King Pale Empire has successfully attained the blessed state," she said, aware her voice was stiff. "But he does not yet require a Voice. Once he does, a new King will rule, and he will retire to the position of honored antecedent. In the meantime, I am merely his servant, and a scientist. I am not of his blood, though in his kindness he adopted me into the royal family, and only women of the royal line may serve as Voices to the Ancestors."

"How can you be sure the Kings are actually saying anything through their Voices that the Voices did not think up themselves? It seems like one of the few ways a woman could get a little power around here."

Lzi had wondered that herself, on occasion. She chose to answer obliquely. "There are stories of Voices who did not do the will of their Kings."

"Let me guess," the Gage said. "They all end in tragedy and fire."

"Stacks of corpses. As must always the ambitions of women."

"So. This old dead King is not dead, but has no living female descendants willing to serve as his interlocutors," the Dead Man said. "He's a King with no Voice. What we are embarked upon, well, sounds like robbery to me, begging your pardon."

Lzi shrugged. "Politics as usual. The voiceless are always powerless."

The Gage said, "And is that the future you desire for yourself?"

Lzi opened her mouth to temporize, and wasn't sure what it was about the Gage's eyeless gaze that paralyzed her voice inside her. Maybe it was simply the necessity of regarding her own face, stretched and strangely disordered, in the flawless mirror of his face. She shut her mouth, swallowed, and tried again, but what came out was the truth. "I have no people beyond the King."

"What became of the family of your birth?" the Dead Man asked, so formally she could not take offense. It was prying in the extreme . . . but the Dead Man was a foreigner, and probably didn't know any better.

"My parents and brother were killed," Lzi said, which was both the truth and devoid of useful information.

"I'm sorry," the Dead Man said. He paused to allow that heavy throbbing sound to rise and fade again, then added, as a small kindness, "I lost my family too."

"Do you miss them?" Lzi asked, surprising herself with her own rudeness in turn. She had, at best, jumbled memories of her kinfolk: warmth, a boy who teased her and took her sweets but also comforted her when she fell and hurt herself. Two large figures with large calloused hands. Sweet rice gruel served in a wooden bowl.

"The first family, I was too young to remember," the Dead Man said without breaking stride. Nimbly, he leaped a branch. "The second family—yes, I miss them very much."

Lzi looked away, wondering how to get out of this one. The Dead Man's voice had been so matter-of-fact . . .

The Gage sank up to the knees in the compost underfoot. Lzi thought it was a good thing brass didn't seem to feel tiredness the way bone and muscle did, or he'd have worn himself out just walking on anything except a paved road.

The Dead Man, kindly, took the opportunity to change the subject. "It's amazing you ever get anywhere." The Dead Man crouched on a long low branch, his soft boots still leaving squelching footprints. The wetness of the soles did not seem to impede his footing.

"I may not get there quickly," the Gage replied, his voice as level as if he sat on cushions in a parlor. "But I have yet to fail to wind up where I intended, and when I pass through a place, few fail to remember where I have been."

Lzi hid a shiver by shrugging her pack off her shoulder. She drank young coconut water. As she capped the canteen, she shrugged to herself. What else had she to spend her life on? More musty, if fascinating, research? More monographs that no one but other naturalists would ever even care about, much less read? More theory on the function of the body and deriving the essential principles from certain plants? More service to an ideal because she had no ambition of her own to work toward?

Perversely, ironic fatalism made her feel a little less empty inside. If she had nothing of her own to live for, it was surely better to find a purpose in life in serving others, rather than increasing suffering and chaos. If you were alone, wasn't it the choice of the Superior Woman to serve those who were not?

The Dead Man shrugged. He stood up on his bough, pivoted on the balls of his feet, and ran lightly along the rubbery gray bark while the branch dipped and swayed under him until he reached a point where another limb crossed the first at midthigh. He stepped up onto the other without seeming to break stride and ran along it in turn, toward some presumed trunk invisible through the foliage ahead. The sound of his footsteps faded into the jungle noise before he vanished from view.

He had the sort of physique that grew veins instead of muscles, and it made his strength seem feral and weightless. In so many ways, the opposite of the Gage.

And yet Lzi could not shake the feeling that in every essential way the two were identical. Except that one wore his armor on the outside, and the other beneath his skin.

She did not desert the Gage. She couldn't have kept up with the Dead Man's branch-running, and it seemed a poor idea to allow their little party to become strung out. She wasn't sure if the Gage noticed, because he labored along without comment.

She was relieved, though, when the Dead Man dropped through the canopy above and ran down a broad bough, his tight-wrapped veil fluttering at the edges. He skidded sideways on his insteps until he was just a foot or two above eye level, far enough away that Lzi didn't need to crane her head back to see him.

"I found the tomb," he announced.

"Palace," she corrected, automatically.

He shrugged. "It resembles a tomb to my eye."

Lzi insisted they pause to eat before pushing any further into unknown dangers—which was easy, in the rich lands of the Banner Islands. They had not even packed supplies: Lzi and the Dead Man simply scanned the earth under the enormous canopy of a breadfruit tree to find ripe, scaly globes, pulled them open, and dined on the mild, custard-like innards. She expected complaints—raw, fresh breadfruit was generally regarded as a bland staple at best—but the foreigner spread a linen cloth that was clean but no longer white across his lap and ate without comment, raising his veil with one hand while scooping morsels from the fruit with the other. Maybe there was no way to eat a ripe breadfruit daintily, but that did not stop him from trying. Lzi wondered what exquisite manners looked like where he came from. Something like this, she imagined.

The Gage didn't seem to care about food.

The Dead Man finished and wiped his fingers daintily on the cloth. He was rolling the cloth so that the soiled portion would not smirch the clean when that searching drone rose once again.

The Dead Man glanced around, cupping a hand behind his veil to better localize the sound. "What *is* that?"

Doctor Lady Lzi had a hypothesis, but she didn't like it very much, and anyway she wasn't confident enough yet to advance it for discussion. One did not become a Lady Doctor by making assertions in public of which one was not confident, and which one could not back up with facts. "Insects?" she asked.

"Well, no maggot curse yet," the Gage said as lightly as a seven-foot-tall brazen bass could be expected to say anything.

The Dead Man shook his jacket clean of nonexistent crumbs. "Mayhap we've not yet gone far enough in."

Lzi followed him through the forest. He stayed on the ground this time, and paused at one point to show her four sets of footprints in a marshy place. They were fresh, filling with water but still sharp-edged. One set was smaller than the others.

The Gage looked at the swampy bit and took the long way around. By the time he rejoined them, Lzi and the Dead Man were already paused behind a screen of greenery, staring across a yard of crushed seashells toward a temple, or a palace, or—she had to admit—a mausoleum. The whole was constructed of pillars—pillars upon pillars upon pillars—stacked in tiers with black basalt in the middle, white coral at the center, and red coral at the top with intermediate shades between so the effect, rather than stripes or bands, was as of the fade from black night to crimson sunrise, only in reverse.

Lzi had expected the palace to be overrun with verdancy, the pillars stumpy and jagged. But it was at least somewhat intact and, if not manicured, she could see where the long knives had recently been at work.

"Maybe King Fire Mountain Dynasty is still aware," she said. "Someone is tending this place."

"Not the people from the canoe?" the Gage asked.

She shrugged. "They probably had machetes."

Something burst into the clearing from the jungle to their left without warning, with such speed and force that Lzi stifled a cry of surprise. It was high up, oil-iridescent, as big and darkly barbed as a bluefin tuna and as sleekly shaped for speed. A blur of glistening wings surrounded it, and Lzi had a confused momentary perception of faceted sapphires glittering as big as her two fists before she realized they were eyes.

She hated being right.

"Well," said the Gage complacently, "that'll be the thing, then, that's been making your buzzing sounds."

"Well, it's better than a maggot curse, right?" the Gage offered, when they had withdrawn a hundred yards or so and were considering their options. Crossing that crushed-shell barren seemed much, much less appealing than it had previously.

"Giant wasps?" The Dead Man shook his head emphatically. "I think not."

"Hornets," said Lzi.

The Dead Man looked at her. The Gage might have also: it was hard to tell in a creature that did not need eyes to see and did not seem to turn his head except when he remembered to.

"They're called corpse-wasps," Lzi said, feeling pedantic even as she embarked upon the explanation. "But taxonomically speaking, they are hornets. They form nests. Colonies."

The Dead Man leaned forward. "So we must expect a great many of these creatures?"

She nodded.

The Gage said, "But they're probably not interested in humans unless you threaten their nest, right? They eat fruit or something?"

"The adults eat fruit," she agreed. "But . . ."

The weight of their attention stopped her, then compelled her to continue.

"...they do sting animals, including people, and carry them back to the nest for the larvae to feed on. That's why they're called corpse-wasps. Although, technically, they're not feeding on corpses, at least not to start, because the prey animals are just ... well, paralyzed."

"Oh, there's your maggots," the Gage said to the Dead Man.

The Dead Man rocked back explosively. "You *knew* about these things?"

"I know they exist," Lzi said defensively. "I didn't know there were any *here*. Anyway, if you separate the infertile workers from the hives, they become really docile."

She had a sense they were both staring at her though with the Gage it was hard to tell.

"They make great pets."

"Pets," the Dead Man said. "People use them like ... watchdogs?"

"Oh, no. They're far too tame for that."

"Ysmat's bright pen," the Dead Man said, and closed his eyes above his veil.

They discussed waiting until nightfall, but Lzi pointed out that many insect species were more active at dusk and after dark, and the hornets could probably sense warmth anyway, so moving by daylight would actually afford them more protection.

"Theoretically," the Gage said.

"Theory is what we have," Lzi answered. "I think it's unlikely, however, that they will be able to carry *you* off, Brass Man."

He chimed like a massive clock: his mechanical laughter. "That does not, however, solve the problem of how to get you two past them."

"Mud," Lzi said, the excitement of an idea upon her. "And more zodia. The pillars of the palace look too close together for the wasps to fly or crawl through, so I think if we reach it, we should be mostly safe inside. But to get us there—"

"Mud," the Dead Man said.

Lzi nodded. "And lots of it."

◆   ◆   ◆

The first half of their approach across the barren to the palace went, Lzi thought, surprisingly well. The green, heady scent of the zodia surrounded them densely, almost palpable on the air, making her light-headed. Their skin was invisible under a layer of pounded plant pulp and mud.

The only problem was that the mud/leaf compound, which had stayed pliable in the moist shade under the leaves, began to dry and whiten almost immediately as they came out into the punishing sun. She thought they would be all right if they hurried, but the mud cracked and flaked off, and they had not thought to plaster the Gage. It might not be possible for the corpse-wasps to sting him or carry him off, but it seemed as if the sunlight dazzling from his brazen hide nevertheless attracted the giant insects.

They had been walking, crouched down under camouflage improvised from handfuls of palm fronds she'd cut with her long knife, the saw-toothed-stem edges wrapped in torn cloth to protect their hands. The heavy thrumming heralded a shadow passing over: first one, then another, and another, until the crushed shells underfoot were darkened with blurry blotches. The corpse-wasps swirled down toward the Gage, who uttered what Lzi assumed was an ungentlemanly word in his own tongue and drew his ragged homespun robes and hood close about his featureless form.

Lzi ducked. "I should have thought of that."

"So should I," the Gage answered. A wasp as long as he was tall veered down, rumbling like a charging elephant, and clanged against his upstretched arm. Lzi stared for a moment. She thought of drawing her knife, then thought how laughable a blade merely as long as her forearm would be against something like that.

Then, as a second shadow swelled around her, she found her feet and glanced over at the Dead Man, who beckoned with an outstretched hand, too polite to grab her elbow and drag her with him. His eyes were white-rimmed, and as she started toward him, bent almost double, he turned and fled beside her.

She was getting the impression that he held no real love for bugs.

Another clang and a heavy, squashing thud followed them. Lzi stumbled while trying to look back and this time the Dead Man did touch her shoulder. "He'll be fine."

She had to trust him. Side by side, they ran toward the completely theoretical safety of the palace.

They were doing all right until they tripped over the corpse. It was just inside the pillars, where the shadow of the roof made it nearly impossible to see through the glare of the sun without. In retrospect, Lzi realized that she'd smelled it before she found it, but between the stench of the tomb, that of the festering mud, and the reek of the zodia her memory hadn't automatically supplied the information that this particular terrible odor belonged to some sort of large and very dead thing.

The body had probably been that of a man, but it was bloated with stings now, the skin stretched and crackling with the products of decomposition. Lzi was startled to see that no maggots writhed through its flesh: surely the smell should have attracted every blowfly on the island by now.

Lzi hadn't fallen, but she'd sprawled against a pillar in the second rank and her palm fronds had gone everywhere. She turned back, the breath knocked out of her, looking for the Dead Man. She wheezed in horror, her spasming lungs unable to shriek a warning, as the corpse lurched and twitched and began to push itself upright behind him.

Fortunately, Lzi's wits, even scattered, were sufficient. With her right hand, she fumbled for her blade and shook it free of the sheath, which fell at her feet. She'd worry about that if she lived. Her bruised and scraped left hand, she raised, waving it frantically to get the Dead Man's attention and pointing past his shoulder.

He had good reflexes, and must have decided she was worthy of at least some trust. He ducked even as he turned, and the corpse's clumsy, club-handed swipe whistled over his head and thudded against the pillar with a noisome splatter.

"He isn't dead!" the Dead Man yelped.

"Oh, he's dead all right," Lzi answered. "And mercifully, too." She could see what the Dead Man could not. The corpse's spine had been eaten away, and beneath the shredding skin pulsated the translucent segments of a great larva.

She hoped he was dead, anyway. Hoped with all the force of her rising gorge even though thick blood welling slowly from some of the fresh tears in the necrotic flesh seemed to give the lie to her desire.

Even as Lzi recoiled, the innate curiosity that had led her to natural philosophy made her focus her attention on the grub. It had a glossy black head like polished obsidian, and Lzi could see the pincery mouth parts embedded in the base of the dead man's skull. The visible part of each was long as her finger, and the gentleness of the taper suggested that they continued for some distance more within the base of the brain. Segmented legs were visible here and there, grasping deep within the festering body.

The larva contracted along its length, a sick, rippling pulse. The corpse convulsed, whirling toward Lzi now in its staggering, seizing dance. The foul arms windmilled and she glimpsed, with ever-increasing horror, that the eyes within the slipping skin were clear, not clouded and dead.

Storm dragons cleanse it with thunder, she thought, and lunged out of the way. She swung with the knife, but the floor under a layer of plant detritus was mosaic, and what had once been smooth was now heaved by roots. Chunks of stone littered it from the collapsing roof. They snagged her feet and slammed her toes so sharp pain shot up her legs. She wasn't sure how she kept her feet, then she wasn't sure how she had lost them. She twisted, falling, and landed on her ass, looking up at the deliquescing face of the horror that pursued her.

The thing staggered like a drunk, dragging one leg and stomping wildly with the other, swaying and wavering. She stuck her long knife out like a ward. Over the blade, she saw the Dead Man raise his right hand. Something glinted bright against the blue of his veil, followed by a stone-cracking retort and the cleansing reek of black powder. The parasite jerked with the impact and collapsed unceremoniously across Lzi's lower legs, twitching faintly.

Lzi screamed through clenched teeth, in disgust as much as pain, and yanked her ankles clear. She huddled, panting, while the Dead Man swiftly reloaded his gun. A shadow fell over her and she looked up, pulse accelerating.

It was the Gage, his robe and brass carapace streaked with fluids of two or three colors. Ichor, she judged, and probably venom. He was wiping his big metal gauntlet-hands on the robe, leaving unidentifiable streaks. Then he bent and picked up her soft leather scabbard from where it had fallen among the litter.

"Well," he said, offering a clean*er* gauntlet to Lzi, "that seems to have got their attention. Get up. There's a flight headed this way and they might be able to squeeze through the pillars."

"Or," said the Dead Man, without holstering his pistol, "there might be more of those." He gestured at the thing on the ground, which still quivered faintly. "There were four sets of footprints."

Lzi pulled herself up with the Gage's help, bruises stiffening. She stowed her knife. Then she bent down and with both hands hefted a sizeable chunk of rubble, one that made her grunt to lift. She thought of the brown, clear eyes in the parasitized thing's melting face.

She lifted the rock to chest height, and threw it toward the ground. It struck the host's skull with a terrible sound and the quivering stopped.

"Now we can go."

The droning buzz of the corpse-wasps grew heavier, more layered, until Lzi felt the vibrations in the hollowness that had been her chest. She imagined she could watch the tremors shimmer across the Gage's surface. If she looked back, she could see that the light was dimming not simply because they picked their way deeper into the palace complex, but also because the bodies of enormous wasps layered one over another blocked the white glare of the sun. The insects had a smell, in such quantities: musty, like dry leaves. But not so clean.

None of the travelers asked how they would be able to leave the palace now that they had won entrance to it, but Lzi was thinking about it. Maybe they could wait until it rained. A soaking thunderstorm was never far, in the Banner Islands, where the dragons roamed the Sea of Storms. Flying insects took shelter in rough weather, lest they be blown out to sea.

She hoped that applied to insects eight feet long.

There was light ahead and they made for it. The Dead Man's teeth chattered behind his veil, but his gun hand was steady. He held a scimitar drawn in his off-hand, and that seemed steady too. The Gage moved with surprising delicacy between the columns, though his carelessness could probably have knocked the whole moldering palace down.

They came to an open space, unroofed, where the drone of the swarm was pronounced but distant, rising and falling like the mechanical noise of cicadas. Litter-filled ornate fountains and statuary bore witness that this had been a formal courtyard. A gigantic tree rumpled the surrounding paving stones and clutched benches it must once have shaded in gnarled roots, as if at any moment it might heave itself free of the earth and come forward, swinging them as weapons. Beyond, a tall building was surrounded by the litter of its own crumbling verandas. Like the pillars, it was shaded from black through white to red. It had once had glass windows, a profound luxury for the era and the place when it was built, and a few unbroken panes still gleamed.

"Can we cross that?" the Gage asked, stopping within the shelter of the penultimate rank of pillars.

"We must," the Dead Man answered, with a glance at Lzi. She was the employer, she remembered. She could call this off right now.

But her life was service. And besides, they could not go back.

"We must," Lzi agreed. And was looking about her for a plan, or at least a cluster of zodia plants, when the painted door up the steps behind the wreckage of the veranda opened, and a woman dressed in a white skirt and twining sandals, her long hair braided back as thick as Lzi's wrist, stood framed against interior darkness.

Lzi touched the hilt of her long knife. "Well, don't just stand there," the woman said. "It's safe to cross the open space right now as long as you move quickly. I spent a long time studying the corpse-wasps. I know a great deal about parasites."

The darkness inside the doorway, once they had scrambled over the rubble of the wrecked courtyard and climbed gingerly up the steps—which settled under the Gage's weight but did not crack—was less absolute than Lzi had anticipated. It was only the contrast with the glare of the direct sun that had made it seem pitch-black behind the woman. In reality, the interior of the palace was comfortably dim and cool.

And the interior of the palace was in much better repair than the courtyard or the pillared colonnade.

Ropes of necklaces and heavy bangles shifted and shone as she closed the door behind them, the gold rich against her brown skin. She was tanned—Lzi could see the paler brown behind the waistband of her skirt—but there were no tan lines behind the jewelry. There were wooden amulets sewn into the wrap cloth, though, and those looked long established, with frayed threads and bits of mud in the fine lines of the designs.

"The Emperor is waiting for you. I am the Lady Ptashne, his Voice." She spoke with awkward dignity, worn like those unaccustomed jewels, and gestured them to follow her.

The woman's feet and ankles were dirty under the sandals, as if she had walked through soupy mud then shod herself without being able to first clean her feet. Lzi saw the Dead Man gazing at them speculatively over his veil, and she knew he was comparing their size to the footprints beside the canoe. She was about to ask how a Voice came to be so presently arrived in a deserted kingdom, but words interrupted her.

Someone spoke . . . her name.

She glanced around. There was no one present except the Gage, the Dead Man, and this Ptashne. They were in an entrance hall of crumbling grandeur, hung with silk brocade so brittle it was shredding under its own weight and stacked with furniture coated in layers of dust. The walls were pale coral in shades of pink and white. They had once been hung with tapestries, but the tapestries had broken their threads and fallen from their rings. No one could be hiding behind them.

And the voice that said her name again was like a rustle of wasp wings in her mind. :*Doctor Lady Lzi. Have you too come to disturb my rest, Granddaughter?*:

She blinked with shock, and though the floors here were smooth, she stumbled so the Gage had to steady her elbow. She saw the Lady Ptashne glance over her shoulder speculatively and frown. Lzi kept her face carefully blank. Experimentally, she thought, *King Fire Mountain Dynasty?*

:*You serve the new King.*:

How is it that you are speaking to me, your majesty? I am not your descendant.

:*Are you sure?*: She could sense his amusement. :*Descent through a mother's line is often forgotten. And what person can say for certain who is his father? You have enough of my blood in you for the palace to awaken to your steps.*:

Lzi considered that for a moment. She allowed herself to drift to the end of the group trailing Lady Ptashne, where Lzi could just follow the shoulders in front of her and not concern herself too much with what her features showed.

Who was the man with the wasp inside him?

:*Lady Ptashne's companion. One of them. There are two others. I think one was her husband.*:

Do you control the wasps? Did you do . . . that . . . to him?

:*The wasps are my guardians, but I do not control them. Long ago, I did bind their ancestors to this place. He and the others trespassed and the wasps defended me.*: He sounded matter-of-fact.

If he was Lady Ptashne's companion, how did he come to trespass?

:*She was yet Ptashne,*: the old King said. :*But not yet Lady when it happened. She brought the men with her as a sacrifice, and she has some little talismans that give her certain powers. Will you be my Voice, Granddaughter?*:

So the Lady Ptashne was, as the canoe had suggested, a recent addition to the royal household. How had she come to pass unscathed through the corpse-wasps, Lzi wondered, apparently alone of her party of four? And why did she seem so calm, despite the deaths?

I spent a long time studying the corpse-wasps. I know a great deal about parasites.

Lzi said—or thought, hard and clearly—*You have a Voice.*

:*So I do,*: the dead King answered. :*One Voice. After a fashion. Is it not better to have a choice, than to have no choices?*:

But . . . you have a Voice. Already.

:*And you have one, too. Do you speak out with it in your own words? Or do you silence it except when commanded to its use by another?*:

It was the same question he had asked before, which she had dodged, but more provocatively phrased this time. Was the dead King needling her? Trying to get her to rise to the bait?

What if I don't have anything to say?

The undead King did not answer. She wondered if she needed to intend to speak to him for him to hear her, or if he were politely ignoring her own interior monologue.

I serve King Pale Empire, she said. *But he does not own my voice.*

:That is good to hear, Granddaughter. Ah, you are nearly to the presence chamber. Do not allow Lady Ptashne to know that you can speak to me, Doctor Lady Lzi. Not yet. It would be . . . unwise.:

Well, *that* painted Lzi with a wash of unease.

Ahead, Lady Ptashne had stopped before an ironbound door. It seemed recently maintained, and there were fresh scratches around the keyhole, which was sized to admit an enormous old-fashioned key. Ptashne lifted just such a key from inside her skirt pocket. A ribbon connected it to the material of her garment: it had been sewn into place with hasty stitches and thread that did not match.

She turned the key, struggled with the weight of the door before prevailing, and led them into another space, shadowy and echoing from its depths.

Nuggets of glass turned under Lzi's feet. She was distracted keeping her balance and watching the Gage pick his way carefully until she realized that if the glass did not crush into powder under his feet, then it was not glass at all, but gemstones. Rubies and sapphires in every color of the rainbow littered the floor: a priceless trip hazard.

Lzi thought with frustration of kingdoms where such riches would not be left uselessly to molder as symbols of the bygone might of dead Emperors, but used to support trade, to buy medicines, to feed the poor. How much had her island home suffered through the centuries because of waste such as this? This . . . all this treasure . . . How much linen could it buy from the mainland for sails? How much hemp for ropes? The Sea of Storms protected the Banner Islands from any raiders more significant than the occasional pirate. But the Banner Islands, though rich in foodstuffs and spices and hardwood, were otherwise natural-resource poor. Trade was their lifeline. This would pay for trade.

As they reached the center point of the hall, lights flared in sconces along both sides. They looked like torch flames but burned strikingly violet and blue, and there were no torches beneath them. Their light stained the Gage's bronze hide a most unearthly color and sent thick, watery, reflected bands of radiance rippling across everything in the hall.

More wealth gleamed on every side, and before them, another fifty steps or so along the enormous hall, was a throne whose golden seat hung suspended between two mammoth ivory tusks that crossed at the top in barbaric splendor.

The throne stood empty.

The Dead Man's step checked. Lady Ptashne, though, seemed to have anticipated it. Without turning her head, she said, "His Majesty is in the Presence Chamber."

She turned them to the right and brought them to a small door, much more human in scale than the one she had struggled with, recessed between two pillars in the side wall. This one was unlocked, apparently, for she simply manipulated the handle and opened it.

It revealed a small, comfortably furnished room that was lit with the same eerie blue flames, but did not need them. At the far end, two multipaned windows big as doors framed a Song-style ox-yoke armchair of carved wood and cracking leather, fragile with age but still strong enough to support the slight weight of the corpse who slouched in it. He was little more than a collection of brown sticks wrapped in moldering silken brocades, decorated with ropes of jewels. Over the robes, the corpse wore a dust-coated cloak. There were places where the heavy, feathery dust had been disturbed—brushed or blown off—and beneath them Lzi glimpsed the iridescent, translucent wings of insects, sewn together in tiers like the feathers of a bird.

The corpse was mummified, the skin glossy brown as lacquered leather. White bits of bone showed through where the fingers had crumpled or been gnawed by rats.

Following Ptashne, Lzi and the others approached. The Gage's footsteps made a heavy careful sound on the flagstones. The dead King smelled of moths and attics, dry fluttery things.

:*I never could stand that throne room,*: said King Fire Mountain Dynasty, and Lzi swallowed and tried not to think too much about the fact that she was in a close little room with his thousand-year-old body. :*Drafty old pile. This is a much better place to wait for eternity.*:

Lzi bowed low before the chair. After a confused glance, the Gage and the Dead Man did as well.

"King Fire Mountain Dynasty bids you welcome, and rise."

Lzi hadn't heard him say any such thing. But perhaps he just hadn't spoken to her.

Lzi turned to the Lady Voice, and said, "Your friend is dead."

Ptashne frowned at her in mild distaste. "My husband?" She shrugged.

How had Ptashne known which of her companions they had encountered? The Gage made his chiming chuckle, and Lzi thought of King Fire Mountain Dynasty's warning about talismans.

Ptashne twisted a hand in the folds of her white skirt. "His majesty commands your assistance. He wishes to be carried from this place, and to the beach."

Lzi held her breath for a moment, gathering her courage. "What are the floats for?"

"Floats?"

"The fishing buoys. In your canoe."

"Oh," Ptashne said. "For floating King Fire Mountain Dynasty back to the big island, of course."

"Back to the big island?"

"Of course," she repeated. "You don't think he wants me to stay here forever, do you? With his treasure and my status as his granddaughter . . ." Ptashne smiled. "We will have a good life. Of course, if you help me, I will share some of my wealth with you. Now, please have your soldier and your"—she waved a hand vaguely at the Gage—"lift him, and carry him down to the lagoon."

:*That is not what I require of you, Granddaughter.*:

And in a flash of comprehension, as if he had shown her a map, Lzi understood what the dead King did require of her. It came on a tremendous warmth, a sense of belonging. Of being part of something.

She rebelled against his request.

I have only found you!

:*And would you, too, use me for power and wealth?*:

She felt deep shame. *Wealth is why I came here. But not for me. For the current King.*

:*And will he not reward you?*:

He has . . . she stopped. Thought. *Given me service. Given me a place.*

:*Well,*: the old King answered. :*If that is all you want, Granddaughter.*:

I want you, she answered. *I have only just found you. Do not make me give you up so soon.*

:*I am tired. And you see what I've had to contend with in certain branches of the family.*:

He didn't move, of course. He couldn't. He hadn't moved in a thousand years. But she still had a sense of a dismissive flick of his fingers in the direction of the Lady Ptashne.

"Pick him up!" Ptashne demanded, increasingly shrill.

"Is that what you require us to do?" the Dead Man asked. "It is you who holds our contracts, Doctor Lady."

You are my only family. She stopped herself from saying it—thinking it—out loud. Whatever she was or was not, she would not guilt-trip a man who had been alone for six hundred years because she was lonely.

"Well, no, actually," Lzi said. She closed her eyes. She *liked* this long-undead ancestor whom she had so swiftly become acquainted with. She felt a great, tearing sense of loss as she took a deep breath and said, "I want you to destroy him."

If she expected an outraged outburst, she didn't get it. The Dead Man just said, curiously, "So there is in truth no curse?"

"Of course there's a curse," she scoffed. "Do you think any of this stuff would still be in there if there wasn't a *curse*? But he wanted to be left alone, not protected. And now, he has been alone a very long time, and what he wants is to be *gone.*"

"How can you know that?" Ptashne said. "*You* can't talk to him. I am his Voice!"

"She's got the contracts," the Gage said tiredly. "Or rather, her King does. Please stand aside, Lady Ptashne."

The Brass Man took a step forward. The lady in the white skirt did not step aside. She wheeled and fell to her knees, clutching the mummified legs of the ancient King. They flaked and crumbled at her touch.

"Let me serve you, ancestor!" Ptashne cried.

Lzi felt her mouth shape words, her throat stretch to allow a voice of foreign timbre to pass. :The only service I require is destruction, child,: she said aloud. :What service you offer is for yourself, and not for the kingdom.:

Ptashne's sobs dried as if her throat had closed on them. She rose gracefully, the cultivated daintiness of a lady. Lzi wondered where she had come from, and what had brought her here. It itched in her conscience and her curiosity that she would probably never know.

Ptashne turned to face the Gage. He towered over her, and she seemed frail and small. Her hands twisted in the waistband of her skirt, clutching at the amulets sewn there.

Her mouth pressed together until no red was left, and Lzi thought if there hadn't been flesh and teeth in the margin, bone would have rasped on bone. It was the expression of an unwanted child who is reminded that there are children for whom parents make sacrifices.

Lzi felt it in her bones, and knew the interior shape of it intimately.

There *are* children for whom parents make sacrifices. It's a thing some take a long while to understand in their hearts even if they see it with their eyes.

Experience is a more potent teacher than observation. And Lzi had never had a sacrifice made for her sake either. A terrible pity took her.

Ptashne looked Lzi in the eyes, forward as a lover, and spoke to her as if to King Fire Mountain Dynasty. "Let me serve you, Grandfather. You are my family. I need you. You are my ancestor, Grandfather. I honor you. I have honored you, and all my ancestors, all my life. With my sorcery and with my search. You owe me this small thing."

Lzi's lips moved around that voice that came not from her lungs, but somewhere else. :I am tired, Granddaughter. Take half my jewels. Make a life with that.:

Why do you speak through me? Lzi asked. *Why not her?*

:She has protections in place for that, as well. I can speak to her, but not through her, and these words need to be spoken aloud.:

"I do not want your jewels, Grandfather." Ptashne straightened up, her muddy feet in their laced sandals set stubbornly on carpet that was more moth-hole than knot and warp. "I want to be your Voice." The hard line of her mouth softened. She looked up at the Gage, who had stopped just out of his own ability to reach her, like a man trying not to frighten a cornered kitten.

She said to the giant metal man, "I've come all this way for him and it's not fair, women are only allowed to hold power through men, why won't he *help* me?"

It was a child's voice. It cut Lzi like a knife. The ridges of wound, gummed cloth on the hilt of her machete were rough against her palm.

And then Ptashne steeled herself, and said, "Then I shall help myself."

She twisted her hands in her skirts. She shouted, a shrill and wavering scream. One of the amulets at her waistband swelled with a green glow like light through young leaves. It streamed between her fingers in rays like the sun parting clouds. The Gage took a step forward, ornate tiles powdering under his foot. The Dead Man reached for his gun.

They were both too late.

The sidelight windows flanking the dead King's chair of estate shattered in a hail of glass and buzzing. Two infected, flailing men stumbled into the room, followed by a half dozen corpse-wasps. The men both waved machetes haphazardly. The wasps brandished daggerlike stingers damp at the tip with droplets of paralytic poison.

Lzi, with her hand on her sheathed knife, froze. She made one startled sound—a yelp of surprise rather than a moan of terror—and then her body locked in place as surely as if the wasps had already had their way with her. She watched her reflection grow in a gargantuan, glossy green-black thorax. The part of the brain that screams *run, run* in those dreams where your body seems immured in glass was informing her calmly that this was the last instant of her life.

The Dead Man stepped in front of her and shot the corpse-wasp between the eyes.

Dust sifted from between the stones overhead. The shot wasp tumbled to the floor and buzzed, legs juddering, the spasms of its wings trembling the stones under Lzi's feet. The sound . . . the sound of the gun was enormous. It filled Lzi's ears and head and left room for nothing else. No other sound, no thought—and not even the paralyzing fear.

She fumbled her machete into her hand. She hacked at the nearest threatening thing—the convulsing wasp's stinger. She severed it in two sharp whacks and looked up to see the Dead Man still standing before her, parrying wild swings by one of the parasitized men. The Gage was fending off two wasps, their stingers leaving venom-smeared dents in his carapace. Ptashne, her hair escaping its thick braid, had fallen back to stand before the chair of estate of the corpse she would have be her

King. She had her own long knife drawn from its sling at the small of her back, but was holding it low and tentatively, as if she did not know how she would fight with it.

And between Lzi and Ptashne were five angry hornets and two pathetically disgusting not-quite-corpses. So that wasn't really a solution.

A wasp came in from the left, furiously intent on the Dead Man as he drove Ptashne's parasitized companion back, step by step. Its wings and the back of its thorax struck the ceiling as it curved, bringing its stinger to bear.

Lzi stepped forward and brought the machete down hard and sharp, as if she were trying to cut a poison-sap vine with one blow. It struck the underside of the heavy chitinous abdomen and stuck there with a sound like an axe buried in wood. Splinters of the insect's carapace and splatters of pulpy interior flew, and the machete stuck fast.

With an angry buzz and a clatter of its mandibles, the sapphire-eyed insect tried to turn on her. Its feet scratched at her face and hair. She ducked to shield her eyes and held frantically to the long knife's handle, locking her elbow and pushing the pulsing, seeking stinger away. The Dead Man was too busy with his maggot man and another of the wasps to come to her aid.

Lzi screamed with all her might and twisted the blade sharply.

The wasp's carapace shattered with a crack, and the stinger twisted and went slack. The thing made a horrible buzz and tried to bite. She hammered at the jeweled eye with the pommel of the long knife, as it was too close to use the blade. Now she screamed, or at least yelled vigorously.

There was a revolting crunch, and the enormous wasp—which was terribly light, she realized, for its size, as if it were mostly hollow inside—scrabbled at her once more and fell away. She looked up into the featureless face of the Gage, smeared with ichor and more nameless things.

"The wasps are protecting the larvae," Lzi said, as sure of the truth behind the inspiration as if she had learned it at her father's knee. "Ptashne doesn't control the adults. Just the larvae in the corpses."

"Destroy the King." The Gage's head did not turn as his left hand flashed out to snatch at the wing of another wasp as it darted toward the Dead Man. He used its own momentum to slam it into the ceiling, his metal body pivoting inhumanly, like a turret, at the waist. He continued in a level tone—or maybe it was just that all its nuances were flattened by her deafness. "If Ptashne has nothing to fight for, she'll stop."

Dragon's breath, I hope so. Lzi thought she might be desperate enough to keep fighting anyway, having nothing else to live for. "Get me through."

The Gage did not respond in words. Instead it turned again, seamlessly, and lurched forward, flailing with its enormous arms. It didn't attempt to prevent the enemies from striking it, and it didn't seem to care if it struck them. It just created a flurry of motion that surrounded Lzi and fended the enemies away. It walked sideways, crabwise, toward the dead King and his Voice.

He turned, still keeping her in the shelter of his parries, and Lzi was next to the place where King Fire Mountain Dynasty slumped in his finery. She could smell him: not rot, but salt and natron and harsh acetone.

Ptashne seemed to realize what they were about and whirled on them. "No," she shouted. She would have rushed at Lzi, but the Gage caught her effortlessly around the waist and held her tight. She hammered at him with the pommel of her long knife, and the room might have rung like a bell if Lzi's ears had not still felt stuffed with wool. Holding on to Ptashne limited the Gage's effectiveness in fending the wasps away from Lzi, but the Dead Man was between her and the enemy, a whirl of blades and faded crimson coat-skirts.

It was hard, so hard, to turn her back on the fight, on the slashing stingers and whirling blades, the clang of machete on scimitar, the screaming and flailing of the would-be Voice. But she did, ran two steps through the chaos, hefting her long knife, and stopped by the chair of the King.

:*That will not do the job, Granddaughter. For this, you need fire.*:

"Fire," she said aloud. She didn't look, but somehow there was a powder horn in her hand, and a flint and steel.

The Dead Man's powder horn.

Fire. Black powder would burn nearly anything.

She poured it over the dead King, his rotting robes, his ropes of gold and jewels, his crooked slipping crown. His face drawn tight to the skull, the nose a caved-in hole. His eye sockets empty with the withered lids sagging into them.

She poured the contents of the horn over him, into his lap, into the tired wisps of his staring hair. She dropped the horn. She clutched the flint and iron and raised them over the corpse of the King.

Behind her, all the sounds of battle ceased. The buzzing continued, but when Lzi risked a glance, she saw that the one remaining parasite host had staggered back and was leaning against the wall by the door, and the two adult wasps that were still alive and mobile crouched in front of him, one on the ceiling and one on the floor, protecting the young of the hive but not, themselves, immediately attacking.

"Please," Ptashne said. She had stopped struggling as well, and now just hung in the Gage's grasp, bedraggled and bruised, her long knife on the floor where it had fallen from her hand.

"All this for a family," Ptashne said, tiredly.

:My family is gone,: King Fire Mountain Dynasty said, through Lzi. :And you gave yours to the wasps in exchange for a weapon, Grandchild.:

The Dead Man looked at him, head sideways. At the mummy, Lzi noticed, and not at the Voice. Used to marvels, this mercenary. "You have family in this room."

I would have given you my life.

:*Keep it for yourself*,: he counseled. :*End this*.:

Lzi struck a spark. She had been too cautious and kept her hand too far away. It fell and fizzled. Ptashne screamed.

Lzi struck again. This time it flared, and the powder caught. She backed hastily away from a shower of sparks and the strange dry smoke of burning mummy. King Fire Mountain Dynasty burned like a torch once he caught, and said nothing further in Lzi's head. Not even the whisper of a *thank-you*.

Well, it was what she should have expected of a King.

"You ruined me," Ptashne said dully. "You have ruined everything."

Lzi glanced at the wasps, which seemed to have no intention of charging these dangerous creatures again. They buzzed menace and held the door. Lzi and her mercenaries were going to have to climb out a window.

"He gave you jewels," she said to Ptashne. "Take whatever you can carry. May you find joy in it."

Lzi sat alone on the beach beside a tree, waiting for the sun to rise and the *Auspicious Voyage* to return. She fretted the edge of her machete with her thumbnail. It was, understandably, dull.

She looked up as two silhouettes approached. "Did you get him?"

The Gage shook his head, which gleamed softly in the moonlight. He sat down on her left, the Dead Man on her right. "We looked. The wasps must have taken their last offspring somewhere safe from the likes of us."

"Poor man," Lzi said.

After a while, the silence of lapping waves was broken by the Dead Man's voice. "So," he said. "We shall collect our pay soon, and be traveling on. And then, where do *you* go from here, Doctor Lady?"

"It's not hard to live here," she said. She gestured to the jungle behind them, the sea before beyond. "Many people are content with the breadfruit, the harvest of the lagoons, the coconuts and mangoes and the pounded hearts of palm. Many people are content to sail, and swim, and find somebody to fight and make babies with."

"But it was never enough for you."

Lzi heard the length of her own pause, and the snort that followed. "Maybe the restlessness runs in the blood like the sea. My parents sailed off in search of an uncharted island and never returned, did you know that? Into the dragon-infested Sea of Storms. They took my brother with them. I was judged too young. They had ambition and it killed them. I had ambition . . . and also I was afraid."

"So you studied the arts of science?"

"I learned to read," she said. "I learned to heal. I learned to kill by poison and by blade, because you cannot learn to create without learning to destroy, and the reverse of course holds true as well. I made a place for myself in the service of King Pale Empire. My life at his command."

The Dead Man nodded, perhaps sympathetically. He leaned against the tree she sat beside. "But."

"But it wasn't enough. I felt like I was scraping mud from the bottom of the well, that it was filling with salt water from beneath."

"You can only give so much from a well until you fill it again. With rain or with buckets, or with time and the water that rises from within. When you are doing something entirely for somebody else—out of altruism, or out of a need to feel some purpose—"

"What else is there?"

"What are you good for?" He might have smiled. In any case, the shadowy stretch of the veil across his face altered. "You could try wanting something. For yourself. For its own sake. Or getting mad enough about something unfair to decide to do something about it."

She considered it. So strangely attractive. Find something worth fighting for, then fight for it.

"But what?"

He blinked sleepily. "Doctor Lady Lzi, if you come to that understanding, you will have exceeded the accomplishments of fully half of humanity. And now please excuse me. It will be day before long, and I am going to look for some dry wood for the signal fire."

She sat on the beach beside the Gage and watched the sun go down. The wind off the water grew chill; the sand underneath her stayed warm.

The Gage spoke before she did. "Do you want to wind up like maggot man back there? That's what service to the unappreciative gets you. Ask a Gage how he knows."

She decided not to. "What if you don't have anything but service?" she asked starkly.

There was a silence. The stars burned through it, empty and serene as Lzi wished she could be.

"I had a family for a time as well," said the Gage, over the hush of the waves.

"You?" Lzi's expression of confusion was making her forehead itch. "But you are . . ."

"Gages are born before we're made," said the Gage. "The Wizard needs something to take apart, to animate the shell when she puts it back together again."

"By the Emperor's wings," Lzi said softly.

"I volunteered."

She stared at him, rude though it was. The light of the moons made blue ripples on his hide.

"Well," the Gage said, reasonably, "would you want something like me around if it hadn't decided it wanted to be made and serve you?"

"Were you dying?" Lzi covered her mouth with her hands. She was catching rudeness from these foreigners.

"Not yet. But I needed to live long enough to exact a kind of justice. For *my* family."

Lzi hadn't heard the Dead Man come up behind her. His voice made her jump. "I did live for service. Very like you. And then the service was taken from me." He thumped a pile of sticks down on the sand. "In this life, one cannot rely on anything."

"What kept you going past that point?"

"For me," the Dead Man said, "it was also revenge."

The Gage had called it *justice*. Lzi asked, "Revenge for your Caliph?"

The naïve might have mistaken his bark of pain for a laugh. "For my daughters," he said. "And my wife."

Lzi couldn't think what to say, and said nothing, for so long that the Dead Man collected himself and went on.

"That desire kept me alive long enough for others to assert themselves."

The Gage tilted his polished head. It gleamed with a soft luster in the tropic dark. "Revenge led me to become a Gage," he admitted. "Since then, I have not met anything that could put a stop to me. So here I am."

"Is that the only effective purpose? The only way to make a space for yourself in the world that is not . . . serving someone else's whim?" Lzi asked. "Vengeance?"

"It is the worst one," the Gage replied. "But it's something to go forward on."

"I don't have anyone to punish." Not even the parents who had abandoned her, she realized. For how do you punish those who are dead and gone? But she realized also that she could never make herself good enough, small enough, useful enough to lure them home. Because they were dead, and they were gone.

"All this for family?" Lzi said, and felt that expression push her mouth thin. "She was right, you know. This is the only power of her own that she would ever have had."

"Yes," said the Gage quietly. "I know."

He was silent for a moment or two.

"Then a harder question. What would you be, beyond a servant?" the Dead Man asked her. "What else would you seek?"

Lzi shrugged. "I am not giving up my service. I am useful where I am."

"What does your soul crave, though, besides being useful?" There was enough light now to see him shift slightly from foot to foot. Morning was coming.

"I suppose the first thing I seek is what I am seeking."

He touched his nose through the veil, which she thought signified a smile. "Write me a letter when you find it."

"You're not staying?"

He shrugged.

The Gage rolled his enormous shoulders, as if settling his tattered homespun more comfortably. Lzi would have to see if the Emperor's gratitude for the sapphires in her pack would extend to a new raw-silk robe for the brazen man.

He didn't turn his polished metal egg, but Lzi had a sense that he was looking at the Dead Man . . . fondly?

"Not here," the Gage supplied for his partner. "He's seeking . . . something else." He waited a moment, watching a pale line creep across the bottom of the sky. "You could come with us. We're short a naturalist."

He's seeking a home, she thought. *Does the destination matter, or is the value in the journey and whom you make it with?* "Let me think about it," she said, and watched the *Auspicious Voyage*'s silhouette approach across the broken mirror of the lagoon.

Lavie Tidhar

· · ·

I had to think hard about whether it was proper to include one of Lavie Tidhar's tales of "guns & sorcery," featuring the bizarre and often ultraviolent adventures of Gorel of Goliris, a "gunslinger and addict" in a world full of evil sorcery and monstrous creatures. Did a story without swords belong in a Sword & Sorcery anthology? But swords or no swords, the Gorel stories are true to the spirit of Sword & Sorcery, and their antecedents are clear—there's the strong influence of Stephen King's Gunslinger stories, obviously, but equally strong are the traces of C. L. Moore, Michael Moorcock, Jack Vance, and Robert E. Howard. The Gorel stories especially remind me of Howard's early Conan the Barbarian stories. What they are is almost the pure essence of Sword & Sorcery—violent, action-packed, paced like a runaway freight train, politically incorrect and socially unredeemable, in your face. They're also a lot of fun, and yet another example, along with the work of many of the other writers here, of the interesting and sometimes surprising directions this particular subgenre is evolving in as we progress deeper into the twenty-first century.

So let yourself be swept along with Gorel on his latest dark and twisted quest, but buckle your seatbelts—it's going to be a bumpy ride.

(Further adventures of Gorel can be found in the chapbook novella *Gorel and the Pot Bellied God* and in the collection *Black Gods Kiss*.)

Lavie Tidhar grew up on a kibbutz in Israel, has traveled widely in Africa and Asia, and has lived in London, the South Pacific island of Vanuatu, and Laos; after a spell in Tel Aviv, he's currently living back in England again. He is the winner of the 2003 Clarke-Bradbury Prize (awarded by the European Space Agency), was the editor of *Michael Marshall Smith: The Annotated Bibliography*, and the anthologies *A Dick & Jane Primer for Adults*, the three-volume The Apex Book of World SF series, and two anthologies edited with Rebecca Levene, *Jews vs. Aliens* and *Jews vs. Zombies*. He is the author of the linked story collection *HebrewPunk,* and, with Nir Yaniv, the novel *The Tel Aviv Dossier*, and the novella chapbooks *An Occupation of Angels, Cloud Permutations, Jesus and the Eightfold Path*, and *Martian Sands*. A prolific short-story writer, his stories have appeared in *Interzone, Asimov's Science Fiction, Clarkesworld, Apex Magazine, Strange Horizons, Postscripts, Fantasy Magazine, Nemonymous, Infinity Plus, Aeon, The Book of Dark Wisdom, Fortean Bureau, Old Venus*, and elsewhere, and have been translated into seven languages. His novels include *The Bookman* and its two sequels, *Camera Obscura* and *The Great Game*, *Osama: A Novel* (which won the World Fantasy Award as the year's Best Novel in 2012), *The Violent Century*, and *A Man Lies Dreaming*. His most recent book is a big, multifaceted SF novel, *Central Station*.

◆　◆　◆

Waterfalling

A Guns and Sorcery Novelette

LAVIE TIDHAR

1.

Gorel of Goliris rode slowly, half-delirious in the saddle of his graal. The creature lumbered beneath him, moving sluggishly. It was a multilegged beast, native to the sands of Meskatel, which lay far to the south. Its tough carapace would turn a pleasing green in sunlight, as it depended on the solar rays for sustenance: but right now its skin was a dark and unhealthy-looking mottled grey, as the storm clouds had been amassing steadily over the deadlands and the creature was starved of nutrition just like its master, in his own way, was. Its tail was raised like the stem of a flower, the better to catch moisture in the air, the sting at its end naked like a spur.

They were much alike, master and beast. Hardy, obstinate, durable, and deadly. Gorel's head hung limp on his chest. His gums hurt and his eyes felt fused shut, and everything ached. His hands shook uncontrollably.

Withdrawal.

He needed it.

He needed the Black Kiss.

What drove him into the deadlands was a mixture of heartache, desire, and need. Somewhere far behind him lay the Black Tor, and its enigmatic master, the dark lord whom Gorel knew only as Kettle. The

Avian mage was a small, slight being, his fragile bones like those of a bird. The two had been together when great Falang-Et fell, and the river Thiamat flooded, its god dead . . .

Kettle had used Gorel, and Gorel could not forgive his onetime lover for that betrayal.

His journey since had taken him far and wide: to the great cemetery of Kur-a-len, where the dead still walk, and to the Zul-Ware'i mountains, where the remnants of an ancient war still littered the glaciers with deadly unexploded ordnance. What drove him, always, was his quest. The search for lost Goliris, that greatest of empires, the biggest and most powerful the World had ever known. His home, from which he had been taken as a child, to which he must return, and claim his throne . . .

Yet in all the World, in all of his searching, throughout the long years, he had never found a trace of his homeland, as though—he sometimes thought, in dark moments—it had been erased entirely from the memory of all living beings.

But the World was large—infinite, some even claimed. And Gorel would not rest until he found it once again.

Goliris . . .

Heartache, then, and need. Yet, what of desire?

It had happened long before, in the jungle lands where the Urino-Dag, the ghouls of the bush, haunt the unwary traveller in the thicket. Where the smell of rotten leaves and decay fills the still air, where a village once stood, where Gorel had come in his search . . . only to encounter the twin goddesses, Shar and Shalin, who bit him, laughing, with the Black Kiss . . . and even as he murdered them both, and all their followers, their curse was in him, and he was forever hooked.

Gods' Dust.

But there were no gods in the deadlands. There were barely any human habitations to attract them, no subsequent illicit transaction of pleasure for faith. And Gorel was driven on blindly, across a land cracked with drought, under a black sky, driven as much *away* as *towards*, growing weak, growing delirious . . .

And in his *delirium tremens*, he remembered.

He remembered Goliris.

2.

The great towers of dread Goliris rose like an infection out of the fertile ground. They were not so much built as *cultivated*, planted there in aeons past by the magus-emperor Gon, the fungimancer. Where he had bought these spores, at what cost, or in what far-flung corner of the great empire of Goliris, was lost to the mists of time, but the towers grew, tall graceful stems with bulbous caps, gills protruding, and a small army of wizard-gardeners tending to their constant maintenance.

Goliris, mother-city, sat atop the shores of a great ocean. Its black ships, unequalled in all the World, departed from its shores to all corners and returned laden with goods and pillage. The hot, humid air was cooled by the sea breeze, and in its wide avenues and canals there strode, flew, and swam the ambassadors of a thousand races, come to pay tribute.

Gorel remembered standing at the top of the palace, holding his father's hand. The room was cool and dark, and through the gills one could see the ocean spread out to the horizon, where a blood-red sun was slowly setting. Its dying light illuminated the great fleet, black sails raising overhead the seven-pointed-star flag of Goliris.

"Where are they going, Father?" the young Gorel had asked.

"To conquer new lands," his father said. "To further spread the fame and power of Goliris. Gorel . . . one day, all this will be yours. For untold generations our bloodline held pure and strong, commanding empire. To rule is your destiny, as it was mine. Will you be ready?"

The young Gorel held his father's hand and stared out to sea. The thought of his future, the terrible responsibility, both excited and frightened him. But he could not disappoint his father, could not reveal his inner turmoil.

"Yes," he said. "Yes, Father, I will be ready."

"Good boy!" his father said. Then he scooped him in his arms, and for one brief, wondrous moment Gorel felt warm, and safe, and loved.

. . . but already their downfall was underway. And that terrible night came not long after, though he could no longer remember the exact sequence of events, what followed what . . . he was only a boy, and they had schemed in secret, in the shadows, the mages of Goliris, servants burning with a hatred of mastery. He remembered that awful night, the screams, the cruel, laughing faces. The stench of wizardry.

Then he was taken. Taken from his home, from his World, from all that he knew and loved. Transported, in the blink of an eye, away from there, the screams still echoing in his ears, and that awful smell, until he woke and found himself in a foreign land, by the side of a hill, and he was crying, for he was only a boy . . .

Now he lolled in the saddle, and his hands caressed the six-guns hanging on his sides. He had fashioned them himself, and each bore the seven-pointed stars of Goliris.

The land he found himself in as a boy was called the Lower Kidron, and the couple who had found and adopted him were gunsmiths. In that wild, untamed land the boy Gorel learned the ancient way of the gun, and it was from there that he set out on his journey, to claim back his ancient throne—though the journey had been taking longer than anticipated, and though he had killed many on the way, he was no closer to his goal . . .

Overhead, the clouds amassed. Somewhere, no doubt, the Avian called Kettle was planning the next stage in his inexplicable conquest of this part of the World. There had always been dark mages, and they were always bent on conquest, yet there was something different about Kettle, a hidden purpose, as though he alone could see some grand and troubling design no one else could discern . . .

But this was no longer Gorel's concern. In truth, he had a job. And, despite all the current set-backs, he was intent on following it through.

The job was simple, as such jobs usually were. Find a man—and then kill him. And Gorel was good at the first, and very, *very* good at the second . . .

3.

The client had tracked Gorel down at an Abandonment on the edge of the deadlands. He was, unusually, an Apocrita.

The Apocrita were benign parasites, starting off small, attaching to a human host's lower abdomen and gradually growing with their hosts until reaching puberty, when they began discarding and changing their humans with some frequency. Other than that unfortunate habit, the Apocrita were considered a highly civilized species, with a fine taste in wine and music and an almost fanatical devotion to the writing of poetry. What one was doing this far away from their natural habitat, a small monarchical feudatory state on the edge of the Yanivian Desert, Gorel had no idea, but nor did he care.

"I say," the Apocrita said. "Are you the gunslinger fellow?"

Gorel was sitting down with a small cup of draeken, that rare wine, from the far western principality of Kir-Bell, which is made by slowly bleeding the indentured tree-sprites of that place and fermenting their blood. He stared at the Apocrita and made a noncommittal grunting sound and struck a match to light his cigar.

"Depends who's asking," he said, at last.

The Apocrita sat down opposite without being invited. He clicked his fingers for service and gruffly ordered, "Whatever that gentleman is drinking." The server, a grave-wraith from Kur-a-len, gave an ugly leer but fetched the drink without comment. The Apocrita had nodal growths spread over the human host's body and its own large, black sack-like mass was fused to the man's back and spread round his hips to the front.

"There's a man," the Apocrita said.

"There usually is," Gorel allowed.

"He stole something from me," the Apocrita said. "The goods would most likely be spoiled by now, but that's immaterial. What is important is that a message is sent. Do you understand?"

"What's in it for me?" Gorel said.

The Apocrita shrugged. From his bespoke tailored jacket he took out a small black money-bag tied with a string. He pushed it across the table, casually and almost contemptuously, at Gorel.

Gorel picked it up, untied it, and stared at the powder inside.

Gods' Dust.

The Black Kiss.

He took a pinch, snorted.

It hit him like an open slap to the face and he rocked back in his seat.

Across from him, the Apocrita dust merchant looked at him with that same mild contempt.

"You will take the job?"

And Gorel said, "Yes."

4.

The man he was tracking was hard to find. Gorel's payment had long ago gone up his nose, and now, away from any gods, withdrawal hit him hard.

But he was nothing if not a professional. He followed the trail, for even in the deadlands there were pockets of habitation, Abandonments and ruins, strange little hamlets where the destitute and the near dead sought shelter in isolation. The man he was seeking had used many names, but he only had four fingers . . .

He'd lost him several times, but he sensed that he was finally close. Gorel always carried a job through. And so now, delirious, half-starved, and in a thoroughly bad mood, he and his graal at last approached the ruins of an old stone building, which might have once been a temple, though who had built it, and for what inexplicable reason, here in the middle of the deadlands, Gorel didn't know.

Not that he cared.

As he approached he slipped softly from the graal's hide. The beast sank gratefully to the ground, folding its legs under itself and withdrawing its head inside the dark carapace. It would remain motionless now until the sun came out again and it could once again absorb enough energy to bring it into waking.

Gorel drew both his pistols. He trod softly on the ground. He crept towards the building. Dark ivy grew in the cracks between the old stones, and inside he could hear murmured voices . . .

The door was nothing but a rotting wooden slab. Gorel kicked it open and went inside, where it was dark and dank.

A figure lying on a mattress scrambled up, said, "What do you—?" and stopped.

"Devlin Fo-Fingga," Gorel said, grinning. His hand was around the man's throat. The man's skin felt slimy. His breath came and went through Gorel's palm. "I *thought* it was you."

"Who—what?" Devlin's small eyes peered up at Gorel's face, panicked. Then—recognition, followed by shock.

"*Gorel?* Is that *you?*"

"Still alive," Gorel said, dryly.

"No, no no no no no," Devlin said, speaking quickly, his hands weaving a dance of denial in the air. "That wasn't my fault, no no no, I wasn't even there when the—"

There had been figures in the mist. Ancient carved totems with malevolent eyes. Buried Eyes, they called those stones. Seeing eyes. Gorel's company had wandered through the mist, but every time it closed, men were missing . . . and the totems had a habit of appearing, out of nowhere, looming out of the mist and staring at you, calling to you . . .

Few had survived the Mosina Campaign.

"You cut a deal with them," Gorel said, flatly. "They let you live—for a price . . ." He smiled grimly and shoved the gun in Devlin's face. "How many did you sacrifice to the old ones of Mosina?" he said.

Beneath him, Devlin Fo-Fingga shook and shivered. Spittle came out of his mouth. "No no no no no," he said, in plea or apology, it was hard to tell. "I never . . . I didn't . . ."

"So imagine my surprise when a certain Apocrita merchant cornered me in a bar and mentioned he was looking for a four-fingered thief. Funny that, I thought. That description tends to stick in one's mind. So I thought to myself, I might take this job. It is good to have friends, isn't it, Devlin? Old friends, from the old days. I wondered, could it be my old friend, Devlin Fo-Fingga, alive after all these years?"

"Gorel, it wasn't—!"

"The only thing I don't quite get," Gorel said, "is what exactly it was that you stole off that tight-ass merchant. He was surprisingly vague on the details. I only ask, because, if it's still worth something . . . I might not kill you *quite* so slowly."

His hands shook suddenly as the craving overtook him, and though he tried to cover it, Devlin's small, sharp eyes noticed it—and suddenly the man was grinning.

"He never said, did he?" Devlin's rotten teeth sucked what little light there was in the room. "Then come, I will show you, I will . . . For old times' sake, Gorel."

Gorel's finger tightened on the trigger, and yet he couldn't shoot. The craving was upon him then, and at last, reluctantly, he released Devlin. The man rose swiftly, like a rat.

"Come," he said. "Come!"

A second, sturdier door separated the antechamber from the main body of the ruined temple. From his belt, Devlin selected a rusted metal key and unlocked the door. When he pushed it open, the darkness beyond was greater still.

Gorel hesitated on the threshold—

But he could feel it.

It lay thick and hard on the air. It suffocated the breath, tantalising and rich, the very scent of it almost enough.

Almost.

But it was never enough.

Ablution. Faith. Call it what you will.

The curse bestowed upon him by the goddesses Shalin and Shar.

Devlin hurried into the darkness. And now lights were coming alive, one by one, small candles being lit along the walls.

In the dim light Gorel could see they were not alone.

It was a large room, and the women and men lying on the floor seemed near death. Only the gentle rising and falling of chests gave indication that they still breathed, still retained a tenuous link to life. He could taste god-sorcery in the air, feel keenly the thin membrane between the two worlds stretching, here . . .

He had crossed it before and could never truly get back.

"What have you done?" he said—but even as he spoke he already knew the answer.

"Come, come come come!" Devlin said. His grin was manic, his eyes dancing wildly in his face. "It is waiting, It is ready, It is near!"

He took Gorel by the hand. The gunslinger followed him, helpless to resist. They walked, deeper into the room, stepping over the sleepers, Devlin putting a finger to his mouth in an exaggerated warning to be quiet. Here and there, groans from the sleepers. One propped herself up and stared at them. "Is it time, Devlin? Is it time, yet?"

"Not for you, Gammy Steel!" Devlin cackled. "Gammy Gammy, ugly Gammy, your time is not yet come!"

"I have money"—the woman said, then—"I . . . I can get some. I can get more."

"Then do so."

Ignoring her, he led Gorel on. The woman's eyes followed them, then, with a sigh, she lay back down. Gorel could hear her stifled sobs.

They came to the end of the hall. Devlin let go of Gorel's hand and knelt down, lighting a semicircle of candles facing the wall. One by one they came alive, and trapped within them was a god.

5.

It was chained to the wall with bands of steel. It had the breasts of a woman, the sex of a man. It was naked. The god's eyes were two dark orbs, and its lips were thick and bruised and glistened wetly. There was no hair upon the body, and the god's cock was a small, shrivelled thing. Sweat glistened upon the god, as fine as grains of dust.

Dust.

Gorel knelt before the god. Devlin's hand was on his head, then, stroking. Gorel stared at the captive god, and the god stared back through eyes like bottomless holes . . .

"Better than dust," Devlin whispered. "You want to know what I *stole*, Gorel? I took only that which was promised to me! Do you like it, Gorel? I see the mark on you, I can taste your need, *old friend*, your desire! Do you *want* it?"

"Yes!" Gorel said. "Yes!"

"Then the Black Kiss itself is yours for the taking, Gorel of Goliris."

He was no longer fully aware of Devlin. The world contracted to the half-circle of candlelight. Gorel could *smell* the god, that rancid, sweet, overpowering scent of dust, and he knew he wanted it, *needed* it, the way he never needed anything else. On hands and knees, slowly, he crept towards the god. If the flames of the candles hurt him, if it burnt his flesh, he didn't know, nor care. The chained god thrashed against his chains but he was held fast. Dimly, Gorel was aware of the others coming alive, felt their desire joining his. He crawled to the naked god and offered him his lips.

The first hit was always the best.

Flashes of light, flashes of consciousness. Gorel was fading in and out of the World. Rarely had it been this good, this . . . *direct*. Even the pain of losing his home, of being vanquished from proud Goliris—the betrayal, the hurt, the fear—they were all gone, and there was only bliss.

Flashing images, disconnected from each other. Strange sensations. The sweet and sour taste of the god's mouth . . . a taste of blood, and sorcery.

He was only briefly aware of hands—Devlin's?—going through his clothes, relieving him of non-essentials, coin and guns. A chuckle, close in his ear, hot rotting breath. A murmur: "Only the first taste is free . . ."

None of these things mattered. His lips fastened on the god's.

Nothing mattered anymore. Nothing but the Black Kiss, the terrible Kiss of the gods.

6.

How long he lay so he didn't, later, know. Time did not matter. Nothing did. The dark hall was Heaven, the only kind of Heaven man could hope for in this World. The dirty mattress that he lay on was his home, grander even than vanished Goliris. He had no need for money, for guns, for knowledge or desire. All was as it should be, here in the Hall of the Naked God.

The naked god . . . the chained god . . . from what dark place did it arise, what primordial bog did it crawl out of, with Fo-Fingga as his prophet and disciple? It was a question unimportant to Gorel—all questions were. He needed nothing, *was* nothing.

Only dimly, therefore, was he aware at last of someone moving through the bodies of the lost, of shouts, and a laugh, and steps again, and a hand reaching down and shaking him roughly awake.

A voice from far-away said, "You stupid fool."

Gorel grinned, or tried to. The hand slapped him, once, twice.

Gorel tried to hit back but couldn't lift his hand.

The voice said, "Devlin, if he's dead, you're next in line."

"He is alive, alive!" a whiny voice replied. "A dead man's no use to me, no use to anyone but the gods beyond the veil."

"Gods," the other voice said. "Save me from gods and their addicts."

"You won't—you won't hurt him, will you?" the wheedling voice, Fo-Fingga's voice, said.

"Gorel?"

"My *god*," Devlin said. "Screw Gorel and those who ride with him."

"Watch your language, little man. Now get him up and sober. I need him."

"He's good for nothing but another dose of dust."

"Then get me dust. And hurry. My patience's running thin."

Hands tugging at Gorel, lifting him. He tried to fight them, but the Black Kiss was upon him again, and he soon enough subsided.

"He'll have to sleep it off. As for the dust—"

"I'll pay the going rate."

"Why didn't you say so to begin with?"

"Just get him ready, or you'll lose another finger."

Darkness, light. He was being carried. The stench of sorcery subsided, gradually. Cold water hit him, made him cry out. He was being scrubbed, none too gently, then hit with cold water again.

Then something soft. A towel.

A voice said, "Dry yourself. Think you can manage that?"

He wasn't sure.

The voice sounded familiar. He dried himself as best he could. Hands dragging him, something soft beneath. A bed, no roaches there this time.

He slept.

◆ ◆ ◆

When he woke up the room was bright with light. Gorel blinked back tears.

"Good to see you back in the land of the living," a voice said.

The voice from his dreams. A familiar voice . . .

He sat up and stared at the small man sitting by his bedside. The man gave him a sardonic smile. His left eye was missing and covered by a plain leather patch. His hair was grey, and bald along the line of an old scar . . .

He was smoking a thin, home-made cigar.

Gorel said, *"Mauser?"*

"Were you expecting Fo-Fingga?"

"I was expecting no one." He examined the smaller man. His fingers bunched into fists. "You took me from *there?*"

"I need you functioning." A curious glance. "When did you . . ."

Gorel shook his head. "An itinerant god. Far south from here . . . it's a long story."

Mauser shook his head. "It's good to see you again, Gorel."

"You, too." Gorel touched his head. It felt sore. His hands, he noticed, were covered in bites. Bed-bugs.

He scratched, half-heartedly. "I thought you were dead."

His friend merely smiled at that. He said, "I heard you were around."

"How?"

"Fo-Fingga tried to sell me your guns."

"That little—"

Mauser gestured with his head. "They're there. Are you fit enough to use them?"

The guns were on the table by the bed, the seven-pointed stars of Goliris shining on their handles. Gorel said, "I just . . ."

"Yes?"

"I need just a little bit."

There was silence between them. Mauser's smile evaporated. He took a drag on his cigar, held the smoke in before releasing it. His face was wreathed in blue smoke.

He said, "Perhaps you're no good to me after all."

"Screw you," Gorel said. He stood up, reached for his guns. Mauser didn't move. Gorel took the guns, began checking first one then the other. Mauser smoked, and watched. After he was satisfied with the guns, Gorel dressed himself, shaved, and stretched. He didn't think he could stomach any food ... but he'd try. When he turned around to Mauser, the smaller man had finished his cigar and in its place was holding a small packet of folded paper. He threw it to Gorel.

Gorel caught it, opened it carefully, and took a pinch of dust. He put it up his nose, snorted it, and smiled.

"What's the job?" he said.

7.

"There's really nothing to it," Mauser said. They were standing outside the ruined temple. Devlin Fo-Fingga was on his hands and knees in the mud, with Gorel's gun pressed painfully against his forehead.

"Please, Gorel ... It's all just a terrible mistake!"

Gorel pressed the muzzle of the gun harder against the man's green-ish skin. "I'm listening," he said, to Mauser.

"A grab and run, a heist. *You* know what it's like."

"Aha. And what's the target?"

"Gorel, *please*, let me go! What happened in Mosina wasn't my fault!"

"Shut up," Gorel said. "Mauser?"

"An ikon, that's all. Look, are you going to finish him off, or what?"

"Haven't decided."

"He could be useful," Mauser said, meditatively.

"A thief's no good, with just four fingers."

"He can still hold a gun, Gorel. You only need one finger to pull a trigger."

"So, a rough job."

"Did you expect anything else?"

Gorel chewed on his cigar.

"A *religious* ikon?" he said.

"You know any other kind?"

"And *where* exactly is this ikon?"

"In a temple, Gorel," Mauser said. "Isn't that where they usually are?"

"I see, I see," Gorel said. He chewed on his cigar, then casually back-handed Devlin on the side of the head with the butt of the gun. The man fell down on the ground holding his face. He stared up in hatred at the muzzle of the gun.

"Oh, get up," Gorel said. "I'm not going to kill you . . . today."

The man slowly got up. He wiped the blood with his fingers, then sucked on them. Gorel looked away in disgust and Devlin grinned.

"You're not?" he said.

"Hey, it's your lucky day," Mauser said.

"You need me, huh?"

Gorel shrugged. "Where exactly *is* this temple?" he said.

"Ever heard of Waterfalling?"

"No, no," Devlin said. He shook his head from side to side and began to back away from them. "No no no no no. I'm not going to no—"

This time it was Mauser's gun pointed at his face. Gorel looked at him, spat out the cigar, and smiled.

"Do you want the job?" he said. "Or not?"

His gun, pointed unwaveringly at Devlin's face, was all the answer anyone needed.

They rode away from that abandoned place that day. They had left the dying god behind, and its worshippers clustered around it, feeding. Who knew, Gorel thought. Perhaps the god would thrive on its worshippers' need. Perhaps it would grow, not diminish, and in years to come that lonely spot would be the birthplace of a new religion.

Stranger things have happened.

Though Devlin complained bitterly and at length about the loss of his property and its derivative income.

They had served together on the ill-fated Mosina Campaign, in the Romango lands far from there. Gorel had been young, had only recently left the Lower Kidron. He'd sought employ with a group of mercenaries, each more savage and unruly than the other. They were a group of young bloods with a taste for murder: there was Gorel, and the half-Merlangai, Jericho Moon, and there was Devlin Fo-Fingga . . .

But as tough as they thought they were, nothing could prepare them for the swamps of Mosina.

. . . where tendrils of fog permeated the air.

. . . where the landscape constantly shifted about them.

. . . where people simply . . . *disappeared*.

You could not fight what wasn't there. And, separated from the main body of troops, their company sank deeper and deeper into the domain of the old ones.

. . . what they were, these *things* which haunted the nightmarish swamps, he never learned. All he could remember was a circle of totemic poles rising suddenly out of the fog, hideous carved faces staring down on them, the eyes alive, and glinting . . . the mouths were cruel slashes, gouged into the wood.

When they got hold of you . . .

There was no getting away, and the screams of their victims pierced the fog and the eternal twilight of that place, lasting for hours, all through their slow and terrible sacrifice.

It was this that he remembered, most of all. The endless screams, across the bogs.

Only one got away.

Devlin got away.

He'd not lost so much as a finger.

Only later did they realise what terrible bargain the thief had struck with the old ones. How he'd paid for his freedom with his comrades' lives.

A rat and a thief and a traitor, and Gorel wanted to kill him, but Mauser was right: they might need him for the job.

They rode away from that desolate place and across the deadlands, heading towards the fertile places beyond.

Gorel was no fool. He knew when he was being sold a dummy. But he owed Mauser, just as Mauser owed him, and the man *had* come looking for him specifically . . . the truth was he was curious. He had heard of this place they were travelling to.

Waterfalling.

8.

They heard it long before they saw it.

The great waterfall which gave the city its name fell down from the high plateau of Tarsh, which borders the deadlands on one side and reaches as far as the Zul-Ware'i mountains. In those mountains, where the twin and ancient races of the Zul and the Ware'i had died in their war of complete annihilation, the glaciers provided the water which fed the Nirian. It was a long, wide, and stately river, which flowed across that vast distance without undue hurry until reaching the sheer drop of rock that led its water, without warning, to plunge for a great distance down until it hit the Sacred Pool. It was not so much a pool, of course, as a wide if miniature lake. From there, the water flowed more gently, away from the Sacred Pool and into a carefully crafted series of canals and water-ways and an ingenious system of locks, around which there formed the numerous islands, embankments, and aits which formed the sprawling city itself.

A rough-hewn path was cut into the side of the mountain, twisting and turning at a steep angle as it rose all the way up to the Tarsh plateau, allowing any resident of the city, when their time was due, to traverse it to the top of the waterfall. That path was long, and tortuous, and steep; and yet it was used. It was called the Path of Ascension.

The sky was calm. The air smelled fresh and clear. A kingfisher flew against the sky. The colour of the water, as one approached, was a startling blue, and against it, the well-ordered flora of the city was in a range of vivid greens. Flowers bloomed everywhere in a cacophony of red and blue and yellow, and their scent filled the air like perfume. The houses were neat and built of wood and stood on stilts, and children ran laughing along the many bridges.

It was, in nearly every way, a peaceful and idyllic scene, and it was only mildly spoiled, Gorel felt, by the still, serene, and perfectly preserved corpses in the water.

But that came a little later.

They approached the city just after dawn. A day's ride away they had come to Mauser's dead drop. There, Gorel found clothes, a stack of weapons that impressed even him, and a small, gaily painted wagon with the legend *Mimes* on it.

Along with the wagon was a donkey.

Gorel stared at the donkey, then he stared at Mauser.

"All this just happened to be here?"

"It pays to be prepared."

"But who's doing the paying?"

Mauser shrugged. "Does it matter, to you? A client's a client."

"I don't like the smell of this job, much," Gorel said. Mauser grinned and tossed him a twisted packet of paper. Gorel unfolded it and stared at the powder . . .

"Besides," Mauser said. "It's an old city, the foundations go back . . . who knows what arcane knowledge they have hidden there? Perhaps they would know of your homeland."

It was bait; Gorel knew it; Mauser knew it; Fo-Fingga, for sure, knew it.

Yet that didn't make it untrue.

Gorel took a pinch, only a pinch of dust; just enough to quiet the craving. "All right," he said. "But what about the wagon? No one is going to believe we're anything other than what we are. Or fail to notice the weapons."

"I've got that covered, too," Mauser said. Gorel stared at him in suspicion as the other man reached into a hidden bag the colour of bark and brought out three amulets. He handed one to Devlin and one to Gorel and kept one for himself.

Gorel stared at the amulet. It was made of a warm metal and was light to the touch, and intricately carved with circles and lines that seemed to spell something to him, if only he could read their meaning . . .

He knew what it was, of course. It reeked of sorcery.

"They're one-use," Mauser said, almost apologetically. "But they'll be enough to get us through. Just don't put it on until we get close to the city."

"And this was provided . . . ?"

Mauser shrugged. "It's not too late to back out," he said. "If you don't want the job."

"And what would you do without me?"

"No one's irreplaceable, Gorel."

They stared at each other, but there was no real question about the outcome.

The next morning, early, three humble mimes made their way in their gaudily painted cart across the plain to the city of Waterfalling. They were pulled by the small and patient donkey. They were not much to look at, three weather-beaten entertainers brought down by life on the road. One of them was missing a finger. They rode in silence and they could hear the city long before they reached it, the never-ceasing sound of an incredible volume of water falling from a great height until it hit the down-below.

There were always rainbows over Waterfalling. The constant spray of water in the air broke the light into joyous colour, while at night one witnessed the silvery form that comes when moonlight interacts with that same fog.

To get to the city one had to cross the largest canal, which served as an effective moat around the city, barring invaders, and it was there that Gorel first saw the corpses. They floated just underneath the surface, their eyes open and serene, their noses pressed against the surface of the water as though ready, at any moment, to rise through and resume their lives. But their skins were leeched white, near translucent, and their depth never varied though sometimes they were pushed by the current as more corpses came down from . . .

"The Sacred Pool," Devlin whispered, and shuddered.

"Shut up, fool!"

Gorel's hand was on the butt of his gun. He hoped the enchantment would do its work and conceal them.

There were guards on the only gate, which blocked entry to the only bridge into the city. The guards were Ebong mercenaries, large beetle-like creatures with great helmet-like heads as opaque as polished black stone, and they held rifles.

"Stop."

The mimes stopped obediently.

"Purpose of visit?"

"We are but humble entertainers, seeking to ply our humble trade—"

"Do a mime."

"Excuse me?"

"I said, do a mime!"

The next five minutes were some of the worst of Gorel's life. Which was saying something. He, Mauser, and Devlin pranced and pretended to be trapped in invisible glass jars and to climb invisible ladders and to go down invisible stairs, and all in silence. They were terrible. Every moment Gorel expected the ruse to be discovered, and to enter a deadly shoot-out with the Ebong. They were not a race he liked to tangle with, at least, not without gaming the odds.

When they were finished, however, there was a short hiss of noxious air which, for the Ebong, must have passed for enthusiastic clapping.

"You can go. Warn you, though, not much call for mimes round here."

"And the rents are steep," added his colleague.

"Ask me, you'd be better off striking for the lowlands," said a third. "Besides, you want to watch out you don't hear the Call."

His colleagues turned their black helmet heads on him at that and the mercenary slunk away, or as much as an Ebong could ever be said to slink. The three mimes thanked the guards humbly, and rode through the open gate and across the bridge and into the city . . .

And Gorel could hear it, now. And he realised he had been hearing it for some time, all through their approach to the city, though it was clearer now.

A sort of faint crystal peal . . .

A little sound of summoning, just at the edge of hearing.

9.

Once they were inside, the talismans began to lose their power. The three would-be robbers found a ramshackle inn that stood on an ait in the confluence of two of the smaller canals. There they checked their weapons while Mauser outlined the plan.

How and when Gorel had met Mauser was a long and not entirely interesting story. It was during that unfortunate episode with the

Demon-Priests of Kraag. Needless to say, both of them had barely escaped with their lives, and Mauser still had a neat little scar to show for it. Where he came from, Gorel was never entirely sure. He was a rare white-face, of a race of barbarians who lived high in the snow-peaked mountains of the Beyaz. Gorel trusted him—as much as he could be said to trust anyone. Devlin he didn't trust at all, but then the man's untrustworthiness was a sort of assurance in itself.

The city was . . . strange.

It was clean and prosperous and ordered, a little haven of peace in a violent world.

He had had a chance to examine the corpses in the canals as they wended their slow way to the inn.

There were the bodies of many races in the water. Human and Avian and Merlangai, Ebong and numerous others. Who could tell where they had come from, or how long they had been lying there, submerged, perfectly preserved in the cold water that flowed from the Sacred Pool?

Even as he watched, he'd see a new body arrive from up-stream, fed into the system of canals, until it found a place and there remained, suspended. And always, at the edge of hearing, there was that faint peal of a bell, a sort of muted laughter, an invitation . . .

And as he watched, he saw a woman stop in the middle of her shopping, and drop her bags, and stand, transfixed. Her child stood beside her, a little girl. A beatific smile filled the woman's face, then she began to walk away, leaving behind both her shopping and her child. The little girl began to run after her mother, but the woman paid her no mind, and a shopkeeper and a flower seller with a kindly face held the girl from following, and tried, awkwardly, to comfort her.

The mother went away.

The plan was simple.

There was only one god in Waterfalling.

The God of the Waterfall had many small temples scattered throughout the city, and one main one. The Grand Temple occupied the entirety of an island high up-stream. The path to the Drop passed close to it as it led farther up until it reached the plateau.

It was not heavily guarded, for who would dare disturb the temple of the god in its own domain?

"The ikon is inside the temple," Mauser said. "It is a small, blue, amorphous shape faintly resembling a human figure. It is made of Ice VII. Some say it holds the soul of the god within it. Others that it is merely an artistic representation. We are going to go on the first assumption. The job's to get in and get the ikon. The ultimate target's—"

"Assassination," Devlin said, and leered.

Gorel stared at the two of them. Devlin's ugly grin and Mauser's grim determination.

"Assassination?"

"Come on, Gorel. It's not like it would be the first god you've killed. In fact, you're almost uniquely qualified."

"Is that why I'm here?"

"Would you rather be somewhere else? Are we keeping you from some urgent appointment?"

Gorel lit a cigar and stared at the two of them. He began to wonder just *who* the mysterious Apocrita merchant who'd first hired him was, and just *how*, exactly, Mauser had then found Gorel . . .

But Mauser was right. A job was a job and, besides, Gorel had his own purpose in being there. So he just nodded, affably enough, and said, "I'm going to look around. You two try to stay out of trouble."

"I think the trouble part's going to come later," Mauser said, and Devlin sucked on his wet, green teeth noisily and leered at Gorel. He left them there, checking and cleaning the weapons.

10.

Of course he'd known about the God of the Waterfall.

11.

Gorel was no fool. And the fame of Waterfalling had spread far and wide . . .

Now he followed the Path of Ascension. Initially the road was paved, as he followed city thoroughfares and traversed small bridges. People stared after him but said nothing. He saw the temple then, a large, imposing complex of beautiful white stone. He skirted the temple and soon reached the first incline and there the city stopped and the Path proper began.

It was cut into the very rock, and it rose steeply, at a sharp incline. Small pebbles rolled underfoot. The climb was slow and hard but there were places to stop and rest along the way, small alcoves cut into the rock. Gorel did not hurry. He enjoyed the climb, the cooler air up there, and when he turned he could look down on Waterfalling and far beyond, across the plains and to the deadlands where, far away, loomed the Black Tor.

He thought of Kettle, then. There wasn't a day gone past when he didn't think about Kettle.

As he climbed he saw almost no people. One he passed, and he realised with some surprise it was the woman he had seen earlier. She was resting in one of the alcoves, with that same happy, vacant look on her face. She didn't seem to see him, and he walked on, discomfited.

The call . . . no.

The Call.

He could hear it more clearly now. And as the Path wound its way up, and up, and up, he could hear the thunder of the waterfall, and feel the spray of its roar on his face, and his eyes were dazzled by an explosion of rainbows; *Come, come!* said the Call but it was faint, still; it was not meant for him but for another. Gorel of Goliris traversed the Path of Ascension until he reached, at last, the Plateau of Tarsh, where the Nirian river flows until it reaches the escarpment.

He saw it all, now. He stood in that place called the Drop. The river moved almost sluggishly as it neared the edge. A series of rocks slowed down the flow of water, and it tumbled over the edge almost reluctantly. When it did, it became a great thundering waterfall. Way down below, he could see the mist rising out of the impact of the water into the Sacred Pool.

He stood there for a long time.

When the woman at last reached the Drop she seemed as beatific as before. Though her journey must have been physically exhausting for her, nevertheless there was no change in her demeanour. For a long moment she merely stood there, smiling that vacant, enigmatic smile. She seemed indifferent to or unaware of Gorel's presence. Then she took one step, and another, until Gorel felt compelled to shout a warning: for she was headed straight for the sheer drop beyond which was the fall. But the woman ignored him as though he weren't there, and when he went to stop her she shrugged him away, not angrily but the way one would shrug off a mild irritant.

Come . . . Come!

For one moment the Call was so clear that it overwhelmed Gorel's senses. Too late, he saw the woman step to the edge of the rocks. Then she took one step more—and, just like that, she was gone.

He crawled to the edge and peered over. He saw her fall. She fell without grace through the air until the waterfall claimed her, the water engulfing her unto itself, then she was gone from sight.

Gorel of Goliris remained at the Drop for a long while more, and his thoughts were troubled. He was not idle, though. When he was done, he wended his way down the Path and returned to the inn, where his two companions waited. It was night, by then. The stars shone down cold and indifferent, and the air was filled with the stench of the Black Kiss. He realised he had not needed a hit since they got to the city. It was all about them, as natural and as plentiful as water.

And he realised they were all, here, as much in slavery to the Kiss as he was.

When the city began, when the first jumper jumped, that no one knew. The city grew, and the god with it. The city prospered, and the god with it. They fed on each other.

And now someone wanted the god dead.

When he had returned, Mauser and Devlin were ready. There was no need for speech. All three men were armed.

They stepped out lightly; and only a fleeting egret saw them pass into the night.

12.

Later, when he was running, with Devlin lying on the canal bank with half his brains blown out and Mauser on his hands and knees trying to crawl away from the Speakers-to-Water as they closed in on him, there was no one to see him then, too. The good people of Waterfalling knew when to close their doors and when to draw the blinds on their windows, and the whole city lay silent and slumbering in the moonlight.

The job was botched from the very beginning. The very air of the city had whispered that this was all folly.

Nevertheless, they went in.

Over the bridge, into the temple complex.

Where the waft of incense and the chanting of priests could be heard . . .

Where ducks and geese congregated in the canals where the dead men lay.

Deep into the temple, searching for the inner sanctum . . .

A novice surprised them, innocently watering lilies, and Mauser shot her, the blast echoing loudly over the islet . . .

Devlin shot two further novices as they emerged, blinking off sleep, to see what was happening . . .

The blue ikon was there just as Mauser said it would be.

A small and amorphous representation of a vaguely human shape that could have been a waterfall.

The three men made for the idol . . .

The Speakers-to-Water emerged then. The priests of the God of the Waterfall. Dressed in flowing white robes, with water flowers in their hair. Their eyes were vacant and they moved in perfect unison. In their hands they held swords of ice.

Their lips moved as one. They said: "You shall not steal."

"Screw that," Devlin said, and he began firing. Blades of ice moved in perfect harmony, deflecting shots. Devlin screamed in rage and snatched the shotgun from his back and fired, once, twice, until he hit one of the Speakers in the guts. The Speaker collapsed to the ground, but his lips still moved, and with his fellow Speakers he said, "You shall not *steal*!"

Gorel and Mauser spread out, and it was then that he saw the corpses. They emerged out of the water, out of the dank canal. One at first, and then another, and another. Humans, Ebong, two Merlangai, an Avian shivering water off her feathers. The perfectly preserved bodies in the water. Now their eyes opened and a single force animated them, and they reached into the canal and pulled out blade-sharp staffs of ice. They advanced on the three men.

"You bring *swords?*" Devlin screamed. "What good are damn swords against *guns?*"

Gorel fired. He fired cleanly, methodically, without emotion. It was a scientific sort of extermination, a matter of numbers, not blood. The creatures in the water must have been living once, but they lived no longer, and the corpses were only that. He shot not to kill but to *destroy*, inflicting damage on skulls and knee-caps and finger bones, shooting to disable, if possible to annihilate. He was good at what he did. He had to be, to have survived this long. Perhaps he wasn't the *best*—the World was filled with the stories of legendary gun masters such as Sixgun Smel of the Upper Kidron, or Yi-Sheng the Unbeatable, who killed the sea serpent, Og, or the wizard, Der Fliegenmelker, who collected the heads of his enemies and whose mound of skulls was said to be taller than a mountain by the time of his disappearance—but these were just that, legends, stories told around the camp-fire in hushed voices. They were of some distant past, and Gorel was of the present. As far as he was concerned, he *was* the best, and would remain so until someone finally managed to shoot him down, if they ever did. He wouldn't have given them odds.

The men kept pulling more guns out of the bags they'd brought with them. But more and more of the bodies came, and their swords of ice flashed cold in the moonlight, and Devlin cried out when one just missed slicing off his arm, and Gorel was pushed back, back as they came, and Mauser fired with a calm intensity on his face, like a card-player calculating the odds of his hand.

There was so very little blood. The things that climbed out of the water had been in there too long, Gorel thought. What ran in their veins, if it ran at all, was a sort of amethyst liquid, and as it left their bodies it congealed and tried to slither back into the canal.

"We can't hold them forever!" Mauser shouted. All the while the Speakers-to-Water were chanting, their lips moving in unison, the canal dwellers between them and the three shooters.

"Cover me!" Gorel shouted, then he was running, bodies blasted on either side of him as Devlin and Mauser fired. Gorel slid in the purple ichor and his forward momentum pushed him along, until he bounced off an Ebong and was through. He came right up to the Speakers in one fluid motion and with his two guns drawn. For a moment he looked into their eyes. What he saw in them it was hard to say.

He pulled both triggers.

With the fall of the Speakers the onslaught abruptly ceased. The preserved corpses did not fall but remained standing, motionless and eerie in the moonlight. The three men looked at one another, their ears still ringing with the sound of gun-shots.

Then they moved as one: racing for the prize, their enemies forgotten.

Gorel got to it first. He snatched the blue idol a moment before Mauser.

When he turned, Devlin had his guns pointed at the two of them and was he grinning his ugly grin. "It's about time we settled this," Devlin said.

Mauser fired but Devlin was quicker and Mauser was thrown back, hurt. The other shot missed Gorel. He had moved behind Mauser and the shot meant for him missed. Devlin's smile dissipated and Gorel's smile bloomed and he fired.

Devlin's body fell back and he lay on the bank of the canal, his skull blown to pieces and his brain leaking slowly into the water.

Gorel was briefly pleased at a job finally brought to conclusion.

"Gorel . . ." Mauser said. He was still alive. The shot had opened an ugly wound in his stomach and he was trying to hold his intestines in. "Help me . . ."

Gorel held up the ikon. He said, "How do you destroy it?"

"I don't . . . know. He said . . ."

"Who bought you off, Mauser? Who hired you?"

"Does it . . . matter . . ."

"It does to me."

"It was him! It was that mage from the Black Tor! The one who brought down Falang-Et and killed Tharat . . . He said you . . ."

Cold fury rose in Gorel. "Kettle?" he said. "Kettle sent you?"

"Gorel, please . . ."

The Speakers-to-Water Gorel had shot rose up from the ground then. They looked at Gorel with broken eyes. And all the corpses that had risen from the water turned, as one, and focused their attention on the two men, the one living and the one dying.

Then the Speakers spoke.

They said: "*Gorel of Goliris.*"

Mauser said: "Help me!"

The preserved corpses advanced one step, then another.

"We *know* you, Gorel of Goliris. Come, now. *Come!*"

"Help me! Gorel, Please!"

Gorel ran.

He ran without destination in mind, yet the destination had always been there, waiting for him. He was not followed. Few saw him pass. And yet his feet led him inexorably upwards, and the voice in his head grew stronger and stronger until it was like a raging storm, and it said, *Come to me . . . come!*

It knew his name. In his hand, the blue idol was still. Gorel's feet would not obey him. He felt a calmness descend on him then, and his face assumed a beatific aspect. He came to the Path of Ascendance and began to climb it.

It has been many centuries since I had last encountered a man of Goliris . . . the voice said.

"You know of Goliris?"

His lips moved, but whether sound emerged or not was immaterial. It was night. He was alone on the Path. Behind him, Devlin lay dead,

Mauser dying. Another botched job in a long line of such. None of it mattered to Gorel.

Many have heard of, yet none had seen, Goliris . . . said the voice in his head. *You seek it, still?*

"Always."

Yet now you must come to rest, Gorel. Let go of desire, of need. I will be all that you require.

"No!" his lips protested. His legs obeyed the orders of the god. "Tell me. Tell me how to find my home."

Sooner or later, all things must come to an end, Gorel of Goliris. All empires pass.

"Including yours?"

But the god was not amused by the retort.

Gorel climbed, and climbed, and climbed. The physical effort of the rise meant nothing to him, for now he truly was under the Black Kiss, and every fibre of his being was bliss, and he was happy; as happy as a man could ever be.

Yet still he resisted. Yet still he fought the insidious Black Kiss of the god. And still: his feet led him on, step by inexorable step.

Until he found himself once more standing at the Drop.

The waterfall thundered nearby. Rainbows of moonlight sparkled in the rising cloud of spray.

Come to me, Gorel of Goliris, said the god. *Come!*

There was no resisting the Call.

And yet he dallied. And it was good, he thought, that he had prepared himself for this eventuality. And he busied himself with the things that he had left there, at the Drop, earlier, for just such an eventuality. And the voice of the god grew mistrustful in his head and it said, *What are you doing?*

But Gorel did not answer. And the Call of the god grew stronger and more insistent, until there was no resisting it further.

For one fleeting moment, Gorel thought of all the countless lives that had come here before him, had worn the rock smooth with the passage of their feet. Then he, too, took those last few, finite steps, to the edge; and fell to his doom.

13.

What did you do? said the god.

14.

The first impact was the worst. He hit the roaring mass of water on his way down and all his protective clothing couldn't stop him from feeling the impact. Then the ropes tied to his harness *pulled*, and he shot upwards then back down and impacted again: but then the bouncing slowed, until he could at last control his descent.

What did you do! roared the god.

The water fell and fell and tried to push him down, down, down into the Sacred Pool, and the rocks beat at him, but Gorel welcomed the pain and used it to his advantage. The Kiss no longer held him. The god's Call was never meant to last beyond the final Drop, and now it had no more power to hold Gorel in thrall. Slowly, slowly, he released more rope, hoping it would hold, and he lowered himself down the cliff.

"Tell me," Gorel demanded. "Tell me what you know of Goliris."

Then join me. Become a part of me! And you will know all that I know.

"No."

Please, the god said. *Please.*

How long he journeyed this way he didn't know. The bottom was a blur far down below. The cliff rose impossibly high overhead. At last he found it. He hit empty air and flailed, then he was through the screen of water and inside a hollow cave, hidden behind the water. He took off the harness and fell to the dry stone floor.

He lay there for some time, breathing heavily.

You have come to kill me! the voice accused. It sounded frightened, now.

"Tell me what I want to know."

It was a natural cave in the rock, Gorel saw. Once, millennia ago, it had been explored, and the skeletons of humans and Ebong still remained in recesses in the wall.

Then, it had become a temple, of a sort. An altar sat against the far wall, and on it was a crude stone figure. Something living hid in the dark behind it, a creature like a ferret or a water rat. Baleful eyes glared at Gorel from the shadows but he paid them no mind. He held the blue ikon in his hand.

"Tell me," he said.

I could only show you.

His mind flickered then. It went through countless rapid lives: he saw an Ebong mercenary arrive at the cliffs and look down, curiously, for the first time; an Avian flying overhead, who plunged down towards the water with a glad cry; an expedition of vanished Zul, searching for a weapon, who had come upon the place and fell victim to the Call; water-dwelling Merlangai who swam down the Nirian, a hunting party, until, too late, they too became a part of the god . . .

He saw the crude village underneath grow and prosper, become a town, then at last a city. The dead resided in the water, their eyes forever open. He saw people drawn from all over to this city, where the Kiss lay like an enchantment over the streets and houses. It was a small price to pay, for happiness, he thought. From time to time some would hear the Call, and climb the Path until they were one with their god. It was a small price to pay.

Do you see? Join me! said the god.

"Show me Goliris."

Then he saw it. A small figure trudging in from the deadlands, a sorcerer of Goliris, and Gorel knew him, then: it was one of his father's servants, a minor war-mage with the fleet—just another face in the corridors of the palace, a man who might have once smiled politely at the boy, this future king.

He came, and he dwelled in the city for some time, then he heard the Call and heeded it.

And Gorel saw deep into his heart, for the man was with the god now, and he saw the hatred and the loathing deep within the man's mind, and he saw that the hatred and loathing were directed inwards, at the traitor's own self. He saw then the sorcerers of Goliris gathered in a dark room, saw them plot the downfall of the royal family. He saw himself, the boy, taken while his father was murdered, saw his mother cry, but soundlessly, and he saw the empty throne, and cobwebs, and bleached skulls.

"How will I find it again?" he said, demanded, of this ghost.

And only the faint echo came back—*You never will . . .*

A great fury took hold of Gorel of Goliris then, and for a time he knew not where he was. Gradually he came back to awareness, and the god's voice, weak, panicked, demanded, over and over, *What did you do? What did you do?*

Gorel sat there in the cave, cross-legged, and looked out at the waterfall. But the water, strangely, seemed to grow less fierce. Its flow was easing. The screen of water slowly parted, and the god's voice cried, *What did you do? You are killing me!*

But Gorel had done nothing.

Beside him, the small, blue ikon was slowly melting.

The waterfall was dying.

As less and less water fell, Gorel could now look out from the cave, into clear air. At last it was all over and he went to the edge and looked down, and saw the pool, no longer sacred, and the corpses below lying still in the water. He looked up, then, and saw no water, falling.

Behind him, behind the altar, the mindless creature that might have been a ferret or a water rat growled, but Gorel paid it no mind. He sat, cross-legged, on the floor and lit a cigar, and he waited.

15.

The small, delicate shape fluttered in the air before coming to rest inside the cave. It leaned against one wall and crossed its arms and cocked its head and looked at Gorel of Goliris.

"Kettle," Gorel said.

"Gorel."

"It was you? You set it up, from the beginning. It was so convenient, how that trader found me, how Mauser just happened to be in the right place at the right time."

"I would have asked you, but you would have turned me down."

"You lied to me. From the very start, you always *lie*."

A look of pain crossed the Avian's face. "Gorel, I . . ."

"You'd tell me you *love* me?"

"You know how I feel."

"And yet you'd use me."

"Isn't that what love is?"

The Lord of the Black Tor looked at Gorel of Goliris and Gorel of Goliris looked away, so that Kettle would not see his tears.

"What was it all for?"

"I needed a distraction. Something to focus the God of the Waterfall's attention on. Something crude and obvious, and effective."

"You used me as *bait*."

"Yes."

"And all the meanwhile you—"

"My engineers had done their work. We dammed the Nirian. My army dug a new channel for the river."

"And starved the waterfall."

"Yes."

"Clever."

Kettle shrugged.

"*Why?*" Gorel said.

"Why?"

"Yes."

Kettle looked at Gorel of Goliris and his eyes were filled with pain.

"There's a war coming," he said. "And an enemy against which even I am helpless. I have been trying to consolidate territories, to prepare . . . Gorel, I *need* you. I need you by my side. Help me. Come back with me."

"Never."

"Will I ever be able to apologise enough? I love you."

Gorel did not reply.

After a time, the small and delicate figure of the mage flew away. After a time longer, Gorel put on the harness, pulled on the ropes, and began the long, slow climb down the side of the cliff, and back towards the ground.

16.

The Dark Mage's army came into the city of Waterfalling at sunrise. They came quietly and with purpose and they were not opposed. The city's residents looked at them with numb surprise, as though waking from a long and pleasant dream that was now, inexplicably, over. Gorel of Goliris was stopped only once, on his way out of the city. But the people who held him must have received orders from high up, for they let him go, and he rode away from there, to continue his search for vanished Goliris.

High above the city, at the place that was once called the Drop, the Lord of the Black Tor looked down on his conquest, but his attention was elsewhere:

Far away, figures moved, numerous beyond count. They marched like shadows but they were not shadows. They marched in rows. They marched upon the World.

He saw them conquer cities, he saw them burn down temples, bring down gods, for gods and sorcery meant nothing to these soulless things. What they were, he didn't know. They moved like automata. They were a wizardry of a sort he'd never known. Something ancient, and deadly, and newly awakened.

They came from the desert. They brought with them the smell of burnt cardamoms.

And as they moved, they spoke.

It was a roar, a cry of triumph, and despair.

A single word.

Goliris.

Cecelia Holland

. . .

Cecelia Holland is one of the world's most highly acclaimed and respected historical novelists, ranked by
many alongside other giants in that field such as Mary Re-
nault and Larry McMurtry. Over the span of her thirty-year
career, she's written more than thirty historical novels, including *The Firedrake, Rakóssy, Two Ravens, Ghost on the Steppe, The
Death of Attila, Hammer for Princes, The King's Road, Pillar of
the Sky, The Lords of Vaumartin, Pacific Street, The Sea Beggars,
The Earl, The Kings in Winter, The Belt of Gold*, and more than a
dozen others. She also wrote the well-known science-fiction
novel *Floating Worlds*, which was nominated for a Locus
Award in 1975, and of late has been working on a series of
fantasy novels, including *The Soul Thief, The Witches' Kitchen,
The Serpent Dreamer, Varanger, The King's Witch, The High City,
Kings of the North*, and *The Secret Eleanor*. Her most recent
novel is *Dragon Heart*.

Here a shipwrecked voyager finds himself in a situation dangerous enough that he might have been better off taking his chances with the raging sea—but a situation in which he must remain if he has any chance to satisfy the thirst for vengeance burning in his heart.

◆　◆　◆

The Sword Tyraste

CECELIA HOLLAND

From the first blow, the iron sang under the hammer. Tvalin sang along with it, pounding out the blade, long and straight and keen. He knew already this would be a noble sword, and it tore his heart to think who would own it.

He thrust the iron back into the forge, and said to his nephew, "Heat it up."

Tulinn worked the bellows. Tvalin wiped his hands on his apron. His shoulders ached. He went to the back of the cave and got a stoop of ale. Galdor at least kept them well fed. Tvalin was soaked with sweat from the work, which felt good, and he loved the smell of the iron heating and the sound of the bellows.

He called the sword Tyraste, darling of the god of battles, but he never said the name aloud, to keep it strong. He said it in his mind often. He drank another long draught of the ale, and going back to the forge, he drew the white-hot blade from the coals. Lifting the hammer in his hand, he beat against the iron, and even through the tongs, the blade's high voice rang true.

High overhead, a door creaked. Tulinn said, "He comes," and backed away into the shadows. Tulinn was afraid of Galdor. Tvalin laid the sword across the anvil, between him and the stairs, and down the steps came the king, massive in his bearskins, his feet scraping on the stone, and his eyes like a snake's. On his forefinger was a red jewel, and he carried a weight of gold around his neck.

The two dwarfs bowed down. Tvalin was cursing himself for allowing them to fall into Galdor's hands. He said, "We are doing the work, King Galdor. We are keeping our end of the bargain." Straightening, he gestured toward the sword on the anvil.

Galdor caught sight of it, and his face flushed red; his eyes gleamed. He said, "Ah, yes." He put out his hand toward it, but the ungripped sword was still hot, and he drew back. Tvalin let out his breath between his teeth. Galdor faced him, narrow-eyed again.

"Finish it. And I will keep you no longer. Is that the bargain?" He looked from one dwarf to the other. Tvalin nodded. Galdor went back up the stair, heavy stepping.

Tvalin went back to the sword, cooling on the anvil, and laid it into the coals again. His chest felt too tight. He knew Galdor was treacherous and the king's last words rang with lies. He turned the sword again in the coals, and drew it out, and worked the fore edge.

With each stroke he thought, Tyraste, be evil. Tyraste, do evil. Tyraste, kill Galdor.

They quenched the blade and honed it, fit on wooden grips and a pommel of a piece of ocean-blood. Galdor would change those anyway to something gaudier. Tvalin lifted the sword in his hand, the balance perfect, the blade eager, and his maker's heart leapt at what he had done. Then the king came down again.

Tvalin laid the sword across the anvil and stepped back. Tulinn hovered next to him, wanting to be gone from here. Galdor threw back his cloak; he took the sword into his hand, and cocking it from side to side, he murmured under his breath.

"A prince of blades," he said. "Tvalin, you are better even than your name."

Tvalin swelled, pleased, and glanced at Tulinn to make sure he had noted that. Galdor said, "Now let's test the edge."

Too late, Tvalin saw what was happening. Galdor swung the sword around and in a single stroke sliced off Tvalin's head and that of his nephew.

"See," Galdor said, up there above them. "Now I don't have to keep you. I'll board this room up, so nobody bothers you." With the sword in his hand, he went back up the stairs.

With his full strength Vagn hauled his oar again through the water. Night was falling, they should have made landfall long ago, and now they were deep into the narrows, here, between two coasts they didn't know, with a storm bearing down on them. Around him his brothers and his friends were rowing as hard as he was, shouting the rhythm. A current fought them, the knarr jerking and bucking. Back over the stern he could see the rain blowing toward them, a shadow over the water. Above them a craggy headland loomed. The first rain struck him in the face. The light was bleeding out of the sky.

At the steerboard, his oldest brother suddenly called out and pointed. Vagn cast a quick glance over his shoulder and saw a light bobbing, in the dark below the headland, a signal, a buoy. His brother was already steering them that way. Vagn flung his body against the oar. The wind helped them, heaved them forward. The rain pounded his cheeks and his wet hair got in his eyes. He bent to his oar and the blade struck something, and just behind his bench he felt the hull shudder. The light had lured them into the rocks.

His brother yelled, "Hold on! Hold on!" Vagn cast his oar overboard and jumped after it.

He went feetfirst into the water, his hands out to fend off the rocks, and sank deep in over his head. When he came up a wave hurled him over, and with him the oar and a piece of a strake. In the murky darkness he could make out nothing but the waves' slap and churn. Then something huge loomed up before him, and his feet touched bottom and he scrambled up onto the side of a rock. The storm wind battered him. He was shivering and he clutched his shirt around him.

Even through the wind and the sea, a scream reached his ears, and shouting. The torch on the shore cast a glow out onto the surging water. He leaned around the side of the rock and saw, against the uncertain light, bare hands raised against swords. He heard his oldest brother calling out, "No, no," over and over. Then nothing. Men thrashed around in the shallows. A sharp voice rose, once, giving orders, directions—they were looking for pieces of the cargo. A keg bobbed in the slack water behind his rock. They would come to get that. He slid down into the rocking waves, in over his head, and waited there. Legs thrashed by him, close enough almost to touch, lifted the keg away, and moved on.

He raised his head above the surface and listened. He could hear voices, in there on the beach, but now they were moving off. He dragged himself up out of the water onto the rock, found a crevice out of the rain, and pulled his shirt around him as well as he could, and waited to die.

He did not die; the woolen shirt, which his mother had made, kept him warm, and this being midsummer, the sun was soon up again. The fierce waves of the night before had passed with the storm. He waded in through little ruffles to the beach. As he came in the seagulls rose in a cloud from his brothers and his friends. The robbers had taken even their clothes away.

He went from one to the other of the dead men, saying each name, noticing the wounds, and pulled them all together on the beach, as they had been on the knarr together. He sat for a while beside his oldest brother, who should have gotten them in to shore sooner, and should not have believed the light. His brother's body was hacked and battered, he had fought hardest of any of them.

Vagn piled up rocks over the bodies, making a boat shape, and putting in what bits and pieces of the knarr had drifted in to the shore. There was nothing left of the cargo, the furs, the salted fish, the casks of honey and wax. As he went around, he stamped on crabs and ate them, ate seaweed, dug up clams, and drank water that seeped out of the cliff.

He did not, for a long while, look up at the top of the cliff.

When he was done, he sat down on the sand, and thought about his brothers and his friends and what had been done to them. Only he was left alive, which put a hard charge on him. Now he stood up, and looked up, at the top of the headland, and the tower there, looming behind its wall. He rinsed the salt out of his shirt, slept a little in the sun while it dried, and in the afternoon, he walked around the back of the headland and made his way up.

✦   ✦   ✦

King Galdor, lord of the Vedrborg, walked out to his high seat and laid the sword on the table before him. Standing there, he looked out over the hall at his men, all on their feet, all their faces turned toward him, and he was still a moment, to feel his power, before he sat, and they could all sit. The slaves brought in the bread and the ale and they fell to feasting.

Galdor thought of his enemies. He wished like Odin he had no use for meat, and did not have to waste time in eating. A great dish came onto the table before him, a mess of fish, likely from the ship they had taken the night before. Peasants' food. He laid his hands instead on the sword in its sheath, with its pommel and grips of chased gold.

The midsummer was on them, when Hjeldric the Dane had sworn to challenge him, to run the strait against his will, and Galdor meant to turn that to advantage. The Vedrborg grew too small for him. He wanted more than mere piracy. He pressed the sword under his hands. A man with his power should have a kingdom and not a rock and a handful of men. He longed to take the sword into his hand, to loose the strength he felt in it, on some cause great enough for him.

In the hall a stirring caught his eye. Someone had come in from outside. He talked to someone, who talked to someone else, the little passage of the words going up the hall along the outside of the table. At his place just below Galdor, his man Gifr heard it, nodded, and stood.

"There is a stranger here who asks to see you."

"A stranger. A messenger?"

"No—just a wayfarer."

Galdor lifted his eyes. In the middle of the hall, a half-grown gawky beardless boy stood, broad-shouldered, with curly black hair, startling blue eyes, in a filthy shirt.

Galdor said, "Come up in front of me. Who are you?"

The boy walked up to stand below the high seat, and spoke out, "My name is Vagn Akason. I have come over the sea because I have heard such of your power, King, that I would join you."

Galdor leaned back in the high seat. He knew at once that this was both true and untrue. In this he sensed some witchwork: the boy was both a danger and an opportunity. He laid his hands on the sword again.

"Vagn: what kind of name is that?" An outlander. Galdor thought again of Hjeldric. He could always use another fighter if this one was apt.

"Well, perhaps you would prove your mettle?" He looked around the table. "Thorulf Grimsson, stand."

At once, they all began to move. Thorulf got to his feet, a bear of a man, all hair and muscle. The others pulled the tables back to make room in the middle of the hall. The boy Vagn stood there looking around him, and when Thorulf lumbered toward him, drawing his sword, the boy wheeled toward Galdor.

"I have no sword."

Among the men now grouped along the wall there gusted some laughter. Galdor said, "What then do you offer me?" He smiled, thinking, for all his big talk, the boy was trying to back out of this. "But there are other ways—bring out staffs, let them fight that way." He nodded to the black-haired boy. "You still have your chance, see?"

He leaned on the arm of his high seat. He thought this could be amusing. Thorulf was a slacker and a stirpot. The boy was brawny and should have one good fight in him anyway. Galdor beckoned to the slave, who came quickly over to fill his cup again.

Vagn stood in the middle of the room, now a much wider space, and gripped the staff in both hands, his knuckles up. He had fought often with sticks with his brothers.

He knew the men who had killed his brothers were all around him.

The lumpy, shaggy man tramping across the floor toward him held the staff crosswise. They batted at each other a few times, shuffling around, and Thorulf didn't change his grip. The men watching began to hoot and call out, spurring them on. Thorulf was already sweating. Vagn took a step to one side and struck, going high, over the upside-down grip, and Thorolf blocked it, and with his counterstroke knocked Vagn flat.

The breath went out of him, but even dazed he knew to keep moving. He rolled. The following blow cracked on the rush-strewn floor beside him. He staggered to his feet. He had dropped his staff. He had made a mistake. He had to be keener. Thorulf was strong and knew how to do this. The big man plunged toward him, jabbing his stick at Vagn's belly, at his face, and Vagn dodged, ducked, jumped, flailing his arms out. The staff whipped past his ear and over his head. In the laughing, jeering crowd someone whistled. Thorulf was red-faced, panting, and his little eyes popped. Big as he was, he was already tired. He lunged around, swinging broad at Vagn's head, and Vagn dove past him into the middle of the room, rolled, and coming to his feet grabbed his own staff up off the floor.

The crowd roared. Thorulf plodded after him, out of breath, and Vagn danced around him, luring him into another rush. When the big man charged Vagn stepped sideways and thrust his staff in between Thorulf's knees and felled him like an ox.

A thundering yell went up from those watching. Thorulf sprawled across the rush-strewn floor, and Vagn bounded after him and battered at him until he crouched down, his knees to his chest, and covered his head with his arms.

Vagn swung the staff up. He knew Thorulf had been there the night before on the beach. He wanted to drive the staff straight through him. The men howling and stamping around him were ready for a death. But then he heard Galdor say, up there, "See if you can kill him."

At that, he lowered the staff. His blood cooled. They were all around him, he couldn't kill them all, now, anyway. He put out his hand to Thorulf to help him up. The other men yelled, disappointed, derisive, and Thorulf swatted away his hand and got to his feet and went off.

The other men were already moving the tables back into place, and the slaves were bringing in more food. Vagn stood watching all this. The others ignored him. He saw how they sorted themselves out, top to bottom, with Galdor up on the highest place. When everybody else had sat down again, he went to the lowest end of the table and sat on the end of the bench. The bread came to him and he ate. The ale came to him and he drank. Nobody paid him much attention.

He thought about what he had to do here. All these men were guilty of his brothers' blood, but it was Galdor who was the head. He looked up at the high seat, where the king sat fondling the sword. Wait, Vagn thought to himself.

◆　◆　◆

He slept the short night on some straw in a corner of the hall. In the morning, he expected someone to come to him with work, as would have happened at home, but nobody was doing much of anything. Men came and went in the hall, rolling up their blankets, talking together, and sitting down at the tables to play chess, and drinking. Galdor did not appear. A slave brought in some bread.

Vagn went off around the place, seeing what was there. As he had marked the day before, on his way here, the tower rose on the high point of the headland. A stout stone wall fenced off a wide half circle of space around the foot of it, running from cliff edge to cliff edge. One high gate, braced and hinged with iron, pierced the wall, closed and barred.

He went around the inside of the wall and found a little stable and some storerooms built along it. In the yard some of the men were pitching axes; they paid no heed to him. Firewood stood in stacks along the foot of the tower and tools lay around the yard. In the far corner, where the wall bent to meet the cliff, he came on the kitchen.

In his experience the three things he needed most, bread, clean clothes, and a warm look, all came from women, and women were usually found in kitchens. This one was a narrow room under a turf roof, with two ovens set in the stone wall and a row of split tree trunks for tables. People came and went through it steadily, and he found a corner at the top of a passageway, at the back of it all, where he lurked around until a wan, sullen girl noticed him.

He wheedled her into giving him some bread; he was glad to see that girls were the same everywhere. Like cats, they loved to be stroked. He stroked her more, and she smiled, and then was pretty. He said so. She flustered and fluttered and went off to her work, kneading dough, her hands dusty white and her cheeks bright red, but a few minutes later she brought him mead in a little flagon.

As he took this, thinking he could kiss her, a rattling sound came up from the passageway behind him. The girl gave a violent start, her hands flying up. He looked around, into the dark throat of a corridor, stacked high with wood for the ovens.

"Where does that go?"

She turned her wide eyes on him. "Nowhere. Stay away from there." She leaned closer. "It's haunted," she whispered, and he kissed her.

Later, he squeezed in past the oven wood into the corridor. As he went he could hear the scurrying of rats and he thought that was the noise he had heard.

The corridor wound down steeply into the dark, but in a niche in the wall, under a dusty veil of cobwebs, he found a rush and a firebox. Someone had come down here often but not recently. He blew the dust off the rush and lit it and took it down into the dark.

Around a corner, he came to a door, blocked with a balk of wood. He moved the wood, and the door swung open. Holding the rush out before him he went down a long flight of steps, and the cold air that came to him smelled of an ancient fire, and of bricks, and of iron. This was a dead forge, hidden under the tower. He reached the last step and turned, looking around him.

Almost at his feet, something moaned.

He went cold. He could not move, every hair staring. The sound came again. Down on the thick dust of the floor lay a shaggy head.

Vagn knelt beside it. The head's eyes were closed. Its long thick hair was filthy with dirt and old blood and its raddled beard trailed away beyond the reach of the rush light. He knew it was a dwarf by its beard and its bristling eyebrows, its plug of a nose. Its lips moved but only a moan came out. Vagn remembered the flagon of mead, and took it from his belt and moistened the dwarf's lips.

The lips moved, greedy, and smacked. They spoke again, but he could not make out what they said, and he fed them more mead.

"Tyraste," the dwarf whispered. "Tyraste, remember."

"What." Vagn put his head down closer. "What are you saying? Who are you?"

"Tyraste, remember," the dwarf said, louder.

The rush light was going out. Vagn looked around to make sure he knew where the stair was. He bent to the dwarf's head again. "Tell me what you mean!"

But all the dwarf said was, "Tyraste, remember."

The light flickered out. Vagn turned and went up the steps, groping along in the darkness. At the top of the stair he shut the door and jammed the chunk of wood against it, and went on up to the light.

Beyond the kitchen a flight of steps went up the wall to a parapet overhanging the sea. Vagn climbed up there, to the highest place, and stood looking out over the strait, where the wrinkled water spread out far into the distance. From here, Galdor had seen the knarr coming, had seen from here that the little cargo ship was struggling, and gone down to lure it in.

A foot scraped behind him, startling him, and he whirled around. Thorulf Grimsson was coming up the stair. Vagn went stiff all over. Two steps from the top, Thorulf stopped and looked up at him, squinting into the sun.

"You're going to need a sword. I'll help you get one."

Vagn said, "Very well. You go first."

The big man turned and went down the steps ahead of him. At the bottom, Thorulf waited for him to catch up, and said, under his breath, "That was Galdor, yesterday, who did that." He put his hand out, and said his name.

Vagn shook his hand. They were walking by the kitchen, by the passageway there. He said, "Who is Tyraste?"

"Is that a name? Some girl?" In the high stone wall beyond the kitchen was a wooden double-sided door. Thorulf pulled the two panels wide open. The sun shone in on a narrow room, the wheels and shafts of a wagon, a pile of round shields, and a barrel of sand. Out of the barrel there stuck up a forest of hilts and crosspieces. Thorulf gripped the barrel and rolled it forward; Vagn saw again how strong he was.

"Try this." The big man pulled a sword out of the barrel and handed it to Vagn.

The hilt was neatly leather-wrapped, with a round pommel, but the blade felt heavy to him. He looked for something to try the sword against and Thorulf pointed him out the door. In the yard just beyond was a stump of wood, notched and splintered, the ground around it caked with sawdust. Vagn hacked at it; the battered chunk of tree was too low and the angle was bad.

Thorulf said, "Here. Use this edge, see, that's the front edge. Try this one."

The next blade was spotted with rust and had a big notch out of the blade near the crossbar, but it felt better in his hand. He struck at the stump again, crouching to get the angle, and Thorulf said, "Good. Stiffen your wrist. Like that." He thumped Vagn hard on the back. "That's it."

Vagn stepped away from the stump, his breath short; he was thinking of his brother. Two other men came over toward them. "What, Thorulf," said one, "teaching him to beat you worse?" And smirked.

Thorulf said, "That's Ketil. Ketil Tooth. And that is Johan, who is not even Norse."

Ketil grinned at Vagn, displaying a jagged eyetooth pointing straight out from the gum. He said, "Don't get too cocky beating up on an old souse like him, boy." The fair-headed Johan, not much older than Vagn, gave him a nod. He stood watching everybody, his eyes sharp, but said nothing.

"You'll need a shield, too." Thorulf went back into the storeroom.

Ketil said, "You won't find much good steel in that barrel, boy." He bumped into Vagn, as if by accident.

"Oh, this suits me," Vagn said. He held his ground, and Ketil had to step back. Big Johan was staring at the sword in Vagn's hand; he pointed at the blade, where below the hilt now Vagn saw some old runes in the iron.

"Gut," Johan said. He nodded vigorously at Vagn. "Gut."

"What is the work here?" Vagn asked.

Johan looked over at Ketil to answer; obviously he had little Norse. Ketil said, "It's easy enough. We keep the narrows. All that come by must give us some of what they carry." Ketil stuck his chin out, pointing east. "The big market lies beyond, where the river flows in. Through here is the quickest way there."

Vagn knew this; he and his brothers had been on their way to this market. He had the sword in his hand. He could kill someone now. Thorulf brought him a leather sheath. Around him three of the men who had killed his brothers.

Then they stiffened, and all three were looking across the yard toward the hall. Vagn followed their eyes.

King Galdor had come out of the hall. He stood upon the threshold, his head thrown back. He wore a black bearskin cloak, a breastplate studded with metal. His sword swung at his hip. He stared at them a moment, saying nothing, and walked off across the yard. As he walked, his hand fell lightly to his sword. Thorulf muttered under his breath and made a sign with his fingers.

Ketil said, "Shut up, fool."

"He's after me," Thorulf said. "He's after me all the time."

"That's a fine sword," Vagn said. "Galdor's sword."

"No other has such a sword," Ketil said. "With that in his hand he does not lose."

In Vagn's mind the weapon in his hand shrank to a twig. A few other men walked out of the hall, yawned, stretched. Ketil and Johan started toward them, calling out. Vagn slid his new sword down into the scabbard. He could not kill them all. Galdor he should hate, not these. The girl from the kitchen was wandering by, a basket on her hip, her eyes not quite finding his. He followed Thorulf off to join the other men.

At undernmeal, he sat between Ketil and Thorulf, halfway up the table. While they were all eating, Galdor called out, "We should have some poetry. Thorulf! Give us a skalding!"

All around the hall the men laughed, and turned to stare at Thorulf, who had turned white as lambskin. He got to his feet. The jug was there and he took a big slurp of the ale. The laughing swelled, expecting some amusement. Galdor was lounging in his place, smiling.

"Give us a poem, Thorulf. Speak!"

Thorulf's chest heaved. He said, "On the swan's road—" and gulped. Around the room, the jeering rose; Vagn sat still, seeing this was an old practice. Thorulf's eyes bulged. "The raven lord came—battle-sweat— unh—"

The yells of the other men rose to a roar, and from all sides they threw bread and bones and cheese at Thorulf, who flung his arms up to ward off the volleys, and sank down on the bench. He covered his head with his arms. The table in front of Vagn was littered with bits of food.

Up there, Galdor said, "Well, that was disappointing."

The room hushed. Everybody waited, breathless, on the king, who looked around them all, and finally said, "Vagn Akason. Perhaps you can do better?"

Vagn stood up; he swiped the crumbs off his sleeves. He said, "Odin's match is the Vedrborg's king—"

A disappointed cheer rose. Beside Vagn, Ketil gave a cackle of a laugh. "Figured it out, did you?" On the high seat Galdor raised his head and beamed.

Vagn said, "Save he has both his eyes, his spears are bread, and his ravens are crows—"

The general mutter of approval broke off. Ketil snorted. Galdor's smile froze. Vagn was cobbling up another line, trying to work in a comparison of Valhalla and the Vedrborg. On either side, Ketil and Thorulf yanked Vagn down onto the bench. Around them the table rumbled up a hard-smothered laughter. Galdor tilted forward from the high seat, staring down at Vagn across the room, and his hands went to the sword lying on the table before him. The laughter stopped.

"Mighty king!" On the far side of the room, another man leapt to his feet. "Ring-breaker, feeder of the eagles—"

Every head in the room swung toward this one, and he went on so, for many lofty words. Vagn sat still; he thought maybe he had shown himself too soon. But he was glad. Already Galdor was making a big point of sending this new poet a golden cup of mead. Next to Vagn, Thorulf clapped him on the shoulder and leaned toward his ear. "Keep watch," he whispered. "Galdor won't forget." He straightened. Up there, Galdor had turned to glare at Vagn again. Ketil handed him the alehorn.

"You need this, fool?"

Vagn drank deep.

Later, he saw Galdor, still on his high seat, leaning on the arm to talk with a balding man, squat as a toad. After that one had gone away, Galdor sent a slave to fetch Vagn up. When Vagn stood before him, Galdor frowned at him.

"You are no skald. You annoyed me. So I want you to go up on the parapet and keep night-watch. It's cold up there, in the wind, and it's likely to rain. You can think about where your stupid tongue has gotten you." He sat back. The sword lay on the table between them.

Vagn said, "Yes, King Galdor," and went off.

There was some weather coming in, as the night fell; he could feel it in the air. He stood on the parapet, looking into the dark, listening to the wind boom and sigh over the walls around him. The rain began, light as a veil. He thought awhile of his brothers, dead down there, and he alive up here, and could not push this into any balance. He knew no one would come down the narrows on a night like this and he went down the stairs again, and away into the back of the kitchen, where the passage started down.

The kitchen slaves were asleep around the banked ovens. He took off his shoes, to make no noise, and kept watch on the yard. In the warmth he dozed a little. He dreamt of the dwarf, just down at the other end of the passage; he heard himself begging the dwarf to help him. He started awake, and heard someone scurry by outside, toward the stair.

He went up to the front of the kitchen, and saw the toad-man climbing up the stair; as he went he drew his dagger. Vagn climbed up two steps at a time behind him, his bare feet soundless. At the top, the toad was peering around.

"Looking for me?"

The toad wheeled, his dagger lashing out, but Vagn was already driving into him, shoulder first, hurling him back across the narrow walkway. The dagger nicked his cheek. The toad hit the waist-high parapet wall and tumbled over into the air. Vagn stood there a moment, and heard a thud. Then he went back down the stairs.

From the kitchen, the girl called him, and he went in there, and lay down with her in the warmth of the hearth.

Galdor came out of the hall door. The rain had stopped, and the sunlight blazed bright and clean over the world. To his surprise, across the yard, hacking at a barrel with a sword, was the black-haired boy Vagn Akason.

The king cast a look all around the yard, looking for his man Gifr, and didn't see him. He called Vagn to him.

"I see you made a night of it," he said, when the boy stood before him.

"Not much happened," Vagn said. There was a fresh cut on his cheek.

Galdor said, "You didn't see anything?"

"No. A blowfly bothered me, once, but I swatted it away."

Their eyes met. Galdor laid his hand on the hilt of his sword. "Where did you say you came from?"

"West of here. From the big island."

"Then how did you get here?"

"I walked."

"On the water?"

The boy opened his mouth with another lie, then, from the tower, the horn blew. Galdor said a round oath. "Get to the ships," he said. "Hjeldric is come at last."

Vagn loved being back on the water, where everything was simple: the stroke, his strength, and the sea. On the bench ahead of him Thorulf swung his oar; Ketil stood at the helm, steering them through the broken water. All around Vagn, the men were chanting the count.

He had rowed all his life, but always clunky little boats like the knarr. Never before a vessel like this one, this sea serpent of a ship, light and supple, skimming over the water. The rhythm carried him like great wings. He added his voice to the count, a glad part of this.

Through the corner of his eye he could see that they were racing to cut off another longship, streaking up the strait from the west. Ketil yelled out and the count quickened. Vagn pushed himself to match it, gasping at the effort; all around him the other men strained at the oars. The ship trashed across a rough current. The oncoming ship was fighting the same surface chop and lost half a length, and then Vagn's ship glided out onto a patch of easy water. The other longship stood up its oars and veered off.

A hoarse cheer rose from the benches around Vagn. Ketil laid them over. The jug came by and Vagn gulped down most of the water in it. His sword lay under his bench. Maybe now they would fight, ship to ship. He longed to try the sword in a real fight. Over there, across the open water, the other longship faced them, too far to see any of those men. He dragged in a deep breath. Thorulf reached around and slapped his shoulder, and someone else gave a random yell. Vagn felt his blood beating through his body; he shook his muscles loose. He looked quickly around at the other men, his crew. His brothers now. He thrust that problem off. He looked out over the water toward the other ship, his hand itching to pick up his sword.

Then a horn blew, behind them.

He twisted to look over his shoulder. Back there, Galdor had his other two ships bow to stern across the narrows. Three more enemy ships lay up the strait, waiting. Lean and low, they were beautiful, and it swelled him to think he would fight in such a one. The horn sounded again and Vagn felt his scalp prickle. This was the beginning of it. But none of the other men even looked up. Back at the helm, Ketil suddenly gave over the steerboard to somebody else and went forward.

Thorulf was sitting back. Another jug came. Vagn said, "What's going on?"

"They're talking." The man across the way from him turned toward him. "Nothing is going to happen for a while."

On the bench behind him, somebody said, "They outnumber us. Galdor doesn't fight against the odds." Thorulf muttered something under his breath.

Vagn looked around them. They were at the narrowest part of the strait. He remembered the rocks that cluttered the water along the shore. It seemed to him Galdor's three ships could hold off the four enemy ships easily enough. Probably there was some piece of warcraft he was not grasping here. Now Galdor was shouting from his ship toward one of the others, and someone there was shouting back. They were arranging to meet on the land. There would still be a fight. Vagn reached down to touch the hilt of his sword.

Galdor had sent most of his men back up to the Vedrborg. The rest he kept below, in a broad meadow just inland of the beach where Hjledric's ships drew up, and he went among them and counted out seven of them. Thorulf was among these seven and so was Vagn. When Ketil was not counted in, he and the others went away. Galdor paced up and down past the men who stayed.

He said, "I am staking the Vedrborg on this. I will reward good work here." His eyes were hot and bright. He drew his sword; Vagn imagined it hissed like a snake, coming out of the sheath. "Thorulf, take the weather edge. I will take the middle."

Thorulf stepped back and leaned on his sword. Around him the other men were gripping each other's hands, drinking deep of the ale-horns. Across the grass Hjeldric's eight men gathered. Vagn looked over his new sword again. He had worked on the rusty parts with sheep's fat and a rag and gotten some of it clean. The notch he could not fix. But the blade felt good in his hand. He took a deep breath. The sun was warm on his cheek. He told himself he might never see another sunrise; this seemed a far-distant, unimportant matter.

Thorulf stood there, swinging his arms back and forth. He said, "Is this the first time you've fought like this?"

Vagn said, "Yes." His voice had a squeak.

Thorulf said, "I think it is my last."

Ketil suddenly appeared again. To Vagn, he said, "Galdor will win this. Keep your sword up." He thumped Thorulf on the back. "You'd better get down there. Feed a few ravens for me." Thorulf walked heavily away across the grass, and Vagn followed.

Vagn could not stop bouncing. He was gripping the sword too tight. Beside him, Thorulf slouched, scratching his beard. He said, "Tonight in Valhalla, Vagn Akason," and spat through his fingers. Galdor came pacing along in front of them, calling their names and jabbing his sword in the air.

He lifted his shield, and the horn blew.

They walked together in a row toward Hjeldric's men, who came toward them in a row, each to each. In front of Vagn was a lanky body behind a big round shield, red hair sticking out all around a leather helmet. Vagn could not quite get his breath. Beside him, Thorulf gave a screech and dashed forward.

The redheaded man lunged at Vagn, striking shoulder high, and Vagn tore his attention away from Thorulf. He swung up the shield and the blow struck so hard it numbed his arm. He slashed out with his sword, low, not seeing much, and felt it bang hard on the redheaded man's shield, and the other man sprang away. Vagn followed him, shield first, wanting him to strike first. Inside the leather helmet, above the thatch of red beard, the man's blue eyes locked with his. He jabbed with his sword, and when Vagn pulled his shield up, turned the stroke low, and hard.

The tip of the sword sliced toward Vagn's knee. He drove his own sword down, and the blades rang together. Vagn saw at once the other man had the longer reach. He crashed forward, shield first, into the tall, gangly body, closing the gap between them. For an instant, they were chest to chest together, the redhead's breath blasting in Vagn's face. He felt the other man's strength coil to throw him off, and as the other man shoved he slid sideways out of the way, laying out his sword. The red-headed man stumbled, fell across the blade and staggered to his knees.

Vagn bellowed, hot with triumph. Then another of Hjeldric's men was charging him, shorter, wider, swinging an axe.

He caught this on the shield, turning the edge a little, so the wide curved blade did not strike full on. With his sword he hacked down at the axeman's head. The axeman ducked back and away, and for an instant Vagn could look around.

The redhead was getting to his feet. Blood smeared his side but he was raising his sword again. Out there on the trampled grass, Thorulf lay in a heap.

The axeman barked some name, and he and the redheaded man fanned out and came at Vagn together. The redheaded man was breathing hard, the blood bright on his breastplate and shield arm. The other man, squatty, with his axe, bobbed back and forth then gave a howl and charged.

Vagn stood fast; he turned the first blow off with his shield and with his sword poked and cut, watching how the other man met that. He knew that the redheaded man was coming in behind him, and he backed up in a rush, getting out from between them. The redheaded man dropped to one knee again. The other one lifted his axe, moving sideways, circling around to Vagn's far side.

The redheaded man heaved himself up onto his feet and stumbled forward. Vagn cocked up his shield; his body felt huge and the shield the size of a pea. From the side the axe sliced at his head and he ducked and lunged and his sword glanced off the axeman's shield. He dodged away from them both again, and the axeman stepped back. The redheaded man lost his balance and fell to his hands and knees.

Vagn cast another look around. They had moved far along the meadow, somehow, almost to the wood; Thorulf's body was a long way back there. Nearer, Galdor and Hjeldric were circling each other. Galdor's sword swung out, and Hjledric dodged, then attacked, going against Galdor's shield hand.

Then from the wood there burst a tide of men.

Vagn stood, startled. They were Galdor's men, and they reached the redheaded man first and hacked him down, and then the axeman went down. Hjeldric wheeled toward them, and Galdor plunged the sword through his back. Vagn did not move. He saw Galdor fling his arms up, triumphant. He saw, down on the beach, two of Hjeldric's ships push away.

Ketil walked up to Vagn. He said, "I told you he would not leave it to chance." His eyes did not quite meet Vagn's. Vagn threw his shield down, and went off to see what had happened to Thorulf.

At undernmeal Vagn sat staring at his hands. Around him the voices purred and muttered but he heard nothing. The food came around and he ate nothing. He drank from the alehorn, which did him no good.

His mind was churning. Thorolf was dead, but Thorulf had died well, of hard wounds taken in front. Vagn thought over and over of the redheaded man, who had fought so hard, even wounded, merely to be cut down from behind like a coward. The gall burned in his belly. Ketil, beside him, spoke to him only once.

"We won, didn't we?"

Vagn grunted at him. After that Ketil said nothing, only glanced at him now and then, and passed him the horn.

In the high seat Galdor shouted out a name, and some warrior stood up, and Galdor pulled one of the gold rings from his arm and a slave brought it down and everybody cheered. Vagn stared at the table.

Then Galdor was calling out his name.

Vagn lifted his head, and all around saw faces watching him. A slave came trotting toward him, holding out a gold ring, and a long yell rose, his name in sixty voices.

He stood up, everybody's eyes turned on him, and hurled the ring across the room.

"No! There was nothing golden on that field, no honor—" He was shaking, the blood booming in his ears. "Better men than you died on that field, Galdor No-King, Galdor Cheat! I would be a better king here than you are."

The hall crashed into silence. Nobody moved.

Galdor said, "This is your end, Vagn Akason." He rose in his place and took the sword up off the table and drew it from the scabbard. Around Vagn the others were suddenly moving, pulling the benches and tables back, and he was alone, standing there. He drew his sword. Galdor was coming toward him down the hall.

He moved away, then Galdor was coming at him, sideways, the keen blade slicing toward him. He bounded backward. He got his sword crosswise of Galdor's and the shock rang up his arm. Galdor was pushing him along, darting here, there, poking at him, laughing. Vagn skittered backward, trying to get some room, and came up against the table.

Hands gripped him from behind. Somebody was holding him for Galdor, and the king moved in fast. Vagn dropped his sword. He reached back and got the wrists holding him, twisted and crouched down, and with all his weight he hauled the man behind him over his shoulder and into Galdor's thrust.

The sword came out through the falling man's chest. While Galdor was pulling it free Vagn grabbed up his own sword again and vaulted onto the table. The other men shied back, toward the walls. Galdor swung hard at his knees, and when he dodged that, the king leapt onto the table after him. Slashing and cutting up and down, he drove Vagn backward, through the bread and the cheese, tipping over the alehorns. Vagn kept his sword up, fending off the king's blows, groping along behind him with his feet.

Galdor stabbed at him, and Vagn saw something; he lunged toward the weakness, but it was a trap. The king wheeled his blow backward at him and struck the sword out of his hand.

A bellow went up. The king's eyes glowed. Vagn leapt down from the table, and raced out the door into the yard. Galdor was hot after him. Just beyond the threshold was a stack of firewood, and Vagn threw a chunk of it at Galdor and saw an axe among the wood. With a bound he caught it up. Galdor was right behind him and he wheeled around and swung the axe waist high, missing Galdor by a finger's breadth.

Galdor howled. His teeth showed. He hacked right, and Vagn dodged, then left and Vagn dodged. The axe was top-heavy and hard to manage. Galdor let him swing and came in behind the swing, and Vagn felt the blade crease his ribs through his shirt. He swung the axe around and hurled it straight at Galdor.

Galdor went down; the axe grazed his shoulder. Vagn raced across the yard, toward the storeroom with the barrel of swords. The doors were shut and barred. Galdor was pounding after him, yelling, derisive.

"Wait, little boy, I'm not done with you!"

Vagn swerved toward the kitchen, where there would be knives. Galdor was on his heels. On the ground out in the middle of the yard he saw a broom, and veered toward it. He could hear yelling, from a great distance; all he saw was the broom, and he snatched it up and wheeled just as Galdor closed with him.

The sword swung at his head; he thrust up the broom and the blade bit the wood and snapped it. Still clutching the short end, Vagn slid back, out of reach of the sword. Galdor stood a moment, the sword raised, the tip circling in the air as if it sniffed for him.

The others, packed up against the walls, were calling and whistling. Vagn watched only the tip of the sword. Sliding his feet along, the stub end of the broomstick poking out before him, he inched his way toward the wall. Galdor shifted as he shifted, the sword blocking him this way, herding him that, moving him backward, backward. Vagn gave a quick look over his shoulder. Just behind him was the stair up to the parapet. The blade ripped at him and he sprang backward, up onto the steps.

Galdor was below him now, but Vagn had no fit weapon. He lashed out with the short piece of the broom and the king coiled back, out of reach, and whipped the sword at his ankles. Vagn leapt up another step, and Galdor came after. The sword jabbed at him. Galdor lunged up the steps and Vagn scurried away across the parapet and came up hard against the rail.

"Nowhere to run now," Galdor said, breathless. He lifted the sword, and Vagn's gaze rose with it. "Aha! You admire my sword? You should. It's beyond price. It longs for blood." He waggled the sword in Vagn's face. "Its first blood was the dwarf who made it, who never made another like it. And now—" He cocked back the sword above Vagn's head. "It will have yours."

The dwarf. The dwarf. Braced against the wall, Vagn cried out, "Tyraste, remember!"

Galdor swung the blade down at his head, and the sword turned in Galdor's hand, struck the wall, and flew across the parapet.

Vagn yelled. Galdor lunged after the sword, both hands stretched out. Vagn was closer. His hand fastened on the sword hilt and without pausing he swung his arm with all his strength around and took Galdor across the body.

Somewhere far off a huge yell went up. Vagn stood. Galdor sagged to his knees, his hands on his ripped belly, his head back. Vagn said, "This for my brothers. And Thorulf. And the dwarf in the cellar." He drove the sword through Galdor's chest.

The yelling went on. Down in the yard the other people were shouting and waving their arms. Vagn stood, panting.

The sword in his hand felt light, quick; its power burned in it. He understood why Galdor had always been touching it. Vagn wanted right away to strike with it again. The dwarf had made it full of charms. He remembered how it had turned on Galdor.

He went on down the stair to the yard, crowded with people. They were all watching him, and when he came toward them they moved back out of his way. He went in through the kitchen. There he found a rush light, and followed the passageway into the dark.

In the forge, at the foot of the stair, he sank down on his heels, and held the rushlight up to see. In the dust was the dwarf's head, but now it was smiling.

Vagn laid the sword down beside it.

"I have brought this back to you."

The dwarf whispered, "Yours. Yours, now."

Eagerly he took it back in his hand. The dwarf's lips bent in a deeper smile. "But beware. It is still evil."

This was how Vagn Akason became king of the Vedrborg. But the life there was not to his liking, and soon he went off to join the Jomsvikings.

George R. R. Martin

. . .

Hugo, Nebula, and World Fantasy Award-winner George R. R. Martin, *New York Times* bestselling author of the landmark A Song of Ice and Fire fantasy series, has been called "the American Tolkien."

Born in Bayonne, New Jersey, George R. R. Martin made his first sale in 1971, and soon established himself as one of the most popular SF writers of the seventies. He quickly became a mainstay of the Ben Bova *Analog* with stories such as "With Morning Comes Mistfall," "And Seven Times Never Kill Man," "The Second Kind of Loneliness," "The Storms of Windhaven" (in collaboration with Lisa Tuttle, and later expanded by them into the novel *Windhaven*), "Override," and others, although he also sold to *Amazing, Fantastic, Galaxy, Orbit*, and other markets. One of his *Analog* stories, the striking novella "A Song for Lya," won him his first Hugo Award, in 1974.

By the end of the seventies, he had reached the height of his influence as a science-fiction writer, and was producing his best work in that category with stories such as the famous

"Sandkings," his best-known story, which won both the Nebula and the Hugo in 1980 (he'd later win another Nebula in
1985 for his story "Portraits of His Children"), "The Way of
Cross and Dragon," which won a Hugo Award in the same
year (making Martin the first author ever to receive two Hugo
Awards for fiction in the same year), "Bitterblooms," "The
Stone City," "Starlady," and others. These stories would be collected in *Sandkings*, one of the strongest collections of the period. By now, he had mostly moved away from *Analog* although
he would have a long sequence of stories about the droll inter-
stellar adventures of Haviland Tuf (later collected in *Tuf Voy-
aging*) running throughout the eighties in the Stanley Schmidt
Analog, as well as a few strong individual pieces such as the
novella "Nightflyers"—most of his major work of the late seventies and early eighties, though, would appear in *Omni*. The
late seventies and eighties also saw the publication of his
memorable novel *Dying of the Light*, his only solo SF novel,
while his stories were collected in *A Song for Lya*, *Sandkings*,
Songs of Stars and Shadows, *Songs the Dead Men Sing*, *Nightflyers*, and *Portraits of His Children*. By the beginning of the
eighties, he'd moved away from SF and into the horror genre,
publishing the big horror novel *Fevre Dream*, and winning the
Bram Stoker Award for his horror story "The Pear-Shaped
Man" and the World Fantasy Award for his werewolf novella
"The Skin Trade." By the end of that decade, though, the crash
of the horror market and the commercial failure of his ambitious horror novel *The Armageddon Rag* had driven him out of

the print world and to a successful career in television instead, where for more than a decade he worked as story editor or producer on such shows as the new *Twilight Zone* and *Beauty and the Beast*.

After years away, Martin made a triumphant return to the print world in 1996 with the publication of the immensely successful fantasy novel *A Game of Thrones*, the start of his Song of Ice and Fire sequence. A freestanding novella taken from that work, "Blood of the Dragon," won Martin another Hugo Award in 1997. Further books in the Song of Ice and Fire series, *A Clash of Kings*, *A Storm of Swords*, *A Feast for Crows*, and *A Dance with Dragons*, have made it one of the most acclaimed and bestselling series in all of modern fantasy. Recently, the books were made into an HBO TV series, *A Game of Thrones*, which has become one of the most popular and acclaimed shows on television, and made Martin a recognizable figure well outside of the usual genre boundaries, even inspiring a satirical version of him on *Saturday Night Live*. Martin's recent books include a massive retrospective collection spanning the entire spectrum of his career, *Dreamsongs*; a novella collection, *Starlady and Fast-Friend*; a novel written in collaboration with Gardner Dozois and Daniel Abraham, *Hunter's Run*; and, as editor, several anthologies edited in collaboration with Gardner Dozois, including *Warriors*, *Song of the Dying Earth*, *Songs of Love and Death*, *Down These Strange Streets*, *Dangerous Women*, and *Rogues*; as well as several new volumes in his long-running Wild Cards anthology series. In

2012, Martin was given the Life Achievement Award by the World Fantasy Convention. His most recent books are *High Stakes*, the twenty-third volume in the Wild Cards series, and *The World of Ice and Fire*, an illustrated history of the Seven Kingdoms.

Here he takes us to Westeros, home to his Ice and Fire series, and back in time for a look at things that happened long before *A Game of Thrones* begins, for the story of an unfortunate sibling rivalry that has tragic and disastrous effects on the entire world.

◆　◆　◆

The Sons of the Dragon

GEORGE R. R. MARTIN

King Aegon I Targaryen, as history records, took both of his sisters to wife. Both Visenya and Rhaenys were dragonriders, blessed with the silver-gold hair, purple eyes, and beauty of true Targaryens. Elsewise, the two queens were as unlike one another as any two women could be . . . save in one other respect. Each of them gave the king a son.

Aenys came first. Born in 7 AC to Aegon's younger wife, Queen Rhaenys, the boy was small at birth, and sickly. He cried all the time, and it was said that his limbs were spindly and his eyes small and watery, so that the king's maesters feared for his survival. He would spit out the nipples of his wet nurse, and give suck only at his mother's breasts, and rumors claimed that he screamed for a fortnight when he was weaned. So unlike King Aegon was he that a few even dared suggest that His Grace was not the boy's true sire, that Aenys was some bastard born of one of Queen Rhaenys's many handsome favorites, the son of a singer or a mummer or a mime. And the prince was slow to grow as well. Not until he was given the young dragon Quicksilver, a hatchling born that year on Dragonstone, did Aenys Targaryen begin to thrive.

Prince Aenys was three when his mother, Queen Rhaenys, and her dragon Meraxes were slain in Dorne. Her death left the boy prince inconsolable. He stopped eating, and even began to crawl as he had when he was one, as if he had forgotten how to walk. His father despaired of him, and rumors flew about the court that King Aegon might take another wife, as Rhaenys was dead and Visenya childless and perhaps barren. The king kept his own counsel on these matters, so no man could say what thoughts he might have entertained, but many great lords and noble knights appeared at court with their maiden daughters, each more comely than the last.

All such speculation ended in 11 AC, when Queen Visenya suddenly announced that she was carrying the king's child. A son, she proclaimed confidently, and so he proved to be. The prince came squalling into the world in 12 AC. No newborn was ever more robust than Maegor Targaryen, maesters and midwives agreed; his weight at birth was almost twice that of his elder brother.

The half brothers were never close. Prince Aenys was the heir apparent, and King Aegon kept him close by his side. As the king moved about the realm from castle to castle, so did the prince. Prince Maegor remained with his mother, sitting by her side when she held court. Queen Visenya and King Aegon were oft apart in those years. When he was not on his royal progress, Aegon would return to King's Landing and the Aegonfort, whilst Visenya and her son remained on Dragonstone. For this reason, lords and commons alike began to refer to Maegor as the Prince of Dragonstone.

Queen Visenya put a sword into her son's hand when he was three. Supposedly the first thing he did with the blade was butcher one of the castle cats, men said . . . though more like this tale was a calumny devised by his enemies many years later. That the prince took to swordplay at once cannot be denied, however. For his first master-at-arms, his mother chose Ser Gawen Corbray, as deadly a knight as could be found in all the Seven Kingdoms.

Prince Aenys was so oft in his sire's company that his own instruction in the chivalric arts came largely from the knights of Aegon's Kingsguard, and sometimes the king himself. The boy was diligent, his instructors all agreed, and did not want for courage, but he lacked his sire's size and strength, and never showed himself as any more than adequate as a fighter, even when the king pressed Blackfyre into his hands, as he did from time to time. Aenys would not disgrace himself in battle, his tutors told one another, but no songs would ever be sung about his prowess.

Such gifts as this prince possessed lay elsewhere. Aenys was a fine singer himself, as it happened, with a strong, sweet voice. He was courteous and charming, clever without being bookish. He made friends easily, and young girls seemed to dote on him, be they highborn or low. Aenys loved to ride as well. His father gave him coursers, palfreys, and destriers, but his favorite mount was his dragon, Quicksilver.

Prince Maegor rode as well, but showed no great love for horses, dogs, or any animal. When he was eight, a palfrey kicked him in the stables. Maegor stabbed the horse to death . . . and slashed half the face off the stableboy who came running at the beast's screams. The Prince of Dragonstone had many companions through the years, but no true friends. He was a quarrelsome boy, quick to take offense, slow to forgive, fearsome in his wroth. His skill with weapons was unmatched, however. A squire at eight, he was unhorsing boys four and five years his elder in the lists by the time he was twelve and battering seasoned men-at-arms into submission in the castle yard. On his thirteenth name day in 25 AC, his mother Queen Visenya bestowed her own Valyrian steel blade, Dark Sister, upon him . . . half a year before his marriage.

The tradition amongst the Targaryens had always been to marry kin to kin. Wedding brother to sister was thought to be ideal. Failing that, a girl might wed an uncle, a cousin, or a nephew; a boy a cousin, aunt, or niece. This practice went back to Old Valyria, where it was common amongst many of the ancient families, particularly those who bred and rode dragons. The blood of the dragon must remain pure, the wisdom went. Some of the sorcerer princes also took more than one wife when it pleased them, though this was less common than incestuous marriage. In Valryia before the Doom, wise men wrote, a thousand gods were honored, but none were feared, so few dared to speak against these customs.

This was not true in Westeros, where the power of the Faith went unquestioned. The old gods were still worshipped in the North, but in the rest of the realm there was a single god with seven faces, and his voice upon this earth was the High Septon of Oldtown. And the doctrines of the Faith, handed down through centuries from Andalos itself, condemned the Valyrian marriage customs as practiced by the Targaryens. Incest was denounced as vile sin, whether between father and daughter, mother and son, or brother and sister, and the fruits of such unions were considered abominations in the sight of gods and men. With hindsight, it can be seen that conflict between the Faith and House Targaryen was inevitable. Indeed, many amongst the Most Devout expected the High Septon to speak out against Aegon and his sisters during the Conquest, and were most displeased when the Father of the Faithful instead counseled Lord Hightower against opposing the Dragon, and even blessed and anointed him at his second coronation.

Familiarity is the father of acceptance, it is said. The High Septon who had crowned Aegon the Conqueror remained the Shepherd of the Faithful until his death in 11 AC, by which time the realm had grown accustomed to the notion of a king with two queens, who were both wives and sisters. King Aegon always took care to honor the Faith, confirming its traditional rights and privileges, exempting its wealth and property from taxation, and affirming that septons, septas, and other servants of the Seven accused of wrongdoing could only be tried by the Faith's own courts.

The accord between the Faith and the Iron Throne continued all through the reign of Aegon I. From 11 AC to 37 AC, six High Septons wore the crystal crown; His Grace remained on good terms with each of them, calling at the Starry Sept each time he came to Oldtown. Yet the question of incestuous marriage remained, simmering below the courtesies like poison. Whilst the High Septons of King Aegon's reign never spoke out against the king's marriage to his sisters, neither did they declare it to be lawful. The humbler members of the Faith—village septons, holy sisters, begging brothers, Poor Fellows—still believed it sinful for brother to lie with sister, or for a man to take two wives.

Aegon the Conqueror had fathered no daughters, however, so these matters did not come to a head at once. The sons of the Dragon had no sisters to marry, so each of them was forced to seek elsewhere for a bride.

Prince Aenys was the first to marry. In 22 AC, he wed the Lady Alyssa, the maiden daughter of the Lord of the Tides, Aethan Velaryon, King Aegon's lord admiral and master of ships. She was fifteen, the same age as the prince, and shared his silvery hair and purple eyes as well, for the Velaryons were an ancient family descended from Valyrian stock. King Aegon's own mother had been a Velaryon, so the marriage was reckoned one of cousin to cousin.

It soon proved both happy and fruitful. The following year, Alyssa gave birth to a daughter. Aenys named her Rhaena, and the realm rejoiced ... save, perhaps, for Queen Visenya. Prince Aenys was the heir to the Iron Throne, all agreed, but now an issue arose as to whether Prince Maegor remained second in the line of succession, or should be considered to have fallen to third, behind the newborn princess. Queen Visenya proposed to settle the matter by betrothing Rhaena to Maegor, who had just turned twelve. Aenys and Alyssa spoke out against the match, however ... and when word reached Oldtown's Starry Sept, the High Septon sent a raven, warning the king that such a marriage would not be looked upon with favor by the Faith. He proposed a different bride for Maegor: Ceryse Hightower, maiden daughter to the Lord of Oldtown (and the High Septon's own niece). Aegon, mindful of the advantages of closer ties with Oldtown and its ruling House, saw wisdom in the choice and agreed to the match.

Thus it came to pass that in 25 AC, Maegor Targaryen, Prince of Dragonstone, wed Lady Ceryse Hightower in the Starry Sept of Oldtown, with the High Septon himself performing the nuptials. Maegor was thirteen, the bride ten years his senior ... but the lords who bore witness to the bedding all agreed that the prince made a lusty husband, and Maegor himself boasted that he had consummated the marriage a dozen times that night. "I made a son for House Targaryen last night," he proclaimed as he broke fast.

The son came the next year ... but the boy, named Aegon after his grandsire, was born to Lady Alyssa and fathered by Prince Aenys. Lady Ceryse did not quicken in the years that followed, though other children came one after the other to Alyssa. In 29 AC, she gave Aenys a second son, Viserys. In 34 AC, she gave birth to Jaehaerys, her fourth child and third son. In 36 AC came another daughter, Alysanne. Each son pushed Prince Maegor further down in the succession; some said he stood behind his brother's daughters too. All whilst Maegor and Ceryse remained childless.

On tourney ground and battlefield, however, Prince Maegor's accomplishments far exceeded those of his brother. In the great tourney at

Riverrun in 28 AC, Prince Maegor unhorsed three knights of the Kingsguard in successive tilts before falling to the eventual champion. In the melee, no man could stand before him. Afterward he was knighted on the field by his father, who dubbed him with no less a blade than Blackfyre. At ten-and-six, Maegor became the youngest knight in the Seven Kingdoms.

Others feats followed. In 29 AC and again in 30 AC, Maegor accompanied Osmund Strong and Aethan Velaryon to the Stepstones to root out the Lysene pirate king Sargoso Saan, and fought in several bloody affrays, showing himself to be both fearless and deadly. In 31 AC, he hunted down and slew a notorious robber knight in the riverlands, the so-called Giant of the Trident.

Maegor was not yet a dragonrider, however. Though half a dozen hatchlings had been born amidst the fires of Dragonstone in the later years of Aegon's reign, and were offered to the prince, Maegor refused them all. His brother's wife teased him about it one day in court, wondering aloud whether "my good-brother is afraid of dragons." Maegor darkened in rage at the jape then replied coolly that there was only one dragon worthy of him.

The last seven years of the reign of Aegon the Conqueror were peaceful ones. After the frustrations of his Dornish War the king accepted the continued independence of Dorne, and flew to Sunspear on Balerion on the tenth anniversary of the peace accords to celebrate a "feast of friendship" with Deria Martell, the reigning Princess of Dorne. Prince Aenys accompanied him on Quicksilver; Maegor remained on Dragonstone. Aegon had made the Seven Kingdoms one with fire and blood, but after celebrating his sixtieth name day in 33 AC, he turned instead to brick and mortar. Half of every year was still given over to a royal progress, but now it was Prince Aenys and his wife Alyssa who journeyed from castle to castle, whilst the aging king remained at home, dividing his days between Dragonstone and King's Landing.

The fishing village where Aegon had first landed had grown into a sprawling, stinking city of a hundred thousand souls by that time; only Oldtown and Lannisport were larger. Yet in many ways King's Landing was still little more than an army camp that had swollen to grotesque size: dirty, reeking, unplanned, impermanent. And the Aegonfort, which had spread halfway down Aegon's High Hill by that time, was as ugly a castle as any in the Seven Kingdoms, a great confusion of wood and earth and brick that had long outgrown the old log palisades that were its only walls.

It was certainly no fit abode for a great king. In 35 AC, Aegon moved with all his court back to Dragonstone, and gave orders that the Aegonfort be torn down, so that a new castle might be raised in its place. This time, he decreed, he would build in stone. To oversee the design and construction of the new castle, he named the King's Hand, Lord Alyn Stokeworth (Ser Osmund Strong had died the previous year), and Queen Visenya. (A jape went about the court that King Aegon had given Visenya charge of building the Red Keep so he would not have to endure her presence on Dragonstone.)

Aegon the Conqueror died of a stroke on Dragonstone in the thirty-seventh year after the Conquest. His grandsons Aegon and Viserys were with him at his death, in the Chamber of the Painted Table; the king was showing them the details of his conquests. Prince Maegor, in residence at Dragonstone at the time, spoke the eulogy as his father's body was laid upon a funeral pyre in the castle yard. The king was clad in battle armor, his mailed hands folded over the hilt of Blackfyre. Since the days of old Valyria, it had ever been the custom of House Targaryen to burn their dead, rather than consigning their remains to the ground. Vhagar supplied the flames to light the fire. Blackfyre was burned with the king, but retrieved by Aenys afterward, its blade darker but elsewise unharmed. No common fire can damage Valyrian steel.

The Dragon was survived by his sister Visenya, his sons Aenys and Maegor, and five grandchildren. Prince Aenys was thirty years of age at his father's death, Prince Maegor five-and-twenty.

Aenys had been at Highgarden on his progress when his father died, but Quicksilver returned him to Dragonstone for the funeral. Afterward he donned his father's iron-and-ruby crown, and Grand Maester Gawen proclaimed him Aenys of House Targaryen, the First of His Name, King of the Andals and the First Men, Lord of the Seven Kingdoms, and Protector of the Realm. The lords and knights and septons who had come to Dragonstone to bid their king farewell knelt and bowed their heads. When Prince Maegor's turn came, Aenys drew him back to his feet, kissed his cheek, and said, "Brother, you need never kneel to me again. We shall rule this realm together, you and I." Then the king presented his father's sword, Blackfyre, to his brother, saying, "You are more fit to bear this blade than me. Wield it in my service, and I shall be content."

Afterward the new king sailed to King's Landing, where he found the Iron Throne standing amidst mounds of rubble and mud. The old Aegonfort had been torn down, and pits and tunnels pockmarked the hill where the cellars and foundations of the Red Keep were being dug, but the new castle had not yet begun to rise. Nonetheless, thousands came to cheer King Aenys as he claimed his father's seat for his own. Thereafter His Grace set out for Oldtown to receive the blessing of the High Septon, traveling by way of Riverrun, Lannisport, and Highgarden on a grand royal progress. His wife and children made the journey with him, and all along the route the smallfolk appeared by the hundreds and thousands to hail their new king and queen. At the Starry Sept, the High Septon anointed him as he had his father, and presented him with a crown of yellow gold, with the faces of the Seven inlaid in jade and pearl.

Yet even as Aenys was receiving the High Septon's blessing, some were casting doubt on his fitness to sit the Iron Throne. Westeros required a warrior, not a dreamer, they whispered to one another, and Prince Maegor was the stronger of the Dragon's two sons. And foremost amongst the whisperers was Maegor's mother, the Dowager Queen Visenya Targaryen. "The truth is plain enough," she is reported to have said. "Even Aenys sees it. Why else would he have given Blackfyre to my son? He knows that only Maegor has the strength to rule."

The young king's mettle would be tested sooner than anyone could have imagined. The Wars of Conquest had left scars throughout the realm. Sons now come of age dreamed of avenging long-dead fathers. Knights remembered the days when a man with a sword and a horse and a suit of armor could slash his way to riches and glory. Lords recalled a time when they did not need a king's leave to tax their smallfolk or kill their enemies. "The chains the Dragon forged can yet be broken," the discontented told one another. "We can win our freedoms back, but now is the time to strike, for this new king is weak."

The first stirrings of revolt were in the riverlands, amidst the colossal ruins of Harrenhal. Aegon had granted the castle to Ser Quenton Qoherys, his old master-at-arms. When Lord Qoherys died in a fall from his horse in 9 AC, his title passed to his grandson Gargon, a fat and foolish man with an unseemly appetite for young girls who became known as Gargon the Guest. Lord Gargon soon became infamous for turning up at every wedding celebrated within his domains so that he might enjoy the lord's right of first night. A more unwelcome wedding guest can scarce be imagined. He also made free with the wives and daughters of his own servants.

King Aenys was still on his progress, guesting with Lord Tully of Riverrun, when the father of a maid Lord Qoherys had ruined opened a postern gate at Harrenhal to an outlaw who styled himself Harren the Red, and claimed to be a grandson of Harren the Black. The outlaws pulled his lordship from his bed and dragged him to the castle godswood, where Harren sliced off his genitals and fed them to a dog. A few leal men-at-arms were killed; the rest agreed to join Harren, who declared himself Lord of Harrenhal and King of the Rivers (not being ironborn, he did not claim the islands).

When word reached Riverrun, Lord Tully urged the king to mount Quicksilver and descend on Harrenhal as his father had. But His Grace, perhaps mindful of his mother's death in Dorne, instead commanded Tully to gather his banners, and lingered at Riverrun as they gathered. Only when a thousand men were assembled did Aenys march . . . but when his men reached Harrenhal, they found it empty but for corpses. Harren the Red had put Lord Gargon's leal servants to the sword and taken his band into the woods.

By the time Aenys returned to King's Landing the news had grown even worse. In the Vale, Lord Ronnel Arryn's younger brother Jonos had deposed and imprisoned his loyal sibling, and declared himself King of Mountain and Vale. In the Iron Islands, another priest-king had walked out of the sea, announcing himself to be Lodos the Twice-Drowned, the son of the Drowned God, returned at last from visiting his father. And high in the Red Mountains of Dorne, a pretender called the Vulture King appeared, and called on all true Dornishmen to avenge the evils visited on Dorne by the Targaryens. Though Princess Deria denounced him, swearing that she and all leal Dornishmen wanted only peace, thousands flocked to his banners, swarming down from the hills and up out of the sands, through goat tracks in the mountains into the Reach.

"This Vulture King is half-mad, and his followers are a rabble, undisciplined and unwashed," Lord Harmon Dondarrion wrote to the king. "We can smell them coming fifty leagues away." Not long after, that selfsame rabble stormed and seized his castle of Blackhaven. The Vulture King personally sliced off Dondarrion's nose before putting Blackhaven to the torch and marching away.

King Aenys knew these rebels had to be put down, but seemed unable to decide where to begin. Grand Maester Gawen wrote that the king seemed unable to comprehend why this was happening. The smallfolk loved him, did they not? Jonos Arryn, this new Lodos, the Vulture King . . . had he wronged them? If they had grievances, why not bring them to him? "I would have heard them out," he said. He spoke of sending messengers to the rebels, to learn the reasons for their actions. Fearing that King's Landing might not be safe with Harren the Red alive and near, he sent his wife and children to Dragonstone. He commanded his Hand, Lord Alyn Stokeworth, to take a fleet and army to the Vale to put down Jonos Arryn and restore his brother Ronnel to the lordship. But when the ships were about to sail, he countermanded the order, fearing that Stokeworth's departure would leave King's Landing undefended. Instead he sent the Hand with but a few hundred men to hunt down Harren the Red, and decided he would summon a great council to discuss how best to put down the other rebels.

Whilst the king prevaricated, his lords took to the field. Some acted on their own authority, others in concert with the Dowager Queen. In the Vale, Lord Allard Royce of Runestone assembled twoscore loyal lords and marched against the Eyrie, easily defeating the supporters of the self-styled King of Mountain and Vale. But when they demanded the release of their rightful lord, Jonos Arryn sent his brother to them through the Moon Door. Such was the sad end of Ronnel Arryn, who had flown thrice about the Giant's Lance on dragonback. The Eyrie was impregnable to any conventional assault, so "King" Jonos and his diehard followers spat down defiance at the loyalists, and settled in for a siege . . . until Prince Maegor appeared in the sky above, astride Balerion. The Conqueror's son had claimed a dragon at last, and none other than the Black Dread, the greatest of them all.

Rather than face his fires, the Eyrie's garrison seized the pretender and delivered him to Lord Royce, opening the Moon Door once again and serving Jonos the kinslayer as he had served his brother. Surrender saved the pretender's followers from burning, but not from death. After taking possession of the Eyrie, Prince Maegor executed them to a man. Even the highest born amongst them were denied the honor of dying by sword; traitors deserved only a rope, Maegor decreed, so the captured knights were hanged naked from the walls of the Eyrie, kicking as they strangled slowly. Hubert Arryn, a cousin to the dead brothers, was installed as Lord of the Vale. As he had already sired six sons by his lady wife, a Royce of Runestone, the Arryn succession was seen to be secure.

In the Iron Islands, Goren Greyjoy, Lord Reaper of Pyke, brought "King" Lodos (Second of That Name) to a similar swift end, marshaling a hundred longships to descend on Old Wyk and Great Wyk, where the pretender's followers were most numerous, and putting thousands of them to the sword. Afterward he had the head of the priest-king pickled in brine and sent to King's Landing. King Aenys was so pleased by the gift that he offered Greyjoy any boon he might desire. This proved unwise. Lord Goren, wishing to prove himself a true son of the Drowned God, asked the king for the right to expel all the septons and septas who had come to the Iron Islands after the Conquest to convert the ironborn to the worship of the Seven. King Aenys had no choice but to agree.

The largest and most threatening rebellion remained that of the Vulture King along the Dornish marches. Though Princess Deria continued to issue denunciations from Sunspear, there were many who suspected that she was playing a double game, for she did not take the field against the rebels and was rumored to be sending them men, money, and supplies. Whether that was true or not, hundreds of Dornish knights and several thousand seasoned spearmen had joined the Vulture King's rabble, and the rabble itself had swelled enormously, to more than thirty thousand men. So large had his host become that the Vulture King made an ill-considered decision and divided his strength. Whilst he marched west against Nightsong and Horn Hill with half the Dornish power, the other half went east to besiege Stonehelm, seat of House

Swann, under the command of Lord Walter Wyl, the son of the Widow-lover.

Both hosts met with disaster. Orys Baratheon, known now as Orys One-Hand, rode forth from Storm's End one last time, to smash the Dornish beneath the walls of Stonehelm. When Walter Wyl was delivered into his hands, wounded but alive, Lord Orys said, "Your father took my hand. I claim yours as repayment." So saying, he hacked off Lord Walter's sword hand. Then he took his other hand, and both his feet as well, calling them his "usury." Strange to say, Lord Baratheon died on the march back to Storm's End, of the wounds he himself had taken during the battle, but his son Davos always said he died content, smiling at the rotting hands and feet that dangled in his tent like a string of onions.

The Vulture King himself fared little better. Unable to capture Nightsong, he abandoned the siege and marched west, only to have Lady Caron sally forth behind him, to join up with a strong force of marchmen led by Harmon Dondarrion, the mutilated Lord of Blackhaven. Meanwhile Lord Samwell Tarly of Horn Hill suddenly appeared athwart the Dornish line of march with several thousand knights and archers. "Savage Sam," that lord was called, and so he proved in the bloody battle that ensued, cutting down dozens of Dornishmen with his great Valyrian steel blade, Heartsbane. The Vulture King had twice as many men as his three foes combined, but most were untrained and undisciplined, and when faced with armored knights at front and rear, their ranks shattered. Throwing down their spears and shields, the Dornish broke and ran, making for the distant mountains, but the marcher lords rode after them and cut them down, in what became known after as "the Vulture Hunt."

As for the rebel king himself, the man who called himself the Vulture King was taken alive, and tied naked between two posts by Savage Sam Tarly. The singers like to say that he was torn to pieces by the very vultures from whom he took his style, but in truth he perished of thirst and exposure, and the birds did not descend on him until well after he was dead. (In later centuries, several other men would take the title "Vulture King," but whether they were of the same blood as the first, no man can say).

The first of the rebels proved to be the last as well, but Harren the Red was at last brought to bay in a village west of the Gods Eye. The outlaw king did not die meekly. In his last fight, he slew the King's Hand, Lord Alyn Stokeworth, before being cut down by Stokeworth's squire, Bernarr Brune. A grateful King Aenys conferred knighthood on Brune, and rewarded Davos Baratheon, Samwell Tarly, No-Nose Dondarrion, Ellyn Caron, Allard Royce, and Goren Greyjoy with gold, offices, and honors. The greatest plaudits he bestowed on his own brother. On his return to King's Landing, Prince Maegor was hailed as a hero. King Aenys embraced him before a cheering throng, and named him Hand of the King. And when two young dragons hatched amidst the firepits of Dragonstone at the end of that year, it was taken for a sign.

But the amity between the Dragon's sons did not long endure.

It may be that conflict was inevitable, for the two brothers had very different natures. Kindhearted and soft-spoken, it was said of King Aenys that he loved his wife, his children, and his people, and wished only to be loved in turn. Sword and lance had long ago lost whatever appeal they ever had for him. Instead His Grace dabbled in alchemy, astronomy, and astrology, delighted in music and dance, wore the finest silks, samites, and velvets, and enjoyed the company of maesters, septons, and wits.

His brother Maegor, taller, broader, and fearsomely strong, had no patience for any of that, but lived for war, tourneys, and battle. He was rightly regarded as one of the finest knights in Westeros, though his savagery in the field and his harshness toward defeated foes was oft remarked upon as well. King Aenys sought always to please; when faced with difficulties, he would answer with soft words, whereas Maegor's reply was ever steel and fire. Grand Maester Gawen wrote that Aenys trusted everyone, Maegor no one. The king was easily influenced, Gawen observed, swaying this way and that like a reed into the wind, like as not to heed whichever councillor last had his ear. Prince Maegor, on the other hand, was rigid as an iron rod, unyielding, unbending.

Despite such differences, the sons of the Dragon continued to rule together amicably for the best part of two years. But in 39 AC, Queen Alyssa gave King Aenys yet another heir, a girl she named Vaella, who sadly died in the cradle not long after. Perhaps it was this continued proof of the queen's fertility that drove Prince Maegor to do what he did. Whatever the reason, the prince shocked the realm and the king both when he suddenly announced that Lady Ceryse was barren, and he had therefore taken a second wife in Alys Harroway, daughter of the new Lord of Harrenhal. The wedding was performed on Dragonstone, under the aegis of the Dowager Queen Visenya. As the castle septon refused to officiate, Maegor and his new bride were wed in a Valyrian rite, "wed by blood and fire."

The marriage took place without the leave, knowledge, or presence of King Aenys. When it became known, the two half brothers quarreled bitterly. Nor was His Grace alone in his wroth. Lord Hightower, father of Lady Ceryse, made protest to the king, demanding that Lady Alys be put aside. And in the Starry Sept at Oldtown, the High Septon went even further, denouncing Maegor's marriage as sin and fornication, and calling the prince's new bride "this whore of Harroway." No true son or daughter of the Seven would ever bow to such, he thundered. Prince Maegor remained defiant. His father had taken both of his sisters to wife, he pointed out; the strictures of the Faith might rule lesser men, but not the blood of the Dragon. No words of King Aenys could heal the wound his brother's words thus opened, and many pious lords throughout the Seven Kingdoms condemned the marriage, and began to speak openly of "Maegor's Whore."

Vexed and angry, King Aenys gave his brother a choice: put Alys Harroway aside and return to Lady Ceryse, or suffer five years of exile. Prince Maegor chose exile. In 40 AC he departed for Pentos, taking Lady Alys, Balerion his dragon, and the sword Blackfyre (it is said that Aenys requested that his brother return Blackfyre, to which request Prince Maegor replied, "Your Grace is welcome to try and take her from me"). Lady Ceryse was left abandoned in King's Landing.

To replace his brother as Hand, King Aenys turned to Septon Murmison, a pious cleric said to be able to heal the sick by the laying on of hands. (The king had him lay hands on Lady Ceryse's belly every night, in the hopes that his brother might repent his folly if his lawful wife could be made fertile, but the lady soon grew weary of the nightly ritual and departed King's Landing for Oldtown, where she rejoined her father in the Hightower.) No doubt His Grace hoped the choice would appease the Faith. If so, he was wrong. Septon Murmison could no more heal the realm than he could make Ceryse Hightower fecund. The High

Septon continued to thunder, and all through the realm the lords in their halls spoke of the king's weakness. "How can he rule the Seven Kingdoms when he cannot even rule his brother?" it was said.

Yet the king remained strangely oblivious to the discontent in the realm. Peace had returned, his troublesome brother was safely out of sight across the narrow sea, and a great new castle had begun to rise atop Aegon's High Hill: built all in pale red stone, the king's new seat would be larger and more lavish than Dragonstone, more beautiful than Harrenhal, with massive walls and barbicans and towers capable of withstanding any enemy. The Red Keep, the people of King's Landing named it. Its building had become the king's obsession. "My descendants shall rule from here for a thousand years," His Grace declared. And thinking of those descendants, in 41 AC Aenys Targaryen made a disastrous blunder, and gave the hand of his daughter Rhaena in marriage to her brother Aegon, heir to the Iron Throne.

The princess was eighteen, the prince fifteen. A royal wedding is a joyous event, the occasion for celebration, but this was the sort of incestuous union that the High Septon had warned against, and the Starry Sept condemned it as an obscenity and warned that children born of it would be "abominations in the sight of gods and men." On the day of the wedding, the streets outside the Sept of Remembrance—built by a previous High Septon atop the Hill of Rhaenys, and named in honor of the fallen queen—were lined with Warrior's Sons in gleaming silver armor, scowling at the wedding guests as they passed by, afoot, ahorse, or in litters. The wiser lords, perhaps expecting that, had stayed away.

Those who did come to bear witness saw more than a wedding. At the feast afterward, King Aenys compounded his misjudgment by granting the title Prince of Dragonstone to his heir Aegon. A hush fell over the hall at those words, for all present knew that title had hitherto belonged to Prince Maegor. At the high table, Queen Visenya rose and stalked from the hall without the king's leave. That night she mounted Vhagar and returned to Dragonstone, and it is written that when her dragon passed before the moon, that orb turned as red as blood.

Aenys Targaryen did not seem to comprehend the extent to which he had roused the realm against him. Thinking to win back the favor of the smallfolk, he sent Aegon and Rhaena on a royal progress, only to find that they were jeered wherever they went. Septon Murmison, his Hand, was expelled from the Faith in punishment for performing the nuptials, whereupon the king wrote to the High Septon, asking that His High Holiness restore "my good Murmison," and explaining the long history of brother/sister marriages in old Valyria. The High Septon's reply was so blistering that His Grace went pale when he read it. Far from relenting, the Shepherd of the Faithful addressed Aenys as "King Abomination," declared him a pretender and a tyrant, with no right to rule the Seven Kingdoms.

The Faithful were listening. Less than a fortnight later, as Septon Murmison was crossing the city in his litter, a group of Poor Fellows came swarming from an alley and hacked him to pieces with their axes. The Warrior's Sons began to fortify the Hill of Rhaenys, turning the Sept of Remembrance into their citadel. With the Red Keep still years away from completion, the king decided that his manse atop Visenya's Hill was too vulnerable and made plans to remove himself to Dragonstone with Queen Alyssa and their younger children. It was a wise precaution. Three days before they were to sail, two Poor Fellows scaled the manse's walls and broke into the king's bedchamber. Only the timely intervention of Ser Raymont Baratheon of the Kingsguard saved Aenys from death.

His Grace was trading Visenya's Hill for Visenya herself. On Dragonstone the Queen Dowager famously greeted him with, "You are a fool and a weakling, nephew. Do you think any man would ever have dared speak so to your father? You have a dragon. Use him. Fly to Oldtown and make this Starry Sept another Harrenhal. Or give me leave, and let me roast this pious fool for you. Vhagar grows old, but her fires still burn hot." Aenys would not hear of it. Instead he sent the Queen Dowager to her chambers in Sea Dragon Tower, and ordered her to remain there.

By the end of 41 AC, much of the realm was deep in the throes of a full-fledged rebellion against House Targaryen. The four false kings who had arisen on the death of Aegon the Conqueror now seemed like so many posturing fools against the threat posed by this new rising, for these rebels believed themselves soldiers of the Seven, fighting a holy war against godless tyranny.

Dozens of pious lords throughout the Seven Kingdoms took up the cry, pulling down the king's banners and declaring for the Starry Sept. The Warrior's Sons seized the gates of King's Landing, giving them control over who might enter and leave the city, and drove the workmen from the unfinished Red Keep. Thousands of Poor Fellows took to the roads, forcing travelers to declare whether they stood with "the gods or the abomination," and remonstrating outside castle gates until their lords came forth to denounce the Targaryen king. Prince Aegon and his wife were forced to abandon their progress, and take shelter in Crakehall castle. An envoy from the Iron Bank of Braavos, sent to Oldtown to treat with Lord Hightower, wrote to the bank to say that the High Septon was "the true king of Westeros, in all but name."

The corning of the new year found King Aenys still on Dragonstone, sick with fear and indecision. His Grace was but thirty-five years of age, but it was said that he looked like a man of sixty, and Grand Maester Gawen reported that he oft took to his bed with loose bowels and stomach cramps. When none of the Grand Maester's cures proved efficacious, the Dowager Queen took charge of the king's care, and Aenys seemed to improve for a time . . . only to suffer a sudden collapse when word reached him that thousands of Poor Fellows had surrounded Crakehall, where his son and daughter were reluctant "guests." Three days later, the king was dead.

Like his father, Aenys Targaryen, the First of His Name, was given over to the flames in the yard at Dragonstone. His funeral was attended by his sons Viserys and Jaehaerys, twelve and seven years of age respectively, and his daughter Alysanne, five. Queen Alyssa sang a dirge for him. The Dowager Queen Visenya was not present. Within an hour of the king's death, she had mounted Vhagar and flown east, across the narrow sea.

When she returned, Prince Maegor was with her, on Balerion.

Maegor descended on Dragonstone only long enough to claim the crown; not the ornate golden crown Aenys had favored, with its images of the Seven, but the iron crown of their father set with its blood-red rubies. His mother placed it on his head, and the lords and knights gathered there knelt as he proclaimed himself Maegor of House Targaryen, First of His Name, King of the Andals, the Rhoynar, and the First Men, and Protector of the Realm.

Only Grand Maester Gawen dared object. By all the laws of inheritance, laws that the Conqueror himself had affirmed after the Conquest, the Iron Throne should pass to King Aenys's son Aegon, the aged maester said. "The Iron Throne will go to the man who has the strength to seize it," Maegor replied. Whereupon he decreed the immediate execution of the Grand Maester, taking off Gawen's old grey head himself with a single swing of Blackfyre. Queen Alyssa and her children were not on hand to witness King Maegor's coronation. She had taken them from Dragonstone within hours of her husband's funeral, crossing to her lord father's castle on nearby Driftmark. When told, Maegor gave a shrug . . . then retired to the Chamber of the Painted Table with a maester, to dictate letters to lords great and small throughout the realm.

A hundred ravens flew within the day. The next day, Maegor flew as well. Mounting Balerion, he crossed Blackwater Bay to King's Landing, accompanied by the Dowager Queen Visenya upon Vhagar. The return of the dragons set off riots in the city, as hundreds tried to flee, only to find the gates closed and barred. The Warrior's Sons held the city walls, the chaos that would be the Red Keep, and the Hill of Rhaenys, where they had made the Sept of Remembrance their own fortress. The Targaryens raised their standards atop Visenya's Hill and called for leal men to gather to them. Thousands did. Visenya Targaryen proclaimed that her son Maegor had come to be their king. "A true king, blood of Aegon the Conqueror, who was my brother, my husband, and my love. If any man questions my son's right to the Iron Throne, let him prove his claim with his body."

The Warrior's Sons were not slow to accept her challenge. Down from the Hill of Rhaenys they rode, seven hundred knights in silvered steel led by their grand captain, Ser Damon Morrigen, called Damon the Devout. "Let us not bandy words," Maegor told him. "Swords will decide this matter." Ser Damon agreed; the gods would grant victory to him whose cause was just, he said. "Let each side have seven champions, as it was done in Andalos of old. Can you find six men to stand beside you?" For Aenys had taken the Kingsguard to Dragonstone, and Maegor stood alone.

The king turned to the crowd. "Who will come and stand beside his king?" he called. Many turned away in fear or pretended that they did not hear, for the prowess of the Warrior's Sons was known to all. But at last one man offered himself: no knight, but a simple man-at-arms who called himself Dick Bean. "I been a king's man since I was a boy," he said. "I mean to die a king's man."

Only then did the first knight step forward. "This bean shames us all," he shouted. "Are there no true knights here? No leal men?" The speaker was Bernarr Brune, the squire who had slain Harren the Red and been knighted by King Aenys himself. His scorn drove others to offer their swords. The names of the four Maegor chose are writ large in the history of Westeros: Ser Bramm of Blackhull, a hedge knight; Ser Rayford Rosby; Ser Guy Lothston, called Guy the Glutton; and Ser Lucifer Massey, Lord of Stonedance.

The names of the seven Warrior's Sons have likewise come down to us. They were: Ser Damon Morrigen, called Damon the Devout, Grand Captain of the Warrior's Sons; Ser Lyle Bracken; Ser Harys Horpe, called Death's Head Harry; Ser Aegon Ambrose; Ser Dickon Flowers, the Bastard of Beesbury; Ser Willam the Wanderer; and Ser Garibald of the Seven Stars, the septon knight. It is written that Damon the Devout led a prayer, beseeching the Warrior to grant strength to their arms.

Afterward the Queen Dowager gave the command to begin. And the issue was joined.

Dick Bean died first, cut down by Lyle Bracken mere instants after the combat began. Thereafter accounts differ markedly. One chronicler says that when the hugely fat Ser Guy the Glutton was cut open, the remains of forty half-digested pies spilled out. Another claims Ser Garibald of the Seven Stars sang a paean as he fought. Several tell us that Lord Massey hacked off the arm of Harys Horpe. In one account, Death's Head Harry tossed his battle-axe into his other hand and buried it between Lord Massey's eyes. Other chroniclers suggest Ser Harys simply died. Some say the fight went on for hours, others that most of the combatants were down and dying in mere moments. All agree that great deeds were done and mighty blows exchanged, until the end found Maegor Targaryen standing alone against Damon the Devout and Willam the Wanderer. Both of the Warrior's Sons were badly wounded, and His Grace had Blackfyre in his hand, but even so, it was a near thing, the singers and maesters are agreed. Even as he fell, Ser Willam dealt the king a terrible blow to the head that cracked his helm and left him insensate. Many thought Maegor dead as well, until his mother removed his broken helm. "The king breathes," she proclaimed. "The king lives." The victory was his.

Seven of the mightiest of the Warrior's Sons were dead, including their commander, but more than seven hundred remained, armed and armored and gathered about the crown of the hill. Queen Visenya commanded her son to be taken to the maesters. As the litter bearers bore him down the hill, the Swords of the Faith dropped to their knees in submission. The Dowager Queen ordered them to return to their fortified sept atop the Hill of Rhaenys.

For twenty-seven days Maegor Targaryen lingered at the point of death, whilst maesters treated him with potions and poultices and septons prayed above his bed. In the Sept of Remembrance, the Warrior's Sons prayed as well, and argued about their course. Some felt the order had no choice but to accept Maegor as king, since the gods had blessed him with victory; others insisted that they were bound by oath to obey the High Septon, and fight on.

The Kingsguard arrived from Dragonstone in the nonce. At the command of the Dowager Queen, they took command of the thousands of Targaryen loyalists in the city and surrounded the Hill of Rhaenys. On Driftmark, the widowed Queen Alyssa proclaimed her own son Aegon the true king. In the Citadel of Oldtown, the archmaesters met in Conclave to debate the succession and choose a new grand maester. Thousands of Poor Fellows streamed toward King's Landing. Those from the west followed the hedge knight Ser Horys Hill, those from the south a gigantic axeman called Wat the Hewer. When the ragged bands encamped about castle Crakehall left to join their fellows on the march, Prince Aegon and Princess Rhaena were finally able to depart. Abandoning their royal progress, they made their way to Casterly Rock, where Lord Lyman Lannister offered them his protection. It was his wife, the Lady Jocasta, who first discerned that Princess Rhaena was with child.

On the twenty-eighth day after the Trial of Seven, a ship arrived from Pentos upon the evening tide, carrying two women and six hundred sellswords. Alys of House Harroway, Maegor Targaryen's second wife, had returned to Westeros ... but not alone. With her sailed another woman, a pale raven-haired beauty known only as Tyanna of the Tower. Some said the woman was Maegor's concubine. Others named her Lady Alys's paramour. The natural daughter of a Pentoshi magister, Tyanna was a tavern dancer who had risen to be a courtesan. She was rumored to be a poisoner and sorceress as well. Many queer tales were told about her ... yet as soon as she arrived, Queen Visenya dismissed her son's maesters and septons and gave Maegor over to Tyanna's care.

The next morning, the king awoke, rising with the sun. When Maegor appeared on the walls of the Red Keep, standing between Alys Harroway and Tyanna of Pentos, the crowds cheered wildly, and the city erupted in celebration. But the revels died away when Maegor mounted Balerion and descended upon the Hill of Rhaenys, where seven hundred of the Warrior's Sons were at their morning prayers in the fortified sept. As dragonfire set the building aflame, archers and spearmen waited outside for those who came bursting through the doors. It was said the screams of the burning men could be heard throughout the city, and a pall of smoke lingered over King's Landing for days. Thus did the cream of the Warrior's Sons meet their fiery end. Though other chapters remained in Oldtown, Lannisport, Gulltown, and Stoney Sept, the order would never again approach its former strength.

King Maegor's war against the Faith Militant had just begun, however. It would continue for the remainder of his reign. The king's first act upon resuming the Iron Throne was to command the Poor Fellows swarming toward the city to lay down their weapons, under penalty of proscription and death. When his decree had no effect, His Grace commanded "all leal lords" to take the field and disperse the Faith's ragged hordes by force. In response, the High Septon in Oldtown called upon "true and pious children of the gods" to take up arms in defense of the Faith, and put an end to the reign of "dragons and monsters and abominations."

Battle was joined first in the Reach, at the town of Stonebridge. There nine thousand Poor Fellows under Wat the Hewer found themselves caught between six lordly hosts as they attempted to cross the Mander. With half his men north of the river and half on the south, Wat's army was cut to pieces. His untrained and undisciplined followers, clad in boiled leather, roughspun, and scraps of rusted steel, and

armed largely with woodsmen's axes, sharpened sticks, and farm implements, proved utterly unable to stand against the charge of armored
knights on heavy horses. So grievous was the slaughter that the Mander
ran red for twenty leagues, and thereafter the town and castle where the
battle had been fought became known as Bitterbridge. Wat himself was
taken alive, though not before slaying half a dozen knights, amongst
them Loadows of Grassy Vale, commander of the king's host. The giant
was delivered to King's Landing in chains.

By then Ser Horys Hill had reached the Great Fork of the Blackwater
with an even larger host; close on thirteen thousand Poor Fellows, their
ranks stiffened by the addition of two hundred mounted Warrior's Sons
from Stoney Sept, and the household knights and feudal levies of a dozen
rebel lords from the westerlands and riverlands. Lord Rupert Falwell,
famed as the Fighting Fool, led the ranks of the pious who had answered
the High Septon's call; with him rode Ser Lyonel Lorch, Ser Alyn Terrick,
Lord Tristifer Wayn, Lord Jon Lychester, and many other puissant
knights. The army of the Faithful numbered twenty thousand men.

King Maegor's army was of like size, however, and His Grace had
almost twice as much armored horse, as well as a large contingent of
longbowmen, and the king himself riding Balerion. Even so, the battle
proved a savage struggle. The Fighting Fool slew two knights of the
Kingsguard before he himself was cut down by the Lord of Maiden-
pool. Big Jon Hogg, fighting for the king, was blinded by a sword slash
early in the battle, yet rallied his men and led a charge that broke
through the lines of the Faithful and put the Poor Fellows to flight. A
rainstorm dampened Balerion's fires but could not quench them entirely, and amidst smoke and screams King Maegor descended again
and again to serve his foes with flame. By nightfall victory was his, as
the remaining Poor Fellows threw down their axes and streamed away
in all directions.

Triumphant, Maegor returned to King's Landing to seat himself
once more upon the Iron Throne. When Wat the Hewer was delivered
to him, chained yet still defiant, Maegor took off his limbs with the giant's own axe, but commanded his maesters to keep the man alive "so he
might attend my wedding." Then His Grace announced his intent to
take Tyanna of Pentos as his third wife. Though it was whispered that

his mother the Queen Dowager had no love for the Pentoshi sorceress, only Grand Maester Myres dared speak against her openly. "Your one true wife awaits you in the Hightower," Myres said. The king heard him out in silence, then descended from the throne, drew Blackfyre, and slew him where he stood.

Maegor Targaryen and Tyanna of the Tower were wed atop the Hill of Rhaenys, amidst the ashes and bones of the Warrior's Sons who had died there. It was said that Maegor had to put a dozen septons to death before he found one willing to perform the ceremony. Wat the Hewer, limbless, was kept alive to witness the marriage. King Aenys's widow, Queen Alyssa, was present as well, with her younger sons Viserys and Jaehaerys and her daughter Alysanne. A visit from the Dowager Queen and Vhagar had persuaded her to leave her sanctuary on Driftmark and return to court, where Alyssa and her brothers and cousins of House Velaryon did homage to Maegor as the true king. The widowed queen was even compelled to join the other ladies of the court in disrobing His Grace and escorting him to the nuptial chamber to consummate his marriage, a bedding ceremony presided over by the king's second wife, Alys Harroway. That task done, Alyssa and the other ladies took their leave of the royal bedchamber, but Alys remained, joining the king and his newest wife in a night of carnal lust.

Across the realm in Oldtown, the High Septon was loud in his denunciations of "the abomination and his whores," whilst the king's first wife, Ceryse of House Hightower, continued to insist that she was Maegor's only lawful queen. And in the westerlands, Aegon Targaryen, Prince of Dragonstone, remained adamant as well. As the eldest son of King Aenys, the Iron Throne was his by right. Prince Aegon was but seventeen, however, and the son of a weak father besides; few lords cared to risk King Maegor's wroth by supporting his claim. His own mother Queen Alyssa had abandoned his cause, men whispered to each other. Even Lyman Lannister, the prince's host, would not pledge his sword to the young pretender though he did stand firm when Maegor demanded that Aegon and his sister be expelled from Casterly Rock.

And thus it was there at Casterly Rock that Princess Rhaena gave birth to Aegon's daughters, twins they named Aerea and Rhaella. From the Starry Sept came another blistering proclamation. These children too were abominations, the High Septon proclaimed, the fruits of lust and incest, and accursed of the gods.

The dawn of the year 43 AC found King Maegor in King's Landing, where he had taken personal charge of the construction of the Red Keep. Much of the finished work was now undone or changed, new builders and workmen were brought in, and secret passages and tunnels crept through the depths of Aegon's High Hill. As the red stone towers rose, the king commanded the building of a castle within the castle, a fortified redoubt surrounded by a dry moat that would soon be known to all as Maegor's Holdfast.

In that same year, Maegor made Lord Lucas Harroway, father of his wife Queen Alys, his new Hand . . . but it was not the Hand who had the king's ear. His Grace might rule the Seven Kingdoms, men whispered, but he himself was ruled by the three queens: his mother Queen Visenya, his paramour Queen Alys, and the Pentoshi witch Queen Tyanna. "The mistress of whispers," Tyanna was called, and "the king's raven," for her black hair. She spoke with rats and spiders, it was said, and all the vermin of King's Landing came to her by night to tell tales of any fool rash enough to speak against the king.

Meanwhile, thousands of Poor Fellows still haunted the roads and wild places of the Reach, the Trident, and the Vale; though they would never again assemble in large numbers to face the king in open battle, the Stars fought on in smaller ways, falling upon travelers and swarming over towns, villages, and poorly defended castles, slaying the king's loyalists wherever they found them. Ser Horys Hill had escaped the battle at Great Fork, but defeat and flight had tarnished him, and his followers were few. The new leaders of the Poor Fellows were men like Ragged Silas, Septon Moon, and Dennis the Lame, hardly distinguishable from outlaws. One of their most savage captains was a woman called Poxy Jeyne Poore, whose savage followers made the woods between King's Landing and Storm's End all but impassable to honest travelers.

Meanwhile, the Warrior's Sons had chosen a new grand captain in the person of Ser Joffrey Doggett, the Red Dog of the Hills, who was determined to restore the order to its former glory. When Ser Joffrey set out from Lannisport to seek the blessing of the High Septon, a hundred men rode with him. By the time he arrived in Oldtown, so many knights and squires and freeriders had joined him that his numbers had swollen to two thousand. Elsewhere in the realm, other restless lords and men of faith were gathering men as well, and plotting ways to bring the dragons down.

None of this had gone unnoticed. Ravens flew to every corner of the realm, summoning lords and landed knights of doubtful loyalty to King's Landing, to bend the knee, swear homage, and deliver a son or daughter as a hostage for their obedience. The Stars and Swords were outlawed; membership in either order would henceforth be punishable by death. The High Septon was commanded to deliver himself to the Red Keep, to stand trial for high treason.

His High Holiness responded from the Starry Sept, commanding the king to present himself in Oldtown, to beg the forgiveness of the gods for his sins and cruelties. Many of the Faithful echoed his defiance. Some pious lords did travel to King's Landing to do homage and present hostages, but more did not, trusting to their numbers and the strength of their castles to keep them safe.

King Maegor let the poisons fester for almost half a year, so engrossed was he in the building of his Red Keep. It was his mother who struck first. The Dowager Queen mounted Vhagar and brought fire and blood to the Reach as once she had to Dorne. In a single night, the seats of House Blanetree, House Terrick, House Deddings, House Lychester, and House Wayn were set aflame. Then Maegor himself took wing, flying Balerion to the westerlands, where he burned the castles of the Broomes, the Falwells, the Lorches, the Myatts, and the other "pious lords" who had defied his royal summons. Lastly he descended upon the seat of House Doggett, reducing the hall and stables to ash. The fires claimed the lives of Ser Joffrey's father, mother, and young sister, along with their sworn swords, serving men, and chattel. As pillars of smoke rose all through the westerlands and the Reach, Vhagar and Balerion turned south. Another Lord Hightower, counseled by another High Septon, had opened the gates of Oldtown during the Conquest, but now it seemed as if the greatest and most populous city in Westeros must surely burn.

Thousands fled the city that night, streaming from the gates or taking ship for distant ports. Thousands more took to the streets in drunken revelry. "This is a night for song and sin and drink," men told one another, "for come the morrow, the virtuous and the vile alike shall burn together." Others gathered in septs and temples and ancient woods to pray they might be spared. In the Starry Sept, the High Septon railed and thundered, calling down the wroth of the gods upon the Targaryens. The archmaesters of the Citadel met in Conclave. The men of the City Watch filled sacks with sand and pails with water to fight the fires they knew were coming. Along the city walls, crossbows, scorpions, spit-fires, and spear-throwers were hoisted onto the battlements in hopes of bringing down the dragons when they appeared. Led by Ser Morgan Hightower, a younger brother of the Lord of Oldtown, two hundred Warrior's Sons spilled forth from their chapterhouse to defend His High Holiness, surrounding the Starry Sept with a ring of steel. Atop the Hightower, the great beacon fire turned a baleful green as Lord Martyn Hightower called his banners. Oldtown waited for the dawn, and the coming of the dragons.

And the dragons came. Vhagar first, as the sun was rising, then Balerion, just before midday. But they found the gates of the city open, the battlements unmanned, and the banners of House Targaryen, House Tyrell, and House Hightower flying side by side atop the city walls. The Dowager Queen Visenya was the first to learn the news. Sometime during the blackest hour of that long and dreadful night, the High Septon had died.

A man of three-and-fifty, as tireless as he was fearless, and to all appearances in robust good health, this High Septon had been renowned for his strength. More than once he had preached for a day and a night without taking sleep or nourishment. His sudden death shocked the city and dismayed his followers. Its causes are debated to this day. Some say that His High Holiness took his own life, in what was either the act of a craven afraid to face the wroth of King Maegor or a noble sacrifice to spare the goodfolk of Oldtown from dragonfire. Others claim the Seven struck him down for the sin of pride, for heresy, treason, and arrogance.

Many and more remain certain he was murdered ... but by whom? Ser Morgan Hightower did the deed at the command of his lord brother, some say (and Ser Morgan was seen entering and leaving the High Septon's privy chambers that night). Others point to the Lady Patrice Hightower, Lord Martyn's maiden aunt and a reputed witch (who did indeed seek an audience with His High Holiness at dusk, though he was alive when she departed). The archmaesters of the Citadel are also suspected, though whether they made use of the dark arts, an assassin, or a poisoned scroll is still a matter of some debate (messages went back and forth between the Citadel and the Starry Sept all night). And there are still others who hold them all blameless and lay the High Septon's death at the door of another rumored sorceress, the Dowager Queen Visenya Targaryen.

The truth will likely never be known . . . but the swift reaction of Lord Martyn when word reached him at the Hightower is beyond dispute. At once he dispatched his own knights to disarm and arrest the Warrior's Sons, amongst them his own brother. The city gates were opened, and Targaryen banners raised along the walls. Even before Vhagar's wings were sighted, Lord Hightower's men were rousting the Most Devout from their beds and marching them to the Starry Sept at spearpoint to choose a new high septon.

It required but a single ballot. Almost as one, the wise men and women of the Faith turned to a certain Septon Pater. Ninety years old, blind, stooped, and feeble, but famously amiable, the new High Septon almost collapsed beneath the weight of the crystal crown when it was placed upon his head . . . but when Maegor Targaryen appeared before him in the Starry Sept, he was only too pleased to bless him as king and anoint his head with holy oils, even if he did forget the words of the blessing.

Queen Visenya soon returned to Dragonstone with Vhagar, but King Maegor remained in Oldtown for almost half the year, holding court and presiding over trials. To the captive Swords of the Warrior's Sons, a choice was given. Those who renounced their allegiance to the order would be permitted to travel to the Wall and live out their days as brothers of the Night's Watch. Those who refused could die as martyrs to their Faith. Three-quarters of the captives chose to take the black. The remainder died. Seven of their number, famous knights and the sons of lords, were given the honor of having King Maegor himself remove their heads with Blackfyre. The rest of the condemned were beheaded by their own former brothers-in-arms. Of all their number, only one man received a full royal pardon: Ser Morgan Hightower. The new High Septon formally dissolved both the Warrior's Sons and the Poor Fellows, commanding their remaining members to lay down their arms in the name of the gods. The Seven had no more need of warriors, proclaimed His High Holiness; henceforth the Iron Throne would protect and defend the Faith. King Maegor granted the surviving members of the Faith Militant till year's end to surrender their weapons and give up their rebellious ways. After that, those who remained defiant would find a bounty on their heads: a gold dragon for the head of any unrepentant Warrior's Son, a silver stag for the "lice-ridden" scalp of a Poor Fellow.

The new High Septon did not demur, nor did the Most Devout.

During his time at Oldtown, the king was also reconciled with his first wife, Queen Ceryse, the sister of his host, Lord Hightower. Her Grace agreed to accept the king's other wives, to treat them with respect and honor and speak no further ill against them, whilst Maegor swore to restore Ceryse to all the rights, incomes, and privileges due her as his wedded wife and queen. A great feast was held at the Hightower to celebrate their reconciliation; the revels even included a bedding and a "second consummation," so all men would know this to be a true and loving union.

How long King Maegor might have lingered at Oldtown cannot be known, for in the latter part of 43 AC word of another challenge to his throne reached his ears. His nephew Aegon, Prince of Dragonstone, had emerged from the west at last to stake his claim to the Iron Throne. Mounted on his own dragon Quicksilver, the eldest son of the late King Aenys had denounced his uncle as a tyrant and usurper, and was marching across the riverlands at the head of an army fifteen thousand strong. His followers were largely westermen and river lords; the Lords Tarbeck, Piper, Roote, Vance, Charlton, Frey, Paege, Parren, and Westerling were amongst them, joined by Lord Corbray of the Vale, the Bastard of Barrowton, and the fourth son of the Lord of Griffin's Roost.

Though their ranks included seasoned commanders and puissant knights, no great lords had rallied to Prince Aegon's cause . . . but Queen Tyanna, mistress of whisperers, wrote to warn Maegor that Storm's End, the Eyrie, Winterfell, and Casterly Rock had all been in secret communication with the widowed queen, Alyssa. Before declaring for the Prince of Dragonstone, they wished to be convinced he might prevail. Aegon required a victory.

Maegor denied him that. From Harrenhal came forth Lord Harroway, from Riverrun Lord Tully. Ser Davos Darklyn of the Kingsguard marshaled five thousand swords in King's Landing and struck out west to meet the rebels. Up from the Reach came Lord Rowan, Lord Merryweather, Lord Caswell, and their levies. Prince Aegon's slow-moving host found armies closing from all sides; each smaller than their own force, but so many that the young prince (still but seventeen) did not know where to turn. Lord Corbray advised him to engage each foe separately before they could join their powers, but Aegon was loath to divide his strength. Instead he chose to march on toward King's Landing.

Just south of the Gods Eye, he found Davos Darklyn's Kingslanders awthwart his path, sitting on high ground behind a wall of spears, even as scouts reported Lords Merryweather and Caswell advancing from the south, and Lords Tully and Harroway from the north. Prince Aegon ordered a charge, hoping to break through the Kingslanders before the other loyalists fell upon his flanks, and mounted Quicksilver to lead the attack himself. But scarce had he taken wing when he heard shouts and saw his men below pointing, to where Balerion the Black Dread had appeared in the southern sky.

King Maegor had come.

For the first time since the Doom of Valyria dragon contended with dragon in the sky, even as battle was joined below.

Quicksilver, a quarter the size of Balerion, was no match for the older, fiercer dragon, and her pale white fireballs were engulfed and washed away in great gouts of black flame. Then the Black Dread fell upon her from above, his jaws closing round her neck as he ripped one wing from her body. Screaming and smoking, the young dragon plunged to earth, and Prince Aegon with her.

The battle below was nigh as brief, if bloodier. Once Aegon fell, the rebels saw their cause was doomed and ran, discarding arms and armor as they fled. But the loyalist armies were all around them, and there was no escape. By day's end, two thousand of Aegon's men had died, against a hundred of the king's. Amongst the dead were Lord Alyn Tarbeck, Denys Snow, the Bastard of Barrowton, Lord Jon Piper, Lord Ronnel Vance, Ser Willam Whistler . . . and Aegon Targaryen, Prince of Dragonstone. The only notable loss amongst the loyalists was Ser Davos

Darklyn of the Kingsguard, slain by Lord Corbray with Lady Forlorn. Half a year of trials and executions followed. Queen Visenya persuaded her son to spare some of the rebellious lords, but even those who kept their lives lost lands and titles and were forced to give up hostages.

The forty-fourth year After the Conquest was a peaceful one, compared to what had gone before . . . but the maesters who chronicled those times wrote that the smell of blood and fire still hung heavy in the air. Maegor I Targaryen sat the Iron Throne as his Red Keep rose around him, but his court was grim and cheerless, despite the presence of three queens . . . or perhaps because of it. Each night he summoned one of his wives to his bed, yet still he remained childless, with no heir but for the sons and grandsons of his brother Aenys. "Maegor the Cruel," he was called, and "kinslayer" as well, though it was death to say either in his hearing.

In Oldtown, the ancient High Septon died, and another was raised up in his place. Though he spoke no word against the king or his queens, the enmity between King Maegor and the Faith endured. Hundreds of Poor Fellows had been hunted down and slain, their scalps delivered to the king's men for the bounty, but thousands more still roamed the woods and hedges and the wild places of the Seven Kingdoms, cursing the Targaryens with their every breath. One band even crowned their own High Septon, in the person of a bearded brute named Septon Moon. And a few Warrior's Sons still endured, led by Ser Joffrey Doggett, the Red Dog of the Hills. Outlawed and condemned, the order no longer had the strength to meet the king's men in open battle, so the Red Dog sent them out in the guise of hedge knights, to hunt and slay Targaryen loyalists and "traitors to the Faith." Their first victim was Ser Morgan Hightower, late of their order, cut down and butchered on the road to Honeyholt. Old Lord Merryweather was the next to die, followed by Lord Rowan's son and heir, Davos Darklyn's aged father, even Blind John Hogg. Though the bounty for the head of a Warrior's Son was a golden dragon, the smallfolk and peasants of the realm hid and protected them, remembering what they had been.

On Dragonstone, the Dowager Queen Visenya had grown thin and haggard, the flesh melting from her bones. Her nephew's widow, the former Queen Alyssa, remained on the island as well, with her son Jaehaerys and her daughter Alysanne. Maegor had made them his mother's wards, prisoners in all but name, but Prince Viserys, the eldest surviving son of Aenys and Alyssa, was summoned to court by Maegor. A promising lad of fifteen years, skilled with sword and lance, Viserys was made squire to the king . . . with a Kingsguard knight for a shadow, to keep him away from plots and treasons.

For a brief while in 44 AC, it seemed as if the king might soon have that son he desired so desperately. Queen Alys announced she was with child, and the court rejoiced. Grand Maester Desmond confined Her Grace to her bed as she grew great with child, and took charge of her care, assisted by two septas, a midwife, and the queen's sisters Jeyne and Hanna. Maegor insisted that his other wives serve his pregnant queen as well.

During the third moon of her confinement, however, Lady Alys began to bleed heavily from the womb and lost the child. When King Maegor came to see the stillbirth, he was horrified to find the boy a monster, with twisted limbs, a huge head, and no eyes. "This cannot be my son," he roared in anguish. Then his grief turned to fury, and he ordered the immediate execution of the midwife and septas who had charge of the queen's care, and Grand Maester Desmond as well, sparing only Alys's sisters.

It is said that Maegor was seated on the Iron Throne with the head of the grand maester in his hands when Queen Tyanna came to tell him he had been deceived. The child was not his seed. Seeing Queen Ceryse return to court, old and bitter and childless, Alys Harroway had begun to fear that the same fate awaited her unless she gave the king a son, so she had turned to her lord father, the Hand of the King. On the nights when the king was sharing a bed with Queen Ceryse or Queen Tyanna, Lucas Harroway sent men to his daughter's bed to get her with child. Maegor refused to believe. He told Tyanna she was a jealous witch, and barren, throwing the grand maester's head at her. "Spiders do not lie," the mistress of the whisperers replied. She handed the king a list of names.

Written there were the names of twenty men alleged to have given their seed to Queen Alys. Old men and young, handsome men and homely ones, knights and squires, lords and servants, even grooms and smiths and singers; the King's Hand had cast a wide net, it seemed. The men had only one thing in common: all were men of proven potency known to have fathered healthy children.

Under torture, all but two confessed. One, a father of twelve, still had the gold paid him by Lord Harroway for his services. The questioning was carried out swiftly and secretly, so Lord Harroway and Queen Alys had no inkling of the king's suspicions until the Kingsguard burst in on them. Dragged from her bed, Queen Alys saw her sisters killed before her eyes as they tried to protect her. Her father, inspecting the Tower of the Hand, was flung from its roof to smash upon the stones below. Harroway's sons, brothers, and nephews were taken as well. Thrown onto the spikes that lined the dry moat around Maegor's Holdfast, some took hours to die; the simple-minded Horas Harroway was said to linger for days. The twenty names on Queen Tyanna's list soon joined them, and then another dozen men, named by the first twenty.

The worst death was reserved for Queen Alys herself, who was given over to her sister wife Tyanna for torment. Of her death we will not speak, for some things are best buried and forgotten. Suffice it to say that her dying took the best part of a fortnight, and that Maegor himself was present for all of it, a witness to her agony. After her death, the queen's body was cut into seven parts, and her pieces mounted on spikes above the seven gates of the city, where they remained until they rotted.

King Maegor himself departed King's Landing, assembling a strong force of knights and men-at-arms and marching on Harrenhal, to complete the destruction of House Harroway. The great castle on the Gods Eye was lightly held, and its castellan, a nephew of Lord Lucas and cousin to the late queen, opened his gates at the king's approach. Surrender did not save him; His Grace put the entire garrison to the sword, along with every man, woman, and child he found to have any drop of Harroway blood. Then he marched to Lord Harroway's Town on the Trident and did the same there.

In the aftermath of the bloodletting, men began to say that Harrenhal was cursed, for every lordly house to hold it had come to a bad and bloody end. Nonetheless, many ambitious king's men coveted Black Harren's mighty seat, with its broad and fertile lands . . . so many that King Maegor grew weary of their entreaties and decreed that Harrenhal should go to the strongest of them. Thus did twenty-three knights of the king's household fight with sword and mace and lance amidst the blood-soaked streets of Lord Harroway's Town. Ser Walton Towers emerged victorious, and Maegor named him Lord of Harrenhal . . . but the melee had been a savage affray, and Ser Walton did not live long to enjoy his lordship, dying of his wounds within the fortnight. Harrenhal passed to his eldest son, though its domains were much diminished, as the king granted Lord Harroway's Town to Lord Alton Butterwell, and the rest of the Harroway holdings to Lord Dormand Darry.

When at last Maegor returned to King's Landing to seat himself again upon the Iron Throne, he was greeted with the news that his mother Queen Visenya had died. Moreover, in the confusion that followed the death of the Queen Dowager, Queen Alyssa and her children found their way to a ship and made their escape from Dragonstone . . . to where, no man could say. They had even gone so far as to steal Dark Sister from Visenya's chambers as they fled.

His Grace ordered his mother's body burned, her bones and ashes interred beside those of her brother and sister. Then he told his knights to seize his squire, Prince Viserys. "Chain him in a black cell and question him sharply," Maegor commanded. "Ask him where his mother has gone."

"He may not know," said Ser Owen Bush, a knight of Maegor's Kingsguard. "Then let him die," the king answered famously. "Perhaps the bitch will turn up for his funeral."

Prince Viserys did not know where his mother had gone, not even when Tyanna of Pentos plied him with her dark arts. After nine days of questioning, he died. His body was left out in the ward of the Red Keep for a fortnight, at the king's command. "Let his mother come and claim him," Maegor said. But Queen Alyssa never appeared, and at last His Grace consigned his nephew to the fire. The prince was sixteen years old when he was killed, and had been much loved by smallfolk and lords alike. The realm wept for him.

In 45 AC, construction finally came to an end on the Red Keep.

King Maegor celebrated its completion by feasting the builders and workmen who had labored on the castle, sending them wagonloads of strong wine and sweetmeats, and whores from the city's finest brothels. The revels lasted for three days. Afterward, the king's knights moved in and put all the workmen to the sword, to prevent them from ever revealing the Red Keep's secrets. Their bones were interred beneath the castle that they had built.

Not long after the completion of the castle, Queen Ceryse was stricken with a sudden illness, and passed away. A rumor went around the court that Her Grace had given offense to the king with a shrewish remark, so he had commanded Ser Owen to remove her tongue. As the tale went, the queen had struggled, Ser Owen's knife had slipped, and the queen's throat had been slit. Though never proven, this story was widely believed at the time; today, however, most maesters believe it to be a slander concocted by the king's enemies to further blacken his repute. Whatever the truth, the death of his first wife left Maegor with but a single queen, the black-haired, black-hearted Pentoshi woman Tyanna, mistress of the spiders, who was hated and feared by all.

Hardly had the last stone been set on the Red Keep than Maegor commanded that the ruins of the Sept of Remembrance be cleared from the top of Rhaenys's Hill, and with them the bones and ashes of the Warrior's Sons who had perished there. In their place, he decreed, a great stone "stable for dragons" would be erected, a lair worthy of Balerion, Vhagar, and their get. Thus commenced the building of the Dragonpit. Perhaps unsurprisingly, it proved difficult to find builders, stonemasons, and laborers to work on the project. So many men ran off that the king was finally forced to use prisoners from the city's dungeons as his workforce, under the supervision of builders brought in from Myr and Volantis.

Late in the year 45 AC, King Maegor took the field once again to continue his war against the outlawed remnants of the Faith Militant, leaving Queen Tyanna to rule King's Landing together with the new Hand, Lord Edwell Celtigar. In the great wood south of the Blackwater, the king's forces hunted down scores of Poor Fellows who had taken refuge there, sending many to the Wall and hanging those who refused to take the black. Their leader, the woman known as Poxy Jeyne Poore, continued to elude the king until at last she was betrayed by three of her own followers, who received pardons and knighthoods as their reward.

Three septons traveling with His Grace declared Poxy Jeyne a witch, and Maegor ordered her to be burned alive in a field beside the Wendwater. When the day appointed for her execution came, three hundred of her followers, Poor Fellows and peasants all, burst from the woods to rescue her. The king had anticipated this, however, and his men were ready for the attack. The rescuers were surrounded and slaughtered. Amongst the last to die was their leader, who proved to be Ser Horys Hill, the bastard hedge knight who had escaped the carnage at the Great Fork three years earlier. This time he proved less fortunate.

Elsewhere in the realm, however, the tide of the times had begun to turn against the king. Smallfolk and lords alike had come to despise him for his many cruelties, and many began to give help and comfort to his enemies. Septon Moon, the "High Septon" raised up by the Poor Fellows against the man in Oldtown they called "the High Lickspittle," roamed the riverlands and Reach at will, drawing huge crowds whenever he emerged from the woods to preach against the king. The hill country north of the Golden Tooth was ruled in all but name by the Red Dog, Ser Joffrey Doggett, and neither Casterly Rock nor Riverrun seemed inclined to move against him. Dennis the Lame and Ragged Silas remained at large, and wherever they roamed, smallfolk helped keep them safe. Knights and men-at-arms sent out to bring them to justice oft vanished.

In 46 AC, King Maegor returned to the Red Keep with two thousand skulls, the fruits of a year of campaigning. They were the heads of Poor Fellows and Warrior's Sons, he announced, as he dumped them out beneath the Iron Throne . . . but it was widely believed that many of the grisly trophies belonged to simple crofters, field hands, and swineherds guilty of no crime but faith.

The coming of the new year found Maegor still without a son, not even a bastard who might be legitimized. Nor did it seem likely that Queen Tyanna would give him the heir that he desired. Whilst she continued to serve His Grace as mistress of whisperers, the king no longer sought her bed.

It was past time for him to take a new wife, Maegor's counsellors agreed . . . but they parted ways on who that wife should be. Grand Maester Benifer suggested a match with the proud and lovely Lady of Starfall, Clarisse Dayne, in the hopes of detaching her lands and House from Dorne. Alton Butterwell, master of coin, offered his widowed sister, a stout woman with seven children. Though admittedly no beauty, he argued, her fertility had been proved beyond a doubt. The King's Hand, Lord Celtigar, had two young maiden daughters, thirteen and twelve years of age respectively. He urged the king to take his pick of them, or marry both if he preferred. Lord Velaryon of Driftmark advised Maegor to send for his niece Princess Rhaena, his brother's daughter and the widow of his brother's son, and take her to wife. By wedding Rhaena, the king would unite their claims and strengthen the royal bloodline.

King Maegor listened to each man in turn. Though in the end he scorned most of the women they put forward, some of their reasons and arguments took root in him. He would have a woman of proven fertility, he decided, though not Butterwell's fat and homely sister. He would take more than one wife, as Lord Celtigar urged. Two wives would double his chances of getting a son; three wives would triple it. And one of those wives should surely be his niece; there was wisdom in Lord Velaryon's counsel. Queen Alyssa and her two youngest children remained in hiding (it was thought that they had fled across the narrow sea, to Tyrosh or perhaps Volantis), but they still represented a threat to Maegor's crown and any son he might father. Taking Aenys's daughter to wife would weaken any claims put forward by her younger siblings.

After the death of her husband in the Battle Beneath the Gods Eye, Rhaena Targaryen had acted quickly to protect her daughters. If Prince Aegon had truly been the king, then by law his eldest daughter Aerea stood his heir, and might therefore claim to be the rightful Queen of the Seven Kingdoms . . . but Aerea and her sister Rhaella were barely a year old, and Rhaena knew that to trumpet such claims would be tantamount to condemning them to death. Instead, she dyed their hair, changed their names, and sent them from her, entrusting them to certain powerful allies, who would see them fostered in good homes by worthy men who would have no inkling of their true identity. Even their mother must not know where the girls were going, the princess insisted; what she did not know she could not reveal, even under torture.

No such escape was possible for Rhaena Targaryen herself. Though she could change her name, dye her hair, and garb herself in a tavern wench's roughspun or the robes of a septa, there was no disguising her dragon. Dreamfyre was a slender, pale blue she-dragon with silvery markings who had already produced two clutches of eggs, and Rhaena had been riding her since the age of twelve. Dragons are not easily hidden. Instead the princess saddled her, and took them both as far from Maegor as she could, to Fair Isle, where Lord Farman granted her the hospitality of Faircastle, with its tall white towers rising high above the Sunset Sea. And there she rested, reading, praying, wondering how long she would be given before her uncle sent for her. Rhaena never doubted that he would, she said afterward; it was question of when, not if.

The summons came sooner than she would have liked though not as soon as she might have feared. There was no question of defiance. That would only bring the king down on Fair Isle with Balerion. Rhaena had grown fond of Lord Farman, and more than fond of his second son, Androw. She would not repay their kindness with fire and blood. She mounted Dreamfyre and flew to the Red Keep, where she learned that she must marry her uncle, her husband's killer.

And there as well Rhaena met her fellow brides, for this was to be a triple wedding. All three of the new queens-to-be were widows. Lady Jeyne of House Westerling had been married to Lord Alyn Tarbeck, who had marched beside Prince Aegon, and died with him in the Battle Beneath the Gods Eye. A few months later, she had given her late lord a posthumous son. Tall and slender, with lustrous brown hair, Lady Jeyne was being courted by a younger son of the Lord of Casterly Rock when Maegor sent for her, but this meant little and less to the king.

More troubling was the case of Lady Elinor of House Costayne, the fiery red-haired wife of Ser Theo Bolling, a landed knight who had fought for the king in his last campaign against the Poor Fellows. Though only nineteen, Lady Elinor had already given Bolling three sons when the king's eye fell upon her. The youngest boy was still at her breast when their father, Ser Theo, was arrested by two knights of the Kingsguard and charged with conspiring with Queen Alyssa to murder the king and place the boy Jaehaerys on the Iron Throne. Though Bolling protested his innocence, he was found guilty and beheaded the same day. King Maegor gave his widow seven days to mourn, in honor of the gods, then summoned her to tell her they would marry.

At the town of Stoney Sept, Septon Moon appeared to denounce

King Maegor's wedding plans, and hundreds of townfolk cheered wildly, but few others dared to raise their voices against His Grace. The High Septon took ship at Oldtown, sailing to King's Landing to perform the marriage rites. On a warm spring day in the forty-seventh year After the Conquest, Maegor Targaryen took three wives in the ward of the Red Keep. Though each of his new queens was garbed and cloaked in the colors of her father's House, the people of King's Landing called them "the Black Brides," for all were widows.

The presence of Lady Jeyne's son and Lady Elinor's three boys at the wedding ensured that they would play their parts in the ceremony, but there were many who expected some show of defiance from Princess Rhaena. Such hopes were quelled when Queen Tyanna appeared, escorting two young girls with silver hair and purple eyes, clad in the red and black of House Targaryen. "You were foolish to think you could hide them from me," Tyanna told the princess. Rhaena bowed her head, and spoke her vows, weeping.

Many queer and contradictory stories are told of the night that followed, and with the passage of so many years it is difficult to separate truth from legends. Did the three Black Brides share a single bed, as some claim? It seems unlikely. Did His Grace visit all three women during the night, and consummate all three unions? Perhaps. Did Princess Rhaena attempt to kill the king with a dagger concealed beneath her pillows, as she later claimed? Did Elinor Costayne scratch the king's back to bloody ribbons as they coupled? Did Jeyne Westerling drink the fertility potion that Queen Tyanna supposedly brought her, or throw it in the older woman's face? Was such a potion ever mixed or offered? The first account of it does not appear until well into the reign of King Jaehaerys, twenty years after both women were dead.

This we know. In the immediate aftermath of the wedding, King Maegor declared Princess Rhaena's daughter Aerea his lawful heir, "until such time as the gods grant me a son," whilst sending her twin sister Rhaella to Oldtown to be raised as a septa. His nephew Jaehaerys, felt by many to be the rightful heir, was expressly disinherited in the same decree. Queen Jeyne's son was confirmed as Lord of Tarbeck Hall, and sent to Casterly Rock to be raised as a ward of House Lannister, and Queen Elinor's elder boys were similarly disposed of, one to the Eyrie, one to Highgarden. The queen's youngest babe was turned over to a wet nurse, as the king found the queen's nursing irksome.

Half a year after the wedding, Lord Celtigar, the King's Hand, announced that Queen Jeyne was with child. Hardly had her belly begun to swell when the king himself revealed that Queen Elinor was also pregnant. Maegor showered both women with gifts and honors, and granted new lands and offices to their fathers, brothers, and uncles, but his joy proved to be short-lived. Three moons before she was due, Queen Jeyne was brought to bed by a sudden onset of labor pains, and was delivered of a stillborn child as monstrous as the one Alys Harroway had birthed, a legless and armless creature possessed of both male and female genitals. Nor did the mother long survive the child.

Maegor was cursed, men said. He had slain his nephew, made war against the Faith and the High Septon, defied the gods, committed murder and incest, adultery and rape. His privy parts were poisoned, his seed full of worms, the gods would never grant him a living son. Or so the whispers ran. Maegor himself settled on a different explanation, and sent Ser Owen Bush and Ser Maladon Moore to seize Queen Tyanna and deliver her to the dungeons.

There the Pentoshi queen made a full confession, even as the king's torturers readied their implements: she had poisoned Jeyne Westerling's child in the womb, just as she had Alys Harroway's. It would be the same with Elinor Costayne's whelp, she promised.

It is said that the king slew her himself, cutting out her heart with Blackfyre and feeding it to his dogs. But even in death, Tyanna of the Tower had her revenge, for it came to pass just as she had promised. The moon turned and turned again, and in the black of night Queen Elinor too was delivered of a malformed and stillborn child, an eyeless boy born with rudimentary wings.

That was in the forty-eighth year After the Conquest, the sixth year of King Maegor's reign and the last year of his life. No man in the Seven Kingdoms could doubt that the king was accursed now. What followers still remained to him began to melt away, evaporating like dew in the morning sun. Word reached King's Landing that Ser Joffrey Doggett had been seen entering Riverrun, not as a captive but as a guest of Lord Tully. Septon Moon appeared once more, leading thousands of the

Faithful on a march across the Reach to Oldtown, with the announced intent of bearding the Lickspittle in the Starry Sept to demand that he denounce "the Abomination on the Iron Throne," and lift his ban on the military orders. When Lord Oakheart and Lord Rowan appeared before him with their levies, they came not to attack Moon but to join him. Lord Celtigar resigned as King's Hand and returned to his seat on Claw Isle.

Reports from the Dornish marches suggested that the Dornishmen were gathering in the passes, preparing to invade the realm.

The worst blow came from Storm's End. There on the shores of Shipbreaker Bay, Lord Rogar Baratheon proclaimed young Jaehaerys Targaryen to be the true and lawful king of the Andals, the Rhoynar, and the First Men, and Prince Jaehaerys named Lord Rogar Protector of the Realm and Hand of the King. The prince's mother Queen Alyssa and his sister Alysanne stood beside him as Jaehaerys unsheathed Dark Sister and vowed to end the reign of his usurping uncle. A hundred banner lords and stormland knights cheered the proclamation. Prince Jaehaerys was fourteen years old when he claimed the throne: a handsome youth, skilled with lance and longbow, and a gifted rider. More, he rode a great bronze and tan beast called Vermithor, and his sister Alysanne, a maid of twelve, commanded her own dragon, Silverwing. "Maegor has only one dragon," Lord Rogar told the stormlords. "Our prince has two."

And soon three. When word reached the Red Keep that Jaehaerys was gathering his forces at Storm's End, Rhaena Targaryen mounted Dreamfyre and flew to join him, abandoning the uncle she had been forced to wed. She took her daughter Aerea . . . and Blackfyre, stolen from the king's own scabbard as he slept.

King Maegor's response was sluggish and confused. He commanded the Grand Maester to send forth his ravens, summoning all his leal lords and bannermen to gather at King's Landing, only to find that Benifer had taken ship for Pentos. Finding Princess Aerea gone, he sent a rider to Oldtown to demand the head of her twin sister Rhaella, to punish their mother for her betrayal, but Lord Hightower imprisoned his messenger instead. Two of his Kingsguard vanished one night, to go over to Jaehaerys, and Ser Owen Bush was found dead outside a brothel, his member stuffed into his mouth.

Lord Velaryon of Driftmark was amongst the first to declare for Jaehaerys. As the Velaryons were the realm's traditional admirals, Maegor woke to find he had lost the entire royal fleet. The Tyrells of Highgarden followed, with all the power of the Reach. The Hightowers of Oldtown, the Redwynes of the Arbor, the Lannisters of Casterly Rock, the Arryns of the Eyrie, the Royces of Runestone . . . one by one, they came out against the king.

In King's Landing, a score of lesser lords gathered at Maegor's command, amongst them Lord Darklyn of Duskendale, Lord Massey of Stonedance, Lord Towers of Harrenhal, Lord Staunton of Rook's Rest, Lord Bar Emmon of Sharp Point, Lord Buckwell of the Antlers, the Lords Rosby, Stokeworth, Hayford, Harte, Byrch, Rollingford, Bywater, and Mallery. Yet they commanded scarce four thousand men amongst them all, and only one in ten of those were knights.

Maegor brought them together in the Red Keep one night to discuss his plan of battle. When they saw how few they were, and realized that no great lords were coming to join them, many lost heart, and Lord Hayford went so far as to urge His Grace to abdicate and take the black. His Grace ordered Hayford beheaded on the spot and continued the war council with his lordship's head mounted on a lance behind the Iron Throne. All day the lords made plans, and late into the night. It was the hour of the wolf when at last Maegor allowed them to take their leave. The king remained behind, brooding on the Iron Throne as they departed. Lord Towers and Lord Rosby were the last to see His Grace.

Hours later, as dawn was breaking, the last of Maegor's queens came seeking after him. Queen Elinor found him still upon the Iron Throne, pale and dead, his robes soaked through with blood. His arms had been slashed open from wrist to elbow on jagged barbs, and another blade had gone through his neck to emerge beneath his chin.

Many to this day believe it was the Iron Throne itself that killed him. Maegor was alive when Rosby and Towers left the throne room, they argue, and the guards at the doors swore that no one entered afterward, until Queen Elinor made her discovery. Some say it was the queen herself who forced him down onto those barbs and blades, to avenge the murder of her first husband. The Kingsguard might have done the deed, though that would have required them to act in concert, as there were two knights posted at each door. It might also have been a person or persons unknown, entering and leaving the throne room through some secret passage. The Red Keep has its secrets, known only to the dead. It may also be that the king tasted despair in the dark watches of the night and took his own life, twisting the blades as needed and opening his veins to spare himself the defeat and disgrace that surely awaited him.

The reign of King Maegor I Targaryen, known to history and legend as Maegor the Cruel, lasted six years and sixty-six days. Upon his death his corpse was burned in the yard of the Red Keep, his ashes interred afterward on Dragonstone beside those of his mother. He died childless, and left no heir of his body.

Nine days later, three dragons were seen in the sky over King's Landing. Princess Rhaena had returned, and with her came her brother Jaehaerys and her sister Alysanne. Their mother, the Dowager Queen Alyssa, arrived a fortnight later, riding beside the Lord of Storm's End at the head of a great host, their banners streaming. The smallfolk cheered. Ravens were sent forth to every castle in the realm, inviting all lords great and small to come to King's Landing to bear witness at the coronation of a new king, a true king.

And they came.

In the forty-eighth year After the Conquest, before the eyes of gods and men and half the lords of Westeros, the High Septon of Oldtown placed his father's golden crown upon the brow of the young prince, and proclaimed him Jaehaerys of House Targaryen, the First of His Name, King of the Andals, the Rhoynar, and the First Men, and Lord of the Seven Kingdoms. His mother Alyssa would act as his regent during the remaining years of the king's minority, whilst Lord Robar Baratheon was named Protector of the Realm and Hand of the King. (Half a year later, the two of them would wed.)

Fourteen years old at his ascent, Jaehaerys would sit the Iron Throne for five-and-fifty years, and in due course become known as "the Old King" and "the Conciliator."

But that is a tale best told at another time, by another maester.

Story Copyrights

"When I Was a Highwayman" by Ellen Kushner. Copyright © 2017 by Ellen Kushner.

"The Smoke of Gold Is Glory" by Scott Lynch. Copyright © 2017 by Scott Lynch.

"The Colgrid Connundrum" by Rich Larson. Copyright © 2017 by Rich Larson.

"The King's Evil" by Elizabeth Bear. Copyright © 2017 by Sarah Wishnevsky (Elizabeth Bear).

"Waterfalling" by Lavie Tidhar. Copyright © 2017 by Lavie Tidhar.

"The Sword Tyraste" by Cecelia Holland. Copyright © 2017 by Cecelia Holland.

"The Sons of the Dragon" by George R. R. Martin. Copyright © 2017 by George R. R. Martin.

If you enjoyed these tales, be sure to look for

the companion volume, exploring the

more mystical side of fantasy:

THE BOOK OF MAGIC

Edited by Gardner Dozois

Coming next fall